By Susan Richards Shreve

A FORTUNATE MADNESS

A WOMAN LIKE THAT

CHILDREN OF POWER

MIRACLE PLAY

DREAMING OF HEROES

QUEEN OF HEARTS

A COUNTRY OF STRANGERS

DAUGHTERS OF THE NEW WORLD

THE TRAIN HOME

THE VISITING PHYSICIAN

Nan A. Talese

DOUBLEDAY

New York London Toronto Sydney Auckland

THE
VISITING PHYSICIAN

Susan Richards Shreve

PUBLISHED BY NAN A. TALESE
an imprint of Doubleday
a division of Bantam Doubleday Dell Publishing Group, Inc.
1540 Broadway, New York, New York 10036

DOUBLEDAY is a trademark of Doubleday, a division of
Bantam Doubleday Dell Publishing Group, Inc.

Book design by Jennifer Ann Daddio
Frontispiece by John Burgoyne

Library of Congress Cataloging-in-Publication Data
Shreve, Susan Richards.
The visiting physician /
Susan Richards Shreve. — 1st ed. in the U.S.A.
p.   cm.
I. Title.
PS3569.H74V57   1996
813'.54—dc20   95-23877
                                          CIP

ISBN 0-385-47701-5
Copyright © 1996 by Susan Richards Shreve
All Rights Reserved
Printed in the United States of America
April 1996
First Edition

1   3   5   7   9   10   8   6   4   2

To Gilbert and Elisabeth and Matthew
with love

The Visiting Physician

I.

The Way Things Are

1.   3

2.   12

II.

Water Damage

The Story of Meridian: Monday, April 9

23

3.   32

4.   40

5.   52

6.   61

III.

Heart Scan

The Story of Meridian: Tuesday, April 10

73

7.   82

8.   89

9.   106

10.   115

IV.

Weather Report

The Story of Meridian: Wednesday, April 11

133

11.   147

12.   163

13.   171

14.   177

V.

Visual Memory

The Story of Meridian: Thursday, April 12

187

15.   201

16.   217

VI.

Do No Harm

The Story of Meridian: Friday, April 13

235

17.   253

18.   262

19.   268

20.   277

I.

THE WAY
THINGS ARE

1.

THE AFTERNOON SUN SPREAD A golden ribbon across the railroad tracks, coloring the faces lining the station platform a deep-crusted yellow. WELCOME TO MERIDIAN, the sign over the stationmaster's door said. Beside it, half obscured by a new poster of a missing child and written in red, were the words "the pure products of America" used to advertise the three-part television series on the town of Meridian broadcast by CBS in early May.

The missing child was a dark-haired angel described as: "Maggie Sailor, age 4, black hair, blue eyes, weight 30 pounds, reported missing May 10. Last seen at Bailey's pharmacy wearing a yellow Big Bird jacket and high tops. There is a strawberry birthmark on her left hip."

Someone, her mother perhaps, according to the stationmaster, had written in pen another "blue" so the information read "blue blue eyes" and had added "curly" with an asterisk before black hair. Someone else had made a Magic Marker mustache and dotted the child's cheeks with red spots. ZITS was written across her small and perfect nose.

"She's late," Reverend Benjamin Winters said, his arms folded tight across his narrow chest. He was a tall, awkwardly put-together man of unexpected temper, older than his pretty wife, whose choice of a profession in the service of God had come not of conviction but of deep misgivings. "What good is a doctor without a sense of time?" he asked of no one in particular.

"She's not late, Benjamin," Edith said, holding their baby daughter, taking the child with her everywhere since Maggie disappeared and now the terrible virus attacking the children of Meridian. "The train is late."

T. J. Wisely had brought the CBS film crew to Meridian in the first place. He sat now in a motorized wheelchair just at the end of the platform, his thick dark hair over the collar of his leather jacket, an eye patch over his left eye giving his strong, handsome face an aspect of practiced menace. Two years earlier, when a television director for whom T.J. was working had been looking for a small-town, preferably Mid-western—"a pure product of America is what I need," he said —T.J. had told him about Meridian.

The platform was crowded; about twenty people were there on the soft afternoon in late May waiting for the train from Detroit. Madeleine and Henry Sailor, the parents of the missing child, young parents, in their teens when Maggie was born, stood at the end of the platform beyond the crowd— stood straight and very close to one another, almost silent, although once Madeleine said, "I hope she is what we need," without looking at Henry, and Henry replied, folding his arms across his chest, "What we need in Meridian is a miracle."

Madeleine brushed imaginary lint from the front of her light cotton dress, a dress she had chosen for the occasion from the few selections in her closet, wishing to appear attractive and solid in spite of her shattered heart.

Henry was wearing the khaki trousers and plaid shirt he had on the day Maggie disappeared. He allowed Madeleine to wash them but otherwise he wore them every day, as if by his dress on the day of her disappearance he could recapture her life.

David Jaspersen, the young chief of police, stood near the Sailors with Winslow—his son Win, his only relation.

He was a large handsome man with extraordinary hands —thick and broad, with short fingers, hands that called attention to themselves; he had been a football player for Meridian and later tight end at the University of Wisconsin. Then he had gone to law school and married and had a son. In Meridian, he was considered a young man with an important future. No one expected him to return to a place of such diminished opportunities. But something happened to him in Wisconsin. He had never said. The year he was thirty-two he returned home with his baby son and trained as a policeman.

As chief of police, he held himself accountable for the silent unraveling of trust since Maggie Sailor disappeared. The generous spirit of good will which had distinguished the town of his birth slipped away daily and he found himself able only to bear witness to what felt very much like the opening of a fault line in the tectonic plates beneath the earth on which Meridian sat.

"I'm surprised you're here to meet the doctor," David said to the Sailors.

"Reverend Winters asked us to come. He asked the congregation at church on Sunday to make her feel welcome," Henry Sailor said. "We didn't want to disappoint him."

"I hear she's very young," Madeleine Sailor said.

"She's young, but good, particularly with childhood diseases," David said. "I read the material sent on her from the hospital in Ann Arbor."

"Does she know she's walking into a nightmare?" Madeleine Sailor asked. "Does she know about Maggie?"

"She knows about the virus. Her specialty is pediatric immunology," David Jaspersen said. "She probably also knows about Maggie. Our bad news has been in the papers as far away as Washington, D.C."

"How come?" Win asked, pulling the brim of his baseball cap over his eyes.

"Since the film, people are interested in us—even our misfortunes," David said. "In the last two weeks, the town is full of tourists."

Since the film aired on the first three days of May, tour buses and bicyclists on day trips and cars full of visitors on their way to Chicago or Cleveland stopped at Meridian to take a look at the town made suddenly famous by "The Story of Meridian" on CBS. It was on such a day, full of tourists taking pictures of Main Street, that Maggie had disappeared.

"The trouble with television is that people believe what they see on the screen and not their own lives," Henry Sailor said. " 'The Story of Meridian' wasn't about us."

"I liked it better before we were on television." Win leaned against his father. "Except the parts when they filmed me playing Little League. That was good."

Meridian had been advertising for a physician since April, when Dr. Hazelton had suddenly gone to Michigan on a family emergency and then written that he would be taking an indefinite leave of absence.

For almost a month they had searched with no success. The letters came back from senior doctors that the town was too small, too isolated, that they should use the hospital in Harrisville, twenty-five miles south, that young doctors no longer wished to work without a partner, especially with the rise in malpractice suits.

But the truth was that the news about Meridian's troubles had appeared in stories released by the AP wires all over the Middle West. First there was Maggie Sailor's disappearance and then the floods, bringing a virus which could cause a perfectly healthy child to die. No young physician was willing to take on the responsibility alone for a small, isolated town suddenly at risk.

And then in May a call came from Dr. Helen Fielding,

a pediatric resident at the University of Michigan, Ann Arbor, saying she was willing to come as a visiting physician until the crisis passed.

Meridian, Ohio, was settled in the early nineteenth century by the Welsh, chosen by them for its hills, like the hills of North Wales, with small valleys, always on the rise or on the fall, so a man standing was at an angle, coming up or going down. It was sheep land and, though the winter came in early and lasted, the summers were spectacular, with dazzling mornings and bright warm long afternoons.

A river ran through the center of town, which was why so small a place had a railway station, where freight trains were loaded with lumber that had been cut up north and floated downstream. The town itself was like a northern Italian town, with a narrow winding Main Street, and houses stacked like building blocks up the hill, rising above the village. The white-steepled Methodist church where Benjamin Winters was the minister was at one end of the main street and a small brick Roman Catholic church where Father Thomas was the priest was at the other, so there was a kind of picture-book symmetry to the place, a quiet simple beauty with the frame houses painted white and lavender and yellow to cheer the spirit during the dark winter. To the hundreds of visitors who had come since the film to see the real Meridian, the town seemed to have fallen asleep. There were no chain stores; the television reception was poor, with only two channels, and cable had not come beyond Harrisville. The shops, even the grocery, were owned by local merchants. There was a small college founded by the Methodists which had been the first college in America to open its doors to women and to blacks, there were two elementary schools and a Catholic grammar school built to educate the Irish population who arrived in the Middle West after the potato famine in Ireland. There were two lawyers, Rubin and Rubin, brothers whose family had been among members of a failed Utopian community of Russian Jews near Philadelphia who had moved west with the railroad. Another descendant of that community owned the dry goods store and another the dry cleaners. There had been a colored section with families who came up from the South on the underground railroad in the nineteenth century before the Civil War and settled just beyond the train tracks. But after the flood of 1917 that section was washed out and everybody in Meridian lived in the houses built on the hills, lived together with a surprising spirit of well-wishing which was the quality the producers of "Meridian" had wanted to capture in the film.

The people of Meridian believed the river was responsible for their spirit of community. It was a long narrow river, almost a stream in the late summer and fall, called the river Meryn for the daughter of one of the Welsh settlers who drowned in it. In the spring, when the snows off the hills melted and spilled into the river, the ribbon of water flooded the banks of the Meryn, sometimes rising above the side roads, over the steps of houses, filling the basements, sometimes surging through

Main Street like an army on the march, taking everything loose on the porches, in the yards, in front of shops, sometimes rising over the furniture, rotting the legs of tables, the must settling in for weeks.

The flooding came regularly in early May. Sometimes it was days of rain, then a small rush of river water over the banks; but there were years when the people of Meridian had to depend on one another like family. There was no predicting year to year how the river would go, so people lived prepared, with a sense of adventure and the kind of trust that comes of necessity.

In the distance, the long sad wail of the twelve-eleven from Detroit, running fifty minutes late, sounded and people along the platform straightened their shoulders, rearranged their clothes.

"Here it comes." David Jaspersen put his hands in his pockets.

"I see the light," Win said.

And the engine of the locomotive appeared curling around the corner, bearing down on the group gathered at the station with terrible speed.

A hundred yards away, the train slowed, crept the last distance, and stopped just at the point where David stood with his son. A conductor opened the door of the first coach, waved at the stationmaster, and lifted a suitcase down.

At the top of the steps a woman, much younger than the people of Meridian could possibly have imagined, with dark brown hair piled loosely on top of her head and an oval olive-skinned face out of another century, looked down at the waiting crowd.

"Hello," she said, not focusing on any one face in particular. She stepped down to the platform. "I believe someone is expecting a visiting physician."

2.

HELEN FIELDING SAW THE ANNOUNCEMENT for a physician on the bulletin board outside of the cafeteria of the university hospital in Ann Arbor in mid-April.

> *Small town in northwestern Ohio in search of a physician as temporary replacement in the practice of general medicine. Physician will be in charge of clinic with assistance from an excellent nurse. Housing provided. Charming yellow clapboard Victorian with three bedrooms and a garden. Contact Director, Medical School, University of Michigan.*

Helen was not in search of a position. In fact just that morning before they got out of bed, Dr. Oliver Hampton had asked her to marry him. She didn't particularly want to marry Oliver, but she daydreamed of her own children. She had spent the morning in the pediatric clinic with telescopic scenes of domesticity interrupting her concentration. This is my daughter Christina, she said to herself as she examined the throat of a young patient, Christina, and my other children are at home, she went on in her mind's story, the fantasy reassuring, the children at home in permanent safety, Oliver at work, Helen capable of doctoring her own daughter, this Christina with a terrible strep throat. Which was how her thoughts were going at lunch break. She washed up, took two Bufferin for a persistent headache, changed to another white jacket and glanced at the bulletin board again. Something about the announcement captured her imagination.

"I believe it's the yellow Victorian house," she said to Oliver at lunch.

"You certainly can't be serious, Helen," he said.

She shrugged.

"I suppose you heard me this morning," he said.

"Of course." She lowered her voice so the other residents at the long Formica table would not overhear them. "It was just the house, Ollie," she said. "You know how I am about houses."

Underneath Helen's bed in the fourth-story apartment near the medical school were the boxes of pictures of houses which she had cut out since she arrived at Michigan from Mackinaw, where she had lived with her mother in a rooming house to which they had moved the year her father left, the year after Emma had died.

At night, before she went to bed, she leafed through issues of *Country Living* and *Home* and *House and Garden* for pictures of houses—whitewashed bedrooms with quilts on the canopy beds and fireplaces, kitchens with round tables, bowls of red apples glistening in the sun, living rooms with couches full of pillows, a table of books with candles, a vase of yellow wildflowers.

The people who knew Helen, who thought they knew her, her fellow students and other physicians at the hospital, found her enchanting, like a child without affectations. There was something unexpected, full of whimsy and unspoken promise: the way she wore her hair in a clumsy halo on top of her head, the way she dressed in long colorful skirts and blouses open at the neck. She had a soft assured voice, a physical ease with people, a generosity of spirit. Not the demeanor of a woman of science.

There was a mystery about her, as if secrets, hormonal in the blood, altered the chemistry of her body, creating a kind of magnet for the imaginings of other people; she was the subject of small observations which accumulated, giving her a force.

Very little was actually known about Helen Fielding's life. She was the only remaining child of a professor of European history in Santa Cruz, California, and a mother who had, in the year Helen went off to college, gone to New York City with a younger man she'd met who was vacationing on Mackinaw Island where she lived. No one in medical school had met Helen's mother, who did not travel except the one trip to New York City. But her father, a man of charismatic warmth similar to Helen's, came once a year and stayed with Helen in her apartment for a week or so during which they would give cheerful dinners for other physicians, ordering in Chinese food.

She seldom lived alone in the small apartment on the fourth floor of Logan which she shared now with Oliver

Hampton but before that for two years with Stephen Bryant and before that at the end of undergraduate school with Peter Tatler. Each man had felt as Oliver did that eventually he would marry Helen. She seemed exactly the kind of woman with whom to make a life. But at a moment of decision she'd slip away.

Oliver was astonished when Helen told him that she wouldn't marry him.

"Not ever?" he asked.

"Not now," she replied.

"But maybe later?" he asked.

"I don't know, Ollie," she said sadly. "There's something that keeps me from making a life."

She knew about falling in love and it worried her, left her in despair; she seemed unable to go beyond the high-spirited drunkenness of early romance. She had fallen in love with Oliver and Peter and Stephen and others but always briefly, a small conflagration that lit up her room and was gone.

Something was absent, as if a painting of Helen Fielding would show a young willowy woman, a stranger, not a face she recognized. Sometimes she'd clean her small apartment, bringing in forsythia, a brightly colored rug and, standing in the entrance, she'd survey the rooms, the living room with its black flowered chintz couch, the white bedroom with yellow freesias in a glass beside the bed, the study with her grandmother's small cherry desk. "This is where Helen Fielding lives," she'd say to herself. "The physician from Mackinaw Island. Do you know her?"

The only time she felt the passion she remembered from

a childhood of strong feelings was when she cut out pictures of the warm crowded rooms in houses. Then she'd have a sudden rush of memory as if she could feel the physical warmth of the soft white comforter in the pictures of *House and Garden*. What she usually felt even in love affairs was an intellectual understanding of emotion, or the physical expressions of a rapid heartbeat, a general anxiety from too much carbon dioxide going out of the lungs, a dry mouth. But she didn't feel the emotion itself.

In May there was another notice on the bulletin board.

> *MERIDIAN. Small town in northwest Ohio in urgent need of a temporary physician. Floods and unusual heat have brought outbreak of a serious virus affecting small children. Contact David Jaspersen, 216-843-2121, Meridian, Ohio 46537.*

Helen sat at a table in the hospital cafeteria, a general sense of weakness overtaking her.

She knew Meridian, Ohio.

She knew Meridian very well, even the wet smell of it in summer, the sound of high wind in the voluminous trees, of the trains from Chicago, the mossy brick sidewalks—she knew the town with the fresh painting of a child's memory, although she hadn't been there since the hot, hot summer when she was four and Emma had been two.

She had a sudden picture of sunflowers against white clapboard and the smell of sugar cookies baking. Until Emma died, her family had spent summers with her father's family in Meridian, her Great-Aunt Martha and Uncle Peter.

Dear Father [Helen wrote on a postcard to her father in Santa Cruz]. I'm moving to Meridian as a visiting M.D. for several months. They have a viral outbreak. It will be so odd to be back there. Will let you know my address, Love, H. P.S. Did you see the TV special, "The Story of Meridian"? They tell me there was a three-part series in early May but I was on rotation and didn't hear about it.

Dear Mother [she wrote to her mother]. I will be moving shortly to Meridian as a visiting physician. They have suffered the loss of children recently—so far one little girl has died from a terrible virus brought on by floods—and one has disappeared. So they are desperate for a doctor. Unfortunately, I am going alone as Oliver Hampton—remember Ollie from your wedding, the one with the wire-rimmed glasses and British?—has met someone else. Love, Helen. P.S. When we visited, you never told me that the river is called Meryn for a little girl who drowned in it.

She thought to cross out the P.S. before she folded the letter and put it in the envelope but did not. Writing to her mother and father made her so anxious that she stopped at the pharmacy after she mailed the letters and bought a pack of cigarettes, smoking several, one after the other, while she stood on the corner leaning against a stop sign, then she threw the pack away.

On the train to Cleveland, Helen had trouble breathing. It was not unfamiliar. She had had trouble breathing before. She sat very still, her hands folded in her lap, her eyes closed. In her role as her own mother, she whispered to herself: "You're fine, Helen darling—it's a big step to return to the place you went as a child, where Emma disappeared— but you'll be absolutely fine, I promise." She held her own hand.

"Are you all right?" the young woman in the seat across from Helen asked.

"Fine," Helen said quickly, her eyes flying open. "I'm perfectly fine," she said without thinking. She reached in her book bag and got out a package of peanut M and M's, peanut butter crackers and two Bufferin.

"Would you like some?" she asked, opening the M and M's, offering them to the young woman.

"Thank you," the woman said. "I love anything choco- late."

And gradually they fell to talking about medicine and the young woman's children, and houses in which the woman also had an interest, having recently bought a new one. Helen was pleased with the ease of conversation, which had the feel of friendship, reassured that she could make a friendship out of nothing, even with a stranger.

When the woman got off the train—they had not ex-

changed addresses, only names: Lynn Sorrell was the one belonging to the stranger—Helen felt an unexpected loss.

In the small foul-smelling toilet of the train south, she
examined her face up close in the mirror, her dark blue eyes
flecked with yellow, familiar eyes, but more pained than she
imagined them when she thought of the face that others saw,
a warm comforting face, as she imagined it, with an expression of an inner peace of mind.

The young woman on the train had seen the film about
Meridian and read the stories about the killer virus in a Pittsburgh paper. Two days ago she had even seen a picture of the
missing child flash on the television screen after the local
news.

"I watch a lot of TV," she said. "You're braver than I
would be. I couldn't be in a town where something is happening to the children."

Helen looked in the full-length mirror on the back of
the door to the toilet, pleased with what the people of Meridian would be seeing soon. She was tall with long legs and full
breasts which she emphasized in her way of dressing in
V-necked shirts and blouses like the one she had on now.
The impression was of a woman too fulsome to be a model
but beautiful with a kind of soft maternal beauty.

The train traveled through hilly farmland, lambing country,
bright in the afternoon sun. Helen opened her backpack
which held mostly books: the May *Country Living* and *House
Beautiful,* a medical dictionary, a Random House paperback

dictionary, *Anna Karenina,* which she always carried, preferring to read a familiar story rather than to start a new one.
She took out the dictionary and opened to the word "meridian." She liked definition 3 particularly: "the great circle of the
celestial sphere that passes through its poles and the observer's
zenith." She looked up "zenith."

One of the important things she had learned as a student of medicine had to do with fate. She was not by nature
accommodating to the forces of fate; rather more likely to
believe in the power of her own will. But science required
certain personal adjustments. What Helen Fielding was doing
on this train headed south toward Meridian, Ohio, felt to her
very much like destiny.

II.

WATER DAMAGE

The Story of

MERIDIAN

THE FILM CREWS HAD ARRIVED in early April and set up shop in the First Methodist Church. They chose it because of the large assembly room in the parish hall next door, and the Sunday school rooms were turned into bedrooms for the crew. The director, a taciturn young man called Peter Forester whose temperament showed no evidence of a childhood in a benevolent small town, liked the church because it had the look of picture postcards, white with a steeple and a simple cross, built at the highest point of Main Street so the cross seemed to float disembodied above the town. A clock was on the tower of the church, stopped, since anyone could remember, at three-fifteen, although Benjamin Winters had tried to get it fixed when Meridian painted all of the buildings on Main Street including First Methodist for the arrival of the crew.

"It's nice the way the clock has stopped at three-fifteen," Peter Forester said to T.J. with the breezy arrogance of a man accustomed to the last word. "It's a metaphor, you know. After all, the film is about stopped clocks."

"I don't like this," Edith Winters said the first night after CBS crews arrived, lying in bed next to Benjamin, keeping her daughter at her breast long after the child had stopped sucking. "It feels dangerous."

"Dangerous?" Benjamin was pleased to have the film crew, pleased with the importance suddenly attending his ministry which, except during the season of floods, was a long repetition of changeless days.

"It's dangerous to have a lot of strangers sleeping in the church at night, making up stories about us." She slid under the covers, turning her back to her husband. "Don't kiss me," she said when he leaned over her.

"The story *is* true," Benjamin said. "We're a small town with an unusual sense of community."

"We were ordinary until they told us we weren't," Edith said. "I feel looked at."

"By people sleeping in the next building? What's the matter with you, Edith?"

"By people who've come pretending to know us," she said crossly.

"Think of it as moral," Benjamin said while she put the baby to bed in the bassinet in their room.

"I don't think of anything as moral," Edith said.

"T.J. tells me the point of his film is moral," Benjamin said. "That people in America have lost their sense of good will toward one another." Benjamin sat up in bed, putting his pillow behind him. "He says the documentary is a call to action, reminding people of the way we used to be."

Edith crossed her arms and sat down in the rocking chair.

"I'm sleeping here tonight in case of a fire," she said.

"A fire?"

"In case they set the church on fire." She pulled her legs up and rested her chin on her knees.

"Suit yourself, Edie," Benjamin said, turning away from the light, staring at the shadows playing across the white walls of the bedroom, waiting for a hint of sleep although there did not seem a chance for sleeping with the rocking of Edith's chair against the hardwood floor.

"Benjamin?" she said after a while. "Are you awake?"

"Quite awake," he said.

"This just feels wrong to me," she said. "I can't explain it."

Days like these with the smell of spring in the air, David Jaspersen ached for a woman. Not a woman he'd go after but one who would take after him, lay her hand on the back of his neck—"I've been thinking about you, David," she'd say—and the touch of her hand was silk.

During nights of this unbearable aching he'd wander the house restless, imagining a woman in his room, imagining the smell of her, her back curved graceful as a willow leaning down to undress.

On the first night the film crew arrived in Meridian, he found himself imagining women again.

He had exhausted Meridian easily when he returned home with Win in September of his thirty-second year. There were the girls he'd known in high school—married now but young enough for a sprinkle of interest. There was Mary

Rubin just out of college, too young for him but pretty and very smart. And there was Sophie. So-phi-a, she called herself. He liked to think of her stretched out on his soft white sheets sleeping, her thick dark hair against the white pillow.

But he had no future with Sophie—she was a child herself, with a child's offhand innocence and the quality of a stray, a wanderer in the backyards of other people's lives. Besides, she had Molly. There was no telling how she and Molly got by day to day, neighbors, probably. Something was askew about her, something wild rattling in her brain, and David knew he ought to steer clear although he had a yearning to save her.

Nevertheless she was recklessly on his mind when T. J. Wisely knocked at the door, wheeled into the living room and dragged himself onto the couch, lifting his legs beside him.

"Jeez," T.J. said. "I killed my back playing basketball with the crew. Do you have a beer?"

"This is my last one," David said.

"What about a whisky?"

David poured Scotch into a glass and sat down across from T.J.

"Maybe you should give up basketball now you're in a wheelchair," he said. "Set some limits on your life."

"I'm good at it," T.J. said. "I'm still very good even on wheels. You ought to come out and play with us. There's a guy on the camera crew who used to play for N. C. State."

"I'm not that good, although I could probably outrun you." David put his feet up on the coffee table. "I suppose you've come over to talk about the film."

"Nope. All that's A-OK. The crew's settled in the good

reverend's church. The reverend is pleased to have some action in the house of God and they're all set on the shoots for tomorrow." He turned over on his side facing David, his arm resting on his hand. "I've come about Sophie," he said.

"Sophie? I didn't know Sophie was in your busy life."

T.J. pulled a cigarette out of his pocket. "In a way, she is," he said.

"Well, you should get her out, T.J.," David said. "You've had a hard enough time as it is without asking for trouble."

T. J. Wisely had arrived alone by train in Meridian when he was three years old, according to the doctor who had examined him shortly after his arrival. The conductor of the train from Chicago had told the stationmaster in Meridian that T.J. had been put on the train in Chicago by a young woman of forgettable description who said his name was T. J. Wisely and he was to get off at Meridian where he would be met by his Uncle Bob. "We have a lot of Bobs here," the stationmaster said but no one of them was there to pick up T.J. when he arrived so he stayed with David Jaspersen's family while the police searched in Chicago for the woman. And later he became a ward of Meridian, a mascot, everybody's child. He was adaptable, assuming the demeanor of the family with whom he happened to be living at the time, the manner of dress, the pattern of speech, the daily mass or weekly church suppers, the standards for studying and behavior, the grades expected. Chameleon-like, he slipped through childhood beloved and then to everyone's surprise, because T.J. had shown no great love of danger, he left just after his eighteenth birthday and went to Los Angeles to become a stunt man in the movies.

"What would you expect from a boy whose mama puts him on a train to nowhere?" David Jaspersen's mother said to him the year T.J. left.

"So tell me about Sophie," David said.

"We've got to do something about her before this film gets going. She doesn't fit the picture."

"I don't get what you mean," David said. "She's a sweet troubled woman."

"Sweet maybe and certainly troubled," T.J. said. "But here we have this story of America like it used to be, pure as the driven snow. That's the idea, right?"

"It's your film," David said.

"So on walks Sophie DeLaurentis with her pouty lips, Eve in the garden of Eden." He rolled his eyes. "I don't think so."

"So cut her out of it after the filming is done," David said. "Most of a film ends up on the cutting-room floor, isn't that right?"

"Usually," T.J. said. "But unfortunately the director of this particular film met her at dinner tonight and WHAMMO. 'She's perfect,' Peter Forester said to me. 'She's a born-again Marilyn with black hair.' "

David shrugged. "You're the film guys," he said. "The rest of us are simply products of your imagination."

Sophie DeLaurentis was still awake when David called.

"Do you have something going with T.J.?" he asked.

"T.J.?" she asked. "What makes you think that, David?"

"Call it a leap of faith," David said.

"Uh-uh," she said, yawning a long-drawn-out yawn. "I don't have anything going on now with anyone but I met the director of the TV show tonight and he sort of liked me."

"So I understand."

"He said he hoped to get me in the show a lot," she said. "And Molly too. He thinks Molly is beautiful."

"Well, be careful," David said.

"Of what?" Sophie asked. "There's nothing to be afraid of."

"Just be careful."

Sophie didn't go back to bed after the chief of police called. She thought of him as the chief of police, liking that he was *somebody* in Meridian and she had seen him naked. Or he had seen her naked. She wasn't sure which she liked better since she knew David Jaspersen no better without his clothes than she knew him in full uniform with his hat on. He was a covered-up man.

She took off her pale pink nightgown with the lacy bib, checking Molly to see if she was sleeping soundly since she didn't want her little daughter to see her looking at her own naked body in the full-length mirror on the closet door.

She had a soft fleshy body with a little round pocket of a belly and downy cushions on her high hips, full wavy hair other women would die for, and large blue eyes. "Wonder eyes," Dr. Hazelton had said to her when he first came back to Meridian from medical school and wanted Sophie to reciprocate his urgent love, which she refused. But she slept with him. That Sophie would do with almost anyone. She picked up the telephone and called him now, keeping her voice soft not to wake Molly.

"Hello, Rich," she said.

"I'm glad you called," Richard Hazelton said coolly. "I saw you at the coffee shop today with the film crew and I wanted to talk to you about that."

"The director wants to make me sort of a star," Sophie said. "That's why I called to tell you that I can't bring Molly to her appointment tomorrow."

"I don't want Molly in this movie," Richard Hazelton said.

"It's not a movie."

"I don't want her in whatever it is," he said crossly.

"She's my child," she said. "It's my choice."

"Not just your child, Sophie."

"I say she is," Sophie said.

"We'll see," Dr. Hazelton said, hanging up. He always was the one to hang up first.

T.J. opened the front door of the parish hall and went in. Most of the crew had already gone to bed, the doors to the Sunday school pulled shut, but at the back there was a small party with Peter Forester and Marina, his assistant, and Pleeper Jones, the new production assistant, sitting in metal chairs with their feet up drinking beers. T.J. took a beer out of the fridge.

"I'm going to like doing this film," Peter said, lifting his glass to T.J. in the gesture of a toast. "Meridian is a lot more interesting a town than I had thought when we came to scout it in the fall."

T.J. pulled a chair up beside Marina.

"What interests you besides Sophie DeLaurentis?" T.J. asked.

Peter rolled his eyes. "I can see creating a real masterpiece in 'Meridian' if we choose the shoots carefully and do some amazing camera work," he said. "So brighten up, T.J. You're a genius to have brought us here."

3.

IT WAS AN ODD LITTLE PARTY that greeted Helen as she got off the train in Meridian. A group, in its earnest formality, out of a different time, more English than American, the way they lined up and shook the doctor's hand, a spirit of expectancy concealing their fragile lives.

Helen had anticipated the person named on the notice would meet her train, the man called David Jaspersen. She hadn't imagined him a policeman, certainly not chief of police, which was how he introduced himself, the first in an assembly line of greeters, then Reverend Benjamin Winters and Edith Winters with their daughter and a professor from the philosophy department at Meridian College, the stationmaster, a banjo player who ran the coffee shop and children from the grammar school, a reporter from the newspaper, the pharmacist, the man who owned the Exxon station and had been the only adult to contact the virus so far but was almost recovered, the widow of a soldier who had died in Vietnam, Madeleine and Henry Sailor.

"I'm the mother of Maggie," Mrs. Sailor said anxiously. "You may have seen her picture on television."

The man in the wheelchair was last but Helen had noticed him as soon as she got off the train. Noticed his extraordinary face, not entirely handsome but so dark and striking that the force of it struck her.

"I'm T. J. Wisely," he said with a small odd wave, but he seemed to be on a mission and wheeled past her, up the hill in front of the station, going quite fast.

"T.J. was one of the producers of the television series about us," David Jaspersen said, taking her duffel bag over his shoulder. "It aired three weeks ago."

"If you haven't seen it, we have a tape," Benjamin Winters said, taking Helen's medical bag and her small backpack.

Helen followed them across the street and down Main Street; even the smell was familiar, a river smell, dank, a little fishy, not entirely unpleasant. She wondered should she tell these new friends that Meridian was familiar to her, that her Aunt Martha lived in the white cottage above the Catholic church on Main Street. Perhaps when she was little Helen had even played with one of them—David Jaspersen didn't seem older than thirty, which was her age.

"I was surprised at the receiving line," she said to David, walking along beside him with Edith Winters, a pretty light-bodied woman, and her bright-eyed baby daughter.

"We wanted to make you feel welcome," Ben Winters said.

"You've made me feel very welcome," Helen said.

But the welcome was weighted with expectation.

"We've had a terrible Spring," David Jaspersen was saying.

"And a hard time persuading a physician to come here temporarily," Ben Winters said.

"We think the film might have discouraged doctors from coming," David said. "There was so much publicity."

"But the film was positive, wasn't it?" Helen asked.

"It's what has happened since the film crews left." David shifted Helen's duffel bag to the other shoulder. "One of our children is missing and now this virus."

Edith Winters stopped at the corner of Lace Street and Main. "She disappeared right here from the front of the drugstore on the tenth of May," Edith said. "Her mother was just in the store getting Advil for migraines and a hot water bottle because their second floor doesn't have heat." She took Helen by the wrist. "Did you see the poster about Maggie in the station?"

"I didn't, although I've heard about her," Helen said. "A woman I met on the train saw the notice of her disappearance on television."

"We've become celebrities," Edith Winters said.

"And now this virus," Helen said. "Tell me about it."

"The virus comes on suddenly," David Jaspersen said. "A child gets up in the morning with a slight fever. By noon she'll be burning with fever and panting for breath."

"Only one child has died," Edith Winters said. "Stephanie Burns died last week. But who knows? You'll see. Some of the children look terrible."

"We've thought of rats, although we haven't seen any in town," David said.

"Or bats," Benjamin Winters said. "I had a cousin die of a fungus from bat excrement and we do have bats."

"Stephanie's brother Kenny came down with it in the

middle of last night," Ben Winters said. "Did you know that, David?"

"I did. I talked to Mrs. Burns this morning," he said. "We have a report of fourteen children ill as of yesterday afternoon," David said. "One was brought into the clinic this morning."

"Who?" Ben Winters asked.

"Beatrice Tallis," David said.

"Who's at the clinic with her?" Helen asked, following David Jaspersen up the hill toward the brightly colored houses along the second tier of houses beyond Main Street.

"A nurse," Edith said.

"Prudential's not exactly a nurse," David Jaspersen said.

"She's as good as a nurse," Edith said. She turned to Helen. "You'll see."

The sun climbed directly overhead, lighting the tops of houses, casting a spider web of shadows on the ground in front of where they were walking.

They passed the market and the dry goods store and the volunteer fire department, a cluster of small houses directly on the street whose front doors opened to the sidewalks as houses do in Eastern European villages.

Aunt Martha's was painted blue now with a peach-colored front door. A young woman with a small child was sweeping the front porch. The woman was tall and slender with soft brown wavy hair, and what Helen saw was her own mother sweeping the front porch while Aunt Martha, in the kitchen, sliced tomatoes for sandwiches and Emma, a powder puff of yellow curls, stood on a chair in the kitchen and crayoned orange and red kittens in her coloring book.

Days, months went by and she never thought of Emma at all; seldom was there even a picture of her sister in her mind—now this lump in her throat as if she were growing a tumor.

They stopped at the end of Main Street at a small Victorian house painted purple with a white front porch and trim, a cheerful, comical house, unlikely as a medical clinic.

"When the film crews were coming, we painted all of the houses along Main Street," Ben Winters said. "We were told that color is good on television so we went all out."

"The purple was Prudential's idea," David said. "She said it was the color of redemption."

"Resurrection," Ben Winters corrected.

"Whatever," David Jaspersen said.

He opened the front door, dropping Helen's bag on a chair. The reception room was empty. It was a large room with long windows and window seats covered in lavender, striped chairs, flowers on the desk, pale peach stock and daisies drooping with age, wicker couches and rocking chairs, baskets of toys lined up against the wall, a worn oriental rug, faded blue and beige. Someplace music was playing. David checked his watch.

"Where's Prudential?" Ben Winters asked.

"I wonder," David said.

"She said she'd be here to meet us when we came," Ben said.

"I know," David said. "I talked to her at ten."

Ben led the way through the reception room, opening the door to the examining rooms.

"You have only one nurse?" Helen asked.

David nodded.

"With a possible epidemic, I'll need more than one nurse," Helen said.

"Wait until you meet Prudential," David said.

Helen followed David and Benjamin Winters down the hall, past a room with a half-closed door, another room, whose door was open—the examining table in disarray, the odor of disinfectant fog-thick in the corridor.

A tiny lavender girl lay on the examining table, her face still damp with perspiration, her pale red hair matted to her face.

"I had a terrible feeling," Benjamin Winters said.

Helen's breath caught in her throat. She went over to where the child lay, hoping to give the impression of competence although she felt as if she couldn't breathe. She examined the little girl, checking her pulse, her ears, her locked mouth, lifting her eyelids, her eyes fixed in death.

She had never worked without a staff, without other doctors or professors of medicine or laboratory technicians. The absolute aloneness of her life in Meridian struck her suddenly with a sweep by doubt.

In her short life as a physician she had seen dead children—there was the child from Archman, Michigan, who died in a fall from a horse—Helen was on emergency room duty when they brought her in and was the only one with her when she died—the farm boy from meningitis and the enchanting Chinese boy from chicken pox and Patricia on the operating table for an appendectomy when Helen was on a surgery rotation. Their small faces, whole scenes of their swift departure, stayed with Helen, rolled through her mind, kept her awake at night—but she didn't feel implicated.

Her deep pleasure as a young pediatrician had to do with the lives she had saved, the children for whom her presence had made a difference. She was considered a gifted diagnostician. She had certainly been responsible for diagnosing Reye's syndrome in Mary Harter, just in time or she would have died, and an unusual stomach cancer in Tom Bruin which probably saved his life, and peritonitis when Rebecca Slade was being treated for constipation.

But here in the sunny room of the Meridian Clinic standing beside the body of a child, no one for miles around with medical authority except the chief of police, who ought at least to have an up-to-date certificate in Emergency Medical Training, but maybe not, Helen was worried.

Behind her there was a shuffle and when she turned around a woman was standing in the doorway, her long-fingered hand on her hip.

"If you're writing up a death certificate, the time was twelve forty-eight and I was with her when she died," she said. "Her mother is on sedatives I gave her."

Prudential—she had no last name that she gave out; too

many husbands over the years, she said—was blue black, with skin that glistened waxy and a large head with a broad forehead. Not a trace of a smile.

"I'm Helen Fielding," Helen said, extending her hand.

"I know who you are," Prudential said, folding her arms across her chest, refusing Helen's extended hand. "I can't touch you. I've got death on my hands."

"So do I," Helen said, conscious of the woman's height, how much taller she was.

Prudential shrugged. "Now you're here, I'm leaving for about fifteen minutes to tend to something at home," she said. "Clinic hours don't start again until two-thirty."

"That's fine," Helen said. "I'll find my way around."

"I called the funeral parlor," Prudential said. "Mr. Rubin will be here shortly." Prudential walked with a limp but she walked fast and she was down the corridor and out the door before Helen had a chance to speak.

"I hope you won't be sorry you came here," David Jaspersen said, pulling shut the door where the child Beatrice lay.

"I won't be," Helen replied.

But following him back down the corridor to the waiting room, lightheaded, her palms cold and damp, she took small drinks of air to keep from fainting.

4.

DAVID JASPERSEN LEFT after Prudential. He said he would be back later to show Helen the house where she'd be living and that Mr. Rubin, the undertaker, would be along to collect Beatrice Tallis.

"Can't you stay?" Helen wanted to ask but he had gone.

At the main desk she skimmed the medical files in a tray beside the telephone, hoping for a call to divert her from the child in the examining room behind her chair, any call requiring her attention.

In the office was a supply closet and she checked what was available—in fact very little for a town of any size—samples of penicillin and erythromycin which she hoped might be useful for this illness but there was only enough for a day or two of sick children. She would order a pathology report on Beatrice Tallis. She telephoned a distributor in Toledo for more erythromycin in case the illness was bacterial and could be treated by an antibiotic.

Then she put in a call to her pediatric professor in Ann Arbor. The child in the examining room had almost certainly died of respiratory failure.

"Legionella," he agreed. A water-borne bacteria washed

into Meridian with a flood in early May could have brought legionella. If the illness was caught in time before the patient's respiratory system shut down, erythromycin was successful.

She called her mother but the answering machine was on with her mother's soft melodic voice. "We hope you'll leave a message after the beep." The answering machine was always on when Helen called. Not that she never talked with her mother. Alice Fielding did call, not often, but she usually returned Helen's calls, sometimes hours later, sometimes days. Helen imagined her standing at her easel in the studio off the kitchen of her New York City apartment listening to Helen's voice—"Mama, just calling to see how you are, I'm here. Call me whenever." She ought to scream, "Mama—Mama, pick up the telephone. I see you there listening to me." But she never raised her voice with her mother, afraid that Allie Fielding might disappear altogether if Helen went after her like that.

"I'm in Meridian at the clinic," she said now. "I'll call you with my new number tonight. Hugs and kisses," she added. "Wherever you are."

Prudential's telephone number was taped to the desk and Helen dialed. It rang twice and the receiver seemed to shake off the cradle but no one spoke.

"Hello," Helen said. "Prudential?"

She waited for a reply.

"Is anybody there?"

There was a shuffle at the other end and then the receiver dropped.

When the telephone finally rang in the clinic, it was

Reverend Winters saying he would be with Beatrice Tallis's family for the rest of the day. He gave Helen the telephone number, which she wrote down, wondering should she go to the Tallises' house, if that's what Ben Winters had wanted from her when he called, as if medicine in a small town required personal contact. She was more concerned by the anticipation of a relationship with the family of the dead child than with the death of the child itself, accustomed to medicine in a laboratory. She had seen parents, of course, standing in the corridor of the Ann Arbor hospital, outside their child's hospital room, and she of course had spoken to them about the condition of their child, but always protected by the limitations of a hospital setting. She was never expected at dinner or required to engage in prolonged conversation of a personal nature with the parents of a child who had died. When she thought of it now, imagining the range of responsibilities in a small town where she was the only doctor, it was as if the opening of this Pandora's box would bring a sufficient flood of tears to drown her.

Mr. Rubin the undertaker didn't come. She went to the window overlooking Main Street, with its line of shops, an ice cream store under a red-striped awning, a toy shop, a laundromat. She didn't remember these shops from her childhood —certainly not the ice cream store. Uncle Peter and Aunt Martha used to take her to a park with picnic tables and swings. Sometimes Emma went along. Not often because her mother didn't trust Aunt Martha. "Aunt Martha is awfully old to watch a two-year-old," her mother used to tell her.

"Something might happen to Emma." She was not too old to swing Helen high over the bank or spread a picnic of fried chicken and biscuits on a bright tablecloth under the willow tree. But Helen didn't remember visits to an ice cream shop. Now she opened the front door, wishing there were someone in Meridian she knew, some friend, someone she could call.

Down Main Street to the left was a small white clapboard cottage next to a playground empty of children, a jungle gym, a basketball court. No doubt the parents of Meridian were afraid to send their children out to play. Beyond, the streets were empty. Next to the white clapboard cottage was a very slender building painted barn red with black shutters and a long yellow banner hanging out the second-story window with MAGGIE written across the length of it.

As Helen watched, the man called T.J. maneuvered his wheelchair out the front door with a pile of papers on his lap. She was glad to see him, glad for company, and waved a shy half wave.

"I heard," he said, wheeling across the street.

"About the child?" Helen asked.

He nodded.

"Beatrice Tallis."

"I know," he said. "It's an awful welcome to Meridian."

"It's why I came here." She sat down on the top step to be at his level. "What do you have there?" she asked.

He handed her one of the bright yellow fliers with a picture of a small dark-haired beauty—a tiny clear picture—and underneath in simple, bold print was written:

MAGGIE SAILOR IS GONE
Contact T. J. Wisely
MAGGIE Headquarters
216-431-0011

"David may have told you," he said. "I used to be in Hollywood until I had this accident."

"He didn't say."

"I was a stunt man and fell," he said. "For the last two weeks I've been looking for Maggie full time."

His voice seemed far away, across the street, in another room. She felt lightheaded.

"You know about Maggie?"

She nodded. "I do," she said.

"Keep some fliers," T.J. said. He touched her arm. "Are you okay? You look gray."

"I must be overtired," she said, handing the flier back to him, "but it's making me faint to look at the picture of her."

"I'm sorry," T.J. said. "You're probably exhausted."

"I can't stand missing children," Helen said.

Emma's body had not been found.

"It makes a difference to see a body," Helen's father had said years later, after the divorce. "To know."

"But you do know," Helen said.

"We assume," her father had said, but he wouldn't continue the conversation and her mother didn't speak of Emma at all.

What they did know was that, on a Saturday in late

June, Helen and Emma had wandered away from the picnic tables in the park, across the field, to the woods along the river Meryn. Helen remembered standing on the bank, throwing pebbles into the river. She remembered Emma sitting on a large root, playing with a stick, her yellow curls wrapped in ribbons.

And then she was gone.

"Gone," Helen said to her mother, running back to the picnic grounds.

"Gone?" her mother said. "Just gone, like that? She can't be."

But she was.

"Try to remember, Helen," her mother said later as the fire department dragged the river, put out alerts in the adjoining towns. "First Emma was there sitting beside you and then she was gone?"

Helen nodded.

"What happened from the last moment you saw her to the moment you realized she was gone?" her father asked.

"I don't remember," Helen said. "I looked down and she was gone."

"T.J. is a peculiar man," Prudential said, her arms folded across her chest, watching Helen pack her medical bag with thermometers and alcohol and cotton and disposable hypodermics and bottles of erythromycin. "Not everybody's cup of tea."

"I like him," Helen said, and it was more than just an attraction, although certainly it was that. "I'm not sure why."

"If anybody can find Maggie Sailor, T.J. will be the one to do it." She shrugged. "It's in his blood."

Prudential checked through the files and pulled the ones for the children they would be visiting.

"So we're doing house calls. Dr. Hazelton never did house calls," Prudential said. "Even when Ben Winters's father had a heart attack, Dr. Hazelton made him come into the office and he died here." She made the list: "Maria Walker, Laura O'Connor, Sallie Durham, Brian Bliss."

"Just four?"

"That'll take two hours," Prudential said.

Helen put a note on the front door that said WILL RE-TURN AT 5 P.M.

"I called you at home," she said to Prudential.

"I wasn't at home," she said.

She closed the door to the office and walked with Helen down the path to the street.

"Someone picked up the phone," Helen said casually, following Prudential away from the center of town.

"Someone did?"

"Maybe a child?" Helen said. "The receiver fell and then the line stayed open."

"I don't have a child," Prudential said. "I'm sixty-five years old."

They went first to Maria Walker's house, a small yellow house next to the Roman Catholic church with a gym set in the front yard and a small boy sitting on the stump of a tree covered with dry ivy, eying them suspiciously.

"Mama's afraid Maria's going to die," the boy said to Prudential.

"Well, she's not," Prudential said. "Dr. Fielding's come with medicine."

The boy, a small-boned, thin boy about four, squinted his eyes and looked up at Helen. "Does it taste terrible?"

"I haven't tasted it," Helen said, "but it's a very good medicine however it tastes."

"Maria will throw up if it doesn't taste good," the boy said.

Maria was a small fragile child, thin like her brother, but she seemed less ill than frightened. Helen sat on the side of the bed and took her pulse, looking down her throat, and at the size of her pupils, her ears, listening to her chest. Her heart was normal, her lungs clear. She left the medication with instructions not to sleep lying down and to drink clear liquids.

"I hear Bea died today," Mrs. Walker said to Prudential as they prepared to leave.

"At twelve forty-eight," Prudential said.

"Before you came?" Mrs. Walker asked Helen coolly.

"She was dead when I arrived. I would've been too late in any case," Helen added, distressed that she felt it necessary to defend herself. "The medication is only successful if you start it before the bacteria attack the respiratory system."

"Did you get Maria in time?" Mrs. Walker asked crisply.

"I'm sure we did," Helen said, shaking Mrs. Walker's hand, following Prudential to the front door. At the door, Mrs. Walker asked Prudential about Sophie.

"Have you heard from her?" Mrs. Walker asked.

Prudential shrugged. "Nothing."

"Nothing?"

Prudential shook her head.

"That's odd, isn't it?"

"I don't know what's odd," Prudential said, walking down the front steps with Helen.

"Did Maria throw up?" the boy, still sitting on the tree stump, asked.

"Not yet," Helen said cheerfully.

The O'Connors, sitting close together next to their daughter's bed, seemed not much older than Laura, who was eleven.

"I didn't go to work today," Mr. O'Connor said, leaning against his wife. "I couldn't."

"He works at the library," Mrs. O'Connor said. "He's the janitor."

"Also at the public grammar school," Mr. O'Connor said. He stood up to let Helen use the chair beside his daughter and she knelt on it, leaning over the fevered girl. "Perhaps we could use cold towels," she said to Prudential. She took out a hypodermic. "This is going to be a little pinprick," she said, "but it will make you feel better by dinnertime."

Mrs. O'Connor was crying when Helen turned around.

"I can't help it," she said, wringing her skirt in her hands.

Helen took out a bottle of erythromycin. "We think this illness is a bacterial infection called legionella but we don't have the confirmed reports yet from the lab. If it is, this will work." She measured out a teaspoon. "Two teaspoons four times a day starting now and going through the night, waking her up every four hours," she said. "Clear liquids, at least one glass every hour." She wiped Laura O'Connor's head and arms and hands with the wet terry cloth towel. "I'm telling everyone to boil their water before you use it. I'll be back tomorrow," she said, laying her hand against the girl's face.

"Thank you, Doctor," Mrs. O'Connor said as Helen left. "We almost died of worry today after we heard about Bea."

"You must be exhausted, Prudential," Mr. O'Connor said. "Up day and night, I hear from David."

"I don't tire easy," Prudential said matter-of-factly, smoothing her cotton uniform with a long-fingered hand dark with age.

"Have you heard from Sophie?" Mrs. O'Connor asked.

"No," Prudential said, opening the front door.

"Nor have I," Mrs. O'Connor said, "and I expected to."

"You never know." Prudential called good-bye to Laura.

"Who is Sophie?" Helen asked as they made their way up the long steep path to the house where Sallie Durham lived at the end of Tea Lane, a dead-end street of old tiny houses, doll-houses.

"She's a woman from this town who left," Prudential said, knocking on the front door of the Durhams' house.

A pretty woman with a lovely open smile answered the door. "You've come for Sallie? It's so nice of you to come." She kissed Prudential on the cheek. "Sallie's better, I think. I'm Ann," she said to Helen, leading her through the brightly decorated narrow house, painted crazily with pinks and yellows, black polka-dotted walls, sunflowers painted alongside the fireplace.

"I'm glad to see you, Pru," Ann Durham said. "I've been wondering how you're doing."

"Same as always," Prudential said. "Same as you."

"And Sophie?"

"Sophie's not in touch."

Helen followed Ann Durham into the bedroom where Sallie sat silent, her eyes unfocused, propped up with pillows, surrounded by stuffed animals as large as she was.

"I don't like doctors," she said, putting a large stuffed rabbit in front of her face.

"You love Prudential, Sal," Ann Durham said.

Sallie shook her head.

Helen leaned over and took the child's pulse, her temperature, listened to her heart.

"I think you're getting better," she said.

Sallie looked at her directly. "I don't like doctors."

"Sallie was premature," Ann Durham said, reaching over to pick Sallie up, but Prudential was already taking her on her lap. "She's seen too many doctors."

"So listen to me, Sallie Durham," Prudential murmured in the child's ear, rocking her back and forth until she relaxed and let Helen look down her throat, listen to her chest.

"She's still got fever," Helen said, "and some fluid in her chest." She gave Ann Durham the medicine with instructions. "I'll be back early tomorrow to check in," she said, "or call me if there's any problem."

———————

By the time they had finished at Brian Bliss's apartment located above the five-and-ten-cent store on Main Street, Helen was too weary to think clearly but, walking with Prudential in the early dusk, she had a peculiar feeling as if she were a part of a story in which she didn't understand her role. She wanted Prudential to talk to her. She wanted a confidant, a friend. She liked this woman Prudential, liked the size and strength and hard resistance of her. But it was clear that for whatever reason, and there did seem to be one, she wasn't going to talk.

5.

WHEN DAVID JASPERSEN ARRIVED at the yellow clapboard house on the road just above the clinic, Helen was asleep sitting on the couch, her feet resting on her luggage, her head dipping toward her chest, a mass of long hair falling out of the hairpins she had stuck in a circle around the bun she wore. The noise he made opening the front door woke her, alarmed her even, and she didn't move, disoriented at first by the unfamiliar place and then by the strangeness of the man standing across the room from her.

"Did I wake you?" he asked.

She brushed her hair out of her eyes.

"Do you remember me?" He laughed.

"I think so." But it took a moment before she did remember where she was: Meridian, Ohio, here as a physician, and this man standing in her living room was the chief of police out of uniform.

"You changed clothes," she said.

"I'm off duty." He sat down on a large overstuffed chair across from her. "It's almost nine."

"At night?" She looked outside at the silver dusk of May. "Oh, brother."

"People have called. The O'Connors, I think, and Edith Winters, the minister's wife, came by to take you to dinner."

"I didn't hear anything," she said.

"They knocked, they said, but you must have been sound asleep," he said. "I'm sorry I'm late."

She stood up, pushing her bags out of the way. Her legs were stiff, weak-kneed, the blood running too thick. "I'm hungry. I feel as if I'll die if I don't eat something."

"I brought something for dinner," he said. "Pasta and some wine. I'll cook."

He'd left the grocery bag on the front step and she followed him while he retrieved it, followed him to the kitchen, which was small and painted a soft peach color with white cabinets and a square farm table in the corner of the room, a vase of yellow freesias in the middle.

"Is this the place where the other doctor lived?" she asked, sitting on one of the ladder-back chairs.

"It is," David said. "He lived here alone with his cat, who is probably someplace in the fields out back. I feed him."

"This doesn't seem like the kind of place for a man to live alone," she said. "It's more like a woman's place."

"Richard Hazelton has an eye for pretty things."

"Did you bring the flowers?" she asked, playing with the petals of the freesias beside her.

"Edith did," he said, filling a pot with water, turning on the stove.

"Wine?"

She nodded.

He poured her a glass of white wine and put it on the table.

"Why did the other doctor leave?" she asked.

"We don't know," David said, taking a jar of marinara sauce out of the bag, a loaf of French bread. "One day he was simply gone with a note that said he had suddenly been called out of town. Then he wrote to say that he wouldn't be returning for some time."

"You all are full of secrets here, aren't you?" Helen said, folding her legs under her, resting her chin in her hand.

"Not really," David said, tasting the marinara sauce bubbling on the top of the stove. "Until Maggie Sailor disappeared, nothing happened here."

"Except you had a television film made about you."

"That certainly happened," David said, taking a saucepan for the pasta, washing the lettuce. "I have the cassette in case you didn't see the film when it aired two weeks ago."

At dinner, across the farm table from David, Helen brought up Sophie.

"Sophie?" David asked, pouring himself a second glass of wine.

"When I was making house calls today, every family asked Prudential about Sophie."

"And what did Prudential say?"

"She said she hadn't heard from Sophie." Helen took seconds on pasta and finished the marinara sauce. "Who is she?"

"Sophie DeLaurentis," David said. "Pru didn't tell you?"

Helen shook her head. "Prudential has nothing to say about anything."

David laughed, getting up to take the French bread out of the oven. "She is close to the vest," he said.

"Actually," Helen said, "she did say something. She said that Sophie had left town."

"That's correct."

"You have a lot of trouble with people suddenly leaving town, don't you?"

David shook his head, a look of bemusement on his face, a sweet look, not confrontational, but he wasn't going to talk about Sophie either except to say that it wasn't so odd Sophie leaving town, she was a fly-by-night woman with little staying power.

There was a meow and David opened the door to a large sleek black and white cat with a bow tie on his mouth and a white tail. "This is Gregory," he said.

The cat walked across the room, his tail perpendicular, swatting at the air. He stopped at Helen and hopped into her lap.

"I hope you like cats."

She shrugged.

"He comes with the house," David said.

After dinner David showed her the house. "Edith cleaned yesterday," he said. "Dr. Hazelton left absolutely nothing except cat food. Even the refrigerator was empty, although he was so thin we used to joke that he lived on antibiotics." This seemed to amuse him. He opened the closet doors. "I see she got you hangers," he said.

The bathroom cupboard had two sets of kelly-green towels with the price tags still on, freesias in the bathroom too; the bedroom was large, almost the full size of the house, with an old painted wooden desk in the window, a double four-poster bed with a blue plaid quilt and starched white pillows up against the headboard, a hanging basket of lavender geraniums in the south window. In the corner of the room was a rocking horse, not a very old one, although the paint was chipped, especially on the bright red saddle, and an old-fashioned doll with a china face dressed in an organdy pinafore, her pink plaster feet unshod, sat on the floor under a window. "I don't know where the doll came from. Not Dr. Hazelton," he said. "Maybe one of Edith's whimsies." He turned on the hall light and she followed him downstairs. "So there you are."

"It's very nice," she said but she was thinking that in Ann Arbor, when the job for a visiting physician was first advertised, there was mention of a three-bedroom house and this house was tiny, with only a living room and kitchen and bedroom above them both. She didn't want to complain, in fact was very pleased to be in this small house with the added company of a black and white cat, but she did wonder, without mentioning it to David Jaspersen, why they should say a three-bedroom house when the house had only one. Did they think it would be so difficult to find a visiting physician without the offer of a large house?

"This street doesn't have a name," David was saying, "but it dead-ends on the top of the hill and you are the second house from Main Street, then, going up, is the pharmacist's house and then the older brother of Mr. Rubin and then T. J. Wisely's house, although why he wants to go up and down that hill in a wheelchair I don't know." He sat back down in the living room. "You know which one T.J. is?"

"I do," Helen said.

"Women find him handsome."

"He came by the clinic today."

"Looking for Prudential?" he asked. "They're very close. She practically raised him." He told Helen about T.J.'s arrival in Meridian, about Prudential, how she had come, maybe in her fifties, from Washington, D.C., where she had been working in a good government job, perhaps on the staff of a senator, he thought, but she had gone to Harrisville, Ohio, with a schoolteacher whom she called her husband but he wasn't, and when he died Prudential moved to Meridian and took a house and a job in the clinic as a nurse, keeping her counsel about her life and business.

"If you'd like to see the film," he said, "Ben Winters brought over that television and a VCR."

"I'd like to see it later," Helen said, sinking into the couch.

"I know you're exhausted."

"You don't have to leave though," she said, feeling a sudden melancholy, wanting him to stay for a while, maybe spend the night—he could sleep on top of the blue and white quilt in the bedroom and then he would be there in the event of an emergency, and though of course she didn't mention to him what she was thinking, it seemed to her a reasonable request. Which was the way her romances often began, quickly with a safe stranger, a fellow student, a physician, a person with whom she had no history, whose own personal history was reliable. She wasn't a woman who gave the impression of need but she knew she was starved for a kind of animal comfort, a physical proximity exempt from matters of the heart. She didn't want to spend a night alone in Dr. Hazelton's pristine and impersonal house. "Would you like to spend the night?" she could say. "I'm accustomed to someone spending the night. I have a small fear of being alone," she could tell him, "especially now, back in Meridian, this place to which I haven't returned since Emma died. Which means that the last time I walked these streets and smelled this peculiar river smell she was alive."

"I have a son," he said.

"I didn't know that you were married," she said.

"I'm not any longer," he said. "But I have a son."

She took the pins out of her hair so it fell to her shoulders, slipped on her shoes. "I suppose you ought to leave then since you have responsibilities," she said. "It's awfully late."

"I do need to leave," he said, showing her where the telephone was, writing down his home number and the number of the Winters house. "If anything comes up, call me. I live only half a mile away."

She walked with him to the door feeling a kind of yearning from childhood, wishing her mother with her, in the room forever.

"In the last three weeks since the film aired people come here as tourists just to see the things they saw on television, although I can't imagine why," he said. His arm against the door, he brushed her hair off her forehead. "In the future, you'll be able to say that you were a doctor in a famous town."

She wanted to tell him she'd been in Meridian as a child but something kept her from saying it, as if her childhood here, of which, until her last visit, she had nothing but sweet memories, might be exposed as something else.

She leaned against the wall, thinking of a way to detain him. "When I was small, I used to be out of the blue lonely; my mother told me that happens with only children."

"I'm an only child too, an only child of elderly parents now dead," David said, confidentially as if there were something not only in common, but exchanged between them, a bartered piece of heart.

"My parents are alive," Helen said, "but we're estranged." She wanted to tell him about Emma, who was crowding her mind.

"I know about estrangement," David said and the remark, the way he said it, was provocative, somehow even romantic.

It was odd, Helen thought later, how small paragraphs of personal stories took on a momentum, propelled a person forward into a territory without parameters.

The first tenet of medicine is "Do no harm." *Do no harm*, Dr. Covington had said in the initial meeting of Human Biology in her first year of medical school. "You must remember that whenever you are dealing with a human life: 'Do no harm.'"

But how was it possible to avoid harm if her own nerve center was in cold storage? Helen had asked herself, slipping out of one relationship into a new one without a change of step. She didn't want another love affair to call to her attention that at some part of herself, some central part essential to living, she couldn't be stirred.

———————

She didn't sleep well in Dr. Hazelton's high pencil-post double bed. She fell in and out of consciousness, turning back and forth, unable to settle. But she was asleep when the phone rang beside her bed and she knocked it off the cradle trying to answer.

"Prudential?" a man's voice said.

"This isn't Prudential," Helen answered.

"What number is this then?" he asked crossly.

"I'm not sure," she said, turning on the light. "This is Helen Fielding," she said. "I've just moved here."

"I'm sorry," the man said. "I must have dialed the wrong number."

Afterward, Helen couldn't sleep. She turned on the light and got up, checking the list of numbers the chief of police had given her, checking the number on her telephone. 693-0468. She dialed her mother in New York City and hung up before it rang.

The bedroom was cold and damp. She took a sweater out of her bag, climbed back in bed, opened *Anna Karenina* and she must have fallen asleep then. When she woke up, it was dawn, she was still sitting with the light on beside her bed and someone was banging at the front door.

6.

SALLIE DURHAM STRUGGLED for breath. Her tiny face was blue, her eyes rabbit wide in terror and she was dying.

"She's dying, isn't she?" Ann Durham hung on the back of Helen, pulled at the neck of her sweater.

"Leave the doctor alone, Ann," Sam Durham said evenly. "Please, Annie, leave her be."

"She's going, I can see it," Ann Durham said. "Tell me she isn't."

"Hush, Annie," Sam Durham said.

"Promise me she won't."

Someone took Ann Durham away, perhaps Sam Durham, perhaps someone else because the Durham house was full of people when Helen arrived just before seven in the morning. "They all came out of their houses with Annie's screaming," Sam Durham had said, rushing ahead, bringing Helen through the house to the back room, too damp and cold for a sick child to be lying in.

"Would someone call Prudential?" Helen asked.

"Prudential," one man said. "You go get her."

"Doesn't she have a phone?"

"I'll call," someone said.

"I'll call," another said.

And in the background, maybe the next room, Annie Durham was crying.

Helen was left alone with the child, losing consciousness, lying in a circle of dampness on her pale blue crib sheet, the morning light through a dirt-streaked window dappled like measles across her face.

She felt the child's throat, just below the Adam's apple, took the small scalpel from her medical bag and in a swift movement made a small incision and inserted a tube, connecting the tube to oxygen.

"Prudential's not there," she heard someone say.

And then, probably Sam Durham behind her, "Prudential doesn't answer her phone."

No one could say why so many people had gathered early in the morning at the Durhams' house, crowding into the living room, the dining room filling up with food on the long table, coffeecakes and doughnuts, toast and jam and Danish, thick, sweet comforting pastries brought in by neighbors who came, some just out of bed, their hair uncombed. The street outside was lined with people, brimming with conversation, carrying coffee in Styrofoam cups from Aunt Amy's coffee house—not a gladiator crowd, the kind at the scene of accidents, pulling at the ropes of human consciousness. But not necessarily a generous crowd either. There was an uneasy feeling of accumulated terror in the air—the last straw for a town unacquainted with collective trouble, selected by the god of bad news to be at the eye of the storm.

"Would you like a cup of coffee?" Sam Durham asked Helen but she shook her head.

"Not yet," she said.

He seemed a nice man and she liked the desperate way he tried to save his daughter by good behavior, maintaining a steady calm, asking after Helen's needs, apologizing for his wife's remarks.

"She's lost her head, I'm afraid," Mr. Durham said. "She doesn't mean what she says."

"Don't worry," Helen said.

Prudential didn't arrive and David Jaspersen had left for Harrisville, where a truck had overturned on a small car.

"Does anyone here have Emergency Medical Training in case I need help?" Helen asked Sam Durham, who came back with the information that three of the people waiting for news were members of the volunteer ambulance service.

After the IV was in, Helen moved the child's bed away from the window, washed her face, her plump hands, brushed the damp yellow curls plastered to her forehead, and waited, standing over the crib, her arms folded across her chest, watching.

"I wonder where Prudential might be," she asked the next time Sam Durham came in.

"Someone says she's at T. J. Wisely's," he said. "Something happened to T.J. in the middle of the night but he doesn't answer his phone, so no one knows. Sometimes he falls."

"It's almost eight o'clock," Helen said. "She ought to be at work soon."

"Prudential lives by her own clock," Sam Durham said, moving a little closer to the crib. "What do you think?"

"I don't know yet."

"Can Ann come in now?"

Helen shook her head.

"She's too upset," she said. "We have to wait to see how things go. Sallie looks a little better."

The child's eyes were open, her pupils dilated, her eyes fixed on Helen. She was a particularly small and delicate child, perfectly proportioned with a broad forehead and large oval-shaped black eyes, like the eyes on the plump-bellied cupids with tiny wings floating across late Renaissance paintings.

Helen reached over and touched her hair, dry now with a life of its own, yellow curls springing to attention even as her body threatened to shut down.

Days after Emma died or maybe it was months later—time had a way of scattering—Helen had an intact memory of an afternoon lunch at her grandmother's in Michigan with lemon meringue pie and the faint smell of honeysuckle in the air.

"I've got work to do for my graduate classes this afternoon," her father was saying to her mother. "I think I'll go to the library."

"And I should pack to go back to Ann Arbor tomorrow morning," her mother said.

"What about you, Helen?" her grandmother asked. "I ought to know a little girl to invite over to play. Maybe the Summers' child."

"I don't want to play with a little girl," Helen said, and

this she remembered clearly because she wasn't a child given to taking emotional risks. "I only want to play with Emma."

The weight of the afternoon dropped on her shoulders. The pale lemon pie left barely touched on her plate grew to enormous proportions, the bodies of the grownups spread across the table in a tidal wave, smothering her until she couldn't breathe.

"Excuse me," her father said and left.

Her mother folded her napkin and stood up.

"Excuse me," her grandmother said, pushing back her chair.

And Helen was left with the sound of her own voice speaking her sister's name.

"Prudential's here," Sam Durham said from the doorway.

Helen turned around.

Prudential was dressed in her nurse's uniform, a white cap perched cockily on her head and a MERIDIAN HIGH SCHOOL sweatshirt tied around her narrow waist. She carried an umbrella although there was no evidence of rain.

"You need me here?" Prudential asked. She walked over to the bed and looked down at Sallie Durham. "Uh-huh," she made a sound in her throat.

"I need you to go to the clinic," Helen said. "I'm staying here for a while."

She walked with Prudential to the door.

"What are all of these people doing here?" Helen asked, looking beyond the front door of the Durhams' house.

Prudential shook her head.

"I don't know," she said.

"I feel as if I'm being scrutinized." Helen folded her arms across her chest.

"You could be," Prudential said without sympathy. "People might be hanging around to see if you're going to bring a miracle or not."

She was a handsome woman with unlined dark skin and eyes too black to see the pupils, a distinguished face, large for the fineness of her long willowy body.

"Is Sallie Durham going to live?" she asked.

"I don't know," Helen said. "I just can't say for sure."

"I'll call from the clinic if there's an emergency," Prudential said.

"Do you have the number?"

"I know every number in Meridian," Prudential said.

"Well, someone in Meridian doesn't know yours because he called in the middle of last night asking to speak with you."

"He found me," Prudential said, swinging her umbrella around like a cane, nodding hello to people as she walked through the small crowd.

Sam Durham pulled a straight-back chair over and sat with Helen in the room, crossing his long legs, resting his elbows on the bed. "You're worried about Sallie?" He was tentative. "Is that why you're staying here so long?"

"I'm less worried than I was," she said.

"I sent Annie over to her mother's for a couple of hours," he said. "Her nerves are bad."

They sat side by side, the morning sun through the window warming their backs, his presence so comfortable that Helen began to wonder had she known him, had he been one of the little boys who spun around on a two-wheeler in front of Aunt Martha's house when she was young or went with her and her father to the drugstore for a double-dip chocolate soda at the counter on thick summer afternoons.

This past year living with Oliver, she had been lonely, struck by the oddness of such isolation in his company. Sometimes she sat up in bed after a particularly long day on the pediatric floor, looking at the pictures in her home magazines, feeling abandoned. She would touch Oliver's sculpted hand to see if it was real. He seemed an unwieldy mannikin in the bed beside her and, though he was a man of British reserve with a surgeon's absence of communication, he was not without force in her life and the loneliness surprised her.

Oliver had a fondness for games and puzzles, jigsaw puzzles in particular, and he kept a large one of fish at one end of the dining-room table, bass and trout, bluefish and scrod, doing a bit of it each night before he went to bed and, when it was completed, undoing it and starting over. For his birthday this past year she had sent a picture of herself to a company she found in the back of *Country Living* which made large jigsaw puzzles from photographs. During the spring, the fish on the dining-room table were replaced by jigsaw bits of Helen Fielding, the corner of a blue eye, shape after shape of brown hair, bits of flesh. Sometimes she worried that she was losing her mind as she watched Oliver sitting at a straight-back chair at the end of the dining-room table, his fine-boned hand moving a piece of jigsaw around the half-shaped reproduction of her face.

"Did you grow up here?" she asked Sam Durham.

"I did," he said. "I left for college but when my father died I came home and took his job." He reached over and touched his daughter's hand.

"Did you ever know Martha Fowler?"

"She was my aunt," he said.

"She was your aunt?" Helen asked, a lump gathering in her throat.

He nodded. "My aunt by marriage," he said. "You knew her?"

"I did," she said. "I knew her when I was little."

"So you've been here before?" he asked.

She didn't reply, turning her attention to the child.

She checked Sallie's pulse, her chest, her temperature. Her temperature had broken. Her breathing was less labored. She didn't want to pursue this conversation with Sam Durham. She wasn't sure why she had decided to keep her relationship to Meridian secret, but instinctively she had, as if to tell put her at risk.

"You know Sallie is in the film," Sam Durham said. "Have you seen it?"

"I haven't," she said. "I've heard about it, of course."

"They have a lot of shots of Sallie. The director liked her," he said. "Her and Molly. They were his favorites."

"Molly?" Helen asked, flattening the thin yellow blanket

over Sallie, checking the IV. She looked up. "I haven't met Molly."

Mr. Durham's face darkened. "Of course," he said. "You wouldn't have met her." There was something peculiar in the way he said it, as if he had surprised himself bringing up her name.

"Who is Molly?" Helen asked Prudential when she arrived back at the clinic just after noon, Sallie Durham out of immediate danger, the crowd in front of the Durhams' house dispersed with the demands of the day.

"Molly?" Prudential looked up from the desk where she was writing on a chart. "I don't know about Molly," she said, taking her cap off, scratching the top of her head with a pencil. "You had a call from the O'Connors," she said. "The medicine is working."

III.

HEART
SCAN

The Story of

MERIDIAN

PETER FORESTER HAD THE REPUTATION of a gifted film director with an eye for the small detail which in its particular describes the whole—like the stopped clock or the crop of hair that fell beneath David Jaspersen's police cap, giving his strong-featured face a vulnerability, or Sophie DeLaurentis's eyes, not large but round, almost perfectly round. The camera caught her straight on looking exactly at the viewer, canceling the landscape. He filmed her in the small garden behind her house, brushing away the debris of winter, exposing the tiny shoots of daffodils, on the front steps with Molly—a frame in which Molly picked up her mother's hand and kissed the fingers—at the playground and the market, buying round pink plush curlers at the pharmacy. Somehow the sight of her soft face checking the selection of hair curlers had a surprising innocence. There was a frame of Sophie and Molly sharing a milkshake at the counter of the ice cream store with Ann and Sallie Durham when David Jaspersen came in with the news that Mona Dickenson had died of liver cancer, earlier than had been expected, giving the film crew an opportunity to make a record of grief.

"It makes a difference that the woman was young," Peter Forester said to T.J. later.

"What do you mean?" T.J. asked.

"She was young and a woman," Peter said. "Heartbreak combination."

"Mona sold tickets at the movies when I was in junior high," T.J. said. "She had the longest legs I've ever seen on a girl. I used to watch the movie imagining her with me."

"Listen, T.J.," Peter said. "To shoot a film in your hometown was your idea; there's no room for sentimentality. Pay attention to the goal and forget the particulars."

The method Peter Forester selected was documentary, filming the town day to day with a kind of randomness, up and down the streets, in the shops, the clinic where Prudential was, at the schools and the churches, inside the houses, along the river. Peter had favorites, not like Sophie but favorites all the same, and there was more footage of David Jaspersen and Prudential and Ann Durham and Mrs. Gunn, whose husband had drowned in one of the floods. Molly DeLaurentis was a favorite and Sallie Durham and Marcie Bliss, who had been born with a clubfoot, and Marcie's Uncle Trip, who had played first base with the Cincinnati Reds until he got Lou Gehrig's disease and lived with the Blisses, writing baseball stories for the Harrisville paper.

"I want to begin with the river," Peter told T.J. and the film crew the morning of the second day, sitting in the front booth of Shirley's Cafe. "Starting north of town where the river is narrow, moving right up as the water widens south to the railroad station."

"Maybe we should have waited a couple of weeks to see if we have a flood this year," T.J. said. "It's the floods that bring this town together."

Peter shook his head. "We can have the illusion of floods," he said. "Television has too much high drama. We're after the genuine in 'Meridian.' "

T.J. was in David Jaspersen's office when David came back with his lunch from Shirley's.

"You aren't who I was hoping to see," David said, checking the list of phone calls which had come in.

"I've come with an emergency." T.J. opened the desk drawer. "No cigarettes?"

"No cigarettes."

He took out a pack of matches and two quarters. "For a Coke," he said.

"What is the emergency?" David asked.

"Sophie is taking this seriously," T.J. said. "She thinks she's a movie star."

"She is," David said. "She's got a camera following her around all day and that handsome small-scale giraffe Forester you've imported from the city of our dreams hanging on her words as if they counted for something near gospel importance. What do you expect?"

"I want you to talk to Peter Forester, David," T.J. said. "I want you to tell him that Sophie isn't really from Meridian and that to have so much of her puss on the screen contradicts the whole point of the film. Right?" he asked nervously. "Don't you think so?"

"I'm not thinking about this film," David said. "It's happening and my job is to keep the town in order."

"Christ, David," T.J. said. "You know what I'm talking about. I'm going a little crazy," he said.

David shrugged.

"It's like we're one of those towns zapped by radiation and we poor dopes haven't got a clue that the camera is shooting invisible poisons."

"If you're so worried about Sophie, tell her. Tell her to clip the wings of her new-found acting career and pay attention to what's valuable in life," David said. "I'm sure she'll be grateful for your help."

"Is that the full extent of your advice?"

"It is," David said. "You know Mona Dickenson died this morning?"

"I heard," T.J. said. "Peter Forester wants to film the funeral."

David shook his head in disbelief. "Film the funeral?"

"He's grateful for the chance to shoot a real-life tragedy."

David sat down at the desk and picked up the telephone. "I have about ten calls to make, T.J. I have to go to the Dickensons' house and to the clinic because a pipe burst in the bathroom and to the grammar school for a meeting with Win's teacher and to court in Harrisville on a robbery at three, all the time keeping my hair combed so I'll look good in your movie." He took the receiver off the cradle and dialed. "I can't worry about Sophie DeLaurentis today."

T.J. flung his head back against the wall, put his hand splayed across his face and when he spoke his voice had a mannered and unnatural quality as if he were imitating the voice of a woman.

"I believe in this film, David. I love Meridian but something in the way Peter Forester is going about it is making me insane."

When T.J. was young, after he lived with the Jaspersens and had moved on to the Wades and the Dickensons and then the Flowers, before Prudential came to town and took him in, he followed David Jaspersen everywhere. He copied the way he dressed, in heavy boots and jeans belted at the waist and wool plaid shirts tucked in, the way he walked, one shoulder lower than the other, a swagger to his hips, his hair kept washed and cut, unlike the hair of the other boys in high school in Meridian.

But after David's parents died, one after the other, of cancer in his junior year of high school, David took after T.J. in a mean way. "Leave me alone," he said. "I don't want to be bothered by you. Drop off the earth."

And he felt bad about that, especially since T. J. Wisely was the only young person in Meridian who knew what it was like to be without parents, first in line for trouble. And so through the years they had developed a closeness as if they knew things other people did not know.

When T.J. headed up Main to join the crew after lunch, Sophie was sitting at the lunch counter of Shirley's, Molly on her lap and Peter Forester right beside her, his thin hip against her flesh, laying claim.

T.J. pushed open the door and wheeled inside.

"Sophie?"

"Hiya, T.J.," Sophie said, turning Molly to face T.J. "Say hi to T.J., Molly."

"Hiya," Molly said.

Shirley's was crowded with citizens hoping for bit parts in "The Story of Meridian," walk-ons, crowd shots. There was a spirit of conviviality. Peter's assistant Marina was sitting next to him smoking a long European cigarette and Pleeper Jones was behind the camera set up in the rear of the diner next to the rest room.

"Sophie," T.J. called. "C'n I speak to you a minute?"

"I'm shooting her, T.J.," Peter called. "Give me a second to set up."

Molly hopped down from her mother's lap and wandered over to T.J., swinging her small arms. She was a classic eighteenth-century child whose wide-browed face and gray eyes had an enchanting solemnity. This afternoon she had been dressed by Sophie for the occasion in an organdy pinafore over a yellow smocked dress which, because of its starchiness, she didn't like to wear and squirmed, pulling at the shoulders.

"Hi, T.J.," she said, standing in front of him, her hand on the arm of his wheelchair.

"Climb up," T.J. said.

She scrambled onto his lap and sat with her plump legs out straight in front of her.

"I want to see your eye," she said earnestly, reaching toward the black eye patch covering his left eye.

"You see my eye," he said. "It's green with yellow flecks."

"I want to see the other eye hiding."

"That eye?" he asked softly. "Are you sure?"

She nodded, folding her hands in her lap.

T.J. reached up to the black patch and lifted it, exposing an empty socket with a thin transparent lid closed over the small space.

Molly caught her breath.

"See?" he said. "No eye."

She raised her hands and covered her eyes.

"I didn't think you'd like it," T.J. said.

She bent her head so she could only see the white organdy pinafore between the spaces her fingers made.

"Molly?"

She didn't reply.

"Look, Molly, I've put the patch back."

But she didn't look up.

"It's okay, Molly." He touched her hair. "The eye hole is gone."

But as he reached under her arms to lift her off his lap she screamed, a long thin ribbon of sound.

When Molly started screaming, Dr. Richard Hazelton, between patients at the clinic, had just come into the rear of Shirley's for lunch. He made his way behind Pleeper Jones and his camera toward the front of the diner, a tall, visibly restrained young man, pale-skinned with soft straight blond hair, thin, too thin, almost unwell-seeming except that he moved with an athletic grace.

"What is going on?" he asked Pleeper.

"Beats me," Pleeper said. "T.J. seems to have created a scene."

"T.J.," Dr. Hazelton said, breaking through the crowd, "what's going on?"

Sophie had already picked up Molly, who wrapped her arms around her mother's neck and hid her face in Sophie's shoulder.

"She wanted to see my eye," T.J. said.

"Poor T.J.," Sophie said to Molly. "He got his eye poked out when he had a terrible fall."

Molly shook her head back and forth, her eyes covered with her plump hands, inconsolable.

"She asked to see what was under T.J.'s eye patch," Sophie said to Richard Hazelton.

"She begged," T.J. said with irritation. "She insisted. So I showed her."

"Don't worry, T.J.," Sophie said. "Children are weird."

"It's nothing so awful to look at," T.J. said. "Just different."

"It's no wonder she's upset with all these television people unsettling our lives," Dr. Hazelton said, stroking her hair.

"I'm sorry, Richard," T.J. said. "I'm sorry about the TV."

"Things have a way of getting out of hand," Dr. Hazelton said.

"But I love the television show," Sophie said. "It's the best thing that's happened since I came to Meridian."

Molly had stopped crying. She tightened her arms around her mother's neck and opened her eyes, looking at T.J.

"I want to talk to you about the television show, Sophie," T.J. said.

"Please, T.J.," Sophie said, laying her hand on his cheek. "I'm having such a nice time, I don't want it to stop."

"Someone will pay for this showing off," Dr. Hazelton said quietly and to no one in particular.

"Hello, T.J.," Molly said tentatively. And then she put one small hand over her own eye, covering it. "My eye is hiding too," she said.

7.

MADELEINE SAILOR CAME into the clinic just before three and sat in a straight-back chair by the front door, a beige cardigan pulled across her shoulders although the afternoon was warm for May.

"Have you come to see the doctor, Madeleine?" Prudential asked. "Do you want to sign in?"

Madeleine shook her head.

"I'll wait," she said.

The clinic was crowded, mostly children sitting at the table in the center of the room with games and books and Fisher Price figures, or leaning against their mothers' arms, their eyes half closed or across their mothers' laps. Brian Bliss was there with his grandfather, holding a matchbox car in his tight fist, and Maria Walker sat with her brother on a small couch, pushing him every time his arm or leg crossed the divide between them.

"I'll wait until everyone has seen her," Madeleine said to Prudential. "I'm not sick."

"She's sick whether she knows it or not," Prudential said to Helen, late in the afternoon after hours of sick children and strep tests and blood tests and thermometers and children in underwear, their legs dangling from the examining table, their expressions solemn.

Since the epidemic began, the clinic had been short on everything—clean paper for the examining tables, the plates for strep tests, alcohol; the erythromycin supply was gone by three, no penicillin or cotton balls or sterile gauze. Maria Walker's cousin Amos came in with a sprained wrist from falling off his skateboard and there were no splints and no Ace bandages.

But as the day progressed, Helen began to feel a lightheaded certainty. She was at a hardship post, out of the United States, a third world country, without supplies or access to them, without hospitals or other physicians. What came to pass was up to her in this back country.

She had never worked as a physician in her own right, always as an assistant following another doctor on rounds, but now she had begun to feel the rush she had remembered as a young child playing at being grown up. She liked having her own nurse, this substantial woman. She actually felt a love for Prudential as if they had worked together agreeably for years and against odds, as if they were friends.

She liked her office—she'd get flowers for the long south window tomorrow, she thought, perhaps a dhurrie rug —another desk, rectangular and less forbidding than the huge mahogany box behind which she sat speaking to the parents after she had examined their children, giving them a lollipop or plastic car or barrette for good behavior.

It was almost five when the waiting room finally thinned and Prudential opened the office door.

"Madeleine Sailor is still here," she said, folding her arms across her chest. "Do you know who she is?"

Helen hesitated.

"You saw the poster of the missing child at the train station?"

"I know about the missing child."

"This is her mother."

"I remember," Helen said. "I met her when I arrived."

Prudential put her hand on her hip.

"You may not be familiar with small towns where people know each other by more than name."

"I grew up on an island," Helen said.

"Then you know you can't believe everything you hear."

Madeleine Sailor was nervous. She sat down in the chair across from Helen, sat very straight, her hands clutching a lavender crocheted bag in her lap, and from the angle where Helen was sitting, it looked as if one side of her face was trembling. She was a slender woman, pretty but hollow-faced and pale-skinned. She could have been beautiful in the flush of health. She carried herself with a presence of someone who has been beautiful once.

"I'm the mother of the child who disappeared after the film crew left Meridian," she said in a speech which seemed rehearsed.

"I remember," Helen said, "I'm so sorry," and she immediately wished she had said nothing, had waited for the woman to deliver her own message, undiminished by Helen's small condolences.

"You know about the film 'The Story of Meridian'?" she asked.

"I know about it," Helen replied. "I haven't seen it."

"CBS people came to Meridian to film us in our daily lives," she said. "The director had been looking for a town in America reminiscent of the way towns used to be and T.J.— have you met T.J.?"

"I have." Helen poured a glass of water for herself and one for Madeleine Sailor.

"T.J. grew up here," she said. "He actually lived with my family for a while until Prudential came to town and took him in."

"I've met him," Helen said. "I know he's working hard to find your daughter."

"He is," Madeleine said, opening her purse, taking out a Kleenex which she didn't use but twisted into little balls, lining them up on the desk in front of her. "T.J. knew the director and recommended Meridian," she said.

"It's a very pretty town," Helen said. "I can understand that he would have."

"The director had a particular fondness for some people in the community. Not us. The only shot of me is with Maggie, standing in line outside a funeral wake." She picked up one of the tiny balls of Kleenex, rolling it between her fingers. "I used to smoke," she said, apologetic. "And then when the film crew left—I think it was April 13," she said, "Meridian had changed."

"How?" Helen asked, leaning forward at her desk.

"Just changed," Madeleine said. "We no longer seemed to wish each other well. In fact," she said, "in the past few weeks, we have begun to wish each other ill." She laced her fingers together.

"And on May 10 I was at the drugstore on Main Street and Maggie was waiting outside. That was perfectly normal in Meridian—nothing out of the ordinary has ever happened here. We didn't lock our doors." Her face was gray and certainly trembling. "When I came out of the drugstore it was maybe six o'clock at night and she was gone." She sat unnaturally still. She had probably made a determination not to belittle the gravity of her situation by tears.

Outside the long south window behind Helen, the day was turning silver, a light wind had picked up, singing through the barely open door.

Madeleine Sailor opened the crocheted bag and took out a rectangular box.

"This is 'The Story of Meridian,'" she said, putting the box on Helen's desk. "If you don't have a VCR in Dr. Hazelton's house, you can use ours."

Helen reached over and put the film cassette beside her. "There is a VCR," she said. "And as soon as this legionella is under control, I want to see the film."

Madeleine's clear blue eyes were direct. "I'd be grateful if you'd look at it carefully," she said. "You're from the outside and might be able to see something I can't." She stood up to leave.

"Like what?" Helen asked softly.

"Maybe a clue about what happened to Maggie," Madeleine said.

"You don't believe she was taken by a stranger?"

"I don't know," Madeleine said. "I have to know."

After she left, cleaning up her little row of Kleenex balls, taking the water glass and pitcher, attempting a smile of gratitude, Helen shut the door. The telephone rang and she heard Prudential answer in the waiting room. It rang again but she didn't bother to inquire.

She was conscious of her own presence in the room, a kind of mad expansion of herself as if she had to multiply in size against a quicksand force seeking to pull her under.

Something must have gone terribly wrong in Meridian, Ohio.

Prudential knocked.

"They are sending a delivery of erythromycin from Toledo by messenger," she said. "It'll be here by seven but I have to leave."

"I'll wait," Helen said. She looked at her watch. Five-fifteen. "I want to do another round of house calls this evening."

Prudential folded her arms across her chest.

"I can't," she said. "I have obligations."

Helen nodded.

"Unless there's an emergency," she said, and there was a

willingness in her voice Helen had not heard before. "A window of opportunity," her father would have said. "You can call me if there's an emergency."

Helen looked up from the chart on which she was writing at Prudential standing in the doorway, tall and slender, her body unwilling to give in to age. She was somehow entirely satisfactory. They would be friends.

She began to mention Madeleine Sailor's visit but Prudential held up a hand to stop her.

"Don't ask me any personal questions," she said, anticipating.

"This isn't personal," Helen said. "I want to know what has happened in Meridian."

"That is a personal question," Prudential said.

8.

THE LATE AFTERNOON WAS WARM and brilliant, the kind of day that seems in its clarity to be permanent. It was still warm at seven in the evening when Helen left for rounds with the new delivery of erythromycin that had arrived from Toledo. But when she finished at the Durhams' house, the temperature had fallen, the wind had picked up, and the trees in the hills above the Durham cottage swished their long skirts. The sky turned suddenly black.

"We don't need rain," Sam Durham said, walking with Helen to the front door.

Helen took the umbrella he offered. "But you've had your flood for this year, haven't you?" she asked. "That's why this epidemic of legionella. I just had a warning issued for everyone to boil the water."

"We did," Sam Durham said. "But it wasn't the kind of flood we sometimes have because there hasn't been enough rain. There could be another."

"I certainly hope not," Helen said, waving good-bye.

In the shadows behind Sam, Ann Durham appeared a ghost on her own front porch. Helen hadn't seen her since the morning when Sallie was so ill.

"Sallie's better," Helen called. "A lot better, I told Mr. Durham. I'll be at home so you can call me there if you need me."

"Say good-bye, Ann," Sam said to his wife loudly enough for Helen to hear him.

Ann Durham folded her arms across her chest and looked out into the evening just beyond Helen.

"I said good-bye," she said to no one in particular, stepping into the light, looking at Helen blankly.

Maria Walker's brother was sitting on the front porch just under the small roof when Helen arrived.

"Papa says we're going to have a flood," he said.

"I hope not," Helen said, stepping over his legs stretched out in front of the door.

"We will," the boy said solemnly, looking at Helen. "You don't look like a doctor," he said. "You look too much like a girl."

"Girls are doctors," Helen said.

"No, they aren't," he said with confidence.

Mrs. Walker was talkative. Maria was much better, she said. The medicine had been a miracle and now if only Timbo, the little boy on the front porch, sickly by nature, didn't get sick, they'd be home free, she said, smiling. She asked about Sallie Durham.

"She was very sick, wasn't she?"

"She was," Helen said, "but she's much better."

Mrs. Walker shook her head.

"I don't like Ann Durham," she said. "We went to high

school together and I didn't like her then either. But," she shrugged, "everybody in Meridian pretends to like everybody else." She put a plate of Oreo cookies on the dining-room table. "Timbo," she called. "You can have one too," she said. "Ann thinks her children are better than other children and they aren't. Children are just children, don't you think?"

Helen nodded, taking an Oreo, hoping to make a quick escape.

"The film made her think that," Mrs. Walker said, pouring Timbo a glass of milk. "Sallie was practically the star. Her and Molly." An odd look crossed her face. "You know the film changed Meridian and I was born here so I know." She split a cookie and licked the white icing. "The film made some people more important than others. And then we started to believe what we saw on TV instead of what was right here on our doorstep." She brushed Maria's hair out of her eyes. "Have you seen it?"

"I haven't but Madeleine Sailor gave me a cassette and I may have a chance to look at it tonight."

"You won't see us," Maria's mother said. "We're not in it, except Timbo. There's a shot of the back of Timbo in the line at nursery school and that's it for the Walker family."

"You must be just as glad," Helen said, not knowing what was expected of her. "I'd hate to be on television."

"I'm just as glad," Maria's mother said but she sounded unconvinced.

It was after nine and very dark when Helen got back to her house. The black and white cat lay curled on the mat, rubbing the back of Helen's legs as she opened the front door, pleased to see her. She went inside, dropped her medical bag, her umbrella, a bunch of limp pale yellow stock the Walkers had given her, turned on the lights.

In the shower, she stood with her eyes closed, her arms stretched out in front of her so the water traveled down to the ends of her fingers, pounded on the top of her head. She could organize her mind in compartments. Empty her brain.

"You have the mind of a man," Oliver had told her early in their relationship when he was still fascinated by her elusiveness.

"Is that better or worse than the mind you had expected?" she asked.

"Neither," he said. "It's simply that you don't let one thing spill over into another like the women I've known do."

Helen's mother had told her that as well when she was young, in grammar school, and her early interest in biology expressed itself in small bottles of formaldehyde with fetal pigs and birds and kittens ordered from a laboratory supply store in LaSalle, Illinois, lined up on the windowsill of her bedroom.

"Sometimes you seem like someone else's daughter with all of your dead animals," her mother had said.

"They're not exactly dead," Helen had said. "They were never born."

"It's not only the bottled animals, Helen, although I certainly wish they weren't living with us," her mother had said with some annoyance. "It's the way you have of doing things, the way you organize, like your father does. Like a man."

"Well, I'm not going to grow up to be a man," Helen had said. "So you don't have to worry."

But the quality of mind had been useful. She had, for example, been able to put the burden of Emma's death completely out of her mind for most of her life until these last few weeks when she had started to think about Meridian again.

She got out of the shower, dried her hair, put on jeans and a man's shirt which had belonged to Oliver, tied her wet hair on top of her head, so it flopped carelessly to one side.

It was almost ten o'clock in the evening and the wind outside was howling when she turned on the television and slipped the "The Story of Meridian" cassette into the VCR.

The film opens without any sound but that of water, with a scene along the river as it narrows, its banks lined with bare slender trees, bending like dancers, some uprooted. Then the river widens broad and fast, moving into the town, and the camera moves up the bank to the railroad station. WELCOME TO MERIDIAN.

"Meridian, Ohio, is located in the northwest corner of Ohio. The border of Michigan to its north and Illinois to its west, west of Cleveland, just west of Toledo, a small hilly town with one main street, a square in the middle without a statue—there have been no famous sons of Meridian to cast in stone—just ordinary people living out their lives in a community remarkable by today's standards for its generosity of spirit. It is early on a Monday morning."

The camera follows Main Street from the station, the

shops opening along the sidewalks around the square, school-children in heavy jackets and scarfs, book bags on their shoulders, on their way to school in groups of threes and fours. The camera stops to focus on a young boy, perhaps eleven, standing precariously on the curb watching three young giggling girls meander up the street. There are other boys in the background, friends of the one on the curb, egging him on. As the girls pass, the young boy makes a leap, landing in a wide puddle in the street, splashing the girls, who scream and laugh and shout, flying back up the street toward home, perhaps to change their clothes. The camera follows the girls as they are lost in an expansive view of the hills of Meridian peppered with brightly colored houses. The girls disappear in the horizon and the camera moves just beyond the square with its shops to a small peach cottage behind the library, where two little girls sit on the steps of the porch, close together, their snow-suited shoulders touching. The smaller one, a dark serious child, has a doughnut squeezed in her tiny hand. The other child is Sallie Durham. The child with the doughnut takes one of Sallie's hands, brings it to her lips and kisses it. The camera moves beyond the girls to two women standing in the doorway. One is Ann Durham bundled up in a coat. The second is a small, dark, voluptuous woman in a man's robe, her long hair uncombed. The camera focuses on her.

Helen stopped the video and rewound, starting again as the camera focused on the little girls.

Sam Durham had told her that the director of the film liked Sallie and Molly. So that must be Molly, Helen thought. The child whose identity had slipped Prudential's mind.

She didn't recognize the lovely-looking woman in the man's robe.

The two women speak. Ann Durham says she will pick the girls up after play group. The front door shuts and Ann Durham walks down the street away from the camera, holding the hands of the little girls.

"It is a cold morning in early April," the narrator is saying. "The smell of winter is still in the air, of early morning wood fires, of rain." The narrator is a bass with a voice that rolls out of his belly, a strong romantic voice, and Helen, sitting in a large soft chair, her knees drawn up under her chin, her arms wrapped around her legs, was pleased by the sound of him.

She didn't hear the knocking on her door at first and, when she did, the wind was roaring along the front of the house with such a force, it was difficult to distinguish sound from weather.

The door flew out of her hand when she opened it, banging against the inside wall. And there, brightly lit by the outside floodlight, was T. J. Wisely, wet and scrambled, his white polo shirt soaked to the skin, his eye patch askew.

"It's a terrible night," Helen said, helping him move his wheelchair over the lip of the front door.

"Awful," T.J. said, shaking his long black hair. "I was at the Durhams' and couldn't make it up the hill. A tree's down."

"I think I heard it fall," Helen said, running up the steps to the linen closet to get a towel.

"We may lose the electricity if this keeps up," T.J. said to Helen when she came downstairs with a brand-new kelly-green towel still with the price tag on it and dried T.J.'s hair. He took his wet shirt over his head, pulling off the eye patch with the shirt.

"Shit," he said, shaking his shirt with one hand, holding his palm over his eye from where the black patch had fallen.

"Here," Helen said. "I'll get it."

She dried the patch and handed it back to T.J.

"How did your eye happen?" she asked.

"I've never been sure," T.J. said, adjusting the string. "I was a stunt man in Hollywood."

"You told me."

"I was doing a leap between buildings," he said. "There was even a net but it didn't hold when I landed. So my back broke and I lost my eye and came back home to Meridian, my stunt man days kaput." He arranged the eye patch. "The eye gives people the creeps."

"I'm a doctor," Helen said.

"You're still a woman and it makes women sick," he said. "Just the idea of an empty socket. I know." He wheeled toward the kitchen. "I'm dying of thirst."

"I only have juices and milk," Helen said.

"No beer?" He helped himself to a banana from a bowl in the middle of the table.

"No beer."

"Juice is fine," he said, comfortable in Richard Hazelton's house as if he had visited often, opening the fridge, taking a glass from the cupboard, agile for a man without the use of his legs, moving gracefully on his strong arms.

"The place looks nice," he said.

"I was told Dr. Hazelton is a fastidious man."

"He is," T.J. said. "You could lick the floors." He wheeled into the living room, lifting Gregory from the sofa to his lap.

"Were you friends?" Helen asked.

"No, we weren't particular friends," T.J. said. "He was extraordinarily quiet and he was the kind of boy that people make fun of."

"But you seem to know his house."

"We all know each other's houses," T.J. said, stretching, lifting himself off the seat of the chair with his arms. Gregory leaped out of his lap and onto the floor.

Helen slid into the couch beside his wheelchair, tucked her long legs under her.

"What were you watching when I came up?" T.J. asked.

"The film about Meridian," Helen said. "I'd just started."

"Turn it on again," he said, sitting in front of the television.

"Haven't you seen enough of it?" she asked.

"I never do." He reached over and turned off the lamp beside the couch.

"I was here," Helen said, turning the play button so the film showed the back of Ann and Sallie Durham, with a wide-angle lens, followed them down the street toward town, disappearing into the village.

"Who is the second little girl, not Sallie?" Helen asked.

"Molly."

"I haven't met her yet."

"You won't," T.J. said. "She left."

Helen laughed. "A lot of people seem to leave Meridian, don't they?"

"I suppose some do," T.J. replied, giving her an odd look.

The camera dances up Main Street, skipping from one brightly painted shop to the next, the pharmacist, the dry cleaners, a dress shop, pale lavender, sunflower yellow, blue. Then stops, holding a still picture framed by the hills of Meridian.

"We painted the houses for the film, you know." T.J. lifted himself out of the wheelchair to the couch next to Helen. "When I moved here, it was nice but not a fairy tale place." T.J. shrugged. He took out a cigarette. "Mind?"

"Yes," Helen said. "I mind."

He put the unlit cigarette in his mouth and settled into the couch, lifting one leg across the other, sinking into the pillows.

Helen was comfortable with men. Not flirtatious exactly but soft and accessible with a slow charm as if a man could slip into her life unharmed.

"The clinic comes next," T.J. said. "The camera's going to pick up Ann and Sallie at the top of Main going into the clinic. You'll see Prudential charging up the hill in a second and then Dr. Hazelton."

Ann is carrying Sallie, crossing the road beside the

barn-red house where MAGGIE Headquarters is, Prudential flying up the street in a turquoise ski jacket and pumpkin-orange scarf, carrying an umbrella, although it isn't raining, waving the umbrella at Ann Durham.

The camera moves in on the meeting of Ann and Prudential in front of the clinic.

"I'm late, late, late," Prudential is saying cheerily. "I overslept in all this gloomy spring weather we've been having." She picks up Molly.

"Which one of you is sick, girl?" Prudential asks.

"It's Molly," Ann says. "She has a sore throat so I've brought her to get a strep test."

The wind had picked up outside, banging the shutters against the house, sailing past the windows as if it had actual shape. There was a crash next to the house and the telephone rang, a half ring, and cut off.

"A hangup?" Helen said.

"The phones are probably out. It happens a lot," T.J. said. "Could you turn up the volume?" he asked, leaning toward the television, fixated, caught up in the narrative as if he were seeing it for the first time. "I can't hear the television with all the wind."

Prudential is opening the door to the clinic, walking with Molly across the waiting room. In the distance Dr. Hazelton, his back to the camera, is looking through the files.

"Prudential?" he calls.

"Good morning, Dr. Hazelton," Prudential says, taking off her jacket, lifting Molly, setting her on the counter.

"Good morning." His head is bent, he riffles through the file drawer. "I'm looking for Jack O'Brien's file. He broke his arm falling in the shower this morning."

Prudential leans down, takes off Sallie's coat and puts her up next to Molly. The camera moves past Prudential over her amazing head to Dr. Hazelton, who turns slowly, a file in hand, and faces the camera.

"Hello, Ann," he says in a pleasant tenor voice. "Who's feeling badly today?"

"Molly," Ann says. "She's not actually sick. Sophie just wanted to have her throat checked."

Dr. Hazelton walks toward the camera, a tall beanpole of a man, pale, pale thin face, pale hair, an inscrutable expression, perhaps indifference but familiar to Helen in his remarkable paleness.

"So that's Dr. Hazelton," Helen said. "Is he actually that white or is it the TV?"

"He's pretty white," T.J. said. "Look at his arms. Have you ever seen such long arms?"

"I can't tell."

"They almost seem deformed."

The lights flickered then, the images on the television screen scattered and disappeared and the living room went dark.

"I knew this was going to happen," T.J. said.

Helen stared out into the blackness, waiting for her eyes to adjust. "Will it last?" she asked.

"Sometimes hours," T.J. said.

They were sitting at either end of the long couch, their arms slung over the back, their hands almost touching.

"Now what?" Helen asked.

"Now we wait," T.J. said.

They didn't speak. For a long time, long enough to make Helen self-conscious, they sat in silence and listened to the wind, the strange sound it made of air forced through a narrow tunnel as the storm traveled through Meridian.

"Do you have children?" T.J. asked finally. His voice in the darkness had a different sound to it, a weight like the voice of the narrator on "The Story of Meridian."

"I'm not married," Helen said.

"I was married once for a few months," T.J. said. "To a stunt woman. Her specialty was fires."

Helen laughed.

"No joke," he said. "I don't know what I was thinking."

"I haven't thought of being married before," Helen said, "but I've thought of having a child."

"That's actually why I got married," T.J. said.

In the distance there was a dull bang, maybe a car.

"I hope it's not an accident," T.J. said.

They listened but the sound seemed to be the wind, steady, unfriendly in its persistence.

"Are you afraid?" he asked.

"Of what?" She suddenly felt his proximity.

"Of the storm," he said.

"Of the dark," Helen said. "I grew up on an island in the North and it was dark all winter and there was just my mother and me. She was always afraid of the dark."

"What's she like?" T.J. asked.

"My mother?"

"Yes, your mother."

"She's a painter," Helen said. "She actually makes collages out of things she finds like bird bones and dried flowers and stones. They're quite nice," Helen said, wishing now she had one of her mother's collages. She especially liked one that Allie had offered her when she went away to college called *Birds in Flight*. But the birds were not in flight. There was a large framed box with the brilliant feathers of birds clinging to the branches of trees made of delicate twigs. Real feathers, real twigs and painted birds in black on white with outsized claws gripping the real branches for dear life.

"I mean what is she like as a person?" T.J. asked. "I take an interest in mothers."

"I never see her," Helen said. "She's afraid to travel."

"I had a mother obviously," T.J. said, "but all I remember about her is smells like cinnamon or cheap perfume."

"David told me how you got here on a train from Chicago."

"I can't imagine putting a child on a train to a place you've found on a map," he said, "but that's what she did."

"Parents do awful things with children," Helen said, suddenly furious out of nowhere, as if she were catching emotion on the fly. "I've seen the worst."

T.J. took her hand, lacing his fingers through her fingers, almost casually, fraternally.

"I get upset about children," he said. "That's why I wanted this film done to honor Meridian, I suppose. In a way the town has been my parents."

The headlights of a car slid over the ceiling, down the wall, across T.J.'s face.

"I think someone's here," Helen said, and before she had

a chance to get up David Jaspersen had come in the front door with a flashlight.

"Helen?" he called, the yellow circle from the flashlight skipping across the floor.

"I'm here," she said.

"God, what a night," David said. "The river's on the rise and trees are down all over town.

"I was wondering where you were, T.J. The beech is down in your front yard. I think it may have been the tree that took the telephone wires down in this part of town."

"I couldn't get up the hill tonight in a wheelchair."

"I guess you couldn't. It's a real mess," David said. "Do you want to spend the night at my place?" He moved through the darkness to the living room.

"I'll go home," T.J. said. "If I come with you, can I get into the house?"

"The tree fell away from the house," David said. "You won't have any trouble."

He walked, following the large circle of light, into the kitchen and then back.

"Is there going to be a flood?" Helen asked.

"It's a storm passing over on its way east," David said, "so I don't think so."

T.J. lifted himself back in the wheelchair.

"I'll come back another night and watch the film with you," he said to Helen.

"I hope so," Helen said, wishing they would stay, wishing at least T.J. would stay with his warm comfortable voice.

"Tomorrow is Beatrice Tallis's funeral," David said. "Prudential told you?"

"She didn't mention it," Helen said, feeling her way to the front door.

"At 10 A.M. The weather better clear." He stopped for a moment, adjusted his flashlight for T.J. to see his way across the living room. "I hope a lot of people come."

"Won't they?" Helen asked.

"People have been less neighborly since the film," David said.

She opened the front door.

Already the wind had abated, the rain thinned to a steady rhythm of pine needles falling from the sky, a hint of moon on the horizon.

"We should have electricity soon," David said, "but I'll check with you early in the morning." He put his hand on her arm awkwardly as if it were a gesture he felt he should make but was uncomfortable making. "Are you okay?"

"I'm fine," Helen said, standing in the door watching them in the small light move down the steps to David's car. "Don't worry," she added. But she was worried.

She had had attacks of nerves since she was young. Panic attacks, her mother called them—their cause elusive. She could be about her business in school or walking along a street with friends or in the market, no known perpetrator around, her body reacting to invisible danger, her mouth dry, her heart beating too quickly, her breath caught in her throat.

Once she had been eating strawberries at a summer lunch with relatives in Michigan when it happened. Once she'd been sitting in algebra class daydreaming of kissing

Peter Samuels and once at the market making a small dinner for other residents at the University of Michigan. She had fled to the street, her basket of eggplant and zucchini and a leg of lamb left in the middle of the aisle. Once the unnamed fear abated, and sometimes that took awhile, she searched for the cause.

The appeal of science to Helen was the reliability of a reality.

"What you get is, by and large, what is," her human biology professor had said early on in the first semester. "So the trick is to see well."

Helen saw very well. Her eyes were instinctual and she loved the reassurance the study of science promised of a measurable reality.

But now, sitting in an alarming darkness in the sterilized house of the pale, long-armed Dr. Richard Hazelton, her hands holding tight to one another to keep from shaking, reality was slippery and Helen wanted to go home, not to Ann Arbor, but home to her childhood, her early childhood, to the time before Emma Fielding died.

9.

THE STORM HAD WEIGHT and density, moving by the front windows of the house with the sound a crowd makes. Helen was curled in the large chair with a safe view, comforted by the company of weather.

The night felt like Mackinaw when she was a child—lonely like Mackinaw where the weather had ongoing conversations and the people whose daily lives were determined by it bore silent witness.

In Mackinaw, Helen and her mother lived in Mrs. Peaches's guesthouse, which in the gray-black Michigan winter was empty—only Mrs. Peaches and her aged mother and Labrador retriever. Allie Fielding's shop was closed in winter and she spent her days in a makeshift studio weaving tapestries to sell in the summer tourist months.

There was a powerful loneliness on the island, a sense of being cast adrift. Often Helen went to school in the dark, home in the evening in the dark. She took piano from Mrs. Peaches's sister and played sports and listened to music at the Barn, where the youth of Mackinaw spent the winter evenings. She wasn't popular with her peers in the conventional sense, not in the center of things, but she was of great interest to them, a subject of private conversations, considered a whimsical figure, as if she were by temperament an expression of the mercurial nature of Mackinaw's weather. But she was an outsider on an island which was by its geography already outside and her daily life felt more like a ballad about a life than the experience of the thing itself. She glided through her years in high school—not unhappy necessarily, but uprooted. When she thought of herself as a child, uprooted was the picture she saw in her mind—a straggly wildflower of a girl overturned, the roots dangling, exposed to the air.

There was a stultifying pattern to her days—school and sports and meals with Mrs. Peaches, stews all winter long, the same stew with beef and too many carrots, grainy potatoes. There were lovely conversations with her mother. Never serious conversations. Her mother refused discussions of personal matters, almost as though she had no interior life to speak of. But in her mother's studio with the smell of paints and lacquer and glue, her mother looking like a girl in blue jeans and a long shirt, her hair tied up in a bandanna, their talks were warm and promising, almost satisfactory. Allie Fielding liked to talk about science although she knew very little scientific. Her interests were color and texture. She kept things in the way a woman with a scientific turn of mind might do—butterflies, dried flowers, bits of cast-off nature, feathers—and over mint tea and cookies they'd talk about things. Allie Fielding liked things. They were personal to her.

"Now see the oval brown spots on the yellow wings of that sweet butterfly," her mother might say. "I love brown and yellow together, especially in winter," or "Feel the softness of this feather on your cheek. Smell the earth on it."

They didn't talk about Dr. Philip Fielding, who had left when Helen was seven, although Allie spoke to him without acrimony when he called for Helen on Sundays. They never talked about the time before Emma died when they lived in Ann Arbor and Dr. Fielding taught at the University of Michigan. They didn't mention Emma at all.

"Nobody talks in our family," Helen said to her father in her senior year of high school, visiting him in Santa Cruz.

"What would you like to talk about?" he asked.

"Anything," Helen said.

"I'm happy to speak to you about anything," her father had said in his self-protective, absent-minded way.

"I want to talk about Emma dying," she had said, hearing, as she was speaking, his sharp intake of breath.

"No," her father said, not cross about it, rather weary and professorial. "You know we don't talk about Emma."

"Why don't we?" Helen had asked.

"It's too difficult for your mother and me," he said. "Much too difficult."

"Maybe later?" Helen asked.

"I don't think so," her father said. "I don't think Emma's death is a subject for our family."

The unspeakable, and by her parents' insistent silence, Helen was accountable, not for Emma's actual death, perhaps, but for the absence of her life.

"Nothing that matters is ever a subject for our family," Helen had said.

———

She must have drifted off to sleep and she awoke suddenly when the lights in Dr. Hazelton's house flickered on. It was just before 2 A.M. by her watch. The wind had stopped roaring by the window and it was raining light as feathers against the pane. Gregory climbed down from the couch, stretched and followed Helen to the kitchen where she turned on the gas for tea. She had awakened weighted by a sense of trouble she couldn't define, as if something specific had happened and she had lost the memory of it.

She made a piece of toast with jam, sitting at the kitchen table, feeling peculiar, the victim of a kind of painless heart attack.

At Aunt Martha's they had picked raspberries in the back garden, not Aunt Martha's garden but one belonging to someone else of whom Helen was afraid. They'd pick the raspberries off their prickly bushes in white cotton gloves which had belonged to Aunt Martha when she was a girl and then, sitting in the white Adirondack chairs, they'd eat them from a cold glass bowl.

The person whose raspberries they had picked was a woman—Helen could hear her voice, as small as the point of a needle, and the woman had a slender face with short curly beige hair, pale white skin and somewhere a purple stripe.

"Why does Mrs. Whatever"—she had lost the last name—"why does Mrs. Whatever with the raspberry patch have a purple stripe across her face?" she had asked her Aunt Martha.

"It's a birthmark," Aunt Martha had told her. "Most everyone has a mark of some kind when they are born."

"I don't," Helen had said.

"But Emma has a tiny tulip on her thumb," her mother said.

They had looked at Emma's plump thumb, at the little red flower on top of it.

"I don't like Mrs. Whatever's birthmark," Helen had said.

"But if everyone had a purple stripe across his face, darling, then you would think it was lovely," her mother said. "You'd want to have one just like it."

"I don't think so," Helen had said.

Sometime later, that evening perhaps, Helen had taken the juice in the bottom of the raspberry bowl and with her finger had drawn a little red tulip on her thumb.

The wind had died and she went upstairs to change for bed. By morning she would be exhausted, she thought, and what if there were an emergency? She ought to sleep. She needed to sleep. She didn't want to change to her nightgown. Perhaps if she slept in her clothes, needing to be prepared as if she could hear an emergency on its way. She lay down on top of the comforter, turned off the lights, closed her eyes but she lay awake, her eyes open, staring into the darkness. And she knew by the irregular stiffness of her back, the tenseness in her belly, that she would be awake for the rest of the night.

At 5 A.M., a slip of dawn lightening the sky, she was wide awake. She got up, put a blanket around her shoulders and went downstairs, turning on the VCR, which was stopped at the clinic with the figure of Dr. Richard Hazelton and Prudential at the clinic.

She replayed Ann Durham walking down the street holding the hands of the two little girls with their backs to the camera. The scene moves across the street, along the backs of the houses which face College Street, their low fences lined with trash cans now loaded on a pickup truck by a young redheaded boy in a navy pea jacket who knows the people in the houses by their first names. He is called Gaven by the narrator and, as the camera leaves him, he has picked up a yellow striped kitten and put him inside the fence of one of the houses.

"They watch over one another's houses and children and kittens," the narrator is saying. "Everyone—Gaven, the chief of police, the reverend of First Methodist—feels himself responsible."

She fast-forwarded the tape to the clinic. Dr. Hazelton turns to face the camera, holding the file. He has a loose, languid body, a way of dangling as if he were hanging from his shoulders instead of standing on his feet, a gentle, limpid face, too soft for Helen's taste. But something about him is familiar, his face perhaps, but maybe it is his long, long arms. His elbows hang below his belt; extended, his arms must hang to his knees.

She knew him. Certainly she knew him. Or did she? Was it just that by a certain age anyone—his face blending with other faces, his arms and gait and voice—seems familiar, seems to be a part of a particular childhood. And he could be, likely is, a perfect stranger.

Before the sun came up on the beginning of a new day in Meridian, Helen was in the pull-down attic of Dr. Richard Hazelton's house with Gregory stretched out on his back beside her. The attic was small and peaked but there was a window and a light, and what she found when she climbed up the narrow stairs was organized in cardboard boxes neatly labeled—COLLEGE BOOKS, MEMORABILIA FROM COLLEGE, MEDICAL SCHOOL BOOKS, FATHER'S PAPERS, LETTERS AND PHOTOS: CHILDHOOD; PHOTOS: COLLEGE AND MEDICAL SCHOOL; PHOTOS AND MEMORABILIA: MERIDIAN.

Helen opened the box marked MERIDIAN. It was organized by the year, beginning in the year of Richard Hazelton's birth, four years before her own, so she could have known him, could have seen him on the street when she visited her Aunt Martha, a man with such long arms. There were pictures of a couple on the front porch of a house, a cottage really, the mother a pale wisp of a woman holding a small baby. "Mother, Father and me: age two months" written in light pencil on the back. Several photos taken the same day with a different perspective, so in some the baby is recognizable as a particular baby, baldish with an expression of indifference on his face, and others, taken at a distance so the perspective allows the inclusion not just of the cottage with the young couple and baby on the front steps but the cottages on either side. On one side, the cottage with its wide front porch, its trellis of wisteria, is certainly Aunt Martha's house.

So this baby, this boy, lived next door. Perhaps she remembered him. Perhaps they played.

There were many photographs in bunches, fifteen, twenty on a particular day and then years passed before another set of photos. The father, smaller than his wife and portly, probably older, maybe a great deal older, had disappeared in the photos by the time the boy was five or six, so the pictures showed the mother, who began to wear her hair on top of her head in a small ball. Often there was a large black dog with floppy ears. Helen noticed that there were no candid shots although the pictures had been taken with an ordinary camera. They were posed, the mother with her arm on the son's shoulder, awkward in the gesture as if the pose had been assumed for the photographer and was unpracticed in daily life, Dr. Richard Hazelton at five or six holding a violin, a book, standing next to a much older woman with a bunch of yellow flowers. There was a whole set of pictures of a grave, or several graves, white slabs of stone evenly lined up with a little flower bed in front—and several closeups of one grave, a new one, the baskets of wilting gladiolus lying on their sides, a picture of a plaque on graceful metal gates: MERCY CEMETERY. There was a group of pictures in front of Meridian Elementary with Dr. Richard Hazelton standing on the front steps, no children anywhere around, just the doctor as a boy, his long arms, long even then, hanging at his side. Stuck in between the files, Helen found an envelope marked MERIDIAN SUMMERS (Boyhood of R. Hazelton) and in the envelope were single pictures from different times—several photographs of the town, of Main Street and the house next to Aunt Martha's, some closeups, quite fuzzy, of a rose garden, of the Methodist church with a man who must have been the minister standing on the steps of the church with Dr. Richard Hazelton at maybe two or three.

She almost slipped by the picture of her own memory since the color in it had dimmed and the picture was a little rumpled but it was a picture of three children and a dog in front of the small cottage covered with climbing yellow roses and wisteria where Aunt Martha lived. The children stood in a line, posed for a photograph, first the boy, Dr. Richard Hazelton, perhaps six or seven years old with a new haircut so his pale face had a ghoulish aspect in the picture, then the dog, a black long-haired dog with a pointy nose, then Helen in white shorts and a T-shirt with writing on it which was illegible, then Emma, holding Helen's hand and with the other hand dragging an upside-down doll with long red hair.

Helen remembered.

Richie, next door to Aunt Martha, the son of Mrs. Whatever with the purple stripe—you couldn't see the stripe in the pictures. She leaned against the attic wall.

By morning she would try her mother once more and perhaps with any luck she could reach her. She was having trouble breathing again.

She lay down on the floor of the attic, waiting for dawn, her eyes closed, concentrating on absence, hoping to breathe.

She had come to Meridian by choice but the consequence of memory restored was like weather, happening beyond her, out of sight but traveling in her direction.

10.

WEDNESDAY WAS SURPRISINGLY BEAUTIFUL after the long night storm. The sun was bright, the air clear although the weather report from Toledo promised a heat wave. The streets were almost completely dry. Families leaving First Methodist Church after the service for Beatrice Tallis talked about the river, how lucky they were to have avoided another flood bringing the possibility of more sickness.

Helen didn't go to the cemetery.

"You go. I'll be in the clinic," she said to Prudential, not wishing to be a stranger in attendance. "You've been here for years and know the family."

"Eleven years in September," Prudential said. "I'm thinking of going home to South Carolina."

"Not before the end of the summer, I hope," Helen said. "Not before I leave."

"Who knows?" Prudential said. "I don't plan far ahead."

They stood apart from the people spilling out of the church, shaking hands with the Tallis family, who had gathered at the top of the steps with Reverend Winters, a formality about the scene surprising in so small and isolated a town, Helen thought.

"I suppose you notice the ill will," Prudential said in a whisper.

"Ill will?" She looked over at Prudential. "Toward me?"

"I notice ill will," Prudential said.

"Is it from someone specific?" Helen asked.

"Who knows? People here expect a kind of miracle and you're just a physician," Prudential said, "nothing more." And then she did the oddest thing, right in front of everyone. She slipped her arm through Helen's in an open gesture of friendship, an act of taking sides.

"I have a nose for bad news," Prudential said. "It's in my genes."

They parted then, Prudential disappearing in the crowd of mourners gathering to walk to the cemetery.

Helen settled in at her desk with the charts. Of course the people in Meridian were suspicious. They were having a terrible time. It wasn't personal. She had to remind herself of that.

She changed the calendar, May 24, and taking the picture of Dr. Hazelton with her and Emma out of her pocket, she looked at it in the full light of day. It must have been taken the summer Emma died. Helen was four, fierce by the look of her picture, and Emma, an angel, had been two. The boy, Dr. Richard Hazelton, had an expression of indifference, no pleasure in the moment. Perhaps he had been required to spend time with the Fielding girls or was shy or sullen or bad-tempered. He had fish eyes—like Oliver, pale wet fish eyes, or so it seemed. His arms, which hung down straight on either side, had an unnatural look, rubber arms pulled to the full length of their potential. But it was the pale aspect of his face which tugged at the back of Helen's memory.

Now that the emergency with legionella was passing, the report of confirmation in from the lab, she needed to go to the hospital in Harrisville to see the patients from Meridian. There had been three of them in the hospital when she arrived. She read the charts. Charles Martel, age fifty-nine, had Dressler's syndrome after a heart attack, a not uncommon reaction of the nervous system to a damaged heart. Karen Read had been hospitalized with acute respiratory distress on Sunday as a result of asthma and Mary Baker had given birth to a premature baby by caesarean section, a boy born at twenty-six weeks, 2 lbs. 5 ozs., with mild respiratory problems. Helen called the attending doctor in Harrisville, Dr. Bartoli, an older man with a careful hesitation in his speech, a slight accent. Mr. Martel had fever and fluid in his lungs, swelling in the sac around his heart, both symptoms of Dressler's syndrome. Karen Read would be released that morning and the Baker infant had been removed from a respirator and was breathing on his own.

Helen loved medicine. She loved the feeling of measurable accomplishment at the end of a day. She had a temperament for emergencies. She needed them, sought them out. Otherwise, there was no definition to her life, no real sense of a life at all. And she had a love affair with the scientific names of things. Mallolus. Malleus. Ossicles. Incers. She repeated them over and over in her head as if she were memorizing for an oral exam—and they seemed like poetry, the way they sounded on her tongue, their precision and clarity.

When she finished speaking with Dr. Bartoli, she called her mother, flushed with the usual anxiety of dialing her mother's number.

If she needed her mother, if she were ill or in distress, Allie Fielding would not come—would not be able to come. Her father would be there, at a remove, there in body, better than nothing. Which was as much as she could expect. It was clear to Helen that her mother's capacity for sustaining others was in permanent retirement.

The answering machine was on again. This time when she left a message her stepfather picked up. He was a lawyer, younger than her mother and quick-witted, maybe even kind, she wasn't sure. But there was something inauthentic about him which put her off and she had never got over the sense that he simply came to Mackinaw on vacation and stole her mother for good.

"Sleeping? At noon?" Helen asked. "Is she ill?"

"No." Her stepfather hesitated.

"Is she avoiding me?" Helen asked crossly.

"She'll call," he said. "Does she have your number?"

"I left it on the machine," Helen said but she gave it to him again.

Her father was chatty and cheerful.

"Hello, hello, my angel," he said when he answered the phone. "And how is the weather in the dreary Middle West?"

He was only interested in the weather in Meridian, not in the town itself nor in Helen's return there. He hadn't seen the film. He didn't remember David Jaspersen or people named Jaspersen at all or the neighbors next door to Aunt Martha called Hazelton.

"We only spent two weeks with Aunt Martha," he said. "We didn't make friends."

He said Allie was not ill but fragile. She had been fragile when he met her as a young girl. Life, he said, had a way of dealing unequally with people. And she never liked to talk on the telephone.

"She got the short end of the stick," he said. "Or the long end. I can't remember which is which."

"Did we have a funeral for Emma?" Helen asked when the conversation was almost over and her father's mind was drifting to the particulars of eighteenth-century European warfare as it tended to do.

"We had a memorial service," he said.

"Where was it? I have no recollection at all."

"Ann Arbor," her father said.

"And was I there?" Helen asked.

"I don't remember. It was a difficult time," he said, changing the subject to a friend's son who had been diagnosed with something called Addison's disease and did she know of any treatments.

Prudential came back shortly after one o'clock just as the clinic was filling for afternoon hours.

"I don't like what's going on," she said to Helen, beckoning for Paula Weller sitting in the waiting room with her daughter Lisa. "Two months ago you wouldn't have a funeral in Meridian without everybody there. And today half the town stayed home and it's not only because of this epidemic."

She turned to Mrs. Weller. "Lisa has a fever?"

"I think she caught the sickness from Maria," Mrs. Weller said.

Prudential took Lisa in her arms and headed to the examining room. "Follow me," she said to Mrs. Weller.

"Before you go back, who do we have today?" Helen asked.

"We have Maria today," Prudential said. "Ann Durham called in about her younger child, Casey. She thinks he's caught it from Sallie."

Helen shook her head.

"It's not possible," she said, washing her hands. "You can't catch legionella from other people."

Prudential raised her eyebrows.

"Anyone else?" Helen asked.

Prudential checked her list. "We have Kathy Bauer with a bellyache, Sandy Case with a high fever, Mrs. Lennon has found a lump in her breast," she said. "And Madeleine Sailor."

Helen nodded. "Is Madeleine ill?"

"Not in body," Prudential said, and led the way down the corridor to the examining room.

Paula Weller sat in the examining room with Lisa on her lap. She was a small, pretty, frightened woman, defended by quick conversation, small talk which went on and on.

"I give her vitamins, three a day, even though she throws

them up," she said, and "My mother lost her hair before she was fifty," and "I wish we got better fruit in the markets here. In New York City the fruit is wonderful and they don't even have trees." Lisa sat quietly on the examining table, her hands folded in her lap. "It's the sickness, isn't it?" Paula Weller asked finally.

"Has she had diarrhea?"

"No," she said. "But she threw up her vitamins this morning."

"What hurts?" Helen asked Lisa.

"Everything," the little girl said.

"Your arms?" She laid her cool hand against the child's cheek.

Lisa nodded.

"Does she have a dry cough?"

"Well, she has a cough but I don't know if it's wet or dry. My uncle got TB when he went to Russia, you know. There's lots of TB in Russia. It's epidemic."

"This isn't TB," Helen said.

"This is the sickness, isn't it?"

"I think it probably is. I'm going to treat her with erythromycin as if she has legionella although her fever isn't at all high."

Paula dropped her head in her hands. "I was afraid of this."

"It's good you got her here today. We've caught it very early," Helen said gently, touching the mother's shoulder. "She's going to be fine."

"I hope," Paula Weller said, holding Lisa, standing in the door ready to leave. "I didn't go to Beatrice Tallis's funeral today because I don't feel friendly toward people like I used to feel and I don't know why." She shifted Lisa to her other arm. "Now I feel bad. Bea Tallis was in Lisa's grade."

"You have a nice way," Prudential said when the Wellers had left. "I like doctors with a nice way."

Kathy Bauer was a tall slender nervous woman, about thirty, with a terrible stomachache. Prudential helped her into the examining room and by the time she was on her back in stirrups for a pelvic examination she was moaning out loud.

"It's not like a stomach flu," she said to Helen. "It's like nothing I've ever had before."

Prudential held her hand.

"It may be a cyst on the ovary," Helen said, examining her.

"Cancer? My mother died of cancer."

"Not cancer," Helen said, helping her lift her legs down. "I'd be surprised if it were more than a cyst."

"Pancreatic cancer. That's what she died of."

"What kind of equipment do they have in Harrisville, Prudential?" Helen asked. "Sonograms? CAT scans?"

"You have to go to Toledo for CAT scans," Prudential said.

Helen called the hospital in Toledo and sent Kathy Bauer in for tests.

Sandy Case had legionella.

"I'm pretty sure," Helen said, giving her a bag of samples of erythromycin and writing her a prescription.

"But I thought it only happened to children," she said. "I'm twenty-six."

"It happens to anyone," Helen said. "Children just seem to have been the ones susceptible in Meridian."

"I know who I caught it from," Sandy said. "I took care of Sallie last week while Ann went to Toledo."

"The doctor says this isn't the kind of disease you catch from people," Prudential said skeptically.

"How do you know?" Sandy asked. "Everybody is getting it."

Helen sat down on a stool, across from her. "What we know about this illness is its symptoms, which are fever and chills, muscle aches, sometimes diarrhea and sometimes a dry cough and pleurisy," she said. "We know it can come from contaminated air cooling systems, which you don't have in Meridian, and from organisms in water."

Helen noticed a look pass between Prudential and Sandy Case but she went on. "We also know, because we have no evidence otherwise, it isn't passed through the air from person to person."

Sandy shrugged. "Maybe not other places," she said, gathering up her medicine.

"In Meridian, we make each other sick," Prudential said.

"You need to go to bed," Helen said, letting the remark go by. "Be sure to boil your water, drink lots of fluids and I'll drop by your house to check on you this evening."

"Mrs. Lennon tells me the lump she found in the shower this morning has disappeared," Prudential said. "So she went home."

Helen pulled off the paper on the examining table, cleaned the counter, dropped the disposable material in the trash can. "Prudential?" She folded her arms across her chest. "I have the sense that you doubt what I say about legionella."

"I doubt what everyone says," Prudential replied with a look of impenetrable calm.

"People asked me to this town because you needed a doctor," Helen said wearily. "If you have all the answers, I should leave."

"Suit yourself," Prudential said.

In her office, Helen opened the window and turned on the fan. It was almost five o'clock, hot and hazy, uncomfortably still. She took off her white starched jacket and unbuttoned her blouse.

When Prudential knocked, she was still sitting in her chair, her feet on the windowsill, half sleeping in exhaustion, but she jumped up with a start.

"Trouble," Prudential said.

"Trouble?"

"Madeleine Sailor is still here." Prudential stepped just inside the door and shut it behind her. "I told her we have house calls to make and she says she only wants a minute of your time."

"Okay," Helen said, buttoning her blouse, putting on her white jacket. "Send her in."

Madeleine Sailor seemed to be drunk. She was wearing a long pale peach silk skirt, a dressy skirt for evenings, and a sweater in the sweltering heat. On her chin she had a small red circle of lipstick exactly the size of the end of a lipstick tube. She sat down in the chair across from Helen, smiling a little cockeyed child's smile.

"You're looking at my beauty mark?" She touched the red circle with her finger. "It's really only lipstick but I'm calling it a beauty mark."

"Are you ill?" Helen asked, standing up, walking around her desk and leaning against it so she was looking down at Madeleine Sailor.

"Oh no, not ill at all," she said. "I'm perfectly fine. Perfectly fine fine fine. Do you remember that song? I used to sing it to Maggie. I'm perfectly fine fine fine," she sang, "all the time time time. Except when I'm blue." She laughed. "No. I came to see you not because I'm sick at all but with a message to you." She opened up her crocheted bag and took out a piece of paper which she unfolded carefully and handed to Helen. "That is my message."

Helen took the note. It was written on white typing paper with red Magic Marker. She read it and handed it back to Madeleine.

WATCH OUT, it said.

"Is that all?"

"That's all," Madeleine said. "I wrote it for you."

"Thank you very much."

"But it's a warning, don't you understand?"

"I do understand."

"I thought you should know there are people in Meridian who are not pleased to have you here."

"Are you one of them?" Helen asked.

"Oh no," Madeleine said. "I'm a friend."

"Then thank you for warning me." She helped Madeleine Sailor out of her chair, walking her to the door, and in such close proximity she could smell the strong odor of alcohol on her breath.

"Have you seen the film yet?" Madeleine asked.

"Some of it," Helen said. "I'll see the rest this weekend."

"Call me if you have any clues," Madeleine said. "I'll be eternally grateful. Eternally. Eternally."

Helen stood at the door and watched her walk unsteadily up the street.

"Drunk?" Prudential asked.

"I think," Helen said.

"I'll call her husband to pick her up," Prudential said. "That's new. I don't think Madeleine ever had anything stronger than lemonade to drink."

"Poor woman. It's too awful for her." Helen packed her bag for house calls. "Where first?" she asked.

"We should go to the Durhams' and the Wellers'," Prudential said.

"What about Maria? Have you spoken to the Walkers?" Helen asked.

"Maria's almost herself again."

"And Sandy Case?" Helen said.

"She lives at the other end of town, beyond the rail station. We'll go there last."

"Have you heard from the hospital in Toledo about Kathy Bauer?"

"It was an ovarian cyst. They're keeping her overnight and want you to call."

Helen telephoned the hospital in Toledo, filled a thermos with ice water and headed out.

"Reverend Winters called to say you can use his car any time you need to go to the hospital."

"I'm going there tonight."

"He'll drive you there so you can find your way the first time."

It was the kind of hot day in which the air takes on weight, a pale yellow haze like a gauze curtain separates the eye from objects in the distance. Helen felt not ill exactly but unlike herself, unfamiliar in her head.

They moved along Main Street without conversation. Helen could tell that Prudential wanted to speak but she wasn't going to make it easy for her.

She opened the thermos.

"Water?" She handed it to Prudential. Then she dipped her fingers in and wiped her forehead. "Ungodly hot."

Prudential had fallen in step.

"You've walked into a hornets' nest," Prudential said finally.

"So it seems," Helen said.

"You're a nice woman and I like women a little edgy." She cocked her handsome head and smiled at Helen. "I'm sorry it's the way it is."

Helen laughed. "What way is it?" she asked, knowing the question wouldn't be answered.

They walked up the steep hill to the Durhams' past Mrs. Barrett feeding her tabby cat on the front porch and Mr. Terry in a large straw hat tending his garden.

"A hornets' nest is fine for hornets as long as you don't walk into it," Prudential said. This seemed to please her. She wiped her damp hands on her cotton shirt, laughing a little to herself.

It was late when Helen got back from the hospital in Harrisville and only slightly cooler.

Ben Winters drove her home. He was a careful driver, apologizing if he made a small mistake, stopping the car too quickly, inching too far in front of a stop sign.

"You don't need to take me all the way home," Helen said. "Stop at your house. It's a nice night and I'd like to walk."

Ben Winters protested, full of good will—"Oh, let me take you, anything could happen."

"Like what?" Helen asked. "In Meridian?"

He laughed. "Of course not. Nothing happens in Meridian," he said. "But it's so dark out tonight, you can't even see the moon."

"I'll be fine," she said.

She walked along the silent, empty Main Street, hearing the river's distant locomotive roar.

The house was dark, a blue-gray darkness of early evening, but even before she walked in the front door she had an overwhelming sense that either someone was there or had been there moments before. She stood in the hall at the arch that led to the living room and turned on the light. On the white wall above a slate-gray couch and beside a large photograph from the turn of the century of Meridian railway station, written in black glossy paint in a large and messy scrawl, was

DR. HELEN FIELDING GO HOME.

And underneath HOME was a funny mark, a kind of frenzied animal with broad brush strokes, a porcupine perhaps, more troubling than the message.

IV.

WEATHER REPORT

The Story of

MERIDIAN

THE THIRD DAY of the shoot of "Meridian," a bleak windy April Wednesday, difficult for filming, Peter Forester woke up early with a strange, unfamiliar euphoria, a kind of pleasant drunkenness, on a day whose weather would generally have put him on the edge of temper. He checked his watch—sixten—got up, dressed, ran his fingers through his long thick hair and left quietly by the back door of the church hall.

The air was damp and cold to the bone so he walked quickly down Main, lit by a line of streetlights, pale yellow circles in the foggy dawn.

Sophie lived on Poplar Street, a long narrow street, straight uphill into the small forest that topped the cone of hills around Meridian. She had a small peach house with white shutters and, as he approached the bottom of Poplar, he was pleased to see a light on the second floor of her house. So she was up too, unable to sleep, thinking about him.

This hadn't happened to him before. He wasn't easily won over, known in his personal and professional life as focused and unflappable, subtle in his energy with unused pockets in reserve. He had been married once briefly and there was always a woman, generally tall and blonde, cool-tempered, witty, intelligent, deceptively fragile. He was predictable that way, predictable too in the excellence of his documentary films, known for his ability to make clear and moving the personal and humane in the flat linear format of documentary. Now suddenly he had this exhilarated sense of slipping.

He had looked at the clips the night before. Sophie, here and there—at the market, in the coffee shop, at the pharmacy, on the front steps of her house with Molly.

"This is absurd," T. J. Wisely had said to him. "If anyone in Meridian saw what I'm seeing, they'd ask us to leave town. Sophie isn't Meridian. She didn't come until a few years ago."

"I take your point," Peter Forester had said. "Don't worry your pretty head. I'm going to be able to make this story work."

But he couldn't help himself. He saw Sophie DeLaurentis as a fallen doe. He wanted to possess her, assume her, as if such union would somehow purify his heart. It wasn't physical or simply physical. But on the third morning of the Meridian shoot Peter Forester's destination was sex.

The telephone rang in the dark but Sophie was already up, propped in her bed, thinking about what to wear for tomorrow's shoot and should she change her hair style. Maybe "up" would be pretty. They had told her to wear makeup, especially with her dark skin. Red, red lips were striking, they said, although ordinarily she didn't wear any color. She turned on the light next to her bed.

"Hello," she said quietly, so as not to wake Molly sleeping at the end of the hall.

"Sophie," Dr. Richard Hazelton said.

"It's too early," Sophie said. "I'm still sleeping."

"I want Molly out of this film," he said. "I spoke to Ann Durham yesterday afternoon and you're making Molly into a little starlet. She's just a baby."

"I'm not doing anything," Sophie said. "The film crew makes the decision."

"I'm coming over today before my office hours to pick her up," Richard Hazelton said. "She can play in the waiting room. Prudential will keep an eye on her."

"Not today, Richard, please," Sophie said. "They're doing play group today and then they're doing your office. They told me I was to bring her to your office with a sore throat."

He hesitated. "Does she have a sore throat?"

"She could have. I mean we're supposed to pretend she has a sore throat. The film needs a story line, Peter says, and Molly and I are sort of it," Sophie said. "Besides, today is Mona Dickenson's viewing. They'll be doing the viewing and I'm not taking Molly there."

"I'm certainly glad to hear that," Richard said. "I'll be over for coffee and we can talk about it then."

"Maybe tomorrow, Rich," Sophie said, "we can have coffee tomorrow." But he had hung up.

Downstairs, she heard what sounded like a knock on the front door. She went to the head of the stairs and looked down. There in the paned window at the top of the door she could see the thick black curly hair of Peter Forester.

She ran to the bathroom, opened the window and called, "I'll be right down in just a second."

David Jaspersen was just making coffee when Richard Hazelton knocked on the front door.

"Trouble?" David asked, leading him into the kitchen. "It's not even seven o'clock yet."

"No trouble," Richard Hazelton said. "No one is sick."

Richie Hazelton had been a strange boy growing up in Meridian, just odd enough with his long arms, his troubling self-consciousness, to be worrisome to people his own age. There was something disturbing about him. In high school he had been ridiculed but his peers were cautious, sensing him capable of unpredictable behavior.

As an adult, he was quiet, without the capacity for small talk, and David assumed he had acquaintances but few friends. This morning, however, David was aware of something different in Rich Hazelton. He sat across from David at the kitchen table in his white physician's coat and tie, thin-lipped, pale, trembling just beneath the skin, a subcutaneous muscle revolution.

"I don't want Molly in the film," he said.

"None of us ought to be in the film," David said. "But there isn't much we can do about it."

They had coffee. David made toast and offered Dr. Hazelton cereal which he refused. Upstairs he could hear Win getting out of bed for school.

"Most everyone in town is pleased this is happening, as I'm sure you know," David said.

"I know," Dr. Hazelton said.

"I don't like it because it's too complicated to have these

extra people around." David poured them another cup of coffee. "And I don't like it because people are willing to do anything to get seen on television." David let the dog in the back door.

"That's it," Rich said, his face filling with color. "Like Sophie." He shook his head. "She's an idiot."

"I wouldn't expect anything else of her," David said.

"But Molly"—Rich Hazelton held his head with his hands—"children shouldn't have to be what their parents make them. If Sophie wants to—" He broke off mid-sentence. "Don't you think?" he asked David. "If Sophie wants to, that's her business but she shouldn't push Molly onto her stage."

David shrugged. "Parents have done that with their children for a long time."

"Well, it's very wrong," Rich said.

Win called and David went upstairs to check on him. When he came back down, Rich Hazelton was in the hall.

"Thanks," he said to David. "I suppose I just needed to blow off steam before I drop by Sophie's for coffee."

"No trouble," David said, and they shook hands.

He watched Dr. Hazelton walk down the steps, across the street, through the Angels' side yard, the shortcut to Sophie's, two blocks directly east of David's.

Then he picked up the telephone and dialed Sophie's number. She answered on the first ring.

"Can I call you back?" she asked in a soft curly voice.

David said not to bother. He had to go to work and would see her later, probably at Mona Dickenson's viewing.

"Do you happen to know the weather for today?" Sophie asked.

"Only what I see outside the window. Not a filmmaker's dream day," David said and hung up.

"So," David said when Win sat down to breakfast. "Has the film crew got many shots of you and your friends?"

Win shook his head. "They're supposed to do a baseball game. We were asked to dress up tomorrow to play on the high school field but they haven't got any pictures of me except maybe one looking at comics at the drugstore yesterday." He finished his cereal and put his bowl in the sink. "Danny O'Neill says the only kids they're filming are Molly De-Laurentis and Sallie Durham." He got his snow jacket, baseball cap, his book bag, kissed his father good-bye and left for school.

Dr. Richard Hazelton walked across the Angels' yard. Danny Angel, who worked in construction in Harrisville, was up and dressed in the kitchen and opened the window when Dr. Hazelton passed by.

"Trouble?" he called.

"No trouble," Rich replied. "I just had coffee with the chief of police and I'm headed through your yard to Poplar." He didn't mention Sophie by name.

"Have you been in the movie yet?" Danny asked.

"Not yet," Rich said.

"Me neither," Danny called and shut the window.

Richard Hazelton had grown up in Meridian, the last child of older parents, his father dead by the time he was six.

For a long time, most of his childhood until he won the state science prize in ninth grade, his mother worried that he was too timid for the world, too strange, that he might in fact never have the emotional strength to leave home. All the way through school, even after the science prize, he was the object of ridicule especially from boys his own age. The only pleasant social time he had was with older ladies in the neighborhood. But the science prize, won for an experiment in chemical properties of weather, focused his floating energy, slipped him onto a track from which he never deviated until he met Sophie DeLaurentis.

He was seventeen when he went to college, twenty-two when he graduated from medical school at the top of his class and twenty-five when he received a Ph.D. in molecular biology. He was offered jobs everywhere, in labs, in teaching, as a scientist at large universities, but what he wanted in his heart and soul was to return to Meridian to his small town where the only doctor was a family doctor, in charge of the health of all of the citizens of the community. He wanted to matter to the people from his lonely childhood.

He was happy in Meridian. People were kind to him, depended on him, invited him to dinner and cookouts and family reunions. He had what passed for genuine friends, which he had never had before. He had his own house, which he organized the way his laboratory had been organized at Michigan, and a straight-spoken nurse in Prudential, who treated him with dignity. He was a part of a life which as a young man growing up had seemed unlikely to ever happen.

———

When Sophie DeLaurentis stayed the night at his small clapboard house early in November just before his thirtieth birthday, he was still a virgin. He had never kissed a woman or held her hand or even been alone with one younger than sixty except professionally. He had thought about Sophie. She was the kind of luscious woman men did think about but he had never expected she would take an interest in him.

And it happened so fast, he could hardly catch his breath. One afternoon she came into the clinic with a fever and by that evening she was lying on top of the sheets of his bed, a soft golden body with large perfect breasts and a mass of black curly hair against his pillow.

At the time, she was married to Mr. DeLaurentis and before the year was out she would be a widow. For weeks afterward, she came to Rich Hazelton's house in secret. She never told him that she loved him or made promises although he spilled out his own declarations of love. But he knew she loved him, must love him, or why else would she come to his bed?

During those months, almost seven of them from the beginning of November until June, two months before Molly was born, they were together. It was almost impossible for Dr. Hazelton to maintain his practice of medicine with the internal explosion of his heart.

He felt as if he flew everywhere, a heavy bird flying low over the branches like an oversize sparkler scattering light.

Sophie never said it was his child. But how not? he asked himself. Certainly the child didn't belong to Mr. De-Laurentis at fifty-nine with a bad heart.

He planned to marry her later, maybe August, after the baby was born and the year of mourning nearly done. And they'd move, maybe to the old Duncan place just north of town with more land and a larger house.

Meanwhile, she came less and less often to visit him. First it was once or twice a week and then once in two weeks. He assumed that was the pregnancy. He was worried but he was too much of an innocent with women to prepare himself for her announcement that the affair was over.

"I planned to marry you," he said. "To raise our child."

"But, Rich," Sophie said, "the baby is Antonio De-Laurentis's baby."

"That's not possible," Richard said. "I'm a doctor. I know it. It's not possible."

She shook her head. "You don't know everything."

She broke his heart.

When Molly was born on the first of August, Richard Hazelton knew. She was his child, his small unclaimed treasure from the love affair of his life—the long almond-shaped eyes, the narrow head and slender fingers; the hair was Sophie's and the coloring and the full lips. But she was his daughter and though Sophie never once agreed that it was a possibility—"I was pregnant before I slept with you," she said —Richard Hazelton laid claim and all the bits and shreds of his shattered heart belonged to that baby.

He walked around the back of the Angels', through the Beeches' yard, across the Durhams' garden and then to Sophie's. Sophie's house was small and the garden fenced to keep wildlife out of the vegetables in summer but as he came up to the side of the house beside the kitchen, looking in the window, what he saw was Sophie leaning against the fridge kissing the tall, slender director from CBS television.

Mona Dickenson's viewing was at home, her mother's house, a white clapboard set back from Main Street on Snow's Court.

David Jaspersen went early although the hours weren't set until afternoon. He wanted to talk to Mona's father about the filming. According to T.J., the family had approved.

But when he walked through the high white gate, T.J. was already there talking to Tommy, Mona's young husband, and her mother.

"The casket's open," Mona's mother said. "She went so quickly, the cancer didn't have a chance to eat her up like it did her father, so she looks just as lovely as she always did."

"She was a beauty," David said, kissing Mona's mother. "The one true beauty we've sent out from Meridian."

"I was talking to Tommy about the film crew," T.J. said to David.

"You're sure you want this to happen today?" David asked Tommy Dickenson.

"I don't mind but I don't want them inside the house." Tommy leaned against the fence, too weary with sadness to stand. "But if the film people are outside—quietly, quietly—I don't want a circus, T.J."

"You don't have to have anything, Tommy," T.J. said.

Tommy shook his head. "That guy, Peter, the director— stopped by last night. He made it seem all right. He said he'd heard from everywhere that Mona was beautiful," and he excused himself with a small complicitous wave to David and T.J. so he didn't break down in their company.

David shook his head. "I can't believe the invasion of privacy."

"Peter Forester's character is not my responsibility," T.J. said, wheeling along the road toward the Catholic church, lit from above by an early morning sun threatening to make a full appearance.

"I'm not holding you accountable for everything, T.J.," David said.

"You're a prince," T.J. said.

The day had turned when the viewing started at three—a clear spring day with a full distant sun, a deep blue sky; the colors of Meridian were spectacular. It was cold, not a harsh cold, so the front door of the house was open, Tommy and Mona's mother, her sister Nora, Tommy's parents, greeting people as they arrived, and the line formed quickly at three. By three-fifteen it was all the way down Snow's Court to Main Street.

The film crew was in the front garden, set up well beyond the assembly, and there was an almost crazy explosive excitement among them.

"It's like a circus," David said to Sophie, coming up behind her in the line of mourners.

She had come alone. The camera had actually followed her from Main Street, up Snow's Court, an angle from the side as she rushed up the street, with tiny steps, constricted by her long straight black skirt, her high, high heels. She had on a white-collared blouse, a long black coat and a brightly colored silk scarf, reds and oranges and yellows.

"Peter said the black and white didn't show too well on color film so he gave me this scarf," she told David when he asked why such a splash of color at a wake.

He wanted to hit her. He actually could feel the clear and urgent sense of picking her up and throwing her down Snow's Court to Main.

Peter Forester, dressed for the occasion, moved in on the crowd, picking up bits of conversation, zooming in on the faces of the community. There was even a still shot of a picture of Mona which Madeleine Sailor had—a lovely black and white head shot from her senior yearbook.

"I remember her when she was very young," Mr. Rubin was saying to Danny O'Connor and his wife. "She looked like an angel then and she looks like an angel now." He shook his head. "I haven't wept to do anyone for years. But when her body came to the funeral parlor yesterday morning, I wept."

"Did she look bad?" Mrs. O'Connor asked.

"She looked beautiful," Mr. Rubin said. "Liver cancer can be fast and merciful and hers was."

On the outskirts of the group of mourners, Mona's golden retriever stood, a black satin ribbon around his neck, a white rose stuck in the tie, and Peter Forester focused on the dog, who cocked his head.

Peter walked to the front of the line where a grim Madeleine Sailor stood with Henry and their daughter Maggie.

"She was in your class, wasn't she, Madeleine?"

Madeleine nodded. "I loved her," she said, restrained,

her voice thin. "She was my closest friend and Maggie's god-mother."

"It was so fast."

Madeleine nodded. "We were always known as the goody girls in class," she said softly. "But no one knew what really went on with us, how we smoked just there in the barn behind Mona's house"—she folded her hands under her chin demurely—"and drank very bad Gallo wine and, once when we were only fourteen, T.J. found us swimming naked in the river and stole our clothes." She smiled. "We had to run home with nothing on."

"They were a perfect couple," Mrs. Rubin said when David Jaspersen came up behind her. "What children they could have had, right, David? And Tommy Dickenson's the only one but you we thought was going to amount to something beyond Meridian."

"He already has," David said, moving back in the line to Sophie, who stood quiet and prayerful, conscious of the camera on her right, scanning her each time she focused on the conversation of a group of mourners.

"Where's Molly?"

"Dr. Hazelton has her in the clinic today," Sophie said. "Prudential is probably looking after her. I didn't want her here of course."

"Maggie Sailor is here and Sallie Durham," David said.

"But their mothers knew Mona. I never did. She had already left for college before I married Mr. DeLaurentis and moved here." She smiled. "Remember?"

T. J. Wisely was in the corner of the garden, his jaw fixed, his arms wrapped tight across his chest.

"Having a blast, T.J.?" David asked.

"Knock it off, David."

"At least your friends from Hollywood aren't disruptive."

"No, but if you pay attention, you'll discover they have about forty shots of Sophie and the rest of the dog."

"I'm sorry, T.J.," David said. "But they're trying to make the most of this dramatic opportunity, right?"

"Shut up."

"How do you get the feeling without inventing the fact?" David asked, leaning against T.J.'s wheelchair. "This film is about feeling, right?"

"This film is important to me," T.J. said quietly, pulling his wheelchair over to a clump of trees. "It means everything. Meridian was my parents."

In the final shot of the finished film after the garden was empty of people, the front door of the Dickensons' house closed, dusk settling, Peter Forester had a frame of the long french doors lined with thin lace curtains in the front of the house, the outline of Mona Dickenson's casket in the background, and in the foreground her golden retriever lay on the front step, the white rose, its petals sheared, beside him.

11.

HELEN STOOD IN THE WINDOW watching for David Jaspersen.

It was almost midnight and when she called he had been sleeping.

"'DR. HELEN FIELDING GO HOME' is what it says," she told him.

"I'm so sorry," David said.

"The paint on the wall is still wet," she said. "Whoever did it must have finished just before I came home."

"I'll be right over."

She was too upset to search the house although she was sure the message had been written by someone who came in the house and left right away. A person wouldn't hide out and wait for her. If he had in mind to hurt her, why would he bother to write a message announcing himself? She thought of Madeleine Sailor with her warning but that poor drunken woman was not capable of the bold statement splashed on the white walls of Helen's house.

She picked up Gregory and pressed him against her. It was taking David Jaspersen too long and the earth seemed to be quaking around her. She had been in an earthquake once in San Francisco with her father in the middle of the afternoon in a restaurant high over the bay. It was not even a large quake but there was no announcement that the earth was about to shift, no warning, just a funny feeling under the floor where her feet were resting, a sense of being a little drunk, the room spinning, some customers spilling out of their chairs, rushing to an archway, and then it was over, not even a rumble, just a momentary alteration. But it felt dangerous to Helen, coming so quickly, just a whisper of danger, a reminder, and then it was gone.

"What was that?" Helen had asked her father.

"A tiny earthquake," her father said. "Wasn't that an earthquake?" He leaned over to the table next to them where a man and a woman were reading their menus. The woman looked up.

"I believe so but who can tell, it was so small."

"I want to go home," Helen said, getting up from the table.

"We're safer here," her father had said.

"I want to leave now," she'd said. "I don't like the earth to change without telling first."

She had grown up with weather, on a comma in the middle of Lake Michigan, buffeted by weather as it rushed up and down and across the United States, and she didn't like it. She wanted to be able to read the weather report in the newspaper and count on what it said. Tomorrow will be calm and sunny, below freezing with no change in sight. Even dependable rain was better than a question mark, the earth slipping underneath her feet as if the planet itself was malleable as a putty ball.

The air in Dr. Richard Hazelton's house was thinning and she leaned against the couch with Gregory, too lightheaded to watch at the window for David Jaspersen to come. The last she remembered, she was thinking she must sit down quickly.

She and Emma had a seesaw at Aunt Martha's—or maybe it was in the backyard of the house in Ann Arbor. She couldn't remember. After Emma died, her mother never returned to the house. They put it up for sale and her father packed the boxes. Helen did remember going with him into the house, which in her memory was very large with long windows opened in summer onto a field. Perhaps that's where the seesaw had been. She knew it was red, that Emma sat on one end and she on the other, but because she was so much heavier than Emma, she was not supposed to sit down with her full weight on the seesaw, keeping Emma up in the air where she might fall.

"Be careful of Emma," her mother would call from the upstairs window. "She might fall."

She did fall once. Helen couldn't remember the circumstances or what happened when she fell or if she was hurt or even cried. But she could see Emma in her mind's eye tumbling through the air as if she had fallen from a great height, tumbling over and over toward the ground.

Helen saw headlights, not headlights exactly, but lights

moving through the trees toward where she was lying, and what she saw in the wide light from a high moon almost at full circle was Emma Fielding tumbling through the dark gray summer sky toward earth.

"I can't stop shaking," she said to David, who sat next to her on the couch where she was lying. "Was I unconscious?"

"You were lying on the floor and your eyes were open," he said.

She took her own pulse. "Rapid," she said. Her mouth was dry and her breathing shallow. "I think I fainted," she said, taking hold of his hand. "A syncopal attack caused by fear." She smiled. "Syncopal has such a nice musical sound. Mmm." She closed her eyes. "I feel weird," she said. "This hasn't happened to me before." She tried to regulate her breathing, to put her mind another place but the all-over shaking wouldn't stop.

David had stood up and was checking the writing on the wall.

"I'm sorry," he said. "I'm truly sorry. Whoever did it was thorough. The paint's enamel."

She kept her eyes closed.

"I have an extra bedroom," he offered. "You can stay there tonight."

"Maybe I will." She sat up on her elbow, resting her head in her hand. "Who do you think could have done it?" she asked.

He shook his head. "I don't know."

"Madeleine Sailor?"

She told him about the warning Madeleine had written.

"It's not in her character," David said, standing back to look at the painted wall. "I've known Madeleine all my life."

Helen stood up slowly, holding onto the side of the couch.

"Something is really the matter in Meridian, isn't it?" she asked. "It's not just bacteria."

"Something seems to be." He put his arm around Helen's waist.

"I'm fine," she said, stepping away from him. "I'd just like to get out of this house before a time bomb goes off."

"There's no time bomb," David said, taking her hand, turning off the lights.

"Who knows?" she said, still lightheaded and a little sick.

"Who do you think wants me out?" Helen asked as they drove down Main Street in the soft darkness, all the houses still as dollhouses. "Everyone?"

"That's difficult to say. I don't know. There are a few people who could be having a hard time with a stranger getting to know people's personal histories, which you do since you're a doctor."

"But they wanted a doctor. You had to get a stranger."

"People aren't necessarily pleased to get what they want," he said, pulling to a stop in front of his house. He put his hand on her cheek.

———

Someone was in Helen's room. It was morning but very early, dawn maybe, and she could feel the presence of another person. Somewhere she heard conversation.

When she opened her eyes, a boy, maybe seven or eight, very blond with a square English haircut and lazy-lidded eyes, stood at the end of her bed.

"Hello," she said, sitting half up, still dressed in the clothes she had on the day before. "I'm Helen Fielding."

"I know," he said. "I saw you when you came on the train from Detroit."

"You must be David's son," she said.

"Are you his girlfriend?"

"No," she said. "I spent the night because there was a problem at my house."

"He told me." The boy made no effort to move. "Maybe he's found the person who messed up your house," he said. "She's downstairs talking to my father."

He sat down on the end of the bed.

"She's crying," he said with a certain pleasure.

"That's too bad." Helen threw off her covers and got up. "Who is she?"

"You know about Maggie?"

"Maggie?"

"Maggie Sailor. The girl who was stolen."

"I have heard about her," Helen said, brushing her hair with her fingers.

"That's her mother downstairs crying."

"And you think she's the person who wrote on the walls of my house?" She could hear a woman downstairs sobbing. "It doesn't seem like the kind of thing she would do."

Win shrugged. "We think a stranger stole Maggie, so Madeleine doesn't like strangers."

Helen went through her things and took out her toothbrush.

"The bathroom's across the hall," the boy said. "It's a little dirty and you can't turn on the cold water, so be careful."

"Could I borrow a brush?"

"I think we have one." Win looked through a dresser. "I don't have a mother, so things are pretty messy."

"Where is your mother?" Helen asked.

"I don't even know her except she has yellow hair like mine and freckles and, when she left us, she married the chief of police in Madison, Wisconsin, where we lived. That's why my father changed from being a lawyer to the chief of police." He lay down on the bed where Helen had been sleeping. "I'll wait till you come out of the bathroom."

In the bathroom Helen washed her face. She decided against the brush, which was thick with beige hair and grease, but she found some mouthwash and a tiny bar of soap, no toilet paper, and the water, as Win had warned her, only ran hot.

Madeleine Sailor sat at the kitchen table with her head in her arms and, when Helen came downstairs, David motioned her away, excused himself and followed her to the front door.

"You may have been right," he said. "It could have been her."

"You think?" Helen said.

"I don't know," he said, walking across the front porch

with Helen, down the steps, along the brick walk to the street. "She called me this morning because someone in Grace, Ohio, claims to have seen Maggie. And just after she called, T.J. called to say he had seen her come out of your house last night."

"But it doesn't seem like a thing she would do, does it? That's what you said last night."

David shrugged. "Who knows?"

Helen checked her watch—seven thirty-five—pinned her hair back up. "Call me if you find out anything."

"I will," he said. "Are you better today?" David asked.

"I'm fine," Helen said.

She wasn't entirely fine. She felt a kind of weakness as if it were her first day up from the flu.

"I'll check in with you later to be sure you haven't died," David said.

"Sweet of you," she laughed. He didn't kiss her but she thought he was going to—it felt as if he wanted to kiss her.

"See you later." He waved. So did Win, who had come out on the front porch, waving and waving.

Prudential was already at the clinic when Helen arrived.

"I heard the news," she said.

Helen slipped into the chair next to her, out of breath after the short walk.

"It's not the town it used to be," Prudential said without looking up but there was genuine sympathy in her voice.

"Things change," Helen said, looking through the folders of patients.

Prudential shook her head. "Not by accident," she said, picking up the ringing telephone. "Meridian Clinic," she said. "Bring her right over." She took out the Hart chart from the file. "Cinder Hart spilled hot water from the stove down the front of her." She hung up the phone. "Last month it was her finger in a light socket."

"Have there been a lot of calls?"

"Four on the machine when I came in—Sallie Durham is coming over during clinic hours, Billie Bliss, Mr. Rubin, the funeral director, has bronchitis and Penny Noels has a rash on her chest." Prudential cocked her head. "Why doesn't a woman like you have a boyfriend or a husband—old as you are and not bad-looking?"

"I tried that," Helen laughed.

"So have I," Prudential said cheerfully. "More than once."

"I don't know about husbands," Helen said, and for a moment before Mrs. Hart flew through the front door of the clinic with Cinder and her baby daughter, the two women were cheerful conspirators, actual friends, and Helen felt a breath of safety in a hostile camp. She moved her chair closer to Prudential on the pretext of checking a chart, moved her arm next to hers, grateful for the comfort of flesh. "I have a lot to know before I'm ready for a husband."

"It's probably not worth knowing," Prudential said.

Cinder was a blond, pale, silent child, burned on her right arm and her shoulder and her neck.

Mrs. Hart sat in a chair across the room, holding her baby. She shook her head.

"I don't know what's the matter with her," she said to

Helen, who was bathing Cinder's burns in ice water. "Every time she touches anything, it's a disaster. She even rode her new bike into a tree and it's got training wheels."

Prudential leaned against the examining tables, took a deck of cards from her pocket and handed Cinder the queen of diamonds.

"You put that under your pillow tonight and don't move it," she said to Cinder as she clutched the playing card. "You know what that card is?"

"Queen," Cinder said.

"Queen of what?"

"Queen of diamonds."

"And if you put her under your pillow, you're going to stop having the accidents you've been having. You understand?"

Cinder nodded. "No more accidents," she said, kissing the plastic double face of the queen of diamonds.

Helen sat down on a stool, pulling it over to Mrs. Hart. "This looks like mostly first-degree burns which involve only the top layer of skin. Except here." Helen pointed to a line of burn from the shoulder to the wrist on Cinder's forearm. "This appears to be second-degree, which is the second layer of skin." She took the ointment Prudential had given her. "I'll dress the wounds with this ointment and you should give her plenty of juices. Not so much water."

"This all started in late April after the film people were here," Mrs. Hart said. "First Cinder just crossed the street in front of Tom Reem's car without looking, didn't you, sweetheart?"

Cinder closed her eyes.

"And then she was bitten by a dog who never bites. Remember, Prudential? The Mullinses' white dog."

She stood up and put her baby on her hip. "And then the bicycle."

Helen lifted Cinder to the ground. "These burns are painful," she said.

"She shouldn't have touched the boiling pot." Mrs. Hart buried her face in her baby's soft hair. "Have you seen the film?"

"A little of it," Helen said.

"Cinder was the lead in *Snow White* and they showed the play on the film. There's also a shot of her at the pharmacy with a lollipop and walking to school with Sallie Durham," she said. "It went to her head." She excused herself and went to the Ladies.

"Does it hurt when I touch it?" Helen asked Cinder quietly. Her eyes were still closed but when she opened them, Helen noticed how clear a blue they were—not a bright blue but clear, and she found herself moved by the pure color of such blue eyes. "Does it?" Helen asked again.

Cinder looked up at her and didn't flinch.

"I hate my baby sister," she said.

Emma was born in early October on a Sunday, wet and cold in Ann Arbor. Helen remembered the weather because her absent-minded father took her to the hospital without a raincoat and she sat in the waiting room with a nurse who took off her wet clothes and put her in a hospital gown while her father went to see her mother. When she first saw Emma, she was wearing that dreadful hospital gown and what would Emma possibly think of her looking so foolish? Her mother, in a wheelchair, held the baby over to her, saying, "Be careful." "Be careful of Emma" as if by touching her Helen would do harm.

DO NO HARM.

She and Emma were someplace dark and damp with the smell of mothballs—maybe an attic, maybe the attic of Aunt Martha's where the pictures of her father as a child were in boxes, where the dolls with china faces from Aunt Martha's childhood were lined up against the wall.

"Be careful of Emma," her mother called from somewhere far off.

Emma sat on the floor of the attic in her yellow sunsuit, holding an old baby doll in her chubby arms.

"Be careful of Emma in the attic," her father called.

Why should she be so careful of Emma? What could happen to a plump smiley little girl with a worrying mother and father? And what about Helen? She could fall out of the attic window, three stories down to the slate patio. She could catch on fire. That didn't seem to matter very much to them. She could die.

"I hate you," Helen said to the plump child, her sister, sitting happily at her feet.

"How bad was that burn?" Prudential asked after the clinic hours were over and Helen was leaving to meet David Jaspersen and go back to her house.

"Not bad," Helen said. "I made a fuss because the mother was being terrible to her child."

"People go bad like peaches," Prudential said. "They start to go bad one place and before you know it they're rotten through and through." She stuck a pencil behind her ear and checked through the appointments for the afternoon. "I'll stay here through lunch," she said.

David Jaspersen was already at Richard Hazelton's house when Helen got there, standing on the front porch with his large hands in his pockets directing the painters who were finishing the wall.

"Let it dry and then go over it," David said to the two young men. "Did you sand it first?"

They nodded.

"Has the writing disappeared?" Helen asked, coming up on the porch.

"Not exactly," David said. "Not yet."

The writing on the wall was dim but still clear enough to read through the paint.

"I don't know what to say." David leaned against the porch railing. "You can stay with me until we can find you another place."

Helen shook her head. "It doesn't seem to matter where I stay," she said. "It's that I'm here at all."

He walked outside and leaned against the porch railing, an expression on his face as if he were about to speak but had changed his mind.

"You were going to say something?" Helen asked softly.

"What would you like to do?" he asked.

"I don't know. Go back to Ann Arbor before long, I suppose," she said. "There're too many secrets here."

David brushed an imaginary insect from her face.

"It's not that secrets are being kept from you in particular. It's that we don't trust strangers, we don't even seem to trust each other." He followed her down the steps. "Your mother called."

"My mother?" Helen asked.

"One of the painters told me."

"What did she say?"

"Just call back."

Helen went inside and picked up the phone.

"You're sure it was my mother?" she said to the painters.

"That's what she called herself," one of the painters said.

Helen dialed the number, her heart racing. She felt the way she used to feel after her father left, after they moved to Mackinaw, waiting on the steps of the island school for her mother to pick her up, her mother late, so often late, and Helen thinking, Will she come soon, will she come at all, has she left by boat for the mainland? Now she could see her mother from years of watching her sitting quietly at the window of her room in Mrs. Peaches's guesthouse, her slender legs drawn up under her chin, looking into the middle distance, hoping for a sign of good news.

It was the answering machine. "Please leave a message at the beep." But Helen did not.

"She also left a message on the machine when I was in the john," the painter said. "I heard her voice. So she called twice."

Helen played the messages.

"Helen, it's Allie." There was a little giggle. "Your mother, Alice Fielding. I have a bad feeling. Your father agrees. I spoke with him just a while ago. We think maybe you shouldn't be in Meridian. Please call."

Helen picked up the telephone again and dialed, waiting for the beep on the answering machine.

"Mama, you never answer my calls and I have to talk to you. I have to talk to you about Emma. Mama? Are you just sitting there listening to me?" She put the phone down and dialed her father, who answered on the first ring and out of breath.

"I have a question," she said, not allowing him the opportunity to frame a careful response. "Do you and Mama blame me for what happened?"

"Of course not, Helen," her father said. "What happened was an accident."

"But I don't really believe in accidents," Helen said. "I see them all the time in the hospital and they're not accidents. They're carelessness."

"Well," her father began, and was he going to say yes, of course, that was true, it had been careless of Helen?

Whatever had gone on by the river when Emma disappeared had been careless, someone's carelessness, and since Helen had been the witness, it must have been hers.

"It was my fault," she said. And the words, spoken like a confession, in the closed dampness of a confessional box, were sufficient for Helen to acknowledge a complicity with fate which had determined the course of her life.

12.

IT WAS AFTER SIX in the evening, not yet dusk, but the sun was sliding over the hills, lighting the sky a soft silver.

The wall in the living room of Dr. Hazelton's house had been painted linen white, coat after coat of paint, and the house smelled of it but Helen could still read the writing, although it wasn't actually visible. The imprint was permanent, whether the words were there or hidden by layers of linen white.

Now, although she knew the house was empty, had checked the closets and under the bed and even the pull-down attic stair, she felt uneasy as if there were always someone in the house just beyond her hearing.

When Emma died, her parents took down the pictures, all the ones of Emma alone and of the whole family and all but one of Emma and Helen, that taken from the back, the girls sitting side by side facing Lake Michigan, their hair lit by the sun like long rectangular halos. They could have been any girls—friends, sisters, a portrait of two girls without a history.

Her parents turned Emma's room into a workroom for

her mother, boxed up her toys and clothes and sent them to the Children's Home in northern Ann Arbor. The space Emma had taken filled in quickly until there was no visible memory of her, nothing to show that Emma Fielding had for a moment occupied a small place in their world.

When Philip Fielding took a job in Santa Cruz, Allie stayed in Michigan. They had no arguments that Helen could remember. Their marriage simply slipped away as Emma had without a trace. That which had been the tangible substance of Helen's life as the first daughter of a mother and father who lived in a white clapboard shuttered house in Ann Arbor, Michigan, was gone as if it had never been.

Helen stood in the middle of the room and listened to the scratching of Gregory's paws on the hardwood floor upstairs, to the soft sound of a light wind in the bushes, a car along Main Street, the sound of a baby crying, nothing out of the ordinary. Satisfied that no one was there, she turned on the tape of "The Story of Meridian." It was Dr. Hazelton she was after—not the whitewashed man she saw on the film but the boy in the picture with her and Emma. She couldn't get him out of her mind.

The camera focuses on the back of Dr. Hazelton in his office, holding the child Molly on his lap and speaking to a woman Helen has not met. He is discussing her husband's heart condition. Molly is happily drawing on the blotter on his desk.

The narrator speaks. "Dr. Hazelton is talking to Adelaide Brown about her husband Max, who suffered a heart attack a week ago and is in intensive care in the hospital in Harrisville."

Fade to conversation between Dr. Hazelton and Adelaide.

ADELAIDE: So you have little Molly today.

Molly looks up and smiles, handing Adelaide a crayon.

MOLLY: Blue.

DR. HAZELTON: Sophie drops her by from time to time when she's very busy so Prudential can watch her.

ADELAIDE: Such a charmer.

DR. HAZELTON (smiling): I saw Max this morning, Addie. He's doing well but no more cigarettes when he gets out of the hospital and no more corned beef on rye at the Harrisville Deli.

ADELAIDE: Max Brown doesn't listen to a word I say.

DR. HAZELTON: Well, I'll tell him tonight he's going to stay in the hospital eating soft vegetables and dry meat until he's ready to listen to you.

ADELAIDE: And no more whiskey, I hope.

DR. HAZELTON: Less whiskey, certainly.

The TV camera fades, blurs, giving the picture an evocative, grainy quality. It focuses for a moment on Molly and then on Richard Hazelton. He leans down and buries his face in Molly's hair and the camera moves out the window, along the sidewalk to Main Street where Sallie Durham is walking along alone eating an ice cream cone and, behind her, Ann Durham, her arm looped through the arm of an older woman, her mother perhaps, they look alike. They are talking although the voice is the narrator's. "It is Tuesday noon and nursery school has just let out. Ann Durham walks with her mother Alice, who grew up in Meridian, the daughter of Mr. Rubin, Sr., the undertaker—who is preparing today for the viewing of Mona Dickenson at her mother's home on Snow's Court."

Outside, Helen heard a noise, a crash, maybe a branch falling. She leaned forward, turned off the tape and listened.

It was just beside the house—footsteps, maybe an animal, but the footsteps were careful, guarded, uneven, more like those of a person. She got up from the floor where she was sitting. The person—it was a person—was behind the hydrangea bushes, next to the house, just beside the large window that looked into the living room. Helen could see that it was a woman wearing a long skirt, a small woman leaning into the hydrangea bushes for concealment.

She went to the front door. "Hello," she called.

The person stood very still and didn't answer.

Helen turned on the outside lights although it wasn't dark enough yet for artificial light.

"Hello," she said again. "Who is that?"

She had taken a step toward the figure in shadows, before she saw that it was Madeleine Sailor flattened against the bushes.

She wasn't entirely surprised.

"Don't you want to come in?" Helen asked. "I was just watching the film you gave me."

"Yes," Madeleine said, stepping into the light. "I do. I'm sorry." She followed Helen into the house.

"Were you looking for something?" Helen asked.

Madeleine folded her hands across her stomach in an

awkward gesture, an attempt to seem comfortable although she clearly was not.

"I was," she said. "I was actually looking for you."

"You could have knocked," Helen said.

"Yes," she said. "Of course. I should have."

She followed Helen into the kitchen while she put on tea.

"I have very little to eat," Helen said. "Animal crackers and cereal. Blueberries. Two bananas. Anything?" she asked Madeleine.

She shook her head. "No, thank you."

Helen sat at the kitchen table and indicated that Madeleine should sit down.

"Where are you on the film?" she asked. "I noticed you watching."

"Still early, Tuesday, I think the narrator said," Helen said. "In Dr. Hazelton's office. He's with Molly."

"Oh yes. You know Molly?"

"She's been pointed out to me."

"I mean, you know about Molly?"

"I know she's Sophie's daughter and Sophie left town with her."

"Yes." Madeleine sat on the edge of the pine ladder-back chair. "That's what I meant."

She had an odd way with her lips, twisting upward as if she were smiling. "Next on the film, you see Maggie," Madeleine said. "There's Ann Durham walking along with her mother and then a very quick shot of Maggie, actually shot from behind so you don't see her face at first and then she turns and smiles."

"Would you like for me to look at it while you're here?" Helen asked.

"Yes," Madeleine said. "Yes, I would."

They went into the living room and Helen switched on the lamp, turned on the VCR.

The camera follows Ann Durham and in the corner of the screen a young leggy girl in a jacket and jeans is bending over, giving a yellow kitten a lick of her lollipop. It is a small innocent gesture charming in its simplicity.

Then the child stands and, realizing perhaps that the camera crew is filming her, she turns toward the camera and smiles, a lovely wide smile, licking the lollipop she has given the kitten.

"I play it over and over," Madeleine said, clasping her hands under her chin.

"She is a beautiful little girl," Helen said. She stood up. "Do you mind?" She turned off the VCR.

"No, of course," Madeleine said. "But next, when you look at it again, comes the drugstore with Mr. Lowry making up a prescription. Remember when I asked you to look for a clue? Have you noticed anything in watching?"

"Not so far," Helen said. "But I haven't seen enough to notice anything."

Madeleine sat twisting her skirt in her hands.

"Did you want something from me?" Helen asked. "Is that why you came?"

Madeleine looked at her, a blank look as if she had suddenly forgotten why she was there.

"You were in the bushes," Helen said. "I think you were about to look at me through the window."

"Yes," Madeleine said.

"You were?"

"Yes, I was. I was going to watch you."

"I'd rather you not do that again," Helen said coolly. "It's upsetting."

"Of course," Madeleine said. "It was wrong but I wanted to see if you were watching the film. I was afraid to knock."

"But you would have been welcome," Helen said.

"I'm sure you think I'm crazy but I have lost a sense of what is real," Madeleine said, standing uncomfortably beside the front door, fingering the lampshade on the hall table. "I ask myself is that film who we are in Meridian? Or are we who we are now, which is really quite different and a lot worse than who we used to be before the film was made." She rested her face in her hands, bending her head just slightly so as not to look at Helen. "You probably think I'm crazy, don't you? Henry does. He's very worried about me."

"I don't know you well enough to answer that," Helen said.

"No, I'm sure." She gave a little laugh. "I don't know myself well enough."

Helen took a deep breath. "Did you write a message to me in black paint on my wall last night?"

"No, I didn't. It wasn't me. David Jaspersen asked me this morning. I said no. I couldn't do that," Madeleine said, wrapping her arms around herself. "Terrible things happen, don't they?" she said. "One minute I was in the drugstore and Maggie was outside. The next minute she was gone. That is what I mean by real. It wasn't real. It couldn't have happened except in a film but it did and it happened to me." She started toward the door. "I shouldn't keep you. I'm sure you want to eat dinner." She turned to Helen with her odd little smile. "Henry's cooking pork chops. That's all he knows to cook."

Helen watched her walk down the path to the road, down the road to Main Street and out of sight. She walked with an awkward coltish gait like a girl. For a moment Helen wanted to run down the road after her.

In her mind's eye she saw herself running. "Wait," she is shouting to Madeleine Sailor. "I know about missing children."

13.

IT WAS LATE, a dusty evening, not dark, Meridian was too far north for late spring darkness to settle until after eight— but a soft gray mist hung like silk sheets on the trees and bushes. Helen had walked alone to the park where Emma disappeared.

"Disappeared" was her father's word. He never said "died" and her mother said nothing at all about Emma. Only Helen said she had died.

Disappeared because there was no body. A missing child.

"Do you think she drowned?" Helen had asked him once.

"I don't think she drowned," her father said. "Your mother does. She thinks she was swept into the larger river of which the river Meryn is a tributary."

"And what do you think?" Helen had asked.

"What difference does it make how it happened, Helen?" he said. "It happened."

"It makes a difference because I was there. I was the only one there," Helen said. "And I don't remember."

On Saturday morning T.J. had called with the news that Maggie had been spotted nearby in Lawrence at a grocery store with a man of no special description. She was wearing blue jeans and looked thinner than she had in the pictures distributed throughout Ohio and nearby states. Someone else had called later Saturday to say that a young girl matching the description of the girl in Lawrence had been seen and, for that matter, Maggie had been seen in the Meridian Park walking along the river.

"I'm going to the park," T.J. said to Helen. "Can you come?"

"I'm not finished clinic hours until four," Helen said. "You ought to go now. She'll be gone by four."

And so he went. He called later to say he was going with David Jaspersen, but by the time he got there the child had gone and the boys playing in the park, the parents of the small children on the playground had not seen anyone who matched her description.

"David says it's pretty common for people to think they've seen someone, to imagine one person is another. Projection, it's called."

"I know about projection," Helen said.

"Anyway it probably wasn't Maggie."

———

All afternoon during clinic hours and sore throats and a gall bladder attack, blood poisoning and stomach flu, Helen found her mind wandering to the park T.J. had mentioned where Emma had disappeared. She hadn't been there since she arrived in Meridian although she knew how to walk there by the railroad station. There was a path which led through the woods and she remembered the lush treed feel of it from childhood.

The river was high, just beneath the bank and moving swiftly, fast even for late May, almost whitewater skipping over the top. The path was narrow, laced with wildflowers, bright in the soft gray light, and thick tree roots pushed out of the earth, spread unevenly across the path, huge stones large enough to sit on right in the middle of the cleared route so she had to walk around them into the thicket. There was the dank smell of wet rotted leaves, of the river thick with bright green ferns along the bank, a wild cacophony of birds chattering.

She walked along the path toward the park, her shoulders brushing the bushes along the side, the trees leaning into the light, bending toward the sun, and in the company of abundant vegetation and especially birds. Helen didn't feel alone, although she was anxious and wished she had asked someone, maybe David Jaspersen, to come along. With human company, she wouldn't have been so attuned to her surroundings as she was now. Her memory would have been softened by the safety of conversation.

The entrance to the park was unmarked, overgrown with

thick black ferns, rancid-smelling in the long heat. Helen's stomach was tight, her hands perspiring, her throat dry. She wanted to run.

In Ann Arbor she had made a point of avoiding the street where they had lived when Emma was alive—afraid the memories would do her in. A living death was what she imagined if the boxes in her brain opened and filled the tiny cranial roads with unbearable news of her past.

She walked through the dense growth, along the narrow path into a clearing which opened with a lovely, lush panorama of green fields, weekend softball players in brilliant white, families in the hushed languid attitude of late spring evenings, packing up after dinner, the smell of wood fires burning, blankets of wildflowers unfolding toward the river. The sun was just below the tree line so the evening had a sudden splash of yellow.

She knew from memory the way the wildflowers peppered the low horizon, the heavy willows, their long-leaved skirts brushing the top of the grass, the way the river smelled and sounded at just this distance along the bank, a small steady rush of water over the rocks. The light from the summer sun dropped over the horizon, dappled the field, a pointillist configuring of soft purples and yellows and periwinkle blues, cattails near the river, high green sheaves of wheatlike vegetation, the long cry of waterfowl in the distance, a pure soft evening, a little damp and gentle, full of romance. It must have been an evening like this one, Helen thought, only a June evening after a heavy rain.

"Tell me," she asked a young boy about seven with straight square blond hair and a dimple. "Can you walk to the river from here?"

"There," he said, pointing to a slender ribbon of clearing in the rich green velvet brush. "It's not too far but I'm not allowed."

The path to the river was narrow, and even at her height, just over five-seven, she was lost to the view of families in the open parkland. Just the top of her head showed above the high sheaves. A child would be invisible here, she thought, and she wondered did her parents allow her at five years old to walk unseen by grownups for such a distance along a path that led to a river. A small child with her baby sister, almost three, three in October. What could they have been thinking? she asked herself, walking out of view of the open field where her parents must have been sitting on the benches around the picnic table.

She is walking with Emma. The sun on its way down in the western horizon falls as the sun seems to do in the evening, dampness in the air promising rain.

Her mother had told her she was a talker when she was small. Always in a story of her own device, taking on the major roles, her mind crowded with narrative possibilities. She didn't remember an imaginative mind—it must have fallen away years ago, replaced by an affection for the specific and literal, for things seen—but a sense of her young mind came back to her now.

"We have to hurry to the river, Em," she is saying. And that is what she called her sister. Em. Not Emma.

"We have to make a pony ride and the ponies will be gone soon. There'll be children for us to play with and animals."

"I can't hurry," Emma says. "I'm too little."

"I'll carry you then," Helen says, lifting her plump baby sister in her own small arms.

"You can be my mama," Emma says happily.

"I am your mama," Helen says. "I am your good mama.

"Here they all are, Em. See. Down at the river waiting for us with lemon cakes and chocolate chip cookies," Helen says. "You can have one cookie and half a lemon cake and yummy mint tea with honey."

The path opened to a grassy bank with birch trees and huge oaks and willows hanging lazily over the river and large rocks down to water which ran surprisingly clear.

Helen leaned against a slender young birch which gave a little with her body, bending away from her.

This was a place where she had been before. There were no specific identifying marks. No rock formations or land cuts or odd designs of trees that she remembered, and she didn't know why she was certain. But she was.

14.

HELEN CALLED T.J. from the rail station on the way home from the park.

"Any more news?" she asked, hoping to seem offhand although she had a reason for the call.

"None," he said. "I think the news about Maggie was bogus."

"But you have to follow any leads, I suppose."

"I feel as if I do," he said. "I did see Madeleine and Henry tonight. I believe she's slipped over the edge."

"Had she been drinking?" Helen asked. "That's what I noticed when she last came by my office, but earlier she stopped over at the house and didn't seem drunk, just odd."

"Crazy?"

"She did, a little."

"That's what Henry says," T.J. said. "He pulled me aside and said he was terribly worried she was losing her grip."

Helen wanted to ask T.J. to come over, to sit around the half-lit living room, half lit to keep her from seeing where the writing on the wall had been. She wanted to watch the film but not alone. It had taken on a quality of menace and she wasn't sure whether that came from the film or whether the menace had to do with the real Meridian.

She was fragile after her visit to the park and, in spite of T. J. Wisely's frank sexuality, he was safer to her with his eye patch and wheelchair, somehow clearer in aspect than David Jaspersen with whom she knew she could easily fall into the thing she always fell into with men, a love affair, embers before she had a chance at something genuine. A love affair wouldn't happen with T.J. He was walled in, as she was. She couldn't get at him. They were equals in that way and, in her life with men which had been as considerable as it was slight, she had never been with a man who seemed familiar as kin.

"Where are you?" T.J. asked. "You sound as if you're outside."

"I'm at a phone booth by the rail station," she said. "I was out for a walk and just decided to call." She caught her breath. "Would you like to stop by?" she asked. "I was thinking of watching the rest of the film."

There was a long pause.

"Maybe you've seen the film enough times," Helen said.

"No," T.J. said but she sensed that he was tentative. "There're scenes on the third cassette from the wake of a young woman who happened to die while the film crew was in town and they actually filmed her wake. Have you seen that part?"

"I haven't," Helen said.

"I'll be over," T.J. said.

———

Helen made pasta, rotelli with a little cheese, no sauce, there was very little in the fridge. But there was a bottle of white wine and half a baguette from lunch and blueberries, so they sat on the gray couch, Gregory between them, the film playing, the sound slightly muted so they could talk.

"Mona died of cancer," T.J. said. "It started in her breast."

Tommy Dickenson moves across the screen, walking down the line of mourners, kissing one and then the other. He shakes hands with T.J., then hugs him, takes Mona's golden retriever by the collar and leads her, in her black ribbon and white rose, up to the front porch where she stands with Mona's mother and sister in the receiving line.

"Mona Dickenson was twenty-seven," the narrator is saying. "She was lovely and talented, a pianist of real promise who studied in New York and had a generous quality of spirit, an angel, so her best friend Madeleine Sailor describes her." The camera focuses on Madeleine standing in line next to Henry with Maggie, who is distracted, her back to the camera, leaning against her mother.

T.J. was pensive.

"She used to play at First Methodist and the sound honest to God broke my heart." He took a cigarette out of his pocket. "I was in love with her." He put the cigarette in his mouth. "Don't worry. I'm not going to light it."

"What is going on with the dog?" Helen asked.

"You'll see what the director does with the dog at the end of the scene," T.J. said. "But here, I don't know. I was in another part of the yard. Peter Forester may have said to Tommy, 'Go get the dog. We want to shoot him standing with the family of the deceased.' Something touching like that." He lifted Gregory on his lap. "My quibble with this film—I shouldn't tell you. I should have you make up your own mind."

"No, tell me," Helen said.

"My quibble has to do with reality. How when you take a little truth and misconstrue it—" T.J. lifted his legs and rested them on the coffee table. "I'm not talking about making up a story. Stories are orderly. What I'm talking about is fussing with the facts to make something better than it is or different, so who knows in the end what's real and what's not." He poured himself another glass of wine.

"It doesn't really seem to be about the town you know?" Helen asked, trying to wind her way into T. J. Wisely's confidence but she wasn't sure of herself the way she usually was when eliciting the stories of other people's lives so they felt an unrequited intimacy with her.

T.J. shrugged.

He fast-forwarded to the end of the scene at Mona Dickenson's wake, the frame of the dog lying on the front porch, a shadowed outline of Mona's casket in the window behind her.

"That's what I mean," he said. "That scene is sentimental. The film crew shouldn't have been at the wake. They didn't know what to make of a real young woman dying in a small town where everybody knew her and so they made something sentimental because the truth is too complicated for television, too ambiguous." He finished his glass of wine. "Now I get mixed up between the town and the story about it."

"It wouldn't be a film without a story," Helen said, taking off her shoes, slipping her feet under her long skirt.

"A town isn't a story," T.J. said. He fast-forwarded the film and stopped at a frame of Sophie DeLaurentis dancing with Peter Forester.

"Do you know who she is?"

"She's Sophie."

"What have you heard about her?" T.J. asked.

"That she bolted just after the film."

"Nobody has said anything about her?" T.J. turned off the light in order to see the film better.

"When I first came, I went on house calls with Prudential and everybody asked had she heard from Sophie." Helen took his plate, poured them both another glass of wine.

"And Prudential said no."

"Prudential said nothing," Helen said. "Who's Sophie with there?" she asked, pointing to Peter Forester, his cheek pressed against Sophie's full black hair. "I haven't seen him before."

"That's Peter Forester, the director, dancing with Sophie." He clicked the rewind button on the television monitor, returning to Mona Dickenson's wake. "Sophie De-Laurentis from Alliance, New Jersey, knows zilcho about Meridian and she is the star of his documentary."

Helen leaned back against the couch pillows, putting her feet on the coffee table.

"There's something I don't understand about you and this film," Helen said.

He broke apart the cigarette he'd been holding, scattering the tobacco in a plate on the coffee table, took another out of the pack in his pocket. "I wanted to honor Meridian because for me, growing up, it was a safe house. And something went wrong."

The camera crew follows the Sailors home after Mona Dickenson's wake, filming at a long distance and from behind. Henry Sailor is walking a little ahead, holding Maggie's hand, Madeleine, willowy and walking at an angle, a little to the left. Maggie stops, pulling her hand free from her father, and turns toward the camera, suddenly self-conscious. She covers her face with her hand and turns away, her arm around her mother's waist, her head burrowing into the side of her. There is no music and the narrator is silent, only the sounds of nature superimposed, bird song, the rustling of small branches, the swish of early spring wind blowing Madeleine Sailor's coat in the direction in which she's walking.

"That's Maggie," Helen said.

"Yes," T.J. said. He stopped the film, rewound and replayed the scene with the Sailors. "That scene rings true," he said.

"Was Maggie your favorite?"

"The reason I'm putting so much time into finding

Maggie is that I'm responsible," T.J. said, replaying the frame with the Sailors. "I brought the film crew to Meridian in the first place and the film brought the tourists who wanted to come to see us for themselves, and one of them must have taken Maggie." He pulled his wheelchair over and moved off the couch into the seat. "My fault she's gone, if you understand."

"I do understand," Helen said and she wanted to say more. She wanted to say that she understood fault exactly. For a moment she thought she would tell him about Emma, but the moment passed and she went into the kitchen to make coffee.

"Don't make coffee for me," T.J. called. "I should go."

"Do you have to leave?" Helen asked, leaning against the doorframe.

"It's late." He turned on the lamp. "Why?"

She shrugged.

"Are you afraid here?" He had a look on his face, a kind of sweetness, and she wanted to say something truthful to him, something undefended about herself. "I can't tell whether I'm afraid to be alone in this house because of someone else," she said, "or I'm afraid to be alone with myself."

He asked her why she had come to Meridian, since certainly there were other places to go.

"I like emergencies," she said.

"But the emergency is over, isn't it?" he asked.

"Legionella is over. At least, it's not an emergency."

"Then go back to Ann Arbor," T.J. said. He said it kindly. "We're not a good place for a visiting physician."

"What do you mean?"

He shrugged. "I'm a fatalist," he said. "Sometimes it's the wrong time and the wrong place."

She helped him wheel his chair down the few front steps of her house. "Are you all right going home in the dark?" she asked.

"I'm fine," he said.

"You didn't do the writing on my wall, did you? Suggesting I go home?"

He laughed. "No," he said, touching her lightly on the waist. "I told you that face to face."

It was late but light enough for Helen to see his shadowed figure wheeling up the narrow street, keeping a grip on the wheels so they did not spin backward, and she was stirred by the power in his arms.

V.

VISUAL
MEMORY

The Story of

MERIDIAN

DR. HAZELTON WAS UP ALL NIGHT before the fourth day of shooting of "Meridian." Sandra Doyle had a baby girl by caesarean section just after 1 A.M. at Harrisville Hospital, and by the time he returned to his house there was a message on his answering machine from Tommy McCollough with a bellyache which turned out to be a bleeding ulcer. When he got back to Meridian a second time from Harrisville, it was 7 A.M. and Sophie was sitting on the top step of his front porch with Molly sleeping in her arms.

Her long black coat was open and she was dressed for an evening in the city, in a blue wool dress, cut quite low, too tight across her breasts, her hair loose and curly around her face, her face bright with rouge, red on her lips, on her cheeks, her eyes circled in black mascara, a pout on her full lips.

He was fragile from exhaustion and tense, his emotions flying. When he saw Sophie, he wanted to kill her.

"Is that what you wear to bed with the director?" He could not help himself.

"Rich." She gave him a little-girl look. "This is business for me. I could have a career." She put a sleeping Molly over her shoulder. "Peter says I might be discovered when people see the film." Her voice went suddenly soft with pleasure. "He thinks I'm talented."

"That you certainly are," Richard said. "Talented especially. Anyone can see that."

"I've come with Molly," she said. "She has a fever so I knew it would be best if Pru took care of her while I'm working."

"A fever?" He opened the front door and held it for her to go inside. "How high?"

"I don't have a thermometer at home," Sophie said.

"You have a three-year-old child and no thermometer?"

"I lost it," Sophie said. She put Molly down on the couch while Dr. Hazelton took her temperature.

"I have to be on the set early," she said. "Eight-thirty, Peter said."

"The set? So now Meridian is a set?" He checked the thermometer. "A hundred and three."

"Oh dear." Sophie was distracted. "Not exactly a set," she said, "but you know what I mean. This morning they're staging a dance sort of like the one we have in the grammar school every Christmas."

"I said her temperature is a hundred and three."

Molly had started to cry. She sat up on the sofa, her small hands covering her face.

"I knew there was something the matter," Sophie said. "What do you think?"

"I don't know." He was exasperated. "I haven't checked."

"Well, it's eight-fifteen and I thought I'd leave her with

you now to check over and then when the shoot is over I'll come back and get her." She picked Molly up and kissed her. "I think it's a virus. Didn't Sallie Durham have a virus last week?"

"Not that I know of." Dr. Hazelton washed his hands. "I'll be at the office with her after nine. If you finish on your set before then, I'll be here," he said coolly. "Should you fancy checking on her."

"Don't be mean, Richard. This could be a break for me." She turned to leave. "You know I've never taken help from you or anyone else. I've raised Molly alone."

"Who knows?" Richard said. "You pass yourself around like a plate of sugar cookies."

But she had gone down the steps, no longer listening, rushing toward Main Street in her slender high-heeled shoes. Molly was crying, her eyes wide, calling after her mother, and the crying put Richard Hazelton in a sudden rage.

"Hush," he said to her.

"I want to get my mama," she said.

"We'll get your mama," Richard Hazelton said. "We'll get her on the double right now."

He saw himself behind the wheel of his yellow Toyota sailing down Main Street after Sophie DeLaurentis in her tight blue dress, sailing over her, down she goes, under the car, flat as a blue sheet on the road.

Almost blind with fury, he picked Molly up, rushing out the front door to the car parked in the driveway. He put her in the front seat, pushed the door shut although it must not have caught, and ran around the back of the car, jumping into the driver's seat, turning on the engine, putting the car in reverse.

It happened in a second, before the car had reached the bottom of the driveway. The front door of the Toyota was open and Molly was no longer in the car. He had not even felt the door fly open—when the car in reverse was going down the driveway.

T. J. Wisely was sitting with Peter Forester, dressed in a dark blue suit and tie, and Pleeper Jones when Sophie came in the diner, went over to the counter and ordered coffee black and plain toast.

"The Christmas dance is not a big deal," he was saying to Peter. "I thought the whole point of this film was the story of the real town—not made-up Christmas dances in the middle of April."

"We need a diversion, some sort of party. A picnic on the river doesn't work in April," Peter said. "The trees are still in bud—people are still in jackets. But a dance does."

"You're dressed for the occasion," T.J. said, ordering more coffee. "I didn't know you owned a tie."

"I don't," Peter said. "The tie belongs to the undertaker and the suit is the chief of police's." This seemed to please him.

"I suppose you plan to be at the dance because of your long personal association with Meridian," T.J. said. "A crowd scene is what you have in mind?"

"I plan to be at the dance because it amuses me to appear in my own work." He leaned across the table and tweaked T.J.'s nose. "And, T.J., I'm the director."

Sophie slid in between T.J. and Peter with her breakfast. "Dieting?" T.J. asked.

"Peter said I might take off some weight," she said, tearing her dry toast in little pieces. "A person looks heavier on film than in real life, right, Peter?"

"That's right, Sophia," Peter said.

"So when do I set up?" Pleeper asked.

"Now," Peter said. "We're doing the dance first thing this morning because we've got the town meeting later and a church supper at the Methodist church."

"So the whole dance deal is made up," T.J. said. "That pisses me off, Peter. If I had known you were going to misconstrue the truth this much, I would have suggested Hollywood."

"Listen, T.J., you'll be happy with this film, and the Christmas dance is not my invention. It's Meridian's. I'm making use of what is already here." He followed Pleeper out of the diner, ruffling Sophie's hair as he passed. "You look terrific," he said.

T.J. ordered more coffee. "Sophie," he began.

"Leave me alone, T.J. I have problems."

"I can see you do." He looked at the shoot schedule which Pleeper had left on the table.

7:30 A.M.   DANCE SHOOT. Duncans,
                      Durhams, Sellerses, Sophie

	(Peter), Brownlees, Fosters, Evans, Grahams, etc. (Story line with Peter and Sophie.)
10 A.M.	TOWN MEETING at Meridian Grammar School on subject of flood control and rat problem
11 A.M.	CATHOLIC LADIES GUILD preparation for St. Patrick's Day Snake Dinner
12 P.M.	LUNCH at the diner. Focus on Ben Winters
12:30 P.M.	Follow Sophie with Molly to the cemetery on the anniversary of her husband's death
1:00 P.M.	2nd grade ball game at the grammar school.

"I see you're taking flowers to the cemetery, Soph. Peach glads and carnations, it says, provided special for the occasion by Bill's Florists. Very nice."

"I'm not kidding, T.J.," Sophie said. "This morning Molly had a high fever and I was up most of the night with her so I'm not interested in your making fun of me."

"I'm not making fun of you, Soph," T.J. said wearily. "I just don't understand how in good conscience you can take flowers to Mr. DeLaurentis's grave in front of a TV crew when you've never done it unattended. Besides"—he took out a cigarette—"I didn't even think you liked him."

"If you weren't a cripple, I'd slap you." She drank the rest of her coffee, left $1.25 on the table and went out the back door of the diner, up the hill to the high school where they were filming the Christmas dance.

Edith Winters was on her way up the hill with her baby girl on her shoulders and Sophie called out to her. "Slow down," she said. "I can hardly walk in these high heels."

"Hello, Sophie," Edith said.

"Are you doing the dance part of the film?" Sophie asked. "That's why I'm so dressed up."

"Benjamin just told me about the dance this morning," Edith said.

"I know you don't think much of this project."

"How do you know?" Edith asked edgily.

"Everybody knows. Peter told me."

"Peter?"

"Peter Forester. You know, the director. He's living in your house." They waved at Mrs. Walker, standing on the front porch of her cottage talking to the postman as they passed.

"He's living in the church hall," Edith said. "Not my house."

"You don't like what's going on, isn't that so?" Sophie asked.

"I think the film is changing people," Edith said quietly. "And I don't like change."

"But we'll be famous, Edie," Sophie said.

"I hope not," Edith said. "I can't think of anything worse."

It was going to be a cool wet April day, a little windy, hovering gray clouds, a distant pale yellow sun. Sophie pulled up the collar of her coat.

David Jaspersen saw T.J. wheeling up the hill and ran to catch up with him.

"I hear the Christmas dance is scheduled for this morning," he said.

"Sure," T.J. said. "I hope you can make it."

"Did I see Sophie here a minute ago?"

"You did," T.J. said. "On her way to fame and fortune, into the arms of Peter Forester."

"Peter Forester's in the shooting today. He's wearing my suit," David said.

"Yes, he is," T.J. said. "Playing the role of the stranger from another town visiting the Meridian dance."

David pushed T.J.'s wheelchair the rest of the way up the hill. "You know, I'm getting very concerned."

"You are!" T.J. said.

"I had a call this morning from *Hometown* magazine saying they wanted to do a story and then *Good Housekeeping* called saying they'd heard about the film."

"It's almost over," T.J. said. "They finish up tomorrow night. They'll be out of here by Saturday morning and we can go back to normal."

"Not a chance we'll go back to normal," David said.

Peter Forester had worked out a story for the dance.

It is Christmas. Sophie is a widow, alone with a child, and Peter, a stranger, a visiting uncle of the Durhams from Chicago. They meet at the dance. No conversation between them. Peter sees Sophie. She is dancing with Sam Durham. Ann Durham tells Peter about Sophie—how she married Antonio DeLaurentis and he died months before Molly was born. Peter cuts in on Sam and dances with Sophie. As the small story progresses through the dance section, there are frames of Sophie and Peter. They do not speak but each frame shows them moving closer together.

"So what's the conclusion of this sweet story?" T.J. asked Pleeper Jones, sitting on the sidelines in the lunchroom decorated for Christmas. "Together forever?"

"Not cool," Pleeper says. "They dance. They say goodbye. The stranger leaves and Sophie returns to life as usual."

"Dumb plan," T.J. said.

"I just shoot the picture," Pleeper said. "I don't worry about the plans."

"I don't get why you did that," T.J. said to Peter after the shooting, on their way to the town meeting in the grammar school auditorium.

"You're getting too excited, T.J.," Peter said. "The trouble with filming what's real is that it misses the spirit of the place. The spirit is in invention and not in fact. Which is why I did the story of a momentary romance."

"I know that," T.J. said. "I have no problem understanding the business of making things up. It's just important which stories you choose to invent."

———

David Jaspersen sat in his office with Win in his pajamas wrapped up in a blanket, sitting on the hard seat across from his father reading a comic with a thermometer in his mouth. David took the thermometer out.

"Normal," he said to Win, who didn't look up from his comic. "How bad do you feel?"

"Bad," Win said.

"Is your throat sore?" David asked.

Win nodded yes. Yes as well to a headache and stomachache and achy muscles.

"So I suppose we should see Dr. Hazelton," David said.

"Maybe," Win replied.

Prudential answered when David called.

"He's not here," she said.

"It's nine-thirty."

"I know what time it is," Prudential said.

"Maybe he's at the hospital."

"I called the hospital," Prudential said. "He hasn't been there yet this morning and he's not at home."

"I'm calling about Win," David said.

"A lot of people have been calling this morning with children who say they're too sick to go to school but haven't got a fever and no symptoms," Prudential said. "I call it Meridian Flu-A strain. Too many cameras in town."

David laughed. "Well, have Rich call me when he gets in," he said and then, reconsidering, redialed the clinic. "And, Pru, if he doesn't come in pretty soon, call me."

He went over and sat down next to Win.

"Other children have the same illness in your class," he said. "I was just speaking to Prudential."

"So?"

"What's going on in your class?"

"A sickness," Win said.

"No, Win. I wonder what is really going on. Are you sick with a real sickness or has something happened to make you not want to go to school?"

"I feel sick," Win said. "Everywhere."

"But has something happened at school?"

Win looked up over his comic book at his father. "A little something," he said.

"What is it?"

"They said I was too small."

"Who is they?" David asked, taking hold of Win's foot affectionately.

"The film people."

"And what did they say you are too small to do?"

"Too small for basketball. Today they are filming a game between the two second grades and they said me and Ricky Martin and John Freemont and Paley Rivers are too small and Oliver Bent is too uncoordinated and Billy Fisher still has the chicken pox on his face." He had started to cry. "Also," he said, "I can't be in the whole school picture."

"What do you mean, you can't be in the whole school picture?"

"I wasn't chosen."

"But it's the whole school."

"Only some people were chosen. It's not really the whole school but it's supposed to feel like it is."

David shook his head.

"I'm certainly glad they're leaving tomorrow."

"Me too," Win said.

Ben Winters stood in the center of the church hall with the assistant director and the cameraman, discussing the filming of the church supper.

They had to remove the cots set up for the film crew, bring the tables out, set up a stage for the Sunday school original musical called *Mercy, Be Kind to the Indians* with Sallie Durham and Molly DeLaurentis playing the nonspeaking parts of Chippewa children and Major Rivers playing an Ohio pioneer with Sara Peace playing his wife Mercy. The crew from the high school was finishing the set of a reservation, covering the flats, lined with blue-black pine trees, a slate-gray lake winding through.

"We'll need about a hundred people," the cameraman was saying. "Any more and I won't be able to move around."

"So explain to me how this will go," Ben Winters asked.

"We'll start around six," the assistant director said. "What would normally happen if this were a church supper evening?"

"People arrive—not just the Methodists—when we have our monthly supper, everybody comes. A lot of people. Well, not everybody, of course, but it's nondenominational. In fact the churches are really community centers for people," Ben said, noticing that he was being recorded. "People come less for God than to mingle around a big living room together." He was pleased with the sound of what he said.

"And then you speak?"

"I usually say a prayer of some kind and I'll make a welcome."

"We'll be following some of the stories of people we've been concentrating on in the last few days—Sophie and Molly, the Durhams—we've been doing a few things with Prudential and she's great on film. Will she be here tonight?"

"You never know with Prudential. She can't be pushed."

"And we'll be doing David Jaspersen as the good cop."

"He's actually a lawyer," Ben said. "Trained in Madison."

"I didn't know," the assistant director said, interested in the information. "Why did he change professions?"

"He's never said but this is his hometown and he wanted to come back."

"I can certainly understand that," the assistant director said. "It's a dream of a town. I wish it were mine."

"Yes," Ben said, filled with a sense of personal victory. "It really is."

He wanted to tell the assistant director his story in Meridian, how he had been born in Oshkosh, Wisconsin, and his father was a drunk and then he'd met Edith, who was a girl when he met her, really a child, but the assistant director was in a hurry to meet the rest of the crew at the town meeting on flood control.

"Later," he said, putting a hand on Ben's arm. "I'd love to hear about it later, Reverend."

Ben surveyed the large assembly room, his room, his place, his church, a small simple white Methodist church in a corner of Ohio, hardly a dot on the detailed map of the United States. Reverend Benjamin Winters, rector, age forty-two, five-eleven, a hundred and forty-eight pounds, fair, thinning hair but no gray yet. People all over the United States, watching television in their living rooms or dens or kitchens, would know First Methodist, Meridian, would know Reverend Ben Winters and his wife Edie and their baby daughter. They would see this room, hear his voice. If he happened to be on vacation in Chicago or Miami or Seattle, people might recognize him on the street and say, "Look, that's the minister from the Methodist church in the film 'The Story of Meridian.' "

He could hardly contain his excitement. He had to be called to several times before he heard Sam Daily from the high school, who was painting the set, shouting for a mop.

"We spilled some paint on the stage, Reverend Winters," Sam called. "Could we borrow a mop?"

"Sure," Ben said. "Of course. I'll get it." He headed to the large kitchen where the broom closet was, still imagining himself on film—"Here is Reverend Winters," the narrator might say, "busy with the details of his daily life as rector of First Methodist, attentive always to matters small as well as matters large." He opened the swinging door and there on the linoleum floor by the stove and lying in a small heap was a child, on her side, facing away from him, in navy-blue tights and a yellow jacket with the hood up.

15.

ON THURSDAY MORNING Prudential called in sick. There was a message on the machine when Helen arrived at the clinic just after seven and, when she tried to call Prudential's house, there was no answer. She sat down at the desk and dialed T.J., who was sleeping.

"I'm sorry to call so early," she said, "I'm looking for Prudential. I need to know where she lives."

"Why?" he asked.

"Because she's not here and not answering the phone and I have to have help at the clinic today."

She could hear T.J. stretch and yawn, perhaps he was sitting up in bed before he spoke. "I'm sorry," he said. "I can't tell you where Prudential lives."

"That's crazy," Helen said. "This is a small town."

"She doesn't want people to know," T.J. said.

"Everyone in town knows where Prudential lives, T.J." Helen said. "People don't want me to know."

"She lives way out of town," T.J. said.

Helen checked through the patient list for Thursday—eleven appointments, with a lot of possible clinic walk-ins. She phoned David Jaspersen.

"Prudential called in sick this morning," she said, "and today's going to be busy."

"If you need it, I'll find you some help. I'm on my way over to the clinic now," David said. "Did you sleep better last night? No invaders?"

"I slept fine," Helen said.

Although it didn't seem as though she had slept at all. The bedroom at Dr. Hazelton's house had a smell from home. A smell of Mackinaw, maybe of her mother. A freshwater smell. "Cucumber" was written on the clear cologne her mother kept on the shelf behind the toilet at Mrs. Peaches's guesthouse. After T.J. had left the night before, Helen hadn't been able to sleep. There was a chill in the air and the smell of cold made her uneasy, like weather change when the outcome is unpredictable.

She had dreams of smothering, face down, someplace soft with the thick damp river smell of Meridian. She couldn't turn her head or lift it, struggling for breath. When she was awake enough to take a breath, a gulp of air, she realized she'd been dreaming about her parents at the river on the evening that Emma died.

Her mother had been thirty, her age almost exactly, her father thirty-three—a handsome athletic couple, taken with each other, pleased with their place in the world. She had seen pictures. Her mother was lovely in a simple vibrant way. Her father was long-legged, slender with a wonderful open face and good bones.

What had her parents been doing that evening at a picnic in the river park? she wondered. Why had Helen been allowed to walk that long path of high wildflowers? She and

Emma must have been out of sight for some time, invisible to the grownups sitting around the picnic tables. They were small and moved slowly, maybe even picking flowers as they walked.

Were her parents worried, she wondered, or didn't they even notice she'd been gone so long?

Helen had just hung up the telephone with Mrs. Walker, sick with the stomach flu, and was collecting the charts for the morning appointments, when David walked in the clinic.

"Henry Sailor called me," he said. "Madeleine never came home last night. He's on his way over here."

People had seen Madeleine. Ann Durham had seen her Sunday downtown on Main across from the library talking to someone from one of the tour buses.

"A bus from Cleveland," Sam Durham said. "I saw the sign on the front."

Tom Walker, Maria's father, had seen her in the pharmacy talking to a woman with bluish permed hair dressed in navy-blue spandex and a white shirt, an older woman with a loud voice. She had gone into the pharmacy with the woman, who was a stranger to Meridian, probably from the tour bus, to buy over-the-counter sleeping pills. They seemed to know each other.

"I don't know what to say," Henry said, sinking down on the couch in Helen's office. "She left early yesterday and called me at the grammar school to cook dinner because she had a late appointment with you," he said.

"I didn't have an appointment with her," Helen said.

"The other day I discovered her looking in my living-room window while I was watching television, but I haven't seen her since."

Henry looked up. "Crazy," he said quietly. "Is that what you think?"

"Distraught is what I think," Helen said.

"What about the people on the tour bus?" David asked. "I hear she goes down in the afternoon and talks to the people from the buses."

"She's been doing that," Henry said. "She goes around lunchtime to see if anyone is parked at the church clock and then she strikes up a conversation." He leaned back in his chair wearily. "I'm sure she's hoping someone will know about Maggie."

"Are you suggesting she could have left with a tour bus?" David asked.

"I don't know what I'm suggesting," he said.

He looked ancient to Helen, sitting with his side to the long window behind her desk so a shaft of morning sunlight painted his face a sickly yellow with lines too deep for the face of a young man.

"David"—he leaned toward David's chair and his voice had a disturbing urgency—"We're disintegrating."

"What did he mean, disintegrating?" Helen asked later after Henry had left.

"Henry believes we shouldn't have allowed the film to be made," David said, "because strangers have started to come since they saw us on TV." He put on his cap and opened the door to the clinic. "It has to do with Maggie."

"But what he said seemed personal," Helen said. "It was directed at you."

"I don't know what he could have meant then," David said coolly. "A man under emotional duress can't be counted on for sense."

The clinic was filling with patients, sitting quietly with magazines or books, their arms folded across their chests, their eyes closed.

"It looks like you have a full day," David said. "Would you like to have dinner?"

She shook her head. "I put the Blake baby in the hospital with pneumonia early this morning. I have to work late."

Helen followed him to the front door, walking out on the porch of the clinic so the patients sitting in the waiting room wouldn't hear her. "Why can't you tell me where Prudential lives?"

"You didn't ask me," David said, pulling away, redefining the borders of their friendship.

"Can you tell me where she lives?" she asked.

David hesitated. "Ask her," he said.

"She won't tell me," Helen said crossly. "Prudential never talks."

Win Jaspersen came by at lunchtime, looking for his father, he said. He sat at the desk across from Helen while she ate lunch between patients.

"You could move into our house if you don't like Dr. Hazelton's," he said. "We have an extra room."

"Thank you very much," Helen said. "But I think I have to stay in Dr. Hazelton's house. It's been given to me for the time I'm visiting here."

Win folded his arms across his chest. "I didn't like Dr. Hazelton," he said.

"You didn't?" Helen said, eating the tomatoes and turkey out of her sandwich.

He shook his head.

"How come?" she asked.

"He gave me the creeps. He had a bad temper." Win shrugged.

"Did he ever lose his temper at you?" Helen asked.

"I saw him lose it once at Sophie," Win said. "I was waiting for a strep test and he lost his temper right here in the waiting room."

"Sophie?" Helen got up, threw out her trash from lunch, took out the files. "I haven't met her yet."

"She doesn't live here anymore. Dr. Hazelton moved too, of course. That's why you're here. Right?"

"He moved because he had a family emergency."

"Nobody told me that," Win said. "He had a cat," Win said, drawing a cat on a prescription pad.

"I know," Helen said. "Named Gregory. He lives with me now."

"I'm allergic to cats."

He moved over closer to Helen, leaning his chin on his hands.

"Are you married?" he asked.

"No, I'm not," Helen said.

"Neither is my dad," he said.

"So he told me," Helen said, checking the clock. She ruffled Win's blond hair. "I have to start clinic hours now, Win, so you'd better go," she said, taking Win's hand, walking him to the door, waving good-bye as he went across the street, where T.J. was wheeling his chair into the ice cream store.

Late in the afternoon Helen called Prudential. It had been a day of ordinary complaints, stomach flus, earaches, a case of strep, a kidney infection, no indication of a new case of legionella. Perhaps if the weather held and there was no more flooding, the epidemic was finished.

Prudential was distracted.

"You heard about Madeleine Sailor?" Helen asked.

"She's lost her marbles plain as day."

"Well, I'm going to borrow Reverend Winters's car and check the hospital and I'll do a run of house calls," Helen said. "Certainly I'll stop by the Durhams' and maybe the Walkers'."

"I'll come with you," Prudential said. "I'll be there in half an hour."

Her father called while Helen was cleaning up the examining rooms. He was cheerful with a familiar false gaiety in his voice, asking how she was and how her work was going, saying he was off on holiday to Belize and wished she could join him but knew she was too busy. And then, as if there had been a sudden shift in emotional altitude, his voice dropped to a lower register, the cheer gone out of it.

"I spoke this morning to your mother," he said. "She thought we should tell you that on the day Emma disappeared we were having a little celebration in the park. It was our wedding anniversary."

"Why didn't she call me herself?" Helen asked.

"You know your mother, Helen. She doesn't like the telephone."

Helen sank into the swivel chair at her desk.

"What are you trying to say to me, Daddy?"

"It's your mother's idea," he said, uncomfortable with this conversation. "She called last night to say that perhaps you didn't know we'd been having a celebration that afternoon."

"I didn't," Helen said. "You've never told me anything about that afternoon."

"It's upsetting to have you back in Meridian, Helen," her father said. "Your mother can't help being nervous about it and I suppose we feel it's almost intentional on your part."

"It is intentional," she said, but she didn't want an argument with her father. Her life felt too slippery to risk the slim hold she had on her parents. So she changed the subject to a discussion of the symptoms of legionella, which seemed to please him, and then she got easily off the phone, resting her head in her hand, trying to catch her breath which had gone suddenly out of her.

A sunny dappled day in late June, champagne-colored as summer days in the northern Middle West can be. In the distance, Helen sees her parents, their heads together, hears their silvery laughter. She cannot get their attention.

"Mama." She goes over to the picnic table and tugs on her mother's soft silky skirt. "I want to go to the river to see the birds."

Her mother, whispering with her father, does not look down.

"Take Emma for a walk," she says or maybe it's her father speaking. "Be careful of Emma."

"Go down the wildflower path to the river. Bring your mama a bouquet of yellow flowers for her anniversary."

Has she made that up? Helen thought. Was her sudden memory playing tricks—the mind dusting off its unalphabetized stories in the brain?

"Now?" she asks.

"Please," her mama says. "Take Emma's hand and pick me lovely flowers."

She goes off down the path with Emma's hand in hers, looking back to see if they are paying attention, if they see her going off. But they don't. Their faces close, their fingers laced, drinking pale yellow champagne, kissing and kissing.

"Good-bye, Mama," Helen calls. "Good-bye, Papa."

But they don't hear her.

Prudential arrived in a temper.

"So let's get out of here," she said. "I don't have all day."

"Are you better?" Helen asked, gathering up her things, her medical bags, a light sweater, pinning her hair back.

Prudential gave her a look. "Better than what?"

In Reverend Winters's car, the women didn't speak, Helen conscious of Prudential's unembarrassed concentration on her as they drove across Highway 15 in the pale orange sunset. She was conscious of the size of Prudential, who though tall was not an indelicate woman. But today she seemed enormous.

"Were you actually sick this morning?" Helen asked.

"No," Prudential said casually. "Why?"

Helen laughed. "Because you said you were."

"Nothing's the way it seems." Prudential folded her hands around her knees, pulling at the hem of her long skirt.

"I suppose," Helen said. She would have liked to talk to Prudential about things that mattered, although she knew Prudential would, like her mother, refuse. But not like her mother either. Silence was a matter of choice with Prudential and, with her mother, it was more like destiny. Sitting in the car next to this woman who seemed to be larger than her actual size, seemed to take up the whole front seat, Helen had a kind of certainty, as if there were unspoken personal conversations between them, no reason to imagine a genuine relationship. But she did.

"I put Nellie Blake in the hospital," Helen was saying. "She has a little pneumonia and she's too tiny to take a risk like that."

Prudential's head was turned away now, watching out

the passenger window at the blanket of yellow wheat. It was a pleasant bright late afternoon, a freshness in the air, a whisper of cool, and Helen had a sense of well-being, even high spirits which had to do with Prudential in the car beside her. Perhaps, she thought, their chemistry was in common like two large dogs who simply smell right to each other.

"What do you think about Madeleine Sailor?" Helen asked.

"I'm not thinking about her."

"But if you were, do you think she's gone off with one of the tour buses?"

"She could have."

"Do you think she's crazy?"

"I think she's playing at being crazy so folks will let her alone with her sorrow," Prudential said. "That's what I'd do in her place."

"I have a question to ask you," Helen began, risking intimacy.

"Don't ask a lot of questions," Prudential said. "We get along good enough as friends."

They stopped by Nellie Blake's room and Nellie was already improved on an antibiotic drip and then they checked on Mr. Marquez, who was well enough to be discharged. They stopped in the hospital cafeteria in the hospital's basement, a green room of long Formica tables with weary doctors bending over their plastic trays, an eerie quiet. They ordered two chocolate milkshakes, drinking in comfortable silence.

"Do you like David Jaspersen?" Helen asked finally.

"Enough."

"I mean do you trust him?"

"Trust?" Prudential gave the subject consideration, lifting her head at an angle. "I don't trust anyone." She took a pen from behind her ear and wrote something on a note pad she kept in her pocket. "Are you thinking of marrying him?"

Helen laughed. "Not likely," she said.

Prudential sat with her shoulders hunched, two fingers like pencils against the high bone of her cheek, her eyes scanning the room suspiciously as if she had reason to expect someone concealing an automatic weapon to materialize. She drank slowly, stopping to stir, to lick the other end of her straw. From time to time she looked at Helen so directly that Helen looked away.

"It looks as if this epidemic is under control with erythromycin," Helen said.

"Uh-huh," Prudential said. "It does look that way."

"So if it's over there's no reason for me to stay on." Helen began hoping for a reaction, for affirmation, a request from Prudential to remain in Meridian. "You needed an emergency doctor, that's all. Isn't that right?"

"After the flood we needed an emergency doctor. That's right." She looked at Helen, her eyes half closed. "So leave."

"I don't want to leave if there's a real need for me," Helen began. "But I had only intended to come as a visiting physician to take care of an emergency situation." She took her glasses off and put them in her pocket. "If you were in my position, would you leave?" she asked.

Prudential shrugged. "I'm not in your position."

"People here seem to want me to leave," Helen said, brushing against the parameters of conversation.

Prudential rested her chin in her hands. "When I was thirteen—young, young, young"—she shook her head—"I had a baby die on me and it was my fault," she said. "You can't say if I were in your position because you are you and I am me and different people in the same position are still different people."

"But you have an opinion."

"My opinion is this," she said matter-of-factly. "I wouldn't leave a place where the children are in danger, and the children in this town are in danger from more than dirty water."

On the drive home Helen wanted to talk, to ask about the baby who died and whether it had been Prudential's own baby. And if it was her baby, how had she found herself with a baby so young? She wanted to know the details of its death and whether it was a boy or girl and was Prudential responsible as a result of carelessness or had it been unavoidable. But Prudential had closed the curtain on conversation.

Helen glanced at her picking her teeth.

"Is it because of the baby dying that you became a nurse?" she asked, turning off Route 15 into a Texaco station.

"I'm not a nurse," Prudential said.

When the car stopped, she got out and went to the public telephone at one end of the filling station. Helen watched her lope across the road, dragging one leg just slightly as if she had had a small stroke. She picked up the phone and leaned against the kiosk. Helen loved the way Prudential moved with grace in spite of her limp, the way she tilted her head just so as if she were lifting an ear to the world so all its troubles could pour in.

And where did that rush of feeling come from? she wondered, her detailed and scientific mind grinding through land mines of emotion.

Prudential climbed back in the car and shut the door. "I had to call home," she said. She had a package of caramels which she opened, offering one to Helen, crossing one leg over the other, lacing her long fingers together.

"Who was at home?" Helen asked.

"I thought your job was answers," Prudential said.

"I'm a young doctor," she said. "I have to ask questions."

It was dusk. The warm air blew between the open windows in a low song, softening their voices, and she felt the weight of Prudential next to her, the long sapling size of her, her dancing brain locked in its skull box buzzing like the sparks off electric wires strung along the road. She wanted a confessional.

"I was wondering," Helen began, ignoring Prudential's comment, pulling out onto the road. "What happened to the baby who died?"

Prudential gave her a look.

Helen couldn't see the look but she could imagine what it was and she didn't continue. What she would have said if Prudential had been willing, what she would say in time, maybe even tonight, was "No wonder we are friends. We have a common history."

And then she'd tell her the story of Emma.

"Who says we're friends?" Prudential would say, knowing all the time that of course they were friends. Their friendship was certain, traveling the air between them like the scent of smoke.

Helen drove along Route 15 through Aimsville, slowed by an Amish wagon outside of Baertown, taking a left off 15 into Meridian, traveling on the narrow road beside the railroad tracks.

"Look out," Prudential said.

"Look out?" Helen asked. "For what? I don't see anything."

"Look out not to knock over Madeleine Sailor walking along the road."

Madeleine Sailor was walking slowly, picking wildflowers beside the road, and what Helen saw was Madeleine holding the hand of a small girl with curly hair who was wearing a short pinafore and no shoes.

"Shouldn't I stop?"

"No," Prudential said. "She might run off if you stop and surprise her. We'll send David Jaspersen after her as soon as we get in town."

Helen gripped the wheel on the windy road, looking in her rearview mirror as the road turned, and she lost sight of Madeleine behind the curve.

But just before she turned, following the road, she caught a glimpse through the mist of the child walking along with a bunch of flowers in one hand and holding the hand of Madeleine with the other. She hadn't seen her for years, a lifetime of days and hours and weeks, but there along the same paths of Meridian where Helen had lost her was Emma Fielding.

16.

HELEN STOPPED THE CAR at the police department. It was warm, a light breeze lifting her skirt, the air sweetly perfumed. As a child, she used to look into the mirror over the sink at Mrs. Peaches's guesthouse until her face lost its familiarity, and now, looking at her hands, her long-fingered slender hands around the steering wheel, she didn't recognize them as belonging to her.

She wanted to ask Prudential about the child with Madeleine Sailor. She wanted to know was it a vision or a real child? And could she count on Prudential? Perhaps Prudential hadn't seen her because she looked too quickly. Perhaps she wouldn't tell the truth. She was selective about what she saw and what she didn't see.

"I'll tell David about Madeleine." Prudential climbed out of the front seat, putting her long legs out first, stretching when she stood up. "You go on. He'll take me home."

"I'll wait and take you," Helen said, not wishing to be alone as if, without a witness to her presence, she was in danger of disappearing.

"Another time," Prudential said casually but Helen knew it wasn't casual.

She leaned in the window, resting her arms on the car door, sticking her head in so she could hear above the sound of the engine.

"I was wondering," Helen began, trying to appear calm. "When you saw Madeleine walking along the road just now, what did you actually see?"

"I saw Madeleine Sailor walking along the road," Prudential said.

"Describe it," Helen said. "I just got a glimpse out of the rearview mirror. Was she picking wildflowers?"

"Not that I noticed," Prudential said. "She was walking along the side of the road and in no hurry and she was wearing a blue and white checked skirt with buttons down the front and a white T-shirt and her hair was rumpled. That's what I saw."

"Oh well." Helen smiled, running her fingers through her long hair, fallen from its knot on the top of her head. "I guess I was wrong about the wildflowers."

She didn't mention the child, although certainly she had seen one. Prudential must have also seen the child, clear as day, a small chubby little girl wearing a pale yellow dress Helen didn't remember on Emma although the face and hair were Emma's. And even if she had imagined the identity of the child out of urgency and desire, she could not have imagined a child where no one existed unless she had lost her mind.

She dropped Ben Winters's car at the church, dropped the keys in the mailbox and walked up the hill, a little breathless although the hill was small.

The house was dark. Gregory was lying on the front stoop and pinned to the door was a note.

I came by. I need to speak to you pronto. News on Maggie. T.J.

She crushed the note in her hand and tossed it in the wastepaper basket in the hall. Gregory followed her from the hall to the living room to the kitchen; an uneasy tomcat, his long black and white tail twitching in the air, lacing through her legs as she opened the fridge—which was full again, a carton of orange juice and cranraspberry, a loaf of whole wheat, sliced turkey and fresh tomatoes, celery and carrots in a plastic container, a carton of 2% milk, a plate covered in aluminum foil with a note from Edith Winters.

"In case you haven't eaten," the note said, and Helen felt a twinge of anger that her house was open to anyone in town; her wall could be defiled, her refrigerator filled. After all, who was to say she wanted 2% milk, and maybe she was a vegetarian. The note had an arrow and she turned it over.

I need to speak with you as soon as possible. Call 863-2143. Edie Winters.

Helen didn't wish to speak with anyone. Something was happening. She felt herself slipping, as if the person inside her body was insubstantial and she was losing herself. If there had been no child walking along the road with Madeleine Sailor, then she was hallucinating children.

———

"I need an emergency," she had told her mother in her senior year in high school when, because the rooming house was full, they had spent the summer in the same room.

"You need a boyfriend," Allie Fielding had said. "A boyfriend feels like an emergency."

"No, Mama, I have a boyfriend. That's easy. I always have a boyfriend if I want." And it was easy—young men wanted Helen—something about her, some promise in her carriage. An agreeable distance. No demands.

"I mean I need a life of emergencies," Helen said. "If nothing is required of me I'll disappear."

"I know," Allie Fielding had said softly.

"How do you know?" Helen had asked, surprised at the confessional tone of her mother's conversation. "I have always thought you wanted a life without emergencies."

"I don't want an emergency," Allie had said. "But I know what it means to feel so empty you can't imagine filling the hole," she'd said. "Only I'd rather disappear."

It was a moment, maybe the only moment, in which Helen could remember the space between her mother and herself close over, heal like an open cut.

She took off the aluminum foil and ate the cold baked chicken and ratatouille and dill potatoes from Edie Winters, standing up.

Perhaps the food was poisoned, she thought. Not the chicken necessarily. That would be difficult. But a little something in the ratatouille, she decided, not unhappily, feeling some small pleasure in Gregory as he wove between her ankles, his soft fur a kind of comfort.

The phone rang and she let it ring, listening for the voice on the answering machine, that of David Jaspersen. And she picked up.

"You sound upset," he said.

"I've been poisoned," Helen said.

"Poisoned?"

"Cyanide in ratatouille from Edie Winters," Helen said. "By the time you get here I'll be dead."

"Helen," David said, unamused.

"This is my first experience with paranoia," she said.

"Are you afraid to stay there tonight? Do you want to be with us again?"

"I'm fine," Helen said. "Did you pick up Madeleine?"

"We took her home," David said. "Prudential went with me."

"Where had she been?"

"Drinking," David said. "She went as far as Harrisville on one of the tour buses and then went into a bar."

"She was alone when you picked her up?" Helen asked, the picture of the child clear in her mind.

"Someone had dropped her off at the Route 15 turnoff," he said. "She was very much alone."

"Oh well," Helen began, not knowing how to finish the thought.

"I might stop over later," David said.

"Actually, I'm exhausted."

"And you're sure you're not afraid?"

"I'm not afraid," she laughed. "Just turning a little crazy in this postcard-perfect small town."

There were calls on her answering machine and after she hung up with David she played them.

The first was from Edith Winters.

"Checking to see if you're back yet and have eaten," she said cheerily. "I hope to speak with you tonight. Call any time," she said, emphasizing "any time."

The second was her mother. "Hi, sweetheart. It's me. Four-fifteen. Could you call as soon as possible? I need to speak with you."

Helen called but there was no one at home, just the soft voice of her mother on the answering machine, as usual. She wasn't going to call Edith Winters. She turned off the downstairs lights, picked up a compliant Gregory and went upstairs. In her bedroom, she took out her medical dictionary.

> *Depersonalization Disorder is an emotional disorder in which there is a loss of the feeling of personal identity. The body may not feel like one's own and important events may be watched with detachment. It is common in some forms of schizophrenia and in severe depression.*

She had felt this way before. One afternoon living with Oliver while he was a resident in surgery, she had come home from the hospital early to find him asleep next to the jigsaw puzzle she had had made for him from a photograph of herself. The face was almost finished except for a triangle that included the temple, a portion of forehead and the right eye

—so the total effect was disturbing, as if the reproduction of her face with its triangular hole was exact. Automatically, she had reached up to feel if a part of her head was missing.

She had awakened him.

"I'm afraid something's the matter with me," she said, holding her head which had no feeling when she touched it. "Am I all right?"

"How would I know, Helen?" Oliver said, not pleased with excesses of emotion.

"I seem to have lost feeling in my head." She showed him the part of her head and face replicated in the jigsaw.

He checked her eyes, her reflexes, took her pulse.

"I'm hallucinating," Helen had said.

"You're overtired," Oliver said. "Take a nap."

She tried to sleep. But every time she closed her eyes she felt a huge space where her forehead ought to be and she couldn't fall asleep.

Often she was plagued by a palpable sense of loss, as if parts of her actual body were in the process of disappearing. Now, sitting on Dr. Richard Hazelton's double bed, she was missing large parts of herself, her arms between her shoulders and her hands, wide empty cavities in her brain, only the small memory of Emma walking along the road to Meridian, a perfect miniature, in the corner of her mind.

Downstairs, she turned on the VCR, putting in the fourth cassette, which opens with children walking to school all over town, down Main Street, and Aspen and Euclid, spilling out of their houses in ones and twos and threes, kissing their mothers on the small front porches of the brightly colored modest Victorian clapboard houses which pepper the Meridian hills. It is the morning of the performance of *Snow White* at the grammar school and the children, walking and skipping, arms laced together, whispering at the street corners, roughhousing on the lawns, are in high spirits. The film is in slow motion, capturing the dance of children playing, their wide-open smiles in slow motion; it moves up Poplar Street to Molly DeLaurentis's house where Molly sits alone on the front porch with a fat stuffed kitten on her lap, her purple mittens on either cheek, her eyes wide. She is waiting, looking off in the direction of the village so she doesn't see Sallie Durham flying down the hill in her bright red jacket, her long hair braided, her cheeks chapped pink. She collides with Molly on the porch and they fall into each other's arms like puppies, kissing and kissing in delight.

She didn't hear T.J. arrive. She hadn't actually fallen asleep with the film of "Meridian" spinning pictures of children but her sense of awareness was so close at hand, so self-conscious, that the outside world was muted in comparison. When she did hear him call to her and realized he was knocking, she leaped out of her chair.

"You frightened me," she said, sitting at the bottom of the steps, wrapping her arms around her legs.

"I'm sorry," T.J. said. "I knocked a couple of times. I guess you were sleeping."

"I was sleeping," Helen said.

T.J. was in shorts, his pale legs loose and dangly like the legs of a child, his eye patch comically askew. "Are you okay?"

"Don't I look okay?" Helen asked, susceptible to suggestions. "I think I'm fine. I hope I am."

"Are you watching the film?"

"I was and then I must have fallen asleep," she said.

"I left a note," T.J. said.

"I got the note," Helen said. "I was so tired I didn't bother to try to call you."

"The news is bad," he said.

She followed him into the kitchen.

"Do you have milk?" he asked. He opened the refrigerator and took out the quart of milk. "I had a call this evening from a woman who works in a gas station in Baertown who saw the newsbreak on Maggie and she thinks she saw her in a car with a pale skinny well-dressed man with a baseball cap on backward."

"You say the news is bad?"

"The woman pumped gas and, while she was doing the windshield of his car, she saw the child lying on the front seat." He poured milk and looked in the cabinet, finding a box of crackers. "She thought the child looked dead."

Helen shook her head.

"A man isn't going to stop in a gas station with a dead child on the front seat, T.J. He'd be crazy."

"I know, but it's the third time I've gotten a call from a person nearby who has seen her." He took bread out of the fridge. "I'm always hungry when I'm nervous. Could I make myself some toast?" he asked. "Jam?" He checked the door of the fridge, taking out a jar. "Edie's own raspberry, not bad."

They were at the kitchen table when David Jaspersen arrived, knocking at the front door, walking in without waiting for anyone to answer. He got a glass of water.

"I'm sorry to barge in like this," he said, checking his watch. "There've been a million things happening tonight."

"Anything about Maggie?" T.J. asked.

"Not about Maggie."

"I had a call from Baertown from a woman who said she saw Maggie lying on the front seat of a car driven by a well-dressed youngish man."

"Dead," Helen said.

David took half a piece of toast from T.J.'s plate. "I got that call too. Not a possibility."

"But it's the third call I've gotten from someone in the vicinity of Meridian who's seen her," T.J. said.

David shook his head. "How many calls do you get a day?"

"Two hundred," T.J. said.

"They've seen her pictures on television. Maybe they've seen 'The Story of Meridian.' It's a miracle you don't get two thousand calls a day." David looked in the fridge. "Do you have a beer?"

"No," she said, going into the living room, stretching out on the couch. "Just half a bottle of wine."

He came into the living room, drinking straight from the bottle, sitting down on a ladder-back chair next to the couch where Helen was lying.

"You seem a wreck," Helen said.

"It's been a hard day." He pulled a notebook out of his

pocket. "Five-fifteen P.M. corner of Aspen and Rowder, Billy Blake lost his temper and hit Callie Blake. Five twenty-seven while I am at Callie Blake's, I receive a call on my beeper that Henry Sailor on his way to the pharmacist's house to get some sleeping pills for Madeleine, which she shouldn't have because she's still drunk, slammed his car into Toby Oler's parked car on Main." He finished the wine and put the empty bottle beside his chair. "And Toby, who was just going into the movies when it happened and is by nature a quiet even-tempered man—I played football with him and know—lost his temper, swung at Henry and told him he was going to kill him."

"Jesus," T.J. said.

"You're under a lot of pressure with the sick children," Helen said. "It's not entirely surprising."

David was silent.

"That's part of it," T.J. said.

"I used to be clear about things," David said. "Rules were rules. Things like that." He stood up and crossed the room. "Who knows what's true and not true any longer? Certainly not me," he said, genuine anger in his voice. "You, T.J.?"

"Shut up, David," T.J. said.

"Please," Helen said. "This has been a very long week."

David turned on television. "Do you have the film?" he asked.

"It's in the VCR," Helen said.

The channel flickered from zigzag lines to salt and pepper, finally surfacing on a picture of Dr. Richard Hazelton walking down the street holding the hand of Molly De-Laurentis and another child Helen didn't recognize.

"Who is that man?" David asked, indicating Dr. Hazelton assuming the pose of an actor.

"Isn't it Dr. Hazelton?" Helen asked, a little frightened at the suddenness of his outburst.

"Exactly. Dr. Richard Hazelton, late of Meridian, Ohio," he said. "But who is he really?"

"Cut it out, David," T.J. said. "Pull yourself together."

"No, no. Listen to me. I'm saying something important, something philosophical. Is this man the good quiet, pale-faced physician we recognize as one of our own or is he some-one else?"

"This is not about the film, David," T.J. said. "What's the matter in Meridian we've done to ourselves."

"I don't know that," David said, turning off his beeper, which was ringing. "I don't know a thing." He picked up the phone on the side table. "Mind if I use your phone?" He dialed.

"Prudential?" He listened.

"I'll be right down," he said.

"Has something happened to her?" T.J. asked, alarmed.

"Prudential's fine," David said, heading toward the front door.

"Do you need me?" Helen asked, sitting up.

"I don't," David said. "It's not that kind of problem. It's personal."

"I'm sorry about all that," T.J. said after David had left. "Sometimes David has a temper."

"Everybody is very much on edge," Helen said.

"That's true," T.J. said. "It's been a difficult spring and then this illness," he said but Helen knew it wasn't the fault of legionella.

After T.J. left, Helen turned off all the lights and sat in the dark in the living room in case a person with a mind to harming her should throw something through the window that faced the front of the house, a large double window with no curtains or shutters or blinds.

When she called her mother, the answering machine was on with her mother's voice. But she had a sense of someone there behind the machine. She could see her mother in her blue jeans and a red bandanna around her head, weaving tapestries. Was she still weaving tapestries in New York City, did they have any interest for a city dweller or were they collecting dust rolled up in the back of a closet in her apartment?

She called her father, who said he'd call back after yoga class.

"Don't bother," she said. "I want to talk to you now. Not after you do yoga. After you do yoga, I may be dead."

There was a long pause.

"Don't be extreme, Helen."

"I'm not extreme. I'm serious. Why doesn't Mother ever answer the phone? You call. Tell her I'm sitting here waiting for her to call me. And do it before yoga."

"I will," her father said quietly. "I'll do it now."

He called back immediately, too soon to have made the call, and waited for the answering machine to complete its information.

"She's out," he said. "I'm sure she'll call you when she gets back home."

Helen waited. She counted to twenty-five. And slowly, she counted to one hundred as her mother used to make her do when she was a child, impatient for time to pass quickly. Then she dialed her mother's apartment again. This time the message had the voice of a man, her stepfather certainly. "You have reached 684-6050. Please leave a message and we will get back to you as soon as possible," he said.

Now her mother wouldn't even allow Helen to hear the sound of her voice.

One more time, she dialed New York. When the message beeper sounded she said in a cool and even-tempered voice, "Mother, this is Helen." She was going to say, "I hate you," in the same cucumber voice, but she couldn't bring herself to do it.

She was six, in Mrs. Dawn's first grade in Mackinaw, and Mrs. Dawn had a baby so Helen refused to go to school with a substitute until she returned.

"You have to go to school, Helen," her mother said at breakfast at Mrs. Peaches's. "I'm taking you to school now."

"I won't go," Helen said.

"You will," her mother said.

"No," Helen said, but she knew the fight was already over and she had lost it.

"I hate you," she said when her mother took her hand and walked with her out the front door. And as they crossed the threshold of Mrs. Peaches's guesthouse it seemed as if the walls fell in, the roof slid into the street and all around them Mackinaw was burning.

When a call came later, Helen thought it was her mother, letting it ring before she answered so as not to seem too eager. But it wasn't her mother.

"I'm calling to ask you to come on over," Prudential said as if it were a normal invitation from an ordinary friend. "I've roasted a chicken."

"It's late," Helen said. "You're sure?"

"I eat late," Prudential said, giving Helen directions to her house. "It's not a long walk from your place."

In the kitchen Helen fed Gregory and finished off the wine, even wishing there were more of it left to quiet her nerves. She wasn't exactly afraid, not enough to refuse the invitation, but she was certainly uneasy.

VI.

DO NO
HARM

The Story of

MERIDIAN

THE FIFTH DAY OF SHOOTING "The Story of Meridian"
was a Friday and the last day because the budget was tight
and Peter Forester had only allowed for five days of camera
crews. He was known in the industry for economy in the use
of time. But without the weekend, he had to make special
arrangements to set up weekend activities on Friday—church
services and ball games and club meetings. It was complicated, particularly church services on Friday, which meant the
shops had to close for a while and the schools miss a day of
classes so half of Friday could be Saturday and half could be
Sunday.

On Friday morning Peter was in a terrible temper. He
came late to the morning meeting in the coffee shop before
the shoot. Pleeper was already there with the rest of the film
crew and his assistant. David Jaspersen was there and T.J.,
Ben Winters, which was unusual for the minister of First
Methodist, and Sophie looking dreadful, her eyes puffed and
red, the whites veiny, her color pallid.

"What is the matter with you this morning?" Peter
asked Sophie, coming in the back door with a cigarette. "You
look like the wrath of God."

"She has the flu," David said.

"Great. Good news. Hours to wrap up and the star's sick."

"It's not my fault," Sophie said quietly, her life entirely altered since Thursday evening.

"I'm sorry. I'm sorry." He took hold of her wrist absent-mindedly. "My patience is thin today. You'll have to excuse me."

" 'S okay," Sophie said. She had lost interest in her film career, so exhausted she could hardly sit on a chair without falling.

"So today we do church in the morning and sports in the afternoon. I'll need a pile of people dressing up for church. School's out, isn't it?" he asked. "You've let school out?"

"It's out," David said.

"First I'm doing the clinic thing I didn't get to do yesterday with Molly," he said.

"You'll have to choose another child," T.J. said evenly.

"I've been tracking Molly. I want to stick to these few familiars. I've got a story going."

"Then do Sallie Durham. You've been following her," T.J. said.

"What's with Molly?" he asked.

"Molly has the flu."

"And, Peter," David began, ordering more coffee and doughnuts all around, "if you're doing the clinic, it will have to be with Prudential because Dr. Hazelton had to leave on a family emergency."

"What?"

"He had to leave," T.J. said. "It was an emergency."

"Shit," Peter said. He leaned over to Sophie and touched her hand. "Don't worry about me, Sophie. I'm a bear on wrap-up day. It's not personal."

Sophie didn't reply.

"Are you okay?" Peter asked her, looking over the schedule with Pleeper.

"Fine," she said. "I'm fine."

By Thursday early evening, Dr. Richard Hazelton had left Meridian, called out of town on a family emergency, the message for Prudential on the clinic answering machine said. But Prudential already knew and so did most everybody else.

Dr. Hazelton drove directly north from Meridian into Michigan, around the waistband of Lake Michigan into the Upper Peninsula, where he checked into a Motel 6. He bought the Friday papers and a stack of mysteries and moved into Room 110 overlooking a parking lot and then the town of Elksville. He had no plans, only a vague notion that he would drop his identity in Motel 6. Or maybe not. Maybe he would return to Meridian, depending on Molly.

Dr. Hazelton realized almost immediately at the bottom of the driveway before he turned toward Main Street that the front door of his Toyota was open and Molly was gone. He stopped the car, got out and dragged himself up the hill to his house, sick with fear. She was lying on the side of the driveway and when he knelt down beside her, his angel, his own, something snapped in his brain.

Molly was unconscious. She had fallen on her head, on the side of her head, although there was no mark. He put her gently in the back seat of the car and drove to the church hall where the film crew was staying, carrying her down the back steps to the kitchen. What he had in mind—in his fractured mind—was a confrontation with Peter Forester and the film crew.

"This is what you have done to my child," he was going to say to them, say to Peter Forester, holding Molly toward them in his long outstretched arms. "You have ruined our lives."

He opened the door and was just walking across the linoleum floor, past the stove and the long table, when he heard someone coming, someone on the other side of the kitchen door, and in a panic, his brain scrambled, he laid Molly gently, gently on the floor and ran. Soon, he thought, driving back to his house, they would pay and pay and pay— the director and the film crew and Sophie DeLaurentis with her cotton-candy dreams.

When Reverend Ben Winters discovered Molly, he assumed she was dead. His first thought as he rushed up to his office with her was that she'd been murdered, maybe raped and murdered by a member of the film crew. He laid her on the couch in the corner of his office, covered her with a blanket, turned off the light, locked the door and rushed downstairs to find David Jaspersen.

Edith saw him first.

"Ben," she said, catching a glimpse of his bone-white face as he rushed by. "What's the matter?"

"Nothing really," he said. "We have a bit of a problem and I need to find David." He grabbed her wrist. "Don't make an issue. It's important with the film crew here to keep up face."

David was dancing with Sophie after the supper, high stepping to Sam Durham's fiddle, and Sophie had her head turned, camera ready.

"I have to go pick up Molly at the clinic," Sophie was saying. "She has a virus but first Rosie Doyle is going to do my hair because Peter wants to do just a couple more shots of me that got messed up. I thought I'd have Rosie do it prissy."

"Whose idea?" David said.

"Peter's," Sophie said demurely.

Peter had come into the church hall with Pleeper, going over the late evening's events.

"Now, Sophie," he began.

"Sophie has to go get Molly," David said for her. "Molly has the flu. But I need to talk with you."

"I have another shoot with Sophie and Molly at Mr. DeLaurentis's grave, so I hope she's okay."

"She'll be fine," Sophie said, hurrying off across the room, disappearing in the crowd of high school students.

"I was talking to my son this morning, Peter," David said. "And he's very upset that you are doing a whole school picture without the whole school."

"You know about film, Chief. I can't do the whole school," Peter said. "There're too many and it wouldn't be aesthetically pleasing to have so many." He slapped his clipboard nervously against his thigh. "The picture of the school will appear several times throughout the series as a leitmotif and I want it to look attractive, not a mob scene." He put his hand on David's arm. "I'll have your son included."

"That's not the point," David said.

"I get the point, David, but I'm a filmmaker, not Dr. Feelgood, so I'm going to do what looks good." He turned away. "You'll be glad. By May, Meridian, Ohio, will be a household name."

David Jaspersen was just walking out the back door of the church hall in a temper when Reverend Winters intercepted him.

"She's not dead," David said, standing up beside the couch in Ben's office after he had examined Molly.

"She's unconscious?" Ben said.

"Yes, but I don't know enough to say anything more." He picked up the telephone and called Prudential.

"Dr. Hazelton isn't here," Prudential said. "He hasn't come back."

"I thought Molly was with you."

"Not with me," Prudential said. "Dr. Hazelton never came to afternoon clinic hours at all."

They—Edith holding Molly—drove the patrol car to the clinic, which was almost empty. Only Prudential was there. Sophie hadn't yet arrived.

Prudential was standing outside when they drove up.

"There's a message on the answering machine," she said. "Dr. Hazelton's been called away on a family emergency."

"Then who was Molly with?" Edith asked, carrying Molly through the waiting room to the back examining room, laying her on the table where Prudential checked her pulse, her eyes, her air passage, unbuttoned her pale blue corduroy dress.

"She obviously hit her head, although I don't see a mark," she said. "We have to get her to Harrisville."

"What do you think, Pru?" Edith asked.

"I don't know what to think," Prudential said. She telephoned the hospital.

"You didn't talk to Dr. Hazelton all day?" Edie asked. "Isn't that odd?"

"More than odd," Prudential said.

"Doesn't Sophie sometimes leave Molly with Dr. Hazelton?"

"She does," Prudential said. "He brings her here for the day. He likes to have her around."

Ben Winters sat on a chair, his head in his hand. "I was afraid something like this might happen," he said.

"Like what?" Edith asked anxiously. "What is this like?"

"Like an accident," Ben Winters said. "When you get careless, there's an accident."

"It's not an accident to find a child lying unconscious in a kitchen," Prudential said.

"We have to find Sophie and get to the hospital," Edith said.

"Did you call T.J., Prudential?" David asked.

"You call T.J.," Prudential said. "He's still at the church hall is my guess."

"I'll call him," Edith said. "And then I'll get Sophie."

"She's not at home," David said. "I called the beauty parlor and she's not there. She's having her hair done at Rosie's and Rosie Doyle doesn't have a phone."

"I'll go to Rosie's," Edith said.

In the back seat of the patrol car on the way to the Harrisville Hospital, Sophie sobbed.

"At seven this morning I took her to Rich's," she said. "He was going to take care of her and then take her to the clinic."

"Was Rich in a bad mood when you dropped her by?" David said.

"A little," Sophie said. "He was a little bad-tempered."

"Someone brought her to the kitchen of the church hall," David said quietly. "She couldn't have come alone."

"Ben thinks it might be someone from the film crew," T.J. said.

"I don't think so, T.J.," David said. "Sophie left her with Rich and what we know about Richard Hazelton is that he's careful to a fault. He wouldn't have let her out of his sight."

"What do you think, Sophie?" T.J. asked.

"Is there any reason to think that Rich could have done something to Molly?" David asked.

"Like what?" Sophie asked. "What do you think could have happened to her?"

"An accident," David said. "Something accidental, and then he panicked and lost his senses."

"How well do you know him?" T.J. asked.

"I don't know," Sophie said. "I sort of know him."

"Sophie?" David began but she was crying now, uncontrollably.

"Don't be mad," she said. "Please, T.J., don't be mad at me."

"Nobody's mad, Sophie."

"Prudential's mad. You're mad at me, aren't you, Prudential?"

"Mad is not the word," Prudential said.

"Rich was mad this morning," Sophie said but only T.J., sitting next to her, could hear her clearly. "He was mad about the film because Molly is in it," she said. And then, almost under her breath, "He thinks Molly is his," she said.

"Is she?" T.J. asked. "Is she his child?" Perhaps the unfamiliar brusqueness of his voice alarmed her.

"Maybe," Sophie said, weeping. "Maybe. I'm not sure."

David sat with T.J. and Prudential in a small room at the Harrisville Hospital waiting for the doctor.

"Are you bowled over?" T.J. asked.

"No, not bowled over," David said. "I never thought of it before—I never thought Rich Hazelton could—but Antonio was pretty sick to be making babies that last year and it does explain Rich's visit to me the other morning."

"Jesus," T.J. said, shaking his head.

"Nothing like television to bring out the truth," David said.

"The truth about what?" T.J. said. "Sophie isn't really from Meridian." He turned to Prudential, who was reading the newspaper. "Are you surprised?" he asked.

"I'm too old for surprises," she said.

Edith and Benjamin Winters arrived before the doctor. It had started to rain, a cold black rain, and they were soaking.

"Do we know anything?" Ben asked.

"We know this," David said and he told the Winterses about Sophia and Dr. Hazelton.

"What are we going to do?" David said.

"What's to decide?" Prudential asked. "We send the police after Dr. Hazelton and tell the film crew to move their sweet bottoms out of this town."

"No, Pru," David said. "That's not how we're going to do it."

Ben Winters sat in the metal chair, his hands together. "I think we're going to keep it a secret," he said.

"Keep what a secret?" Edith Winters said.

"What happened to Molly."

"Why would we keep it a secret?" Prudential asked.

Ben Winters lowered his voice, speaking as if people were listening in the next room. "A child found unconscious in the church hall." He shook his head. "Absolutely not. They'll film this," he said, indicating the door to the room where Molly was being examined. "We'll be known everywhere as the place where a thing like this can happen."

"This isn't the right way to go about it," Prudential said. "I don't like it at all."

"It's the moral thing to do."

"Moral?" Edie said. "I don't understand you, Ben Winters. What's moral about telling a lie?"

"We're not telling a lie. We're not telling anything," Ben said, standing now, in charge of the situation. "We're protecting our town."

Prudential shook her head. "I'm going home to South Carolina by the weekend," she said. "This isn't a place for a decent person to live."

David folded his arms across his chest, leaned against the door.

"Ben is right," he said, surprised at his own calmness. "We'll get together tonight at my house after the film crew's gone to bed, someone from every house involved in the filming."

"And what are we going to say to the film crew about what happened?" Edie asked.

"Nothing. We'll say nothing," David said. "Dr. Hazelton has been called away on a family emergency. Molly has the flu."

The doctor came into the waiting room with Sophie, who sat in a chair on the other side of the room, turning away from them, facing the window.

"I believe she simply hit her head falling from a distance," Dr. Bartoli said. "You just found her on the sidewalk, is that right?"

"That's right," David said.

Prudential slid deep into the blue plastic couch on which she was sitting and closed her eyes.

"It's a head injury, a broken arm and possible internal injuries. She has lapsed into a coma—on the Glasgow coma scale." He showed them the motor responses. "Not good but not the worst by any means."

Riding back from the hospital to Meridian, T.J. in the front seat, David was sick with nerves. He turned off 15 into Meridian.

"I used to be so sure of what I thought and I've lost that," he said.

"Who doesn't lose it?" T.J. asked.

"Worse than that. I'm about to do something which I know is wrong and I'm going to do it anyway."

"You're the chief of police protecting your town."

"I ought to go after Richard Hazelton. That's the law."

"So?"

"I'm not going to do it."

There were thirty people at David Jaspersen's house at midnight. The news had slipped by osmosis into the houses of Meridian like an airborne virus carried by the winds. People spoke in low voices, worried that their conversation could be heard seven blocks south at the church hall where the CBS film crew was sleeping.

"What is our story then?" Ann Durham asked.

"That Molly has pneumonia."

"What about Sophie?" Edie asked.

"She's at the hospital now," David said. "But she'll be here tomorrow to do the filming."

"Peter Forester seems to have fallen in love with Sophie," Sam Durham said.

"I've worked with Peter Forester for a few years," T.J. said. "What you've been observing is called lust."

"Sophie might tell," Henry Sailor said. "She's human."

"She won't tell," David said. "She promised and she's terrified of what will happen."

"What will happen?" Edie asked. "I mean what will ultimately happen after the film crew leaves?"

"What do you mean, happen?" David asked.

"Richard Hazelton must know something," Madeleine said. "You'll try to find him, won't you?"

"Rich has been called away on a family emergency," David said. He hesitated. "I have no reason to go after him."

"He was taking care of Molly," Madeleine said. "He was the last person to see her."

"We don't know that," David said.

"As if that makes any difference," Madeleine Sailor said quietly from the corner of the room where she was sitting on the floor.

"What do you mean, Madeleine?" David asked.

"I just don't like lies," she said. "They grow. I've seen them grow fat with blood like wood ticks."

"This isn't a lie," T.J. said. "It's a concealment."

"I don't like concealments either," Madeleine said. "Something will happen."

"You have to make these kinds of choices," Mr. Rubin, Sr., said. "Though I certainly understand your concern, Madeleine. I'm concerned too. The film crew wanted to come into the funeral home when Mona was being fixed up Tuesday. They're not entirely likable."

"But the point is what do we do about this?" Sam Durham said. "And what we do is protect ourselves."

"This is the lesser of two evils," Henry Sailor said. "Always my father used to tell me, choose the lesser of two evils."

"Our lips are sealed," Henry Sailor said to David, who stood at the back door of his house, embracing his fellows, his childhood friends, watching them wind into the dark moonless night.

"What do you think?" T.J. asked, lighting a cigarette, after everyone had left.

"I don't know what I think," David said, sinking onto the living-room couch.

On Friday they filmed church school in the rooms the film crew had been using, classrooms with large round tables and small chairs.

"I want Molly," Sallie Durham pouted. "I don't want to sit with Maria and Tommy Blake. He hits."

"Molly's sick," Ann Durham said to her. "You'll be fine, darling." She turned to Peter Forester. "How do you plan to do this?" she asked.

"I'm trying to capture the children thinking about ethical questions," Peter said, "like what is the meaning of family or what is death or what is good and bad—the adults will be talking about the same thing, so we'll have a sense that in this community important things matter." He picked Sallie up and put her on the edge of the table. "What happens in your Sunday school classes?"

"We have a story like 'The Good Samaritan' and children relate the story to their own lives," Ann Durham said. "Even children small as Sallie."

"I'm trying to get across that your lives are more substantive, more humanistic, less materialistic than the lives of most Americans."

"We live good lives," Ann said. "I know that sounds unsophisticated but we are a kind of tribe and careful of one another."

Sallie looked up at Peter Forester suspiciously.

"Molly got run over by a car," she said in the middle of their conversation.

"Molly what?" Peter asked.

"Molly has the flu, Sallie," Ann Durham said. "Remember I told you?"

Sallie closed her eyes.

"Daddy said that Molly got run over," Sallie said after Peter Forester had gone to the other side of the church hall.

Peter Forester slipped his arm over Sophie's shoulder.

"I really want to do that shoot at the cemetery, Sophie.

Do you have something black to wear—maybe that long coat of yours and very little makeup? The gray light today will give your face a nice color and you ought to look pale."

"Okay," Sophie said.

"Right after the Sunday school shoot, I'll do you walking from your house with the flowers—and then wherever your husband's buried, I want you to pass by Mona Dickenson's grave. You can put one flower of yours on her grave, then go on to your husband's grave." He was pensive for a moment. "What do you think about the dog following you there—Mona's yellow dog?"

Sophie looked perplexed.

"Following me?"

"Never mind," he said. "Probably a dumb idea."

Benjamin Winters arrived at the church hall in full dress.

"Is everybody going to be at church?" Peter asked.

"Everyone was notified," Ben Winters said. "They'll be here."

"Do you have a sermon prepared for this?" Peter Forester asked.

"I have an old sermon about grace."

"Grace—that's a big seller," Peter Forester said. "We'll shoot a few seconds of grace straight on—you in the pulpit, Reverend Winters, for all of America to see," he said.

Peter Forester joined T.J. to pick up Sophie for the cemetery shoot.

"This has gone very well, T.J. I'm glad I came," he said. "I've had a good time."

"I'm glad you've had a good time," T.J. said.

"And you've not?"

"You bet I've had a great time, Peter," T.J. said.

The camera crew followed Sophie. She came out of her small cottage like a dark-eyed gloomy bride carrying a bunch of peach gladiolus and white roses, walked up the hill to Aspen and turned left to Highpoint Way where the cemetery was, built high because of the floods. From the angle of the camera focused up, the hill was powdered with light snow and white tombstones, bare slender birches and maples graceful against the horizon.

She did look lovely, T.J. thought, in her long black coat and black hair falling a little from the lavender ribbon holding a mound of curls in a loose cushion. She looked appropriately weary.

"Do you know her well?" Peter Forester asked, directing the crew to get a different angle as she entered the cemetery, walked past Mona's fresh grave—the Dickensons' plot immediately to the right—took a white rose out of the center of her own bunch of flowers and leaned over Mona's grave, putting the white rose on the bare, newly turned black earth.

"Mmm," Peter said. "Perfect shot, I think."

Then Sophie walked along a narrow, damp path to a

new section of the cemetery, knelt down beside a simple high slab of marble with ANTONIO DELAURENTIS and the dates, put down her flowers and to everyone's complete surprise, certainly T.J.'s, she wept.

Pleeper Jones turned around and raised his eyebrows.

"Is she still heartbroken?" Peter asked, bemused.

"How do I know?" T.J. asked. "Maybe she adored him."

"You could have fooled me," Peter Forester said.

He looked in the camera lens. "Good. That's nice, Pleeper. We'll be able to use that at the end of one of the hours."

T. J. Wisely turned his wheelchair and started down the hill. He heard Peter Forester call him and then Sophie but he didn't turn around. He kept his head up, high up, tilted toward the sky, over the black peaked roofs of the houses, the brilliant rainbow of colors, brighter for the gray afternoon, the sprinkling of people along Main Street; he couldn't find it in his heart to look down at the perfect beauty of his beloved town.

17.

THE DIRECTIONS TO PRUDENTIAL'S HOUSE were simple but Helen couldn't imagine the place. A ten-minute walk, she had said. "Turn left when you leave your house, straight up the hill past the Rubins' and T.J.'s at the very top and then keep going although the road will seem to end, you'll be on a path through the woods which opens to a small clearing and a house. Not even ten minutes," she said.

The night was cool with a light wind, the sweet smell of honeysuckle in the air, a slender crescent of moon just ahead, a silver cookie low in the sky. There was very little light and, although the road was paved, Helen felt uncertain walking in such darkness.

The light was on in the Rubins' house and she could clearly see Mr. Rubin in his bedroom wandering back and forth in his pajamas, packing to go away perhaps. Mrs. Rubin opened the front door and called the cat, "Kitty kitty kitty," in a high cat-calling voice, and the cat, a fat gray one, dashed across the road in front of Helen. She didn't remember who lived in the next house—David had told her and she had forgotten but it was a modern one-story house unlike most of the houses in Meridian. There was only one light in the bedroom but through the window she could see the posts of a four-poster bed. T.J.'s house was dark inside but the yard and porch were lit by floods and she knew it was T.J.'s house although she had never been there because there was a ramp onto the front porch for a wheelchair.

After T.J.'s, it was very dark and she had difficulty seeing what actually was ahead but the paved road ended and she went into a woods which seemed less dense than ordinary woods although there was a lot of pine—a clean evergreen smell, the floor of the path crunched with sharp dry pine needles.

The scratching of pine needles reminded her of something particular. Some clear memory perhaps of Michigan in late summer. She thought of memories in white cardboard jewelry boxes, the size for a ring or a pair of earrings, obscured in the soft cotton filling—a wealth of jewels stacked in a corner of the top drawer of her mind. And it seemed now with the strong scent of Mackinaw as if one of these boxes was opening with news she wasn't certain she wanted to know.

The path went on for longer than she had expected, although halfway to the clearing the light from Prudential's house slipped through the trees, lighting the path where she was walking. Reaching the clearing, she was amazed at the tiny size of the house and its simplicity, a small wood house, two stories, one on top of the other, and lit top to bottom.

Prudential was on the porch. "Did you have trouble finding it?" she called.

"No trouble," Helen said, walking across the high grassy field, waving to her.

"So you haven't had a chance to come to my house," Prudential said, suggesting time constraints were what had made Helen's visit impossible.

"No, I haven't," Helen said.

She climbed up on the porch, high without steps, almost a jump, and Prudential grabbed her hand, leading her in the front door.

The main room was furnished in old furniture with brightly colored Indian throws and mayonnaise jars full of wildflowers on every table and walls of theater posters, a cheerful lighthearted room surprising for a woman like Prudential of no small spiritual darkness.

In the middle of the room a table was set for four with blue and white striped cloth and candles already lit.

"I don't do much entertaining," Prudential said and she seemed nervous about Helen being there. "Just last-minute like tonight when I get a chicken and it looks better than the chickens I usually get. So I call T.J. or the Winterses and, tonight, you."

The kitchen was small, with all kinds of pots and pans and pottery and pictures of vegetables and fruit on the wall and dried flowers in glasses and little jars of fresh herbs stuck in water, a cozy crowded kitchen but organized, spoons with spoons in a crockery jar, yellows with yellows, greens with greens—exactly the opposite kind of kitchen from the one Helen would have expected from Prudential, more like a kitchen in her *Country Living* magazine, with the promise of home.

The sink was full of spinach leaves soaking, a pot boiling on the stove. Prudential emptied the drain and shook the spinach.

"I love fresh spinach," she said, "cooked just so, only a minute." She smiled. "You want a beer?"

"No, thank you." Helen shook her head.

"I don't drink," Prudential said. "I used to. I'd drink and dance all night but I had to quit."

She wiped her hands on the back of her madras cotton dress.

"David's coming," she said. "At least so he said if there isn't an emergency."

She turned off some of the lights and lit the other candles in the room, lots of them, big ones. "Candles remind me of church, the smell of them does." She patted the couch. "Sit down," she said. "I'll be sitting down soon." But she didn't sit. She moved from one part of the room to the next, fussing with the table and the wildflowers in the mayonnaise jars, dusting off the back of the couch. And Helen wanted to say, "Have you gone crazy, Prudential? Who are you this evening and what is this busy charade?" But she sat on the edge of the couch, not a comfortable couch, not one made for sitting, and watched Prudential—a woman accustomed to long languid movements and slow ones—scurry around the room.

It occurred to Helen even before she heard a noise in the back room behind the kitchen that all the fussing Prudential was about had to do with making noise. That she was trying to keep Helen from hearing someone in the back room. And there was someone. Helen heard a door open just behind her.

Prudential was in the kitchen, taking the roast chicken

out of the oven, mashing potatoes, but when the door opened, she stepped out of the kitchen into the main room.

"Why, hello, sweetheart," she said. "That was a very long nap."

The child was maybe three, small with a circle of black curls around a china-white face, a delicate, beautiful face, the child from "The Story of Meridian," the child Molly.

Helen caught her breath.

"You come on in now," Prudential said. "And say hello to Dr. Fielding, the new doctor I've been telling you about."

Prudential went back into the kitchen then as if nothing out of the ordinary was going on, picked up her bowl of potatoes, mashing them with her strong slender arms.

The child was in a thin nightgown, white with tiny yellow flowers, and her face was wrinkled with sleep. She folded her arms across her chest and didn't move.

"Hello," Helen said, smiling.

Molly's eyes grew round and she fixed on Helen.

"You must be Molly," Helen said.

"How did you know her name out of the blue like that?" Prudential asked.

Helen gave Prudential a look. "From the film," she said.

"I'd forgotten you've seen the film," Prudential said disingenuously.

"Enough of it to recognize Molly," Helen said.

Molly slid around the wall without turning her back on Helen, slipping into the kitchen with Prudential.

"Where's Mama?" she asked.

"Visiting," Prudential said. "Still visiting." She looked at Helen.

"We had her l-e-a-v-e," Prudential said, spelling the words so Molly couldn't understand them. "When you came to town, we said o-u-t until the visiting physician goes home."

"How come?" Helen asked.

Prudential shrugged. "You tell one lie and, before you know it, all you tell is lies."

Headlights ran over the wall before Helen had a chance to think, to accommodate to the situation, to know what to say. Prudential picked up Molly and went to the door.

"Here comes David, sweetheart."

"T.J. too?" Molly asked.

"Just David, darling," Prudential said. "T.J.'s working."

David was as cheerful as Prudential—striding into the house, kissing Molly and Prudential, kissing Helen, acting as if dining in this company was a familiar occurrence. He sat down next to Helen and took Molly on his lap, playing "Here's the church and here's the steeple," with her. And not for a minute did he betray a sense of oddness in the situation, as if the terms for this scene at Prudential's secret house were set.

They sat around the table eating chicken and mashed potatoes and spinach and hot rolls and strawberry shortcake with piles of whipped cream. The conversation was warm and pedestrian—what's up on the police blotter and who's sick and how's the garden doing, the strawberries must be from out back.

Helen began to think that she was making too much of things, that in fact Prudential had just gotten around to asking her to dinner, trusting her enough to let her in her house and she oughtn't worry about Molly. She was even having a good and easygoing time when Prudential turned to her and said in her old familiar sharp voice and attitude, "You're not a stranger to Meridian, are you?"

Helen drew her legs up under her chin, buried her face in her knees.

"Sam Durham knew you," David said, and he was gentle about it, not confrontational but clear. "When Sallie was ill and you spent the day there, you had a conversation with Sam about your Aunt Martha and then he remembered you. We looked it up."

"Looked what up?" Helen asked.

"We remembered the name Fielding from somewhere. In a town as small as Meridian, people remember when a child dies," David said.

Helen was suddenly lightheaded. She cupped her hands, breathing the same air in and out to keep from hyperventilating.

"The name Emma Fielding means something to us," he said. "She was your sister, wasn't she?"

"I didn't mean to keep it a secret," Helen said, getting up, moving around the room, folding her arms across her chest.

Later Helen couldn't remember what happened next. T.J. arrived and Molly sat on his lap, pulling off his eye patch, hiding behind her hands. Prudential did the dishes, singing church music with the radio in the kitchen, and she and

David talked about nothing in particular, sickness in Meridian, a little about Madeleine Sailor's drinking. Prudential took Molly to bed, made coffee, blew out the candles and finally they were all four of them sitting in the living room, almost silent, in the light spring air.

"So you know who I am," Helen said. She was sitting in a high-backed wooden chair, uncomfortable. She folded her legs under her. "Now you tell me what's going on in Meridian."

David did most of the talking. He sat in the hardwood chair across from Prudential, who was humming along with the conversation as if her role was musical accompaniment.

"Prudential wanted you to know about Molly," David said. "She insisted you come here tonight. She's been insisting all the time."

"It's a crazy place that keeps a child hidden from a doctor in a town," Prudential said.

"As soon as we found out you had been here when you were a little girl, that Emma Fielding, whom we all had heard about, was your sister . . . somehow it seemed out of control." T.J. shook his head. "It was as though you'd been sent here to find us out."

"Find out what?" Helen asked. "What is it that's happening?"

"What happened," Prudential said, folding her arms across her chest, throwing her great head back, "is suspicion—that's what you've been seeing with the hateful way people act to one another, creeping around, looking at their neighbors through eye slits like anybody could be carrying an automatic weapon. Tell the doctor what happened, David."

"It's not as simple as I'm going to say it," he said. And he told her about T.J. and the decision to choose Meridian for the film about an American small town. "It's probably not at all simple," he said, and he told her about Sophie and Peter Forester and about Dr. Hazelton. He was generous about Dr. Hazelton.

"We were cruel to him when he was young," David said. "I was cruel. He was thin and girlish and awkward and we treated him terribly."

He told her about Molly and Dr. Hazelton.

"I think he lost his head when he was taking care of Molly that morning."

"But why did you hide her?" Helen asked.

"We hid her until the film crew left so they wouldn't know our secret. We didn't want them to know that we were anything less than the town they had invented for the television film. And then when we had to have a doctor because of the children getting sick, we hid her from you," he said. "A doctor gets to know everything about a small town and we didn't want you to know about Molly."

They stayed up late talking and talking. Finally Prudential went to bed and T.J. said he had to go home or he'd die of exhaustion.

It was dawn when David took T.J. to his house and then drove Helen. She was almost asleep on her feet as he walked her up to the door. She leaned against him with her body weight, hard against him as if this evening he were large enough to carry her weight and his own.

"Whew," she said, lifting his large hand, kissing his fingers.

18.

HELEN WAS HALLUCINATING CHILDREN.

It is a soft measured sunny day—a spread of lawn, maybe the back garden of her childhood home in Ann Arbor. The lawn checkered with sprinklers watering the grass with children, tiny children popping out of the holes in the sprinkler, ballooning upward and upward, flying children spilling on the long green lawn, rolling over and over as they hit the earth. The garden is filling with children and Helen cannot breathe.

She woke up in bed in Dr. Hazelton's house, lying flat without a pillow, the room spinning as if she were drunk, and she grabbed the side, pulling herself to a sitting position, turning on the light.

It was 4 A.M., she thought, and she was unraveling again. She could see her mind like a tight ball of twine, undoing itself, slipping across the hardwood floor.

She made a mental list of the last few hours. She'd been

at Prudential's for dinner and there was the child Molly and David and T.J. and she drank too much wine.

She had said she was too tired to walk home and David had driven her in the patrol car, stopping first to let T.J. out at his house.

The next thing Helen remembered, he was leaning down over her face and she was sleeping.

"You're at home," he'd said.

Home, home, home, home, came through her sleep.

"Come home, Helen, hurry, Helen," her mother is saying. "I'm here on the front porch waiting for you."

And swinging across her vision is a faded color photograph of her mother on the front porch of their house in Ann Arbor before Emma died—her lovely mother, just out of girlhood, in a yellow dress, her hair long and breezy, a small sunflower stuck behind her ear.

She got out of bed, showered and dressed for the day although morning would not begin for several hours. But anxious to erase the images of raining children crowding her brain, she went downstairs, turned on the television and put in the third cassette of "The Story of Meridian," fast-forwarding to Dr. Richard Hazelton. It was easy to find him even with the images flashing across the screen—he was a white, white figure dancing by and she stopped the moving picture and examined it as if under a microscope, looking at each detail of his face—Dr. Hazelton on the front steps of the clinic, Dr. Hazelton with Molly on his lap, the back of him, and Dr. Hazelton recognizable from the long, long arms, standing in line at the pharmacy, bending to speak to a small young curly-haired woman with a lollipop.

Summer in the shade under a leafy tree, Helen sits on the ground with a stick making pictures in the dirt in the triangle made by her outstretched legs. She can see her parents from where she is sitting and they're laughing like bells.

Emma is standing beside her mother, pulling on her long lavender skirt, a striped skirt, lavender and white stripes and shiny. Helen sees her but she keeps her head down, pretending to look at the Bengal tiger she has drawn in the dirt on the ground in front of her.

"Helen," her mother calls, looking over at the tree where Helen is sitting. But she keeps her head down and doesn't answer. "Helen?"

"Helen," her father calls. "Helen."

Her mother is barefooted, pretty bare feet with red polish on the toes, a lavender and white striped skirt, just above the ankles, but Helen doesn't look up.

"Darling," her mother says, "I'd love it if you'd take Emma for a little walk just now so your father and I can finish our supper.

"Helen?"

She looks up. Her mother is holding Emma in her arms, Emma's plump arms wrapped tight around her neck.

"No," Helen says.

"Helen." Her father's voice drops like a rock on her small head. "Take Emma for a walk down the wildflower path to the river. Bring us back some flowers."

"By the time you get back, we'll be finished supper and we can do something lovely with you," her mother says. "Here." Her mother puts Emma down beside her. "You take Emma's hand and I'll take Daddy's."

They are walking back to the picnic table, hand in hand, her father bending toward her mother, bending over her, kissing her hair. "Be careful of Emma," he calls.

"Be careful of Emma," her mother calls but they don't turn around or wave or smile or notice that Helen has gone down the wildflower path to her destiny.

On television, there is a story of two little girls, familiar girls to Helen, she has seen their pictures. The older, the larger, a tall dark-haired whimsy of a girl, is holding the hand of the younger, plumper, sweet-faced, yellow-haired girl. The camera focuses on the hands laced together. The older girl lifts the hands of both, turning them so the soft plump baby hand is on top. And then the camera moves up the body of the dark-haired older girl, close up so she fills the screen in pieces, to her face on which there is a look of—is hatred too strong a word? The angle changes and what Helen sees in the soundless landscape is a closeup of both children, the older one looking down without affection at the plump baby hand on top of her own.

———

Helen dials her mother in New York. It is so late at night or so early in the morning that there is a chance her mother will by accident answer the phone and then she can capture her, hold on to her voice at the other end.

It rings again and again and then, in her mother's small musical voice, out of sleep, "Hello."

"Mama," Helen says and she is a child again, pure child, no distance on her broken heart and no defense. "I am going crazy. You have to help me."

There's a hesitation. A brief hesitation, a split second to throw a net over her mother's head and drag her in. "Please talk to me."

Maybe you will have no daughters, Mother, Helen thinks but she doesn't say anything. Maybe I will die of grief unless you can help me now. She is silent, waiting, waiting.

"I'm going to change phones," her mother says.

There is a pause, a long silence and then a click.

"I know you've called because you want to know what happened on the day that Emma died," Allie Fielding said and her voice was stronger, more certain than Helen had heard it for years.

"I would be grateful," Helen said, her heart beating so fast, she thought she would die of it before she heard what her mother was going to tell her and she knew that this time she was going to find out.

From the other end of a tunnel, a long sewer pipe to eternity, her mother's voice. "I don't know what happened that day," she said. "It was a lovely, warm evening, my anniversary, and I bought champagne and wanted to be alone with your father. I wanted for you and Emma to go off and play." Her voice was soft and clear. "I don't remember what went on at all because I was drunk." From a great distance, but distinctly, clearly, "What happened to Emma was my fault."

19.

THE TELEPHONE WAS RINGING AND RINGING. Helen heard it somewhere in the back of her brain but she was sleeping too soundly to separate the ringing from sleep. When she woke up she was sitting in a chair in front of the television, the television blank, the last cassette of "The Story of Meridian" playing while she was sleeping in front of it. It was daylight, after 6 A.M. She picked up the telephone. There was no voice on the other end. She knew in her sensible brain that no one was there, although in her ear the voice she heard was Richie Hazelton's, Dr. Richard Hazelton's voice before it had changed to the voice of a man.

"Hello, Helen Fielding?" he said.

Helen is standing on the bank of the river Meryn, her arms folded, Emma in the dirt making pictures with a stick. Kneeling beside her is a young boy about ten—Helen remembers—not a boy she likes particularly, rather a strange boy and one who worries her with his long, long arms and white skin and way of staring at Helen as if he wished to harm her.

He has come out of the bushes beside the bank, out of nowhere.

"I was fishing," he says. "What are you doing by the river?"

"Mama made me walk Emma to the river," Helen says.

He takes Emma's plump hand. "Hi, Emma," he says.

Emma looks up without speaking. Perhaps she isn't talking yet.

"Wanna go swimming?" he asks her.

"She can't swim," Helen says. "I can't swim either. I can't put my head under."

"I'm just going to have her wade," he says, picking Emma up. "Just pretend swimming."

Helen watches him walk down to the river, Emma cooing happily, gripping the back of his shirt with her small fist. He holds her over the water, letting it lap and tickle her bare feet. She is squealing with excitement and delight.

"Be careful of Emma," she says over her sister's happy cries.

"I'll be careful," he calls.

She doesn't see the next moment, blinking or looking over Richie Hazelton's head or to the side, only a split second, the speed of light, of sound, no time to change the course of their lives.

And Emma is swimming downriver, her yellow sundress a bright moon in the middle of the gray-black hurrying water.

"She's swimming," Richie Hazelton says and his voice has the cry of hysteria.

"No," Helen screams. "She can't swim. Please get her. Please catch her."

"I can't catch her," he calls, running down the path in the direction that Emma is tumbling and tumbling downriver, away from them. Helen cannot run after her. Standing on the path with her hands over her eyes, she cannot breathe.

Years later, it seems years later, a lifetime, Helen, still standing on the bank with her eyes covered, hears Richie Hazelton coming toward her through the leaves littered on the path.

"She's gone," he says flatly.

And he kneels down beside her at eye level, looks at her directly with his cold blue eyes.

"If you tell," he says coolly, "I'll kill you."

Helen was screaming. She couldn't help herself. A sound roared out of her belly that she had never heard before, shattering the morning. It came and came and she stood in the living room of Dr. Hazelton's house, unable to change directions, an odd witness to her own unstoppable grief.

She picked up the telephone and called David Jaspersen.

"I believe Dr. Hazelton has Maggie Sailor," Helen said.

"Dr. Hazelton?" David said.

"I have a feeling he's at the river with her, maybe even right now."

"What makes you think that?" he asked.

"I have a reason to think it," Helen said, and even now in her mind she could see him on the riverbank with Maggie and he was going to put her in the water to see if she could swim.

There was a moment of silence.

"All right," David said quietly. "We'll go check. I'll call Prudential. If you're right, we should bring Prudential."

The night before, after her call to her mother, Helen had fallen asleep almost immediately, drugged by the conversation. It was her instinct to sit still as if she were too fragile, actually fragile, with breakable arms and legs. So she waited for sleep. She had no dreams but rather a sense of weightlessness, in a tiny corner of the earth from which gravity had slipped and, though the absence of weight was joy in its pure freedom, it was too close to death for pleasure. She felt as if she were tumbling into an open space with nothing to hold her feet on the ground.

In the patrol car she sat next to Prudential, pressing against her as if the back seat of the car was too small for both of them. Prudential's flesh was compensatory and gave Helen a feeling she longed to have of confinement, holding her down, keeping her insides from escaping the thin protection of her own skin.

Prudential lifted her head up, looking out the window away from Helen.

"I apologize for lying," she said matter-of-factly.

"You didn't actually lie," Helen said. "You just didn't tell the truth."

"I lied," Prudential said. "You asked me the first day you were here did I know a Molly and I said no when Molly was living in my house. I apologize for that."

They drove on in silence. The sun was rising as they drove east, blinding through the windshield, and Helen closed her eyes.

"We'll park just at the entrance," said T.J., who sat with David in the front seat.

"It's a big park," David said. "I'll let you out and drive along the road periphery to the park and, T.J., you can go through the open fields since I don't think the wheelchair will go down the path to the river."

"I'll go down the path to the river," Helen said.

"You know that path?" David asked. "It's been there since I can remember."

"We weren't allowed to go down alone because someone died there once. Do you remember that, David?"

"I remember," David said.

"We didn't know who died," T.J. said. "Someone. Parents said someone. I used to ask and nobody seemed to know."

"It was probably my sister," Helen said.

It was just before seven when they left the car, the air clear and lovely, the sun flooding the horizon with a bright silky light, shimmering over the purple field, the path to the river cheerful with the sounds of insects chattering, the cries of birds.

The two women walked along briskly, Prudential taller but walking slightly perpendicular to the ground, dragging her foot, so their heads from a distance were even, just skirting the tops of the unmowed grasses sprinkled with color.

"We made a mistake," Prudential said.

"You mean about Molly?"

"I mean about lying," Prudential said to settle the score, heading down the path to Judgment Day. "I don't believe in sin but if I did, what we did was sinful."

"Who is we?" Helen asked.

"The town," Prudential said. "We got taken away with the picture of things and didn't want bad news in the film."

"You don't seem like the type," Helen said. "I'm sure it wasn't your fault."

"I didn't do anything to stop it." She picked a long reed and stuck it in her mouth, pulling it through her teeth. "Do you believe in God?" she asked.

"No," Helen said. "But I believe. I'm afraid if I didn't believe, I'd be struck dead." She laughed. "So if I'm afraid, then I must believe," she said. "Do you?"

"Uh-huh," Prudential said. "I don't believe in God."

Helen let her hand swing to touch Prudential's.

"Scared?" Prudential asked.

"A little," Helen said.

"I don't think we're going to find anything except the river," Prudential said.

"But listen," Helen said.

They stopped.

"Can you hear it?" Helen asked. "The water was high when I was here earlier and now you can hear it rushing over the rocks."

"I don't like water," Prudential said. "I like the earth and not the air and not the sea." She folded her arms across her chest. "Maggie's not at the river," she said sourly. "I doubt she's still alive."

"You really think not?" Helen asked.

"That's what I think."

They were coming to the clearing. Helen could tell by the sudden suffusion of light.

"Shh," Prudential said, taking hold of Helen's arm. They stopped and stood very still.

Helen listened. She heard the insect life and birds and was it voices, she wondered, holding her breath to listen above the sound of her own breathing.

"Quietly," Prudential said, moving ahead just a little, and they crept slowly along through the thick grasses swishing by them as they went.

It was strange, Helen thought later, how you know the unseen even though it's invisible, as if the presence of everything desired is in the mind as a suggestion, a whisper of truth.

She knew before the path opened like stage curtains onto the banks of the river Meryn that a child would be on the riverbank. She felt her presence and, lightheaded, too faint to catch her breath, she took hold of Prudential.

What Helen saw was Emma Fielding on the ground beside the river, her legs stretched out, making a triangle of dirt on which she was drawing with a stick. She was larger than Helen remembered, maybe five, Helen's age at the time she had disappeared, and she was wearing a sunny yellow dress, her hair tied up in a ribbon.

Leaning against a tree just behind her, watching her draw in the dirt, was a tall pale-skinned man with long arms.

"Dr. Hazelton," Prudential said.

He turned, his hands in his pockets, in no hurry. He ran his fingers through his hair.

"Hello, Prudential," he said.

The child looked up toward the field where Helen and Prudential were standing but she didn't move or show any recognition of Prudential at all. She simply sat with her legs out and looked at them curiously.

"Maggie?" Prudential said in a soft velvet voice.

The child tilted her head.

"Your mama's been looking for you."

Helen took a step toward him and they were looking at each other directly across the space of land.

"Dr. Hazelton?"

He crossed his arms tight over his chest.

"I'm Helen Fielding," she said. "Do you remember me?"

She couldn't tell from his face whether he remembered her. His expressions moved through surfaces like developing photographs.

"I'm a doctor here now," Helen said. "Since this legionella epidemic. Since you left."

"I see," he said. His face looked shattered, reflected in a mirror of broken glass. He put his hand up to cover his mouth as if he were about to scream.

"Are you Emma Fielding's sister?" he asked. "I remember Emma."

"Do you remember what happened to her?"

He nodded. "Of course. I remember," he said. "I let her go."

A brilliant yellow sun moved over the horizon, drawing

a shaft of light between them, too bright for Helen to see Richard Hazelton's face washed bone white in the sunlight. But she could see him sinking to the ground, folding in on himself as if he were made of strips of cardboard. And she heard him across the distance before she turned to follow Maggie and Prudential down the path to the park.

"It was an accident, Dr. Fielding," he said. "I didn't mean to harm her."

20.

Dr. Hazelton was dead.

He was discovered by a member of the Harrisville police force in a thicket beside the river. An autopsy conducted in Harrisville revealed that he had died of an overdose of a combination of drugs taken shortly after Helen and Prudential walked with Maggie down the path back to the park. He must have concealed himself in dense brush, taken the drugs and lain down, for he was found lying on his side with his knees up and his arms twisted as if at the last moment and in spite of his intentions he had thrashed for air.

Maggie Sailor said that Dr. Hazelton had been kind to her, reading her stories, buying her ice cream, taking her to the movies.

"He wouldn't let me come home and I was homesick," she said. "But he wasn't ever mean. He said I'd get to go home someday, not long from now, and that nothing bad would happen to me with him."

Sometime in the spring Dr. Hazelton had bought a truck because on the day of Maggie's disappearance he had come with a truck to Meridian. Maggie said she was standing outside the drugstore waiting for her mother when he leaned out the window and said, "Hi, Maggie," and she was glad to see him and climbed into the driver's seat with him when he asked her if she'd like to see the instruments on his new truck. That was all she remembered. He did something to her that made her go to sleep. But he didn't hurt her.

In Meridian, in spite of what had happened, Dr. Hazelton was mourned.

The church hall at First Methodist filled up, people arriving with food: fruit pies and chocolate cakes and potato casseroles and noodles, chicken and sausage, macaroni and cheese, bottles of Gallo wine and beer. After the news of Dr. Hazelton's death had traveled through town, they gathered in the church hall. By that afternoon the church hall was full, as if the flood dikes of suspicion dominating the spirit of Meridian since the film crew left had given way, spilling the population down the hills to the large cup at the bottom of town where First Methodist was located.

"I don't understand it," Helen said to Prudential after Maggie was found. "He kidnapped a child. And what about Molly?"

"Things aren't so simple," Prudential said. "I suppose we feel to blame for what happened to him, how he got in such a state of mind to do what he did."

"If you say so," Helen said, sitting in a swivel chair in

the waiting room across from Prudential, eating a chicken sandwich.

"It's hard to know very much about a person or a place," Prudential said, braiding her long hair. "There's going to be a funeral tomorrow afternoon."

"David told me," Helen said.

"My guess is that the whole town will turn out," Prudential said solemnly. "Even the Sailors."

Helen was bone weary but well—better than she had been for many weeks, maybe for years. She felt a kind of internal settlement as if the myriad cardboard shapes that filled in the jigsaw face of Helen Fielding—the one that Oliver used to keep on the dining table, half finished—were in place. She was lightheaded, lifted off the ground.

She had written to her parents, sending the same letter to both of them.

> Dear Mama and Daddy,
>
> I don't know if what I imagined happening when Emma disappeared is what actually happened but this is what I saw in my mind's eye on the bank of the river the evening of your anniversary, June 28, twenty-five years ago.

And she told the story of Dr. Hazelton.

At the end of the letter she wrote:

> I'm not sure why I couldn't remember Richie Hazelton was there. I suppose I was so afraid he would kill me as he promised he would do if I did tell that I forgot until I came back to Meridian and all the memories flooded in.

P.S. Thank you for telling me about the circumstances of your anniversary, Mama. That news has made all of the difference in my life.

I'll be going home soon. Maybe this week. The epidemic is over in Meridian and they no longer need a visiting physician.

"I'm going back to South Carolina soon," Prudential said, sensing a wind change, brushing the crumbs off her lap.

"You can't," Helen said.

"I beg your pardon." Prudential got up, stacked the files of the morning's patients and started to put them away.

"They need you here," Helen said.

"They've got you."

"No," Helen said, leaning against the desk, her arms folded. "I'm the one who should go home. I've done what I came here to do."

Prudential shrugged. "Well, don't worry about me," she said combatively. "I was fine before you came so it won't break me in two for you to leave."

She got out the files for the afternoon clinic patients. "So will you go to Dr. Hazelton's funeral?"

"What time is it?"

"One-thirty tomorrow," Prudential said, opening the folders, making the list of afternoon patients.

"I'll be there," Helen said.

She had not told Prudential she was leaving tomorrow, going home, back to Ann Arbor on the three forty-eight to Detroit. She would tell her maybe later, but no one else. She wanted to slip away quietly, no gestures of appreciation from the town, no ceremonies, just a quick sail through town like weather as if she'd never been or was returning in another form or would come back later, predictable as rain.

David Jaspersen was sitting on her front porch reading the Harrisville paper when Helen came home from the clinic.

She kissed him on the lips. She had wanted to, planned to kiss him all the way down the block and up the steps, knowing that the gesture would be an announcement. She saw him from a distance sitting on the top step of her porch with the newspaper and she was moved to see him there, feeling a kinship as if there were something similar between her and this man David Jaspersen, the chief of police—who had made an error in judgment, a wrong decision, and hurt people who mattered to him. And though, of course, there was nothing similar and she had been a child when Emma died, making no decision except perhaps the wish in the darkest of her dreams not to be careful of Emma, she felt close to him, struck by the ambiguity of the film's heroic policeman and the young troubled man on her front steps who would not resign from his job although he had failed at it. In a peculiar way, he seemed to her blighted and salvageable— heroic in his humanness.

"I bought dinner," he said. "T.J. may come later. He's at the Sailors' talking to Maggie." He followed her into the house. "Fresh salmon," he said, taking the pink fish out of the grocery bag. "We never get fresh salmon in Ohio."

Helen peered into the bag.

"Champagne?"

"It's a celebration."

"Of what?" Helen asked.

"Of the miracle doctor."

She laughed. "That's lovely, David, even though it isn't true."

They cooked together, Helen washing asparagus, scrubbing potatoes, chopping dill, David cleaning the salmon, opening champagne.

She took off her shoes, slipped into a chair, lifting her glass of champagne to him.

"Who will live here when I leave?" Helen asked.

"You're not leaving," he said.

"In case I leave," she said.

"Probably Prudential. She'll be the doctor here if you go and this is the doctor's house." He put the salmon under the broiler and sat down next to her, taking her hand, inspecting it, turning it over in his as though he had not examined a hand before.

"I want to know one other thing," Helen said. "Did you paint my wall?"

David laughed. "Me?" He shook his head. "I'm too chicken for that."

"So who did it?"

"Madeleine," David said.

"Madeleine?" Helen asked. "Did you know all the time?"

"I found out today," David said. "She's written you a letter of apology and called to read it to me."

Helen put her head down in her folded arms.

David touched her hair. "You must be exhausted," he said.

"A little, I suppose," she replied.

There was something she wanted to say to him, not yet formed in her mind, which had to do with the future, with seeing him later but just wishing for that, something she had never wished for in her hello-good-bye love affairs, made her suddenly shy.

He pinched out the candles with his fingers.

"I suppose you think I'm awful because of all this," he said.

She looked over at him through the smoke.

"I wasn't there so I don't know," Helen said. "I don't understand why you didn't go after Dr. Hazelton."

"At the time it seemed crucial to protect the reputation of the town," David said. "We seemed to be in an emergency situation."

Helen shrugged.

"I guess you'll leave soon," he said. "Everything's in place here."

"I will," Helen said. "Probably soon. Prudential can handle things."

"It's too bad." He poured her another glass of wine.

"That I'm leaving?"

"Just the way things fell out."

Later, after dinner, sitting in the living room, her brain slippery from champagne, she turned on the television to the last cassette of "The Story of Meridian."

They sat on the couch, Helen leaning against David's shoulder.

"When they filmed this section, it was Friday and Molly had been found and was in the hospital," David said. "They filmed all the weekend events and then packed up and were gone by Saturday morning."

"Whatever happened with Sophie and the director?" Helen asked.

"Nothing," David said. "As far as I know, they've never been in touch. We asked Sophie to leave town when you came because Sophie's a talker and we didn't want a stranger to know what had happened here."

The last day opens with a baseball game on the high school grounds, the boys in bright red and white uniforms, playing without jackets, although it is clear even from the film that it is cold outside. The game fades to a meeting of the choir and then a frame of Ben Winters in the pulpit of First Methodist speaking on grace and the Sunday school classes with Sallie Durham talking about Easter and what happens when a person dies and what happened to Jesus when he died and did he die after all, and is dead dead or not.

"I remember my Grandmother Durham," Sallie is saying matter-of-factly. "She had blue hair and made me ginger cookies with white icing and now she's dead."

After church, after the closeups in the church hall of all of the people who had principal roles in the film, the camera slips over their heads, over the trees and up the eastern hills of

Meridian, over the rooftops, sliding down to a peach frame house into the garden where Molly DeLaurentis leans against a tree, holding a stuffed animal, maybe a bear, face in against her jacket and looking off into the middle distance.

And then the camera follows her gaze down Poplar Street, over Main behind the railroad station to the river Meryn, a creek at first, growing wider and wider, filling the television so the credits as they roll down the screen appear over the whitecaps and there is no sound but that of the river headed south.

At the services for Dr. Hazelton, Helen sat next to Prudential at the back of the church. She was weepy. She couldn't help herself.

The church was full, people in the aisles, children in their parents' arms—the Durhams were there, Sallie Durham gave Helen a little wave, and Maria Walker stood with Laura O'Connor. Edie Winters walked up the aisle with the Sailors, Maggie between them, beaming and beaming—they couldn't help themselves.

"I'm surprised at all these children coming," Helen said to Prudential.

"Dying shouldn't be any more remarkable than living is what I think," Prudential said.

"And Maggie?" Helen asked. "Do you think she knows how Dr. Hazelton died?"

"No, not that," Prudential said.

T.J. came just as the opening hymn began and stopped

his wheelchair next to the aisle where Helen was sitting, blowing her a kiss.

The organ rose above the congregation and everyone was singing and then David Jaspersen got up to speak. He spoke about Dr. Hazelton. Saying good things about his work in Meridian, and telling of the way he was treated sometimes with cruelty by other boys, including himself, because he was different. He talked about Meridian and Maggie and the Sailors and Molly, he thanked Helen for coming and then he talked about "The Story of Meridian."

"Before the television crew came here," he said, "we had a sense of who we were, neither more nor less than other people, and that seemed satisfactory and safe. And then we fell in love with our image on film, losing sight of what was real in our lives and what was not.

"It wasn't the fault of television or even the television's portrayal of us. It was our fault for believing it."

And then he walked down the steps to the pulpit, down the three short steps from the altar and sat down.

It was a long service, with memorials and the children's choir and Sandy Case singing "Amazing Grace" and finally Henry Sailor reading a prayer for the congregation.

Helen slipped out during the final hymn just before the recessional. She kissed Prudential's hand, touched T.J. on the face as she crossed by him and left by the side door into a brilliant cool late spring afternoon.

She looked back to see if David Jaspersen had come out but he had been at the front of the church and would be among the last to leave. She had written him a note.

Dear David, I'm going back to Ann Arbor today. I hope you'll come. Love, Helen.

She had told only Prudential that she was leaving but it seemed the right thing to do, to leave silently and quickly while Meridian, Ohio, shaken by the long passage of spring, folded inward to recover. Maybe she would return. Maybe she would be a visitor again.

She hurried up the hill from First Methodist, past Aunt Martha's, no longer Aunt Martha's. There was no Emma in her mind's eye on the front porch, no child at all, only a familiar house belonging to a stranger. She rushed past her offices at the clinic, the police station and pharmacy and library and ice cream shop, arriving at Meridian railway station glittering in the pure light of late May just as the three forty-eight to Detroit lumbered into town.

The stationmaster handed her the bags she had left with him earlier in the day. "See you later," he called. "Hurry, Dr. Fielding. Trains only stop for a minute in Meridian."

And she ran to the platform, climbing up the steps into the coach, which was empty except for a young girl in a pale rose sundress who sat in the middle of a seat, her hands folded, a wrapped lollipop in her fist.

Helen looked around and sat down on the seat beside her.

"Mind?" she asked.

The young girl shook her head. "I'm glad," she said. "I've been alone since Louisville."

The train moved slowly out of town past the town's sign

WELCOME TO MERIDIAN, the CBS advertisement for "The Story of Meridian," half hidden by the poster of a missing child. At the end of Main Street it picked up speed, hurtling past the fields outside of town and along the river as it widened and widened through the dusky gray windows beside Helen, filling her view.

MANAGING
STRATEGIC
CHANGE

Wiley Series On
ORGANIZATIONAL ASSESSMENT AND CHANGE

Series Editors:
Edward E. Lawler III and
Stanley E. Seashore

Assessing Organizational Change:
The Rushton Quality
of Work Experiment
   by Paul S. Goodman and Associates

Measuring and Assessing Organizations
   by Andrew H. Van de Ven and Diane L. Ferry

Organizational Assessment: Perspectives on the Measurement of
Organizational Behavior and Quality of Working Life
   edited by Edward E. Lawler III, David A. Nadler and
   Cortlandt Cammann

Perspectives on Organization Design and Behavior
   edited by Andrew H. Van de Ven and William F. Joyce

Work and Health
   by Robert L. Kahn

Managing Strategic Change: Technical, Political
and Cultural Dynamics
   by Noel M. Tichy

Managing Creation: The Challenge of Building
a New Organization
   by Dennis N.T. Perkins, Veronica F. Nieva, and Edward E. Lawler III

Assessing Organizational Change: A Guide to
Methods, Measures and Practices
   edited by Stanley E. Seashore, Edward E. Lawler III, Philip
   H. Mirvis, and Cortlandt Cammann

FORTHCOMING

Human Stress and Cognition in Organizations:
An Integrated Perspective
   edited by Rabi S. Bhagat and Terry A. Beehr

MANAGING STRATEGIC CHANGE

Technical, Political, and
Cultural Dynamics

NOEL M. TICHY

The University of Michigan

A WILEY-INTERSCIENCE PUBLICATION

JOHN WILEY & SONS
New York   Chichester   Brisbane   Toronto   Singapore

This publication is designed to provide accurate and
authoritative information in regard to the subject
matter covered. It is sold with the understanding that
the publisher is not engaged in rendering legal, accounting,
or other professional service. If legal advice or other
expert assistance is required, the services of a competent
professional person should be sought. *From a Declaration
of Principles jointly adopted by a Committee of the
American Bar Association and a Committee of Publishers.*

Library of Congress Cataloging in Publication Data:

Tichy, Noel M.
  Managing strategic change.

  (Wiley series on organizational assessment and
change, ISSN 0194-0120)
    "A Wiley-Interscience publication."
    Bibliography: p.
    Includes index.
    1. Organizational change. I. Title. II. Series

  HD58.8.T5 1982   658.4'06   82-15941
  ISBN 0-471-86559-1

Printed in the United States of America

20 19 18 17 16 15 14 13 12

To the Memory of my Father,
Milton Tichy

Series Preface

The ORGANIZATIONAL ASSESSMENT AND CHANGE SERIES is concerned with informing and furthering contemporary debate on the effectiveness of work organizations and the quality of life they provide for their members. Of particular relevance is the adaptation of work organizations to changing social aspirations and economic constraints. There has been a phenomenal growth of interest in the quality of work life and productivity in recent years. Issues that not long ago were the quiet concern of a few academics and a few leaders in unions and management have become issues of broader public interest. They have intruded upon broadcast media prime time, lead newspaper and magazine columns, the houses of Congress, and the board rooms of both firms and unions.

A thorough discussion of what organizations should be like and how they can be improved must comprehend many issues. Some are concerned with basic moral and ethical questions—What is the responsibility of an organization to its employees?—What, after all, is a "good job"? —How should it be decided that some might benefit from and others pay for gains in the quality of work life?—Should there be a public policy on the matter? Yet others are concerned with the strategies and tactics of bringing about changes in organizational life, the advocates of alternative approaches being numerous, vocal, and controversial; and still others are concerned with the task of measurement and assessment on grounds that the choices to be made by leaders, the assessment of consequences, and the bargaining of equities must be informed by reliable, comprehensive, and relevant information of kinds not now readily available.

The WILEY SERIES ON ORGANIZATIONAL ASSESSMENT AND CHANGE is concerned with all aspects of the debate on how organizations should be managed, changed, and controlled. It includes books on organizational effectiveness, and the study of organizational changes that represent new approaches to organizational design and process. The volumes in the series have in common a concern with work organizations, a focus on change and the dynamics of change, an assumption that diverse social and personal interests need to be taken into account in discussions of organizational effectiveness, and a view that concrete cases and quantitative data are essential ingredients in a lucid debate. As such, these books consider a broad but integrated set of issues and ideas. They are intended to be read by managers, union officials, researchers, consultants, policy makers, students, and others seriously concerned with organizational assessment and change.

The present volume addresses issues of organizational assessment and change at a very broad level. The focus is upon organizational response to changes in the environment or in managerial priorities that require changes of a strategic kind—changes that are substantial in their effects and often irreversible. Small, incremental changes will not do. The author proposes a model of organizational functioning that incorporates factors commonly overlooked or undervalued by managers under the stress of approaching critical organizational decisions. While the central topics of the book are rather grand in scope, the treatment is brought to the ground level by inclusion of case examples, and of operational methods and instruments, that have a strong action orientation. It is a how-to-do-it book as well as one that offers a broad theoretical framework and orientation. The volume is an invitation to managers to rethink their strategies for strategic decision making. It is an invitation to scholars to rethink their ways of studying the processes of organizational transformation.

EDWARD E. LAWLER III
STANLEY E. SEASHORE

Ann Arbor, Michigan
August, 1981

Preface

Getting back to basics is a theme of this book. Managing strategic change requires raising questions about the fundamental nature of organizations: What business(es) should we be in? Who should reap what benefits from the organization? What should be the values and norms of organizational members? The answers to these questions do not come easily and require a great deal of hard-headed soul searching.

My own exploration as an academician and as a consultant working with organizations on these questions over the past 14 years has led to TPC theory, the conceptual framework presented in this book. It provides a vehicle for sorting out and managing basic dilemmas and problems facing organizations in the technical, political, and cultural areas.

It should be made clear that TPC theory is not a formal theory. It is a meta-theory, a framework for working with organizational problems. Coupled with the organizational model presented in Chapter 3, it is, hopefully, a pragmatic tool as well as a conceptual framework for conducting research and building a body of knowledge in the field of change. "Theories are intellectual tools for organizing data in such a way that one can make inferences or logical transitions from one set of data to another; they serve as guides to the investigation, explanation, organization, and discovery of matters of observable fact" (Deutsch and Krauss, p. 6). Even though TPC theory generally meets these criteria, it is not explicit enough about its assumptions; the mode of logical inference and the empirical referents are not worked out; and there is no ability to unambiguously test the theory's implications. As a theoretical orientation, however, I hope it will stimulate work that will move it from a meta-theory to a more formal theory.

Before looking into the future of TPC theory and strategic change management, it is instructive to look at how these concepts evolved. It has always been my feeling that in order to understand a behavioral science theory, one must understand the theorist because there is usually something autobiographical in the theory. For example, Kurt Lewin's quest for scientific principles supporting democracy can be related to his escape from the totalitarian fascist Hitler regime. Warren Bennis' modification of his thesis on the inevitability of democracy in large organizations was tempered by his experience as president of a large university, where he dealt with a multitude of political forces.

TPC theory is also autobiographical. It reflects a summary of my own development as an agent of change and as an academician interested in change.

There are three major foci with regard to change management: (1) technical aspects of work, (2) power, and (3) values. These correspond to the three strands—technical, political, and cultural—of the strategic rope presented in Chapter 1. As mentioned in this chapter, change agents are often fixated on one to the exclusion of the others. If I look back at the evolution of my own work, I can see that it went through a series of phases, each of which had its own set of priorities and emphases.

Initially, both my consulting and my academic work were value-driven. In 1966 I worked at Bankers Trust Company and became involved in their Blake and Mouton Managerial Grid program. This experience got me excited about experience-based learning and the value of good interpersonal relationships. I decided that studying T-groups and organization development based on the use of sensitivity training and team building was a way to change organizations and make the world a better place in which to live. I decided on the social psychology program at Teachers College, Columbia University as research in this area was being done by Matthew Miles; in addition, faculty such as Morton Deutsch and Harvey Hornstein were interested in social change and value-related issues.

For several years my consulting and academic work centered around the National Training Laboratories oriented T-group and organization development. At that time many of us were actively involved in the 1960s issues of civil rights and the Vietnam War. One of my first pieces of research as a graduate student was a study of the impact of the Columbia student strike of 1968 on the attitudes and values of faculty and students.

During this time my wife and I teamed up to do T-groups and experience-based training activities with hard-core unemployed groups and Peace Corps trainees; we were also involved with black/white confrontation and team building in Middletown, Connecticut with Herb Shephard from Yale as well as work with teenager and couples groups. The driving force was a focus on values. The technical aspects of work existed, but I wasn't very interested in them and did not attend to them. Power was given lip service but not understood or emphasized in my change work.

By the end of my Ph.D. experience it was clear that I wanted to be a change agent and a change agent scholar; therefore, my dissertation consisted of an empirical study of different types of change agents, trying to understand how they diagnosed organizations, what strategies they employed, their values, their use of different change techniques, and their change goals. After spending up to half a day interviewing each of 133 change agents, ranging from radical interventionists such as Minutemen, Black Panthers, and a radical anarchist, to McKinsey consultants and organizational development consultants, I felt I had a map of the world of professional change agents (Tichy, 1974, 1975). Despite my commitment to understanding change from various perspectives and my intellectual grappling with power and the technical aspects of what these change agents worked on, my personal theory of change was still largely value-driven.

A focus on the *technical* strand began to emerge when I took a job at the Business School at Columbia, which, at the time, had an element of value conflict because, as the symbol of the establishment, the business school had been the focus of a lot of student unrest. I defined my mission in those days as bringing behavioral science enlightenment and humanistic values to the technocrats. I did have to be able to grapple with the "bottom line" implications of the behavioral sciences, so I began to learn more about management, organizational design, and the functions of marketing, finance, accounting, and so on.

I also went into a value-driven change agent endeavor at this time. My wife and I and two other couples purchased some property about 50 miles north of New York City in a rural area. There were a main house, a farm house, and a guest cottage, along with 50 acres of beautiful woodland, streams, and a pond. We were committed to building a community and a professional growth and development center where we could run programs and bring groups for one- and two-week residential programs. We never actually created the conference center but we did own the property together and work together on many projects for five years. We initially wanted to demonstrate to ourselves and others how work and life-style could be integrated. In the long run, the financial realities of running a conference center and our shifting interests made the dream a bit out of reach. Nevertheless, the five years was a successful cooperative effort.

During this time period, the value focus remained, but my focus on work increased. In 1972 I began work with the Martin Luther King Health Center in the South Bronx. My help was needed with technical issues, management systems, planning, organizations design, and a host of technical work problems. The values were given. We were all there to do two things: (1) provide better health care for the impoverished South Bronx and (2) provide jobs and develop community people so they could run the Martin Luther King Health Center.

Two activities during the early 1970s altered my change theory to incorporate more of the technical strand. One was the start of work in Sweden with a group of Swedish OD consultants. This has continued through the present and includes involvement with the work innovation projects at Volvo and Saab. I also was involved with General Motors' first work in organization development, when they trained about 120 internal OD consultants in 1973 and 1974. With both the Swedish and the GM experience it was clear that productivity and the organization of work on the shop floor, as well as organizational design, were important change levers. Thus, my change theory now had technical and cultural strands (Tichy, 1976).

By 1975 I had what I felt was a pretty integrated change theory, one that combined a focus on values and integrated technical aspects of work ranging from strategic planning to organizational design to job design. I felt so confident of this that I launched two endeavors to communicate to a larger audience how well I had integrated some thoughts about change.

One was the launching of the Columbia Advanced Program in Organizational Development and Human Resource Management, which was built around the notion that experienced OD practitioners needed to develop more technical skills—for example, in organizational design, strategic planning, and personnel systems—to be coupled with their soft skills in survey feedback, team building, process consultation, and training and development. The second was an agreement to write a book on change.

As fate would have it, a unique opportunity came along about a year later which would slow up my writing task. I had been working with a health group in rural Appalachia—Hazard, Kentucky, to be exact —to help set up an outreach program and a clinic to deal with children. The Hazard area had one of the worst infant mortality rates in the country in the early 1970s. A young pediatrician, Dr. Gregory Culley, had some ideas about how to deal with these problems. He set out to organize an interdisciplinary team of health providers, nutritionists, social workers, nurses, and himself to go out in the "hollers" and deliver care to pregnant women and infants. This group was set up, and after a few years of working with them on a monthly basis and seeing them grow, I was given the challenge by the Robert Wood Johnson Foundation to help make the Hazard Children's Health Services into something that would survive in the long run.

The challenge was to help them become financially viable, to establish a network of clinics to serve the whole family and develop a model for other parts of Appalachia and the Appalachian Regional Hospital chain, to which this clinic was associated. They said that to do this I would have to go down and live there for about a year. I agreed. This was my chance to be the "lone ranger" change agent and, at the same time, to write my book on change. What better way to write a book on change than during a project that was putting me to the test of all my skills and knowledge? Well, it did not work out that way; that is why the book is being completed in 1983.

I learned about power and politics in Kentucky. I went in and did all the correct management- and organization-oriented things; I did a thorough diagnosis of the system; I analyzed what its problems were, what its capabilities were, and how to develop a strategy to make it viable. I did this for both the Hazard clinic system and the larger hospital system. My recommendations and plans for working with the clinic and the larger hospital system to which it was associated were based on my value system and on the logic of a technical orientation which assumed people wanted to efficiently and effectively deliver health care to poor people in Appalachia.

Not so. Part of my role as change agent did succeed. That is, with the clinic network I had sufficient political control, and there was minimal political uncertainty, so I was able to help them technically reorganize and succeed. However, the hospital system was in turmoil. It was insolvent two days before I arrived. A letter from the president of the chain was waiting for me, a temporary employee of the system, saying that the payroll could not be met that week and everyone would have to wait. The hospital system went to the Secretary of Health, Education, and Welfare, then Joseph Califano, and asked for money to bail it out. Mr. Califano said he would have a task force look into it. This task force came and studied the system. They found out about me and my managerial studies and wanted my opinion. I saw an opportunity to be a helpful change agent by bringing the federal government forces in to help straighten up the hospital system. I also saw that I could keep the Feds from being too harsh on the hospital system, which after all was doing good things for people. I drew elaborate plans for joint committees and collaborative vehicles with which HEW could work with the hospital system to save it from bankruptcy while also working to change its management, planning, and organization systems so that it would be more efficient and effective. My proposals all grew out of my change theory. *Values* were important; people wanted to deliver high-quality care to those in need and do it in an organization where the employees were fairly rewarded and participated maximally in decisions that affected them. *Work* was also important. After all, the hospital system could have avoided bankruptcy had it been more professionally managed.

For about six months I kept working at this task, talking to HEW people and having meetings with the president and senior managers of the hospital system. I even had the chief operating officer of the hospital chain attend my Columbia executive program to gain more technical skills. I tried to get everyone to cooperate and solve this important problem, but I kept being frustrated by things like a report that got leaked to the press on what the HEW task force would recommend—it indicated that it would recommend that HEW not bail them out. This would have meant the loss of many jobs and the loss of the major provider of health services in this part of Appalachia. Acrimonious letters went back and forth from the president of the hospital system and undersecretaries at HEW and Joseph Califano himself. I had worked hard to get both sides to agree to a collaborative, problem-solving session. The meeting turned into a fiasco, from my point of view, with both HEW and the hospital group fighting and calling each other names.

Ultimately, the solution was quite simple. The governors of three states and members of Congress, such as Carl Perkins, put the heat on Joseph Califano to stop stalling and find the money to bail out the hospital system. This was done, but not directly. By some strange coincidence money that exactly matched the amount needed to keep the hospital system afloat was found in other government programs. In essence, the money was laundered so that it didn't look as if HEW had caved in to pressure. Another interesting part of the game was that the president of the hospital system resigned under a great deal of pressure, having been held responsible for bad management. This was a positive indication to HEW that the hospital system was serious about improving its management. An interesting fact is that this same scenario had happened three times in the previous 15 years, that is, the system got into financial trouble, went to the federal government, got bailed out, and replaced the president but kept all the rest of corporate management.

There were other events, but this should give you enough information about why my book was stalled. Theory didn't help; all of my change tools were useless in this endeavor. How could I write a book about organization development, the use of open, collaborative, high-trust interventions coupled with a great deal of technical know-how, when I had just failed in their application? I had to rethink the nature of organizations and the problems they faced. Thus, the missing strand, the *political* problem. I needed to develop a way of integrating the political problem into my theory of change because politics was obviously the arena in which HEW and the hospital system people were playing. As a matter of fact, when I looked at the hospital events in this political framework, it had a logic to it. I was able to make a coherent and logical analysis of the situation the same way Graham Allison had in his *Essence of Decision* analysis of the Cuban Missile Crisis, making a logical picture through three frames of reference, one a political frame. The leaks to the press, the confrontations, the lying, the laundered money, and the symbolic removal of the hospital system president fit well with a political analysis.

As a result of this experience, there was no way any theory of organizational change was going to ignore political dynamics. Thus, the TPC framework is as much a reflection of my experiential development as it is a product of rigorous scholarly work. I find that it stands up to scholarly criticism and can be useful in formulating research on organizational change. During the next several years a program of research is being carried out at the Institute for Social Research and the Graduate School of Business at the University of Michigan, which is committed to the empirical development of the TPC framework.

Because of the complexity of the phenomena and the difficulty of carrying out systematic large-scale longitudinal research, the continued development of change theory will rely on a mixture of clinical experience, action research, and conceptual thought. My change theory, as well as others', will thus continue to be somewhat autobiographical.

NOEL M. TICHY

Ann Arbor, Michigan
March 1983

Acknowledgments

My interest in organizational change began in 1966 while I was working in the personnel department of Bankers Trust Company. Otis Brown was then heading the bank's organizational development effort. He invited me to attend the Phase I Blake and Mouton Managerial Grid Session held at the Thayer Hotel at West Point. This experience, as well as others at Bankers Trust, launched my interest and involvement in organization development and change. It was also Otis Brown who recommended that I look into the Ph.D. program at Columbia where Matthew Miles was working, as Matt had been involved with evaluating change at Bankers Trust Company.

While working at Columbia University, as both a graduate student and a faculty member, I had a number of outstanding colleagues who influenced the thinking I present in this book. A very central figure is Charles Kadushin, who pushed me into the sociological arena and has continued to be my most supportive and horizon-expanding colleague. My major advisor, Harvey Hornstein, started me looking at change in new ways while he was completing his book *Social Intervention* in 1969 and 1970. This led to my doctoral dissertation research on change agents. We have remained close friends and colleagues, and I was thankful when he provided helpful comments on an early version of this book.

I benefited from work with other Columbia colleagues, especially Amitai Etzioni, whose commitment to organizational and societal change provided new ideas and directions for my work. In addition, my work at The Center for Policy Research, which Amitai founded and directed, provided a stimulating environment in which to pursue my early change-related work. Another important colleague is E. Kirby Warren, who provided me with an ideal environment for my many action research projects, which provided a basis for learning about change. This includes his help in arranging my year off from Columbia to work on a change project in Hazard, Kentucky, in 1977 and 1978. Michael Tushman provided me with very helpful comments on an early version of the book.

The two Columbia colleagues who played the most significant role with regard to this book are Mary Anne Devanna and Charles Fombrun. They struggled through numerous meetings discussing and debating many of the ideas and concepts in this book. Those discussions were invaluable, and, even though we are still unresolved on some of the positions I take in the book, I'm thankful for their support and friendship.

A funny thing happened on the way to publishing this book. Initially it was planned as a textbook for another publisher. As I became involved in the project, though, my editors and I began to realize that what I was producing was not a textbook but a more theoretical, academic treatment of organizational change. This change was never consciously planned. I am thankful for Dick Fenton at West Publishing for his support and understanding in the evolution of this book. Both John Slocum and Don Hellriegel are to be thanked for their very helpful criticism and skillful editorial feedback on several earlier versions of the book. All three were very helpful in making the transition to Wiley as the publisher.

There are many nonacademic colleagues to whom I owe a debt of gratitude, as they were the source of much learning. By carrying out applied research projects and consulting with clients in a variety of organizations, I have been able to test myself and my concepts. At Chase Manhattan Bank, both Frederick Hammer and Arthur Bennett provided me with a research opportunity to further my work. Both have been influential in my thinking. I owe a special thanks to Cynthia Haddock from Imperial Chemical Industries, who provided me with challenging and enhancing ideas throughout an earlier version of the book and whose enthusiasm for the project was helpful in motivating me to complete it. A continuing source of enthusiasm and encouragement for the book came from Thore Sandstrom, whose friendship and colleagueship provided me with a Swedish angle of vision.

Dick Beckhard remains the organizational change practitioner I continue to respect as the best source of clinical insight into the process of complex system change. Discussions, collaborative work, and my reading his work influenced the ideas presented in this book.

My move to Michigan brought along with it a change in publishers. I want to thank Stan Seashore and Ed Lawler for their strong support and guidance in carrying out this transition. Andy McGill provided very useful comments and ideas on earlier versions of the manuscript. At Wiley, John Mahaney has been a model editor, constructively pushing this book through to completion.

Production of anything I work on is difficult, as I revise, and revise, and revise. I was lucky to have had Dixi Wheat at Columbia to master the word processing system there and not only do an outstanding job of word processing but help significantly with editorial changes and substantive contributions. At Michigan I was greatly helped by Susan Majcher, who diligently tracked down references, prepared indices, and tried to keep me organized. Carole Barnett pitched in at critical moments and kept the rest of the store in order while the manuscript was completed.

My wife, Monique, deserves the greatest thanks, as she is my best critic. She and I have struggled together on change projects, starting with the Dr. Martin Luther King Health Center and including living in the hills of Kentucky. These experiences, as well as our many discussions of our experiences and ideas about change, have greatly molded my thinking and influenced this book. She has also unselfishly done more than her share in providing me the time to work on this book, often at the expense of family time. Thus, I thank my three daughters, Michelle, Nicole, and Danielle, for their patience in letting Daddy write. Finally, I thank my mother for encouraging me to challenge the status quo.

N. M. T.

Contents

PART ONE A FRAMEWORK FOR STRATEGIC CHANGE   1

**Chapter 1. Strategic Change Management:
Organizational Development Redefined**   3

Introduction, 3
Improving Change Management, 5
The Need for New Models, 7
Ongoing Organizational Dilemmas, 9
Some Assumptions and Definitions, 14
When Strategic Change Becomes Necessary, 18
Overview of Coming Chapters, 20
Appendix, 22

Chapter 2. Organizational Models   37

Introduction, 37
Why Models Are Needed to Overcome Managerial Myths, 37
Formal Organizational Models for Change, 42
Conclusion, 49
Appendix, 50

Chapter 3. The Role of Social Networks   69

Introduction, 69
The Network Model, 70
The Components of the Model, 74
Conclusion, 94
Appendix, 94

Chapter 4. Organizational Model: Dynamic Aspects   117

Introduction, 117
Change Over Time, 118
Strategic Alignment, 124
Interrelationships Between Model Components, 126
Overall Technical, Political, and Cultural Alignment, 137
Conclusion, 138
Appendix, 138

**PART TWO   STRATEGIC ISSUES:
DIAGNOSIS AND STRATEGY DEVELOPMENT**   145

Chapter 5. Diagnosis for Change   147

Introduction, 147
Diagnosis: Three Orientations, 152
Analysis of Alignment, 164
Conclusion, 168

Chapter 6. Application of Diagnostic Strategy   169

Introduction, 169
Two Case Examples, 169
Diagnosis as Part of the Change Process, 178
Resources Required for In-Depth Organizational
    Diagnosis, 181
Conclusion, 183

Chapter 7. Change Strategy   185

Introduction, 185
Development of Integrated Technical, Political, and
    Cultural Strategies, 187
Case Examples, 188
Guidelines for Developing a Change Strategy, 193
Conclusion, 202

Chapter 8. Technical Change Strategies   203

Introduction, 203
The Environmental/Mission and Strategy Interface, 204
Changing People as a Change Strategy, 220
Emergent Networks, 225
Conclusion: Guidelines for Technical Strategy
    Development, 225

Chapter 9.   Political Change Strategies   227

Introduction, 227
Developing Political Strategies, 231
Politically Mechanistic Strategies, 232
Politically Mixed Strategies—Manipulation, 235
Participative Management Strategy, 240
Politically Organic Strategies, 241
Guidelines for Developing a Political Strategy, 249
Summary, 250
Conclusion, 251

Chapter 10.   Cultural Change Strategies   253

Introduction, 253
Cultural Content, 256
Managing Cultural Uncertainty, 273
Matching the Culture to the Political and Technical
    Systems, 282
Conclusion, 283
Appendix, 284

PART THREE   IMPLEMENTING STRATEGIC CHANGES   289

Chapter 11.   Change Technologies   291

Introduction, 291
What Are Change Technologies?, 292
Categorizing Change Technologies, 293
Current Change Technologies, 296
Network Change Technologies, 319
Deciding Which Change Technology to Use When, 326
Conclusion, 329

Chapter 12.   Transition Management   331

Introduction, 331
Some Characteristics of Change, 332
Transition Management, 332
Review the Current and Desired State, 335
Resistance to Change and Transition Management
    Guidelines, 343
Political Transition Management, 346
Developing an Integrated Transition Management Plan, 355
Conclusion, 360

PART FOUR   MONITORING CHANGE AND THE
FUTURE OF STRATEGIC MANAGEMENT   361

Chapter 13.   Monitoring and Evaluating Strategic Change   363

   Introduction, 363
   Basic Orientations to Monitoring and Evaluating Strategic
      Change, 368
   A Framework for Carrying Out the Evaluation, 373
   The Case for Explicit Organization Models for Evaluating
      and Monitoring Change Efforts, 375
   A Case Illustration of an Organizational Assessment
      Approach, 380
   Summary and Conclusion, 385

Chapter 14.   Strategic Change in the Future   387

   Introduction, 387
   Transforming Organizations in Turbulent Times, 388
   Back to Basics, 393
   The Focus on Human Resource Management, 401
   The Future of TPC Theory, 412

References   416

Author Index   423

Subject Index   427

MANAGING
STRATEGIC
CHANGE

A FRAMEWORK
FOR MANAGING
STRATEGIC CHANGE

Chapter One

Strategic Change Management

Organizational Development Redefined

The accelerating rate of change is producing a business world in which customary managerial habits and organizations are increasingly inadequate. Experience was an adequate guide when changes could be made in small increments. But intuitive and experience-based management philosophies are grossly inadequate when decisions are strategic and have major irreversible consequences (Henderson, 1979).

INTRODUCTION

In light of the discontinuous, large-scale changes facing the world, organizations will be required to undergo major, strategic reorientations. These reorientations will involve changes in products, services, markets, organizational structure, and human resources. This book provides a set of concepts for managing strategic change. Several dramatic examples of strategic change are presented as follows.

AT&T is involved in a massive strategic change to evolve from a regulated telephone monopoly to a competitive, broad-based information service company. Such change is due to the Federal Communications Commission decision to allow other companies to sell products once monopolized by AT&T, and also to market electronic communications equipment which bypasses the telephone via satellite networks. The change involves a corporate strategy focused on new markets, services, products, and new ways of doing business. The organization of one million people is being restructured as its 22 regional operating companies are divested. Key people are being hired from outside of AT&T, and new hiring and promotion criteria are being adopted along with new reward and development systems. The company will be transformed into an innovative, profit- and competition-oriented com-

3

pany capable of competing with IBM and other computer and information companies.

General Motors is also undergoing a massive strategic change. The once all-powerful U.S. automaker is in the process of transforming itself into a competitive worldwide automaker. Past practices and assumptions about auto design and production are no longer relevant. Quality and energy efficiency have replaced superficial design changes. The company must alter its strategies, change its product, restructure major portions of the organization, and introduce rewards for managers and workers which stress quality and energy efficiency. In addition, GM must learn how to compete in terms of productivity in world markets where the Japanese have a $1000 to $1700 per car production advantage, only about $450 of which is due to wage and benefits differentials, the remainder due to management practices such as inventory and automation (*New York Times*, B-1, February 27, 1982).

The banking industry is facing a revolution brought on by the electronic technology which permits national electronic banking networks as well as a blurring of lines between banks and nonbanking institutions. For example, Sears Roebuck, Merrill Lynch, General Electric Company, and other nonbanking institutions offer consumer financial services such as loans, checking accounts, and credit cards. Following these changes are changes in federal banking laws which will eventually allow interstate banking. The result is that banking is becoming a very competitive and innovative business. New services and delivery mechanisms will require totally new organizational structures such as new types of employee rewards for a new set of behaviors. For example, Citibank's president, Mr. William Spencer, states that the aim of his bank is "to provide all financial services to every place in the world where it is legal, moral, and on which we can make a profit." This has led Citibank to establishing "nonbanking financial subsidiaries across the country which provide a wide range of loans to both businesses and consumers (*The New York Times*, 28 December 1980, p. B22)." The strategic change occurring at Citibank and other major banks is critical to their long-term viability.

When faced with conditions calling for strategic organizational changes, managers often focus on small components of the overall change problem. This can lead to a fixation on tactical concerns such as:

Should we change from a functional structure to a matrix structure?

Should we centralize or decentralize?

Should we launch a company-wide "quality of work" program or not?

Should we individualize or collectivize the incentive system?

Should we attempt to do a better job of relating business strategy to organization design?

These and other concerns are "tactical" if they do not fit into an overall framework for change. Change within such a framework has a profound effect in the overall reshaping of the organization. All too often, fad, fashion, or personal proclivity guide decisions about change rather than hard-nosed, systematic analyses of the organization and managerial conditions.

In the past, and in simpler organizations with less turbulent environments, there was more room for trial and error approaches to these concerns. But now, we are proceding further into the era of discontinuous change brought on by energy problems, finite resources, environmental limits in the absorption of industrial wastes, the cleavage between developed and underdeveloped nations, and a world economy which does not function effectively or efficiently. In this context, we encounter ever increasing organizational complexity. For example, it becomes increasingly difficult to manage the multinational corporation which operates simultaneously in dozens of markets around the globe. Public service organizations such as hospitals, schools, and welfare agencies are enmeshed in conflicting federal, state, county, and city planning systems, brought on by various government requirements and by the diversity of funding sources. Organizations facing these increasingly turbulent and often hostile environments will need more systematic and informed means of making the major strategic changes required for organizational survival and viability. In this book, I will try to develop specific aids so that those charged with managing complex organizations can better carry out organizational diagnosis as well as plan and implement large-scale organizational changes.

IMPROVING CHANGE MANAGEMENT

Change Levers

Managers and consultants have frequently limited their approaches to the management of change. However, this book will attempt to broaden the definition of change management. Contemporary change management practice is limited because managers and consultants tend to focus attention on a restricted set of organizational change levers. That is, regardless of the nature of the problem, they tend to employ the same levers. Some always restructure the organization. Others always try to improve communication. Others always replace people. And others always alter production and control systems.

What narrows the focus? It is that managers tend to view the change process from only one perspective. That is, some view change solely as a technical problem. Others see it solely as a political problem. And still others see it as solely a cultural problem. By limiting their viewpoint, they limit their use of different change levers.

Strategic change involves all three of the preceding problems. At AT&T for example, there are such technical problems as selection of markets, product development, pricing, and organization design; political problems of altering regulatory requirements, providing new power bases for people in AT&T, altering who gets ahead and who stays behind career-wise; and cultural problems of changing a noncompetitive, service oriented, noninnovative organization into an aggressive, marketing-oriented and profit driven organization. All three sets of problems need to be managed. In order to strategically manage change, the following change levers must be equally available for use.

1. *External Interface.* As the environment becomes more complex and turbulent, the task of identifying and predicting pressures becomes more difficult to understand. It is also more difficult to map environmental pressures. The development of new environmental scanning and information processing capabilities is often required.

2. *Mission.* In times of relative environmental stability and surplus resources, it is possible with nebulous, shifting goals and priorities. But as the economic, political, and social pressures mount, so does the need for clear statements of organizational mission to guide the organization in strategic decisions.

3. *Strategy.* The development of a strategic plan with operational objectives at multiple levels in organization is a vital requirement. Installing such a process requires a new set of management techniques and processes.

4. *Managing Organizational Mission/Strategy Processes.* As planning and decision making become more complex, it will be necessary to develop more sophisticated processers which realistically engage the relevant interest groups.

5. *Task.* A shift in strategy may entail the introduction of new tasks and technologies to the organization. This requirement may result in the introduction of new professionals into the organization, or the training and development of existing staff.

6. *Prescribed Networks.* Adjustments are required in the networks of communication and authority to deal with new tasks and/or technologies. The introduction of a new task requires management to plan and prescribe the necessary network of communication. This includes specifications of the communication, of who works with whom to accomplish which tasks, as well as who reports to whom.

7. *Organizational Process: Communication, Problem Solving, and Decision Making.* Post-industrial organizations have multiple authority-managerial/professional splits, and matrix splits. Therefore, lines of decision making become blurred. This makes it imperative that managers understand and utilize consensual decision-making approaches as well as conflict bargaining procedures.

8. *People.* Any organizational change entails altering individual behavior. Thus, an explicit focus on motivating people becomes part of the managed change process.

9. *Emergent Networks.* A major part of an organizational change process is to manage the informal communication and influence-networks which exist throughout the organization. Coalitions and cliques in these networks can facilitate or hinder the change effort and thus require explicit attention.

These nine change levers represent the agenda for this book. But first, the question must be asked: How can one determine which lever needs to be adjusted? What are the approaches and techniques available to adjust each of the levers?

Currently, very few managers and consultants are trained to work with all nine levers. This book attempts to help managers acquire that training.

THE NEED FOR NEW MODELS

This book will build on the notion that three dominant traditions have guided thinking about organizations and the practice of change and that these traditions should be brought together in order to provide managers of change with the necessary set of strategic tools.

1. One tradition views organizations and change from a technical perspective and prescribes change strategies based on empiricism and enlightened self-interest. This will be called the *technical view.* As Arygris and Schon (1978) point out:

> The viewpoint is instrumental and rational . . . the focus is upon the acquisition and application of the knowledge useful for effective performance of organizational tasks, and the organizational world is conceived as fundamentally knowable through scientific method (p. 323).

2. Another tradition views organizations as *political entities* which can only be changed by the exercise of power by the dominant group over those with less power or by bargaining among powerful groups. This will be called the *political view.*

3. Another tradition views organizations as cultural *systems of values* with shared symbols and shared cognitive schemes which tie people together and form a common organizational culture. Change comes about by altering the norms and cognitive schemes of the members of the organization. This will be called the *cultural view.*

Practicing managers, students of organizations, and change theorists tend to think in terms of only one of the above traditions. The result of such one-dimensional thinking often leads to unanticipated negative consequences. Figure 1.1 summarizes these three perspectives.

1. **The Technical Design Problem**
   Organization faces a production problem.
   Social and technical resources must be
   arranged to produce desired output.
2. **The Political Allocation Problem**
   Organization faces an allocation of
   power and resource problem.
   The uses to which the organization is
   put as well as who reaps the benefits
   must be determined.
3. **The Cultural/Ideological Mix Problem**
   Organizations are held together by
   a normative glue—shared beliefs.
   Organizations must determine what
   values need to be held by what people.   **Figure 1.1**

Management scientists and production engineers frequently view work and organization design essentially as an engineering or technical problem. This can lead to problems. An example of the dysfunctional consequences of such a perspective was the General Motors' Lordstown, Ohio plant which was built to produce the Vega automobile in the early 1970s. The plant was billed by General Motors as the most modern and technically efficient auto assembly plant in the world. Actual performance, however, fell far below the expectations of management, the production engineers, and plant designers. There was high absenteeism and low quality control. Productivity was below target and a wildcat strike eventually erupted.

A brief analysis of the events at Lordstown disclose that in 1972 workers struck against the requirement to perform unchallenging tasks, and speed-up attempts by management. It is obvious that psychological and sociological factors were ignored in the organizational design which was inappropriate for young workers who did not function according to the purely technical view of the production engineers. The GM Lordstown experience can be contrasted to the managerial concepts which prevailed in the design of the new Volvo Plant built in Kalmar, Sweden at about the same time. The Volvo plant was planned with both a strong cultural and technical orientation in mind, and demonstrated concern for the values and needs of the work force, as well as a strong technical perspective (Tichy, 1976). The result was a successful new plant start-up.

A purely *political* orientation to organizational life and change is also likely to be dysfunctional. It can lead to low levels of trust, cynicism, and a view that all interactions are win/lose bargaining situations. Many large public agencies, such as the U.S. Department of Health and Welfare, are dominated by this orientation. For example, at the Department of Health and Welfare it would not be unusual for internal program staff to bargain programs to save the hungry children in Appalachia against inner-city adolescent programs. In the bargains, the substantive aspects of the programs, the technical dimension, would be irrelevant to the power brokerage practice of *who* controls *how much* of *which* budgets. The dysfunction which results leads to a situation in which the potential for cooperative links within the organization is greatly diminished. The goal is to win the political struggle and to keep your budget and staff as large as possible. The ultimate goals of the organization are thus lost in day-to-day political brokering.

The *cultural* orientation can also be overemphasized. As can be seen from the following quote from Bennis (1969), organization development's reliance on truth, love, and collaboration avoids the problem of power and the politics of change.

> Organization development practitioners rely exclusively on two sources of influence: truth and love. Somehow the hope prevails that man is reasonable and caring, and that valid data, coupled with an environment of trust (and love) will bring about the desired change . . . Organization development seems most appropriate under conditions of trust, truth, love and collaboration . . . there seems to be a fundamental deficiency in models of change associated with power, or the politics of change . . . unless models can be developed that include the dimensions of power conflict in addition to truth-love, organization development will find fewer and narrower institutional avenues to its influence. And in so doing, it will slowly and successively decay (pp. 78-79).

Many organization development practitioners' overreliance on a purely cultural orientation has limited their use of other change approaches, especially those derived from the organization design and management fields (Tichy, 1978).

It is this tendency to subscribe to one dominant mode of change strategy which is a major reason for the current view among many researchers and managers that we know little about how to manage change. A more balanced perspective will result in greater capacity to manage change.

ONGOING ORGANIZATIONAL DILEMMAS

A more comprehensive view acknowledges all three approaches and the fact that organizations must continuously make adjustments in order to resolve three basic dilemmas:

1. *Technical Design Problem.*   All organizations face a production problem. That is, in the context of environmental threats and opportunities, social, financial, and technical resources must be arranged to produce some desired output. In order to solve this problem, management engages in goal setting, strategy formulation, organizational design, and the design of management systems—all to solve the technical problem.

2. *Political Allocation Problem.*   All organizations face the problem of allocating power and resources. The uses to which the organization will be put, as well as who will reap the benefits of the organization, must be determined. Decisions around these issues get reflected in compensation programs, career decisions, budget decisions, and the internal power structure of the organization. Unlike the technical area, in which there are formalized tools such as strategic planning and organization design, in the political area, the concepts and language are less formal and often less obvious. Nonetheless, a great deal of management time and attention are given to strategic political issues, such as before and after a chief executive officer or key executive change takes place, when a major acquisition occurs, or if relationships with unions and management are altered.

3. *Cultural Problems.*   Organizations are in part held together by a normative glue that is called culture. Culture consists of the values, objectives, beliefs, and interpretations shared by organizational members. One of the most important and most difficult tasks of top management is to decide the content of the organization's culture, that is, to determine what values should be shared, what objectives are worth striving for, what beliefs the employees should be committed to, and what interpretations of past events and current pronouncements would be most beneficial for the firm. Having made these decisions, top management's next task is to communicate these value laden messages in a memorable and believable fashion, which will not be instantly forgotten or easily dismissed as corporate propaganda. Note that these decisions are not always made explicitly. Decisions about culture are often made implicitly, intuitively, and by trial and error.

Technical, political, and cultural problems are portrayed in Figure 1.2 as three interrelated strands of a rope.

The Strategic Rope.   The metaphor of a rope is used to underscore several points. First, from a distance, individual strands are not distinguishable. This is true in organizational settings; it is not clear from casual observation what is technical, what is political, what is cultural. Nevertheless, the three strands are there and they need to be understood and dealt with in order to understand the nature of the organization.

Second, ropes can become unravelled, and when they do, they become weakened. Organizations can also come unravelled. Their technical, political, and cultural strands can work at cross-purposes, and as a result, the organization can become greatly weakened. For example, if a traditional single product organization introduces a variety of new products for new markets, and changes its organization design from a functional structure to one focused on new products and markets, then fundamental changes will be required in the political and cultural areas. The political decisions (promotions, budgets, decision-making prerogatives) must

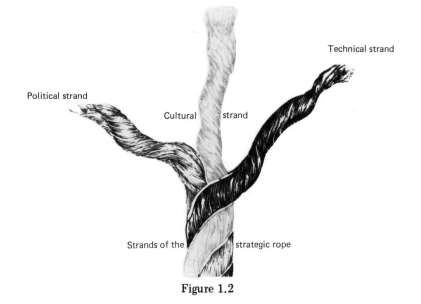

Technical strand

Political strand

Cultural   strand

Strands of the   strategic rope

Figure 1.2

reinforce the marketing and design changes. Furthermore, the culture, which may have been focused on economies of scale in a dominant, single-line business, must be altered to reflect the new product and market orientation of the firm. Otherwise, the three strands of the rope will become unravelled, the organization will be working at cross-purposes and will therefore cripple its own ability to capitalize on the desired changes.

Strategic management is the task of keeping the rope from becoming unravelled in the face of these technical, political, and cultural problems.

Organizational Cycles.   Because organizations are perpetually in flux, undergoing shifts and changes, none of the three problems is ever resolved. They are ongoing dilemmas. At different points in time, any one of them, or some combination, may be in need of adjustment. Adjustments are managed by implementing a range of strategies. These include self-adjustment through benign neglect or purposeful avoidance, slight massaging of the problem, concerted managerial effort focusing on changes in the organization's mission and strategy, redesign of the organization's structure, or alterations of the human resource management systems.

Adjustments in each of these three problem areas can be conceptualized in cyclical terms. Thus, there are technical, political, and cultural adjustment cycles in organizations. Organizations vary over time in the amount of energy invested in making adjustments during these cycles.

These cyclical manifestations overlap and interact with each other. Such interaction may be beneficial or problematic for the organization.

Figure 1.3 portrays the cycles in terms of peaks and valleys. Peaks represent high stress and a high need for adjustment in one of the three problem areas. The valleys indicate a smooth, non problematical period for that cycle. Thus, the left axis of the figure indicates both.

When, due to high stress and a strong need for adjustment, management attempts to resolve one or more of these problems, systems are developed. There are technical systems to resolve production problems, political systems for allocation problems, and cultural systems to express, reinforce, challenge, and change ideological values. All of these systems have an internal logic. All three types of systems are interdependent and, if an organization is strategically well managed, all three are congruent.

If one were to plot the GM Lordstown example, it would start with a technical peak. At that time, most attention was focused on designing a highly rationalized assembly plant. However, the technical cycle triggered a rise in both the political and cultural cycles as workers resisted the overly mechanized plant. The political cycle peaked with the wildcat strike. The cultural cycle peaked with workers wanting a work culture that was more meaningful and enriching. Obviously, the political and cultural cycles required different managerial approaches from the technical. Managing change involves making technical, political, and cultural decisions about desired new organizational states, weighing the trade-offs, and acting on them.

Figure 1.4 depicts the process of managed change. The concepts derive primarily from a transition management model developed by Beckhard and Harris (1977). Change is triggered by a threat and/or opportunity which is of sufficient magnitude that organizational members cannot ignore it. This occurs at Time A. It is followed by a period of disequilibrium indicated by Time B. Time B is the period during which change occurs.

The AT&T case provides a good example because the company simultaneously became aware of a threat and an opportunity in their environment. On the one hand, their position in the communication field

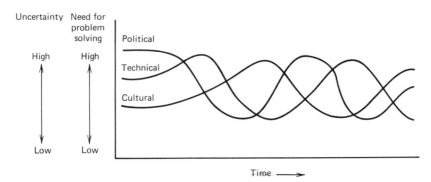

Figure 1.3

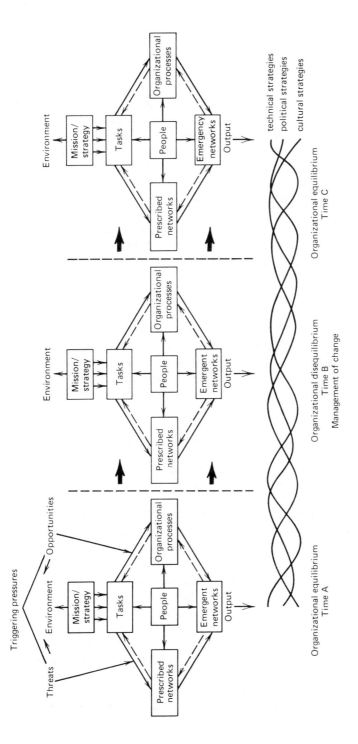

STRATEGIC CHANGE MANAGEMENT

Figure 1.4

13

would slip if they remained solely in the telephone business as new electronic information and communication systems were becoming competitive. Examples include two-way interactive cable television, computer networks, and satellite systems. This was the threat. On the other hand, AT&T had the capability both technologically and financially to capitalize on these new developments. These forces triggered action. The technical cycle was triggered at Time A. The management of AT&T developed a strategic plan to move the company from a regulated telephone monopoly to an information processing company. As this strategy was moved forward, AT&T and the federal government agreed on a plan for AT&T to divest its 22 regional operating companies and move out from under the regulated umbrella. The company is now in Time B, the time of disequilibrium, as indicated in Figure 1.4.

In the following chapters we will see how organizations can (1) more effectively assess their current states, (2) develop a desired state, and (3) manage the transition from current to desired.

SOME ASSUMPTIONS AND DEFINITIONS

Change alters the way people behave and alters the patterns of relationships and structures within organizations. Thus, assumptions about people and organizations which we make here are important determinants of how we implement change. Our core assumptions for managed change are discussed in this section.

People, Motivation, and the Contract

It is assumed that people in organizational settings are engaged in an exchange relationship. They decide to provide the organization with certain behaviors (labor) in return for the organization's rewards (money, prestige, self-esteem). March and Simon (1958) refer to an inducement–contribution contract, Schein (1970) refers to the psychological contract, and Etzioni (1961) refers to compliance. In all three definitions, the reference is to an *exchange relationship.* Understanding this exchange relationship is the core to understanding how to change people. For change requires some implicit or explicit renegotiation of the exchange relationship. That is, when individuals are called upon to engage in new behaviors in an organization, their inducement–contribution contract is also altered.

For example, the strategic change which occurred at Chrysler Corporation required members of the United Auto Workers (UAW) to accept less wage increases and more layoffs. Other examples include changes which require people to change jobs and learn new skills, such as must occur at AT&T.

The nature of the contract between employee and organization is dominated by assumptions about motivation which are held by management and which are in turn derived from society at large. Schein (1970) traces the history of shifting trends in industrial organizations beginning with Adam Smith's technical economic assumption, "Fair day's work for a fair day's pay." Then Schein modifies this definition by citing contemporary contracts which include "fullfillment of needs for meaningful work in return for a fair day's work." The behavior of the Lordstown GM workers revealed the existence of this assumption. They did not strike for more pay but for more meaningful work. These contemporary contracts are based on the assumption that individuals are self-actualizing (Maslow, 1968) and personal growth-oriented (Herzberg, Mausner, and Snyderman, 1959). For our purposes, both the traditional Adam Smith technical-economic assumptions and the self-actualization assumptions are excessively simplistic, each implying a universalistic "one best way" approach. The model of motivation used in this book is based on a more complex view of human relationships which enables managers to continuously reanalyze and readjust management's psychological contract with the members/workers within the organization. Some of the assumptions follow:

1. People have a "dominating will to live, reproduce, and maintain society; the ability for reciprocal interaction with others, including the ability to communicate and to establish relationships based upon trust, confidence, and love; and the ability to collaborate in 'primary activities' such as work (Jacques, 1976)." It is the characteristics of the organizational settings which facilitate or hinder the fulfillment of these human potentials.

2. People in organizations make conscious decisions about the nature of their contract with the organization. That is, what behavior they are to give in return for what inducements. These decisions are based on their own perceptions of how likely it is that their work efforts will result in desired performance and how likely it is that desired performance will obtain outcomes or rewards which they value (money, power, prestige, friendship, a sense of achievement, etc.) (Porter, Lawler, and Hackman, 1975).

3. People differ in the outcomes that they value. These differences are assumed to be related to an individual's underlying personality. In other words, individuals differ in terms of which needs are most important to them.

Three needs are considered important in organizational settings: the need for power, the need for affiliation, and the need for achievement (McClelland, 1961). All of these needs are found to some degree in all people. However, they vary in their strength among different individuals and within the same individual depending on the circumstances.

Organizations

The abstraction called "organization" has been defined in conflicting ways by managers, management scientists, and social scientists.

Figure 1.1 presented three of the dominant traditions. Each focused on a different aspect of organizational reality. It is almost as if each tradition wore its own set of rose-colored glasses. Figure 1.5 presents a summary of the academic literature most closely associated with the various perspectives. The technical view restricts much of its sight to organizing most effectively and efficiently to get work accomplished. The management, bureaucratic literature, and organization design literature support this view. The political perspective views power and the allocation of rewards as the dominant concern. Finally, the cultural view restricts much of its sight to value and normative concerns.

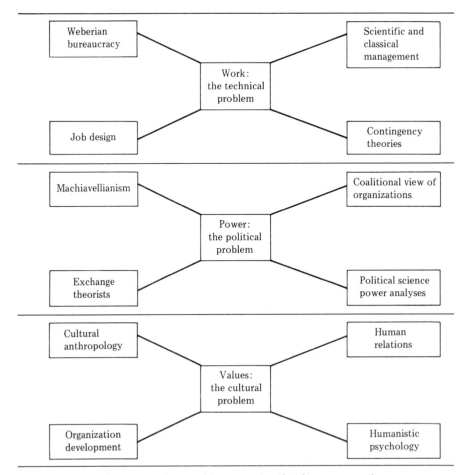

Figure 1.5   Summary of literature on the three perspectives

All three views are valid and not mutually exclusive. They often seem so, but that is because the political, technical, and cultural aspects of organizations are dialectical in nature. Organizations constantly juggle trade-offs between these three areas and create interrelated cycles of uncertainty. Thus, the nature of organizations is a paradoxical one. They are all three points of view at once.

Definitions of the Change Process

Organizational change is defined by Schein (1970) as the "induction of new patterns of action, belief, and attitudes among substantial segments of a population." All definitions of change are problematic. This is because they assume that we can differentiate between states of change and stability. This turns out not to be so simple. For organizations are always changing, often in subtle and incremental ways. Nevertheless, change is a core characteristic of all social systems.

This book is concerned with a *specific type of organizational change*, that is, change which is both of a large magnitude or strategic in nature, and change which is or can be managed. In contrast, much change can take place as a consequence of evolutionary forces. This is the result of events which are generally out of the control of any managerial action.

Strategic change refers to nonroutine, nonincremental, and discontinuous change which alters the overall orientation of the organization and/or components of the organization. For example, this kind of nonroutine change occurred after Philip Morris acquired the Miller Brewing Company. The Miller Brewing Company was transformed into an aggressive market-oriented organization through a massive change effort. Quantitatively, the phenomenon that occurred was different from small-scale change in that it entailed larger shifting of resources, the change of more components in the organization, and altering more behavioral patterns of people. Qualitatively, it was more complex, had a longer time frame, included more discontinuity in moving from State A to State C (see Figure 1.4). The exact boundary between strategic and nonstrategic change is blurred. Despite this blurring, we will retain the distinction and will provide examples where it is necessary to differentiate between the two.

Once the change process has been triggered it may be managed in various ways. Most technical prescriptions call for organizational change to be based on strategies which are explicit, purposefully developed, and planned in advance. This often turns out to be both unrealistic and not empirically representative of managed change efforts. As with organizational strategy, labelled by Mintzberg (1976) as both "intended" and "realized," managed change has both intentional (explicitly planned for) and realized (emerged out of the situation) aspects.

Managed change is assumed to reflect the organization's attempts to manage uncertainty via the decisions of leadership in the technical, political, and cultural areas. Leadership here is referred to as the dominant coalition, that is, those organizational members able to control allocation of resources, maintain control, and deal with uncertainty (Thompson, 1967). Uncertainty can be caused by external events and/or internal problems. For example, the U.S. Army is often faced with increasing uncertainty due to its peacetime shift to an all-volunteer organization. As a result, large-scale change efforts have had to be instituted to deal with technical, political, and cultural uncertainty.

The process of strategic change is started when problems, crises, or opportunities are recognized by means of a *threshold* phenomenon. "From the plethora of data received by managers, certain unique kinds of information exceed a threshold of perception and galvanize strategic responses" (Wieland and Ullrich 1976, p. 422).

Five areas can be compared to determine whether a certain piece, or cluster of information, exceeds threshold. According to Wieland and Ullrich (1976), these are:

1. Historical (comparison of current data with past)

2. Planning (comparison of current data with projections)

3. Extraorganizational (comparisons with other organizations)

4. Other people's expectations (compare with other managers)

5. Scientific (compare with theoretical predictions)

WHEN STRATEGIC CHANGE BECOMES NECESSARY

Problems, crises and/or opportunities emerge in the following areas:

1. *Environment.* Increasing competitive pressures can be the trigger for strategic change especially in quickly changing high-technology industries. Changes in the economy such as shifts in commodity prices, energy costs, resources, inflation, or employment legislation may all add up to a volatile environment which may easily trigger change. The auto industry was triggered by energy costs and foreign competition. AT&T was triggered by technology change in the communication and information processing field. The banking industry was triggered by electronic and communications changes as well as new competition from nonbanking institutions and foreign banks.

2. *Diversification.* The diversification of an organization into new areas of business generally requires a strategic change. This often includes a shift from a functional to a divisional structure (Chandler, 1962). For example, a relatively small medical instruments company organized by functions—sales, marketing, research and development, and production—decides to diversify into the business of tools for repairing electronic equipment. Such a firm might reorganize into two

divisions: (1) medical, and (2) electronic, with each division having its own functions.

3. *Technology.* Rapid shifts in technology impose new data and behavior requirements on organizations. Again, depending on how rapidly the change takes place, it can lead to either incremental or strategic change. For example, the microprocessor is having a major impact in some industries in the 1980s. The auto industry will be able to automate engine self-adjustments for greater efficiency. Appliances such as ovens already use microprocessors.

4. *People.* Another trigger for strategic change is change in people. That is, the types of people entering the organization may change in terms of education, expectations, or status, such as previously excluded minorities. Or the people already in the organization may change as the result of education, or shifts in attitudes or expectations.

Figure 1.6 identifies some of the key elements and phases of a managed effort. They are presented in sequential fashion, and much of what is prescribed in the planned change and organizational development literature involves a careful adherence to these ordered stages. Of course, strategically managed changes, including well-managed changes, are never so neatly sequential. They may go through all of the phases in Figure 1.6, but most often in an overlapping and nonsequential fashion. The organization may be continuously clarifying, redefining, and modifying as it evolves toward a new state of equilibrium—building that equilibrium a piece at a time (Mintzberg, 1976).

Again, the process is made dynamic and complex to a large extent because of the mixture of political, cultural, and technical forces which come into play. *Politically*, individuals readjust their power relationships and establish a new equilibrium. *Cultural* readjustments are made to support new behaviors. And *technical* processes may provide the leading edge, for example, someone found a better mouse trap; or technical processes are invoked after the fact to provide a rationale for a political or cultural change.

An example of how political and technical strategies become intermingled in the management of change was Henry Ford II's firing, in July, 1978, of Lee Iacocca, then the president of Ford Motor Company. The firing was a "managed strategic people change." It is interesting, however, to note that Henry Ford presented the dismissal in terms of its importance for organizational effectiveness and efficiency—a seemingly *technical* strategy. However, an examination of the actual events which led up to the change indicates rather clearly that there were other more *political* processes involved. In April, 1977, the Ford Motor Company created the so-called Office of the Chief Executive. Henry Ford II formed a three-man office including Lee Iacocca as president, Philip Caldwell as vice-chairman, and himself as chairman with "an extra vote." A year and three months later he dismissed Mr. Iacocca after expanding the office of chief executive to include his younger brother, William Clay Ford.

No data have come to public light indicating that Iacocca's performance was below par. However, there are data indicating that "there were other signals of possible change, including manifestations of Ford's own sense of dynasty (*Fortune*, August 14, 1978, p. 13)." In 1976, after recovering from an attack of angina he said, "I think the public wants, after I go, to see somebody called Ford somewhere right at the top of the company." The change was therefore quite likely not in pursuit of organizational effectiveness and efficiency (*technical* strategy) but rather in pursuit of adjusting the power group, the dominant coalition, to make certain that the allocation of power and resources was acceptable to Henry Ford II and the "family" (*political* strategy). The *technical* strategy was invoked after the *political* to justify the change.

Another way to express the contrast between the technical and political views of the change process is that the technical approach assumes that change occurs in response to economic requirements, even in the case of organizations not directly linked to market mechanisms—such as public service organizations. The *political* view, however, assumes that organizational design is

> the determinant of governance and control of the organization, the allocation of rewards and benefits, and the serving of certain interests, design, and changes in design are outcomes of political contests among various interest groups and subunits both inside and outside the organization. . . Change in the formal structure is thought of as quasi-revolution rather than a process guided by technical or instrumental technicality (Pfeffer, 1978, p. 176).

These opposing views become obvious in most change situations, and present us with a major dilemma. That is, changes are brought on by multiple factors, making it hard to clearly identify causes. There is, in fact, multiple causation. A technical strategy tends to develop regardless of the real cause for change. This is the result of the prevailing organizational mythology and terminology, which is generally managerial rather than political, and is therefore used to explain the causes of the change. The result is often: ". . . first the change and then the planning (Pfeffer, 1978)."

OVERVIEW OF COMING CHAPTERS

Regardless of the mix of technical, political, and cultural elements in a managed change situation, three ingredients must be present for successful change management: (1) A *diagnostic capability* to probe potential future courses of action and to determine the current state of organizational and managerial affairs, (2) a *capacity for developing change strategies* and for selecting the appropriate organization and management techniques for carrying out the strategy, and (3) a cluster of *skills and competencies required to implement* and carry through the effort.

Figure 1.6 summarizes the change process as it will be discussed in the following chapters.

At the heart of the process is a *comprehensive organizational model.* The model provides guidelines for selecting diagnostic information and arranging that information into meaningful patterns. This forms the basis for evaluating dysfunctional aspects of the organization. Chapter 2 explores some of the problems associated with current organizational models. Chapter 3 proposes an alternative model which becomes the central focus of the book. Chapter 4 presents the conceptual tools for treating the model dynamically. The model is then used to develop diagnostic plans which are presented in Chapter 5. Chapter 6 demonstrates how a diagnosis can be carried out. After the diagnosis is made, the model guides the selection of appropriate strategies for change. Chapter 7 presents guidelines for strategy development. Chapters 8, 9, and 10 deal with technical, political, and cultural strategies in that order. Chapter 11 presents an array of organizational change technologies ranging from matrix organization designs to sensitivity training and job enrichment. The task of Chapter 11 is to guide the managers of change in the appropriate matching of technologies to the overall strategy of change. Chapter 12 deals with the dynamics of implementing change. Chapter 13 provides readers with a set of guidelines to plan for the ongoing evaluation and monitoring of a change effort. The final chapter

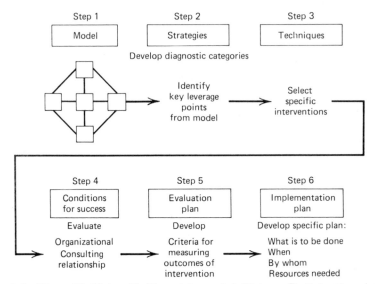

Figure 1.6 (From N. Tichy, H. Hornstein, and J. Nisberg, Participative organization diagnosis and intervention strategies. *Academy of Management Review,* 1976, 2, Figure 3.)

discusses future trends and unresolved dilemmas for the strategic management of change.

Recurring Themes

The following core themes emerge from most chapters of the book:

1. Change can be managed in all three of its modalities: technical, cultural, and political.

2. Change is multifaceted and paradoxical.

3. Change management is a major portion of the manager's role and as such calls for the development of requisite concepts and skills.

4. Effective use of professional change consultants is an important part of the strategic management of change.

APPENDIX TO CHAPTER ONE

The 1980s provide managers with an uphill battle of major organizational and managerial chances. The following article provides a criticism of U.S. management as we enter the 1980s. The remainder of this book develops a framework and set of tools for addressing many of the problems identified in the article.

Overhauling America's Business Management*

STEVE LOHR

The French journalist Jean-Jacques Sevan-Schreiber warned his readers in the late 1960's that Europe was in grave danger of economic invasion by the United States. The Old World, he said, might soon become a subsidiary of the American multinational companies and vanish as an autonomous civilization. These American invaders were superior, in Servan-Schreiber's view, not because of their money, resources or technology but because of their corporate organizational ability—and the genius behind it all was the American corporate manager. He was the real key to American power.

Not only in Europe were American managers and American management held in awe. The Japanese, too, regularly came to the United States to attend its business schools and tour its factories, and they used to joke that a B.A. degree meant Been in America. To Asians, this supremacy was often explained in terms of the West's Faustian spirit of aggressive individuality in rationalizing and conquering the forces of

---

*©1981 by The New York Times Company. Reprinted by permission.

nature. The reasons suggested for the American success varied from country to country, but the general drift did not: The American manager was the nonpareil—revered, even feared, throughout the world.

How quickly and dramatically, it seems, things have changed. Today, when foreign executives speak of their American counterparts, they are apt to be more scornful than awe-struck, and, indeed, the United States appears to be strewn with evidence of managerial failure. Whole industries—autos, steel, consumer electronics and others—have fallen victim to more aggressive, more efficient overseas competitors. The American economy is afflicted with stagnating productivity, high unemployment and the debilitating combination of surging inflation and high interest rates. The average age of the nation's plant and equipment is about 20 years, twice as old as Japan's. The rate of investment in research and development, the rate of new capital investment and the value of the dollar are all sliding with tangible consequences: a declining standard of living, more inflation and too few jobs.

No one seriously blames the country's corporate managers entirely. Government regulation, tax laws, pollution-control expenses, misguided economic policies, labor costs and the lofty price of imported oil have all played a part. Still, there is now a growing consensus, both at home and abroad, that the performance of American management of late has been sorely lacking; that, to some extent, the management policies, which served America so well and were admired the world over, are now being ignored in the country that created them; and that, worse, American corporate leaders have been slow to adapt to the rapidly and profoundly changing world of high energy costs and resource scarcity.

This indictment is heard not only from the traditional critics of business—the Ralph Naders and the like—but from top corporate executives as well. Reginald H. Jones, chairman of the General Electric Company and head of the Business Council—a collection of the chief executives of most of the nation's largest corporations—was asked, during a recent interview, about the perceived shortcomings of American management. "The indictment, in many cases, is justified," he replied. "It should be taken very seriously." From the ivy halls of the Harvard Business School to the executive spires of Manhattan to the low-slung plants of California's Silicon Valley, the criticisms are being taken very seriously. There seems, too, to be a growing willingness, even eagerness in some instances, to get going on important innovations that must be made to return American management to its position of preeminence.

At his desk in New York at 8 A.M., Akio Morita, the small, elegant, slender 59-year-old chairman and co-founder of the Sony Corporation, is engaged in an overseas telephone call. He is discussing business with a colleague, speaking in rapid, clipped cadence. Upon finishing the call, he rises to greet a visitor and quickly launches into a highly informed discussion of American politics. Akio Morita has become a man of two cultures—Japanese and American—and he also happens at the moment to be the very symbol of the kind of change in business-management techniques that has successfully occurred in one culture and, many people believe, must take place in the other.

Indeed, the prevalence in the United States of all manner of Sony merchandise—televisions, radios, tape recorders, video-cassette recorders and the like—is testimony to the triumph of his approach, and indirect confirmation that American business is in need of repair.

For years, Morita says, he was one of those who regarded America as "a teacher," a nation whose management methods were to be emulated as much as possible. Now, however, he believes that, "for much of the trouble of the American economy, American management has to take the responsibility."

Not that Akio Morita's highly admired achievements—in marketing, product development and quality control, for example—were arrived at with perfect ease. He was long regarded as something of an outsider in his country, apart from the traditional Japanese establishment, one of a handful of aggressive entrepreneurs who emerged after World War II and whose brazen style was considered un-Japanese. Morita, along with his partner, Masaru Ibuka, started a small electronics business in Tokyo back in 1946.

In the 1950's, when American consumers saw the tag "Made in Japan," it was a stigma—a code phrase for shoddy merchandise. Sony, more than any other company, was responsible for reversing that image. The turnabout was so substantial that, by 1972, when Sony opened its first American manufacturing plant in San Diego, California, to construct color televisions, its dealers were concerned that its American-made television sets wouldn't match the quality of those made in Japan. The company now has a second factory in the United States, located in Dothan, Alabama, which in 1977 began producing magnetic tape cassettes for the Betamax recorder and audio tape. Today, Sony's American arm is nearly a $1 billion-a-year operation employing 4,500 workers, and the quality seems to have held up fine.

In Morita's view, the trouble with a large segment of American management is attributable to two misguided attitudes: American managers are too worried about short-term profits and too little concerned about their workers. These two mistakes, Morita says, are connected and go a long way toward explaining productivity problems.

"A lot of American companies know they have old machines," he says. "But the manager figures he'll keep the old machines as long as they still run, make a big profit one year, and take that record as an advertisement to get a job elsewhere. So productivity here declines."

Most American managers, according to Morita, take a shortsighted view of their workers. Indeed, it is the antagonism between management and labor in America that Morita thinks is most counter-productive. Here lies one of the greatest contrasts between the United States and Japan, with its tradition of corporate paternalism and life-time employment. Morita argues that the Japanese approach to labor management is not a cultural eccentricity, applicable only in Japan. He says it can be transplanted, in a slightly watered-down form, into America. As evidence, he points to Sony's plants at San Diego and Dothan, where, he says, productivity has risen steadily so that it now is very close to that of the company's factories in Japan. "The workers in San Diego and Dothan are terrific," says Morita.

It is difficult for an outsider to gauge the success Sony and other Japanese companies have had in bringing their type of management into the United States. But those who have studied the Sony experience here agree for the most part that it has gone fairly well and that American managers should be taking notes.

Sony has tried, as much as transient Americans are willing to import its system of lifetime employment. "We never lay off workers in a re-cession," Morita notes. "When we select someone, the person becomes part of the Sony family."

Bonuses are a democratic affair for Sony in Japan. They are paid to everyone, production workers and top management alike. Everyone shares the prosperity in the good years, and shares the grief in bad ones. In the United States, some adjustments have been made for the local culture. For instance, Morita admits that top executives in Sony of America are in a profit-sharing program.

Critics contend that one reason Sony has been able to install much of its system here is that it has fought so strenuously, and successfully, to keep unions out. Wages aren't the issue, says Morita, though Sony wages are generally competitive. "We want to keep the union out to maintain our philosophy," says Morita. "We want to keep our family whole and not have a third party interfering."

In all the current American discourse about economic "re-industrialization"—that unfortunate locution at once evocative and vague—there is agreement that something must be done to close the chasm between management and labor in this country, an often need-lessly adversarial and counterproductive atmosphere that management has in good part brought upon itself. As one auto executive noted: We're all in this together, plant workers and management alike. And, frankly, for too long we didn't recognize that or try to create a working environment that makes everybody want to pull in the same direction."

Certainly, there are significant differences between Japan and the United States in Government policy, culture, capital markets and taxes. The cultural homogeneity in Japan and the extremely strong citizen association with national purpose are examples. Yet it seems that Amer-ican management could certainly take a page back from the modern

Japanese workbook. "Teamwork historically is, I think, the American way," Morita says. "But your managers too often forgot that. They got greedy; they viewed the worker as a tool. That has not been good for American products or American companies, and it has hurt your competitive stature in the world."

There is a fairly broad agreement, in retrospect, among executives, academics and others on what went wrong in American management in the 1970's. After the oil embargo in 1973 and the Arab-led cartel increased petroleum prices fourfold, American corporations were slow to recognize the full significance of the new energy economics and respond. With a single stroke, the old order was sundered. True, both Japan and Western Europe had never had such cheap or plentiful energy, and, thus, had the advantage of not having to adjust to the shock. Nor did they have the physical space of America to encourage a greater use of energy, in heavier automobile usage, for example. Nevertheless, American business leaders seem to have delayed too long in making difficult, costly adjustment. Even Thomas A. Murphy, the just-retired chairman of General Motors and the perennial optimist of the auto industry, concedes that the 70's were "all but a disaster. We seem to have spent most of our time not making decisions."

This managerial inertia cost American industry dearly in terms of its competitive standing. Yet the related and deeper problem, observers agree, is the set of managerial approaches and attitudes that is widespread but serves business poorly in the current setting. For management, as the author-consultant Peter F. Drucker has written, is not just a discipline but also a "culture," with its own values, beliefs, tools and language. To assess the past failures of management and, by inference, to suggest the direction of needed change, one must identify some of the distinguishing characteristics of the current American management culture.

First, as Morita points out, most corporate managers in the United States are now oriented to short-term profit, which tends to discourage them from making important investment in new plants, equipment and research and development. It is often noted that much of the highly efficient steel-making technology employed with such effect today by foreign competitors was actually developed in the United States. But the American steel companies did not undertake to refashion their plants years ago, when it was a good deal less expensive to do so. Yet, the failure to do so, even now at higher cost, is stealing from the future. Second, the freewheeling entrepreneur, the Henry Ford or the Andrew Carnegie, seems to have fallen in short supply, at least among the denizens of big corporations. It was Ford, of course, who had such an unshakable faith in himself and in the notion of inexpensive mass-produced automobiles that he told his customers they could have cars in whatever color they wanted, as long as it was black. Again, the current emphasis is more on safeness, certain profitability, than on boldness, ingenuity, innovation—old American trademarks. Observes Robert H. Hayes, a Harvard Business School professor: "You don't have much of the spirit anymore of the top manager who simply looks at something and says: "Dammit, this is a good product. Let's make it even though the payoff isn't apparent yet.'"

Third, too many top corporate positions are filled by people who are financial wizards, but who know too little about the fundamentals of the very businesses they run—the markets, technologies, production processes and workers. These people, usually with financial or legal backgrounds, are the breed of self-styled "professional managers" that so often occupies the executive suites in large corporations. Critics contend that these managers run businesses by the numbers, period. What is needed today, they argue, is less of the Olympian detachment of the 50th floor and more nuts-and-bolts undertanding of the factory floor.

Fourth, some of the financial yardsticks that managers rely upon so much in deciding whether to make investments may yield results that are badly distorted in the current period of high inflation. The validity of some of these yardsticks like "discounted cash flow" or virtually indecipherable formulas for figuring "return on investment," is being called into question to some extent. "It may be that some of the basic tools we've been teaching in business schools for 20 years are inordinately biased toward the short term, the sure payoff," said Lee J. Seidler, a Wall Street securities analyst and professor at the New York University Business School. That suspicion, in turn, raises doubts about the almost theological commitment of corporate managers to financial analysis.

And finally, American managers have often been chauvinistic, not seeing the growing internationalization of business, not learning the tricky art of selling abroad. "We had this huge homogeneous market in the U.S. for so long that American industry was spoiled," says Reginald Jones of General Electric. Too few companies did what G.E., in fact, has done: more than doubled its international business over the past decade to 37 percent of the corporate total, so that G.E. by itself generates a trade surplus (exports minus imports) of more than $2 billion.

Though the American horizon has been gloomy, it has also had its bright spots in the past decade—particularly in the computer and semiconducter industry. The rapid pace of technological change in this area is truly difficult to comprehend. Modest folk in the industry are fond of citing the following by way of helpful illustration: If the aircraft industry had progressed as rapidly as the semiconductor or computer business in recent years, the Concorde would now hold 10,000 passengers, travel at 60,000 miles an hour and a ticket would cost 1 cent. Others maintain that what is happening is virtually tantamount to a second industrial revolution.

How did these businessmen triumph when so many others around them were not doing well?

"Unlike steel, autos and some others, this industry has never been an oligopoly," Robert N. Noyce says of the field of semiconductors. "It has always been intensely competitive. And it has always been a brain-intensive industry, rather than a capital-intensive one. It has been an industry where, if your key people don't agree with you, they take off, start their own businesses and become your competitors."

Robert Noyce knows whereof he speaks. In 1968, he and Gordon E. Moore, two scientists working for Fairchild Semiconductor in northern California, split off and, with a grubstake of $2 million in venture capital, founded a fledgling outfit called Intel (for Integrated Electronics). Soon afterward, they were joined by Andrew S. Grove, another former Fairchild scientist. By 1970, Intel, of Santa Clara, Calif., reported sales of $4 million. By 1980, the sales were increased to $900 million, and the work force had reached 15,000. Ironically, though short-term profit has not been its chief goal, Intel has managed to keep its pretax profit margins safely above 20 percent—twice the average of its major competitors—during booms and recessions alike. Accordingly, Intel is probably now the company held in highest esteem in a highly esteemed field.

There's more to Intel's story than a willingness on the part of intelligent employees to disagree with their boss—though that's an important part of it. The whole story tells a good deal about where alert American corporations may be headed in the future, and, by way of contrast, about what many firms have failed to do in the recent past.

First, Noyce, Moore and Grove were not shy about charging ahead with controversial new technologies—initially with the computer memory chip and then with the microprocessor, or computer on a chip. By introducing slight impurities onto a wafer of silicon, used in the manufacture of semiconductors for computers, and etching microsopic patterns on its surface, the Intel manufacturers were able to place many thousands of electronic circuits onto a "chip" smaller than a dime.

The managers have been willing, too, to pour an unusually large share of the proceeds back into the business. They invest roughly 10 percent of yearly revenues in research and development. The company's capital-spending program for new facilities and equipment totaled about $150 million last year.

Intel is not the largest supplier in the industry; it is No. 4—smaller in size than Texas Instruments, National Semiconductor and Motorola. However, the company has not tried to be the biggest, concentrating instead on staying at the technological frontier. Intel has been there first with the most, technologically speaking, and it has done so more consistently than its competitors. Typically, the company will experiment and test-market a new product, then later will have experience in producing it more efficiently and more cheaply than the competition.

All the while, Intel is striving to ferret out the next technological leap needed to renew the cycle. Indeed, the company is now in the midst of another long-range jump in technology, developing devices that will eventually be complex enough to put the computing power of an entire mainframe computer (the nation's largest and most powerful computer) on a handful of silicon chips. Should it slip in this effort, the company would suffer greatly. But based on Intel's track record so far, competitors aren't betting that it will fail.

In combining technological mastery with extraordinary business success. Intel has been a management innovator, both in style and structure. The central management problem for a fast-growing high-technology company is to solve one riddle: how to stay flexible and nimble, in tune with emerging technologies and markets, even as its very growth tends to make the concern sluggish and bureaucratic. The answer may lie both in structure and philosophy.

Intel has a three-man executive office, made up of Noyce, Moore and Grove. Simply put, Noyce is the "outside man," who spends nearly half his time on things not directly connected with Intel, such as speaking to the financial community, Government policy makers and serving as a member of the National Academy of Science. Moore is the company's long-range thinker, charting its product strategy. Grove, a scientist-turned-manager, is the person who runs Intel day-to-day.

Intel is organized to avoid the bureaucratic hierarchy that is characteristic of most corporations. Workers may have several bosses, depending on the problem at hand. Instead of staff specialists for purchasing, quality control and so on, Intel has several dozen committees, or "councils," that make decisions and enforce standards in specialized fields. These groups are overlaid on a grid of about 25 so-called strategic business segments that do product planning.

"What we've tried to do is to put people together in ways so that they make contributions to a wider range of decisions and do things that would be thwarted by a structured, line-type organization," Noyce explains.

But more than structure, it is Intel's "culture," as Drucker puts it, that sets it apart from most American companies. There are no "offices" at Intel, only shoulder-high partitions separating the work space of individual white-collar employees. White collars, for that matter, are scarce as well; there is no dress code and very few of the men wear ties. There are no reserved parking spaces for executives, no limousines, no separate dining rooms. Top managers eat in one of the company cafeterias, along with everyone else, or in lunch-hour meetings with one of the ad hoc problem-solving groups. Everyone is espected to report to the job at 8 A.M. sharp. "I can justify my salary, just as I can justify the salary of a production operator, a technician or an engineer—it's a function of the market," says Grove, the company's 44-year-old president, who wears an open-necked beige shirt with a gold chain underneath. "But I can't justify why I should get a reserved parking space. There's no justification for that at all."

At the council sessions, it is expected that all will participate as equals, with new employees challenging senior executives. Ultimately, the top managers must pass judgment on the projects that will consume the many millions of dollars needed not merely to keep up but, more important, to set the pace of technological development. "But we go through the discussion as equals," says Grove.

Many of the elements of Intel's management approach strike skeptics, especially those familiar with traditional corporate practices, as empty symbolism and affectation. Neither is the case, Grove argues. "It isn't symbolism at all," he says. "It's a necessity, I think, for this company in this industry with the technology shifting so fast, and that rapid change will continue."

He explains: "I can't pretend to know the shape of the next generation of silicon or computer technology anymore. That's why people like me need the knowledge from the people closest to the technology. That's why we can't have the hierarchical barriers to an exchange of ideas and information that you have at so many corporations."

Grove has an example of what is wrong with many companies. He presents a newspaper clipping that described an incident leading to the dismissal of William A. Niskanen Jr., chief economist at Ford. In late 1979, Niskanen had advised his bosses that Government-imposed quotas on Japanese cars would not solve Ford's problems, and this view was not popular among the company higher-ups. "In the meeting in which I was informed that I was released," Niskanen told a reporter, "I was told, 'Bill, in general, people who do well in this company wait until they hear their superiors express their view, and then contribute something in support of that view.'"

"That," says Grove, "is precisely the kind of attitude that we cannot afford here."

To perpetuate the philosophy and culture of the company, Intel conducts a series of training courses for many of the employees, who then, it is hoped, carry it out and pass it on to others.

By now, outsiders have studied Intel's management and, generally, they agree that it has worked. Some have said that the company's egaliterian, flexible structure approximates the futurist Alvin Toffler's notion of an "adhocracy." Others say it is a kind of American version of the Japanese management style. "What a lot of it boils down to is creating an environment in which people want to cooperate with each other and it is in their interest to do so," says William G. Ouchi, a professor at the University of California, Los Angeles.

Ouchi has written a book, to be published in April, entitled "Theory Z Corporations: How American Business Can Respond to the Japanese Challenge." In it, he says that the answer lies in converting American companies into what he calls "type Z" concerns—ones whose management approach and corporate culture are something akin to Intel. Many other corporations, particularly General Motors, are making a major effort to try out or perfect Theory Z, which essentially projects a broader base of interlocking corporate authority and encourages more wide-spread participation in company decisions at the plant level than the more traditional Type A, with the boss at the top.

Ouchi says that one trouble with Type Z is that its "managers are often heard to complain that they feel powerless to exercise their judgment in the face of quantitative analysis, computer models and numbers, numbers, numbers. Western management seems to be characterized for the most part by an ethos which roughly runs as follows: Rational is better than nonrational, objective is more nearly rational than subjective, quantitative is more objective than nonquantitative, and thus quantitative analysis is preferred over judgments based on wisdom, experience and subtlety. Some observers, such as Prof. Harold Leavitt of Stanford University, have written that the penchant for the explicit and the measureable has gone well beyond reasonable limits, and that a return to the subtle and the subjective is in order.

"In a Type Z company, Ouchi says, "The explicit and the implicit seem to exist in a state of balance. While decisions are informed by the complete analysis of facts, they are also shaped by serious attention to questions of whether or not this decision is 'suitable,' whether it 'fits' the company. A company that consists of isolated subspecialities which do not effectively communicate with one another is hardly capable of achieving such fine-grained forms of understanding. Perhaps the underlying cause is the loss of the ability for disparate departments within a single organization to communicate effectively with one another. They are forced to communicate in the sparse, inadequate language of numbers, because numbers are the only language all can understand in a reasonably symmetrical fashion."

To itemize the missed opportunities is not to explain them. To do that, one must look at the larger arena that helps shape the actions of corporate managers.

To raise money, public companies in the United States are heavily dependent on the stock market. This is not the case in West Germany or Japan, where banks (often backed by the Government) supply most of the capital for companies. Consequently, while foreign corporate managers have to answer to a relative handful of investors who have a long-term stake in companies, their American counterparts play to Wall Street and the often fickle tastes of institutional stock players.

Rare is the American chief executive who, in a philosophical moment, away from the daily fray, will not say that corporations should focus more on the future. However, in the next breath, many of these same executives will say that the verdict of Wall Street—and, hence, their survival in office—depends on producing the steady quarter-to-quarter increases in profits that so please the financial community. This is known as the tyranny of Wall Street. "Our top corporate managers are in the same boat as baseball managers," explained Norman E. Auerbach, chairman of Coopers & Lybrand, one of the so-called Big Eight accounting firms, which has mostly big corporations as clients. "You'd better win, produce those higher earnings quickly, or you're out."

Consider, too, the social side of these pressures. The typical chief executive of a major corporation is about 60 years old. The top job is the pinnacle of his career, something that he has worked a large share of his life to achieve, often requiring considerable personal and family sacrifice along the way. His salary is probably $200,000 or more. His community and social position are tied to his job. Assuming retirement at 65, he has five years in the top office, that is, if all goes well. How likely is such a person to reduce this year's profits to invest in some costly new project, the payoff for which is several years down the road, and uncertain even then?

But this shortsightedness of management and Wall Street seems to be changing. Increasingly, investment analysts are using measurements other than reported earnings to gauge corporate performance. When General Motors reported a loss of $567 million in the third quarter of 1980, the comments from Wall Street were generally upbeat. One reason was that, despite the slump in auto sales, General Motors had not pulled back from its five-year $40 billion capital-spending program, designed to give the company a full array of smaller fuel-efficient cars by 1985. If it had cut down on spending. General Motors could have at least reduced its third-quarter loss. Rather, it took the long view and invested in the future. The company is seen as an awakened giant.

For an ever-growing number of corporate managers, the two-year stint at a graduate school of business has become an initiation rite into the managerial culture. Today, the degree granted by these schools, a masters in business administration, or M.B.A., is seen as a sine qua non of upward mobility in many large corporations. Probably none is more influential or has more highly placed alumni than the Harvard Business School. And indeed the schools have in the past taught and helped formulate some of the important theories of management, such as statistically based quality control or the early ideas of Alfred P. Sloan (G.M.'s head for many years) on promotion from within or openness among top management. But it is a widely held view that the M.B.A. might be part of the current problem. The charge is that even the leading business schools such as Harvard or Stanford have been teaching how not to manage a modern American company; that they have simply taught business as business has been practiced, and not helped lead the way to necessary change.

John H. McArthur, the 46-year-old dean of Harvard Business School, a large, robust man with an informal manner, talks openly about this criticism. Seated in an overstuffed chair beside a fireplace in his office along Boston's Charles River, he concedes that it has some merit. He agrees, for instance, that "too often analysis has meant being able to shove a problem quantitatively through the computer nine different ways and come out with a printout the size of the Manhattan phone book." Also, he generally agrees that in the past too little attention has been paid at the business schools to the handling of workers, production management and international business.

"I don't think these are things that we in business schools are passing along very well yet," says McArthur. "But bear in mind that the economic world changed drastically and irrevocably in the 1970's. American management and business schools are now in transition, struggling to respond to the changes. We do have a serious problem in this period of transition, but this nation also has enormous resources. I think the shift is under way, both out there in the corporate world and at business schools like this one."

In a nearby office, there is an example of this shift. He is Prof. Robert Hayes: "Look, I'll admit it. I was one of the guys teaching all the quantitative methods with such vigor. I was part of the problem." Hayes has recently been quite critical of some aspects of American management, and his views have been widely circulated in management and academic circles. In particular, he has questioned the wisdom of having managerial ranks filled with financial practitioners cast in the "professional manager" mold—that itinerant band of job-hopping executives applying their skills at one company for a few years before moving on to the next, rarely learning the fundamentals of the specific business they run. Instead, Hayes suggests that managers with more firsthand experience would be more likely to make the decisions necessary to insure the long-run health and survival of the business, focusing on production management—the side of the "art of organization" that attends directly to business operations.

Generally, John McArthur contends, that, not only in the notions of Robert Hayes, but also in the attitude of the business schools in general, a changed response is beginning to take shape.

If, despite the acknowledgment of serious problems, there seems to be a new optimism in the business community, it may be in part because of the improved political and social milieu in the United States. It is impossible to say with much certainty just what the long-range effect will be of having Ronald Reagan in the Oval Office and more Republicans in Congress. But with the economy a key issue in the election, the results do reflect increasing popular support for the traditional economic goal of conservatives—the creation of wealth—and away from the liberal objective—the distribution of wealth.

The Reagan Administration, by all accounts, is expected to curb Government regulation while providing investment incentives for the private sector. The New President and his advisers are well aware that the healthiest foreign economies, such as those in Japan and West Germany, are ones which strongly encourage saving and investment with Government tax allowances. Reagan has promised to free the economy from the inhibiting influence of Government, which he says will unleash the nation's productive capacity. In Reagan's scenario, corporate management will then be largely responsible for bringing about the hoped-for surge of productivity and, with it, lower inflation, increased employment and a rising standard of living.

The new Administration itself has a managerial caste, with several top corporate executives in the Cabinet. Reagan, it is said, will run the executive branch of Government like a corporation, with himself as chairman. Where corporate management is concerned, Reagan is a believer.

The basic optimism comes, however, from the new attitude of management itself. There is a lengthening of corporate sights, now that, as one Japanese executive said privately, "your managers are beginning to recognize many of their industries are engaged in a global fight for survival." He offered the following elaboration: When Japan attacked Pearl Harbor, he said, the United States had the seventh largest navy in the world. By the end of World War II, the American fleet was the biggest. "When forced to," he said, "Americans can respond vigorously. Ultimately, that is what your nation will probably do about its current economic problems, and your corporate managers must lead the response."

Based on talks in recent months with a broad spectrum of representatives and observers of American management, it appears that the response is coming. The past failures and current weaknesses are recognized and accepted, and there is a readiness to try corrective techniques. At present, it is impossible to discern the precise contours of the expected transformation—just how American corporations will be structured and run differently a decade or two from now. Nonetheless, certain harbingers are clear.

Given the ever-quickening pace of change, companies can only benefit from a broader participation in decision making by their increasingly educated workers. To stay attuned to fast-changing markets, technologies and production techniques, it helps to have the information and cooperation of those closest to the operation—the workers. Companies that do this effectively are what Ouchi of U.C.L.A. would call "type Z" concerns. However, the label attached to such companies is relatively unimportant; what is significant is that more and more corporations are trying it. And it is not just the Intels or Hewlett-Packards, relatively young companies dwelling in the rarefied realm of futuristic technology. General Motors has completed a project in an assembly plant in Brookhaven, Miss., to increase worker participation in the corporate decision-making process. The company is so pleased with the results—that it is now undertaking 160 organizational changes at plants throughout the country, with the full support of the United Automobile Workers. And at plants throughout the auto industry, workers have been given the authority to shut down the assembly line if they think that, for whatever reason, quality control standards are not being met—a revolutionary change. The particular corporate milieu, or culture, within which the worker is given greater authority and responsibility will vary from company to company. This changing character in boss-worker relations, becoming more a two-way street, seems one representative example of the shift in traditional management perceptions and practices that is now apparently underway. The changes are, in a sense, a return to elemental American values, to more democratic organizations and away from the hierarchical class structure found in so many large corporations today.

Similarly, the task of corporate management is to fashion solutions to the problems of business that are firmly in the American mold, to borrow perhaps from other cultures but not mimic them. American society is individualistic, pluralistic and enterpreneurial. These are the historic sources of generative energy that largely explain the economic rise in the United States and, most agree, constitute this nation's greatest potential advantage in the unfolding competition for global markets. To renew, encourage and channel these energies is a challenge facing American management today.

Chapter Two

Organizational Models

INTRODUCTION

In the folklore of the Middle East, there is a story of Nasrudin and his friend. The friend found Nasrudin on his knees looking for something and asked him:

"Nasrudin, what have you lost?"

"My key," said Nasrudin.

The friend went down on his knees and began searching as well. After a time, with no success, the friend asked:

"Exactly where did you drop the key?"

Nasrudin replied:

"In my house."

"Then why are you looking here for your key?"

"There is more light here than inside my house."

This well-worn but timeless story (Mintzberg, 1976) is useful here. It identifies a puzzling reality of human thought. We are not always logical, and we often make absurd assumptions and associations. The appeal of the story lies in self-recognition. That is, in making us aware of how we often trap ourselves by focusing on a problem in the wrong context. The decisions about where to look to diagnose organization problems are guided by our underlying assumptions about and models for organizations. The objectives of this chapter are to help you explicate your own model, and examine several alternative models. Together with your model, these various inputs and the model presented in Chapter 3 may help you avoid looking in the wrong place when engaged in strategic change management.

WHY MODELS ARE NEEDED TO OVERCOME MANAGERIAL MYTHS

Evidence regarding the commonly held myths about managerial behavioral patterns (Mintzberg, 1973) provides us with support for advocating more explicit and comprehensive organization models. Three of the more significant myths which were found when Henry Mintzberg (1973) observed senior managers at work are:

1. *Managers Are Systematic Planners.* This, according to studies of managerial behavior, is myth number one. The findings indicate that although managers work at an unrelenting pace, their work is characterized by fragmentation and brevity. Senior managers have been observed to spend an average of less than ten minutes on any one task. There is little evidence that managers spend much reflective, uninterrupted, and systematic planning time.

2. *Managers Rely on Formal Computerized Management Information Systems.* This is myth number two. The reality is that most managers prefer live action, that is, telephone communication, face-to-face interpersonal communication, and unscheduled meetings. These personal encounters average 6 to 12 minutes in length. The preference for this kind of information collection means that information will be stored in the brain of the manager and not in a computer. Unless the manager has a method of recording this data and entering it into a computerized information system, it remains his/her personalized information system. This lack of systematic information gathering seems to be pervasive.

3. *Management Is Fast Becoming a Science.* This is myth number three. If management were becoming formalized as a science, then we would see evidence of managers following formal propositions and programs to guide the allocation of time and resources, delegation, control, and organizational design. The reality is that managers tend to rely largely on intuitive and implicit theories.

Given this mythological view of managerial behavior, the implications for the management of change are quite profound. First, we can predict that most managers will *not* do much systematic planning prior to launching a change effort. Second, we can assume that the data base for making decisions about the change will be generated via many *personal interactions*, and that the data are not likely to be formally recorded anywhere. This means that the diagnosis will tend to be personalized and unstructured. Finally, the development of a change strategy and the implementation of the change will be based on the manager's intuitive and implicit models of organization and change.

The use of the term "model" refers to a set of assumptions and beliefs which together represent reality. These models or theories guide action. They are often very personalized and intuitive. However, they may at the same time be widely shared and explicit. But even when widely shared and explicit they may also be intuitive. For example, at one time, a theory about the earth being flat greatly influenced the behavior of explorers. It caused them to worry about falling off the edge. Another example: The physiological model which guided physicians several hundred years ago was based on the assumption that the body was made up of fluid humors which needed to be kept in balance. This model led to remedies such as leeching and bleeding.

Such a state of affairs is acceptable if the manager's intuitive and implicit models are (1) consonant with the problems that need resolving, and (2) consonant with the models of the other people with whom he or she must collaborate. Organization models are at the core of all organizational change. They provide guidelines for selecting diagnostic information and for arranging the information into meaningful patterns. The organizational model for a manager or a consultant functions much like a physician's model of the human system. The physician conducts tests and collects vital information with the model as guide. After the diagnosis is made, the model guides the selection of appropriate medical intervention. In a similar fashion, the organizational model is used to guide the conduct of a diagnosis and the development of change strategies.

Problems Created by Implicit Models

Managers who work with each other often use "implicit models" composed of their own somewhat subjective and biased views of the managerial problem. This can easily bring on conflict about what course of action to take in a change effort. Such implicit models create a great deal of difficulty in resolving differences. The differences generally emerge during disagreements over what to do. This is because in the absence of an accepted model, it is difficult to explore the underlying reasons for various actions. For example, a group of managers in one company struggled over how to organize. One group advocated reorganizing by product line, another group by geography, and a third group fought for a matrix organization which focused on both product and geography. At no time during the arguments was there any examination of the underlying reasons for why one structure might be superior to another. That is, the disagreements were over *what* to do . . . not *why* to do something. The result of these haphazard negotiations was a matrix structure that did not work.

Another example of the use of implicit instead of explicit models occurred when the management of another company faced serious morale problems. Some of the managers advocated an "off-with-their-heads" solution based on replacing people, firing key supervisors, and hiring new ones. Other managers advocated training the existing staff, and offering human relations training to the supervisors. Until groups like these find a way to deal with the differences in their underlying implicit models, they will have trouble reaching any kind of accord. Another reason for explicating one's model is to examine it for weaknesses, omissions, and blind spots. As long as the model is intuitive and implicit it cannot be subjected to any rigorous analysis.

Several research studies provide strong evidence that managers do have different perceptual models of organizations, and that these models lead to different conclusions about managerial action. In a study by Dearborn and Simon (1958), executives from different parts of an organization were asked to analyze a case study and indicate whether the problem was (1) a sales problem, (2) a need to clarify the organizational structure problem, or (3) a human relations problem. The resultant diagnoses were related to the executive's departmental position. Five out of six sales managers reported that the problem was one of not clarifying the organizational structure. Three of four accountants saw the problem as a sales problem. The only executives who called it a human relations problem came from the personnel office. In studies of professional consultants, it has been found that what they view in diagnosis is related to what they try and change (Tichy, 1976).

Organizational models filter and focus perception. They underlie and guide our perceptions about organizations. It has been shown that thinking about and working with models runs counter to much of managerial reality. Therefore, in practical situations, I have found it necessary to stress *model generation*. In such cases, managers and students of organizations are requested to "willingly suspend disbelief." That is, they are urged to begin exploring models before resisting the notion.

It is my belief that in order to properly influence managerial behavior, the change manager must examine and ultimately alter the underlying conceptual frameworks used to make decisions about organizational change. This requires calling a temporary halt to managerial action and explicating underlying conceptual frameworks. The approach I use to do this is presented in full with a case illustration in Appendix I. The steps are briefly outlined here.

1. *Read.* Read case so as to have an organization in mind.
2. *Choose Elements of the Model.* Identify the diagnostic information you would require to plan a change effort in that organization.
3. *Develop Model Categories.* Organize the information areas identified in Step 2 into clusters of broader categories. These represent the components of your model.
4. *Specify Interrelationships Among Model Categories.* Examine the interrelationships between the categories developed in Step 3 so as to make the model dynamic.
5. *Share Models with Group.* If you are working with a group, share the model and discuss the underlying assumptions and reasons for the interrelationships. Agree upon a common model. (Skip Step 5 if working alone.)

6. *Apply the Model.* Apply the model to carrying out a diagnosis of the case in Appendix 1. Use the model to determine what information to look at and determine the problems of the case.

7. *Compare.* Compare your model to the one applied in Appendix I. How does it differ? How is it similar? What conclusions do you draw?

In response to the problems of implicit organizational models, managers of change are encouraged to develop emergent pragmatic theories of change. These models are developed in an inductive fashion. They start with an exploration of an individual's pre-existing assumptions and implicit theories, and make them explicit. They then can be compared to other theories and tested against reality. In the process, they can be modified by exposure to expert input and organizational readings. Figure 2.1 summarizes the emergent pragmatic theory process.

The emergent pragmatic theory which results from the process is one which is personally and pragmatically meaningful to users as they plan diagnosis, develop change strategies, and evaluate success. Appendix I includes the activities necessary to develop an emergent pragmatic theory. Readers are encouraged to do these activities now.

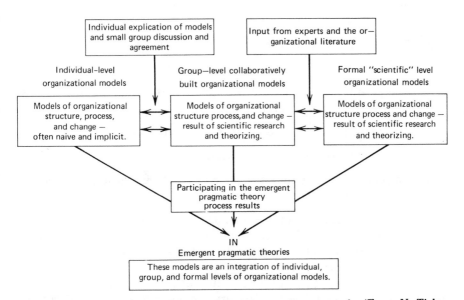

Figure 2.1 The objective of the emergent pragmatic approach. (From N. Tichy, H. Hornstein, and J. Nisberg, Participative organization diagnosis and intervention strategies. *Academy of Management Review,* **1976, 2,** Figure 2.)

FORMAL ORGANIZATIONAL MODELS FOR CHANGE

Chapter 3 presents a model which is based on findings from research and theory in the behavioral and management sciences. This model provides the framework for the remainder of the book. However, since there is no one accepted model of organizations for use in the management of change, several precursors to this model are presented in this chapter. The purpose is to demonstrate the strong influence a model can and should have on managerial behavior as it is related to change.

Classical/Mechanistic Model

Figure 2.2 presents a traditional view of organizations which demonstrates the classical aspects of organizational structure, namely the chain of command and span of control. It is based on the scheme originated by the classical management theorists (Taylor, 1923; Fayol, 1949; and Urwick, 1943) who developed a set of rules for the proper structuring of organizations. These rules have turned out to be quite similar to the principles of bureaucracy developed by the sociologist Max Weber. The model is referred to as a mechanistic model of organizations (Burns and Stalker, 1961), and the rules prescribe that the organization should be:

1. Differentiated into specialized functional tasks.

2. Subordinates should pursue individual tasks with concern only for the completion of their narrowly stated tasks.

3. Rigid chain of command (one man, one boss).

4. Detailed and exhaustive job descriptions.

5. The overall picture of the organization is only relevant to those at the top of the hierarchy.

6. Interaction follows vertical lines along the chain of command.

7. Behavior is governed by superiors.

8. Emphasis is on narrow, specialized knowledge rather than general, complete knowledge.

The implicit strategy for the management of change demonstrated here is a technical one. That is, the goal is to make changes that move the organization toward a better fit with the mechanistic principles listed above. Presumably, the closer the fit, the greater the organizational effectiveness and efficiency. Much of the planned change carried out by organizations in this century, including most contemporary work, falls into this category. Measures taken to secure such change include time and motion studies, job analysis and job description

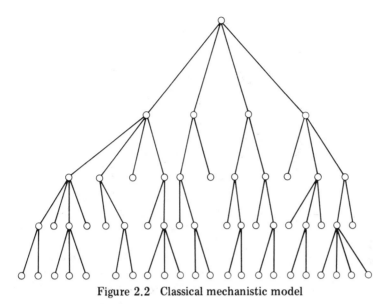

Figure 2.2 Classical mechanistic model

studies, as well as design of mechanistic control systems, and revisions of the formal organizational chart. In most cases, the change is worked out by technocrats, then legislated from the top and implemented through the hierarchy. Underlying this concept is the belief that technical considerations will prevail and lead to greater effectiveness and efficiency.

Human Resources Organic Model

The second model, graphically portrayed in Figure 2.3 has its roots in the now famous Hawthorne Studies carried out in the late 1920s in which Roethlisberger and Dickson (1939) discovered the important impact of social factors and informal groups on job satisfaction and performance. Following World War II, social psychologists, largely from Kurt Lewin's group, began to respond to what they felt were dehumanizing and dysfunctional consequences of mechanistic organizations. They were supported by the work of sociologist Robert Merton (1957) who spoke of the "bureaucratic personality." He argued that this phenomenon is exhibited among people in bureaucracies when they become fixated on the means rather than the ends of their work. Thus the petty bureaucrat, more concerned with how you filled out the form or whether you followed a confusing array of rules rather than whether you were served, can be viewed as a victim of a social system that fosters rigid behavior. The mechanistic system was seen as authoritarian, unresponsive to individual needs, as well as unable to change and adapt. The humanistic behavioral scientists felt that these

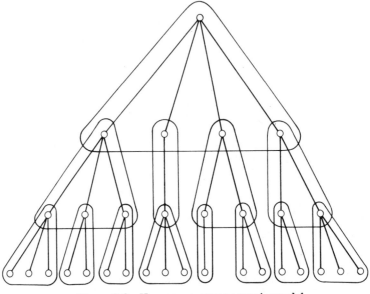

Figure 2.3   Human resources organic model

authoritarian mechanistic structures were taking a severe psychological toll on organizational members (Argyris, 1962).

The organic model emerged from the humanistic movement which held a set of cultural beliefs opposed to mechanistic systems. McGregor's (1960) Theory X and Theory Y formulations drew the battle lines. Theory X assumptions support the mechanistic model. Theory Y assumptions support the nonmechanistic model and reflect the organizational development orientation to change. The beliefs underlying the organic model are:

1. Democratic leadership and supportive leaders are most effective.

2. Employees are most productive when they can participate in decision making.

3. Openness, honesty, and trust facilitate the transfer of information.

These beliefs are backed by a fair amount of research (Coch and French, 1948; Herzberg, Mausner, and Snyderman, 1959; Likert, 1961). One of the most articulate and prolific spokesmen of this group was Rensis Likert (1961). His viewpoint is based on the following principles:

1. Individuals are motivated by higher-order needs as well as by economic needs.

2. Individuals derive their primary work satisfaction and motivation from work groups (they provide a source of norms, values, and security).

3. Therefore, work groups should be developed instead of manipulated.

4. The role of the supervisor is to develop cohesive groups and motivate them by including group members in decision making. The object would be to set high, but attainable goals and by being supportive of individual and group needs. Likert stated that: Leadership must be such as to insure a maximum probability that in all interactions and in all relationships within the organization, each member will view the experience as a supportive one which builds and maintains his sense of personal worth and importance.

5. Likert conceived of an organizational structure as pictured in Figure 2.3. It is a set of overlapping work groups with the supervisor of one group functioning as a participant in another group. The supervisor acts as the *linch pin* which holds the organization together.

Likert's ideal organization, which he calls System 4, is an organic organization which is characterized as having (Burns and Stalker, 1961):

1. A network structure of control, authority, and communication.

2. Continual adjustment of tasks through interaction with others.

3. Commitment to the organization as a whole.

4. Lateral as well as vertical interaction.

5. Communication of advice rather than orders.

6. Sanctions derived from within the community (peers and superiors) indicating a concern for the whole organization.

7. Jobs not formally defined.

Organization development grew out of this tradition and subscribes to a similar set of cultural beliefs. The method of management of change derived from this model is based on the following line of thought:

1. *Assumptions About Individuals*
(a) It is becoming increasingly true in modern societies that individuals will assert their needs for personal growth and development. These needs are most likely to be satisfied within a supportive and challenging work environment.
(b) Most workers are underutilized and are capable of taking on more responsibility for their own actions and of making a greater contribution to organizational goals than is permitted in most organizational environments. The job design, managerial

assumptions, and other factors in formal organizations frequently "demotivate" individuals.

2. *Assumptions About People in Groups*

(a) Interactive groups are highly important to people. And most people satisfy many of their needs within groups, especially the work group. The work group includes both peers and the supervisor and exerts powerful influences on the individual within the group.

(b) A work group, as such, is essentially neutral. Depending on its nature, the group can either be helpful or harmful to the organization.

(c) Work groups can greatly increase their effectiveness in meeting the needs of the individual and requirements of the organization by working together collaboratively. In order for a group to increase its effectiveness, the formal leader cannot exercise all leadership functions at all times and under all circumstances. Group members will then become more effective in assisting one another.

3. *Assumptions About People in Organizations*

(a) Since the organization is a system, changes in one subsystem (social, technological, or managerial) will affect other systems.

(b) Most people have feelings and attitudes which affect their behavior, but the culture of the organization tends to suppress the expression of these feelings and attitudes. When feelings are suppressed, problem solving, job satisfaction, and personal growth are adversely affected.

(c) In most organizations, the level of interpersonal support, trust, and cooperation is much lower than is desirable and necessary.

(d) Although "win/lose" strategies for dealing with change can be appropriate in some situations, an overreliance on "win-or-lose" approaches is destructive to both employees and the organization.

(e) Many personality clashes between individuals or groups are caused by the organizational design rather than by the individuals involved.

(f) When feelings are regarded with respect, additional avenues for improved leadership, communication, goal setting, intergroup collaboration, and job satisfaction are opened up.

(g) Shifting the emphasis of conflict resolution from manipulative "edicting" or "smoothing" to open discussion of ideas facilitates both personal growth as well as the accomplishment of organizational goals.

(h) Organizational structure and the design of jobs can be modified to meet the needs of the individual, the group, and the organization (Huse, 1975; Beckhard, 1969).

These assumptions lead to organization development change efforts which aim to achieve an organic culture in the organization. This change requires an adjustment in the values, beliefs, and attitudes of the organization's members who subscribe to mechanistic model assumptions. The focus is therefore on solving the value, ideological, or cultural problems of the group and its leader.

Early in the organization development field, a great emphasis was placed on techniques derived from T-groups or sensitivity training to "unfreeze" individuals from their mechanistic beliefs and to expose them to alternative belief systems.

Recently, organization development has shifted from this focus by first emphasizing the creation of organic structures, and then working to change the culture so that people may function better within it. In conjunction with the structural changes, team building and process consultation activites (as described by Schein, 1969; Merry and Allerhand, 1977) have become popular techniques of effecting these cultural changes These activities have their roots in sensitivity training. Such team-building activities were found to be extremely useful in the aerospace company, TRW Systems, as it implemented its complex matrix structure. Groups of managers had an organization development consultant help them learn about group dynamics as well as receive guidance in how to structure and run their teams effectively.

The weakness with this approach is that it, like the earlier mechanistic approach, implies that there is one best way for the development of an organization's structure and process. Evidence is weak that this "one best way" leads to happier people or to greater productivity in a wide range of organizations (Porras and Berg, 1978).

The Political Model

A model which captures the political nature of organizations is presented in Figure 2.4. Organizations can be viewed as political arenas in which multiple coalitions vie for control of the organization's resources and the uses to which they will be put. Cyert and March (1963) developed a theory which asserted that multiple coalitions vie for control of the organization through ongoing processes of bargaining and coalition formation.

Henry Mintzberg (1977) developed a framework for analyzing organizations as political systems in which he divides the participants into an external coalition and an internal coalition. The external coalition is made up of the participants listed in Figure 2.4 who vie for power from outside the structure. The internal coalition is made up of full-time employees or organizational "members who have responsibility and take actions (Mintzberg, 1977, p. 4)." In addition, there is a role called peak coordinator (PK) made up of top management.

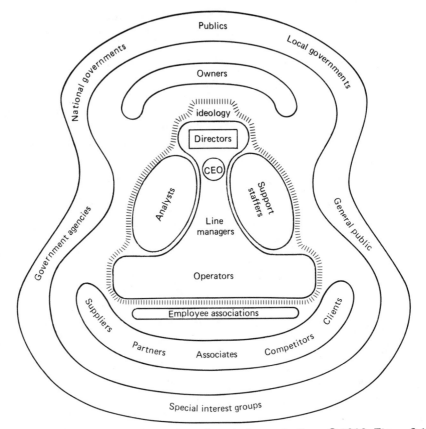

Figure 2.4   (H. Mintzberg, *Power in and around organizations.* © 1983, Figure 3.1. Reprinted by permission from Prentice-Hall.)

Mintzberg developed a typology of power configurations that defines an organization according to its dominating coalitions. The six types are:

1. *Commander power configuration*, in which the organization is the instrument of the founding entrepreneur. The peak coordinator is the center of power, possesses dominant control over the internal coalition, and deals with a weak external coalition. Henry Ford, the founder of the Ford Motor Company, operated this way throughout his reign as CEO.

2. *Continuous chain power configuration*, "in which a dominant external influence, usually the power and the peak coordinator (Mintzberg, 1977, p. 24)" are the dominant coalition. Examples include closely held corporations or subsidiaries of larger organizations.

3. *Closed system power configuration*, in which the external coali-

tion is passive. The power passes to the internal coalition with a peak coordinator willing to "rely largely on bureaucratic control." Top and middle management design the organization and bureaucratic controls. Examples include "widely-held corporations, public service bureaucracies, and government itself (Mintzberg, 1977, p. 25)."

4. *Missionary power configuration*, in which "an ideology, centered on a mission and usually a charismatic leader (present or past), dominates all organizational decisions and actions (Mintzberg, 1977, p. 27)." The dominant coalition is made up of the peak coordinator and the internal coalition who identify strongly with their mission. Reverend Sun Myung Moon's Unification Church represents this type of organization.

5. *Professional power configuration*, in which the professionals who perform the key organizational work are dominant. These members of the internal coalition are the center of power leading to much political activity with "empire building being the most popular game (Mintzberg, 1977, p. 28)." Examples include hospitals, schools, research laboratories, etc.

6. *Conflictive power configuration*, in which both the external coalition and the internal coalition are divided and politicized. "The organization is a political arena that at best satisfies a whole set of constraints, at worst, spins its wheels intensely in futile political activity" (Mintzberg, 1977, p. 29).

The political model of organizations leads to change strategies based on making political adjustments between coalitions. Negotiation and bargaining become the focus of change activities. The weakness of this model is that it leaves the technical production problem and the cultural problem unresolved. Thus, the need for an organizational model which incorporates all three problems. Chapter 3 presents such a model.

CONCLUSION

This chapter has argued that models are needed for a systematic approach to strategic management of change. In this chapter, the reader was urged to construct his/her own model for viewing an organization. Three models which represent major points of view in the management and organizational literature were presented to function as comparison templates for the reader's own model and for the model to be presented in the following chapter.

APPENDIX TO CHAPTER TWO: BUILDING YOUR OWN ORGANIZATIONAL MODEL

Pre-step One.   The Westinghouse Corporation Case*†

During the 1970s, Westinghouse Corporation, a 95-year-old company with an international reputation in appliances, power products, and industrial equipment, faced some tough times. One calamity after another seemed to strike the corporation; not only had it made a series of bad acquisitions, it had also become involved in a nasty bribery case. To make matters worse, it lost a great deal on consumer appliances and is still suffering smartly from a costly agreement to supply uranium under fixed-price contracts which some estimate will cost the corporation close to a billion dollars in the end.

During the 1970s, the corporation organized itself into four major companies—International, Power Systems, Industry Products, and Public Systems—and consequently eliminated the unprofitable appliance business from its fold. By 1978 Westinghouse was able to pull itself up by its bootstraps and achieve a modest income-before-taxes of $402.9 million.

Seriously concerned about his company's competitive strengths and position, Vice Chairman Danforth at the annual senior executive meeting in 1979 appointed T. J. Murrin, President of Westinghouse's Public Systems Company, to chair an ad hoc committee, the purpose of which was to explore ways to increase productivity. Corporate funds totaling $22 million were allocated for this effort.

Murrin, a former college football player in the mid-1950s, commands a lot of respect at Westinghouse; he turned the corporate "dog," Public Systems Company, an unpromising collection of defense electronics, soft drink bottling, real estate, and other operations, into the fastest growing company in Westinghouse. Realizing the need to size up the competition, Murrin, along with Bill Coates, President of the Construction Group in the Public Systems Company, undertook a worldwide analysis of competition practices and states of the art in productivity improvement. From this information both short and long-term strategic plans were to be formulated for Westinghouse.

A year later, with some productivity programs in progress, Murrin convened the senior management staff and delivered the following address:

---

*This case has been written for classroom use and is based on actual organizational situations. Case written by Chet Borucki, under the direction of Professor Noel Tichy.

†Pre the first step in the model building activity is to read the Westinghouse case. This is so that you will have an organization in mind when building your organizational model. *Read the case before proceeding to Step 2.*

During the past year I was able to observe first-hand how productivity improvement (PI) was developing across the corporation. I have a good feeling, a feeling that we are embarking on a decade of determination in productivity improvement. The $22 million we have committed to 84 PI projects has resulted in the organization of more than 600 quality circles in our plants, with three being added every day. Our Robotics subcommittee is targeting 200 robots for on-line activity by the end of the year. And our Value Engineering Sub-committee is exploring techniques which may potentially reduce costs by 30%. You are to be congratulated for your efforts.

At this point, Murrin's tone turned chilly:

Frankly, gentlemen, my perspective of our competitive strength and position is tempered with caution and concern after gazing about the boardrooms, offices, laboratories and factories of our competition over the past year, from Fairfield, to Dallas, to Munich, to Tokyo, and around much of the rest of the world. What I see is both exciting and alarming, in particular, findings in Japan scare the hell out of me.

First, on the home front, General Electric posted a 50% gain in their production rate from 1978–80, increasing productivity from 2.5% in 1978 to 6% in 1980. Their program is supported by computer aided design, robotics, microelectronics, and advances in new plastics and materials.

Then there's Texas Instruments. Their PI is running at a 9.5% annual level. T.I. has one module of computing power per exempt employee and furthermore possesses a worldwide electronics mail and communications network capable of handling 25,000 messages daily at the extremely economical cost of 4¢/message. T.I. projects savings alone from electronic mail for fiscal 1980 to be $31.3 million, with the largest savings of $13.6 million coming from the management and administration area.

What is truly astonishing is this international pace of productivity improvement. In Germany, Siemens in 1979 invested $140 million in manufacturing technology, providing for a 50% increase in manufacturing process, engineering, and R&D expenditures. Siemens also uses electronic mail and may eventually become a major supplier in office automation in the 1980s. The Dutch, French, and Italians are following suit, forging ahead in electronics and robotics.

Looking to the east, the Koreans also represent exemplary competition. The Hundae shipyard in South Korea contracted for the delivery of four supertankers even before ground was broken for the shipyard. By the second year, the shipyard facilities were completed, and the first supertanker was delivered on schedule in the third year. The same company, Hundae, contracted for transformers for a Nigerian power station before the facility was built, again delivering on schedule.

In terms of productivity, Japan is currently the world benchmark, stressing high quality and masterfully integrating technology, people, and value engineering. Toyota produces 2,700 cars per day, utilizing 1.6 man days of labor per car compared to Germany's 2.7 and America's

3.8 man days. Toyota now has 220 robots in operation with 700 more due to be added to production lines over the next three years. Robotics are a key part of the Kanban system, which has effectively reduced the backlog of work in process by 85% with capacity for responding quickly to consumer volume and mix desires. This payoff has caused sharp pains in the U.S. auto industry in the first half of 1980 Toyota alone produced as many units as the total United States.

Murrin, in a worldwide analysis of electronics and computer productivity discovered these results:

1. Fujitsu, a leading computer outfit, predicts it will be the world leader by the end of the 1980s. Its overseas sales have increased by 36% accompanied by a 20% productivity improvement.

2. Japanese printed circuit board production (PCB) has a productivity rate ten times greater in terms of area of board per month workers than our Baltimore facility. When Baltimore produces 1,200 styles of PCB, using 15 mil spacing and 15 mil lines, Nippon electric can produce up to 17,000 styles of PCB using 4 mil lines and 4 mil spacing and in smaller lot sizes. "The good news," says Murrin, "is that U.S. Defense Department will upgrade our specifications and technology to match or better the Japanese in PCBs. Nevertheless, some 70% of integrated circuits currently used in defense systems are actually manufactured in Thailand, the Philippines, Malaysia, Singapore, and Hong Kong. Motorola alone has 25,000 employees in Malaysia."

Terming typical U.S. productivity gains of 2 to 3% in industry as "inadequate" compared to the average of 10% in Japan, Murrin went on to cite specific reasons why Westinghouse's sights should be higher.

1. Sony's plant outside of San Diego achieved a worldwide record of 200 days of assembly-line productivity without a major defect, all accomplished with a 100% American labor force.

2. Matsushita recently took over a Motorola plant in Chicago, and, with the same direct labor force minus 50% of the white collar staff, doubled the daily rate of Quasar sets from 1,000 to 2,000 units, and also reduced the in-plant rejection rate from 60 to 3.8% with a foreseeable target of 1%. Annual warranty costs reduced from the astronomical level of $17 million to $3 million with consistent improvement. The major element responsible for these incredible improvements was a $20-million investment in simple mechanization aids. Matsushita gave their employees good tools. They planned and analyzed processes and equipment extremely carefully. Any new equipment, once installed, was reexamined thoroughly to make sure it was being used optimally. One hundred percent incoming inspection for components, parts,

and materials was enforced, stressing defect prevention versus defect detection. Suppliers readily responded to changes in quality philosophy.

The process and manufacturing engineers work hand in hand with design engineers with open lines of communication and training from the top down through rank and file, promoting quality awareness and excellent employee atmosphere. A 40-year service employee, when asked about what it's like to work for the Japanese, responded; "After noting that you could eat off the factory floor, they're just great! They've given us pride in our work." Viewing the Japanese style of management, Westinghouse executives think participation is a secret of Japanese success. Coates exclaims:

> When you visit Japanese factories and see everyone, but everyone, working like tigers to make that product more reliable at a lower cost, it's awesome. They even come back early from breaks. In factory after factory, everyone inside is trying to whip us. If we don't get that attitude, we literally won't survive.

As a result of his travels and observations, Murrin formed his plan of what Westinghouse must consider:

1. Raise sights; higher goals can be achieved. The 5.1% target for productivity improvement doesn't have to be our limit.

2. Stress quality; the Profit Impact Marketing Strategy (PIMS) shows us that companies with higher quality products than their competitors are the most profitable in all business climates, even in a recession (Figure 2A.1).

Secrets to Japanese success in quality and productivity lie in four basic areas: (1) facilities, (2) materials, (3) training, and (4) methods.

1. Facilities
   We must provide our employees with the best tools and equipment possible.

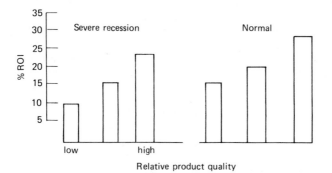

Figure 2A.1 Profit Impact Marketing Strategy (PIMS)

We must study the state of the art both at home and around the world.

We will have 12 productivity improvement subcommittees mandated to do this.

We will invest $2 billion in plant and equipment over the next five years, which must be spent to improve productivity as much as possible.

2. Materials

    The Japanese almost universally practice 100% incoming inspection.

    Stress defect prevention as opposed to defect detection. It costs much more to replace failed parts than to pay a little more for reliable ones.

    Westinghouse currently is sent *second-line* products because they meet our acceptable quality levels. Japan gets *first-line* products.

    We measure defects per thousand, Japan measures defects per million.

3. Training

    In Japan, employees are trained for weeks. Each employee is taught why as well as how.

    The importance of quality is stressed: "If there is top quality, all else will follow—productivity, profitability, security." Japanese quote: "We train people, people will grow, and the company will grow with the growth of its people."

4. Methods

    Have close liaison among engineering, manufacturing, and marketing.

    "Value engineering should be a way of life in U.S. business disciplines."

Murrin concluded his address with the following mandate:

The Management Committee, as you all know, implemented the seed fund concept so initial productivity improvement efforts would not be restricted by established budgeting constraints. However, corporate seed monies available next year will be less than monies available this year. You are expected to include productivity improvement programs in your profit and strategic plans. You should start now, if you haven't already, to

1. Describe your productivity improvement programs.

2. Justify the necessary funding and other resources.

3. Incorporate these into all of your future profit and strategic plans.

You must be challenged and hopefully motivated by our recent findings of competitive capabilities and trends. Your mission is to:

1. Raise your PI objectives to at least 6.1% per year.

2. Expand substantially the technology, people, and value engineering efforts.

3. Greatly increase emphasis on top quality by applying proven Japanese practices.

Though headquarters help will be available for the short term, the great majority of your funds must be justified in your respective profit and strategic plans. Your future success will increasingly depend on your productivity improvement and operating margin performance.

Good Luck, Gentlemen!

Diagnosing Complex Organizations: A Model Building Exercise

You are to follow the steps in the exercise to build your own organizational model. Once this is complete you may share this model in a small group discussion.

Introduction. Organizations are complex. They offer a rich array of data even for casual observers. When people are working to improve organizational conditions this array of data becomes even more obvious. In order to adequately diagnose current organizational conditions one is forced to select information from all that is available. Different people choose different kinds of information, and that selection has profound consequences on the diagnoses they make.

It is as if a room were surrounded by keyholes, each providing a different perspective. Because of limited time and resources and our own biases, each of us chooses just a few keyholes. The purpose of this activity is to help you understand the keyholes you use in diagnosing organizational situations. By identifying the keyholes you use, hopefully you will be able to question them, explore alternatives, and recognize your own idiosyncrasies in diagnosing organizations and planning strategies for the organization's improvement.

This exercise goes beyond simply helping you explore the way you look at organizations; it provides you with a way to understand and further develop your own personal model of organizational functioning. Your personal model of organizations is based on your experience of organizational reality. The exercise will help you organize and systematize this experience.

There are four steps to this exercise; each requires some tough-minded self-analysis. The result of these four steps will be a greater understanding of how you approach organizational diagnosis.

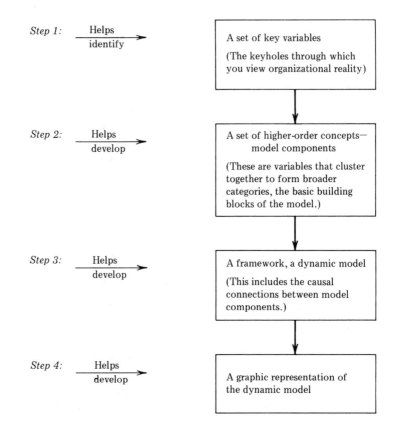

Step 1: $\xrightarrow[\text{identify}]{\text{Helps}}$ A set of key variables

(The keyholes through which you view organizational reality)

Step 2: $\xrightarrow[\text{develop}]{\text{Helps}}$ A set of higher-order concepts—model components

(These are variables that cluster together to form broader categories, the basic building blocks of the model.)

Step 3: $\xrightarrow[\text{develop}]{\text{Helps}}$ A framework, a dynamic model

(This includes the causal connections between model components.)

Step 4: $\xrightarrow[\text{develop}]{\text{Helps}}$ A graphic representation of the dynamic model

Consolidated Statements of Income and Retained Earnings Westinghouse Electric Corporation			
Year Ended December 31	1980	1979	1978
Statement of Income (in millions)			
Sales and operating revenues	$8,514.3	$7,443.1	$6,779.8
Cost of sales	6,486.4	5,706.2	5,152.6
Distribution, administration and general expenses	1,352.7	1,163.7	1,030.0
Depreciation	185.0	160.0	149.0
Operating costs and expenses	8,024.1	7,029.9	6,331.6
Operating profit	490.2	413.2	448.2
Equity in income of finance subsidiary and other affiliates	24.0	15.7	44.5
Other income	104.0	74.1	17.6
Interest expense	(61.7)	(43.7)	(41.4)
Income before income taxes and minority interest	556.5	459.3	468.9
Income taxes	(151.5)	(125.7)	(154.4)
Minority interest	(2.1)	(2.5)	(3.2)
Income before extraordinary loss	402.9	331.1	311.3
Extraordinary loss from uranium litigation, net of income taxes of $367.0 and $69.9	—	(405.0)	(67.9)
Net income (loss)	$ 402.9	$ (73.9)	$ 243.4
Earnings per common share:			
Income before extraordinary loss	$ 4.71	$ 3.85	$ 3.59
Extraordinary loss, net of income taxes	—	(4.72)	(.78)
Net income (loss) per common share	$ 4.71	$ (.87)	$ 2.81
Statement of Retained Earnings (in millions)			
Retained earnings at beginning of year	$1,546.7	$1,704.5	$1,545.5
Net income (loss)	402.9	(73.9)	243.4
Dividends declared on preferred stock	(.6)	(.6)	(.6)
Dividends declared on common stock	(119.0)	(83.3)	(83.8)
Retained earnings at end of year	$1,830.0	$1,546.7	$1,704.5

Certain Statement of Income amounts for years prior to 1980
have been reclassified for comparative purposes.

Consolidated Balance Sheet Westinghouse Electric Corporation

At December 31 (in millions)	1980	1979
Assets		
Cash	$ 111.0	$ 65.9
Marketable securities at cost, which approximates market	742.3	851.7
Customer receivables	1,475.2	1,462.1
Inventories	1,013.1	1,092.3
Costs of uncompleted contracts in excess of related billings	254.0	258.7
Income taxes refundable	33.9	145.2
Uranium settlements assets	45.4	52.1
Deferred current income taxes	68.7	126.4
Prepaid and other assets	374.6	313.0
Total current assets	4,118.2	4,367.4
Investments	704.0	712.8
Plant and equipment	1,714.1	1,463.0
Other assets	276.3	278.0
Total assets	$6,812.6	$6,821.2
Liabilities and Stockholders' Equity		
Short-term loans and current portion of long-term debt	$ 138.1	$ 109.1
Accounts payable	470.9	559.8
Accrued employe compensation	278.3	251.3
Income taxes currently payable	99.1	107.2
Billings on uncompleted contracts in excess of inventoried costs	1,273.9	1,380.3
Estimated future costs of uranium litigation	81.3	147.7
Other liabilities	921.4	824.0
Total current liabilities	3,263.0	3,379.4
Estimated future costs of uranium litigation, non-current	353.8	538.6
Other non-current liabilities	233.8	177.9
Debentures and other long-term debt	326.7	344.1
Deferred non-current income taxes	59.4	84.6
Minority interest	29.9	30.5
Redeemable preferred stock	16.1	16.1
Common stock	277.1	277.1
Paid-in capital	503.9	498.1
Common stock held in treasury	(81.1)	(71.9)
Retained earnings	1,830.0	1,546.7
Total common stockholders' equity	2,529.9	2,250.0
Total liabilities and stockholders' equity	$6,812.6	$6,821.2

Certain 1979 amounts have been reclassified for comparative purposes.

Consolidated Statement of Changes in Financial Position Westinghouse Electric Corporation

Year Ended December 31 (in millions)	1980	1979	1978
Source of funds			
Income before extraordinary loss	$ 402.9	$331.1	$311.3
Depreciation	185.0	160.0	149.0
Equity in income of finance subsidiary and other affiliates	(24.0)	(15.7)	(44.5)
Deferred non-current income taxes	(25.2)	(14.3)	(37.6)
Minority interest	2.1	2.5	3.2
Funds from operations before extraordinary loss	540.8	463.6	381.4
Extraordinary loss from uranium litigation, net of income taxes	—	(405.0)	(67.9)
Estimated future costs of uranium litigation, non-current	—	414.4	96.8
Reduction in non-current marketable securities	79.3	(2.7)	(133.9)
Issuance of common stock to employes	32.4	30.4	29.6
Transfer of prepaid pension contributions, non-current	16.0	28.8	(59.9)
Fixed asset reduction to realizable value	—	—	80.0
Other non-current items, net	82.2	98.3	122.1
Decrease in current assets:			
Income taxes refundable	111.3	(145.2)	—
Inventories and costs of uncompleted contracts			
in excess of related billings	83.9	(62.5)	(69.5)
Deferred current income taxes	57.7	(150.5)	(7.6)
Uranium settlements assets	6.7	(52.1)	—
Increase in other liabilities, current	106.0	11.9	187.7
Other current items, net	47.8	57.4	22.1
Total source of funds	1,164.1	286.8	580.9
Use of funds			
Expenditures for new and improved facilities	446.0	317.0	235.0
Reduction in estimated future costs of uranium			
litigation, non-current	184.8	—	—
Dividends	119.6	83.9	84.4
Reduction of debentures and other long-term debt	51.3	33.4	64.0
Increase in investments	46.5	(90.8)	47.4
Purchase of common stock for treasury	35.7	45.7	43.4
Decrease in current liabilities:			
Billings on uncompleted contracts in			
excess of inventoried costs	106.4	(102.4)	(181.1)
Accounts payable	88.9	(27.4)	(94.1)
Estimated future costs of uranium litigation	66.4	(108.9)	(4.5)
Income taxes currently payable	8.1	24.2	(67.9)
Increase in current assets:			
Prepaid and other assets	61.6	45.7	(25.2)
Customer receivables	13.1	85.6	183.1
Total use of funds	1,228.4	306.0	284.5
Increase (decrease) in cash and marketable securities	$ (64.3)	$(19.2)	$296.4

Westinghouse Consolidated Balance Sheet

Assets

(Amounts in thousands)	At December 31	
	1977	1976
Current Assets:		
Cash	$ 116,910	$ 116,390
Marketable securities at cost, which approximates market	523,538	469,110
Customer receivables (less $26 million and $25 million doubtful account allowances)	1,193,412	1,169,376
Inventories (Note 7)	915,500	992,552
Costs of uncompleted contracts in excess of related billings (Note 8)	303,491	177,297
Prepaid and other current assets (Note 4)	292,423	312,010
Total current assets	3,345,274	3,236,735
Investments (Note 9)	559,342	386,505
Plant and equipment, net (Note 10)	1,353,104	1,375,028
Other assets (Note 11)	269,908	320,074
Total assets	$5,527,628	$5,318,342

Liabilities and Stockholders' Equity

(Amounts in thousands)	At December 31	
	1977	1976
Current Liabilities:		
Short-term loans and current portion of long-term debt (Note 12)	$ 74,692	$ 115,819
Accounts payable—trade	438,304	407,076
Accrued payrolls and payroll deductions	206,112	220,998
Income taxes currently payable	63,428	135,616
Deferred current income taxes	31,723	24,861
Billings on uncompleted contracts in excess of inventoried costs (Note 8)	1,096,778	984,099
Other current liabilities	658,767	547,330
Total current liabilities	2,569,804	2,435,799
Non-current liabilities	90,070	42,251
Deferred non-current income taxes	136,461	127,449
Debentures and other long-term debt (Note 13)	408,528	500,913
Minority interest	28,852	73,495
Stockholders' Equity (Note 16):		
Cumulative preferred stock	16,092	16,092
Common stock	277,108	277,108
Capital in excess of par value	497,715	494,165
Retained earnings	1,545,536	1,380,033
Less: Treasury stock, at cost	(42,538)	(28,963)
Total stockholders' equity	2,293,913	2,128,435
Total liabilities and stockholders' equity	$5,527,628	$5,318,342

The financial information on pages 31
through 43 is an integral part of these
financial statements.

Westinghouse Financial Information by Segments

(Amounts in thousands)

Earnings Information for the Year Ended December 31:	1977	1976	1975	1974	1973
Sales to unaffiliated customers:					
Power Systems	$2,254,238	$2,052,537	$1,983,103	$1,803,389	$1,623,259
Industry Products	2,256,737	2,083,846	1,939,249	2,010,849	1,635,344
Public Systems	1,404,971	1,315,826	1,297,842	1,405,672	1,387,732
Broadcasting	175,821	172,350	145,816	138,354	123,075
Other	45,894	520,593	496,737	440,249	331,713
	$6,137,661	$6,145,152	$5,862,747	$5,798,513	$5,101,123
Intersegment sales:					
Power Systems	$ 109,436	$ 100,659	$ 91,863	$ 94,361	$ 75,140
Industry Products	60,292	54,237	56,870	123,139	68,175
Public Systems	10,692	10,250	18,794	23,508	9,142
Other	29,151	25,718	32,491	17,351	57,176
	$ 209,571	$ 190,864	$ 200,018	$ 258,359	$ 209,633
Total revenue:					
Power Systems	$2,363,674	$2,153,196	$2,074,966	$1,897,750	$1,698,399
Industry Products	2,317,029	2,138,083	1,996,119	2,133,988	1,703,519
Public Systems	1,415,663	1,326,076	1,316,636	1,429,180	1,396,874
Broadcasting	175,821	172,350	145,816	138,354	123,075
Other	75,045	546,311	529,228	457,600	388,889
	6,347,232	6,336,016	6,062,765	6,056,872	5,310,756
Eliminations	(209,571)	(190,864)	(200,018)	(258,359)	(209,633)
	$6,137,661	$6,145,152	$5,862,747	$5,798,513	$5,101,123
Operating profit:					
Power Systems	$ 113,700	$ 113,095	$ 67,443	$ 43,739	$ 143,839
Industry Products	220,591	198,865	193,782	186,029	166,371
Public Systems	68,853	49,298	59,837	66,554	62,456
Broadcasting	52,444	52,000	41,705	39,626	38,733
Other	(15,313)	6,522	(4,525)	5,731	(11,773)
Adjustments and eliminations	(10,744)	(13,518)	5,747	(3,618)	(4,688)
	429,531	406,262	363,989	338,061	394,938
Equity in income (loss) from non-consolidated subsidiaries and affiliated companies	34,001	21,050	(4,513)	(32,285)	3,341
Other income	128,000	88,089	70,374	71,890	63,567
General corporate expenses	(118,517)	(101,849)	(78,514)	(60,237)	(60,566)
Interest expense	(46,107)	(52,347)	(76,425)	(111,261)	(69,317)
Income before taxes	$ 426,927	$ 361,205	$ 274,911	$ 206,168	$ 331,963

Asset Information at December 31:	1977	1976	1975	1974	1973
Identifiable assets:					
Power Systems	$2,034,111	$1,741,644	$1,652,565	$1,651,332	$1,542,014
Industry Products	1,101,559	998,810	970,790	1,002,317	923,045
Public Systems	662,809	696,345	731,198	759,716	886,554
Broadcasting	103,845	99,909	103,773	88,890	96,858
Other	95,529	509,315	526,969	520,180	323,655
Adjustments and eliminations	(76,131)	(67,486)	(58,489)	(60,433)	(43,813)
	3,921,722	3,978,537	3,926,806	3,962,002	3,728,313
Investments	559,342	386,505	289,188	226,209	183,575
Corporate assets	1,046,564	953,300	650,292	625,407	696,799
	$5,527,628	$5,318,342	$4,866,286	$4,813,618	$4,608,687

61

Financial Information by Segments Westinghouse Electric Corporation

Earnings Information (in millions)	1980	1979	1978
Sales and operating revenues:			
Power Systems	$2,998.2	$2,675.7	$2,541.7
Industry Products	3,227.4	2,907.9	2,641.3
Public Systems	2,245.2	1,805.8	1,562.9
Broadcasting	266.5	218.9	202.5
Other	115.4	105.0	95.0
	8,852.7	7,713.3	7,043.4
Intersegment sales	(338.4)	(270.2)	(263.6)
	$8,514.3	$7,443.1	$6,779.8
Operating profit:			
Power Systems	$ 272.6	$ 234.7	$ 210.9
Industry Products	218.8	199.7	235.7
Public Systems	114.6	90.3	106.5
Broadcasting	64.4	59.3	58.3
Other	(2.2)	(13.2)	(9.0)
Adjustments and eliminations	(16.0)	(14.6)	(19.7)
Segment operating profit	652.2	556.2	582.7
General corporate expenses	162.0	143.0	134.5
	490.2	413.2	448.2
Equity in income of finance,			
subsidiary and other affiliates	24.0	15.7	44.5
Other income	104.0	74.1	17.6
Interest expense	(61.7)	(43.7)	(41.4)
Income before income taxes			
and minority interest	$ 556.5	$ 459.3	$ 468.9

Asset Information (in millions)	1980	1979	1978
Segment identifiable assets:			
Power Systems	$1,899.7	$1,979.1	$2,087.4
Industry Products	1,576.4	1,487.9	1,259.9
Public Systems	1,069.2	893.5	753.9
Broadcasting	204.5	135.4	113.9
Other	19.6	68.0	65.5
Adjustments and eliminations	(120.1)	(113.5)	(92.5)
	4,649.3	4,450.4	4,188.1
Investments	704.0	712.8	785.2
Corporate assets	1,459.3	1,658.0	1,320.2
Total assets	$6,812.6	$6,821.2	$6,293.5

Sales and Operating Revenues and Operating Profit for 1979 and 1978
have been reclassified for comparative purposes.

62

Step One. Key Variables

In beginning to diagnose the effectiveness of the organization you described, you would find yourself looking at certain variables and ignoring others. In other words, you'd be asking questions, reviewing records, observing behaviors, and so on—performing activities you believed were central to assessing the effectiveness of the organization.

An initial list of variables is presented below. Place a check mark beside any of the items you would actually use in beginning to diagnose the effectiveness of the organization. Add variables of your own if the list is incomplete from your viewpoint.

1. _____ Formal authority structure

2. _____ Informal reward system

3. _____ Span of control

4. _____ Work process—technology and organization of tasks

5. _____ Informal groupings

6. _____ Relation of system to external factors—market/government

7. _____ Formal reward system

8. _____ Selection of staff

9. _____ Training

10. _____ Organizational culture; norms and values of system members

11. _____ Fiscal characteristics—assets, profits

12. _____ Turnover

13. _____ Satisfaction of members with their jobs

14. _____ Performance evaluation; individuals

15. _____ Performance evaluation and appraisal of organizational units

16. _____ Satisfaction of members with interpersonal relations

17. _____ Goals of system

18. _____ Resource limitations

19. _____ Information channels

20. _____ Political leadership

21. _____ Informal leadership

22. _____ Control systems

23. _____

24. _____

25. _____

26. _____

27. _____

28. _____

29. _____

30. _____

31. _____

32. _____

33. _____

34. _____

35. _____

Step Two.   Forming Higher-Order Concepts/Categories

Refer to Step One while working on Step Two. The task in Step Two is to arrange the information you have listed as necessary (those items you checked and added) into categories. Look over the items you checked to see if they fall into groupings. Place the items which seem to you to "hang together" in the spaces provided. Finally, give each grouping a descriptive name in the space provided.

1. New category name: _____ (Include information items below) Briefly state why items fall into this group: _____ _____ _____	2. New category name: _____ (Include information items below) Briefly state why items fall into this group: _____ _____ _____
3. New category name: _____ (Include information items below) Briefly state why items fall into this group: _____ _____ _____	4. New category name: _____ (Include information items below) Briefly state why items fall into this group: _____ _____ _____
5. New category name: _____ (Include information items below) Briefly state why items fall into this group: _____ _____ _____	6. New category name: _____ (Include information items below) Briefly state why items fall into this group: _____ _____ _____
7. New category name: _____ (Include information items below) Briefly state why items fall into this group: _____ _____ _____	8. New category name: _____ (Include information items below) Briefly state why items fall into this group: _____ _____ _____

Step Three. Dynamic Relationships of Organizational Components: Developing an Organizational Model

Individual Portion (estimated time: 30 minutes). Refer to the preceding pages during this activity. In Step Three, you are interested in the relationships between the categories you have just created. Sometimes these categories affect each other in such a way that if one changes others may change also. Now is the time to consider the effects that a change in one category has on each of the other categories.

First, list each category name in the appropriately numbered space in the left-hand column below. Then imagine that the elements in Category 1 have undergone a major change; assign each of the other categories (writing in the category name) to one of the three spaces to the right of Category 1 to indicate the likely effects of the change in Category 1. Do this for all the remaining categories you have listed.

	Assign other categories to these three columns		
Write each of your category names (from the previous pages) in the spaces below	Likely to show a great deal of change	Likely to show moderate change	Likely to show little or no change
1.			
2.			
3.			
4.			
5.			
6.			
7.			
8.			

Step Four.   Mapping Your Organizational Model

You are now ready to graphically depict your personal organizational model.

Procedure

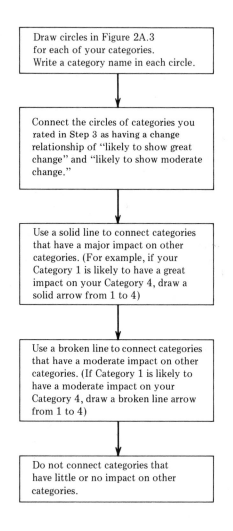

Draw circles in Figure 2A.3
for each of your categories.
Write a category name in each circle.

Connect the circles of categories you
rated in Step 3 as having a change
relationship of "likely to show great
change" and "likely to show moderate
change."

Use a solid line to connect categories
that have a major impact on other
categories. (For example, if your
Category 1 is likely to have a great
impact on your Category 4, draw a
solid arrow from 1 to 4)

Use a broken line to connect categories
that have a moderate impact on other
categories. (If Category 1 is likely to
have a moderate impact on your
Category 4, draw a broken line arrow
from 1 to 4)

Do not connect categories that
have little or no impact on other
categories.

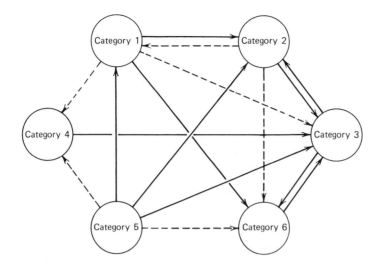

——→ Likely to show moderate change.
——→ Likely to show great change.

Figure 2A.3 Example of how to map your organizational model (draw circles to represent categories).

Step Five.   Applying Your Model to the Westinghouse Case

In this section you will use your new organizational model to analyze the Westinghouse case.

Part I of the Diagnosis.   Specify the findings relative to the categories of your model. In order to accomplish this, list the categories of your model in the left-hand column below, keeping in mind the specific items of information within each category (refer back to the labels you included in each category). List the key findings from the case.

Categories of My Model	Key Findings

Part II of the Diagnosis. Assess the degree of fit or alignment between the categories of your model. That is, looking at the model as a dynamic set of interrelated components, how well does it fit together? Which components carried out in Part I of the diagnosis and in the model in the model building exercise.

Draw your model below in a diagram fashion. Using the findings in the case in Part I, assess the alignments and list them below the diagram. Where you have components out of alignment specify the nature of the problem you have uncovered.

Summary of Alignments, Alignment of:	Need for Alignment (yes/no)	If Alignment Needed, Specify Nature of Change Required
Components 1 and 2		
Components 1 and 3		
Components 1 and 4		
Components 1 and 5		
Components 1 and 6		
Components 1 and 7		

Chapter Three

The Role of Social Networks

INTRODUCTION

Social networks play an important role in business organizations:

> Lee Iacocca was ousted as Ford Motor Company President, insiders say because he failed in Henry Ford's view to develop support through presence and grace and social relationships. It is said that Iacocca didn't like the passive role of deferring credit to Henry Ford II and he didn't like socializing and small talk.

> His successor was No. 2 man of Ford, Philip Caldwell, who developed social and professional contacts that helped lead to influence (McGill, 1978; Kadushin, 1978).

and in service organizations such as New York University, in which Baldridge (1971) found that:

> The decision process, then, is taken out of the hands of the individuals (although there are still many who are powerful) and placed into a network that allows a cumulative build-up of expertise and advice . . . A complex network of committees, councils, and advisory bodies grows up to handle the task of assembling the expertise for reasonable decisions . . . one of the most important practical implications emerging from this study is the importance of maintaining the "decision network" (pp. 190, 206).

as well as in communities, in which it was found that:

> a core group of 47 people . . . emerged as the group that runs Detroit . . . almost all 47 persons who hold Detroit power have at least one-third of their partners in common, and the proportion of overlap at the very top of the power list is even greater . . . . This leadership circle can be split into two circles. One circle consists of the usual men or power-businessmen, corporate leaders, and the socially prominent . . . The second circle includes some politicians and lawyers who many experts would expect to form the core of government . . . This tightly knit second group is more than half black and includes a number of labor union leaders with a consistent background of militant, left-of-center unionism.

> The two circles in many cases have diametrically opposed interests and views. And yet, lest their city disappear altogether as a place where human beings

can thrive, they have locked into a series of coalition organizations . . . (McGill, 1978; Kadushin, 1978).

Organizations can be viewed as social networks. That is, a social system composed of social objects (people and groups) which is joined by a variety of relationships. Many are not directly joined. Others are joined by multiple relationships. The social network perspective is concerned with the patterning of these relationships, such as the coalition relationships in Detroit or the decision networks at New York University. The perspective also seeks to identify both the causes and consequences of relationships (Tichy, 1980). Thus, how the Detroit coalitions came about is as important as their description.

A social network organizational model is presented in this chapter. It aims to:

1. Integrate political, technical, and cultural orientations.

2. Point to pragmatic diagnostic questions.

3. Help in the formulation of specific change strategies and, specifically, to help in the selection of change techniques in the political, technical, and cultural areas.

THE NETWORK MODEL

In this model, organizations are conceived of as clusters of people joined by a variety of links. These clusters transmit (1) goods and services —raw materials, marketing research support, and financial and accounting services among groups within a company; (2) information—exchange of ideas and knowledge among people in an organization; (3) influence —giving orders and direction both formally and informally; and (4) affect—exchanges of friendship among individuals. These clusters of people are both *formally structured* (prescribed), such as departments or work groups, and *informally structured* (emergent), such as coalitions and cliques. Prescribed networks are typically represented in organizational charts. Clear distinctions are made here between prescribed and emergent networks to emphasize the point that, within organizations, there exist a multitude of interpersonal work arrangements which arise out of many possible types of relationships. Only a portion of the organizational structure is prescribed. Thus, unplanned structures and behavior patterns generally emerge in all organizations.

Among some managers, and in much of the management and organizational literature, these emergent structures and behavior patterns have been misleadingly labeled the "informal organization" and often assumed to be something undesirable. They are, in fact, neutral and take on desirable or undesirable characteristics depending on how they are managed. For example, in some research and development laboratories, prescribed organizational charts are not maintained because all the work is done through emergent networks, that is, groups of people who interact in a variety of ways depending on the demands of the task.

Figure 3.1 presents some of the salient features of a network approach to organizations:

1. There is a focus on the formal organization—the prescribed network—thus incorporating the classical/mechanistic organization model. In addition, however, individuals are shown to have various additional links to each other and to the external environment.

2. Influence, information, affect, and goods and services are potential modes of exchange between individuals. Thus, lines in Figures 3.1 can be further specified to identify the transactional content (affect, influence, information).

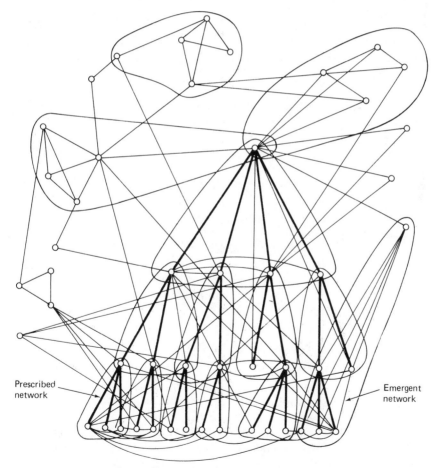

Figure 3.1   Network contingency model

3. Clusters within the network are identified by who is linked to whom (clique members, for example are all directly linked to each other via affect links).

4. The links in Figure 3.1 represent a simplification of the actual number found in most organizational settings. There is clear need for methods to formalize the interrelationships which are important aspects of networks.

The analysis of influence networks—seeing who influences whom about what—provides the concepts and tools for political analysis. Thus, in the Ford Motor Company case, Henry Ford's action to fire Lee Iacocca undoubtedly involved the formation of a coalition of board members to support Henry Ford's position. To fully understand the event one would need to map out the networks around Henry Ford. The analysis of information networks—who exchanges information with whom—provides the concepts and tools for technical analysis. In order to understand how research gets accomplished in R&D organizations, it is necessary to map the informational exchange networks. When this is done, it is possible to discover such problems as externally well-linked scientists—those who exchange information with outside scientists who have new ideas which could contribute to the R&D effort—but who are not well-linked internally. That is, scientists who don't share information with their colleagues because they do not interact with them.

Finally, the culture of an organization is best analyzed by uncovering the friendship relationships. It is through these relationships that the values and norms of the culture are largely disseminated and reinforced. Therefore, a model that represents who talks to whom about what can guide designs to alter the culture.

Figure 3.2 presents the components of the network model which guide the proposed strategic change management process. It is built on the assumption that organizational effectiveness (or output) is a function of the characteristics of each of the components of the model, as well as a function of how the components interrelate and align into a functioning system.

The Interrelationships Among Components

As has been shown, organizations are systems in dynamic interplay with their environment and their own internal parts. Although systemic thinking in organizations is the current vogue, it is very difficult to apply. To do so requires simultaneous attention to a mind-boggling array of variables. A useful analogy is to conceive of organizational components as parts of a machine. In order to analyze the machine, a systems perspective is required. The analysis should not be based on the characteristics of each machine component examined one at a time,

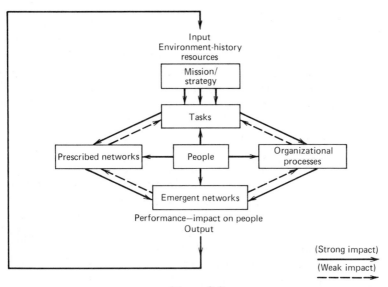

Figure 3.2

but on how well the components serve together (do the gears mesh?, are they of similar quality?, etc.). The machine's value is not based on the strength of any one component but on the combined strength of them all.

The dynamic interrelationships among the parts of the organization and the degree to which the organization fits or is aligned with its environment must be simultaneously analyzed from the three perspectives: technical, political, and cultural. The analysis is necessary for the purpose of generating answers to the following four key questions:

1. How well are the parts of the organization aligned with each other for solving the organization's *technical problems*?

2. How well are the parts of the organization aligned for solving the organization's *political problems*?

3. How well are the parts of the organization aligned for solving the organization's *cultural problems*?

4. How well aligned are the three subsystems of the organization, the *technical*, *political*, and *cultural*?

More detailed guidelines are presented in the following chapter for analyzing each of the three types of alignment. In addition, there are guidelines for assessing the relationships between the technical, political, and cultural systems.

THE COMPONENTS OF THE MODEL

This section will examine each component of the organizational model. We will start with a discussion of organizational *output* in terms of the effectiveness of an organization. Then the focus will shift to the *input* side of the model, or the organization's environment, and will be followed by a discussion of each of the remaining model components.

Output

The first focal point is *organizational effectiveness*. What is it? And how is it determined? A scanning of the literature and a brief exposure to the practical experiences of various managers will quickly lead you to the conclusion that what constitutes organizational effectiveness is certainly controversial. The discussion criteria range from adaptability-flexibility to productivity to job satisfaction of members to profitability to the ability to acquire scarce resources to control over external environment to growth to survival. The method in which I approach effectiveness is derived from the work of Richard Steers (1977), who proposed that effectiveness consists of three related components: (1) goal optimization, (2) a systems perspective, and (3) a behavioral outcome perspective. Let us look at each one:

1. *Goal optimization* evaluates organizations in relationship to their behavioral intentions. It assumes that organizations may have multiple and at times conflicting goals which require trade-offs. An example would be a trade-off between productivity and job satisfaction. In this case *goal maximization* is not possible nor even desirable. Instead goal *optimization* is appropriate. The important questions for evaluating effectiveness with regard to goal optimization are:

(a) Is the organization applying its resources toward the attainment of its goals? Or are there "unfunded" goals and "funded nongoals?" A commercial bank which professes to provide complete retail banking services and then cuts back the budget, closes branches, and pulls resources from retail banking is an example of an unfunded or *under*funded goal. This same bank may exhibit a funded nongoal by opening offices and doing a great deal of commercial business in the Mid-East when this is not one of its planned goals.

(b) Is there a clear relationship between the amount of financial resources the organization spends on a particular goal and its importance? Are behavioral intentions which are weighted as equally important receiving equal resources? Academic institutions are constantly struggling with the balance between research goals, teaching goals, and service goals.

(c) What kind of return on investment, per goal, is the organization getting on its resources?

(d) Are all parts of the organization working toward at least one of the organization's behavioral intentions? Are parts of the organization working toward goals which do not align with those of the rest of the organization?

(e) Is the organization's environment changing, and if so are the goals being readjusted?

2. *Systems perspective* emphasizes the importance of viewing the organization as an open system with interdependent parts. These parts —the components of the organizational model presented in Figure 3.2 —must be relatively consonant if effectiveness is to be achieved. There must be an alignment in each of the three subsystems: political, technical, and cultural. And these must be mutually compatible. That is, a *well-designed organization should exhibit alignment between its cultural, its political, and its technical subsystems.*

3. *Behavioral emphasis* focuses on the interface between the organization and its members, that is, the impact of the organization on its members in terms of satisfaction, quality of working life, and opportunity to grow. These all contribute to behavior and therefore to overall organizational effectiveness.

Input

Now that we have discussed the output side of the model, we will shift our focus to the input side. History and environment are two major categories of input. The third category is resources.

History.   Organizations are in some respects prisoners of their history. As a result, history can uncover material which not only helps explain why things are the way they are today but can also help us predict the future. Once, before I became aware of the importance of organization history, I made the mistake of only examining current events. For example, a hospital was close to bankruptcy. The president called me in as a consultant. I diagnosed the situation and attempted to help him and his management deal with the crisis. Ultimately, the hospital had to be bailed out by the federal government. In going to the federal government, the board of trustees implicitly admitted that poor management was one of its problems and forced the resignation of the president. My efforts had no impact on the hospital because, rather than correct the failing of the management team, the board merely fired the president—much like professional sports teams which fire the coach and leave the team intact.

Had I examined the history of the hospital, I would have observed that this had happened three other times in a span of 12 years. That is, the hospital found itself in financial trouble, went to the federal government for help, and forced the resignation of the president as a symbol of change. That is all that changed. The rest of the management remained largely intact. Organizations frequently recreate their own histories because the conditions which led to a particular behavior pattern in the past usually remain in place. This was certainly the case for the hospital, where the technical, political, and cultural systems were all historically quite stable.

These historical behavior patterns represent the way in which the organization resolves its technical, political, and cultural problems. In the case of the hospital, a technical problem of serious financial magnitude kept triggering a political response in which the hospital argued for federal funds while making a political gesture of firing its chief. Other organizations might have focused on resolving the technical problem and not on masking it as a political problem.

Historical analysis starts with an examination of the economic, political, and cultural forces which have acted on the organization in the past. For example, the coal industry operated in a boom and bust economy, which led to great technical uncertainty in the coal companies. This contrasts with a company like AT&T which historically operated in a steadily growing economy and thus developed a very certain internal technical environment. The political and cultural environment can be similarly analyzed. In the coal industry, there have been very turbulent political activities surrounding the early days of unionization and the establishment of safety regulations. In contrast, Bell Telephone has had a rather stable political environment.

The historical focus then shifts to the internal organization: to an analysis of its pattern of technical, political, and cultural cycles. These patterns help in analyzing and predicting organizational behavior. For example, even though all organizations can be said to pass through a developmental stage in which managers must mobilize people to invest energy and decide how best to harness this energy, there are substantial variations among organizations during this stage. Starting a new MacDonald's franchise is basically a *technical* problem, that is, training and organizing people to mass-produce food efficiently. Starting an innovative, idealistic health center would be primarily a cultural problem which would require finding a core group of true believers. It can be predicted, though, that an overemphasis on the cultural or ideological aspect of an organization will lead to technical problems. For example, if everyone is a true believer in the new health center, but no one has figured out how to deliver effective and efficient health care, a technical cycle will be triggered. Solving the technical problems might, in turn, trigger a political cycle because technical leaders may gain more control and upset the balance of power. These patterns are often repeated over a number of years.

In other words, depending on which cycle—technical, political, or cultural—is dominant at the organization's birth, different organizational adjustments must take place. An organization which starts at a *cultural* cycle peak will be characterized by a great deal of focus and energy invested in values. Often this cycle is managed by the actions of a highly cohesive core group following a charismatic leader. Most religious movements began this way. Other examples include innovative social welfare and health delivery organizations started by individuals committed to social change.

An organization which starts with a *technical* cycle peak, such as a manufacturer of computer terminals, must focus on the solutions of technical production problems. These solutions involve the best way to organize the work, as well as the capital and management needed to produce computer terminals.

A *political* cycle peak at the beginning of an organization's life would be characterized by a great deal of coalitional bargaining and exchange activity in determining the allocation of resources and decisions regarding organizational goals. Such is the case in organizing a union or a political party.

The predominance of any particular cycle at birth leads to predictable problems in the other cycles. An organization dominated by cultural adjustments at birth will be faced with *technical* problems when issues arise such as who does what with whom in order to produce organizational outputs. This occurred at the Martin Luther King Health Center, which was born as an idealistic innovative health delivery system (Tichy, 1977). An organization dominated by *political* adjustments at birth will soon have to come to grips with *technical* and *cultural* problems. Likewise, the technically dominated organization will end up having to make political and cultural adjustments. This often happens when the organization struggles to shift power from the entrepreneur founder to a professional management cadre.

In order to understand some of the problems faced by an organization at any given moment in time, we must look to history to find the antecedent causes. For example a massive effort to alter the technological work processes of an organization—such as the introduction of automated work procedures requiring massive reorganization, retraining, layoffs, and hirings—which was carried out in a very autocratic manner may appear to be successful in the short run but will often lead to a long-term counterreaction in the political cycle. The result might be the eventual unionization of the work force or a future inability to change work procedures.

Organizations are peppered with time bombs planted inadvertently with decisions made using a short-term perspective. They are apparently dormant at the outset, but they blow up some time in the future after another cycle has been triggered. Often, the key figures of the earlier cycle have left the scene. This is particularly true in organizations which operate under considerable managerial mobility. Managers are generally measured on short-term performance. If they want to move up rapidly, they must produce quick results. Thus, there are strong positive incentives for being expedient in the short run. These actions light the fuses for future major organizational time bombs.

Akio Marita, chairman of Sony Corporation, noted this time bomb phenomenon in *The New York Times Magazine* (4 January 1981, p. 42):

> A lot of American companies know they have old machines. But the manager figures he'll keep the old machines as long as they still run, make a big profit one year, and take the record as an advertisement to get a job elsewhere. So productivity here declined.

In sum, three aspects of history are important to analyze: (1) the political, economic, and cultural context within which the organization has operated; (2) the pattern of technical, political and cultural cycles of the organization; and (3) the identification of any planted time bombs.

Environment. Organizations are embedded in environments which provide both opportunities and constraints. The importance of environmental context to the life blood of an organization is underscored by several studies which indicate that perhaps as much as 90% of the variance in organizational performance is due to environmental context rather than administrative action or internal organization (Lieberson and O'Conner, 1972; Salancik and Pfeffer, 1978). This figure seems extreme and is as yet only supported by a few studies. Nevertheless, it provides a reminder that much of the organizational literature and conventional managerial wisdom regarding organizational performance focuses on managerial action and internal organization, and ignores environmental context. I suggest the need to return managerial attention to the environment. It is especially important in times of organizational change, when shifts in the environment often provide the major triggering impetus for change.

It is assumed that organizations are driven to seek predictability and control (Thompson, 1967). Thus, they seek to reduce uncertainty in the environment. "Uncertainty refers to the degree to which future states of the world cannot be anticipated and accurately predicted (Pfeffer and Salancik, 1978, p. 67)."

In order to analyze the performance of an organization in terms of mental context, analytic dimensions are needed for mapping environmental uncertainty. Figure 3.3 presents the relationship of several environmental dimensions to uncertainty. The first set of dimensions are categorized as structural characteristics of the environment.

1. *Concentration.* Refers to the extent to which power and the authority to control desired organizational outcomes in the environment

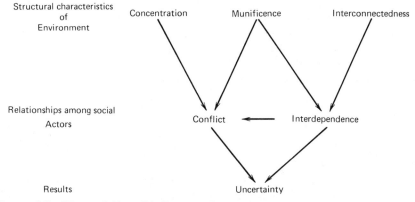

Figure 3.3 (From **Jeffrey Pfeffer** and **Gerald Salancik**, *The external control of organizations: A resource dependence perspective*, **New York: Harper & Row, 1977, p. 68.**)

is dispersed (Pfeffer and Salancik, 1978). For example, uncertainty is reduced in oligopolistic situations due to the fact that control over pricing is made easier. Thus, low concentration, non-oligopolistic situations increase uncertainty for the organization. The auto and steel industries are organizations with high concentration, whereas the consumer electronics industry—hi-fi equipment, home computers—is low on concentration.

2. *Munificence.* Refers to the availability of critical resources for the organization. An environment with scarce resources is a more uncertain environment. The scarcity of specialized labor for some industries creates uncertainty as does the availability of critical raw materials.

3. *Interconnectedness.* Refers to the extent to which organizations in the environment are linked to each other. The larger the number of the interconnections the greater the uncertainty. This is because a disturbance anywhere in a highly interconnected system will cause disturbances elsewhere in the system. It is analogous to a highly integrated electrical power system in which a blackout in one section can quickly cause a large-scale blackout in the total system. The oil industry is quite interconnected, as was shown when oil-producing OPEC nations disrupted supplies. This sent ripples all the way to the neighborhood gas station.

These structural characteristics affect the relationships among the social actors. These are the individuals and organizations with whom the organization directly interacts. As noted in Figure 3.3, these relationships can be evaluated in terms of:

4. *Interdependence.* Refers to the extent to which the organization depends on other organizations and therefore must coordinate its

actions with others. Interconnectedness of the wider environment increases the interdependence among units. Within the auto industry one can find variations. GM is not as interdependent with other organizations as is American Motors Corporation. This is because GM is much more self-contained, producing more of its own parts and components than AMC, which has to purchase parts from GM and Ford.

5. *Conflict.* Refers to the amounts of dissension over goals existing between the organization and those with whom it is in direct contact. As noted in Figure 3.3, concentration is negatively related to conflict. This is because the more concentrated the environment the more coordinated, and hence, the less conflict.

6. *Uncertainty of the Environment.* As experienced by the organization, this is directly influenced by the level of conflict and the level of interdependence.

It is important to note that the environment's impact on the organization is only partially determined by objective reality. Karl Weick (1969) points out that "the human being creates the environment to which the system then adapts. The human actor does not react to the environment, he enacts it (1969, p. 641)." People have a perception of reality which they act out. The organization's perception of its environment is a representation, therefore it can vary in its completeness and accuracy. Because the environment is so complex and can never be totally comprehended or represented, the information processing capacity of the organization and its members determines which aspects of the environment are enacted.

The major determinant of what is enacted is attention. Individuals must attend to something in order to perceive it. The attention process is largely channeled by the organization's information structure which, as Cyert and March (1963) claim, dictates what the organization members believe are the important aspects of the environment.

The characteristics of the environment presented in Figure 3.3 provide categories for focusing managerial attention on the organizational environment.

An analysis of the environment for use in managing strategic change should be based on an adequate model which addresses such questions as:

1. What is the organization dependent on?

2. When should it respond and when should it not respond to its environment?

3. How should it avoid limiting its actions in the future?

4. What are managers attending to in the environment and what are they ignoring?

Resources.   Resources represent the third category of organizational input. Four categories of resources are focal: (1) An assessment of how much capital the organization controls in terms of space, equipment, inventory, accounts receivable, and cash. (2) An assessment of the organization's technological capability for carrying out its tasks, e.g., how "state of the art" is the organization? (3) An assessment of its people resources in terms of numbers, demographic characteristics, and skills. (4) An assessment of the reputation and level of goodwill attributed to the organization. This is a subjective measure, but one which often is a critical organizational resource accounting for the overall effectiveness of an organization.

Mission/Strategy.   Figure 3.2 shows a component labeled "mission/ strategy." The mission is the organization's reason for being, and the strategy is its basic approach to carrying out the mission. Such a strategy includes a set of guidelines, which determine the organization's future objectives. These, however, are often not explicit and not agreed upon by organization members. For example, the organization may have multiple missions and strategies due to the fact that multiple coalitions or stakeholders already exist, each with a different set of priorities. And each group lays claim to the organization's energy and resources. Much of the management literature argues for systematic "technical" strategic planning, defined as "the determination of the basic long-term goals and objectives of an enterprise, and the adoption of courses of action and allocation of resources necessary for carrying out those goals (Chandler, 1962, p. 19)." Such a prescription calls for organizational strategy that is explicit, developed consciously with a purpose, and in advance. This is often not the case.

For example, organizations often have strategies by virtue of the fact that a series of decisions related to some important aspect of the organization maintained consistency over a period of time. Yet, the organization never consciously or in advance developed such an intended strategy. An example of this can be found in many medical centers. Here the determination to support research rather than teaching have been reflected in budget decisions, staffing patterns, and the formulation of policy. Yet there is no formally stated strategy which stresses research. Many large commercial banks have operated this way, and have been for the most part driven by historical precedent. They have not had formal, planned strategies. Therefore the term "strategy" in this book includes both planned and unplanned strategies.

Organizational strategic decision making entails the dynamic interplay of three factors: organizational environment—its degree of uncertainty; organizational momentum—the push by the operating system for stability and the pressure to minimize uncertainty; and organizational leadership—whose role it is to mediate between the environmental constraints and opportunities and the bureaucratic momentum.

An example of this type of decision making occurred at AT&T when John D. deButts, former chairman, assessed the competitive and technological environment for AT&T as highly uncertain, thus requiring a strategic change. He had to mediate between environmental pressures which on the one hand indicated that healthy survival of AT&T in the information processing world of the future required a move out from under the monopolized, regulated telephone business and into information processing, and on the other hand, pressures which involved the internal bureaucratic inertia of close to a million employees trained and developed to run a telephone system.

Strategy formation is assumed to reflect the organization's attempts, via decisions made by the leadership, to maintain control and deal with uncertainty (Thompson, 1967). This leadership is often referred to as the dominant coalition, which consists of those organization members who are able to control the allocation of resources.

An analysis of mission and strategy for use in strategic change management should be based on an understanding of how strategies are formulated. The fact that strategies change over time should be recognized when making an analysis of the actual substance of the organization's strategy.

For example, General Electric has an elaborate formalized strategic planning system. The strategies for the overall company and each of its businesses are formulated via a set of managerial and staff problem-solving steps. The strategies are characterized as being very complex, explicit, well-integrated, and proactive. In the same industry is Westinghouse, which does not have such an elaborate, formalized, strategic planning system but rather has strategies which can be characterized as less complex, more implicit, more fragmented, and less proactive than GE's.

Tasks. The task component of the network model represents those specific activities which the organization must perform in order to carry out its mission and strategy. For example, the training of students, part of a university's mission, involves the tasks of professors teaching and students learning. An auto manufacturer's mission involves the task of assembling cars. The task represents *what* needs doing while technology represents *how* the task is carried out. The technology for a teaching task might include lectures, tutorials, field projects, readings, etc. The task of assembling an auto includes sequential assembly line technology. The technologies of each organization differ greatly in the extent to which they affect other aspects of the organization. This includes the kinds of people needed to operate the technology as well as the best ways to design the organization's structure.

The analysis of an organization's task and technology is divided into three dimensions. First, there is the notion of the degree of *task interdependence*. That is, how the units of goods or services are combined into finalized output. Thompson (1967) identified three types of task interdependence:

1. *Pooled.* The tasks can be carried out independently and then pooled together for a final output, such as the case in most universities where students take a range of separate courses which are pooled to add up to a degree.
2. *Sequential.* Tasks must be accomplished in a particular order, such as in an assembly line where one task builds on another.
3. *Reciprocal.* The tasks must be done simultaneously with feedback between tasks, such as on a research project in which a new product is being developed.

The second dimension is task *predictability*, defined as the number of unexpected exceptions encountered in the work. Assembly line work is highly predictable whereas high technology research is highly unpredictable.

The third dimension is problem analyzability, which is the difficulty of finding a solution when an unexpected exception comes up. These latter two dimensions are illustrated in Figure 3.4 along with examples of industries dominated by tasks of each category.

The analysis of an organization's tasks should lead to a set of conclusions regarding the overall degree of task uncertainty. The highest level will include tasks which are reciprocal and have many exceptions with unanalyzable problems. The level of task uncertainty will in turn influence the selection of people, the design of the prescribed networks, and the organizational processes. Let us now go back to our organizational model to examine the next component.

Prescribed Networks. The prescribed network component refers to the definition of jobs and the expected interrelationships among jobs. This becomes management's means to map out who does what and with whom.

There are two major dimensions of prescribed networks, differen-

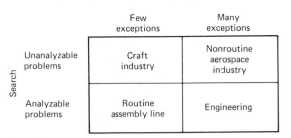

Figure 3.4 (From Charles Perrow, A framework for the comparative analysis of organizations, *American Sociological Review*, 1969, 32, Figure 1, p. 200.)

tiation and integration (Lawrence and Lorsch, 1967). Differentiation refers to the way in which the organization is divided into subunits. This represents decisions about the division of labor and is mainly influenced by the nature of the technology and the environment. Integration refers to the way in which the differentiated subunits are coordinated to lead to accomplishment of common goals.

Four major organizing dimensions can be found in large businesses:

1. *Functional structure* is most often found in one-product companies with rather repetitive technologies that can be sequentially organized. The company is divided into such functions as engineering, production, sales, and financial control. Integration is accomplished by use of hierarchical management decision making, planning, and control systems which coordinate the work of the various functions. For example, steel production is functionally organized.

2. *Geographic structure* reflects the company's desire to get closer to the markets, so that response time can be reduced and distribution can be handled more easily. This structure is often found in companies with one internationally distributed product, such as large oil companies. The organization is differentiated into separate functional organizations with geographic locations in, for example, Europe, Latin America, or Asia. The integration occurs via an overarching corporate management structure along with supporting control and planning systems.

3. *Product structure* is more decentralized. It is found in companies with multiple product lines, each one requiring a different distribution pattern and manufacturing process. The organization is differentiated into *product* units, each with a general manager, such as in the elevator business, the aircraft engine business, as found within United Technology. Within a product unit there may be a functional or geographic organization structure. Integration occurs through an overarching corporate management structure along with supporting control and planning systems.

4. *A matrix structure* can handle complex technologies by utilizing more than one of the preceeding dimensions. In a matrix structure, it is possible to combine functions such as chemical engineering, physics, and medicine with products such as automated blood analyzers. Each person on a team reports to a functional head and a product head. Matrix designs are typically found in the aerospace industry, in the consulting field, and within the entertainment industry, where two dimensions of the business are of equal importance.

Once the overall structure is set around the above dimensions, subunits can be created within the organization. Each level of the organization makes decisions about the appropriate differentiation. For example, a personnel department of 40 individuals can be organized into functions such as recruitment, compensation, development, and employee appraisal. Or it can be organized into market teams such as a unit for R&D staff, a unit for production staff, or a unit for marketing staff. Or, in a matrix structure, the organization can reflect both dimensions. In the latter case, there are functional representatives who combine efforts with personnel generalists to service R&D, production, marketing, etc. Once the organizational networks have been divided into subunits they must be tied together or integrated.

The second dimension, integration, refers to the prescribed structure or networks for coordinating the different subunits of the organization. Integrating mechanisms can be divided into three levels, each having differential capacity for coping with uncertainty. Capacity is increased by enhancing the information processing capability of the organization. As information processing capacity increases, so does the cost and complexity. Therefore, it is important to match capacity carefully with actual need for information processing so as to avoid excess cost and complexity on one hand or inadequate information processing on the other.

The three levels of integrating mechanisms are presented as follows (Galbraith, 1973):

1. *Simple mechanisms* are those which are cheap and can handle low levels of uncertainty, that is, which have low information processing capacity. These include the use of rules and procedures, the decision-making hierarchy, and joint goal setting. For example, telephone operators' work is coordinated largely via standard rules and procedures. However, when there is too much uncertainty, that is, a problem not covered in the rules, they rely on the hierarchy (a supervisor) to solve the problem. Production lines work in a similar fashion. Goal setting can be used to supplement the use of the hierarchy.

2. *Intermediate level integrating mechanisms* reduce interdependence and hence reduce the need to coordinate activities. These include providing subunits of the system with slack resources to enable them to operate with reduced interdependence and less coordination. For example, MacDonald's sets up identical franchise operations often within a few minutes travel from each other. In each case, the fast-food store operates on its own without coordination from the other franchise stores. Branch banks are generally run this way, that is, each operates as a separate entity. Chase Manhattan Bank, with over 200 branch banks, altered its design because management felt the company had too many self-contained units and was losing economies of scale. They created 23 clusters of branches, called zones, which in turn were self contained.

3. *Complex integrating mechanisms* enhance the capability of the system to engage in complex interdependent problem solving and coordination. They include information systems for providing greater

information processing capability as well as lateral relation mechanisms such as liaison roles for coordinating units. Other mechanisms for coordination between different subunits are: task forces—made up of individuals from different differentiated subunits; teams—which are permanent work groups made up of members from differentiated subunits; and finally, a matrix structure which combines differentiated subunits within one organizational design.

The liaison role is found in consumer goods companies where a product manager is given responsibility to integrate across subunits, that is, to see that a product makes it from development to production to sales. Teams are often used where there are complex problems which either a liaison person or a temporary task force can't handle. For example, a team made up of individuals from different departments may exist in an R&D setting to work on interdisciplinary problems with a new product. The matrix structure is an organization design which provides a framework for permanent team work. The matrix grew up in the aerospace industry where it was equally important to manage projects efficiently—see that parts of the plane were completed on time and within budget—and to ensure a high quality of innovation and engineering. To do this, interdisciplinary teams are managed by two bosses, one to see that the quality and engineering is sharp, and the other to see that the project is within budget and on time. Authority and power are split in a matrix. By doing so, more complex tasks can be managed.

People. Motivation and leadership are the two central issues in the people component of the network model. In order to achieve improved organizational performance and to be able to strategically change an organization, people must be motivated. Motivation is the willingness of an individual to invest energy in specific activities. Thus, getting workers to produce a certain number and quality of widgets per day is largely a motivational problem. Also, when management wants change, such as introducing a new set of work processes, or working with robots to produce widgets, workers must be induced to invest energy in new behaviors. A motivational framework is presented as follows.

Motivation is analyzed according to the *expectancy theory* of motivation (Lawler, 1973). Expectancy theory posits that people make conscious decisions regarding how much effort to give to work in an organization. These decisions are based on the following calculations:

1.   The likelihood that their effort will lead to a desired performance. For example, people calculate a probability estimate as to the likelihood that hard work will lead to a desired performance. Thus, a design engineer thinks about the likelihood that working hard at a set of drawings will result in high-quality products. An assembly line worker calculates

the expectancy that working hard will lead to the desired level of production. A professor estimates the probability that if he or she worked hard for six months writing an article that it will lead to a worthwhile product. This expectancy is referred to as the E (effort) to P (performance) expectancy. It can range from 0 to 1. If it is too low it decreases an individual's motivation. If one expects that hard work will not lead to good performance then it does not take too long to question the worth of banging one's head against the wall. The E to P expectancy is affected by the individual's ability as well as by the organizational setting. For example, the design engineer's performance is affected by his or her ability as an engineer as well as the work environment and tools provided by the organization. A bad work setting can interfere with a skilled engineer by making it almost impossible to accomplish high-quality drawings. The E to P expectancy is then multiplied by the following expectancy to derive the overall motivational score for an individual.

2. The likelihood that a desired performance will lead to various outcomes, is referred to as the P (performance) to O (outcome) expectancy. Each outcome is given a value, either positive or negative. For example, one outcome might be a salary increase, another a promotion, and still another praise from management. People place different values on each of these outcomes. It is assumed that we have expectancy values relating performance to the various outcomes. These expectancies are multiplied by the values we place on the outcomes. Therefore, if a design engineer believes that good drawings (performance) lead to salary increases (outcome), and if he places a high value on money, then this will contribute more to the engineer's motivation than a situation in which money is highly valued but good performance is not believed to be related to salary increases. Such would be the case where seniority, not performance, determined salary increases. In the expectancy model all the possible outcomes for a given performance are added together along with their valences. The formula is presented in Figure 3.5.

The expectancy theory can be applied to individuals as well as groups. For example, it was used in one engineering company to assess the motivation of groups of employees. Figure 3.6 presents the results of an assessment of the total engineering firm using the expectancy framework. The results do not include the calculation of the expectancies in the formula. Instead it presents the data required for such a computation. Nevertheless, it provides a clear example of the expectancy application.

First, it can be noted that the majority of the staff, 75%, indicate a high probability that effort will lead to performance. This means that it is reasonable to assume that most individuals have the ability and that the organization provides a reasonably good work setting. The

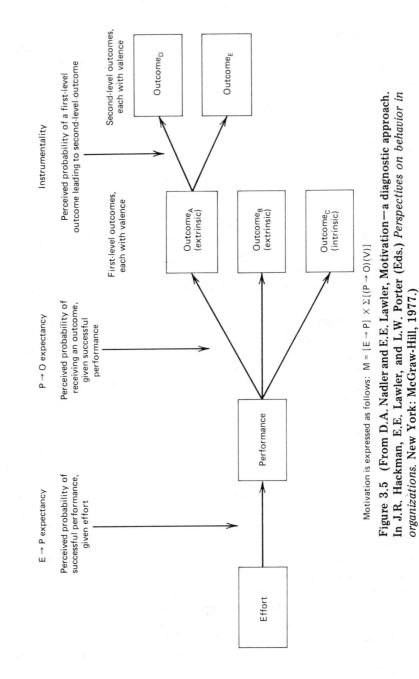

E → P expectancy

Perceived probability of successful performance, given effort

P → O expectancy

Perceived probability of receiving an outcome, given successful performance

Instrumentality

Perceived probability of a first-level outcome leading to second-level outcome

First-level outcomes, each with valence

Second-level outcomes, each with valence

Effort

Performance

Outcome$_A$ (extrinsic)

Outcome$_B$ (extrinsic)

Outcome$_C$ (intrinsic)

Outcome$_D$

Outcome$_E$

Motivation is expressed as follows: $M = [E \rightarrow P] \times \Sigma[(P \rightarrow O)(V)]$

Figure 3.5 (From D.A. Nadler and E.E. Lawler, Motivation—a diagnostic approach. In J.R. Hackman, E.E. Lawler, and L.W. Porter (Eds.) *Perspectives on behavior in organizations.* New York: McGraw-Hill, 1977.)

P to O expectancy was measured by asking staff to indicate the likelihood that good performance would lead to each of the outcomes listed in Figure 3.6. Only 46% expected good performance to lead to pay increases, 35% expected it to lead to promotion, and 34% to management praise. The next column in Figure 3.6 represents the valence of the outcome. It is clear that pay is highly valued with 82% of the staff, indicating that it is very important. Finally, the last column in Figure 3.6 presents the satisfaction with each outcome. It is not surprising that satisfaction with pay is a low 26%. In order to improve

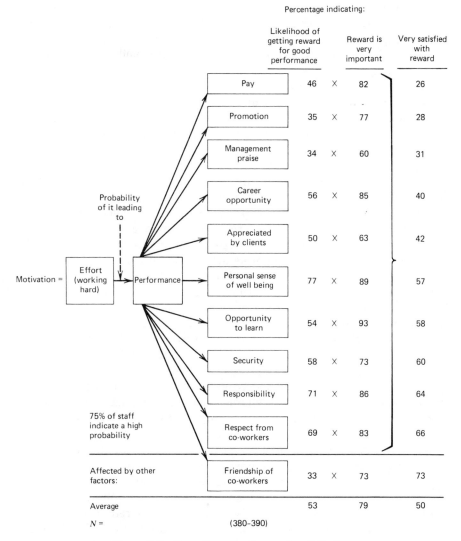

Figure 3.6   Overall motivation and satisfaction

motivation of the staff, the management of the company can alter several expectancies. First, pay raises can be linked to performance, promotion, management praise, and other outcomes the staff value. Second, the company can continue to monitor the perceptions of the staff so as to insure that both the expectancy and, presumably, the motivation changes.

Leadership. Two elements of leadership are considered in this framework. The first is the degree to which the organizational leaders make use of professional management techniques. For example, many organizations are dominated by managers who achieved managerial positions because of technical expertise. As a result they have no training or experience in management. Examples include scientists and engineers who get promoted to management, physicians who become administrators, bankers who become managers, etc. Often these managers are never given any additional training or experience with which to develop professional management expertise. As a result they operate in a "seat of the pants," trial and error fashion. In assessing an organization's leadership, it is crucial to examine this problem because, as pointed out by Henderson (1979) in Chapter 1, "intuitive and experience-based management philosophies are grossly inadequate when decisions are strategic."

The other element of leadership involves the actual style of management. Two extremes are presented in the following, both of which are usually mixed in most organizations. One style is called "mechanistic management style." It is characterized by managers who rely on a highly structured and highly restricted flow of information, and strict adherence to the chain of command; by pressure for uniform managerial style of all managers; by authority for decision making strongly rooted in the formal line managers; by insistence on holding fast to tried and true management principles despite changes in business conditions; by personnel having to follow formally established procedures; by tight control of operations through rigid control systems; and by strict adherence to on-the-job behavior as set down in the job descriptions. It is similar to MacGregor's Theory X style.

The opposite end of the spectrum in terms of style is the "organic management style" which is characterized by managers who rely on open channels of communication throughout the organization; by encouragement of individual managing styles; by authority for decision making rooted in situational expertise; by free adaptation by the organization to changing circumstances; by an emphasis on getting things done rather than on following formally established procedures; by loose, informal control with an emphasis on cooperation; and by allowing on-the-job behavior to be shaped by the requirement of the situation and personality of the individual doing the job (Khandwalla, 1977). It is close to MacGregor's Theory Y style.

Organizational Processes. For people to carry out their prescribed tasks in organizations there must exist dynamic processes of communication, control, problem solving, reward, and conflict management. Processes of communication are the central lifeblood of the organization. One view of organizations holds that they are information-processing mechanisms. That is, in order for organizations to combine the resources of technology, capital, and people into products or services they must use information as the dynamic glue. In addition to the need for information processing to accomplish tasks, organizations are made up of people who have social needs which must be met through communication. Therefore, organizations are vast communication networks with people exchanging all types of task and social information. Communication processes are greatly influenced by the organization's prescribed and emergent network structures. The networks deal with the channels of communication; there is an additional aspect of communication which involves quality and content of what travels over the network.

The major qualitative elements of organizational communication are the degrees of openness, timeliness, distortion, and reciprocality. The more complex the tasks of the organization, the more open, timely, and distortion-free should be the communication. To create these conditions, organizations must train employees, especially managers, in communication skills and must establish a culture (norms) which encourages this type of communication. Such a culture is often found in companies with more stable work forces, such as in Japan. It also exists in some companies in the United States where openness is encouraged.

Control processes exist in all organizations as a tool for observation and for providing information to make necessary adjustments when problems arise. There are two basic types of control processes found in organizations. One is aimed at catching errors, that is, checking for quality mistakes on a production line or auditing systems in banks. The other is aimed at collecting problem-solving information, that is, capturing information which will enable the organization to learn from errors and make improvements. Such control processes are more developmental. An example is the use of quality-control circles derived from Japanese management and beginning to be used in the United States. Workers get together on a regular weekly basis to generate ideas for improving the quality of the products or services. The control process is focused not on catching and punishing mistakes but on learning from errors and mistakes so as to improve future performance.

The most prevalent use of control processes in organizations has been aimed at capturing mistakes. As a result, the control processes often foster "game-playing" to avoid detection of errors. At Volvo, a worker showed me how he and the other workers in an engine assembly plant had developed a way of beating the control system. The engines which were completed move on little electric trolleys past an electric eye at the end of the assembly area. The trolleys, however, were not on a fixed assembly line and could be moved backward and forward by the workers. He showed me how he could move the trolley back and forth through the electric eye and fill a day's quota of engines in about 20 minutes.

W.T. Grant went bankrupt, in part because its control processes encouraged managers of individual retail stores to misrepresent their inventories in order to provide the control system with false performance data. By doing this the store managers were able to increase their own bonuses.

In order to develop more effective control processes it is important to identify its primary purpose—error catching or error problem solving. Once this is done the following guidelines are characteristic of the more effective control processes: (1) establish controls with the participation of those being controlled; (2) make control measurements explicit and realistic; (3) identify proper people for monitoring performance; (4) establish procedures and responsibility for evaluating performance; and (5) determine by whom and how corrective action is taken when performance does not match standards. At W.T. Grant, the individual store managers did not participate in the control measures, only some of the measures were realistic, a very inadequate central auditing staff was responsible for monitoring the standards, and no one was given any responsibility for taking corrective action.

Problem-solving and decision-making processes vary from mechanistic to organic. Mechanistic problem solving and decision making is that which is characterized by use of limited and structured information, low levels of participation, and adherence to the prescribed chain of command. It is best suited for routine problems and decisions. Organic problem solving and decision making is characterized by the use of a great deal of information which is unstructured, high levels of participation without regard for prescribed hierarchy, and is best suited for nonroutine, complex problems. Therefore, mechanistic problem solving and decision making are best for simple production situations whereas organic processes are best suited for research and development, high technology, and highly professional settings.

Reward system processes are crucial for driving motivation in the organization. As shown in the early example of the engineering company presented in Figure 3.6, organizations often do a poor job of using the rewards they control to enhance employee motivation. In the case of the engineers, the use of expectancy theory could have guided the organization to redesign the reward system to make a clearer link between good performacne and the rewards engineers valued such as pay increases, promotions, management praise, etc. The reward system provides an important tool for strategic change management, as it can be used to motivate key managers toward new change goals. All too often in U.S. companies the pressure for short-term profitability creates a conflict with long-term strategic change. It has been argued that this in part created the myopia of the U.S. auto industry; senior executives' bonuses were tied to annual sales figures which encouraged them to delay switching over to small cars until it was almost too late. In contrast, the Japanese automakers were more willing to mortgage the present for the future as evidenced by Datsun's willingness to continue with losses for a number of years in the United States until it gained a foothold in the market.

In recognition of this problem, companies are beginning to split rewards for senior executives between short-term profit rewards and long-term strategic rewards. This can happen once the organization has developed an explicit strategic course.

Another problem with reward systems is tailoring them to different subpopulations in the organization. Not all people value the same rewards. Rewards motivate to the extent that they match what is valued by the parties being rewarded. Expectancy theory provides a way to profile the valence of different outcomes for different subpopulations. This in turn provides the rationale for altering the rewards system.

Emergent Networks. Only part of the organization is prescribed explicitly. Organizations develop extensive informal or *emergent structures* and processes as a result of human interaction. These networks of relationships and processes emerge because individuals tend to formulate, reformulate, and interpret the mission; understand, abide by, and/or change the prescribed organization and organizational processes; use, abuse, and alter the technology; and differentially respond to changing environmental conditions. As a result, a new set of unplanned and often unanticipated structures and processes emerge.

These emergent networks have double-edged consequences. They may either facilitate or hinder the accomplishment of an organization's mission. Yet, they are necessary in most organizations to accomplish the work. This is because most organizations are so complex that no blueprints or plans can be developed for all contingencies. Emergent networks come into play as a result of informal luncheons, or even phone calls, then more complex formations of coalitions take shape to develop new strategic directions for an organization. At the same time, emergent networks can emerge that hinder organizational effectiveness or foster dysfunctional political battles.

Emergent networks may be examined in terms of what they accomplish. This may include everything from the transfer of information and friendship to the exercise of power. Their emergent structure is analyzed by examining who is linked to whom and what subgroups exist within the networks. Various configurations of networks may be more or less effective in task accomplishment. For example, in organizations facing highly uncertain environments and tasks, vast emergent networks are needed to collect and process information. Vast emergent networks are not needed for getting the work accomplished in environments with less uncertainty. In the latter case emergent networks appear more frequently for social reasons.

CONCLUSION

This chapter has been built on the premise that models must be at the core of strategic change management. The network model is one framework for guiding the change process. The model: (1) explains factors affecting organizational effectiveness; (2) takes into account organizational history and cyclical forces; (3) consists of interrelated components, each of which was defined and briefly described.

APPENDIX TO CHAPTER THREE

This appendix presents the analysis of an organization using the Network Model presented in Chapter 3. The case provides an example of how the model can be used to:

1. Diagnose specific aspects of an organization.

2. Identify areas needing improvement.

3. Guide the development of a strategic change plan.

The Swift Engineering Case

Overview. The Swift Engineering Company is an engineering consulting firm which provides mechanical, structural, electrical, heating, and ventilation engineering services to the construction field. They are a company of approximately 400 engineers and about 100 support personnel. They have offices in four major U.S. cities; the home office has close to 300 hundred of their 500 personnel.

The management of Swift Engineering called in a consultant to do a diagnosis of the organization to help them develop a strategic plan for the next decade based on a careful assessment of current organizational and managerial strengths and weaknesses.

Organizational Assessment

During the late spring and early summer of 1980, an organizational assessment of SE was conducted by a team from the Graduate School of Business, Columbia University. The goals of the assessment were:

1. To provide Swift Engineering with strategically useful information to aid in the preparation of its long-term business plans.

2. To provide a systematic summary of current organizational problems with a view to short-term organizational improvements.

Framework for the Assessment. An organizational framework was used to guide the organizational assessment efforts. The framework is based on the premise that organizations are open systems that use inputs of capital, people, and materials to create outputs. Some of the outputs are tangible, such as specific client services, and others are less tangible, but no less real, such as measures of the morale and satisfaction of SE personnel.

The organizational framework is presented as follows along with definitions of each of the components of the framework. (See Figure 3A.1). Swift Engineering is depicted as an organization with inputs and outputs. Its mission and strategy require a set of tasks, such as specific engineering services for various clients; people are hired to accomplish those tasks and are assigned to certain positions in the formal organization where they make decisions, get into conflicts, and build networks. The result is a distinct set of organizational outputs. Clients evaluate these outputs and thereby affect the future behavior of the organization. The core assumption of the organizational assessment is that an organization is more successful with a greater degree of "fit" or alignment between its environment, mission and strategy, tasks, people, formal structure, processes, and emergent networks. The organizational assessment ultimately aims to help the organization address the following strategic concerns:

1. Is Swift Engineering's organizational mission and strategy designed in keeping with its environment?

2. Does the design of the Swift Engineering organization enhance its ability to accomplish its strategy?

3. Are the kinds of people in Swift Engineering appropriate for the ongoing tasks, structures, and processes?

Conducting the Organizational Assessment

The data collection involved two distinct steps. The first was an assessment of how key Swift Engineering personnel viewed the organization's environment and future strategic opportunities. Data were collected from more than 100 Swift Engineering professional staff in two- to three-hour group interview sessions.

The second step consisted of a survey of the total staff of Swift Engineering. Approximately 90% of the staff completed the survey. The survey included questions which covered most of the categories

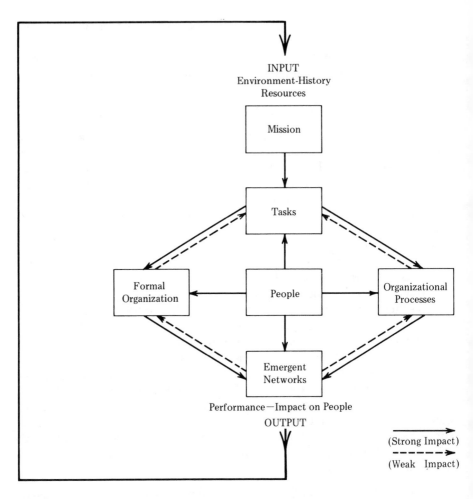

INPUT
Environment-History
Resources

Mission

Tasks

Formal
Organization

People

Organizational
Processes

Emergent
Networks

Performance—Impact on People
OUTPUT

⟶ (Strong Impact)

------➤ (Weak Impact)

Description of Components

Mission/Strategy: This includes
the organization's reason for being,
its basic approach to carrying out
its mission, its strategy, and its
criteria for effectiveness.

Tasks: This refers to the technology
by which the organization's work is
accomplished.

People: This includes the characteristics of the members of the organization
including background, motivational
patterns, managerial style.

Formal Organization: This refers to
the explicitly designed social structure of the organization. It includes
the organization of subunits, communication and authority networks, as well as
structural mechanisms for integrating the
organization.

Organizational Processes: These are the
mechanisms (communication, decision
making, conflict management, control, and
reward) which enable the formal organization to carry out the dynamics of work.

Emergent Networks: These are the
structures and processes which, although
not planned or formally prescribed,
inevitably emerge in the organization.

Figure 3A.1

of the organizational framework. Table 3A.1 summarizes the questions of the assessment.

Summary of Organizational Assessment

Table 3A.2 summarizes the analysis of the components of the model. Each of these components is discussed in more detail in the remainder of this Appendix.

Table 3A.3 presents an analysis of the current alignment or fit between components of the framework. This table also includes some suggestions regarding change implications. Which are also explored in more depth in the rest of the Appendix.

Detailed Analysis of SE Components

In this section of the case a more detailed analysis of each of the model's components is presented, including some of the questionnaire results.

Environment. The first component analyzed was the environment, which includes the social, political and economic factors which provide opportunities and/or constraints to SE.

The degree of complexity and expected amount of change was measured by asking respondents to rate how they would characterize their environment. As noted in Table 3A.4, the majority of the respondents do not see the environment as very heterogeneous, changing, unpredictable, etc. The highest rating, 34% of the respondents, was for a "technically sophisticated" environment.

Staff at SE were asked to rate the impact of a number of external forces as their degree of positive or negative impact on the effectiveness of the firm both for 1980 and for 1985. Figure 3A.2 presents these results. First it is interesting to note that the majority of the forces are seen as positive both in 1980 and 1985, with the labor market and economic trends being the two exceptions. The other interesting observation is that all of the forces become more positive in 1985 than in 1980, when the survey was conducted. Thus, they see their environment as becoming more munificent. The two major environmental impediments appear to be the *labor market*—the difficulty of recruiting and retaining good engineers in a tight market—and the *economy*.

When SE staff was asked to rate constraints on future growth and development, a similar picture emerges. Table 3A.5 presents a summary of the responses which indicate that there is not any factor which more than 50% of the staff feel is very constraining on SE. The one that is considered the greatest potential constraint is the "shortage of technical manpower," which 50% rate as an important constraint.

Table 3A.1 Diagnostic Plan

Components of the Organizational Model	Specific Information Sought	Method of Data Collection
Environment	How complex is the environment in terms of the number of domains and organizations which personnel must actively deal with?	Documents/interviews
	How stable is the environment—how quickly is change occurring?	Documents/interviews
	How predictable are changes in the environment?	Documents/interviews
Mission/strategy/ objectives	What do key actors in the system perceive as the mission/strategy and objectives of personnel?	Questionnaire (open-ended written response)
	How do members rate possible system goals?	Questionnaire ratings
	What are managers' concepts of strategy?	Interviews
	How are strategic decisions actually made? (use tracer decisions)	Interviews/observation
People (Management Style)	What is style of managers—risk taking, "seat of pants," participative, open communications, flexible?	Interviews and observation
	Do the key managers possess basic management competence?	
Prescribed organization component	What is the overall formal organizational design?	Documents and interviews
	What integration mechanisms exist and how do they function?	Interviews and questionnaire ratings
Organizational processes	What are the characteristics of communication—openness, distortion, time lag, quantity?	Interviews/observation
	How is conflict handled in the organization? (norms and behavior)	Interviews/questionnaire ratings
	How is decision making handled by personnel, that is, degree of participation, how systematic, how flexible?	Interviews/observation
Emergent networks	Who most frequently speaks to whom for information, for influence, and for fulfilling affective needs?	Interviews using sociometric questions/observations
Output	What is the organization's performance over time and in comparison to comparable systems?	Documents/interviews
	What is the level of individuals' satisfaction?	Questionnaires

Table 3A.2 Summary of Assessment for Components of Framework

Component	Summary Diagnosis
Environment	Perceived to be quite complex and changing. Becoming more competitive. New market opportunities opening up.
Mission/strategy	No formally written and agreed upon mission for firm. Disagreements among key actors regarding scope of services and markets which should be incorporated in mission of firm. Strategy dominated by historical precedent and incremental change directed from the top. Strong desire among top managers for more explicit and comprehensive strategy.
Tasks	Range from very routine to moderately complex. Perceived to have moderate variety, freedom, and uncertainty.
Prescribed organization	Differentiated by function, geography, and project. Integration mechanisms not perceived to be effective —especially the matrix structure.
People	Professionally oriented, highly involved in work at the operational level, not managerially or strategically oriented. Managerial style is nonparticipative and unsupportive of innovation and new ideas, yet fair and encouraging short-term productivity. Motivation is driven by a combination of extrinsic (pay, promotion, career) as well as intrinsic rewards (sense of well being).
Processes	Communication is not perceived to be open across hierarchical levels. Decision making is nonparticipative. Control is subjective and primarily based on supervisory judgments, no standards of performance are part of system or used by project teams to assess their own performance. Reward system not well matched to motivational profile of the staff (good performance is not seen as tied to pay, promotion, or career opportunities by many).
Emergent networks	Existence of old boy networks. Operationally focused—few informal interactions which encourage talking and interacting over managerial and strategic concerns.
Output	The firm is perceived to be quite effective with regard to quantity of work and reputation in the market place. It is not perceived to be very innovative. The satisfaction of personnel is mixed. A fairly high proportion of the firm are considering looking for jobs outside the firm in the short run, and/or do not think they will be with the firm in five years.

Table 3A.3   Alignments

Alignments	Action Implications
Environment to mission and strategy Not well matched as the environment is complex and changing and the mission and strategy are not clearly articulated or comprehended.	Need to systematically assess the environment for long-term threats and opportunities. Need to align mission to environment. Develop comprehensive strategy for implementing the mission.
Mission/strategy and tasks The fit with the historical mission and strategy is OK. Future strategy may require introduction of new tasks.	Need to articulate and develop tasks as future strategy is developed.
Tasks and prescribed organization The current organization design is suitable for the current tasks, however, some of the integration mechanisms are not working effectively. If the strategy changes and new tasks are developed, then the organization design will have to be redesigned.	Need to make adjustments to the integrating mechanisms, especially the management information. Reexamine the organizational design as part of the strategic planning process.
People/prescribed organization/processes The managerial style is not supportive of innovation and open communication. The motivational needs of staff are not well met by the organizational reward system. Control is subjective and supervisor based.	Develop more open managerial style. Adjust reward systems so as to better match motivational needs. Develop more explicit performance standards and develop less subjective control systems.
Emergent networks/prescribed organization/processes Fit is not supportive of managerial and strategic activities.	Develop ways of fostering more task-relevant networks by placing people on task forces and committees.

Mission/Strategy

The key senior staff of SE were asked to define SE's core mission. It was found that there was substantial disagreement among the staff. One of the major controversies was whether SE could continue to have as its mission to be the elite, custom design firm in the face of an increasingly competitive environment challenging the marketability of their services.

In the strategy area staff at SE were asked a number of questions to determine the current strategy, how strategic decisions were made, and what the firm should be doing strategically.

Table 3A.6 presents a list of strategic activities which the firm could be engaged in. Each respondent was asked to rate the extent to which

Table 3A.4   Current Environment:
Characterizing the External Environment
Within Which Swift Engineering Functions

Characteristic	Percentage of Agreement
Very heterogeneous	22
Dynamic and changing	16
Risky	14
Unpredictable	11
Rapidly expanding	23
Strong cyclical fluctuations	24
Hostile and stressful	7
Technologically sophisticated	34
Dominant, overpowering	18
Restrictive	14
	$N = 108$

the firm was doing each, and the extent to which he or she felt the firm should be doing each. It is interesting to note that there is very little agreement on what the firm is currently doing with number 5, and that "Working to maintain current level of activity" has the most agreement, 34%. When we look at the ratings for the future, numbers 3 and 7 have a great deal of consensus, namely improve the quality of services and upgrade the technical competence of professionals in the firm.

Table 3A.7 indicates a desire on the part of most of the SE staff to shift the way in which strategic decisions are made in the firm. According to Table 3A.7 the dominant mode as seen by 50% of the top staff at SE is that of one person at the top without much explicit direction. The majority, 77%, would like it to shift to a more professional and explicit form in which there are rather detailed, written strategic plans.

Finally, the SE staff members are asked to generate a list of strategic responses to the key environmental pressures. Table 3A.8 presents the list of responses which came up most frequently. These became candidates for strategic elements of the overall firm plan.

Tasks at SE

Staff members were asked a number of questions regarding the nature of their tasks. First, it was found that they face a moderate level of task variety and complexity. They reported that there is a big degree of task interdependence. That is, over 40% of the staff report that in order to get their work done they must work in team settings interacting with a number of other professionals, such as mechanical engineers, electrical engineers, air conditioning, and ventilation engineers, draftspersons, and other support personnel.

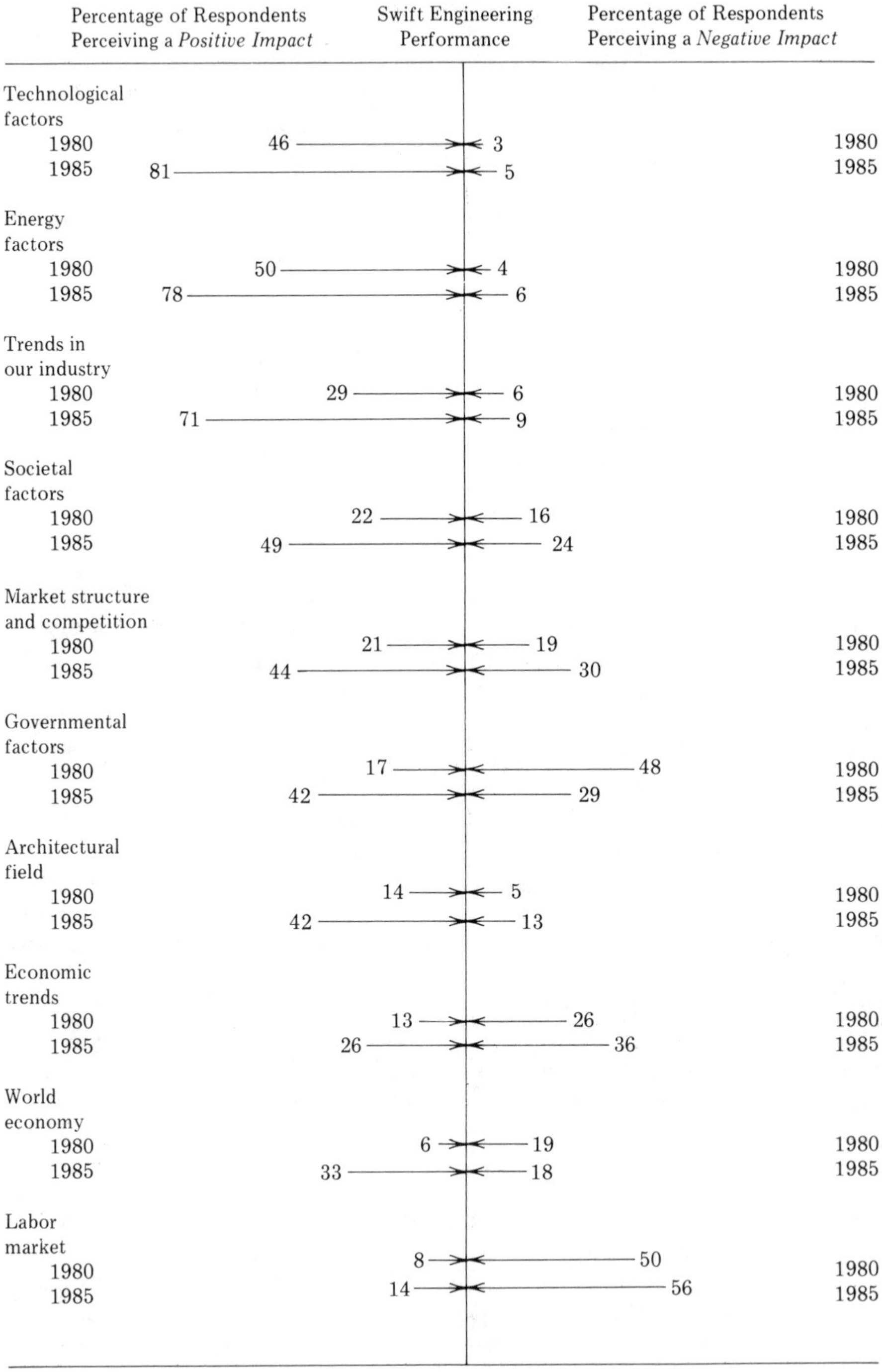

Percentage of Respondents Perceiving a *Positive Impact*	Swift Engineering Performance	Percentage of Respondents Perceiving a *Negative Impact*

Technological factors
- 1980: 46 ← 3 (1980)
- 1985: 81 ← 5 (1985)

Energy factors
- 1980: 50 ← 4 (1980)
- 1985: 78 ← 6 (1985)

Trends in our industry
- 1980: 29 ← 6 (1980)
- 1985: 71 ← 9 (1985)

Societal factors
- 1980: 22 — 16 (1980)
- 1985: 49 — 24 (1985)

Market structure and competition
- 1980: 21 — 19 (1980)
- 1985: 44 — 30 (1985)

Governmental factors
- 1980: 17 — 48 (1980)
- 1985: 42 — 29 (1985)

Architectural field
- 1980: 14 — 5 (1980)
- 1985: 42 — 13 (1985)

Economic trends
- 1980: 13 — 26 (1980)
- 1985: 26 — 36 (1985)

World economy
- 1980: 6 — 19 (1980)
- 1985: 33 — 18 (1985)

Labor market
- 1980: 8 — 50 (1980)
- 1985: 14 — 56 (1985)

Figure 3A.2

Table 3A.5 Constraints: To What Extent Are the Following Factors Constraints on the Future Growth and Development of Swift Engineering?

Constraint	Percentage of Agreement
Insufficient capital	15
Shortage of managerial talent	42
Lack of growth opportunities	18
Lack of cooperation of employees	33
Shortage of technical manpower	50
Government regulations	2
Resistance to changes needed for growth on the part of the managers	31
	$N = 108$

Table 3A.6 Strategies: For the Following Activities Use the Scale Below to Indicate the Extent to Which Swift Engineering Is Currently and Should in the Future Engage in Each Activity.

Activity	Percentage of Agreement	
	Done Now	Should Be Done
Working to increase the number of similar clients.	28	56
Working to look for new types of clients.	13	79
Working to improve the quality of existing services.	8	87
Working to develop new services.	9	62
Working to maintain current level of activity.	34	54
Working to develop managers for the future of the firm.	6	81
Working to upgrade the technical competence of professionals in the firm.	6	87
Working to make full utilization of the computer for producing engineering services.	9	74
		$N = 108$

Table 3A.7 Strategic Decision Making: Rank Order the Following Descriptions in Terms of (a) How Your Firm Makes Strategic Decisions and (b) How You Would Like it to Make Strategic Decisions.

	Percentage of Agreement	
	How It Is	How I Would Like It to Be
. . . good managers don't make policy decisions. . . rather they give their organization a sense of direction, and they are masters of developing opportunities. . . the successful general manager does not spell out detailed objectives for his organization. . . he seldom makes forthright statements of policy. . . he is an opportunist, and he tends to muddle through problems.	50	10
. . . a master strategy sets the basic purpose of an enterprise in terms of the services it will render to society and the way it will render these services. . . it includes systematically and explicitly; (1) establishing the service market in niches that are propitious in view of society's needs and the organization's resources, (2) selecting the underlying technologies, (3) expressing plans in terms of targets. . . (4) setting up sequences and timing of steps toward these objectives which reflect the organization's capabilities and external conditions.	24	77
A strategy is not a fixed plan, nor does it change systematically at prearranged times at the will of management. . . the aggressive proactive strategy maker—the hero of virtually all normative literature—can sometimes do much more harm than the careful reactive one. . . and making strategy explicit in an uncertain environment with an aggressive bureaucracy can do great harm to an organization.	26	13
		$N = 108$

Table 3A.8   Strategic Responses

	Overall Responses
Societal factors	More minority hiring
	Greater local community involvement
	Public education
Governmental factors	Lobby for more work from government agencies
	Become known by government as experts in the field so as to influence rules and regulations
Technological factors	Need for more computer use in both design and word processing
	Staff education in technology and computers
Structure of our market	Diversify by exploring new markets:
	Retrofit
	Design build
	Alternative energy
	Multimaterials
	Real estate speculation
World economy	The firm should continue to expand where profitability has been assessed
Labor market for staff	Raise salaries and benefits to competitive level
	Increase in-house education programs
Energy factors	Greater emphasis on research in energy alternatives
	Become active with the government to influence government legislation
Architectural field	Closer relations and more joint ventures
Economic trends	Diversify by broadening technical competencies
	Cost efficiency and high productivity
Trends in our industry	Diversify by broadening base of operations

Prescribed Structure at SE

SE is organized into three major subgroupings: (1) functional departments reflecting engineering disciplines; (2) project groups, and (3) geographical groups covering different regions of the country.

Integration of the organization is accomplished via a number of integrating mechanisms ranging from standard operating procedures through a complex matrix organization design. Table 3A.9 reports the results of the survey questions asking individuals to rate the effectiveness of the various integrating mechanisms. The responses are in terms of the percentage rating the mechanisms as *not effective*. The matrix was rated by 41% of the staff as not effective. There are other mechanisms, such as management information systems, task forces, and project teams, which were rated as not effective by 30% or more of the staff.

Table 3A.9 Prescribed Structure: The Effectiveness of Simple and Complex Integrating Mechanisms

Integrating Mechanism	Percentage of Each Level Rating Mechanisms Not Effective[a]							
	Overall	Principals	Associate Partners	Associate and Directors	Senior Engineers and Consultants	Staff Engineers	Project Engineers and Designers	Others
Simple mechanisms								
Rules and procedures (Q21)	19	8	11	22	34	21	20	13
Hierarchy (Q22)	18	10	8	14	48	33	20	11
Planning and goal setting (Q23)	23	7	21	46	28	28	21	19
Management information system (Q24)	33	33	40	45	44	33	41	21
Complex mechanisms								
Liaison people (Q25)	21	7	6	25	40	28	23	17
Task forces (Q26)	31	30	28	45	50	17	31	25
Project teams (Q27)	14	8	13	14	40	25	11	14
Matrix (Q28)	26	15	29	28	41	43	26	31
	N = 200-316	[b]N = 10-14	N = 15-20	N = 21-37	N = 17-29	N = 7-17	N = 53-89	N = 75-163

[a]Not effective = 1 or 2 rating on the scale.

[b]The values of N vary because respondents could indicate that mechanism was not used.

It is also interesting to note the discrepancies among staff members at different levels of the firm regarding their assessments. The principals are generally less critical than lower-level staff.

Table 3A.10 may provide an explanation for some of the problems with the matrix for lower-level staff. This reports the percent of staff who indicate that the mechanism is *not being used* at SE. The matrix response is particularly interesting because 56% of the staff engineers who in fact do work in a matrix organization report that the firm does not have a matrix organization. This probably represents poor communication from the top as to the actual nature of the organization's structure and a rationale for the matrix design. It was found that many of the junior staff had never been given the full picture and thus were often confused, which further contributed to the *not effective* ratings.

People Component

Expectancy theory was used to guide the collection of data on what people valued in their work setting. Table 3A.11 presents a summary of these data. It can be seen that the most valued reward for staff is "opportunity to learn," which 93% rate as important, with management praise being the least important reward. (Sixty percent said that it was important.) Other findings presented in Table 3A.11 indicate that in SE, generally, 75% feel that if they put in effort (work hard) it will result in good performance. This generally indicates that staff members are competent to do the job and have adequate organizational tools and resources to get the work done. Overall, however, SE staff do not perceive much link between good performance and many of the rewards presented in Table 3A.11, namely, pay, promotion, and management praise, each of which is rated by less than 50% of the staff as being linked to good performance. The satisfaction scores also indicate some problems. Motivation can be enhanced by more closely linking things people value with their level of performance. Thus if they are performing well, they should be able to perceive a link between that and pay, promotion, and other valued rewards.

Management style was appraised by asking staff to rate their supervisor on such dimensions as how helpful they were, how well they planned, how fair and open they were, and their degree of flexibility. The finding was that the reviews were very mixed. There was no consistent SE style, and many supervisors got pretty low marks. Thus, the need was identified to deal with trouble spots, define what the appropriate style should be, and work out a management development program to improve things in this area.

Processes

The first area looked at is communication. Table 3A.11 presents the results of the two communication questions, broken down into different

Table 3A.10 Prescribed Structure: The Use of Complex Integrating Mechanisms

| | | | | | | | Percentage of Each Level Rating That Mechanisms Are Not Used |
	Overall	Principals	Associate Partners	Associate and Directors	Senior Engineers and Consultants	Staff Engineers	Project Engineers and Designers	Others
Complex mechanisms								
Liaison people (Q25)	26	0	24	40	31	12	20	29
Task forces (Q26)	43	36	33	49	45	56	40	44
Project teams (Q27)	31	7	33	27	32	19	28	37
Matrix (Q28)	41	7	29	46	39	56	36	47
	$N = 369$	$N = 14$	$N = 21$	$N = 37$	$N = 29$	$N = 17$	$N = 89$	$N = 163$

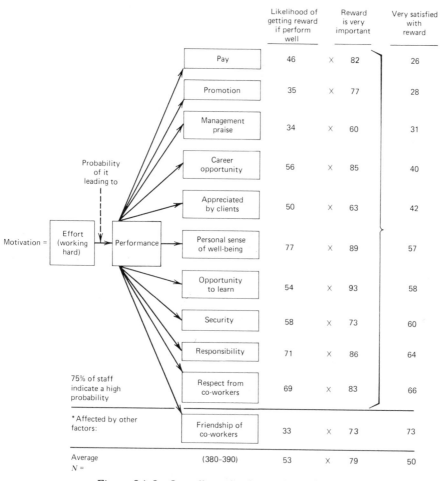

Figure 3A.3 Overall motivation and satisfaction

levels of the organization. The results indicate very little openness and little sharing by management of information about the business with employees.

The findings regarding participation in the firm, as presented in Table 3A.12, are also problematic. The principals seem to have a more positive view of participating than almost everyone else in the firm. The groups in the middle of the organization see the least amount of participation with regard to decisions at SE.

Emergent Networks

The SE staff were asked to nominate the most influential individuals in the firm when it came to budget decisions, personnel decisions, and

Table 3A.11 Percentage Indicating Open and Effective Communication

Factor	Principals	Associate Partners	Associates and Directors	Senior Engineers and Senior Consultants	Staff Engineers	Project Engineers and Designers	Others
Willingness among people. . . to say what they really think to people above their supervisor	20	29	14	21	6	19	23
Management shares information about business employees	13	33	25	10	24	25	23
	$N = 15$	$N = 21$	$N = 36$	$N = 29$	$N = 17$	$N = 86$-87	$N = 164$-168

Table 3A.12 Degree of Participation as Reported by Different Levels: Percentage Indicating Participation in Decision-Making Factor to a Considerable or Great Extent

Decision-Making Factors	Principals	Associate Partners	Associate and Directors	Senior Engineers and Senior Consultants	Staff Engineers	Project Engineers and Designers	Others
When management decision is needed. . . persons affected by the decision are asked for their ideas. . . .	33	14	11	7	6	19	20
Employees are encouraged to try out new ways of doing things.	27	19	17	3	12	17	21
Employees are encouraged to make suggestions, participate in work decisions.	53	24	45	24	18	30	32
Managers and supervisors are given power to make decisions and don't have to check with higher levels	53	62	44	38	50	37	30
	$N = 15$	$N = 21$	$N = 35$–36	$N = 29$	$N = 16$–17	$N = 85$–88	$N = 157$–170

111

technical decisions. In each case the result indicated that the prescribed network was where the real power was perceived to reside. No emergent influence networks were uncovered.

Performance

Staff were asked to rate their firm in comparison to its competition on a number of measures. Table 3A.13 presents some of these results, reported by level in the organization. The results in this table indicate the two items for which the people in each level *least* agreed with the statement that SE was better than its competition. In other words, these are the items for which SE is rated lowest with regard to performance. For example, for the principals and associate partners,

Table 3A.13 Perceptions of Swift Engineering Capabilities and Performance Compared to Competitor: Percentage Rating Swift Engineering Somewhat or Far Better Than Competition—Top Three and Lowest Two Choices, by Level (Part 1).

Principals	Associate Partners	Associates and Directors
Top three choices		
. . . is developing plans for the future in a sensible and realistic fashion. 87% (Q160)	. . . has good business prospects. 81% (Q161)	Reputation for work excellence. 78% (Q157)
. . . has good business prospects. 80% (Q161)	Reputation for work excellence. 71% (Q157)	The quantity or amount of work produced. 65% (Q154)
The number of innova- or new ideas introduced.	The quantity or amount of work produced.	. . . has good business prospects.
73% (Q156)	67% (Q154)	59% (Q161)
Lowest two choices		
Efficiency of operation. 13% (Q158)	Efficiency of operation. 14% (Q158)	Morale of personnel. 16% (Q159)
Morale of personnel.	Morale of personnel.	Efficiency of operation.
40% (Q159)	19% (Q159)	21% (Q158)

Table 3A.13   Perceptions of Swift Engineering Capabilities and Performance Compared to Competitor: Percentage Rating Swift Engineering Somewhat or Far Better Than Competition—Top Three and Lowest Two Choices, by Level (Part 2).

Senior Engineers and Senior Consultants	Staff Engineers	Project Engineers and Designers	Others
The quantity of work produced.	The number of innovations or new ideas introduced.	. . . has good business prospects.	Reputation for work excellence.
62% (Q154)	53% (Q156)	64% (Q161)	47% (Q154)
. . .has good business prospects.	The quantity of work produced.	Reputation for work excellence.	. . .has good business prospects.
59% (Q161)	47% (Q154)	58% (Q157)	47% (Q161)
. . . is developing plans for the future in a sensible and realistic fashion.	. . . has good business prosects.	The quantity of work produced.	. . . is developing plans for the future in a sensible and realistic fashion.
52% (Q160)			
Morale of personnel.	Morale of personnel.	Efficiency of operation	Efficiency of operation.
7% (Q159)	6% (Q159)	33% (Q158)	21% (Q158)
Efficiency of operation.	. . . is developing plans for the future in a sensible and realistic fashion.	Morale of personnel.	Morale of personnel.
10% (Q158)	11% (Q160)	36% (Q159)	24% (Q159)

"efficiency of operations" is not one of SE's strong suits, nor is "morale of personnel."

Part 1 of Table 3A.13 presents the items that staff at different levels feel SE does better than its competitors. Note that there is quite a bit of variation among levels.

A final performance measure is what the firm does to its people with regard to their commitment to stay. Table 3A.14 reports the results of two such questions. One question is whether the staff member will be looking for another job next year. It is clear that many will be, with 70% of the senior engineers saying that they will look. This is the group that gets most of the work done for the firm. In a tight labor market it is pretty costly to lose these people because they have completed their initial training and are the backbone of the firm.

Another interesting finding in Table 3A.14 is that many of the higher-level staff indicate that they will *not* be at SE in five years, 47% of the principals, 55% of the associate partners, etc. In the lower levels the senior engineer group again stands out, with 62% indicating that they will not be at SE in five years.

Table 3A.14 People Looking for Other Jobs or Who Do Not Plan on Being at SE in Five Years						
	Principals	Associate Partners	Associates and Directors	Senior Engineers and Consultants	Staff Engineers	Project Engineers and Designers	Others
Looking for a job in the next year (3, 4, 5) (Q63)	7	31	37	70	50	46	53
Do not plan to be at SE in five years (1, 2, 3) (Q222)	53	45	50	38	47	38	24

Chapter Four

Organizational Model:
Dynamic Aspects

Complex systems differ from simple ones in being "counter-intuitive," i.e., not behaving as one might expect them to. They are remarkably insensitive to changes in many system parameters, i.e., resist policy changes... Intuition and judgment generated by a lifetime of experience with the simple systems that surround one's every action create a network of expectations and perceptions that could hardly be better designed to mislead the unwary when he moves into the realm of complex systems. (Forrester, 1969, p.150).

Organizations serve as social means through which people attempt to accomplish technical, political, and cultural ends. They are complicated, difficult to design, difficult to manage, and even more difficult to change, once they are set in motion. As has been stated, this book is concerned primarily with the management of change. However, managing change and the redesign of the organization is often closely intertwined with the initial design and the ongoing management.

A major premise of my argument has been that there are three core areas or sets of problems which face those attempting to design, manage, and change organizations. These problem areas are what contribute to the complexity of organizations and to the counter-intuitive behaviors described in the previous quotation by Forrester.

Chapter 1 identified the three core problems that must be managed in organizations. Chapter 3 identified a set of organizational components which can be manipulated to make adjustments in the technical, political, and cultural systems. The organizational model can be viewed as the set of factors which management can control to affect the three systems. Thus, changes can be made in the organization's mission and strategy, prescribed networks, people, etc. in order to affect the technical, political, or cultural systems.

The strategic change management task is to keep the organization internally aligned and aligned with its external environment. This alignment may occur quite unconsciously on the part of the organization and its members and may be viewed by some, such as the organizational ecology advocates (Aldrich, 1979), as an evolutionary process. On the other hand, it may be a very proactive, planned process. Regardless of whether or not it is explicitly and consciously aligned, organizations are proposed to be effective to the extent that there is alignment within each system—technical, political, and cultural—and across the three systems. Figure 4.1 presents a matrix of strategic tasks illustrative of what needs to be managed to achieve alignment.

Across the top of the matrix are the components of the organizational model presented in the previous chapter. These are the tools which can be used to work on the three core systems. The matrix highlights a weakness of previous organizational models dating back to Leavitt's (1965) framework; it lacks a rationale for calculating the "goodness of fit." The models of Galbraith and Nathanson (1978), Tushman and Nadler (1978), Pascale and Athos (1981), and Kotter (1978) all are quite imprecise about "goodness of fit." They implicitly appear to limit their calculations to the first of the three systems—the technical system. The aim of this chapter is to explicitly state how goodness of fit, or alignment, is calculated for each of the three systems, and how it is calculated across the three systems.

The challenge for those attempting to change organizations is to recognize that the task is best represented as a dynamic jigsaw puzzle of 18 pieces, as presented in Figure 4.1, which must be aligned with each other. These pieces will never be perfectly aligned. They require ongoing attention and adjustment. How much adjustment depends on factors which lead to uncertainty in each system and between the systems.

CHANGE OVER TIME

Figure 4.1 represents what needs managing. Before presenting the concepts for alignment in each system, I would like to discuss the dynamics of change over time. A concept which was introduced previously is the notion of uncertainty. It has been argued that organizations attempt either to reduce or manage uncertainty. There are three types of organizational uncertainty which need management—technical, political, and cultural. Examples include uncertainty about markets, production capability, and technical innovation; uncertainty about candidates for success, power distributions, and the politics of reward allocations; and uncertainty about the appropriate value system for the organization, or the existence of conflicting value systems. As previously indicated, adjustments in each of these three areas can be conceptualized in terms of cycles.

Once uncertainty in any one of these systems is perceived, a response is triggered. At that time, managerial problem-solving attention is invested in either reducing the uncertainty or figuring out how to cope

Managerial Tools

Managerial Areas →

Managerial Areas	Mission and Strategy	Tasks	Prescribed Network	People	Processes	Emergent Networks
Technical System	Assessing environmental threats and opportunities; Assessing organizational strengths and weaknesses; Defining mission and fitting resources to accomplish it	Environmental scanning activities; Strategic planning activities	Differentiation: organization of work into roles (production, marketing, etc.); Integration: recombining roles into departments, divisions, regions, etc.; Aligning structure to strategy	Selecting or developing technical skills and abilities; Matching management style with technical tasks	Fitting people to roles; Specifying performance criteria for roles; Measuring performance; Staffing and development to fill roles (present and future); Developing information and planning systems to support strategy and tasks	Fostering the development of information returns which facilitate task accomplishment
Political System	Who gets to influence the mission and strategy?; Managing coalitional behavior around strategic decisions	Lobbying and influencing external constituencies; Internal governance structure; Coalitional activities to influence decisions	Distribution of power across the role structure; Balancing power across groups of roles (e.g., sales vs. marketing, production vs. R&D, etc.)	Utilizing political skills; Matching political needs and operating with organizational opportunities	Managing succession politics (who gets ahead, how do they get ahead); Decision and administration of reward system (who gets what and how); Managing the politics of appraisal (who is appraised by whom and how); Managing the politics of information control and the planning process	Management of emergent influence networks, coalitions, and cliques
Cultural System	Managing influence of values and philosophy on mission and strategy; Developing culture aligned with mission and strategy	Use of symbolic events to reinforce culture; Role modeling by key people; Clarifying and defining values	Developing managerial style aligned with technical and political structure; Development of subcultures to support roles (production culture, R&D culture, etc.); Integration of subcultures to create company culture	Utilizing cultural leadership skills; Matching values of people with organization culture	Selection of people to build or reinforce culture; Development (socialization) to mold organization culture; Management of rewards to shape and reinforce the culture; Management of information and planning systems to shape and reinforce the culture	Fostering friendship and affective networks, coalitions and cliques to shape and reinforce the culture

Figure 4.1

119

with it. At the time this book was written, another whole industry, the computer chip industry, was facing tremendous technical uncertainty because of Japanese innovations. In this case, the 64K Random Access Memory Chip, which represents the new generation of computer chips, has been taken over by the Japanese who threaten to dominate not only this particular product but also the succeeding generations of chips. The technical uncertainty is extremely high in silicon valley and other parts of the computer chip industry.

Uncertainty creates a need for adjustment; management attempts to resolve these problems by making changes in the components of the organizational model presented in the previous chapter. One way to view change over time is in terms of the interaction of the technical, political, and cultural cycles. This chapter presents a set of concepts for understanding and managing each of these cycles.

A *Case Illustration:* Before presenting the concepts needed to manage each cycle, a concrete case illustration will be offered. In 1981 a group of executives from 15 chemical companies were interviewed regarding their strategic tasks for the 1980s. These executives were either presidents or division presidents within major chemical companies in the United States. The results of some of their interviews are presented to illustrate the need for uncertainty and problem-solving concepts in the technical, political, and cultural areas.

First, each executive was asked to identify the strategic changes which they expect to occur within their companies during the 1980s. They were asked to predict changes: (1) in the technical system, such as changes in product mix, opening up of new markets, major restructuring of the organization, and the introduction of new production technologies; (2) in the political system, with examples such as succession issues for the CEO and other key jobs, shifting of power from an old guard to a new guard, revamping reward systems to further the lot of some groups and not others, shifting centers of decision making; and (3) in the cultural system, with examples including how cultural values need to be aligned with the strategy of the organization, how subcultures need to be integrated or managed when old and young subcultures clash, or when technical versus managerial cultures compete.

An examination of strategic technical changes presents a picture of industries facing a decade in which they must completely revamp production processes. Most will be shifting from almost total dependence on gas and oil to a mix of raw material (feedstocks) which will include greater use of coal and biomass (fermentation).

1. The specific changes which were identified as critical technical system changes in the 1980s by these executives were:

(a) *Technology Changes.* Altering the feedstock and the production processes so as to be able to use coal and biomass requires totally new plants and technologies.

(b) *Structural Changes.* Because of slow growth in the U.S. and European markets, there will be increasing expansion to other world markets, thus necessitating organizational design changes which will make the organizations more multinational. There will be more decentralization in an effort to set product lines closer to their markets and to make them more responsive.

(c) *Strategy Changes.* In order to be effective in a more turbulent environment, there will be a need for more effective strategic planning and further diversification—especially into specialty chemicals to avoid the oil companies and OPEC who will dominate the low value added, commodity end of the business due to their control of oil and gas feedstocks (note: the exception might be DuPont, which bought an oil company—Conoco). Finally, a part of the strategy will aim at increased productivity, because profit margins will be squeezed by the companies inability to pass feedstock costs on to customers.

(d) *Management Changes.* In order to carry out the kinds of changes previously outlined, companies will look for a more "hands on" type of manager—one who will have to be trained to manage across different cultures. The 1980s will be a decade requiring a great deal of management development.

2. Strategic political system changes in the 1980s were reported to include:

(a) *Promotion/Succession Issues.* All the companies identified significant personnel changes at the top.

(b) *Reward Issues.* In several of the companies, executives reported that the bonus systems would be adjusted to open it up to more people. They all indicated that rewards would have to be more explicitly and closely linked to performance for all employees.

(c) *Shifts in Power Centers.* It was generally felt that the technical people would have increasingly more power over strategic decisions and running the company than their financial and marketing counterparts. This was argued as a reasonable shift due to the tremendous technological changes occurring during the 1980s.

(d) *External Control Issues.* Many of the executives indicated that their boards would exert increasing control over the company. Also, many indicated that there would be increasing numbers of external takeover attempts.

(e) *Other Political Issues.* These included such things as political resistance to new organizational structures and to new managerial styles.

3. Strategic cultural system changes in the 1980s were predicted to be:

(a) *Performance-Related Values.* The culture of the organization would be more driven by performance and accountability. This contrasts with a culture which many of the executives painted as being quite comfortable and tolerating a great deal of performance mediocrity.

(b) *Decision-Making Values.* Managers would be required to take a more long-term view regarding their decisions. In addition, decisions would be more decentralized and would have to be made more quickly.

(c) *People-Oriented Values.* These executives indicated that people will be an increasingly important competitive advantage. Even though the chemical industry is very capital intensive the major companies are all quite equal in terms of capital, technology, and products; therefore, the key difference will be in the quality of the people. They indicate that the culture will become less "nice guy" and more performance oriented with an emphasis on team work and delegation. This may sound paradoxical, but what they were referring to was the end of an era where mediocrity was tolerated, and a shift to a time when one plays nice guy only to those who perform.

(d) *Management Style.* They see a need to become much more entrepreneurial and proactive in their styles. This is also reflected in a more proactive stance toward their environment, especially the regulatory environment.

Each respondent was asked to draw his view of how each of the three cycles would play out over the coming decade. Figure 4.2 presents the technical cycles as drawn by this group of chemical company executives. Each line represents a different person and a different company. It is interesting to note that only two companies reflect a relatively certain decade in terms of the technical cycle. This means they are not predicting any major alteration in markets, products, organization design, or production processes. Most executives predict the decade will bring increasing technical uncertainty as industries gear up for new production processes, new products, and new markets.

Figure 4.3 presents the political cycles drawn by these executives. They are quite idiosyncratic. For example, the line running across the top reflects a view of a decade of political turbulence. The executive who drew this line said he envisioned a totally new power structure, reward system, etc. for the coming decade and predicted a great deal of infighting all the way along. Others presented lines which had peaks and valleys. Very often a peak was associated with the retirement of a group of key executives or a planned reorganization. Again, there

TECHNICAL CYCLE

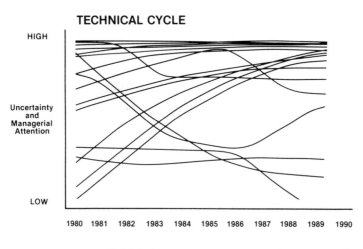

Technical = focus on the production problem · efficiency & effectiveness

Figure 4.2

POLITICAL CYCLES

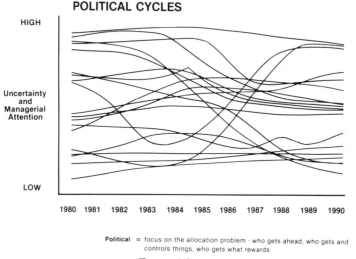

Political = focus on the allocation problem · who gets ahead, who gets and
controls things, who gets what rewards

Figure 4.3

were a couple of organizations reporting relative political stability
in the 1980s.

Finally, Figure 4.4 presents the cultural cycles for the decade. They
tend to trail the technical cycles. The executives talked about them in
terms of the kind of culture needed to make the organization work
in the 1990s. They were very conscious of the need to alter the norms
and values of their organizations over the next 10 years. Whether
or not these projections will make their companies effective is open to
debate and will not be our concern here. What is of concern is helping

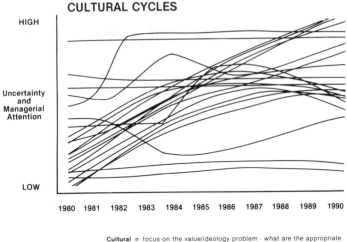

CULTURAL CYCLES

Cultural = focus on the value/ideology problem · what are the appropriate
norms and values for this organization

Figure 4.4

managers of change develop concepts and skills for managing each of
the three cycles. As reflected in Figure 4.1, the tasks needed to manage
the technical system are distinct from those required for the political
and cultural systems. The remainder of this chapter presents guidelines
for managing each system.

STRATEGIC ALIGNMENT

The goal of strategic change management is to align the components
of an organization technically, politically, and culturally. The argument
is made that an effective organization is one in which there is good
strategic alignment, that is, the organizational components are aligned
with each other and the political, technical, and cultural systems are
in good alignment with each other. For example, up until the end of
the 1970s, the auto companies were generally in pretty good strategic
alignment. Change was first triggered in the technical area because of
the energy crisis and the fuel-efficient and higher-quality Japanese and
European cars which cut into the sales volume. The uncertainty in the
technical area spurred massive changes in corporate strategy and organizational design, people, and processes which will take five or more
years to implement fully. These changes, in turn, triggered political and
cultural changes. In the political area, the relationship between union
and management will undergo massive readjustment. Chrysler Corporation has included union representatives on the board, and AMC
has proposed that workers loan some of their cost-of-living increases

to the company. General Motors and Ford are involving workers in quality of work-life programs. The managerial ranks will be weeded out, and there will be uncertainty in the future about what it takes to get promoted. Finally, a culture that values quality, efficiency, and participative management must be developed to support the new strategies.

Four strategic alignment tests will be discussed in this book: (1) a technical one, (2) a political one, (3) a cultural one, and (4) one which tests consistency between the three systems. Because organizations are dynamic and exist in changing environments, none of these alignments will ever be stable. They reflect ongoing dilemmas for the organization. At different points in time, any one, or combination, may be in need of adjustment. These adjustment processes tend to trigger a new organizational cycle in another area, such as the automakers' technical cycle triggering a political and cultural need for alignment. It should be noted that even though strategic alignment is discussed in terms of being a conscious, managed activity, there are other possibilities. These include adjustment by benign neglect or purposeful avoidance. For example, a strong leader may choose to ignore an attempted coup d'etat. Often such an action can make the opponents look weak and ineffectual and ultimately lead to their own demise without the leader having to expend political energy. Other avoidance approaches could include riding out a business downturn rather than altering the company's markets, products, or production efficiencies. This book is dedicated to suggesting direct approaches to managing uncertainty and achieving strategic alignment.

Achieving strategic alignment is the responsiblity of the leaders of an organization. Guidelines will now be presented for managing the technical, political, and cultural problem areas. In doing so, the following points should be kept in mind:

1. Organizations must deal with the three problem areas simultaneously; (a) during the initial organizational design, (b) as the organization is managed, and (c) when efforts to change the organization are undertaken.

2. Various mechanisms exist to *temporarily* resolve each of these problems. They never stay permanently aligned.

3. Management's prime task is to attend to all three problem areas outlined at the beginning of this chapter.

4. The management of change poses unique and extreme demands on the resolution of the three problem areas.

5. Organizations proceed through cycles which are determined by how these problem areas are managed.

INTERRELATIONSHIPS BETWEEN MODEL COMPONENTS

Technical

The first alignment we will discuss is technical. It is designed to manage uncertainty with regard to the financial, business criteria outputs. The concepts presented in this section draw heavily from the contingency organizational design theorists who strove to match organizational designs to the complexity and uncertainty of environments and the organization's technologies (Galbraith, 1977; Lawrence and Lorsch, 1967; Tushman and Nadler, 1978).

Technical alignments assume that the components of the organization are to be interrelated in such a fashion as to achieve organizational effectiveness and efficiency in the marketplace. Figure 4.5, adapted from Tushman and Nadler (1978), presents a basic scheme for technical alignment. The following principle applies: *An organization is technically effective to the degree that the uncertainty it faces matches its capacity to process information and to eliminate the uncertainty.* (It should be noted that too much information processing capacity is as dysfunctional as too little, because the management of information processing capacity is costly and complex.

1.   Uncertainty arises because the information required to complete tasks exceeds the information possessed. There are three major sources of uncertainty in an organization:

(a)   *Environments.* Changing and complex environments engender uncertainty; the electronic and information processing industry faces such an environment.

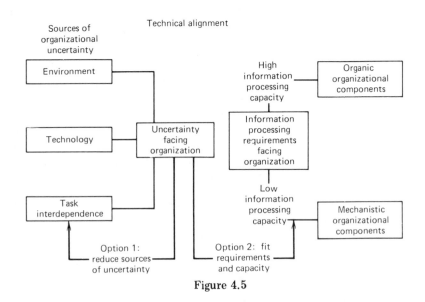

Figure 4.5

(b) *Tasks.* Simple routine tasks such as found in basic manufacturing produce low levels of uncertainty, whereas nonroutine complex tasks such as those found in high technology research industries, create high levels of uncertainty.

(c) *Task Interdependencies.* Work tasks which must be closely linked are highly interdependent and create greater uncertainty (Tushman and Nadler, 1978).

2. As uncertainty increases—from any combination of sources—so does the need for information-processing capacity. For example, if an organization suddenly becomes more uncertain about the status of one of its environments—for example, a market or a governmental agency—pressures build to process information about this environment. The additional information processing components include marketing research departments and governmental affairs offices.

3. Different organization configurations—of networks, people, and processes—have different capabilities of processing information. As information processing requirements change, organizational components should be adjusted. Figure 4.6 compares the characteristics of purely mechanistic configurations with organic ones. Organic configurations, in which people interact with many others, have high information-processing capacities, whereas mechanistic configurations, in which people have strict reporting relationships and limited interaction, have low information-processing capacities.

4. Organizations will be more efficient and effective from a technical point of view when there is a good alignment between the information-processing requirements facing the organization and the information-processing capacity of the organizational components.

5. Finally, there is a time dimension implicit in Figure 4.5. Organizations never maintain static equilibrium, although they may reach a temporary equilibrium. As time passes, information-processing requirements change, and organizational configurations should evolve to match these new requirements.

Two options are available to deal with a poor match between uncertainty and information-processing capacity. Option 1 is to reduce the uncertainty. This might be accomplished by changing the relationship with an uncertain environment by formation of foreign cartels, lobbying for protective legislation, or withdrawal from certain markets.

Option 2 is to change tasks or task interdependencies, that is, alter information-processing capacities. Automation is one way of simplifying tasks, for example, having machines and computers handle the uncertain tasks as has been done in banks, where loan officers are replaced by computers which analyze consumer loan applications by point-scoring systems. These systems match an applicant's scores on 10 to 20 items with a set of criteria programmed into the computer, thus replacing the judgment of a loan officer. Task interdependence can

Components of Model	Mechanistic	Organic
	Nature of Environment	
	Certain (Stable)	Uncertain (Turbulent)
Mission/strategy	Simple implicit fragmented	Complex Explicit Integrated
People—management style	Conservative Seat of the pants Nonparticipative	Risk taking Optimization of performance Participative
Prescribed networks	Simple integration mechanisms	Complex integration devices
Organizational processes	Minimal communication Conflict avoided Nonparticipative Decision making	Open communication Conflict confronted Participative Decision making
Emergent networks	Friendship, non-task related cliques	Extensive task related networks Task coalitions

Figure 4.6   Technical organizations

be reduced by creating autonomous work groups. At Volvo, each work group assembles a total engine rather than one piece on a long assembly line. As is indicated by 4.6, changing the organizational components to more organic forms will enhance information-processing capacity. One way to effect this change is to connect people more fully in the prescribed networks in order to facilitate communication. Thus, people can be prescribed to interact with others via formal committees, task forces, etc., in order to increase information-processing capacity.

Strategically aligning an organization to be more technically organic may trigger political and cultural cycles of adjustment as people's budgets, careers, and power bases shift, and as new sets of norms are required to make the system function.

Political Alignment

The second type of alignment deals with the political aspects of the organization. March observed,

> a business firm is a political coalition and . . . the executive in the firm is the political broker. The composition of the firm is not given; it is negotiated. The goals of the firm are not given; they are bargained (1962, p. 672).

Cyert and March (1963) support this view and argue that a coalition's members constantly reevaluate the rewards they receive for participating in the coalition. A coalition's members therefore make continuous adjustments to enable them to fare better.

Political alignment is based on the view of organizations as coalitions (Cyert and March, 1963; March, 1962) altering "their purposes and domains to accomodate new interests, sloughing off parts of themselves to avoid some interests, and when necessary, becoming involved in activities far afield from their stated central purposes (Pfeffer and Salancik, 1978, p. 24)." As a result, organizational behaviors are shaped by political bargaining which will guide the allocation of organizational resources. The political drive is for survival and growth, as contrasted with technical effectiveness and efficiency; survival and growth from a political perspective require an organization to pursue the interests of the guiding coalitions. Survival and growth depend on continuing exchanges which induce members of the organization—with money, prestige, and threats—to contribute labor, money, or support. The more an organization depends on the contributions of an individual participant, the more power that participant exerts on the allocation process.

The political test of alignment is similar to the technical test in that the objective is to reduce or manage uncertainty. The difference is that here the focus is on the uncertainty surrounding the power to allocate resources and decide on the organization's goals. An organization faces political controversies or uncertainties which require political bargaining and conflicts. These requirements should match the organization's capacities for political bargaining and conflict.

1. Organizations vary in their degree of political uncertainty. Political uncertainties result from controversies regarding the power to

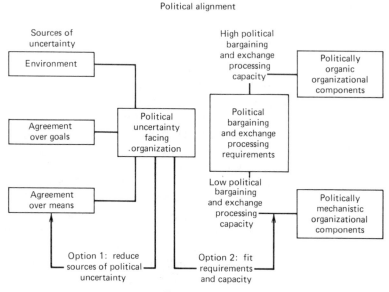

Political alignment

Figure 4.7

allocate resources and to set organizational goals. These controversies express disagreements among coalitions vis-a-vis allocations of resources, power, and prestige.

At a societal level, an argument has been made by Lestor Thurow (1980) in his book *Zero Sum Society*, that such economic problems as inflation, energy, and unemployment cannot be solved without some parts of society winning and some losing. The *technical* or economic problems in the United States have triggered great political uncertainty. Thurow argues that the United States does not have the capacity to deal with the high level of uncertainty generated by the severe economic (technical) problems. He states that:

> The problem with zero-sum games is that the essence of problem solving is less allocation. But that is precisely what our political process is least capable of doing. When there are economic gains to be allocated, our political process can allocate them. When there are large economic losses to be allocated, our political process is paralyzed. And with political paralysis comes economic paralysis. (p. 12)

Political controversies vary because of:

(a) *Changing and Complex Environments.* An example of environmentally induced political uncertainty is the change brought to American organizations by Equal Employment Opportunity legislation: The guiding coalitions which excluded women and blacks suddenly lost legitimacy, and women and blacks acquired the right to file suits for financial redress. Both AT&T and GE have had to make large settlements of back pay and promotional advancements in class action suits.

(b) *Changing Organizational Goals.* Political uncertainty increases when there is disagreement among organizational members regarding goals. Goal disagreement splits organizational members into competing camps. For example, in medical centers, there often exists competition between those groups with research goals, and those with teaching goals, and those with service goals. Large commercial banks have coalitions supporting different lines of business, for example, consumer banking versus institutional banking. There was a fair amount of turmoil at Bankers Trust Company when the company made a strategic decision to sell its branches and get out of consumer banking.

(c) *Changing Means for Achieving Organizational Goals.* When members of the organization disagree about the best means for accomplishing the organization's work, political uncertainty is increased. For example, conflicts often erupt over whether to centralize, decentralize, or organize geographically (Thompson and Tuden, 1959).

2. As political uncertainties increase, so does the need for political bargaining and exchange.

3. Different organizational configurations have different capabilities for political bargaining and conflict. Figure 4.8 contrasts politically mechanistic configurations, which have lower capacities for bargaining and conflict, with politically organic configurations, which have higher capacities. Politically mechanistic organizations for the most part are locked into a particular set of power allocations for resource relationships; there is little opportunity for changing these relationships without revolution or mutiny. Martin Luther had to revolt against the mechanistic Catholic Church. A sailor must commit mutiny to question a ship's power relationships and a worker in a mechanistic organization must form a powerful coalition to counter the power of management. In contrast, organizations with democratic mechanisms, such as some less power-centered churches, are much more politically organic as they allow for voting to alter the power relationships. Worker owned firms or professional organizations are generally politically organic.

4. Organizations will manage the political bargaining and exchange processes and will be more politically effective to the extent that there is a match between the requirements of bargaining and exchange and the bargaining capacity of the organization's components.

Two options are available to deal with a poor match between political uncertainty and the organization's bargaining and exchange capacity. Option 1 is, again, to alter the uncertainty. This can be accomplished by attempting to change the environment by forming political coalitions, or using interlocking directorates to maintain control. Another way is illustrated by governmentally regulated firms which have captured the governmental agencies that are supposed to regulate them—by supplying key personnel, by exerting influence through legislators, and by hoarding technological expertise (Kohlmeier, 1969).

Politically Mechanistic

> Power relations formally prescribed
> Little capacity for managing shifts in power
> Examples: Military organizations, the Catholic Church,
>   family owned business organizations

Politically Organic

> Power relations prescribed and emergent
> High capacity for shifting power bases
> High capacity for managing ongoing bargaining
> relationships
> Examples: Political parties, kibbutzim, democratically
>   managed labor unions, participationally managed
>   organizations

Figure 4.8   Political organizations

Option 2 can be exercised by developing a goal and/or means consensus. For example, consider a group of medical centers which traditionally pursued three goals: research, teaching, and service delivery. Faced with environmental shifts in the early 1970s which included major cuts in federal support as well as rapidly rising costs, the medical centers were faced with the necessity of making choices among goals. This created great political uncertainty. Which goal would dominate under win—lose conditions of scarce resources? The dominant coalition of one medical center decided that their core goal would be research, for which they developed a specific research strategy. Another center decided that teaching medical students was its core goal. In both cases, political uncertainty— in other words, fighting over goals and means—was reduced by developing a consensus over goals and means. It required adjustments in the fit between political bargaining needs and political bargaining processing capacity. This is done by making adjustments on the mechanistic/organic scale for the organization as outlined in Figure 4.8. When such options are not feasible, then Option 1 must be followed.

5. Finally, as with the technical alignment, there is a time dimension. As time passes, there will be changes in the political bargaining, and processing demands; the organization must make adjustments to meet these new demands. A *political* adjustment cycle is triggered which can in turn trigger technical and cultural cycles of adjustments.

Cultural Alignment

Of the three systems, the cultural is both the most pervasive and the most ambiguous. This is because norms and values are not always explicit and clearly identifiable in the way a technical organizational structure or production technology is. One writer on organizational culture (Jay, 1971, p. 183) said that an organization resembles a tribe and proposed that "a good way to find the central faith of a tribe is to get its members to see who can formulate the biggest blasphemy." For example:

> In the BBC: "I admit it wasn't really true, but the Home Secretary was very keen we should say it." In Rolls Royce: "It's a lousy bit of engineering but it will sell like hotcakes." (pp. 182-183).

Culture is too critical to strategic management to rely simply on identifying blasphemous statements about organizations. Poorly managed culture had led companies into pretty serious problems. Two oil companies were led into such serious problems by their CEOs:

> Five years ago the chief executives of two major oil companies determined that they would have to diversify out of oil because their current business

could not support long-term growth and faced serious political threats. (*Business Week*, 27 October 1980, p. 148)

In both cases the oil companies were unable to successfully diversify. The result was that they ended their forays outside of the oil industry and have returned to their dominant business.

> Each of the CEOs had been unable to implement his strategy, not because it was theoretically wrong or bad but because neither had understood that his company's culture was so entrenched in the traditions and values of doing business in oil that employees resisted—and sabotaged—the radical changes that the CEOs tried to impose. (*Business Week*, 27 October 1980, p. 148)

Other examples of how cultural differences can create serious organizational problems include the experiences of some companies with sensitivity training. In many organizations during the 1960s, managers who had participated in this training rejected traditional, power-oriented beliefs. Yet, they went back to their organizational settings and confronted a culture in which their bosses were still the cultural guardians of the traditional norms.

Vandivier (1972) described the maneuvering inside the B.F. Goodrich Company after an engineer designed an aircraft brake incorrectly. The company's values and norms dictated that the brake should be delivered as designed and that false data should be submitted about the brake's performance. The values of the engineering profession held that performance data should be accurate, and governmental agencies raised the spector of civil or criminal liability. Consequently, two low-level members rejected the company's norms and talked to the Federal Bureau of Investigation.

One of the most important and difficult tasks of top management is to decide the content of the organization's culture; that is, to determine what values should be shared, what objectives are worth striving for, what beliefs the employees should be committed to, and what interpretations of past events and current pronouncements would be most beneficial for the firm. Having made these decisions, management's next task is to communicate these values in a memorable and believable fashion which will not be instantly forgotten or easily dismissed as corporate propaganda. Note that these decisions are not always made explicitly. Decisions about culture are often made implicitly, intuitively, and by trial and error.

Obviously, although organizations generally have dominant sets of beliefs, subcultures and countercultures may develop. For example, the subculture in research and development may be visibly different from the more staid and conservative atmosphere in the financial department or the more action-oriented production department. A powerful executive with an independent sphere of influence, such as John DeLorean at General Motors, may successfully develop a counterculture which challenges some, but not all, of the values of the dominant culture. Hierarchy also may affect the culture. It may be essential for blue-collar workers in an organization to share the same values and commitments as the professional and/or managerial members of the organization.

There are two critical issues regarding culture. First, the content of the culture and subcultures of an organization. Second, the means by which cultural processes are managed, that is, what vehicles are used for molding and shaping culture and for incorporating subcultures into the organization. This chapter focuses on the second of these issues: the processes of managing culture. The content of culture will be dealt with in the chapter on cultural strategies, Chapter 8.

Katz and Kahn (1978) proposed two conditions for cultural congruence among members of an organization: (1) a majority of the active organizational members should accept the beliefs, endorse the values, and abide by the norms; and (2) individual members should be made aware that the beliefs, values, and norms have collective support. However, cultural congruence in an organization varies over time. This is perhaps because of environmental value shifts or perhaps because new members bring diversity into the culture. Therefore, organizations must have ways of either reducing cultural incongruence or developing capacities for managing cultural incongruence. Incongruence is used in this case so as to make a parallel with the concept of uncertainty discussed in the beginning of this chapter.

There are a set of concepts for analyzing the amount of cultural uncertainty which an organization faces, and there are managerial responses to cultural uncertainty. The following guidelines for assessing the cultural alignment of an organization can be used to deal with these phenomena. They are outlined in Figure 4.9.

1. Organizations vary in their degrees of cultural congruence. Congruence is defined as the degree of consistency among organizational members with regard to values and organizational norms. Congruence varies as a result of:

   (a) Environment—cultural value shifts in the wider environment are reflected within the organization and thus create cultural incongruence.

   (b) Diversity of backgrounds in the organization along such dimensions as ethnic background, education, professional identification, sex, and age contribute to greater cultural value incongruence. In addition, differences in functional background, such as finance, marketing, R&D, and production also creates diversity.

2. As organizational value/cultural incongruence   increases, so does the *need for increased amounts of cultural/value adjustment*

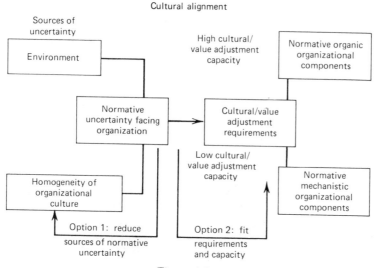

Figure 4.9

Culturally mechanistic
  Little capacity for incongruent
  values/ideologies
  People fear being vulnerable
  Relations are manipulative
  Defensive interpersonal relations
  Defensive norms
Culturally organic
  High capacity for managing
  differences in values/ideologies
  People oriented towards facilitative/
  collaborative relations
  Minimally defensive interpersonal
  relations
  Learning-oriented norms

Figure 4.10   Cultural organizations

and hence the need for greater organizational capacity for dealing with cultural/value shifts.

3. Different organizational configurations (networks, people, processes) have varying capabilities for facilitating cultural/value adjustments. Figure 4.10 contrasts the components of an organization which has low cultural/value adjustment capacity with one which has a high capacity. The mechanistic versus organic distinctions are used for analysis of cultural alignment as well.

4. Organizations will manage the cultural/value adjustment process and be more culturally effective to the extent that there is a match between the cultural/value incongruencies facing the organization and the adjustment capacity of that organization's components.

5. Finally, as with both the technical and political alignments, there is a time dimension. Adjustments are required over time as new cultural incongruencies emerge. These adjustments may trigger cultural cycles which in turn may trigger technical and political cycles.

When there is a poor alignment between cultural/value congruence and the cultural/value adjustment capacity in the organization, there are two basic options for changing the situation. Option 1 is to change either the environment and the organization's relationship to the environment, or to change the diversity of people in the organization. An example of this option occurs when an organization develops selective criteria which lead to a homogeneous worker population. This can be found in a variety of industries ranging from publishing to investment banking where there are Jewish organizations, White Anglo-Saxon Protestant organizations, and Catholic organizations. The implicit goal is homogeneity of culture. Often the locations of manufacturing plants have been based on assumptions of the cultural values of workers in the local workforce, rather than on technical grounds.

Option 2 is to alter the alignment between the value/cultural adjustment demands and the organization's value/cultural adjustment capacity. This entails making adjustments on the mechanistic to organic dimensions for the organizational components as outlined in Figure 4.10.

The culturally mechanistic organization is one in which there is little opportunity for people to explore differences in values and constructively coexist. Extreme forms are radical political groups and tightly knit social fraternities with discriminatory membership. Less extreme cases include business organizations which, through staff selection, socialization, and firings acquire members with very homogeneous values and ideologies. An example of such a case, presented in the next chapter, is Texas Instruments.

The culturally organic organization is one in which there is a high capacity for people to express value differences and coexist with such differences. The culture is one in which interpersonal openness is actively supported. Often, there is widespread use of various experience-based interpersonal group technologies such as T-groups, sensitivity training, and team building to help individuals learn to function and grow through such openness. Organizations which have offered consciousness-raising for women and minorities, confrontation meetings between men and women and among minority groups, and, have focused sensitivity training sessions on value orientation are exhibiting culturally organic characteristics.

OVERALL TECHNICAL, POLITICAL, AND CULTURAL ALIGNMENT

This chapter focused primarily on tools for managing each of the three systems. As I indicated at the start of this chapter, the total matrix in Figure 4.1 must be aligned like a dynamic jigsaw puzzle. Thus we will need to provide managers of change with some tools for managing down the columns of Figure 4.1. This requires the concepts and skills for keeping the technical, political, and cultural strands of the strategic rope woven together. Alignment across the three systems is actually the most strategic of the tasks and is the primary focus of Chapter 6, which will deal with the development of an overall change strategy.

The basic task for change managers is to ensure that there is alignment within each of the three systems and then between the systems. A well-designed organization should exhibit harmony between its cultural, political, and technical systems, and each of these systems should be internally aligned.

Many organizations have systems in which one part supercedes the others. For example, cultural systems often dominate in religious organizations, political systems in labor unions or political parties, and technical systems in business firms.

Imbalances, and hence the need for redesign, are likely to occur in the subordinate systems. If members are constantly attending to technical issues and pursuing solutions to technical problems, they are likely to give too little attention to cultural or political systems. This was the case in the two oil companies mentioned earlier, in which cultural issues were ignored and ultimately led to a political upheaval which removed the CEOs. This appears to have also happened at Citibank in New York City (Seeger, 1977). The bank brought in a team of production managers from Ford Motor Company to turn its paper processing into a factory operation. This was done very technically. However, some political time bombs were activated. The traditional bankers became angry with the power that the new factory managers were able to exert over them. Power struggles arose, especially over the future top management control of the bank.

The foregoing suggests a rule of thumb for change managers: Dominant systems are likely to be in balance, and subordinate systems are likely to be out of balance. A word of caution: What is explicitly presented as dominant may, in fact, be subordinate. One previously cited example was the firing of Lee Iacocca by Henry Ford, which was publically explained as a technical problem and not the political problem that it really was. In the firing of the two oil CEOs, the public pronouncement did not address the real problem, which was the inability of the CEOs to manage cultural change.

Overall organizational effectiveness is a multidimensional concept. It includes the organization's ability to adapt and survive; this is possible only if there is a reasonable degree of alignment both within and between the technical, political, and cultural subsystems.

CONCLUSION

This chapter provided certain conceptual tools for making the organizational model dynamic. These conceptual tools enable one to evaluate the dynamic interplay between the organizational model components from each of the three perspectives—technical, political, and cultural.

The concept of alignment provides the guideline for the development of a change strategy. Bad alignments necessitate change. The management of change consists of technical, political, and cultural adjustments among the components of the organization.

APPENDIX TO CHAPTER FOUR

A Case Illustration of Organizational Change: Technical, Political, and Cultural

The Dr. Martin Luther King, Jr. Health Center (MLK) is a neighborhood health center located in the South Bronx, New York. MLK serves one of the most blighted urban areas in the United States. The problems of deteriorating housing, widespread unemployment, lack of educational opportunity, crime, and drugs have contributed to a complex of socially related health problems that defy conventional medical solutions. The center was founded in 1966 with the help of a federal grant administered by Montefiore Hospital and Medical Center. MLK has grown to a health care center with a staff of close to 400 and serves 39,000 residents of a section of the Bronx which has 75,000 residents.

The center is known for its innovative primary health care; it developed the family-oriented primary health care team, utilized community health workers, and nurse practitioners in unique ways, developed a matrix organizational design, and developed an internal structure which was managed all the way to the top by community members.

The MLK case illustrates one way that organizational cycles can operate in one setting over a 10-year period. The discussion of the case is divided into four phases. These are not meant to be constructed as developmental stages, but are created as post hoc descriptions of the organization's activities. The titles of the phases were created to reflect the major activity of that time period.

Figure 4A.1 presents two sets of concerns: MLK's organizational cycles over a 10-year period in relation to the four phases, and a description of the salient characteristics of each component of the organizational model during each phase.

Phase 1: Start-Up

As Figure 4A.1 indicates, the dominant cycle in the start-up phase for MLK was the cultural cycle. This cycle was triggered by the environmental offering of a major opportunity. The Office of Economic Opportunity sprang into life in the mid-1960s. It made large grants available to build neighborhood health centers. The availability of this resource triggered Harold Wise to develop an ideology for organizing a critical mass of people to start the MLK Center. This core group started with a vague idea of a future organization. The key problem to solve was the value/ideological problem. That is, Harold Wise and the core group worked to develop a common ideology and sense of mission. This provided the normative glue for the organization.

The core group saw it as their moral duty to organize the community around this ideology. The professional outsiders identified the informal community leaders and built an alliance with them. The outside professionals were highly committed to the ideology and formed a social contract with the community members to carry out this ideology. For the community members, the ideological commitment was preceded by a desire for jobs.

The condition which facilitated cultural problem solving included an environment which was munificent (money readily available), a highly charismatic leader, and an organization with a great deal of fluidity. Figure 4A.1 presents the conditions which were predominant during this phase.

The first year saw the health center begin as a social movement. There was a central charismatic leader and a core of socially committed professionals who moved into the community as organizers. Authority was exercised through normative rewards, and members' involvement with the MLK Center involved high personal commitment to the intrinsic value and mission of the organization (Etzioni, 1961).

During the first year the center was being set up, the leader/founder, Harold Wise, encouraged people to do "their own thing," to get projects started, to try things out and not worry about how well they would work or who would pay for them. The organization was dominated by a moral feeling that what they were doing was right and that innovation was the important mode of operation.

During this phase political uncertainty developed. Although the community board was a benign factor during the first two years of the center, conflict later developed between board and staff over control of the center and patronage (jobs for family and friends of board members)

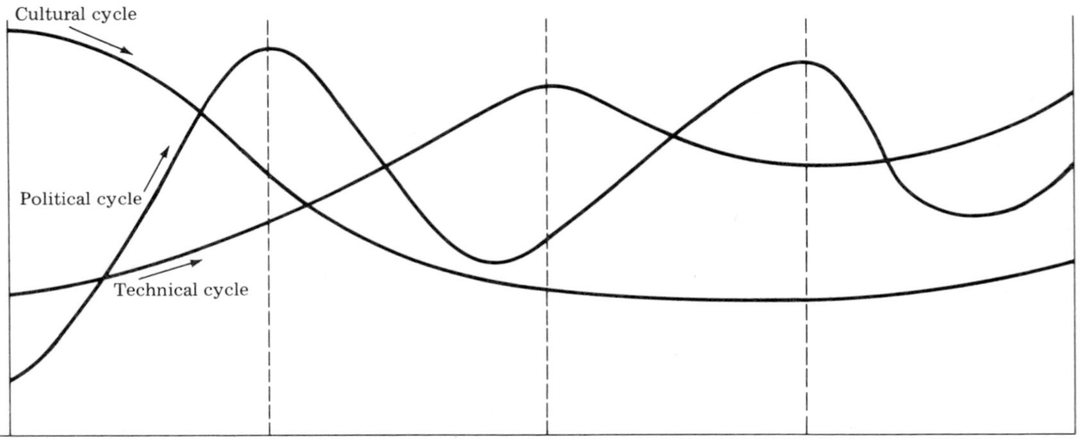

Organizational Components	Phase I Start-Up	Phase II System Development	Phase III Stabilization	Phase IV Self-Renewal
Environment	Benign, supportive, internal community control	Pressure for more internal community control	Moderate pressure for internal community control	Strong pressure (by opportunity and/or threat), external community control
Mission/strategy	High commitment	Rationalized, explicit	Continuity of strategy with piecemeal changes	Reformable, explicit, and rational
Sociotechnical	Adaptive, experimental	Rationalized formalization	Stabilized, little change from Phase III	Redesign
Organizational processes	Fluid, commitment over time or quality, error-embracing	Systematized, more of a balance between error-embracing and avoiding	Routinized, error avoidance dominant	Redesign
People	Innovators, idealistic	Pushers in charge	Good followers needed	Innovators and pushers needed
Emergent networks	Extensive internal and external social linkages	Supportive of management efforts	Variety of social networks	Reenergize to support the top

Figure 4A.1 Organizational cycles and trade-offs. (From Noel M. Tichy, *Organization design for primary health care*. Copyright © 1977 by Praeger Publishers, Inc. Reprinted by permission of Praeger Publishers.)

during the third year. At this point, major cleavages among the board, the middle-class professional staff, and the community workers emerged. Since the community was lacking in institutions as well as other resources, the MLK community board meetings became one of the few forums for political activities. It, therefore, attracted a variety of community activists with various political agendas. One of the major issues on the board was the struggle for power between blacks and Puerto Ricans. Thus, the political cycle climbed toward a peak after a couple of years.

The situation within the center differed from that of the community board as community workers and professionals became increasingly concerned with health delivery and less involved with broad political and social problems. They attended more to the technical cycle. Although the majority of the center's workers were black, ethnic conflicts were reduced by on-the-job camaraderie. There was increasing divergence in the relationship between board members and community workers. Initially, they had held a common point of view. But, as the workers became more technically competent and career oriented, they began to view the board members, who served part-time without pay, as uninformed about health matters and unqualified to make decisions about the center. Furthermore, the workers wanted to cool down ethnic conflict, and regarded the playing out of the Puerto Rican/black struggle on the board as a threat to the center.

The political problems were managed by Dr. Wise and the community workers planning the eventual takeover of the center's management by the community members. Thus, rather than turn control over to an external board, MLK would develop an internal community worker cadre. This originally would include the community workers and professionals who originally resisted control by the external community board. The coalition developed and the external board became a weak political force at the MLK Center for much of the following 10 years.

The emphasis on the cultural and political cycles triggered the technical cycle. By the end of the start-up phase a crisis of confidence developed toward the charismatic leadership. The crisis was not resolved until pressure was exerted from both the internal and environmental arenas. Without this pressure the organization would have floundered. In the MLK Center's case, individuals from the outside, two young physicians and a management professor from MIT, were major conduits for external pressure, each telegraphing the message that the ship was not in good order and required a technical overhaul. The resolution of the crisis in the next phase was facilitated by managerial attention and rational problem solving. The technical organizational cycle was triggered and resulted in the explicit and systematic reexamination of mission and strategy, system design, development, and implementation. The information-processing capacity of the organization was increased to match uncertainty. At the health team level, a much more organic system including a matrix organization structure was designed.

The start-up phase ended with the organization facing confusion, internal conflicts, and frustration. The dominance of cultural, and then political concerns had left little attention for the technical concerns; yet the technical cycle had reached a peak.

Phase II: Systems Development

The second phase of the MLK Center's development was dominated by the development of managerial procedures to provide a semblance of order out of the confusion created in Phase I. The organization invested heavily in developing systems and procedures. The conditions which facilitated development in Phase I—experimenting, creativity, entre- preneurial leadership—actually hindered development during the second phase. The decision making and leadership required for Phase II in- volved rational planning and a less participative, forceful managerial style.

The pressure for change was sufficiently intense for Harold Wise to seek outside help from Professor Richard Beckhard of MIT's Sloan School of Management.

Beckhard brought management and organizational design expertise to the MLK Center, thus providing the group with new models for deal- ing with their problems. Professor Beckhard worked with the top man- agement and the community heirs apparent, Deloris Smith and Sonia Valdez, in clarifying the Center's mission and strategy. Once this was done, it was clear to Beckhard and the Center's managers that the struc- ture and management was ineffective. It did not provide effective team- oriented health care with maximum community and worker involvement and control.

Beckhard proposed a new organizational design and management structure. The result was that the MLK Center became a matrix type of structure; team development and planning work were carried out with each team; and plans were developed for training and preparing the community heir apparents to take over the Center.

The system development phase resulted in reducing confusion, frus- tration, and ambivalence, and improved management of the technical cycle, yet it triggered a new dilemma: doubt and cynicism about management.

The implementation of these rational plans was left to the leadership of Dr. Edward Martin, the director of health services. He was relentless in his determination to follow the rules, encourage the Center to pull its own financial weight, and provide quality health care.

By the end of Phase II the organization had been driven hard. Not only had new systems been designed and implemented, but also the community managers had completed their training and had moved into positions of authority. The organization ended this phase with a sense of accomplishment. The technical cycle was decending into a valley. Even though the changes were accompanied by a sense of accomplishment, the organization had been pushed hard and power had become more centralized, resulting in a general reaction against control and a cynicism about management. A greater we/they dynamic between managers and workers set in. As Figure 4A.1 indicates, even though the technical cycle was dominant during this phase, the political cycle had started climbing as efforts were made to develop managers from the community. The cultural cycle remained stable throughout this period.

Phase III: Stabilization and Consolidation Phase

This phase provided the MLK Center with time to test the newly designed and implemented technical solutions to the production and efficiency problem, and to make minor alterations and improvements. This phase had the added significance of including the testing of newly promoted community managers who were given total responsibility for managing the Center. The dominant organizational activities of this period involved making small adjustments and changes. Cultural problems received minimal attention as people became increasingly concerned with jobs, careers, and instrumental rather than ideological concerns. By the end of this phase the political area began requiring attention. The cycle was heading toward another peak as pressure increased from HEW (the grant was shifted to HEW when OEO was dismantled) and Montefiore to turn the Center over to a community board. This meant that new community managers had to deal with the political uncertainty of creating a working board. This was difficult because the existing board had some powerful members who were not very supportive of the existing management, and there was the very real danger that a community board would alter the Center's goals and replace key managers. The community managers justifiably feared that their jobs might be in danger if the currently constituted board took over.

Over a period of a couple of years a new working board with total responsibility for the center was developed. Montefiore turned over all control to the community board early in 1978.

Self-Renewal Phase

While undergoing the transition to a new board, the Center experienced tremendous pressure from the environment which included demands for cost effectiveness, a migration of patients away from the MLK Center's service area, and a reduction in federal grants to cover deficits. This phase was the prelude to a struggle for survival in an increasingly hostile environment. Both the technical and political cycles approached peaks as the Center faced two problems: (1) how to manage more efficiently and effectively, and (2) how to capture a greater allocation of HEW and other resources for the Center and the South Bronx. The managerial response possible under such circumstances is to trigger either political and/or technical activities. Political activities focus on capturing more financial resources from various government agencies. The technical activities focus on mapping the environment via marketing and financial studies, reformulating the mission and strategy, and mobilizing the organization for action around the redesign and change of strategy. The MLK Center first focused on the technical theme. However, the political cycle could not be held in check during this phase; the major political uncertainties involved the balance of power between the internal community managers and the external community board. At the writing of this paper, the two cycles—political and technical—had peaked simultaneously. The organization faced a major, financial production problem—how to survive with tighter financial resources. At the same time, the external board had forced the resignation of the director, a community manager who was very technically competent, for political reasons. This mobilized an internal coalition of community workers to fight the external board.

Another rather ominous sign appeared: The cultural cycle began to rise. That is, differences in values and ideology increased among the staff. One group represented a radical Marxist ideology, another was committed to the ideology of community-based preventive health care, and another group focused on instrumental material gain—how to make more money.

The simultaneous peaking of two cycles creates enormous strain on an organization; if all three cycles peak simultaneously, the survival of the organization comes into question. The cycles at the MLK Center may all peak simultaneously.

PART TWO

STRATEGIC ISSUES: DIAGNOSIS AND STRATEGY DEVELOPMENT

Chapter Five

Diagnosis for Change

INTRODUCTION

Strategic change becomes necessary when certain events create intolerable turbulence for some portion of the organization. This necessity for change is felt and acted on by key people. These individuals mobilize for action to deal with the turbulence or uncertainty. Because strategic change is large-scale change, it will be triggered by a large-scale uncertainty—in the form of either a *threat* or an *opportunity*.

One consequence of such uncertainty is the creation of stress. Stress can restrict perception and lead to hasty, unconsidered action. As an illustration:

> The highly stressed change manager can end up in trouble. As the pressures build, he starts to run, figuratively, and literally. He becomes a familiar sight running to the airport, to the factory, and back to the airport. He becomes notorious for cancelling appointments because of "the crisis." Then last month's cancellations become next month's crises.

> In his secret Walter Mitty mind, he may see himself as the captain of his ship in desperate straits. Only his maneuvers will keep her afloat. When the messenger wakes him with the warning, "inventories are too high," he responds by bellowing through the voice tube to the bridge, "cut the damn inventories." Next month, because of the skimpy inventories, the lookout reports, "volume is down." Now the captain knows the storm is getting worse. Raising his voice so he can be heard above the gale, he calls the sales manager in the engine room. "All engines ahead flank: Emergency." The following month, because of the extra sales expense, the report from the lookout is "Profits are way off." Bracing his legs to keep his balance on the heaving deck and holding onto the voice tube with both hands, the captain shouts, "Cut the payroll: Slash advertising and research" (*Fortune*, 1976).

To avoid management by crisis, managers must be able to control stress as they encounter it and develop effective ways of carrying out diagnosis and planned change. Decision makers under stress are driven by forces which undermine thorough analysis and planning.

This chapter is about diagnosis. Diagnosis involves a technical process of coolly calculated information collection and analysis. The trouble is that human information processing is carried out by humans who:

> programmed as they are with emotions and unconscious motives as well as with cognitive abilities, seldom can approximate a state of detached affect-lessness when making decisions that impact their own vital interests or those of their organization (Janis and Mann, 1977, p. 54).

Strategic change management decisions are made on the basis of vital interests. The core dilemma is not how to achieve a coolly detached, totally technical process, but how to manage the process of diagnosis, strategic planning, and implementation so as to avoid the Walter Mitty high-stress syndrome as well as other dysfunctional modes of decision making.

Modes of Decision Making Under Stress

The psychological, organizational, and managerial conditions necessary for avoiding dysfunctional diagnosis under stress will be discussed before the steps and guidelines for diagnosis. Table 5.1 presents five possible modes of decision making in response to a triggering event. These five coping patterns characterize managers in strategic change situations. The first four are extremely dysfunctional and can severely hamper effective information processing. They are:

1. *Unconflicted Adherence.* No change results because the triggering event did not lead the participants to see any serious risks in continuing to do what they have been doing. Examples include the early warning signals in New York City prior to its serious financial crisis in 1976 which were not perceived to be above the threshold level for change. Another example is the U.S. government's approach to dealing with the "energy crisis." The risk in such situations is that no adequate diagnosis is carried out and few if any alternatives are explored.

The ultimate dysfunction of unconflicted adherence is the "boiled frog" phenomena (described to me by Professor Karl Weick of Cornell University). A frog placed in water which is gradually heated to boiling will not jump out as long as the rate of change is below the frog's noticeable difference threshold. The result is a boiled frog, even though the frog appears to have had the option of jumping out of the pan at any time. So it is with organizations and managers. Problems may gradually heat up below threshold. The problems or opportunities do not trigger action until it is too late. The result is organizational or managerial failure because of a persistent problem or missed opportunity.

2. *Unconflicted Change.* This concept is based on a perception that some change is called for, but that the chosen course is merely

Table 5.1 Predecisional Behavior Characteristic of the Five Basic Patterns of Decision Making

Pattern of Coping with Challenge	Criteria for High-Quality Decision Making							
	(1) Thorough Canvassing of Alternatives	(2) Thorough Canvassing of Objectives	(3) Careful Evaluation of Consequences		(4) Thorough Search for Information	(5) Unbiased Assimilation of New Information	(6) Careful Re-evaluation of Consequences	(7) Thorough Planning for Implementation and Contingencies
			a. Of Current policy	b. Of Alternative New Policies				
Unconflicted adherence	-	-	-	-	+	-	-	-
Unconflicted change	-	-	+	-	-	+	-	-
Defensive avoidance	-	-	-	-	-	-	-	-
Hypervigilance	-	-	±	±	±	-	-	-
Vigilance	+	+	+	+	+	+	+	+

Source: From I.L. Janis and L. Mann, *Decision Making: A Psychological Analysis of Conflict Choice and Commitment.* Copyright © 1977 by the Free Press, a Division of Macmillan Publishing Co., Inc. Reprinted with permission by Macmillan Publishing Co., Inc.

KEY: + = The decision maker meets the criterion to the best of his ability.

- = The decision maker fails to meet the criterion.

± = The decision maker's performance fluctuates, sometimes meeting the criterion to the best of his ability and sometimes not.

All evaluative terms such as *thorough* and *unbiased* are to be understood as intrapersonal comparative assessments, relative to the person's highest possible level of cognitive performance.

149

a slight variation of the existing course of action. This can best be called "incrementalism." Again, if strategic change is called for, this approach is dysfunctional since it lacks a thorough diagnosis and consideration of major alternatives to the organization's current course of action. W.T. Grant's demise is an example of this. Long before this organization declared bankruptcy, triggers for strategic change were apparent. But the changes launched by the management only included minor course adjustments when major strategic change was called for.

3. *Defensive Avoidance.* The organizational members perceive serious risks for both the current and the new courses of action and feel that no solution can be found. The people have lost hope for a better solution and thus avoid dealing with information about the issue. This is the "head in the sand" approach.

4. *Hypervigilance.* This occurs when the actors perceive serious risk both from the current course of action and from change, and feel that better solutions might be found—but that there is no time to act. As Janis and Mann state:

> The person is constantly aware of pressure to take prompt action to avert catastrophic losses. He superficially scans the most obvious alternatives open to him and may then resort to a crude form of satisfying, hastily choosing the first one that seems to hold the promise of escaping the worst danger. In doing so, he may overlook serious consequences, such as drastic penalties for failing to live up to a prior commitment (1977, p. 74).

The following method is preferred for dealing with stress that requires strategic change management.

5. *Vigilance.* This is a condition in which the participants perceive serious risk from the current course as well as the new course, yet believe a better solution can be found and have sufficient time to search for and evaluate it. Stress is kept under control and operates as a motivating force and not a stimulus to defensive avoidance or hypervigilance.

The approach to diagnosis for strategic change management advocated here is designed to foster decision-making procedures that approach the following ideal procedural criteria (Janis and Mann 1977):

1. Thoroughly canvass alternative courses of action.

2. Survey the full range of objectives to be fulfilled and the values implicated by each choice.

3. Carefully weigh the costs and risks of negative consequences which could flow from each alternative.

4. Intensively search for new information relevant to further evaluation of the alternatives.

5. Correctly assimilate and take account of new information or

expert judgment, even when that information or judgment does not support the course of action initially preferred.

6. Reexamine the positive and negative consequences of all known alternatives, including those originally regarded as unacceptable, before making a final choice.

7. Make detailed provisions for implementing or executing the chosen course of action, giving special attention to contingency plans that might be required if various known risks were to materialize.

The further the diagnosis and the strategic change planning is from meeting these criteria the more defective the process.

Conditions for Vigilant Change Diagnosis

Time pressure, political processes, and a lack of management experience with strategic change all work against vigilant decision making. The following guidelines are recommended for use by practicing managers and consultants who are preparing to carry out the diagnostic steps outlined in the remainder of the chapter.

1. Begin to conceptualize managerial decision making in terms of strategic and nonstrategic change decisions. Set up time and resources to facilitate strategic change decision making. Don't focus all the attention on day-to-day fire fighting or on long-range strategic problems. Balance the attention given to the organization's problems.

2. Be aware that operational problems and immediate crises create "time traps" which draw managerial behavior into hypervigilance, unconflicted change.

3. Develop management triage systems to help filter the type and level of change problem to be dealt with at upper levels. One way to minimize decision-making overload, and thus reduce stress, is to ensure that only the appropriate level of decisions reach the upper levels. Triage systems built on standard operating procedures, administrative aides, and secretaries, can be used to allocate managers' time for strategic change problem solving.

4. Another important managerial practice for fostering vigilant strategic change decision making is the buffering of management. This buffer can be created by the decentralization of decisions and limiting management's "open door policy" by interposing other people to protect managerial time.

5. Create strategic change advocates. Such individuals can be given the role in the organization of advocating that attention be given to strategic change activities. Often the internal organizational development staff can play this role.

6. Monitor time allocation. A norm should be established and

supported for monitoring the allocation of management time to strategic and nonstrategic activities.

Once the time and commitment is found for vigilant diagnosis, the process can take place in the several forms to be discussed as follows.

DIAGNOSIS: THREE ORIENTATIONS

Diagnosis takes place once awareness is triggered by an event or activity that creates organizational uncertainty. Diagnosis is guided by the use of an organizational model such as was presented in the previous two chapters. The object of diagnosis is to gather sufficient information to determine which organizational alignments (which components in the model) need adjusting, and whether the adjustments are political, technical, or cultural.

Triggering the Change Process

As indicated in Chapter 1, the change process is triggered when members of the organization, ultimately the dominant coalition of the organization or a subunit, make decisions to cope with uncertainty by managing the change.

The triggering information can be interpreted according to the following factors:

1. Historical comparisons between current performance and past performance may trigger action, such as when production, productivity, or absenteeism rates worsen over time.

2. Planning comparisons of current performance against future projections. It may be felt that in order to accomplish projections, major organizational changes are required.

3. Extraorganizational comparisons with firms in the same industry. It is frequently not the absolute performance of a firm that motivates managerial action as much as its performance relative to competitors.

4. Other people's expectations often trigger change in organizations. This is particularly so in situations where managers are attempting to make an impact in order to enhance their own careers. Being a good status quo manager does not result in the visibility or recognition necessary for upward career mobility. Thus, managers often start change projects based on what they envision will be positive career outcomes of the change.

Triggers for Change. Two types of events trigger uncertainty and cause cycles to peak. One group represents events and activities which occur independently of the cycles. The second set of events are cycles themselves which trigger each other. That is, a peak in one cycle—be it cultural, political, or technical—will eventually trigger a peak in one or both of the other cycles.

Regardless of the event which causes a cycle to peak, the process is the same. Some core groups in the organization may feel uncertainty and respond to it, thus resulting in stress and a felt need for adjustment.

The set of triggers include:

1. *Environmental changes* such as increased complexity, unpredictability, and competition. The U.S. auto industry was triggered by such an environmental change.

2. *Technological changes* which result in the potential for new products or services and/or new methodologies for producing existing products and services. Genetic engineering and related developments have triggered DuPont to orient itself more toward life science products.

3. *Shifts in agreement among organizational members over the goals of the organization,* such as when splits erupt among members of the dominant coalition(s) regarding the future mission of the organization.

4. *Shifts to agreement among organization members over the means of getting the work done.* These shifts occur when different factions support different forms of production or organizational structure.

5. *Changes in people.* This occurs when recruits are brought into the organization, especially those who differ in some significant way from existing members. An example: women and minorities brought into white, male-dominated organizations.

Figure 5.1 presents these trigger events. A disturbance or uncertainty created by one of the above triggers leads to a need for adjustment in one or more of the cycles. The shaded cells in Figure 5.1 represent the

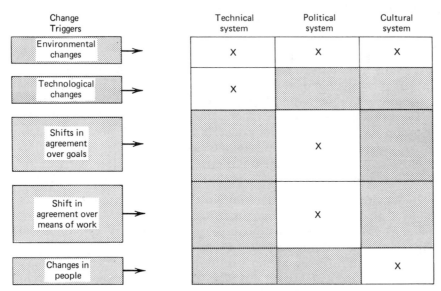

Figure 5.1   Triggers of change

cycles which are affected most by each of the triggers. Note that the environment is shown to impact all three of the cycles simultaneously. This means that major environmental uncertainty often leads to stress and a simultaneous need for adjustment in the technical, political, and cultural subsystems. This does not mean that the organization must attempt to make such adjustments simultaneously. It simply means that the peaks occur at the same time. For example, in the Southwest Hospital case, which will be presented later in the chapter, a financial crisis brought on by the environment triggered all three cycles; the change was managed, however, by dealing with only one of the cycles.

The other triggers are likely to have different impacts on the cycles. For example, technological triggers affect the technical cycle more than the other two cycles. Yet shifts in agreement over goals and means affect the political cycle. Conflicts often erupt in medical centers between factions who variously consider the core mission of the organization to be research, teaching, or service. This conflict creates high political uncertainty.

The second set of triggering events for cycles are the cycles themselves. Except for major environmental triggers, it may be assumed that triggering events begin by first creating uncertainty in one cycle. The cycles are loosely linked to each other, thereby causing counter reactions. Thus, a major technical adjustment, such as a reorganization, generally triggers a political realignment as people vie for power in the new structure and as various individual's careers are altered. This in turn can trigger a cultural cycle so as to alter the values and norms to fit the changed technical and political environments.

Diagnosis starts with an analysis of the trigger and its impact. It proceeds to survey the total organization in order to provide the basis for a strategic change plan. In addition to providing the information base for planning a change approach, the diagnosis also (1) creates an awareness of the need for change, and (2) can generate motivation for change. The organizational model is used to guide diagnosis.

Figure 5.2 presents the steps involved in an organizational diagnosis.

Diagnosis is useful to the extent that it contributes to the important criterion identified by Thompson (1967), that of focusing not on what the organization has accomplished but on its fitness for future action.

Now that we know what the diagnosis must disclose, let us look at some diagnostic approaches.

Radar Scan Diagnosis. This entails the employment of the model to guide a quick and somewhat superficial scan of the organization with the purpose of identifying possible trouble centers, or "blips." The blips signify potentially bad alignments in the model.

An example of such a blip occurred in one organization when the regional president identified a lack of alignment between the organization's strategy and the people it employed. As the organization moved to introduce new products into a region, it became clear to the presi-

Steps in diagnosis

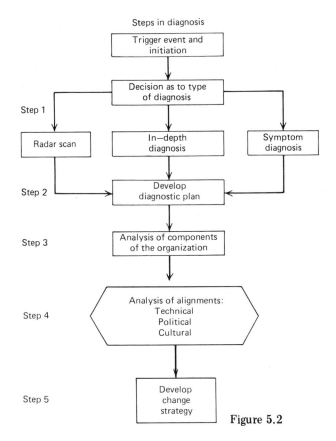

Figure 5.2

dent that his regional managers, who were oriented to the old, traditional products, would have trouble introducing new product lines requiring aggressive, entrepreneurial tactics.

Radar scanning should be an ongoing managerial activity. It also represents one method of diagnosis for the start of a strategic change process. An event may trigger management to carry out a quick scan of the organizational components to assess alignment. Depending on the time and resources available and the nature of the blips found, this scan can immediately lead to change activity or to a deeper, in-depth diagnosis along the lines of either of the following approaches.

Symptom Focused Diagnosis. Often an organization clearly "hurts" in one area. An example might be in the people area. A typical symptom is high turnover or absenteeism. Another symptom might be a sudden increase in environmental uncertainty brought on by new competition or an event such as the energy crisis. Management's attention becomes focused on one component of the model, on the component in which the symptom is located. However, there should also be a scanning of other components to discover whether or not any other "blips" or trouble centers can be found. This occurs in good medical practice when a patient is diagnosed to have a heart attack. A diagnosis of other systems might uncover diabetes or other "blips."

Symptom focused diagnosis may be misleading because it can result in the treatment of symptoms rather than causes. For example, an absenteeism or turnover problem may not be a people problem but a problem in the organization's design. Leaving this problem untouched would be a mistake. To guard against this possibility, it is recommended that, at a minimum, any diagnosis which begins with a focus on a symptom should be supplemented by a radar scan of the overall organizational model. An in-depth general diagnosis is preferred.

In-Depth Diagnosis. This involves a systematic analysis of each component of the model as well as an analysis of the alignment between components. The steps which should be undertaken are as follows:

1. *The Trigger Event and Initiation.* The diagnosis is undertaken with an awareness that change may be necessary to deal with a perceived threat or opportunity. First, one must decide which subsystem is appropriate for diagnosis. That is, what is the unit to be analyzed? Is it the total organization, a division of the organization, a functional area such as marketing, R & D, or production? This decision is guided by the following considerations:

(a) How localized or pervasive is the perceived uncertainty?

(b) Is it possible to place a boundary around the focal unit, that is, can the unit be reasonably studied by itself? Or must other units be part of the diagnosis? Focal units can be divisions or departments of larger organizations.

(c) Given the time and resources available, how extensive can the diagnosis be?

For example, in one medical instruments company the root of the company's inability to develop new products lay in the R&D division. It was thus possible to put a boundary around R&D and focus the diagnosis on that subunit.

2. *Develop Diagnostic Plan.* Once the unit for study is determined, the diagnostic plan can be developed. It should outline the specifications of data collection that is, methods, personnel, and the time frame. One important decision is who should participate in the diagnosis. The greater the number of people participating the deeper their eventual commitment to the outcomes of the diagnosis. On the other hand, the more participation, the longer the process will take, and the greater the likelihood of conflict between groups.

3. *The Analysis of Components.* The overall diagnosis based on the organizational model begins with an analysis of the organization's environment and an assessment of its history and its output. This is followed by an analysis of each of the organizational components.

The analysis of the components is carried out in a sequential fashion. Each component is described in terms of the following dimensions:

Diagnostic Plan

Diagnostic Focus	Specific Information Sought	Method of Data Collection
I. Input		
A. History of organization	(1) What were the critical events in the organization's history, are there identifiable phases of development?	Documents, interviews, and surveys
	(2) What is the service/product mix history of the organization (sequence of development, relative success and performance)?	
B. Environment of organization	(3) With whom or what is the organization interdependent for services, goods, information, influence? (Identify external network.)	Documents, interviews, and surveys
	(4) How fluid are elements in the environment (economy, markets, competition, labor market, etc.)?	Interviews, documents, and surveys,
	(5) When there is environmental change how predictable is it?	Interviews
C. Organizational resources	(6) What capital does the organization control?	Interviews, documents
	(7) What is the state of the organization's technical capability?	Interviews, documents
	(8) What are the overall people resources (numbers, skills, etc.)?	Documents
II. Mission/Strategy Analysis		
A. Mission	(1) What is the formal view of the mission?	Documents, interviews

Diagnostic Focus	Specific Information Sought	Method of Data Collection
	(2) How do members describe the mission?	Interviews
	(3) How is the mission formulated (who is involved, doing what, when)?	Interviews
B. Strategy	(1) Is there a formal strategy? If so what is it?	Interviews, documents
	(2) What do members perceive to be the strategy?	Interviews
	(3) How is strategy arrived at (who does what, when)?	Interviews
C. What are the perceived goals?	(1) What are the goals as perceived by key staff?	Interviews
D. Organizational processes surrounding mission/strategy formation	(1) Who are the key people with regard to strategy formation, how do they work together to influence mission/strategy?	Interviews, documents
III. *Task Analysis*		
A. What are the basic tasks?	(1) What are the core tasks?	Interviews, documents (job descriptions, management by objectives, documents, etc.)
	(2) Who performs what tasks?	Interviews, observations, documents
	(3) What is the nature of the core tasks? Expertise required. Standardization of tasks. Discretion of task performers.	Interviews, documents

158

Diagnostic Focus	Specific Information Sought	Method of Data Collection
	Task variability.	
B. How do the tasks interrelate?	(1) Integration of core tasks—Who is interdependent with whom for what?	Interviews, observation
IV. *Prescribed Organization Analysis*		
A. *Differentiation—* What is the overall configuration of the organization?	(1) How is the organization differentiated: vertically, horizontally, spatially,	Organizational chart, documents, interviews
	(2) What is the distribution of authority over budgets, personnel, tasks?	Interviews, documents
	(3) What are the characteristics of individual units? Number of job titles. Number of tasks. Heterogeneity of people skills. Interchangability of roles.	Documents, interviews, observation
B. *Integration—* What is the overall configuration of the organization?	(1) Which simple integrating mechanisms are in use and how effective are they? Rules/programs. Hierarchy. Planning.	Interviews, documents
	(2) Which mid-level integrating mechanisms are in use and how effective are they? Slack resources. Buffering. Self-contained units.	Interviews, documents
	(3) Which complex integrating mechanisms are in use:	Interviews, documents

Diagnostic Focus	Specific Information Sought	Method of Data Collection
	vertical information systems, liaison personnel, task forces, teams, matrix structure?	
V. *People Analysis*		
A. What are the demographic characteristics of the staff?	(1) Education and skill levels of staff?	Documents, questionnaires
	(2) Personal characteristics—sex, age, etc.	Documents
B. What are the managerial styles of key staff?	(1) Risk taking?	Interviews, observations
	(2) How much use of professional management technology?	Interviews, observations questionnaires
	(3) How participative?	
	(4) How open and flexible?	
C. What are the motivational forces driving various staff?	(1) How do staff perceive their own ability to control their effectiveness?	Interviews, questionnaires
	(2) What outcomes do staff members value (money, security, challenge, career mobility, etc.)?	Interviews, questionnaires
	(3) What is the perceived match between what employees value and what they feel they get?	Interviews, questionnaires
VI. *Organizational Processes Analysis*		
A. What are the characteristics of communication?	(1) How open is communication and for what issues?	Interviews, observation, questionnaires
	(2) Is there much distortion?	Interviews, observation

Diagnostic Focus	Specific Information Sought	Method of Data Collection
	(3) What is the quantity and quality of communication relevant to task accomplishment?	Interviews, observation
B. What are the characteristics of decision making?	(1) Are there different modes of decision making for different issues? What are they?	Interviews, observation
VII. *Emergent Organization Analysis*		
A. What is the overall emergent organization?	(1) Who shares information with whom (types of information specified)?	Interviews, observation, questionnaires
	(2) Who influences whom regarding what issues?	Interviews, observation
	(3) Who is friendly with whom?	Interviews, observation
B. Which coalitions form?	(1) Are there identifiable clusters of people who cooperate in order to exert influence? If so, around what issues?	Interviews, observation
C. What are the cliques which exist?	(1) Are there relatively durable small clusters of friends within the departments?	Interviews, observation
VIII. *Output Analysis*		
A. What is the degree of goal optimization in ER?	(1) Are they applying their limited resources toward the attainment of goals or are there "unfunded" goals and "funded" nongoals?	Interviews, documents (analysis of budgets)
	(2) Is there a clear relationship between the amount of resources spent on the various goals and the importance of the goal?	Interviews, documents

161

Diagnostic Plan

Diagnostic Focus	Specific Information Sought	Method of Data Collection
	(3) What kind of return on investment are they getting on resources (return on staff time etc.)?	Interviews, documents
	(4) Are all parts working toward at least one of the goals?	Interviews, documents
	(5) Are goals adjusted with environmental changes?	Interviews
B. What are the behavioral impacts of the organization?	(1) How satisfied are members with their work, each other, their careers, etc.?	Interviews, questionnaires

The organizational diagnosis as proposed in the preceding outline can be applied to different levels within the organization. It can apply to the total organization, divisions, or departments. It is important to specify the unit of analysis in advance and then to consistently apply the diagnosis at that level.

Data Collection Procedures. Five basic approaches for collecting diagnostic information are presented. Table 5.2 summarizes the five approaches and includes advantages, disadvantages, and references for further reading. The choice of diagnostic procedure should be guided by an assessment of the trade-offs involved in any given situation. However, it is generally desirable to use multiple diagnostic techniques. Examples of diagnostic data collection approaches include:

1. *Survey.* A hospital administrator and his department head decided to conduct a hospital-wide survey of the 1500 staff members using a structured questionnaire. The results were fed back to work groups throughout the hospital in order to isolate ways in which they might improve their functioning.

2. *Interview/Observation.* The head of a management team for an international division of a large bank decided to hire a consultant to interview each member of his division. The consultant also observed them at work and studied the operation of several committees. A one-day "feedback session" followed. This was done to begin developing a strategy for improving the effectiveness of the unit.

Table 5.2 Data Collection Procedures

Procedure	Advantages	Disadvantages	Further Reading
Questionnaire	Data from large number of people Standardization for measuring change over time Relatively inexpensive Quick	Measures attitudes not behavior Questionable validity Requires honesty on part of respondents	Price, *Handbooks of Organizational Measurement* (Lexington, Mass: D.C. Heath & Co., 1972)
Observation	Rich behavioral data Deep understanding of an organization's culture Build relationships with members of the organization	Takes a great deal of time Sampling bias (may get biased view of system because everything can't be observed Subjective, therefore measurement of change over time difficult Requires a great deal of trust to be accepted into groups to be observed	Schatzman and Strauss, *Field Methods* (Englewood Cliffs, N.J.: Prentice-Hall, 1973)
Interviews	Combines some advantages of questionnaire with a chance to observe some behavior and establish relationships with organizations	Limited data on actual organizational behavior Time consuming Sampling problems in large systems	Cannel and Kahn, "Interviewing," in *Handbook of Social Psychology*, (Reading, Mass.: Addison-Wesley, 1969)
Workshops and diagnostic meetings	Mobilizes organizational groups to take action Quick Makes data real for everyone involved Reinforces the "action research" process	Requires high committment to take action May lead to superficial, biased diagnosis	Beckhard, *Organizational Development* (Reading, Mass.: Addison-Wesley, 1969)
Documents and records	Often readily available Provides good unobtrusive measures Provides data over time Inexpensive data source	Limited number of relevant diagnostic areas recorded in documents and records	Webb et al., *Nonreactive Measures in Social Science* (Boston, Houghton-Mifflin, 1981)

Source: From *Management Handbook for Public Administrators*, edited by John W. Sutherland. Copyright © 1978 by Van Nostrand Reinhold Co., Inc. Reprinted by permission of Van Nostrand Reinhold Company.

163

3. *Workshop.* The manager of a small manufacturing plant decided to have his five first-line supervisors participate in a diagnostic workshop to identify key organizational problems. At this workshop, a consultant helped the group identify issues which (1) management alone should examine, (2) top management in collaboration with first-line supervisors should work on, and (3) first-line supervisors should resolve themselves. The workshop ended with explicit action plans.

Once data has been collected for each component shown in the outline given earlier, a diagnostic summary is written for each component. For example, in one study the characteristics of several of the components were described as follows (Devanna, et al., 1981):

> *Mission/strategy*—Formally written statement quite comprehensive and integrated, however, not fully understood or agreed to by many staff and not seen as accurate by many of the organization's customers.
>
> *People*—Technically competent, yet people had motivational needs which were not well matched with organizational rewards, especially career mobility. People also lacked a strategic orientation.

Once the components are described, the analysis shifts focus to the relationships between components. The purpose is to determine how well the components are aligned with each other. This analysis of alignment provides the change manager with the information required to develop a change strategy; wherever alignment is poor, a change is implied. Alignment is analyzed for each system: technical, political, and cultural.

ANALYSIS OF ALIGNMENT

The analysis of alignment is the most complex aspect of the strategic change management process. Figure 5.3 provides a format for summarizing the analysis of alignments. Based on the diagnostic data collected, a judgment is made for each cell of the matrix regarding the amount of change needed to create alignment. Working across the matrix, the alignment is within a system: technical, political, or cultural. Working down the matrix, the alignment is between systems. The 0, 1, or 2 ratings represent the amount of change needed to align that component.

Figure 5.3 presents an illustration of how an analysis of alignments can be summarized. A judgment was made for each cell of the matrix. The two marginals of the matrix provide the key information. From the right margin we can see that the major realignment required is in the cultural system (11 points) versus 6 points for the political and 5 for the technical. From the bottom of the matrix, we can see that the component requiring the most change is organizational processes (5 points) followed by people and emergent networks.

Organizational components

Core systems	Mission/ strategy	Tasks	Prescribed network	People	Processes	Emergent networks	Amount of within-system alignment
Technical system	0	0	1	1	2	1	5
Political system	1	1	1	1	1	1	6
Cultural system	2	2	1	2	2	2	11
Amount of required organizational component change	3	3	3	4	5	4	Total alignment score = 22 (Minimum 0 → 36 maximum)

Diagnosed need for change
0 = No change 1 = Moderate change 2 = Great deal of change

Figure 5.3

165

In order to carry out the analysis effectively it is useful to organize a committee of individuals who represent both the key power figures and the groups which are likely to be affected by a strategic change. The goal of the committee is to agree upon an analysis of alignment and to recommend where the change process should begin.

It is desirable for the committee to begin by having each individual complete a private assessment of the analysis of alignments using the framework provided in Figure 5.3. These individual assessments can then be shared in committee. The committee should work until it reaches a consensus on the analysis of alignments. Some guidelines for the final diagnostic assessment follow:

Guideline 1

The analysis of alignments follows the description of components. The analysis should be carried out one system—technical, political, or cultural—at a time and then across systems. This can be facilitated by working first across rows then down the columns in Figure 5.3.

Technical analysis of alignment is conducted by focusing on the concept that the organization wants to maximize effectiveness and efficiency. The judgment of alignment is based on how well the organizational components are aligned for processing the information necessary to deal with the overall uncertainty caused by (1) the environment, (2) the nature of the tasks, and (3) the amount of task interdependence. The steps in this analysis were presented in Chapter 4, Figures 4.4 and 4.5.

An example of the type of analysis which occurs at this stage involves a division of a manufacturing company. The division's environment began to change quite rapidly when the parent company entered new markets and began producing new products. At the time of the diagnosis the division had not yet adjusted to these environmental changes. Therefore the mission and strategy were technically out of alignment with the environment. Mission and strategy had to become more organic—that is, more complex, more explicit, and more attuned to a changing environment. In turn, the other components of the organization were in alignment with the old mechanistic mission and strategy. If the division adopted a new mission and strategy, then the other mechanistic components would also have to become organic. The technical alignments were therefore all in need of adjustment. This would have resulted in 2's across the technical row of Figure 5.3.

Political Alignment. Once the technical alignment column has been analyzed, a different conceptual focus must be applied. This focus is based on the view that organizations are driven to survival and growth as a means for allocating power and resources. The uses to which the organization is put, as well as who reaps the benefits, must be determined. There is an ongoing bargaining process among competing coalitions, both internal and external, which exchange money, labor, and political contributions to the organization for some desired outcome. The political alignment should match political uncertainty with political bargaining and exchange capacity. Figure 4.8 provides a set of distinguishing characteristics of politically mechanistic (low bargaining and exchange capacity) and politically organic (high bargaining and exchange capacity) to guide the analysis. An overall assessment of political uncertainty is made to determine the political cycle's position.

For example, in a company faced with new competitive pressures requiring a change in products or services, conflict often erupts between the old guard and the new staff. The young push either for new goals or new means of accomplishing the goals. The political uncertainty which is created can be reflected in conflict over task priorities, production means, and interpersonal career rivalries.

Cultural Alignment. This analysis is based on the view that the organization is in part held together by belief in a set of norms which make up the organization's culture. The major concern when evaluating the cultural alignment of the organization is to determine the degree of cultural homogeneity; that is, to what extent the organization is dominated by a single culture or multiple cultures. The Chase Manhattan Bank was traditionally a bastion of conservative, gentlemanly culture. The Chase culture through the early 1970s emphasized style and appearances leading to a homogeneous culture which was not geared toward agressive competition in the banking industry.

> The typical Chase executive in those days was a well-groomed functionary who did not drive himself hard to set high standards for his own performance (*Business Week*, 27 October 1980, p. 158).

Implementing a new culture in the late 1970s was not an easy task as management had to replace many of its top executives with outsiders, revamp its salary and incentive program to provide greater reinforcement for high performers, conduct an advanced management program designed to reinforce strategic thinking and the new culture. By the early 1980s the new culture at Chase was beginning to dominate, yet there was still a fair amount of cultural uncertainty as there were still managers at the bank who supported the old culture. The diagnostic point is that the old values still contribute to moderately high cultural uncertainty. Yet the new culture is clearly predominant. Several years ago a similar analysis would have shown the reverse, that is, the old culture still dominant with the new performance culture creating cultural uncertainty.

Guideline 2

The final step in diagnosis is to determine the degree of alignment between the technical, political, and cultural systems of the organization. To what extent do the three systems reinforce each other and thus drive the organization forward?

The two oil company examples included in Chapter 4 point out the following aspects of fit between technical, political, and cultural subsystems. First, the CEOs faced technical uncertainty and thus made a technical adjustment by altering the corporate strategy toward greater diversification away from oil. This change, however, altered the fit between the technical and the cultural systems and triggered cultural uncertainty. The traditional oil culture was based on long-term investment for rewards in which success came from wildcatting. This conflicted with a new culture based on marketing, market share, new products, and innovation. The cultural uncertainty was not resolved in favor of the new culture. Rather, it ended up triggering political uncertainty. The political cycle peaked and the uncertainty was resolved by powerful coalitions in each company firing their CEO. Once the CEO was fired, political uncertainty receded, and the cultural uncertainty was reduced by reverting back to the old culture. It should be noted that the potential technical uncertainty these CEOs attempted to deal with still remains. The future of oil is uncertain for the oil companies. However, in the short run, these two companies have managed their technical, political, and cultural uncertainty by avoiding the future, long-term problems of technical uncertainty. The critical point of diagnosis is that the three subsystems must be viewed in relationship to each other.

CONCLUSION

Diagnosis is the basis for action in any managed change effort. This chapter dealt with the conditions necessary for conducting an effective organizational diagnosis. Three types of diagnosis were discussed: (1) radar scan—diagnosis which entails a quick and somewhat superficial diagnosis of the organizational components and their alignments, (2) a symptom diagnosis which entails significant analysis of organizational components felt to relate to the symptom, and (3) *in-depth diagnosis*, which is rarely carried out in total due to time and resource requirements. It is a mode worth trying, however, when conditions allow. The chapter included a step-by-step set of procedures for carrying out an in-depth diagnosis. The same procedures can be modified to conduct both the radar scan and symptom diagnosis.

Chapter Six

Application of Diagnostic Strategy

INTRODUCTION

The previous chapter provided a general strategy for conducting an organizational diagnosis. This chapter presents two case examples which illustrate the application of that strategy. The first case is of a hospital chain which was experiencing severe financial problems. The second examines the efforts of Texas Instruments to develop strategic management.

Following the case illustrations is a discussion of the conditions necessary for successful management of in-depth organizational diagnosis. This includes a look at organizational and consultant resources which might be of use.

TWO CASE EXAMPLES

These case examples demonstrate how the diagnostic approach can be applied in two very different settings. One is a chain of hospitals, the other a multinational corporation in the electronics field.

Case 1: Southwest Hospital System

The organization is called Southwest Hospital System (SHS). It consists of a chain of 12 small- to medium-sized nonprofit hospitals and three primary-care clinics. The total operating budget for the system in the fiscal year 1976–1977 was $76 million. The chain serves a population characterized by poverty, unemployment, and dependence on welfare.

The chain's top management staff is located in a central headquarters remote from any of the hospitals. The director is a physician who was a private practitioner before he assumed the directorship.

The system has always had financial difficulties. At the time this diagnosis took place, it was operating at a deficit of over $2 million a year. On top of this, it faced an additional and extraordinary financial pressure: One of the major employers in the area cut back on his insurance benefits. The reduction, which required employees to share in previously covered health costs, resulted in the immediate reduction of hospital utilization as well as nonpayment of bills by employees of this company. Consequently, as this case unfolded, the system was thrown into a major fiscal crisis, requiring staff cutbacks, reduction in work hours, and curtailment of services.

The network organizational model was used to diagnose the system and develop a strategy for long-term organizational viability. The immediate financial crisis was viewed as a severe manifestation of more serious underlying managerial and organizational problems.

Trigger for Change.   The trigger event was the extreme financial pressure exerted by the reduction in revenues. It was an environmental trigger which affected all three cycles.

Method of Diagnosis.   Using multiple data collection methods, each component of the model was analyzed. The focus of the analysis was the overall management and organizational design of SHS. The basic format of the diagnosis followed the outline in Figure 5.3. Interviews and questionnaires were completed for 40 of the SHS staff. This included all hospital administrators, heads of nursing, medical directors, and central headquarters management.

The Environment.   Many of the performance or output problems of SHS are traceable to environmental pressures. These pressures threatened long-term organizational viability and effectiveness. The environment was a rural poverty area in which SHS was the dominant health provider. There is a high level of nonpayment of fees among patients (ranging as high as 20% for one hospital with patients who do not qualify for Medicaid and have no way of paying for care). There was also great uncertainly regarding eventual receipt of as much as 30% of the system's revenues because of the forementioned employer's cutback on health benefits. In addition, management claimed that it was reimbursed by Medicaid for only 95% of its actual costs. The great physical dispersion of the system through 12 communities added to the complexity of the environment. Finally, fluctuations in the area's economy further contributed to the system's instability.

The Diagnosis.   Severe financial pressure facing the system caused the highly unstable and uncertain state of the SHS environment.

System Output.   In addition to the immediate crisis, there were other, longstanding problems that confronted SHS. This was evident from an examination of certain performance indicators. First, the organization had operated at a chronic deficit in the last decade, resulting in almost no capital improvements and in minimal maintenance.

Second, the system's occupancy rate of 61% was well below what was needed to break even financially. Third, the percentage of heavy debt, uncollected bills, and the necessity to supply free care to the indigent was higher than the regional average of 4.1%. The total for this amounted to a cost of over $3 million a year. Fourth, the system had a very controversial image in the area; the local communities did not trust a big, centrally managed corporation headquartered in a distant city. As a result, neighboring communities provided little support, financial or otherwise, to the hospitals. Finally, turnover among health professionals and administrative personnel was substantial.

SHS Strategy. This reflects the organization's attempt through management decisions to maintain control and to deal with the uncertainty created by a changing and turbulent environment (Thompson, 1967).

The SHS strategy was determined from written documents and interviews. It became obvious that top management and administrators were conceptually confused about the strategic plans and how they had been formulated. SHS did have 5-year plans. These, however, as required by government planning agencies, were merely an extension of the budget estimates. They were merely extrapolations of the next year's budget which included adjustments for inflation. Thus, there was no formal procedure for articulating the organization's mission or for devising an explicit strategy.

Interview responses further illustrated the confusion. After the interviewer had given a definition of strategic planning, that is, setting the basic long-term purposes and course of the organization, the respondents were asked whether SHS systematically carried out such an activity. Some typical responses were:

"Strategic planning? No, not to my knowledge."

"Not formally set up. There is a development committee made up of members of the board of trustees, but no one really doing strategic planning."

The consultants concluded that SHS's strategic planning was mechanistic: fragmented, simple, implicit.

People Component. The major focal point for analysis in the people component was the management group. In particular, this included the top people who acted as decision makers, mediators, and brokers between the organization and the environment.

As was noted in earlier chapters, the effectiveness of managerial styles has been found to depend, in part, on variations in the environmental uncertainty facing top management (Khandwalla, 1977). High levels of uncertainty (a turbulent environment) call for an organic style. Conversely, when there is low uncertainty (calm, stable, predictable environment) a mechanistic style is more effective.

As has also been noted, the consultants concluded that the SHS top management style was predominantly mechanistic. More detailed data from interviews and direct observation revealed the following:

1. The SHS Director's style was characterized as:
(a) a "seat-of-the-pants" approach (he had no formal management training) to planning, organizing, and controlling;
(b) nonparticipative (not oriented to human relations); and
(c) not oriented toward scientific management.

2. The two deputy directors demonstrated very different managerial styles:
(a) the deputy director of finance was more mechanistic than the director;
(b) the deputy director of operations was more organic in style than either of the other two.

3. When it came to strategic decision making, the top three managers did not function as a team. The director solicited some ideas and commented on a one-to-one basis. But then he made unilateral decisions, often without notifying his deputies.

4. Systematic and formal management planning techniques were not used at the strategic level although they had been used at the operational budgeting level.

Prescribed Network Component. In the SHS case, the diagnostic focus for the prescribed network components was on organization-wide integrating mechanisms. These mechanisms consist of coordination and control structures for tasks and for people. The analysis, based on Galbraith's (1977) three-level categorization scheme for integrating mechanisms, was:

1. *Simple Mechanisms Which Are Cheap and Can Handle Low Levels of Uncertainty.* These include the use of rules and procedures, the decision-making hierarchy, and goal setting.

At SHS the simple mechanisms were found to be out of adjustment. Rules, the hierarchy, and goals all require explicit, agreed-upon understanding in order to be useful as integrating mechanisms. Rating-scale data for all three of these mechanisms indicated that the SHS people had widely differing views of these simple mechanisms. For example, when asked whether there were rules for hiring a new department head, some administrators said yes and others said no. It is obviously very difficult for a rule to be used for integration if some members of the organization do not even know it exists. Similar discrepancies were found with regard to the use of the hierarchy. Some administrators and managers indicated that certain budget and personnel decisions could be made at their level, whereas other administrators, working at the same level, indicated that the same decisions needed to be made at the vice-presidential level. The existence of such varied perceptions means that the use of these integrating mechanisms at SHS was inefficient and ineffective.

2. *Intermediate Integrating Mechanisms Which Reduce Interdependence and Hence the Need to Coordinate Activities.*   These include providing subunits of the system with resources to enable them either to operate with reduced interdependence and less coordination or to create totally self-contained subunits.

These devices were in use. Each hospital unit ran by itself and was largely self-contained. There was virtually no need to coordinate between units.

3. *Complex Integrating Mechanisms Which Enhance the Capability of the System to Engage in Complex Interdependent Problem Solving and Coordination.*   These include vertical information systems and "lateral" relations mechanisms such as liaison roles, task forces, teams, and the matrix structure.

The complex mechanisms were also largely undeveloped at SHS although it had a very complete computerized management information system. The system did not function as an integrating mechanism because it was primarily used for the fulfillment of financial reporting demands: reports for leading agencies, regulatory bodies, trustees, and the public.

> The information provided in these reports is not particularly helpful to management in its governance of the organization. From an information system point of view, it is important to segregate financial accounting from managerial information (Grossman and Rockart, 1976, p. 162).

This had not been the practice at SHS. Also, there were virtually no formal lateral integrating mechanisms, such as liaison roles, task forces, or teams, in existence at SHS.

Organizational Process Component.   The consultants concluded that organization-wide communication, problem solving, and conflict management were quite mechanistic and failed to encourage communication, conflict avoidance, and nonparticipative problem solving. Our interviews found:

1. There was poor communication between hospitals and headquarters (mentioned by over 50% of the administrators).

2. Conflict existed between the hospital administrators and headquarters staff. This conflict has been unresolved and not openly confronted for a number of years, according to over 50% of the respondents who mentioned it.

Emergent Network Component.   Emergent networks or relationships are inevitable in all social systems. They vary greatly, however, in their capacity to process task-relevant information. In effective mechanistic systems, there is little need for networks to process task-relevant information. This is because the networks emerge to fulfill personal social needs and compensate for the highly structured and controlled aspects of the sociotechnical component.

On the other hand, in organic systems, emergent networks must exist in order to get work accomplished. Complex integrating devices such as lateral relations, teams, and the matrix structure require that each individual develop work-related networks for acquiring task information and exercising influence. Such networks emerge because the complexity of the organic system precludes planning of all task relationships.

The SHS emergent network findings were based on sociometric interview questions. Few task-related emergent networks were found among the SHS administrators. Thus, it was concluded that the networks were mechanistic in nature.

The major problems of alignment were found to be (1) between environment and mission/strategy in terms of the technical alignment; and (2) between mission/strategy and people in terms of political alignment. There were also a series of secondary analyses of alignment which required attention.

1. *Environment–Mission/Strategy.* The SHS environment was assessed to be highly uncertain. The organization's strategy had, however, been very mechanistic, that is, simplistic, implicit, fragmented, rigid, and reactive. From an information processing perspective, a more appropriate approach to such an uncertain environment would involve a more organic mission and strategy. That is, one which is complex, explicit, integrated, flexible, and proactive (Khandwalla, 1977).

2. *Mission/Strategy–People.* This problem of alignment was a political one. The director at the time of the case diagnosis had control of the dominant coalition in the organization. His implicit, simplistic, and fragmented mission/strategy had helped the organization get into trouble. Altering the mission/strategy required reducing his dominance and hence his power to influence the allocation of resources and the direction of the system. An organic mission/strategy would have required altering his managerial style from one which was authoritarian to one that was more participative, flexible, and less "seat-of-the-pants." The alternative was to replace him.

The second-order problems of alignment in the SHS case were:

3. *Mission/Strategy–Prescribed Networks.* Both were assessed to be mechanistic. This means that at the time of the analysis they were congruent with each other, but the uncertain environment called for a change in strategy to a more organic style. This in turn required that the prescribed networks become more organic as well. In other words,

the information processing capacity of the networks would have to be increased. This alignment represents a *technical* alignment, that is, how to make the organization more task-efficient and effective. Such technical readjustments would have an impact on the *political* or *cultural* alignment.

4. *Prescribed Networks–Organizational Processes.* As indicated in the previous alignment evaluation, both were mechanistic, and both needed to be adjusted to match environmental uncertainty. Individual employees' power bases would be affected.

5. *Prescribed Networks–Emergent Networks–Organizational Processes.* These three components were jointly mechanistic and required shifts to become organic.

Developing a Change Strategy. The overriding factor in the SHS case was pressure for change brought on by an unstable environment. This in turn required major readjustments in the organizational model. The lack of an organic strategy and a strategic decision-making capability severely hampered the organization's ability to cope with its environment. The technical alignment between the organization and its environment was kept out of balance by the political, vested interests of the current, dominant coalition.

In order to bring about change, an uncoupling of the technical, political, and cultural systems were all in poor alignment and were reinforcing each other's dysfunctions. Uncoupling means that the three systems—technical, political, and cultural—must be pulled apart and adjustments made in each so that a new mutually reinforcing combination can be created. The SHS case will be further discussed in later chapters in terms of how the changes were in fact implemented.

Case 2: Texas Instruments

Texas Instruments (TI) began a major change effort in the early 1960s to prepare itself for long-term fast growth in an increasingly turbulent environment. The company now prepares for the expected Japanese dominance in the consumer electronics business of the 1980s. In 1979, TI had sales of $2.5 billion. This was up from less than $400 million in 1964. There were 68,000 workers in 45 plants in 18 countries. The company is a fast-growing (15%–20% per year), high-technology concern. This case provides a sharp contrast to the SHS case, in which a troubled organization faced basic survival. TI is a very successful organization which is actively developing itself for future growth and viability.

Trigger for Change. The early 1960s was a time when the semiconductor industry went through a major shake-up. At that time, TI found itself faced with the loss of some major contracts. The future promised to be bleak unless TI could manage both innovation and tight production control. The technical cycle peaked at this time.

Diagnosis. Each of the organizational components are briefly described as they were in the early 1960s.

History. The company began as a builder of oil exploration equipment and then moved into the electronic component business, primarily as a supplier of end products. Prior to the 1960s, however, it became clear to management that they had a chance to play a major part in the growth of the electronics field.

Environment. The early 1960s found TI facing an uncertain and turbulent environment. There was increasing competition in the field and the firm had just lost several important government contracts.

The environment which the organization was to face throughout the 1960s was described by one manager of TI in terms of the role of obsolescence: "At the moment when a newly designed electronic component or end product enters production for the first time, it is already obsolete." He went on to say: "Markets are equally explosive."

As a result of this seesaw market, sales oscillated through wide volume ranges. In addition, there was a lot of raiding for scarce experts among firms in the electronics field. One way to secure a flow of innovations was to hire people away from firms which were innovative. Thus, there was uncertainty in the area of keeping innovative people within the structure.

Mission/Strategy. The major strategy of TI from the early 1960s through today has been to adhere rigidly to what they refer to as the "learning curve theory." Simply put, it states that manufacturing costs can be brought down by a fixed percentage, depending on the product, each time cumulative volume is double. Such a strategy involves constant redesign and improvement of products and production processes so that prices can drop as fast as possible.

In the early 1960s, strategy was formulated by the top management group and then implemented through the divisional structure at TI. This was problematic. Innovation was stifled as managers focused primarily on their particular functions, not long-term innovation. The learning curve could be implemented, but the other important strategy of TI was to keep innovating so that they would have products on which to apply the learning theory.

Prescribed Networks. In the early 1960s, TI was organized in a standard divisional structure, as shown in Figure 6.1. This structure created decentralized Product Customer Centers (PCCs). They worked well for short-term production purposes. However, the PCCs brought duplication of resources and a lack of integration for long-range projections needed to operate across the board at TI. In other words, to develop innovations for the future it was important to have a way of

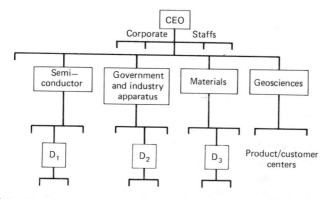

Figure 6.1 (Reprinted by permission from Jay R. Galbraith and Daniel A. Nathanson, *Strategy implementation: The role of structure and process.* Copyright © 1978 by West Publishing Company. All rights reserved.)

bridging the prescribed networks, but they were divided into separate PCCs.

People. The organization has always had a high percentage of technical personnel. However, in the early 1960s, they were not driven toward innovation as much as they are now. The technicians focused more on short-term improvements of existing capabilities of incremental expansions.

Organizational Processes. The communication, decision-making and conflict-management processes were very much influenced by the prescribed PCCs which supported the production side of the organization but did not support innovation and long-range planning. Participation by middle-level personnel was low, communication was mostly from the top down on important matters, and lacked feedback at other levels.

Emergent Networks. As with the SHS case, there was little use of emergent networks to foster task accomplishment, especially in the area of innovation. As a result, these were the alignments which required readjustments in the 1960s:

1. *Environment–Mission/Strategy.* The basic strategy was sound: It emphasized innovation and the application of the TI learning curve to the electronics field. However, the strategy-formulation and the strategy-implementation processes were weak.

2. *Mission/Strategy–Prescribed Network.* This alignment represents the major problem in the case. The PCC structure supports learning curve activity and efficient high-volume production. But it works against innovation by focusing on short-run efficiency concerns. The prescribed networks needed to be adjusted to support both aspects of the organization's strategy.

3. *Mission/Strategy–People–Organizational Processes.* Because of the need to change the prescribed network, the other two components also required readjustment. The people and the processes were only operating in support of the PCC prescribed network.

4. *Prescribed–Emergent Networks.* This alignment, prior to the change effort, was congruent. But once the prescribed networks were changed to support innovation, the emergent networks required modification.

5. *Technical–Political–Cultural Alignments.* The major uncertainty facing TI in the early 1960s was in the technical cycle. That is, in order for TI to derive more effectiveness and efficiency, its capacity to deal with greater uncertainty had to be increased. Changing the environment and/or task or task interdependence (See Figure 4.5) was not a viable option. Thus, Option 2, increasing the information-processing capacity, was required. The *political* and *cultural* cycles were not problems. However, once TI began its change strategy and resumed its phenomenal growth, the political and cultural cycles were readjusted via such means as self-selection, strong monolithic political leadership, and an organizational development program which strove for homogeneity of values.

Summary. The diagnosis of TI in the early 1960s led to the identification of a need for strategic, long-range planning processes supported by an organization that closely monitored technology and market, was adaptable, flexible to product/market changes, able to foster design of production facilities, reinforce major research and development efforts, and encouraged creativity.

DIAGNOSIS AS PART OF THE CHANGE PROCESS

All diagnostic activities create turbulence in the organization. Often, there are undesirable consequences. The diagnostic process therefore must be carefully managed, not just in terms of the generation of data but also in terms of its own impact on the organizational members. Diagnosis can lead to the following consequences:

1. *Diagnosis Signals People to Focus Attention on Issues Which May Not Have Been Thought About in the Past.* For example, it is not unusual to find that the organization's members, often in management positions, have not given much serious thought to what the organization will face in terms of future external opportunities and constraints. Questions about these issues in an interview and questionnaire signal people to begin thinking about such issues.

2. *Diagnosis Triggers Individual Problem Solving.* People are often stimulated not only to pay attention to new issues, but also to actually enhance the quality of relationships among workers, their supervisors, and/or themselves.

3. *Diagnosis Triggers Group Problem Solving.* Not only can individuals be stimulated to work on issues which may have been triggered by diagnosis, but groups can also be triggered. The interesting thing is that this triggering—both for the individual and the group—comes prior to an analysis or feedback of the data. It is stimulated by the data collection process which provokes individuals to think about organizational issues.

4. *The Diagnosis Sets the Tone for the Remainder of the Change Process.* Depending on how the diagnosis is handled, it can start a negative cycle of events which encourages employees to resist change. Individuals may develop serious mistrust for management and consultants who appear to be spying. The change effort may seem to be aimed at catching them napping, or they may see it as threatening to manipulate them. On the other hand, diagnosis can start a positive cycle in which people begin to develop greater trust for each other, for management, and for the consultant. Employees might begin to feel that they can improve things in the organization. The diagnostic activities set a tone of openness and direct confrontation with problems.

5. *Diagnosis Raises Questions of Anonymity and Access to Data.* No matter how benign the data collected from individuals in the organization, there will always be concern over who will see it and whether any individual response will be attributable to a particular person.

How these issues are managed can determine the success or failure of the total change effort. Decisions related to the management of these issues should be made in terms of impact on each of the three organizational perspectives. Depending on the triggering circumstances, different ways of managing the diagnosis are appropriate.

Let us observe some of the diagnostic criteria which prevail in the technical, cultural, and political arenas.

Technical Perspective: Implications for Diagnosis

The purpose of diagnosis from a technical perspective is to look "scientifically" for better ways to carry out the tasks of the organization in light of its environment. As such, the diagnostic activities are evaluated in terms of the validity of the data, and how the data relates to the conceptual framework guiding the change effort. Therefore, the key criteria are:

1. Developing valid data collection instruments.

2. Sampling the right units and people in the organization.

3. Careful analysis of the data.

4. Fitting the data to predictive models.

5. Improving organizational effectiveness.

Political Perspective: Implications for Diagnosis

The purpose of diagnosis from a political perspective is to identify, uncover, and eventually resolve conflicts over goals, means, or other problems from the environment. Diagnostic activities are thought of in terms of their impact on various interest groups and coalitions in the organization. The key criteria are:

1. Developing valid ways to identify conflicts.

2. Inducing interest groups and coalitions to uncover the real conflicts and issues at stake.

3. Managing the consequences of making problems explicit, which may itself, however, start unmanageable fights.

4. Developing a political map of the organization.

Cultural Perspective: Implications for Diagnosis

The purpose of diagnosis as viewed from a cultural perspective is to identify the core norms and values held by various members of the organization. Diagnostic activities are thought of in terms of their ability to uncover and explicate the norms of organizational members. The key issues are:

1. Developing data collection tools for identifying such norms.

2. Creation of a felt need, a desire, for dealing with cultural aspects of the organization, (Argyris, 1970, talks about the importance of valid data, free choice, and commitment as conditions for cultural change in the organization).

Guidelines for Managing the Diagnostic Process

The following guidelines provide the strategic change manager with an initial planning framework. These guidelines are aimed at helping the manager cope with the change implications of diagnostic activity.

1. *Identify the Trigger Event and Its Primary Area of Impact.* The first step in planning the diagnosis should be based on a clear understanding of why change is being triggered, and in which area—be it technical, political, or cultural. The primary area of impact largely determines the goal of the diagnosis. If it is technical, then the diagnosis is focused more on valid "scientific" data in order to determine a better alignment between uncertainty and information processing. This would contrast greatly with a situation in which the dominant impact was in the political area.

2. *State the Purpose of the Diagnosis in Each Area.* Set specific

goals for the diagnostic activities related to the technical system, the political system, and the cultural system. It should be made clear to change managers which system is dominant with regard to diagnosis.

3. *Develop a Plan for Managing the Diagnostic Phase.* The plan should include the following elements:

(a) List of diagnostic areas for investigation from an organizational model.

(b) A list of specific information sought for each diagnostic area.

(c) Specification of the method of data collection.

(d) List of people responsible for specific activities.

RESOURCES REQUIRED FOR IN-DEPTH ORGANIZATIONAL DIAGNOSIS

This section provides some guidelines for estimating managerial, employee, and consultant resources necessary for conducting an in-depth diagnosis.

One factor which makes this resource estimation process more complex is that in reality it is often difficult to separate diagnostic activities from actual change intervention activities. Even in situations where there is a clearly delineated diagnostic phase of activity, there frequently are other more advanced change activities taking place, often because of the impact which the diagnostic activities have exerted on the structure. The result is that additional resources may be needed beyond those principally needed for data collection.

For example, the administration of an attitude survey involves much more than the time to design, prepare, administer, and analyze the questionnaire. It includes the time needed to prepare employees for the questionnaire, time to deal with employee resistence to such a survey, time for follow-up activities, and for the management of activities triggered by the employees' reactions to the questionnaire. These contingencies should be anticipated and financial arrangements should be incorporated into the plan for resources.

Use of Consultants

Most large-scale change efforts involve the use of change consultants. This is especially true of the diagnostic phase in which a variety of specific experts may be called for.

The range of consultants include:

1. **Operations Researchers.** These are management science experts who take part in such diagnoses as analysis of control systems, management information systems, and production systems.

2. **Industrial Engineers.** These are consultants with skills in analyzing task/technology demands and production planning.

3. **Human Resource Management Consultants.** Generally, these consultants are specialized in some aspect of personnel or human resources management. For example, there are compensation experts, job classification experts, affirmative action experts, selection/placement experts, and labor relations experts.

4. **Organizational Design Consultants.** These consultants have skills in helping analyze the formal, prescribed structure of the organization and the ability to provide guidance in the redesign of the structure. These consultants are generally found in the traditional, management consultant firms.

5. **Survey Analysts.** These are consultants with expertise in the design, administration, and analysis of questionnaires.

6. **Strategy Consultants.** Strategy consultants focus on the organization's position in its market or environment—specifying its products or services with regard to different markets.

7. **Organization Development Consultants.** These consultants focus primarily on improving management's ability to solve problems and communicate effectively. Some are beginning to include in their work some activities in the organizational design and strategy area.

These, then, are the kinds of human resources available to a manager of change during the diagnostic phase of the effort. Selection of the consultant should occur after an initial set of diagnostic plans are formulated. It may be desirable to use the consultant in finalizing such a plan, but without some initial homework on management's part, it is hard to select the appropriate expert(s).

Another important issue is whether to use an internal or an external consultant, or both. Internal consultants or staff resources are generally found on the staffs of large corporations. They often function in departments with names similar to the ones used to describe the different types of consultants above. Many organizations have departments of organization development, industrial engineering, organizational design, and strategic planning. Internal consultants are often highly skilled in their areas of expertise. They thus offer excellent service at a much lower price than a comparable external consultant. But some other considerations must be taken into account before deciding whether upcoming diagnosis is to be handled "in-house" or not.

First, each has advantages and disadvantages. The advantages of internal consultants, besides their lower cost (in some companies, the client is charged the same for internal resources as for an external consultant), is that they tend to know the organization better, have an easier time being accepted by many of the employees, and are more available. On the negative side, the internal consultant is often part of the internal political struggle in the organization. Thus, they are not objective. They suffer from trying to be prophets in their own land and lack the credibility of the external consultant.

The advantages of external consultants are that they tend to have broader exposure to organizational problems because they have worked in many varied organizations. They are considered to be more objective.

The ideal procedure is to mix internal and external consultants. The optimal approach, then, is to examine ways to have teams of internal as well as external consultants simultaneously working on a project.

In terms of actual consultant time for diagnosis it may be realistic to plan on a 5- to 10-day span of time. For example, in the SHS case described above, 10 consultant-days were required to conduct the 35 necessary interviews. In addition, 5 days were needed to analyze the interviews and produce a final report. In the Texas Instruments case, an internal organizational development department had existed since the mid-1960s. This department had worked with many external consultants over the years on a variety of diagnostic projects. Some TI projects had involved man-years, rather than man-days, of consultant resources.

Managerial time is the most valuable resource and the one most often under-budgeted until managers find themselves trapped in a project much bigger than they anticipated. During the diagnostic stage, it is true that managers must invest twice as much time in the process than do consultants. They must think of diagnosis as something in which they participate actively, not something which the hired hands, the consultants, can do for the organization.

Employee time is used less than either consultant time or managerial time during diagnosis. Sometimes, completion of a questionnaire or interview will be the extent of participation asked of employees. However, even this period should be carefully planned ahead of time so that internal problems do not arise.

CONCLUSION

The case examples were presented to demonstrate how the diagnostic approach and organizational model can be used to diagnose an organization. The final section provided a set of guidelines for planning and managing the diagnostic process. In so doing it was again pointed out that diagnosis is a change intervention which affects all three systems—technical, political, and cultural.

Chapter Seven

Change Strategy

INTRODUCTION

We now shift our attention from diagnosis to the actual management of the change process. Change management may be divided into three separate topics. Each topic focuses attention on a unique set of conditions necessary for the successful management of change. The three are: (1) the development of the overall strategic change plan; (2) the selection of appropriate change technologies for carrying out the strategy; and (3) the development of a transition or implementation process. In order to understand these distinctions more fully, a medical analogy will be used.

Strategic Plan

For the physician, the strategic plan for treatment of a patient emerges from a diagnostic work-up which uncovers areas out of "alignment," or areas which are in need of treatment. The strategic plan represents the physician's opinion of the desired state for the patient. It is the point toward which the physician strives. Thus, a physician who has just diagnosed a heart attack, may develop a strategic plan which includes an altered life style, a new diet, and a changed physiological state. The strategic plan identifies *what* needs changing but does not indicate *how* it is to change.

Change Technology. Continuing with our heart-attack patient, the physician must now make decisions as to what medical technologies or tools to use in order to carry out the strategic plan. An array of technologies or tools is available to the physician and patient for making changes in his lifestyle, diet, and physiological condition. For example, lifestyle can be altered via chemotherapy (using drugs such as sedatives, tranquilizers, etc.) via individual and/or group psychotherapy, or via persuasion of the physician: "If you don't change your lifestyle you will die." Diet can also be changed via different technologies: chemotherapy (diet pills), psychotherapy, surgery (cutting out a section of the large intestine), and persuasion. Finally, with regard to the desired

185

physiological change, an array of techniques ranging from biofeedback to treatment with drugs is available. The choice of technologies is guided by an understanding of how various technologies work and the conditions necessary for their effective utilization.

Transition and Implementation Plan. The third element in change management is the transition, or implementation plan. In our medical example, this would refer to the specific steps for carrying out the treatment, such as how often to take the pills, or the specific therapy regime to follow. The plan also deals with the handling of the inevitable lapses in the pursuit of prescribed treatment, such as missing therapy sessions, not following a diet, etc., because of the patient's resistance to treatment. In medicine, as in organizational change, it turns out that a major hindrance in carrying out a strategic plan is due to inadequate management of implementation. Lack of commitment as well as unmanaged resistance often leads to sabotage and blocking.

This chapter will provide a broad framework for the development of the strategic plans. The following three chapters deal with the more detailed technical, political, and cultural strategies which will fill in the framework.

Any change strategy has as its principal purpose the spelling out of a desired organizational state. This is an image of the organizational components in good technical, political, and cultural alignment. The components which need to be adjusted to achieve this improved alignment will be identified along with the nature of the required adjustments.

The desired state is developed from an analysis of alignments. The alignment tests presented in Chapter 4 for each of the three systems will guide the strategy formulation process. Two basic options were presented for an organization faced with a condition of bad alignment. The first option is to remove or reduce the cause of the disequilibrium without changing the organizational components. The second option is to alter the organizational components. Each can be a viable approach and the decision on which one to employ should be made carefully.

An example of some of the difficulties which may be encountered in deciding which option to choose is the case of the U.S. auto industry, which faced simultaneous governmental regulations on pollution standards and gas efficiency. Option 1 focuses on eliminating the environmental pressures; this meant attempting to change the environment through lobbying and direct efforts to change the law. Option 2 involved altering the organizational components to respond to the new environment. In actual fact, the auto industry has pursued both options. Much effort has gone into lobbying and has resulted in more lenient government timetables and the lowering of some of the original standards. As the auto industry realized that the regulations on pollution and combustion efficiency were becoming an unalterable part of their environment, Option 2 was carried out. Internal changes also began to be made. The results are seen in GM's new cars as well as new models emerging from Ford and Chrysler. Currently, both options are being pursued, with Option 2 being given more attention and managerial resources.

Another example of what happens when the possible trade-offs are made between Options 1 and 2 occurred in an organization which was faced with cultural incongruence because of a change in hiring practices. This brought in a large number of young workers whose cultural values were at odds with the older parts of the workforce. Option 1 would be to revert to the old hiring practices and select only value-congruent workers. Option 2 in this case might include use of sensitivity training or intergroup confrontation workshops. The object would be to allow the two different groups to make mutual adjustments so as to be able to manage the value incongruence.

The actual change strategy is selected after an examination of both options. This chapter presents a set of guidelines and steps to follow in developing a change strategy based on such options.

DEVELOPMENT OF INTEGRATED TECHNICAL, POLITICAL, AND CULTURAL STRATEGIES

The development of a change strategy involves simultaneous attention to the three systems—political, technical, and cultural. The future desired state must be thought of in terms of these three systems. What must be considered is how good the alignment is within a system as well as how good it is between the systems. Again, a medical analogy might be helpful. A person's health is thought of in terms of the interdependent systems of the body. These would include the respiratory system, the circulatory system, the nervous system, etc. A desired state of health not only involves each individual system in good alignment, but also all of the systems functioning smoothly and in concert. In the same way that it is absurd to think of a healthy person with only one of these systems in good alignment, it is absurd to think of a healthy organization with only one of its major systems in good alignment.

The issue of alignment between systems is a complex one. This is because most systems are only partially interdependent. They are what some theorists call "loosely coupled" (Weick, 1976). The consequence is that change in one system may or may not be directly felt in the other system. This is also true of our medical analogy, where major changes in the respiratory system will affect the circulatory system and may also affect the nervous system. However, because these systems are only loosely coupled, it is hard to predict the exact nature of their interdependence or the impact one change would have on the other. In medicine, as in organizations, the interrelationships between subsystems require that intervention proceed with experimentation and constant adjustment. For example, in medicine it is important to monitor the treatment given to improve one system for side effects on another. What may occur is that when a drug is used for calming the nerves, the drug may also raise blood pressure or speed up breathing.

A useful metaphor, presented in Chapter 1, is to think of organizations in terms of loosely woven ropes. The strands can be dealt with individually—the political strand, the technical strand, and the cultural strand, but they are also interdependent and the ropes' supportiveness and load-bearing capacity is based on the combined strength of the strands.

Following are some principles to provide guidelines for developing integrated technical, political, and cultural change strategies.

1. *Technical, Political, and Cultural Systems Are Loosely Coupled.* First, it must be recognized that these three systems are interdependent but in a loose and, at times, haphazard way. An effective organization is one in which there is a reasonable degree of congruence among the three systems.

2. *Strategic Change Requires Uncoupling or Unbundling of the Three Systems.* Organizations tend to evolve to states in which the three systems are mutually reinforcing. For example, the technical system—the way in which work is organized and products are sold—is generally supportive of the political structure within which it operates. There is generally a culture present within organizations that rewards and encourages behavior congruent with technical and political systems. For strategic change to occur, it is necessary to be able to unhook or uncouple these systems from one another, much as it would be necessary to pull the strands of a rope apart to work on a single strand.

3. *It Is Necessary to Develop an Image of the Organization with Its Loosely Coupled Technical, Political, and Cultural Systems.* The desired state must include an all-encompassing view of the technical, political, and cultural systems. The desired state should not be developed according to an image of only one system, or even all three dealt with individually. For example, it will be pointed out that Texas Instruments' change strategy involved not only major technical, political, and cultural changes but also adjustments between the three systems to ensure their coordinated functioning.

4. *Plan for Recoupling the Systems.* Explicit attention is required so that the three systems can be helped to recouple with each other. A major part of a strategic change process involves reconnecting the three strands.

CASE EXAMPLES

To illustrate the use of guidelines which we have just established, let us turn our attention to two case examples. In the previous chapter, diagnoses of the Texas Instruments and Southwest Hospital System cases were presented. Now we will examine the development of change strategies for each of these cases.

Texas Instruments

As indicated in the previous chapter, the diagnosis of TI in the early 1960s led to the identification of a need for a strategic long-range planning process supported by an organization that monitored technology and market closely, was adaptable and flexible to product market changes, was able to foster design of facilities, reinforce research and development efforts, and encourage creativity among its people. This turned out to be a tall order.

The change strategy that was developed enabled TI to maintain a growth rate of 15–20% in a high-technology business committed to a strategy of continually pushing down its production costs to achieve price reductions. As noted previously, tightly controlled production, which TI was successfully implementing at the time of the diagnosis, and innovation which it was unsuccessful in managing, were required.

Strategic Plan for TI. The desired state for TI was a system which was continuously able to formulate and implement long-range strategic plans while simultaneously motivating its Product Customer Centers (PCCs) to maximum performance. The solution was to design a new prescribed organization which was then to be draped over the existing PCC structure. This strategy moved the TI organization, from a technical perspective, to a more organic form.

The name given to the new prescribed organization was Objectives, Strategy, and Tactics (OST). The OST organization was put in place to provide strategic, long-range planning and support of innovation. The company's total expenditures are divided between OST and the PCCs.

Very simply, the OST and Product Center Organization combination requires that individual senior managers at TI work in two separate organizations, or wear two hats. One hat is the product hat. For sake of illustration, let us say that manager Smith is responsible for production of 64K RAM computer chips. Wearing his product hat he may spend 60% of his time as production manager seeing that computer chips are produced with proper quantity and quality. 60% of his bonus comes from this activity. His other hat, 40% of his time, is devoted to a long-term objective for which he is held accountable. He is monitored on his work in this area and 40% of his bonus is allocated to this hat. The OST process operates as follows (See Figure 7.1):

1. Business objectives (a total of 9 of them) are designated at the top and represent the major businesses in which TI will operate for the long run.

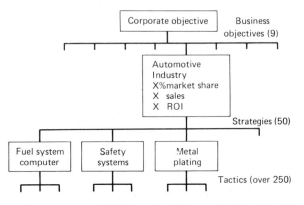

2. Each objective states such factors as listed in Figure 7.1, namely, percent of market share, sales volume, and return on investment. Each objective is to be carried out by a manager who is also a manager in the PCC structure. 20–50% of the manager's time is spent on OST work.

3. Each objective is established by means of several strategies which are stated in terms of 5- to 10-year goals. Each strategy also has a manager. These managers have individual roles and each has two bosses, one for the OST and one for PCC.

4. Each of the stated strategies have several specific tactics associated with them. In turn, realization of these tactics is broken down to 6- to 18-month checkpoints. Control is assigned to the PCC units. These are monitored on a monthly basis. This is how the strategic thinking of the OST network is tied into the production organization.

5. The prescribed organizational networks are supported by changes in other components of the organization:

(a) An extensive planning process includes a week-long objective and strategy session at which all strategies and objectives are to be reviewed for the benefit of the top 400 to 500 managers.

(b) Budgets are integrated between the two systems.

(c) Reward and management information systems are established to monitor and reinforce both the PCC and OST systems.

(d) Career development paths rotate managers through line, then staff, then line, etc., positions. This prepares them to understand more thoroughly both the PCC and OST networks.

6. They foster the development of emergent networks to support innovative activities.

An example of fostering such emergent networks is the TI plan to counter overly deterministic planning processes which might actually stifle some creativity. This is because with these processes in place, managers began to set excessively safe and conservative goals.

One mechanism to foster more creativity and combat conservatism is part of the formal OST method. It involves a method for funding the more speculative programs which were showing signs of underfunding in the initial OST system. The device is called the "wild hare." It allows managers to rank speculative projects separately and hence give them more funding.

Another mechanism for fostering innovation is to provide any organizational member(s) with a chance to obtain a grant from a pool containing several million dollars to fund innovative projects. The result has been the emergence of coalitions which apply for grants from the innovations pool, which then attempt to produce viable products. It was through this procedure, called IDEA, that some TI staff got together and developed the $19.95 digital watch.

The above sketch represents the revised strategic change plan for TI, that is, an outline of the desired state which in reality took 10 years to implement. This strategic change plan was revised and reformulated over the 10-year period. However, the basic blueprint was developed in the early 1960s. The implementation process, the transition management phase, will be discussed in more detail in Chapter 12.

The TI Change Strategy. In terms of our model and of our guidelines the TI case illustrates the following:

1. Environmental and technological triggers caused uncertainty in the technical cycles. The question was, how to remain competitive in a rapidly changing technological environment with major demands for innovation—while at the same time maintaining extremely efficient production.

2. The current state of TI in 1963 indicated a poor alignment in the technical system for encouraging or promoting innovation.

3. The desired state strategy involved making the technical system more organic. This became the OST structure.

4. The technical, political, and cultural systems were uncoupled and attention was first paid to the technical system.

5. A plan evolved for a new fit between the technical, political, and cultural systems. The desired technical system was accompanied by changes in the political and cultural systems.

6. Change strategy implementation took several years of recoupling the technical, political, and cultural systems, that is, changes were required on all three so as to make them mutually reinforcing.

Southwest Hospital System

Table 7.1 presents a summary of some of the key diagnostic findings in the SHS case presented in the preceding chapter, along with implications for change. The overriding factor in the SHS case was pressure for change brought about by an unstable environment. This in turn required

Table 7.1   SHS Diagnosis and Implications

Diagnostic Finding	Change Implication
Environment/Strategy/Management Style Alignment The SHS environment is high in uncertainty, yet has a strategy and a management style which are mechanistic.	Management development effort to alter style and/or replace managers with more organic style managers. Introduce and develop a systematic strategic planning process.
Strategy/Prescribed Network Alignment The SHS strategy ideally should be organic, requiring an organic prescribed network component. SHS has no complex, organic integrating mechanisms, and the simple mechanisms need adjustment.	Adjust simple integrating mechanisms (clarify rules and programs, hierarchy and goals). Develop more complex lateral integrating mechanisms for specified complex interdependent tasks. Redesign management information system to meet the organization's information processing capacity, not external accounting needs.
Prescribed Network/Process Alignment SHS processes are mechanistic. If the integrating mechanisms are made more complex in parts of the SHS system, then the fit between sociotechnical and process will worsen.	For areas of the organization in need of more organic processes, provide training and development support for improved communication, conflict management and problem-solving effectiveness.
Prescribed Network/Process/Emergent Networks Fit SHS has few task supportive emergent networks. Thus, the emergent networks have low task-relevant information processing capacity.	Facilitate the development of task-relevant emergent networks by developing reward system for informal lateral (cross-hospital) problem solving, etc.

Source: Reproduced by special permission from *The Journal of Applied Behavioral Science,* Noel M. Tichy, "Diagnosis for Complex Health Care Delivery Systems: A Model and Case Study," Vol. 14, 3, p. 316, copyright 1978, NTL Institute.

major readjustments of the components of the organizational model. The lack of an organic strategy and of strategic decision-making capability severely hampered the organization's ability to cope with its environment. As a result, the technical alignment between the organization and its environment became poor largely because of the political vested interests of the dominant coalition. In addition, the culture of the management and board had been too intimately coupled to the mechanistic technical system. The culture had a missionary orientation. The chain was originally established by a group of church people and wealthy business and political leaders as a charitable effort to do good for the rural poor. The culture supported a highly centralized structure by a board and management who believed it was their duty to take care of poor people who could not manage their own hospitals.

The basics of the plan for SHS are outlined in Table 7.1. This strategic plan triggered a confrontation with the political support base of the director, whose personal vested interests were linked to a dysfunctional strategy. The fact that the director was an extremely powerful figure in the influence network and had close ties to members of the board of trustees, as well as politicians in the external environment, created a situation in which the management of change required a political strategic plan along with a technical strategic plan. The political strategy was based on an individual analysis of the influential "stars" on the board of trustees as well as of the influential stars within the managerial ranks, some of whom had strong ties to the board as well. These influential people eventually were induced to form a coalition to force the resignation of the director. A new director was selected to implement the strategic plan.

Both of these cases demonstrate a number of important factors in change management. First, the need for a comprehensive organizational model to facilitate the development of a change strategy; second, the necessary interplay between technical, political, and cultural perspectives; and third, implementation may be complex and time consuming: The TI readjustment process took place over a period of 10 years. These two cases will next be used to demonstrate the guidelines which must be observed in developing a complete change strategy.

GUIDELINES FOR DEVELOPING A CHANGE STRATEGY

Guideline 1: Keep the Stage Set for Vigilant Decision Making

As was true in the diagnosis, when formulating strategy, the stage must be set for effective decision making. Change managers must continue to allocate their time properly and focus on long-range strategic issues as well as their immediate tasks. The same seven procedural criteria presented in Chapter 5 are relevant for strategy formulation. A summary of these criteria follows. It is useful for the organizational members involved in strategy formulation to review them and develop a set of procedures for insuring that they are in fact adhered to.

1. Thoroughly canvass a wide range of alternative courses of action.

2. Survey the full range of objectives to be fulfilled and the values implied by the choices.

3. Carefully weigh the costs and risks of negative consequences that could flow from each alternative.

4. Search intensively for information relevant to further evaluation of the alternatives.

5. Correctly assimilate and take account of new information or expert judgment, even when not in support of the course of action initially preferred.

6. Reexamine the positive and negative consequences of all known alternatives, including those originally regarded as unacceptable, before making a final choice.

7. Make detailed provisions for implementing the chosen course of action. Pay special attention to contingency plans that might be required if various known risks were to materialize.

Guideline 2: Summary of the Diagnosis

The diagnostic activity must be summarized in a form which can be usefully translated into strategic action. This is difficult because massive amounts of information must be boiled down to a few analytically sound, key conclusions. The start of this process was described in Chapter 6. The following specific steps are suggested to aid in developing the diagnostic summary:

Step 1: Analyze the Impact of the Diagnostic Activity. Often times the actual data collection and diagnostic activities have created predictable turbulence in the organization, and it becomes necessary to include a method for dealing with change created by the diagnosis itself. The impact of diagnostic activity may be assessed by answering the following questions:

1. What issues have been made salient to employees and executives as a result of the diagnosis?

2. Have individuals or groups been provoked into action by the diagnostic work?

3. What is the level of trust among organizational members with regard to the overall organization's climate and to the diagnostic activities?

4. How did the diagnostic activities affect the political system; the technical system, and the cultural system?

The answers to these questions should be followed with a statement of implications for the change process. In the SHS case, the diagnostic activity resulted in the following:

1. *Salience of Issues.* Managers and hospital administrators became more aware of the lack of strategic thinking in the organization and the problems attendant to the information systems.

2. *Level of Trust.* The diagnostic activities contributed to an increased gulf between the director and one of his deputy directors and the rest of management. The diagnosis was perceived by some as spying on the part of these two. It decreased trust and contributed to a climate of cynicism.

3. *Impact on Systems.* The diagnosis affected the technical system by uncovering poor alignments between the organization and its environment, and also with the complexity of the tasks and the organizational design's capacity for dealing with the complexity. The political system was affected by the mobilization of competing internal coalitions who began to blame each other for bad management. The cultural system was affected because the organization had an ideology of being the charitable guardian of health care in the region. Thus, when management was questioned, there was a sense of moral indignation by some, and a sense of pragmatic concern for better management by others.

The implication of the diagnostic activities on the management of change at SHS was that it created a political cleavage among powerful members in the organization, and necessitated that the resulting strategic plan be equipped to contend with these adversary forces.

Step 2: Summarize Trigger Events. As indicated in Chapter 5, the trigger event plays a key role in determining the nature of the diagnosis. Figure 7.2 provides a framework for summarizing the trigger's impact. In the TI case, the trigger was both the environment (increased competition in the semiconductor industry) and technology (rate and complexity of change). These triggers most directly affected the technical cycle. This, in turn, needed to be readjusted to have more information processing capacity so as to be able to engage in more creative innovations and long-range planning. Finally, this triggered the political and cultural changes which took place once changes were seen to be necessary in the technical arena.

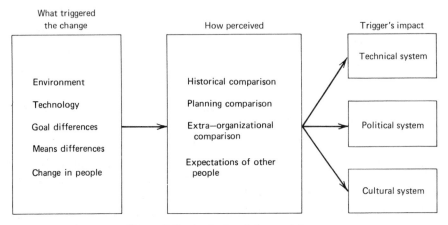

Figure 7.2   Analysis of change triggers

Figure 7.2 provides a handy checklist to allow for a quick visual survey of change triggers.

In SHS, the trigger event was the environment, which meant, because of historical comparison and past performance: a large deficit. The impact was felt simultaneously in all three cycles. In the technical area it was felt because of the need to have a more responsive and adaptive organization. In the political phase, it was felt because of the resulting indictment of the current dominant coalition. And the cultural area was affected as the result of the split between "missionaries" and "pragmatists" caused by the crisis.

The diagnosis—whether radar scan, symptom focused, or in-depth —is summarized using the organizational model categories. The diagnostic plan presented on pages 156-162 provides the questions which are further summarized in Figure 7.3. The summary consists of an evaluative statement entered in the chart for each category along with any implications for change. This is done in much the same manner as a physician might make an entry in a medical record—or chart—when conducting an overall health evaluation or in an attempt to diagnose a disease. This diagnostic data-base summary is used to help generate a list of change priorities. This provides the tools for developing a data-informed change strategy. The most difficult part of this task is the discipline needed to advance systematically through the steps without jumping ahead to the formulation of solutions.

Step 3: Summarize and Record Analysis of Alignments. Chapter 6 provided analytic guidelines for analyzing the alignments among the organizational components for each of the three perspectives using the principles presented in Chapter 4. After this analysis is carried out, the results should be summarized in the format presented earlier for the SHS case.

Guideline 3: From Diagnosis to Strategy

Now the diagnosis must be translated into a change strategy. This phase is a mixture of intuitive problem solving along with the application of the heuristic principles of analysis for the technical, political, and cultural alignments. There is no precise formula to help one move from diagnosis to change strategy. Nevertheless, it is useful to use the analysis of alignment principles.

General Statement of Required Changes

The change strategy should include two major components. The first is an overall statement of the nature of the changes required in one, two, or all three systems. This is stated in very general terms. For example, in the TI case, there was a strategic change plan to alter the technical

Key Findings

	1.	2.	3.
I. Input			
A. History of organization			
B. Environment of organization			
C. Organizational resources			
Change implications ➤			
II. Mission/strategy			
A. Mission			
B. Strategy			
C. Perceived goals			
D. Processes surrounding Mission/Strategy			
Change implications ➤			
III. Task analysis			
A. Basic tasks			
B. Task interrelationships			
Change implications ➤			
IV. Prescribed organization			
A. Overall configuration— differentiation			
B. Overall configuration— integration			
Change implications ➤			
V. People			
A. Characteristics of staff			
B. Managerial styles			
C. Motivational forces			
Change implications ➤			

Figure 7.3 Summary of diagnostic data base

VI. Organizational processes			
A. Characteristics of communications			
B. Characteristics of control			
C. Characteristics of decision making			
D. Characteristics of conflict management			
Change implications →			
VII. Emergent organization			
A. Overall emergent organization			
B. Coalitions			
C. Cliques			
Change implications →			
VIII. Output			
A. Degree of goal optimization			
B. Behavioral effects			
Change implications →			

Summary Change List-Based on diagnostic change priorities and diagnostic support

Change	Data Base
1.	
2.	
3.	
4.	
5.	
6.	
7.	
8.	

Figure 7.3   (continued)

system so as to make it more organic. The starting point in 1963 might have been portrayed in Figure 7.4 as Point A. The desired state—the strategic plan—being Point C in the technical area. This strategy was based on information processing principles which indicated that in 1963, TI was a largely mechanistic organization which was not capable of handling the complexities of problem solving and decision making necessary to deal with such a fast-changing market and technological environment. Thus, the decision was made to make TI more technically organic. Strategy had to be developed for the political and cultural areas as well. Once innovation and creativity were stressed, and the

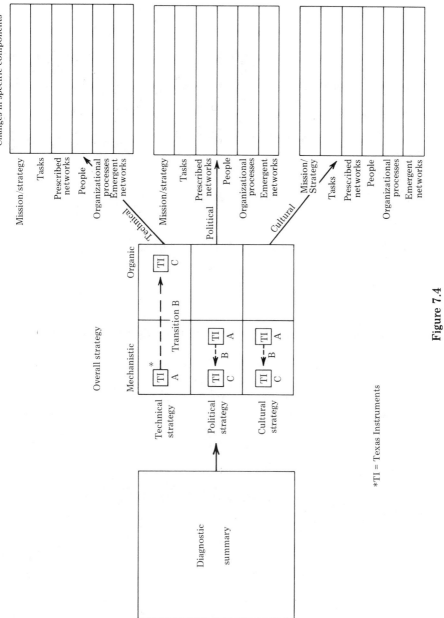

Figure 7.4

*TI = Texas Instruments

status quo was challenged, new political coalitions were turned into viable future controllers of TI. Also, splits between production people and R&D people appeared. Value/ideological splits were thus triggered.

In looking at TI retrospectively, the strategies appear to have been as listed in Exhibit 7.3. Politically, they became more mechanistic, leading to more monolithic control at the top. Culturally, they became more homogeneous. There were fewer value/ideological differences amongst the staff.

The SHS strategy included a technical shift to a more organic configuration. But unlike the TI case, the strategy in the political and cultural spheres pointed toward a more organic configuration. Politically, the system had to be able to deal with conflicts over how to accomplish SHS goals, differences among its stakeholders, i.e., community groups, doctors, administrators, and central headquarters. In the cultural area, the missionaries and pragmatists had to be induced to coexist. Thus a strategy was needed which allowed for the required value/ideological mix.

Detailed Statement of Needed Changes

The second component of the strategy is to specify in detail those changes which are required in specific components of the organizational model. It is at this stage that changes associated with each of the components of the organizational model are specified. The three mechanistic-to-organic tables presented in Chapter 4 provide examples of the types of changes that can be made. For example, in the TI case, Figure 4.5 can be used as a guide for describing the components' changes which were required to implement the technical strategy. In implementing the more organic technical strategy, TI made the following changes in components:

1. *Mission/Strategy.* This became more complex, explicit, integrated, flexible, and proactive (See Exhibit 4.6). The OST process was designed to produce such mission/strategy characteristics.

2. *People Management.* Style moved toward more risk taking, optimization of performance, flexibility, situational expertise, and more participation. Through selection, training, and development, the managerial style changed dramatically.

3. *Prescribed Networks.* There was increased use of complex integration mechanisms (vertical information systems, matrix structures, project teams, etc.) The OST structure added a great deal of complexity to TI and increased the need for information processing.

4. *Organizational Processes.* More open task-related communica-

tion flows, and capacity for conflict management had to be built into the formal negotiation over resources and plans. Again, the OST structure and process were explicitly designed to enhance communication and open negotiation. Finally, there is participative decision making regarding technical plans modification.

5. *Emergent Networks.* Extensive task-related networks and task coalitions became necessary. The use of the special project fund IDEA to encourage emergent coalitions to work on innovative projects is one example of the task-related emergent networks encouraged at TI.

In the case of TI, the change strategy can be described as having involved changes in the following components:

1. *Prescribed Networks.* A very tightly controlled top management dominant coalition was formed. It gave monolithic support to the OST structure.
2. *People.* A great deal of selection, socialization, and termination activity would likely take place. This was a part of the political strategy. It was deemed necessary to employ only those people at TI who would support management.
3. *Emergent Networks.* Non–politically supportive emergent networks were discouraged from forming and destroyed when found.

For the cultural system, much the same pattern emerged as found in the political system. TI pursued a strategy which made the cultural system more mechanistic. The organization looked for ways of creating homogeneity among the population with respect to values and norms. The major components to change were: people—selection, socialization, and termination—and emergent networks, which encouraged TI employees to socialize and live similar life styles.

By observing the following steps the change manager creates a change strategy:

1. Understand trigger and impact.
   a. What triggered the change?
   b. How was the trigger perceived?
   c. What was the trigger's impact?

2. Summary of the analyses of alignments.
   a. Technical system alignments.
   b. Political system alignments.
   c. Cultural system alignments.

3. Sequence of change strategies.
   a. Technical strategy.
   b. Political strategy.
   c. Cultural strategy.

4. Development of strategic change plan.
   a. What needs doing?
   b. How will the organization look?

A good test to see whether an adequate strategy has been formulated is for the change manager to involve a team in the strategy formulation process. One activity for such a team is creating a snapshot or scenario of the future organization. This "snapshot" is partly created by means of the procedures outlined above. However, what is suggested here is a more realistic scenario, one which is less abstract. The strategy team members are each asked to write brief descriptions of the future organization, giving specific examples of "who would be doing what with whom." These "snapshots" of the future help explain the strategy to each other. The team then develops a common strategy. As the strategy changes over time, the "snapshots" should also be updated and changed. The following three chapters give examples of technical, political, and cultural strategies.

CONCLUSION

This chapter discussed the development of change strategies. The strategic plan identifies what needs changing and is developed in terms of major changes in alignment for the technical, political, and cultural systems. The development of a strategic change plan is carried out by following these guidelines:

1. Keep the stage set for vigilant decision making; make certain that guidelines for effective problem solving and decision making are followed.

2. Summarize the diagnosis; the change strategy is developed from the diagnosis. This includes both the diagnostic findings and the turbulence and expectations created by the diagnostic activities.

3. Move from diagnosis to strategy. This involves the development of an overall profile of the planned movement from the organization's current state to a desired state in each of the systems—technical, political, and cultural. The planned change is conceptualized in terms of the mechanistic-to-organic continuum and includes specific changes related to each of the model's components.

Chapter Eight

Technical Change Strategies

INTRODUCTION

Technical change strategies alter the information-processing capacity of the organization. The strategies involve adjusting components of the organizational model. These adjustments are made either to increase or decrease the organization's capacity to deal with uncertainty brought on by changing environmental conditions, new technological developments, or complexities in the tasks.

In the 1960s, Dow Chemical needed to attend to information and decisions in three areas: products, geography, and functions. They needed to enhance their information-processing capacity. The result was the development of a very organic structure, one which they felt would give them greater information-processing capacity. They developed a three-dimensional matrix structure. One dimension had product managers, another had geographic managers, and the third had functional managers; each had interdependent responsibilities. In theory, this matrix design provided tremendous information-processing capacity. Even though the matrix provided a good technical system solution for Dow Chemical's information-processing needs, it proved too difficult to manage due to the lack of supporting political system and cultural system changes. The matrix decomposed in 1970; it went to a two-dimensional structure, product and geography, and a decade later ended up as a geographic structure (Davis, 1976).

Another example of a technical change strategy was the development of increased information-processing capacity for environmental analysis at General Electric. As part of its strategic planning process, GE required information and analysis of its future worldwide environment, thus GE created staff groups to monitor the economic, political, and social trends and changes occurring worldwide.

Another interesting technical shift was Union Carbide's move away from the matrix structure to a product-line structure. One Union Carbide executive observed that:

Now that we have a division which is responsible for all functional activities from R & D to production and sales, we are able to respond more quickly to conditions in the coatings marketplace. This enables us to be more sensitive to the requirements of our customers.

Lines of communication within our organization between top management and operating personnel are much shorter. Decisions can be made faster (*American Paint Journal*, 1980, p. 15).

The Union Carbide example shows how information processing can be enhanced by creating self-contained units. It means that the company must have more of the resources for running a business within each division; it thus loses some economies of scale possible with companywide functions but gains the advantage of increased information-processing capability within each division.

In order to illustrate the variety of technical change strategies available to organizations, a series of case illustrations will be presented; each highlights strategic changes possible for the components of the network model. The changes to each component will be examined in terms of the shifts along the mechanistic to organic continuum initally outlined in Figure 4.6. Figure 8.1 presents a summary of the types of component changes discussed in the remainder of the chapter.

THE ENVIRONMENT/MISSION AND STRATEGY INTERFACE

The technical alignment of the organization with its environment is essentially a task of seeing that the organization's mission and strategy are appropriately matched to the threats and opportunities which face the organization. The organization which operates in a relatively stable environment can operate quite effectively with a mechanistic strategy: one that is not complex, not very explicit, and fragmented. On the other hand, when the environment becomes increasingly uncertain the mission and strategy require more attention.

The 1970s witnessed the burgeoning growth of strategic planning systems and staffs. By 1980 most of the Fortune 500 corporations had some form of systematic strategic planning. The purpose of the strategic planning systems and staffs were to provide the organization with a higher information-processing capacity vis a vis its technical alignment with the environment. The success of these strategic planning efforts in terms of better alignment of the organization to its environment is variable. Nevertheless there are a few stellar examples of strategic planning in which it has become the driving force in making the company perform better than its competitors. On the other hand, there are many companies which have done a miserably poor job at strategic planning, often because they treated it as a gimmick and something for staff to work on rather than a central aspect of line management.

Organizational Components

Managerial Areas →	Mission and Strategy	Tasks	Prescribed Network	People	Processes	Emergent Networks
Technical System	Assessing environmental threats and opportunities Assessing organizational strengths and weaknesses Defining mission and fitting resources to accomplish it	Environmental scanning activities Strategic planning activities	Differentiation: organization of work into roles (production, marketing, etc.) Integration: recombining roles into departments, divisions, regions, etc. Aligning structure to strategy	Selecting or developing technical skills and abilities Matching management style with technical tasks	Fitting people to roles Specifying performance criteria for roles Measuring performance Staffing and development to fill roles (present and future) Developing information and planning systems to support strategy and tasks	Fostering the development of information networks which facilitate task accomplishment
Political System						
Cultural System						

Figure 8.1 Technical strategic management

Even though the pitfalls were identified at the start of the decade, the majority of companies which tried strategic planning stumbled over at least some of the following 10 mistakes (Steiner, 1972):

1. Top management's assumption that it can delegate the planning function to a planner.

2. Top management becomes too engrossed in current problems and doesn't spend sufficient time on long-range strategic problems.

3. Failure to develop company goals suitable as a basis for formulating long-range plans.

4. Failure to assume the necessary involvement in the planning process of major line personnel.

5. Failure to use plans as standards for measuring managerial performance.

6. Failure to create a climate in the company which is congenial and not resistant to planning.

7. Assuming that corporate comprehensive planning is something separate from the entire management process.

8. Injecting so much formality into the system that it lacks flexibility, looseness, simplicity, and restricts creativity.

9. Failure of top management to review with departmental and divisional heads the long-range plans which they have developed.

10. Top management's consistent rejection of the formal planning mechanism by making intuitive decisions which conflict with with formal plans.

The early 1980s appear to be a time when companies will need to learn to do it right. This means those who have tried and failed will have to try again, and some that are just learning will have to go on an accelerated track. The reasons are quite obvious, as pointed out in the introductory chapter: U.S. industry is undergoing major transformations which will require strategic planning and decision making at the core.

A more organic strategy formulation process was called for in the SHS case presented in the last two chapters. The hospital system had been relying on muddling, informal, adaptive processes for setting strategic long-term direction. Members of the board would develop pet projects, or the president might decide to try out some new ways of organizing and delivering new services. Coalitions supporting strategic shifts would be formed over cocktails or through informal meetings. The result was a mechanistic strategy which did not bode well for the hospital system in a changing and hostile environment.

At Texas Instruments, prior to the initiation of the OST system, strategy formulation was very unsystematic and excessively decentralized. The OST system is one example of an organic strategic process. Such a process aims to provide organizations with the capability to:

1. Adequately map its external environment—now and in the future (markets, economy, relevant social and political trends, etc.)

2. Have the information processing capability to use the environmental mapping data to support strategic decision making.

3. Develop the capability to assess current and future organizational strengths and weaknesses relevant to strategy.

4. Develop a strategic decision-making process which utilizes the relevant data about the environment and the organization.

5. Develop the capacity for implementing and following through on the business strategy.

Creating the conditions for these five approaches is no simple task. It requires basic reorientation of the managerial process. For example, at SHS the change was initiated by focusing on the way managers thought and spent their time. There was a need to change managerial activities—which had been dominated by crisis-oriented operational problems—toward investing in strategic issues. The approach developed by the consultant involved:

1. Getting management to distinguish between operational issues and to accept the notion that it is important to take time to do both well.

2. Developing mechanisms for protecting managerial time and resources for strategic decision making, following many of the principles presented on page 151: developing managerial triage systems, buffering time, decentralizing, and creating strategic advocates.

3. Developing a strategic-planning and decision-making structure. This includes both top-level (the board included) and lower level (hospital administrators) training and design of supporting systems. The implementation of a strategic planning process at SHS will take at least 3 years, as it requires major reorientation of managers at all levels, will require changes in process (reward processes must shift from crisis management to rewards for strategic management) and changes in the ability to deal with conceptual complexity of strategic issues.

Altering Strategic Decision Making. Processes and Analytic Tools

Process changes in strategic planning refers, for example, to the types of changes which were introduced at TI in their OST process and in SHS in organizing and structuring themselves for more systematic strategic decision making. The process includes the following activities (Naylor, 1980):

1. Review of the external environment

2. Assessment of the situation

3. Formulation of objectives

4. Formulation of goals

5. Formulation of strategies

6. Specification of project plans

7. Development of operating plans

8. Implementation of a control function.

Analytic Tools.   There are a growing array of analytic tools to help in the process of strategy formulation. These tools are meant to aid managers in processing complex, uncertain information to facilitate strategic, resource-allocation decisions. The tools fall into two major categories: (1) strategic portfolio models and (2) computer based planning models.

Strategic Portfolio Models.   These assume that the company has a portfolio of businesses, and that decisions must be made regarding how to allocate the company's scarce financial resources across them. The most popular version of this approach is the Boston Consulting Group's (BCG) matrix. It categorizes a company's businesses or products in a growth share matrix indicated in Figure 8.2. One dimension refers to the business attractiveness in terms of the expected annual growth of sales in constant dollars. The other dimension refers to the market share held by the business under consideration. There are four basic types of businesses:

Figure 8.2

1. *Cash cow.* High market share with low growth potential. These frequently generate more cash than is required to maintain market share so that the excess cash is available to make investments in long term R & D, in start-up businesses, etc.

2. *Star.* High-growth and high market-share businesses which are beginning to show profits but may not yet show a positive cash flow.

3. *Question mark.* High market-growth potential but the business has a small market share, and requires a large infusion of cash to grow market share so that it can become a star; without the cash it will become a dog.

4. *Dog.* Low market share and low market-growth potential— these are worthless drains on the company and should be divested.

According to the BCG, a balanced portfolio calls for:

1. Heavy investment in stars where high share and high growth assure the future.

2. Protection of cash cows that supply the funds for future growth.

3. Selective investment in question marks to be converted into stars.

4. Liquidation of dogs.

Another important element in the BCG set of strategic concepts is its idea of the experience curve, which is a revision of the learning curve. The learning curve was first developed by economists during World War II to describe the concept of unit costs declining with increased volume. The BCG experience curve predicts that unit costs of manufacturing a product decline approximately 20–30% each time accumulated experience is doubled. The factors which account for the declining costs are:

1. Improved labor efficiency (learning).

2. New processes and improved methods (specialization).

3. Product redesign.

4. Product standardization.

5. Economies of scale.

6. Factor input substitution.

The experience curve is used to guide strategic decisions in the following areas: market share, growth, debt capacity, cost control, product design, make or buy, procurement negotiation, market potential, and product line breadth (Henderson, 1974).

Another technical tool for strategic decision making is the PIMS (Profit Impact of Market Strategy) program of the Strategic Planning Institute. PIMS includes a number of models based on multiple regression analysis for studying the impact on profitability of various factors such as rate of growth, degree of market share, market concentration, product quality, and productivity of capital and labor. PIMS has a data base of over 1000 product-line businesses with which to run comparisons.

Business planning models are also used for strategic planning purposes. These are simulation models which enable the managers to ask "what if" questions. Simulation models developed for marketing, production, and financial planning purposes can be used in conjunction with other analytic tools such as data from macroeconomic models which examine "what if" issues at the societal level.

All of these analytic tools are adjuncts to the planning process. No matter what the strategic decisions, they are fraught with uncertainty, and require good clinical judgments on the part of management. Thus, the process is more important than the fanciness of the analytic tools.

Altering the Prescribed Networks: Organizational Design Changes

Perhaps the most popular change strategy is to reorganize. Managers are often obsessed with redoing organizational charts. Often these changes are as much political as technical. The focus in this direction is on the technical aspects of altering the prescribed networks.

The Macro Worldwide Structure. The structuring of worldwide, multinational companies offers some interesting information-processing dilemmas. There are five basic worldwide structures; each has a capacity for processing different amounts and types of information. The five are:

1. International divisions—set up to parallel the domestic divisions but instead focus on worldwide markets

2. Worldwide product divisions in which products are managed worldwide

3. Area or geographic divisions, each able to deal with its own marketplace fairly independently of the other divisions

4. Matrix organization, which has two dimensions working together such as product and market

5. Focused market units which are focused on markets rather than products; they focus on serving a particular market without concern for geographic lines.

Table 8.1 identifies the trade-offs involved in choosing one structure over another. For example, an international division does not do a

Table 8.1 Suitability of Basic MNC Organizational Structures to Corporate Concerns

Area of Corporate Concern	Level of Suitability				
	International Division	Worldwide Product Division	Area Division	Matrix	Focused Market Units
Rapid growth	M	H	M	H	H
Diversity of products	L	H	L	H	H
High technology	M	H	L	H	H
Few experienced managers	H	M	L	L	L
Close corporate control	M	H	L	H	H
Close government relations	M	L	H	M	M
Resource allocation:					
Product considerations should dominate	L	H	L	M	M
Geographic considerations should dominate	M	L	H	M	M
Functional considerations should dominate	L	M	L	H	M
Relative cost	M	M	L	H	M

Source: From John Hutchinson "Evolving Organizational Forms." *Columbia Journal of World Business*, Vol. XL, 2, 1976, p. 51. Reprinted with permission.

KEY: H = high
    M = medium
    L = low

good job managing "diversity of products," whereas the matrix and the focused market units do. Obviously, the matrix and the focused market units have the highest information-processing capacity of the five worldwide structures.

Organizational Design. The redesign of prescribed networks is facilitated by employing the guidelines for technical alignment prescribed in Chapter 4. In the TI case, we see that the need for greater information-processing capacity led to the OST structure. This, coupled with the PCC structure, resulted in a complex matrix organizational design. Each manager works for two separate bosses, has two distinct sets of work objectives, is evaluated, monitored, and rewarded for these two sets of activities. The result is an organizational design with extremely high information-processing capacity—able to facilitate short-term production control and efficiency while also promoting long-term innovation and product development. TI's OST system is not without its problems. By 1982 it was being blamed for some of TI's business problems. The real problem may reside in TI's mechanistic political and cultural systems.

New organizational designs can be created by following the logic built into the technical alignment mode. The remainder of this section outlines a number of alternative prescribed network strategies, (1) adjusting the integrating mechanisms, (2) the matrix design, and (3) principles for organizational design and subunit design.

Adjusting Integrating Mechanisms. In the Southwest Hospital Systems case, as indicated in Chapter 6, the prescribed organization was analyzed in terms of its use of integrating mechanisms. Integrating mechanisms represent the means by which the organization achieves coordination and control over its tasks and people. The mechanisms vary in their capacity to process information, and in how simple, how complex, and how costly (see Figure 8.3) their use may be.

As noted in Figure 8.3, there is a considerable range of integrating mechanisms. The technical organizational design problem is to match low uncertainty with simple and cheap mechanistic integration devices and to save the expensive, complex devices for those situations with high uncertainty. Complex devices are appropriate when there are high information-processing requirements and complex interdependence, such as in top-level strategic planning. Galbraith's (1973) categorization scheme for integrating mechanisms provided the basic tool for diagnosis and strategy planning in the SHS case.

1. *Simple Mechanisms at SHS.* Questionnaire items were administered to SHS managers to assess their perceptions of the use of rules and standard programs, the hierarchy and goals, as integrating mechanisms. For each integrating mechanism respondents gave their opinions/ ratings on whether it existed and, if so, in what form.

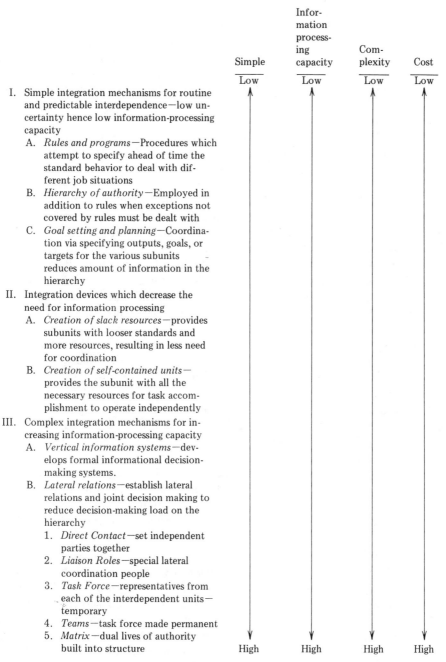

	Simple	Information processing capacity	Complexity	Cost
	Low	Low	Low	Low

I. Simple integration mechanisms for routine and predictable interdependence—low uncertainty hence low information-processing capacity
  A. *Rules and programs*—Procedures which attempt to specify ahead of time the standard behavior to deal with different job situations
  B. *Hierarchy of authority*—Employed in addition to rules when exceptions not covered by rules must be dealt with
  C. *Goal setting and planning*—Coordination via specifying outputs, goals, or targets for the various subunits reduces amount of information in the hierarchy

II. Integration devices which decrease the need for information processing
  A. *Creation of slack resources*—provides subunits with looser standards and more resources, resulting in less need for coordination
  B. *Creation of self-contained units*—provides the subunit with all the necessary resources for task accomplishment to operate independently

III. Complex integration mechanisms for increasing information-processing capacity
  A. *Vertical information systems*—develops formal informational decision-making systems.
  B. *Lateral relations*—establish lateral relations and joint decision making to reduce decision-making load on the hierarchy
    1. *Direct Contact*—set independent parties together
    2. *Liaison Roles*—special lateral coordination people
    3. *Task Force*—representatives from each of the interdependent units—temporary
    4. *Teams*—task force made permanent
    5. *Matrix*—dual lives of authority built into structure

High	High	High	High

Figure 8.3 Galbraith's integrating mechanisms

For example, the managers were asked whether or not standard operating procedures existed at SHS in 12 different areas, such as hiring nurses, capital budgeting, and medical policy, and in those situations where they existed, how specific they were. When it came to evaluating the hierarchy as an integrating device, respondents were asked their perceptions of the levels at which different types of decisions, such as personnel transfers, budget reallocation decisions, etc., were made at SHS.

Regarding both of these integrating devices, SHS managers registered a great deal of disagreement. This provided the decisive basis for the conclusion that these mechanisms were in need of readjustment. Such simple mechanisms do not work unless they are adhered to consistently. Yet, they cannot be consistently adhered to if the people using them have vastly differing views as to their functions. For example, if administrators of a hospital do not think there is a rule for "entering new areas of service" they will invent their own procedures, often to the dismay of the vice-president at corporate headquarters. Likewise, if the top-level hierarchy is to be used to integrate the overall organization, the administrator and corporate vice-president must agree upon which decisions are to be made and at which level.

Goals are also useful as integration mechanisms to the degree that they are commonly shared. Again, there were significant variations among SHS managers as to goal priorities of the system.

2. *Intermediate-Level Integrating Mechanisms at SHS.* Self-contained units and slack resources reduce the need for joint problem solving and decision making. They are a more complex form of integration than rules, programs, the hierarchy, and goals. SHS was composed of a group of self-contained units, namely 12 separate hospitals. However, in deciding on their decentralization, the planners made no explicit analysis of the costs and benefits of self-contained units as opposed to the economies of scale and balancing of resources possible by providing uniform and centralized services to the 12 hospitals. Such an analysis was needed to determine how much integration was needed.

3. *Complex Integrating Mechanisms at SHS.* As noted in Figure 8.3, one type of complex integrating mechanism is the vertical information system. SHS had a very complex, computerized management-information system. However, this system did not provide sufficient information-processing capacity for the organizations's integrating requirements. This was because the system was dominated by financial accounting demands. However, with respect to such demands for:

> reports for lending agencies, regulatory bodies, Trustees, and the public ... which express how well or badly the organization has been directed

toward its financial objectives . . . the information provided in these reports is not expected to be particularly helpful to management in its governance of the organization . . . from an information system point of view it is important to segregate financial accounting (Ackoff, 1974).

This was clearly not done at SHS. The result was a vertical information system which the managers reported as not being very useful for making managerial decisions. It was used primarily in generating external reports and making some corporate-level managerial decisions. Thus, it was of little help in integrating SHS.

Lateral integrating mechanisms are the most complex and have the capacity for enabling management to integrate multiple interdependencies simultaneously. SHS did make use of direct contact among the administrators by setting up meetings with the vice-president of operations once every couple of months. In addition, the central administration staff had occasional meetings. In neither case were they used for integrative problem solving and decision making as much as they were for information sharing and venting of gripes. Thus, much of their potential integrating function was missed.

The organizational design was assessed to be mechanistic at a time when the strategy was becoming more complex and organic. There was a need for higher information-processing capacity and a need to move the prescribed organization toward the organic end of the scale. What made the situation even worse was the fact that the more mechanistic integrating devices never functioned effectively. The poorly functioning simple mechanisms coupled with the lack of more complex mechanisms meant the system had very little information-processing capability. The hierarchy was constantly overloaded with crises piling up on corporate-level managers, problems which could have been solved lower down in the system via rules and programs, goals, a better information system, or, best yet, lateral integrating devices.

A part of the change strategy was to make the organizational design more organic and to improve its information-processing capacity. The steps began with adjusting the simple integrating mechanisms. An organizational design task force headed by two corporate vice-presidents with representatives from the hospital administrators followed the steps listed below:

1. Identify the problems with existing integrating mechanisms —lack of understanding, conflicting views, etc.

2. Bring key parties together to clarify and develop simple integrating mechanisms.

3. Assess the information-processing needs which exist after effective simple mechanisms are in operation.

4. Develop more complex integrating mechanisms in collaboration with those managers affected by them.

5. Implement complex mechanisms and monitor their effectiveness.

The Matrix Design

An organizational design strategy which deserves special attention at this point is the matrix structure. It is often "sold" unrealistically as the panacea of organizational design. As a result, it is often inappropriately selected by many large corporations as their basic organizational design strategy.

Intuitively, the matrix design makes a great deal of sense. However, as a strategy of choice, it must be used only when the following conditions are met (Davis, 1976):

1. There is diversification of products, functions and/or markets, requiring balanced and simultaneous management of two out of these three.

2. The opportunities lost and difficulties experienced by favoring either a product, function, or market should be a major factor. Unity of command cannot be ignored.

3. Environmental pressure to secure economies of scale require the shared use of scarce human resources.

4. There is a need for enriched information-processing capacity because of uncertain, complex, and interdependent tasks.

5. Information, planning, and control systems operate simultaneously along different dimensions of the structure.

6. As much attention is paid to managerial behavior as to the structure. The organizational culture and ethos must actively support and believe in negotiated management. In other words, they have to "think matrix."

The pros and cons for the matrix structure might look like this (Davis and Lawrence, 1977):

Cons	Pros
More organizationally induced conflicts.	A great deal of flexibility in complex environments.
Requires a managerial style which includes good interpersonal skills and ability to make consensual decisions.	Provides a means for managing two organizational areas simultaneously, that is, function and product or product and market, etc.

Relies on multiple bosses and is therefore a source of conflict and confusion.	High flexibility to shrink or expand according to need.
Time consuming and expensive due to complex information and control systems and consensual decision making.	Forces interaction and conflict resolution.
More ambiguity.	Involves critical components in decision making.
Matrix problems are costly.	Accountability is more closely related to responsibility and authority.

Power struggles

Anarchy

"Groupitis"

Collapses during economic crises

Excessive overhead

Decision strangulation

As can be seen from the list of cons for matrix design, its use involves more than the technical system. The political and cultural systems are greatly affected. Power relationships are dramatically changed as are the norms and values covering the areas of performance, conflict, and communication. Thus, a successfully implemented matrix design requires an accompanying political and cultural strategy. This was the case at Texas Instruments, where the dominant coalition consolidated its power in the design and worked to make the culture of the work force homogeneous. The end result was that the personnel either supported the matrix structure or left the organization. Over time, people were brought along to believe in the structure as a basic part of the work culture.

Sub-Unit Design—The Volvo Kalmar Case

Part of the design strategy implemented at lower levels in the Volvo Kalmar assembly plant in Sweden included organic subunits. In the late 1960s, Volvo made a commitment to improve the work environment in order to deal with morale, absenteeism, and turnover problems. The Kalmar plant was created to provide an environment that encouraged teamwork. This was part of the Volvo president's stated strategy:

> A way must be found to create a workplace which meets the needs of modern working man for a sense of purpose and satisfaction in his daily work. A way must be found of attaining this goal without an adverse effect on productivity. (Per Gyllenhammer, 1977).

The design is *technically* organic. Yet the Volvo design also altered the political and cultural systems. The work is organized between teams of 15 to 25 workers, each of which has responsibility for a different work process, for example, electrical systems, brakes, wheels, etc. There is no assembly line. Each team establishes its own work rhythm. There are 600 day-shift employees; the factory's maximum two-shift capacity is 60,000 cars a year.

Figure 8.4 depicts two work-team areas in the Kalmar plant. The center of the diagram discloses the central storage area (1). Between each of the work areas there are buffer zones for storing work completed by one team and ready for further processing by the next team (2). Instead of an assembly line, cars are transported on self-propelled electric trolleys. Members of each team retrieve cars from buffer zones when they are ready to work on them. Thus, two teams working next to each other can work at different rates without interfering with each other. Material procurement from stores is also controlled by the team. Material intake is by electric trucks (3). Each team must manage its own inventory of parts. The work area includes a pre-assembly area (4) next to the material area. The cars move along the area labelled (6) where the team may work on them either in a stationary position or while the automobiles are in motion. Also, the trolleys have a tilting arrangement which enables the car to be turned over on its side to facilitate working on the underside. The remaining portion of each work area includes its own rest zone (7),

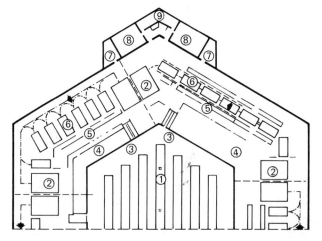

Figure 8.4 Workshop in Volvo's car assembly plant at Kalmar. *Key:* 1. stores; 2. body buffers; 3. material intake by electric trucks; 4. pre-assembly; 5. materials; 6. bodies—on the left stationary, on the right moving; 7. pause over; 8. toilets; 9. changing room. (From N.M. Tichy, Organizational innovations in Sweden. *Columbia Journal of World Business.* Summer, 1974.)

toilet facilities (8), and changing rooms (9), as well as a separate exit. The construction of the outer walls allowed for clearly defined work areas for each team. Attempts were made architecturally to make the work settings pleasant and included the extensive use of windows to provide daylight and contact with the out-of-doors.

As part of the political system's change strategy, the work teams have considerable say in the total management of the plant through a joint council. Teams are also responsible for a portion of the selection and training of new members as well as for the management of problems related to the productivity of its own members.

The plant construction cost an estimated 10% more than a comparable conventional plant. Management justifies its investment by the benefits received. These have included greater employee satisfaction reflected in decreased absenteeism, turnover, and increased productivity.

The approach taken in this case is based on the assumption that technology and environmental conditions constrain and limit the design of an organization and the management structure, but do not fully determine it. It is further assumed that alternative structures have different social and psychological effects on organizational members. The organizational design solution is aimed at finding a technical and organizational arrangement which produces a desired effect on individual members and work groups.

The cultural system principles which guided the Volvo design effort and other similar sociotechnical systems strategies are:

1. Participation in decision making increases the commitment and motivation to carry out the decision.

2. People are motivated to work for many different reasons including material rewards, social rewards, self-recognition rewards, and growth rewards.

3. The core unit for improving employee satisfaction and performance is the work group, not the manager or the individual worker.

4. A sense of completeness and satisfaction with a task accomplished is enhanced when individuals participate in a total task.

5. Tasks should be organized to give teams maximum control over them.

6. The physical environment is important in securing satisfaction and productivity.

The Volvo solution did not represent a purely technical strategy. It incorporated both political and cultural change strategies which, as pointed out in Chapter 2, may account for the success of the change as contrasted with change strategies which are excessively dominated by technical concerns.

Guidelines for Design of Prescribed Networks

Nadler, et al. (1979) provide a set of guidelines for designing an organization's prescribed networks:

1. Identify the most critical information-processing needs—those tasks which require the most interdependence and are important.

2. Group critical roles into units which have the highest information-processing needs—those which must process the most information because of their interrelationships.

3. Each unit should be analyzed in terms of the amount of environmental, task, and interdependent uncertainty which it faces, thus defining the information-processing capacity needed. The more organic the unit structure, the more information-processing capacity will be required.

4. Analyze the interunit needs for information processing, that is, which units are interdependent with which others. Develop appropriate integrating mechanisms to link units together.

5. Keep aggregating units and interunits using the above design procedures, until the total organization is structured.

CHANGING PEOPLE AS A CHANGE STRATEGY

Another component of the model is people. There are two basic ways to alter the people component (1) selection and (2) socialization. The most basic change strategy is obviously the hiring and/or firing of people to alter the characteristics of the people component. Training and developing of individuals is a more difficult process. Before exploring these approaches, a continuum of organizational managerial style is presented.

Managerial style can vary in terms of the mechanistic to organic continuum. Figure 8.5 presents a comparison of organic versus mechanistic management styles. One goal of the change strategy is to appropriately match managerial style with the demands of the role to be filled by the manager. Thus, more mechanistically oriented tasks and organizations fit better with people who have needs for security, stability, and lower tolerances for ambiguity, complexity, and uncertainty. Organic settings fit better with people who have greater growth needs, less need for security and stability, and are capable of dealing with uncertainty, complexity, and change.

Organic	Mechanistic
top management style ⟵————————⟶	top management style
Open channels of communication; free flow of information throughout the organization	Highly structured channels of communication and highly restricted flow of information
Managers' operating styles allowed to vary freely	Uniform managerial style insisted upon
Authority for making decisions rooted in situational expertise	Authority for making decisions rooted in formal line managers
Free adaptation of the organization to changing circumstances	Insistence on holding fast to tried and true management principles despite changes in business conditions
Emphasis on getting things done rather than on following formal procedures	Personnel to follow formal procedures
Loose, informal control; emphasis on norms of cooperation	Tight control of operations through sophisticated control systems
On-job behavior permitted to be shaped by the requirements of the situation and personality of the individual doing the job	On-job behavior to conform to job descriptions

Figure 8.5 (From Pradip N. Khandwalla, *The Design of Organizations* Copyright © 1977 by Harcourt Brace Jovanovich, Inc. Reprinted by permission of the publisher.)

In order to achieve an appropriately aligned management style, one can choose between two basic approaches. First, through screening and selection, people can be closely compared with the organizational context. An example of how this might be done at a senior management level is in deciding who is to run which businesses in a multibusiness company such as GE. In such an integrated firm it is worthwhile to give priority to the technical strategic alignment of its personnel. One way of accomplishing this is to use a framework such as the Boston Consulting Group's typology of businesses for categorizing types of managers.

Cash cows are generally more mature businesses, with more stable environments and hence a more mechanistic structure. They can be "milked" to provide a steady supply of cash. This calls for managers who can coordinate such mechanistic situations.

Question marks or problem children are businesses of high potential which, however, require a great deal of entrepreneurial management to turn them into performance stars. Thus, in selecting managers for these organizations it would be important to find those who fit into the organic end of a corporate continuum, don't have strong needs for security or stability, and who can deal with change, complexity, and uncertainty.

The stars may require a mixture of managerial styles. The dogs call for more mechanistic managers who are able to liquidate or divest the business.

An example of matching managerial style to technical configurations occurred at Chase Manhattan Bank. Here the organization had a strategy of moving a low-margin operation oriented to keeping its costs down to one which would aggressively compete in a more broadly defined consumer financial services market. In order to launch this strategy the bank conscientiously looked for an executive with the requisite entrepreneurial skills. They went outside the bank and hired Mr. Frederick Hammer who had a track record of entrepreneurial activities in banking, computer services and as division chief for an industrial firm overseas. He replaced a manager who fit the traditional Chase retail banking strategy who was then matched to a business setting more congruent with his style, namely the Chase European operation. (*Business Week*, 25 February 1980, p. 166).

Texas Instruments also looks to match managerial style to the type of business within which the manager operates. They attempt to change managers according to the product life cycle so that in startup situations they have the risk-taking entrepreneur type who they move out when the business matures and needs more of a cost-conscious type to help harvest the business.

Finally, technical style matching can be carried a step further, as is being done by General Electric.

> At GE, an adherent of product portfolio analysis, strategic objectives for the company's wide-ranging products are defined as "grow," "defend," and "harvest" depending on the product life cycle. Now its general managers are being classified by personal style or orientation as "growers," "caretakers," and "undertakers" to match managerial type with the product's status (*Business Week*, 25 February 1980, p. 173).

As mentioned earlier, there are two basic strategies for fitting managerial style to the task demands. The hiring, firing, or internal transferring of people is the quickest and the most effective means. At Chase it was reported that such matching of styles was not painless. Alan Lafley pointed to this in stating that between 200 and 300 people left the bank "at least half of whom were encouraged to leave because their skills didn't fit our strategies."

The second approach to people alignment is to socialize and develop managers who will operate successfully within the organic or mechanistic demands. For managers, this may be an implicit part of their rotation through positions in the organization. The higher a position is in any organization, the more organic it becomes. Activities which help to generate such organically oriented managers include specific assignments, management training, and interpersonal and leadership training, etc.

Development or socialization would appear to be the alternative approach. Companies such as GE and Texas Instruments, in addition to personnel selection, pay much attention to the development of managers whose styles are suited to their potential future tasks. This includes selecting managers with mechanistic styles to operate "cash cows," and bringing in those executives with experience in organic structures to run "question mark" or "star" units or companies. In addition, management development programs can be used to provide training methods to alter managerial styles.

Altering Processes

The process component includes such organizational activities as communication, reward, decision making, and conflict. These processes can all be adjusted along the mechanistic to organic continuum.

Control Processes. These are composed of mechanisms such as plans, budgets, rules and regulations, job descriptions, and reporting systems which guide corporate employees in certain directions. The more mechanistic the organization, the more the control processes become standardized and fully specified. They also tend to be characterized as "error-avoiding" in focus, thus, they foster top-down control and emphasize predictability and correctness (Hrebiniak, 1978). The response on the part of organizational members is typically one of resistance, low trust, and ritualistic behavior.

Organic control processes are characterized more as "error-embracing" and place greater emphasis on self-control; they employ fewer constraints and support risk taking by employees. The two types of control processes are contrasted in Table 8.2.

The means by which the two control processes are made to function involve a series of calculated reward mechanisms.

Reward Processes. These are extrinsic and intrinsic rewards which members of the organization receive as reinforcement for certain positive behaviors. Extrinsic rewards include pay, promotion, status symbols, fringe benefits, and social recognition. Intrinsic rewards encourage feelings of accomplishment and self-realization in the employee. Mechanistic reward systems are characterized by a close linkage between narrowly specified job behaviors and specific extrinsic inducements, such as pay and promotion. The reward system is simple and routine in contrast to organic structures which are characterized by more flexible reward systems tied to a wide range of perquisites, such as rewards for innovation, creativity, and entrepreneurial activities. Organic reward systems are also more sensitive to emotional and motivational needs. There is more customization of reward systems in the organic scheme.

Communication Processes. These are the paths taken by information throughout the structure. In mechanistic settings the information

Table 8.2 Behavioral Manifestations in Control Systems

Events, Climate, Attitudes	Avoiding Error	Embracing Error
Control	Primarily top-down; reactive or constraining; emphasis on predictability and correctness	Primarily self-control; less constraining; emphasis on learning; few rules
Allege or accuse of an error	No error occurred; it was unimportant or someone else's fault	Admit the error; examine the causes and learn for future
Emphasis on	Being right; defensibility of action	Risk-taking innovation
Acceptance of responsibility	Ritualistic	Realistic; shared
Goal setting	Top-down; monocratic; stability of goals (*Type A*); goals are set standards	Shared; norm that goals must constantly be revised (*Type Z*); goals reflect conditions which are constantly changing
Decision making	Analytical; less concern with the intuitive	Intuitive; creative; less concern with analytical
Perceptions of power/authority	Fixed-pie	Power expansion and sharing
Faced with uncertainty	Avoidance; seek out controllable situation	Confrontation; seek out uncertainty
Attitude toward change	Resistance	Embracing change as necessary
Interpersonal orientation	Guarded; low trust; others are enemies; Social Darwinism and Machievelianism; alienation	Open; less or no concern with enemies; higher levels of trust and helping attitude; psychological involvement
Assumptions regarding man	Man-machine model; Theory X; little emphasis on responsibility; "infant" end of continuum	Sociotechnical systems; Theory Y; emphasis on responsibility; "adult" end of continuum

Reprinted by permission from *Complex Organizations* by Lawrence G. Hrebiniak, Copyright © 1978 by West Publishing. All rights reserved.

224

flow is more restricted and standardized. Communication is less frequent. Organic communication processes tend to be more reciprocal and open. They take many forms: writing, telephone, face-to-face talks, and conferences, among others.

Conflict Processes. Conflict is a frequent by-product of social interaction within organizations. The mechanistic conflict resolution process attempts to reduce or alleviate conflict by avoiding it, by buffering it, or when necessary, by using authority to mediate and legislate conflict abatement. Mechanistic conflict processes are found in many large bureaucracies built on the classical model of organizational design and behavior.

Organic conflict processes focus on the productive management of conflict. In organic settings such as a matrix organization, conflict is purposely made manifest as a powerful productive force for innovation and enhanced performance. Thus, organic conflict processes entail open and direct confrontation and airing of differences. The use of various bargaining and negotiating techniques becomes part of standard managerial practice.

Decision-Making Processes. As indicated in Chapter 4, the mechanistic processes are nonparticipative whereas the organic ones are participative.

EMERGENT NETWORKS

The final component of technical change management is emergent networks. In mechanistic systems, emergent networks are not relied upon to enhance the task effectiveness of the organization. Rather, they exist to fulfill non-task-related needs. In contrast, organic emergent networks tend to be task related. Texas Instruments uses a reward system to foster the emergence of task-related coalitions, which thereby prompts employees to work on new, innovative projects. Task-emergent networks are a necessity in organic settings. This is because the organization is so complex that the prescribed network cannot begin to handle all the information processing which becomes necessary in so complex an interactive system.

CONCLUSION: GUIDELINES FOR
TECHNICAL STRATEGY DEVELOPMENT

The development of technical change strategies should follow the framework presented in Chapter 4 for an information-processing perspective to alignment analysis. One must examine the alignment between the components of the model with a set of technical criteria. This is done by following these steps:

1. Examine the alignment between the environment and the mission and strategy. This becomes the first area for the adjustment. Once adjustment is completed, the internal components should be adjusted in the following sequence:

2. Adjust the alignment between the mission/strategy component and the tasks of the organization. Make certain that what is espoused in the strategy is attainable in specific activities and tasks. That is, if management states that it is engaged in certain businesses and has a market and product strategy which will pursue X, Y, or Z, make certain that the specific tasks are written down for use.

3. Adjust the prescribed organization to align with the tasks.

4. Adjust the processes to align with the prescribed organization and the tasks.

5. Adjust the personnel and staff to align with the prescribed organization and the processes. Or make adjustments in the prescribed organization and processes to align with the people. (This is a two-way street. If the people can't be changed, then the organization will have to be adjusted).

6. Adjust the alignment between the emergent networks, the prescribed organization, processes, and people.

This chapter presented guidelines for developing a technical change strategy. In addition, specific examples for each component of the organizational model were presented.

Chapter Nine

Political Change Strategies

INTRODUCTION

Political uncertainty is triggered by a variety of factors. Among them are:

1. *Succession Concerns.* The pyramidal structure of large organizations becomes exaggerated in political conflicts. Only one CEO emerges from the ranks of senior management. Succession-generated political uncertainty often increases as the time draws close for a key executive to retire. It is much like the heightening of political activity leading up to a national presidential election. Campaigning increases dramatically as the election draws near. Political uncertainty surrounding succession in business organizations is much the same.

For example, at General Electric, political uncertainty regarding the successor to Chairman Reginald Jones began to heighten fully eight years prior to his retirement. In 1980, as the time drew very close for his retirement, political uncertainty among the three or four contenders was intense. Almost every major business decision had an undercurrent of "what will this mean for so and so's chance of becoming chairman?" Once the decision was made and John F. Welsh got the position, political uncertainty subsided.

At Chase Manhattan Bank, the year 1980 was marked by political uncertainty regarding which of three contenders would rise to Mr. Willard Butcher's position as president when he completed his scheduled move to the chairmanship upon David Rockefeller's retirement in early 1981. Once it was announced that Thomas LeBrecque would become the president, one of the former contenders resigned from Chase to become the CEO of another bank, First Chicago.

Uptown from Chase, at Citicorp, a similar political process was unfolding among a handful of contenders for Walter Wriston's position, which is to be vacated by the mid-1980s. It is not unusual in such campaigns to see early contenders for the top spot leave the company as it becomes clear they will not get it. There have been several such exits from Citicorp. The process is very much a political campaign, with a March 12, 1982 *New York Times* article focusing on the leading candidate, Thomas Theobald. The *Times* states that "Mr. Theobald's chief rivals appear to be the company's two other senior executive vice presidents, Hans Angemueller and John S. Reed" (p. 34).

An even more overtly political process is reported to have taken place at McGraw-Hill in 1975 when Harold McGraw became Chairman. In a November 13, 1977 *Business Week* article, it was reported that both of Harold's cousins, John and Donald Jr., were more likely candidates for the job in part because they were both sons of the former chairman whereas Harold's father had not worked for McGraw-Hill. Harold was able to get support from other members of the family, which controls 25% of the stock, and pushed his two cousins aside. After a year as chairman Harold eliminated his cousin Donald's group president job and offered him an amorphous job which Donald declined and then left the company. After Donald resigned he kept what power he could and is quoted as having said "I'm still a director of this company. I'm still in the wings."

2. *Goal concerns.* This is another kind of political uncertainty which needs to be examined. Which of various alternative goals an organization decides to pursue is often the result of a lengthy political-bargaining process among competing coalitions.

For example, a medical center which faces constrained environmental funding opportunities must set priorities among goals for teaching, health care, and research. Inevitably, competing coalitions representing each of these goals vie for political power to push the organization in the direction they desire. The result is high political uncertainty.

Another example: a large engineering company faced high political uncertainty due to a lack of consensus about goals. This became acute when the top 20 executives divided themselves into three competing coalitions over the future direction of the firm. This led to a great deal of political uncertainty among the top group as their views of the core mission led them to set vastly different priorities. This created friction over budgets, staffing, marketing, etc.

The following comments were made to me by executives in this firm during the course of a study conducted to analyze the strategic planning process.

The three groups were:

(a) The energy group whose members perceived the market scope of the firm to be the domestic energy industry and desired to limit the scope of services to construction-related services. In response to the question: "As I see it, the firm's reasons for being are as follows . . ." a typical executive response was:

to service the electric utility market by providing those services necessary to engineer, construct, maintain, and operate generating stations and associated facilities.

(b) The industry group which had a broader view of market scope that included domestic industries in addition to energy industries. A typical executive statement of the firm's mission was:

to provide professional services—primarily engineering and construction—to clients engaged in mining, converting fuels to energy, or converting raw material feedstocks to usable products in the production cycle.

(c) The international group had the broad view of the firm's mission. It included services to both domestic and international clients, both private businesses and governments. A representative of this group stated the mission as:

To provide counseling services, consulting engineering, engineering, and design and construction services to the private and public electric utility sectors in the US and abroad with the basic objective of achieving a profit for our owner that is commensurate with a reasonable return on our owner's investment. Further, to provide these services to other than the utility industry thereby achieving the necessary diversification to maximize profit potential and growth of profits.

Because of these diverse perceptions of the firm's goals, managers made conflicting decisions regarding organizational priorities and the allocation of resources. These three groups fought with each other to gain control of the firm's goals.

3. *Means of Doing the Work Concerns.* A third area for creating political uncertainty is diversity of opinion regarding how best to carry out the organization's goals, that is, disagreement about means not ends. Here, too, competing coalitions emerge to advocate different means. We can return to McGraw-Hill for an example of political uncertainty over means. In this example it is differences among managers concerning how best to manage *Business Week*. Harold McGraw wanted it to be more closely controlled and less autonomous. He indicated that it was living too "high on the hog." In order to change the way things were done, Harold put Gordon Jones in charge. Mr. Jones wanted to make it clear that he was in charge and let it be known that if anyone stepped out of line they would be fired. In order to make this point to the *Business Week* staff, he took on a key subordinate, James Randolph, the publisher. Because *Business Week* was performing well, with large advertising gains, it would not have been politically wise to fire him directly.

Instead, in 1976, Jones deftly executed a classic ploy of corporate maneuvering; he promoted Randolph from *Business Week* to a new job. (*Business Week*, 14 November 1977, p. 61).

After Jones had hired a new publisher, Randolph, who had been led to believe he would still have a role, soon discovered that he had no followers. Shortly thereafter, following a good deal of confusion and frustration, Jones fired him.

4. *Environmental Changes.* Another major factor in creating political uncertainty is brought about by environmental changes. Hickson *et al.* (1971) explain why the environment triggers political uncertainty:

> Strategic contingencies theory of organizational power makes it clear that changes in the environment affect the balance of power among the various coalitions within the organization, because skills and/or resources which were once unimportant become highly valued. Participants whose power is threatened are apt to respond defensively and/or aggressively. Those who gained power are apt to seek to consolidate their position. Consequently, the response of the total organization is not the technical adaptation of a harmonious system, but is the resultant vector of conflicting interests, distorted information, and struggle . . . The more turbulent the environment, the more pervasive and strong the resulting internal strife may be (Nord, 1978, p. 675).

This in turn can trigger differences among organizational members with regard to the goals of the organization and with regard to the means for accomplishing goals (two other sources of political uncertainty). One example of how environmental conditions lead to a political change inside the organization is found in many multinational corporations where a new position with substantial political clout has been created.

> Faced with revolution, rising nationalism, and economic troubles all over, more companies are methodically assessing the political and economic risks of investing abroad. For that job, many of them are hiring political scientists and former foreign service officers full time . . . the political analyst needs clout within the company to make the machinery stop and listen and then apply what he's saying to the nitty gritty decisions . . . (*Wall Street Journal*, 30 March 1981, p. 1).

5. *Reward Reallocations.* Perhaps the most political of all issues is that of allocating the rewards of the organization. U.S. corporations have the greatest salary differentials between levels of all industrialized countries. This is reflected in such phenomena as having some employees earn $15,000 a year while the CEO earns $1.2 million. Such pay differences are maintainable when all parties feel they are getting their fair share. Given the history of economic growth in this country during this century, political turmoil around distribution of rewards has been surprisingly minor given the pay differentials. The union movement has been the most visible countervailing political force for altering the distribution of rewards.

There will undoubtedly be a great deal of political uncertainty concerning rewards as a result of several forces. First, there is no longer a general trend of economic growth. We are facing a flat or declining economic future in many sectors of our economy. Thus, the pie to be divided up is shrinking and money allocation will involve more zero-sum decisions. The auto industry provides a dramatic example of this.

For the past couple of years, though, the big auto companies have been struggling to survive in a new, energy-conscious world that demands smaller, more fuel efficient cars. To protect them and to continue competing with aggressive foreign automakers the U.S. industry believes that it must cut its labor costs, which run into tens of billions of dollars a year, and that it needs the savings so urgently that the current labor contracts should be revised before they expire . . . a step backward by this blue collar elite could presage a radical change in labor's traditional, relentless drive for "more." (*Wall Street Journal*, 24 April 1981, p. 1).

The changes which have already occurred in the auto industry are cutbacks in white collar benefits; these are meant to signal the unions that everyone will share in the re-allocation of rewards.

Second, there are reward problems being created by shortages of certain technical workers, especially engineers. This, along with inflation, has resulted in pay compression at the lower end of the pay scale, creating political uncertainty. This is due to the small, often nonexistent differentials between starting workers and ones who have been on the job three to five years. Starting salaries for new, Bachelors-level engineers might be $27,000, whereas those hired three years ago might only be getting $29,500.

Third, reward issues leading to political uncertainty will arise more frequently due to the drive for productivity improvements in U.S. companies. Workers are asked to participate in quality circles and other productivity improvement efforts. As these efforts unfold, they naturally lead to the issue of who reaps the rewards of increased productivity. Thus, gainsharing, profit sharing, or cost savings bonus systems will be considered. Historically, profit sharing was resisted by many management groups:

What both GM and Ford say they are willing to offer is profit sharing, something that the union has been demanding since 1958 (*Wall Street Journal*, 24 April 1981, p. 20).

Once uncertainty has been triggered, by whatever source, there is need for a change strategy to either reduce the uncertainty or manage it.

DEVELOPING POLITICAL STRATEGIES

The development of political strategies for change is governed by the principles outlined in Chapter 4 for managing levels of political uncertainty. Political uncertainty was defined as "the degree of stability and predictability with regard to the bargaining and exchange relationships among interest groups over the allocation of resources, power, prestige, etc." Organizations must either minimize political uncertainty or else develop mechanisms for managing it.

Political change strategies must address the managerial issues listed in Figure 9.1. For each component of the organizational model there are mechanistic and organic alternatives. For example, in the mission/strategy component, a mechanistic alternative is to totally limit the involvement in mission/strategy formulation to the top, whereas, an organic alternative would be widespread democratic involvement of organization members.

Figure 9.2 presents the range of strategic responses which exists when dealing with political uncertainty. One end of the spectrum represents politically mechanistic strategies, that is, situations characterized by power relations which are very formally prescribed, with little capacity in the organization for managing shifts in power. These are, in other words, autocratic strategies. The other end of the spectrum represents politically organic strategies, that is, prescriptions for situations where power relations are more fluid and tend to be both prescribed and emergent. There is, in such a situation, a high capacity in the organization for shifting power bases, and there is a high capacity for managing ongoing bargaining relationships. These are democratic strategies. In the middle, we have a mixture of strategies which we have labeled politically mixed–manipulative strategies. Even though the possible change strategies fall within a continuum as indicated in Figure 9.2, we will discuss them in three major categories for illustrative purposes.

POLITICALLY MECHANISTIC STRATEGIES

These strategies are most familiar to many of us. They represent the classic bureaucratic organizational design found in the Catholic Church, military organizations, and the majority of business firms. As Thompson (1967) pointed out and as is reflected in Michel's "iron law of oligarchy," there are pressures in organizations for the powerful to consolidate their power. By doing so, they reduce their political uncertainty. The examples from McGraw-Hill tend to support this notion.

This consolidation often results in a tendency for power to become an end in itself. This is reflected in a statement by Kahn (1964, p. 5–6):

> If a person seeks power only for instrumental purposes, we can predict that his search will be bounded; he wishes to control other people only in so far as that control will contribute to the attainment of other goals. If, on the other hand, he finds the experience of controlling others intrinsically rewarding, there may be few limitations on the number of people over whom he will strive for power, the magnitude of power to which he will aspire, or the kinds of activity over which power will be sought.

One strategy for consolidating power is to:

> attempt to design structures which reduce the discretion of lower level participants. Power is limited by explicit decisions made by authority but more

Managerial Areas →	Mission and Strategy	Tasks	Prescribed Network	People	Processes	Emergent Network
Technical System						
Political System	Who gets to influence the mission and strategy Managing coalitional behavior around strategic decisions	Lobbying and influencing external constituencies Internal governance structure Coalitional activities to influence decisions	Distribution of power across the role structure Balancing power across groups of roles (e.g., sales vs. marketing, production vs. R&D, etc.)	Utilizing political skills Matching political needs and operating with organizational opportunities	Managing succession politics (who gets ahead, how do they get ahead) Decision and administration of reward system (who gets what and how) Managing the politics of appraisal (who is appraised by whom and how) Managing the politics of information control and of the planning process	Management of emergent influence networks, coalitions, and cliques
Cultural System						

Figure 9.1 Political Strategic Management

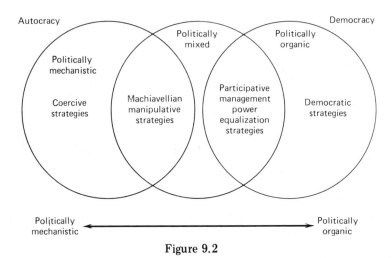

Figure 9.2

subtly and often more effectively by the power of nondecision, that is, the ability to suppress and/or thwart challenges by preventing an issue from being considered subject to a decision (Nord, 1978, p. 676-677).

Using nondecision as a political strategy is a very powerful and effective tool. For example, in some organizations, it is a nondecision for secretaries to think about managerial careers. The built-in caste system represents a means for enforcing such a nondecision. In most organizations it is a nondecision for lower level employees to be involved in policy decisions and in the strategic direction of the organization.

In order to develop politically mechanistic strategies for change, managers can follow the mechanistic principles articulated by Burns and Stalker (1961):

1. Differentiation into specialized functional tasks.

2. Subordinates pursue individual tasks with concern for task completion.

3. Rigid chain of command.

4. Exhaustive and detailed job descriptions.

5. Overall picture relevant only to those at the top of the hierarchy.

6. Interaction follows vertical lines along chain of command.

7. Behavior is governed by superiors.

8. Emphasis is on narrow, specific knowledge rather than general, complete knowledge.

The politically mechanistic model fosters tighter control and allows the dominant coalition to control because:

> The superior has the power or tools to structure the environment and perceptions of the subordinate in such a way that he sees the proper things in the proper light. The superior actually appears to give few orders . . . instead, he sets priorities ("we had better take care of this first"; "this is getting out of hand and creating problems, so let's give it more attention until the problems are cleared up") and later the flow of inputs and stimuli (March and Simon, 1958; pp. 151-52).

In the extreme, the politically mechanistic organization is a monolithic dictatorship. However, the more frequently adopted strategy is to create a tightly controlled bureaucratic structure. In such a structure, commands are followed and it is not necessary to coerce compliance as it can be manipulated or cajoled. There are very few purely political, mechanistic organizations; the mixed strategies discussed next are more common.

POLITICALLY MIXED STRATEGIES—MANIPULATION

Most strategies used in the strategic management of change fall in this second category rather than to either end of the spectrum. There are two subcategories: (1) strategies which are Machiavellian in nature, and (2) strategies which are participative management in nature. The distinction lies in the intent and degree to which power is actually shared. Machiavellian strategies are essentially veiled, politically mechanistic, coercive strategies, whereas participative management strategies grow out of a belief that greater democratization is desirable. Yet, as we shall see, there will be manipulative elements in any structure to the extent that power is not really shared.

Machiavellian Strategies

The historic roots of these strategies extend back in time long before Machiavelli, the 16th century Florentine who wrote *The Prince*, and the *Discourses*, which are, in fact, handbooks for acquiring and keeping power. It was Machiavelli who first tried to systematize the principles guiding the effective acquisition of power. In organizational settings, there are modern-day versions of Machiavelli's work represented in writings such as Anthony Jay's *Management and Machiavelli.*

Wrapp (1967) describes how effective Machiavellian managers work:

> Good managers don't make policy decisions, rather, they give their organizations a sense of direction, and they are masters of developing opportunities . . . the successful general manager does not spell out detailed objectives for his organization . . . he seldom makes forthright statements of policy . . . he is an opportunist, and he tends to muddle through problems—although he muddles

with a purpose. He enmeshes himself in many operating matters and does not limit himself to the "big picture."

The successful manager is sensitive to the power structure in the organization. In considering any major current proposal, he can play the position of the various individuals and units in the organization on a scale ranging from complete, outspoken support down to determined, sometimes bitter, and oftentimes well-cloaked opposition. In the middle of the scale is an area of comparative indifference. Usually, several aspects of a proposal will fall into this area, and here is where he knows he can operate. He assesses the depth and nature of the blocs in the organization. His perception permits him to move through what I call corridors of comparative indifference. He seldom challenges when a corridor is blocked, preferring to pause until it has opened up.

Related to this particular skill is his ability to recognize the need for a few trial balloon launches in the organization. He knows that the organization will tolerate only a certain number of proposals which emanate from the apex of the pyramid. . . . As the day to day operating decisions are made, and as proposals are responded to both by individuals and by groups, he perceives more clearly where the corridors of comparative indifference are. He takes action accordingly (p. 93–94).

A more systematic statement of Machiavellian strategies for managers is as follows (Wieland and Ullrich, 1976; p. 300).

1. Use caution in taking council. Advice can be useful, but can easily become pressure.

2. Avoid creating superior-subordinate relationships which are too close—the door may be "open" but not too far.

3. Maintain maneuverability—don't commit yourself completely and irrevocably.

4. Use passive resistance when necessary. Stall or initiate action in such a way that the undesired program suffers delays and ultimately fails.

5. Don't hesitate to be ruthless when to be so is expedient—"no one really expects the boss to be a 'nice' guy at all times. If he is, he will be considered a softy or patsy and no longer deserving of respect (McMurray, 1973, p. 144)."

6. Limit what is to be communicated. Many things should not be revealed if they will create anxieties or conflicts between parts of the organization.

7. Recognize that there are seldom any secrets. Don't reveal matters "in confidence."

8. Don't place too much dependence on a subordonate unless it is clearly in his or her personal advantage to be loyal.

9. Compromise on small matters to obtain power for further movement.

10. Be skilled in self-dramatization and salesmanship. Be an actor, capable of influencing audiences emotionally as well as technically.

11. Radiate self-confidence.

12. Give outward evidence of status, power, and material success.

Machiavellian political strategies work best in certain types of systems. One such system is what Cohen and March (1974) termed an "organized anarchy." These are organizations characterized by ambiguities regarding organizational mission and strategy, power relationships, and evaluation of performance. In an "organized anarchy" such as a hospital or university the following characteristics vis-a-vis decision making exist:

1. Most issues most of the time have low salience for most people. Professionals are not all that interested in what goes on organizationally.

2. The system has high inertia. Nothing requiring organized effort either to start or stop is likely to be started or stopped.

3. Any decision can become a garbage can for any other issue. Whether it happens depends on what alternative arenas or garbage cans exist for handling the problem at the moment it arrives.

4. System processes are easily overloaded. As the load builds, decision outcomes become increasingly separated from formal mechanisms.

5. The organization has a weak information base. Information about past decisions is hard to retain or retrieve.

In terms of the organizational model, a political strategy for transforming an organization into an organized anarchy would involve moving toward the following characteristics:

1. *Mission/Strategy.* Keep both ambiguous, set the strategy by muddling with a purpose, look for corridors of relative indifference and be opportunistic.

2. *Tasks.* Varied tasks work effectively in low energy systems in which high-level professionals perform individualistic tasks. These professionals view the organization as a workshop for carrying out their tasks rather than as their employer. Thus, professors, physicians, and scientists in research and development settings identify primarily with their tasks rather than the organization.

An example of this is an incident with Dwight D. Eisenhower on his first day as president of Columbia University. It appears that on that day Ike was introduced to a group of faculty members. Being still a bit innocent of academic protocol, he said something about how pleased he was to meet "the employees of Columbia University." After a stunned silence, a senior member of the faculty arose and said stiffly, "With all due respect, sir, we are not employees of Columbia University. We are Columbia University."

3. *Prescribed Organization.* There should be multiple and ambiguous power structures. For example, in a hospital which has both an administrative and medical hierarchy, the boundaries between the two should be kept blurred and ambiguous. This allows organization members to play one structure off against the other. This is often the case when a medical director argues with administration over a budget: "I need an increased budget to save lives of my patients" when the real reason is for expanding operations to control more turf. This also occurs in university settings. To foster this type of political jockeying, it is important to keep the prescribed organization underdefined so that there is always some confusion and room for manipulation.

4. *People.* The managerial style best suited is obviously Machiavellian, with individuals at the controls who have considerable needs for power being most effective. Motivationally, a good fit is for the rank and file professionals in nonmanagerial roles to have relatively high needs for achievement while the managers have high needs for power.

5. *Processes.* Verbal and written communication should be informal and kept to a minimum on organizational matters.

Decision making is done unobtrusively so as to take advantage of corridors of relative indifference; garbage can issues should be provided so as to draw organizational members away from the really important issues (in universities the grading system is a popular form of such "garbage"; in hospitals, patient satisfaction is a popular one); and persistance is required to take advantage of the low energy within the system. Here, professionals do not have much endurance in dealing with organizational issues.

Conflict is generally avoided. Or, if confrontation is necessary it is best for it to be directed at noncritical issues, such as the grading system.

6. *Emergent Networks.* As much as possible, the system should reward and reinforce dividing and manipulating emergent networks and coalitions so that no strong and stable emergent coalitions come into being which can consistently control the organization. This is best done by playing coalitions off against other coalitions via budgets, space, and personnel decisions.

The management of organized anarchy systems is best accomplished by following the rules identified by Cohen and March (1974, pp. 208-

212.* The authors focused particularly on university presidents—however the rules have generalizability to business settings as well):

1. *Spend time*—The kinds of decision-making situations and organizations we have described suffer from a shortage of decision-making energy. Energy is a scarce resource. If one is in a position to devote time to the decision-making activities within the organization, he has considerable claim on the system.

2. *Persist*—It is a mistake to assume that if a particular proposal has been rejected by an organization today, it will be rejected tomorrow. Different sets of people and concerns will be reflected each time a problem is considered or a proposal discussed.

3. *Exchange status for substance*—Specific substantive issues . . . have low salience for participants. A quite typical situation is one in which significant numbers of participants and groups of participants care less about the specific substantive outcome than they do about the implications of that outcome for their own sense of self-esteem and social recognition.

4. *Facilitate opposition participation*—The high inertia of organizations and the heavy dependence of organization events or processes outside the control of the organization make organizational power ambiguous . . . In an organization characterized by high inertia and low salience it is unwise to allow beliefs about the feasibility of planned action to outrun reality . . . on the whole, the direct involvement of dissident groups in the decision-making process is a more effective depressant of exaggerated aspirations than is a lecture by the president.

5. *Overload the system*—As we have suggested, the style of decision making changes when the load exceeds the capabilities of the system. Since we are talking about energy-poor organizations, accomplishing overload is not hard. In practical terms, this means having a large repertoire of projects for organizational action; it means making substantial claims on resources for the analysis of problem discussion of issues and political negotiation.

6. *Provide garbage cans*—One of the complications in accomplishing something in a garbage can decision-making process is the tendency for any particular project to become intertwined with a variety of other issues simply because those issues exist at the time the project is before the organization . . . the prime procedure for making a garbage can attractive is to give it precedence and conspicuousness.

7. *Manage unobtrusively*—A central tactic in high-inertia systems is to use high leverage minor actions to produce major effects—to let the system go where it wants to go with only minor interventions that make it go where it should.

8. *Interpret history*—In an organization in which most issues have low salience, and information about events is poorly maintained, definitions of what is happening and what has happened become important tactical instruments . . . Minutes should be written long enough after the event so as to legitimize the reality of forgetfulness.

*From C. Cohen and J. March, *Leadership and ambiguity*, Copyright © McGraw Hill, 1974. Reprinted with permission.

These politically mechanistic strategies lead to organizational conditions which have minimal capacity for managing political uncertainty. An overload of political uncertainty in an organized anarchy quickly brings the organization to a halt. This was the case with a number of universities in the late 1960s, among them Columbia University, which took several years and a change in administration, along with a calming of the external environment (the end of the Vietnam War), to stabilize.

PARTICIPATIVE MANAGEMENT STRATEGY

Participation in decision making is a double edged mechanism of social control. Participation, of course, has been advocated on the basis that it improves the motivation, understanding, and commitment of participants in the decision-making process. But there is a social control aspect to participative decision making as well. By participating in decisions about proposed alternatives one becomes vulnerable to persuasive techniques. As Mulder (1971) suggests, when individuals participate but lack adequate information or expert power, their participation causes them to lose power (by being "open" and subject to influence) and they are worse off than had they not participated (Wieland and Ullrich, 1976, p. 281).

Participative management change strategies can be both political and cultural strategies. The cultural strategy is based on the belief that participation leads to greater motivation, understanding, and commitment. The same change strategy, participative management, can also be viewed as political when it deals with the allocation of power.

Participative management mixes elements of democratic and manipulative strategies. Most often, the espoused goal of participative management is increased democratization of the workplace. In reality, participative management falls short of actual democratization, as it does not include voting mechanisms or checks and balances. The real power rests with the managers who make the decisions regarding delegation and retain the power to take back the delegation.

Rosabeth Kanter (1977) developed a strategy for moving organizations toward more participative managements. She labels her changes "empowering strategies." She points out that: "It is always hard to get at real power issues or make impactful changes in a power structure, since, almost by definition, those in power have a stake in keeping it for themselves (p. 276)." Nevertheless, she proposes the following empowerment strategies:

1. *Flatten the Hierarchy.* This involves removing levels and spreading formal authority. It adds to "the power components of jobs" (the nonroutine, discretionary, and visible aspects) along with increasing the contact among managers. Kanter concludes that flattening the hierarchy can simultaneously enhance the power of those below as well as above (p. 277).

2. *Decentralization.* "Any structural change that increases an official's discretion and latitude and reduces the number of veto barriers for decisions is, in general, then, empowering (p. 277)."

3. *Team Concepts and Projects Teams.* This structure is empowering when the group has control over the total work process.

4. *Providing Access to the Power Structure.* It is possible to build in points of access to the power structure via the opening up of communication channels and providing access to information such as budgets, salaries, and minutes of key meetings. As Kanter (p. 279) points out, "Access to operating data and formerly restricted information is a must, furthermore, for any decentralized team or team-oriented system."

5. *Providing Artificial Sponsorship.* That is, in order to empower lower level employees for career mobility it is necessary to have the sponsorship of higher level senior people. Kanter proposes that the organization can artificially establish sponsors by linking certain disenfranchized groups and individuals, such as women, to powerful senior people who are given responsibility for sponsoring these lower level people for better jobs.

Participative management as a strategy for enhancing management of political uncertainty is limited because it stops short of actual democratic strategies which allow for changes in leadership and allocation of power. Kanter points this out in her statement:

> Organizational reform is not enough. It is also important to move beyond the issues of whether or not concrete individuals get their share to questions or how shares are determined in the first place—how labor is divided and how power is concentrated. The solutions to such questions form the backdrop that places an ultimate limit on how much can be accomplished by changing organizational structure alone (p. 285).

POLITICALLY ORGANIC STRATEGIES

Unlike the strategies described heretofore, the strategies in this category do have a high capacity for managing political uncertainty. They enable the organization to manage major disruptions triggered by the environment which alter strategic contingencies within the organization. The politically organic organization is able to manage goal conflicts, conflicts over the means for goal accomplishment, and succession issues through democratic procedures.

These strategies force us to focus on several important societal value/ideological issues. One issue becomes apparent when we think about the irony that in a democratic society such as the United States, democratization of the workplace is considered a radical idea. In political organizations, we adhere strictly to public democratic exercise of power, yet in the same society, the exercise of power in economic organizations is left to owners and managers. Robert Dahl (1970) has observed:

> The prevailing ideology prescribes "private" enterprise, that is, firms managed by officials who are legally, if not de facto, responsible to private shareholders ... It is widely taken for granted that the only appropriate form for managing economic enterprise is a privately owned firm ... Ordinarily technical arguments in favor of an alternative must be of enormous weight to overcome the purely ideological bias in favor of the private firm (pp. 117–118).

Patemen (1970) extended Dahl's thinking to include a total democratization of the work setting as a necessity for a democratic society. She wrote:

> The aim of organizational democracy is democracy. It is not primarily increased productivity, efficiency, or better industrial relations (even though these things may even result from organizational democracy); rather it is to further justice, equality, freedom, the rights of citizens, and the protection of interests of citizens, all familiar democratic aims (pp. 18–19).

Societal Positions on Democracy in the Workplace

In most of Western Europe, the ideas of Pateman (1970) are far from radical. They are mere reflections of existing legislation which have been passed to ensure steps toward organizational democracy. Steps have been taken toward industrial democracy or codetermination in most Western European countries. In these countries, there are societal mandates regarding democratic control of organizations. Table 9.1 presents a summary of these laws and some of the organizational characteristics associated with them. Such changes represent a more politically organic strategy than the participative management strategies just discussed. However, the codetermination strategies fall short of the purely political organic strategy. This is because, as argued by Elliot Jaques in reviewing forms of participation:

> Four main types of participative arrangement will be critically examined. First, the common type of advisory joint consultation. Second, so-called participative management and functionally autonomous work groups. Third, the currently popular but abortive conception of workers' directors. Fourth, the syndicalist type of arrangement associated with workers' councils in Yugoslavia and the small industrial units of the Israeli kibbutzim.
>
> Each of these arrangements is unsatisfactory because of a failure to differentiate adequately between the employeeing association, the bureaucratic hierarchy, and the associations formed by the employees. In so doing, all these arrangements fail to give attention to the realities of the power relationships and social conflict between the employeeing and employee associations as interacting power groups (p. 190).

Table 9.1 Industrial Democracy in Europe: Analysis by Country

Country	Co-Determination	Works Councils	Shopfloor Participation	Collective Bargaining	Financial Participation
Austria	1973 law provides that 1/3 of board represents employees.	First established in 1919, abolished in 1934; reestablished works councils strengthened by 1973 law.	Few experiments; some successes in steel industry.	Nongovernmental Austrian Parity Commission rulings normally determine bargaining results harmoniously.	OCP presented union plan in 1975; union fund managed by workers and management.
Belgium	Little interest, but will probably accept EEC proposals.	1948 law made mandatory, with management representation; 1973 decree provides that employers must share information with councils.	Lagged behind other countries, but some union and government interest and experiments.	CSC bargains for shopfloor democracy, FGTR wants only information, not decision making responsibility.	Little interest.
Denmark	1973 law provides for two employees on board.	"Cooperation councils" established under agreement between LO and employer association; elected by all employees, with shop stewards ex-officio.	1976 law on work environments gave workers more control.	Main Agreement of 1960 regulates relations between LO and employers confederation, with centralized bargaining and few strikes.	LO pushes plan for investment fund managed by unions and government thus far without success.
France	Government's Sudreau Report included co-determination, but union and management opposition forestalled action.	Comities d'enterprise instituted in 1945; generally insignificant.	Sudreau Report recommended increased shopfloor democracy; many voluntary projects, often with government support.	Low unionization and ideological unions lead to little successful bargaining.	1967 law established mandatory fund with limited individual withdrawal rights after five years; few workers benefit significantly.
Italy	Little interest, except as analogy to rights gained through bargaining.	1969 labor disturbances led to spontaneous "factory councils" to replace old and ineffective "internal commissions," recognized by employers in 1972.	Innovative agreements reached through bargaining, including plant design and elimination of fixed-speed assembly lines in some plants.	Almost all industrial democracy achieved through bargaining.	No interest in legislation.

243

Table 9.1 (Continued)

Country	Co-Determination	Works Councils	Shopfloor Participation	Collective Bargaining	Financial Participation
The Netherlands	1973 law made supervisory board mandatory, with members "coopted" by board from nominees of shareholders and employees.	Established in 1950, strengthened in 1971, 1976; consulted on major changes, co-decision rights on some employment matters; second only to German councils in strength.	Among leaders in voluntary action, with projects sponsored by employers, unions, government.	Unions moving to left, abandoning postwar cooperative attitude.	Unions propose profit-sharing fund from "excess profits" managed by unions; limited withdrawal rights by individuals after seven to ten years.
Norway	Union plan in early 1960s dropped, resurrected in 1971, statute providing 1/3 of board members (minimum of two) be worker representatives; also a "company assembly" with 1/3 workers to approve major employment decisions.	1945 agreement created works councils as essentially consultative forums.	Decade of experimentation led to 1976 law on work environments requiring maximum job variety, interest, safety, and worker contact.	Highly centralized unions cooperate in shopfloor projects, favor industrial democracy, but not devoted to parity co-determination by statute or agreement; amazingly peaceful, harmonious.	Not high legislative priority.
Sweden	1972, 1976 statutes provide two employee places on board; no significant drive for parity; used predominantly for communication.	1946 agreement created works councils, strengthened in 1966 but seldom strong; importance depends on management attitude, not legislation.	Innumerable experiments, projects, styles; leader in field; government, managements, unions cooperate.	1976 Democracy at Work Act expands (and does not limit) areas subject to bargaining; all industrial democracy subjects now can be bargained about.	1975 LO plan (Meidner Plan) takes some profits for fund to buy stock, support union projects and activities; stirred up great opposition.

United Kingdom	Government's Bullock Committee reported in 1977 recommendation of unitary board with equal number shareholder and employee representatives, with coopted third group; employers oppose, mixed reactions from labor.	No mandatory councils; shop stewards fill many of their normal functions.	Various projects springing up voluntarily, some with government support; Tavistock theories not applied as elsewhere.	Nonlegislated system of bargaining by unions (not TUC) occasionally leads to major disruptions in certain industries; more than 100 unions.	Not high legislative priority.
West Germany	1947 agreement in coal and steel for parity codetermination, made permanent by 1951 legislation; 1976 law for all industries (except coal and steel) provides equal numbers of members from employees (including middle management and white-collar) and shareholders.	1952, 1971 Works Constitution Acts produced strongest councils in Europe; arbitration or judicial action available if recommendations ignored; wide ranging powers.	1974 government humanization of work program responded to strikes, emphasis by workers; $30 million annually, covering work structure, safety, noise, ergonomics.	Highly organized DGB coordinates national bargaining strategies; only 16 sector unions.	Decade-long DGB push for participation in form of union-administered fund with limited individual withdrawal rights after seven to twelve years; no immediate passage likely.

Source: Ted Mills and David Jenkins. *Industrial Democracy in Europe: A 1077 Survey.* Washington, DC: American Center for the Quality of Work Life, 1978. Reprinted with permission.

Or as Katz and Kahn (1966, p. 412) point out:

> Some degree of employee representation does not mean that the organization is a democratic political system. In such a system the constituent members elect their officers and legislators, who in turn appoint executive officers; policy on all matters is determined by the constituents or their duly chosen representatives.

The industrial democracy outlined in Table 9.1 does not provide for perceived democratization of the workplace. It is necessary to "layer in" representative democratic structures throughout an organization to accomplish this.

Jaques makes the statement that:

> Participation has to do with the right to take part in the control of change by taking part in formulating and agreeing on new policies or modifications to existing ones. It is this control of the setting, the rules and the limits within which social relationships will be carried on (within which the social structure will function) that is so very important. It is important not so much for any immediate effect upon output or productivity: there is little evidence to support the notion that the introduction of opportunities to participate will act as a form of incentive system. Opportunity for participation is an essential element for the survival of democratic industrial society itself (p. 191).

The politically pure organic strategy is the creation of a true democratic work organization. Two democratic blueprints for organizations are presented, one by Elliot Jaques and one by Russell Ackoff.

Jaques' Constitutional Democracy

Jaques argues for a constitutional right to participation. By this he means "a right made explicit and manifest in a constitutionally established institution with known and agreed procedures (Jaques, 1976, p. 199)." There are six conditions necessary for the creation of a constitutionally based representative organizational democracy:

1. Policy and executive action must be kept distinct. Policy indicates "the direction or the limits within which action shall take place if the need for action should arise (p. 207)." Policies can be negotiated, whereas executive decisions cannot be negotiated in the same way but are open to challenge via elected employee participation.

2. All significant employee power groups are recognized as having the right to participate through elected representatives; a significant power group is any organized group which through collective action can exercise effective coercive power to cause the enterprise to stop.

3. The matters in which participation is to be allowed are defined as any matters whatever which are of concern to any significant power group—no so-called management prerogative can be allowed.

4. The members of power groups must accept as binding upon them the agreements arrived at on their behalf by their elected representatives.

5. Employees and their representatives must be kept informed of changes which the governing body or chief executive are contemplating so that they can determine whether those anticipated changes need explicit consensual acceptance or not.

6. The establishment of a constitutional body or council on which elected representatives of all significant employee power groups can meet with one another and with the chief executive acting for the governing body. Voting on such a council must be unanimous, to express the fundamental principle that no power group can impose changes on any other nor can it have unacceptable changes imposed upon it.

The second blueprint for politically organic strategy is one proposed by Russell Ackoff (1974).

Russell Ackoff's Circular Organization

Ackoff argues that worker participation on boards of directors has not worked particularly well. This is because it does not foster what Ackoff calls "self-control." Self-control is the ultimate aim of democracy. He defines industrial democracy as "humanization." Any one who is controlled by someone else is controlling him in a humanized industrial democracy. There is no way to avoid the traditional hierarchy. The question is: How can it be made democratic? The circular organization proposes to do this.

Ackoff urges that if a board of directors is good for the chief executive officers, why not for everyone in the organization? Therefore, in the circular organization (see Figure 9.3) the board would include:

1. The incumbent,

2. His or her supervisor, who would be chairman of the board,

3. All immediate subordinates.

Each person also meets with his or her own superior's board. Thus, each person interacts with five levels of management, (1) own level, (2) the boss' level, (3) the boss' boss' level, (4) subordinate's level, and (5) subordinate's subordinate's level. Thus he is embedded into a sys-

Humanization of corporations

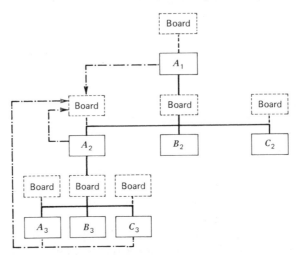

Figure 9.3 Ackoff's circular organization (From R.L. Ackoff. *Redesigning the future.* New York: Wiley-Interscience, 1974, Figure 3.2, p. 51. Reprinted with permission.)

tem of multiple levels of decision making. The board controls whether incumbents hold jobs. But it cannot fire them from the organization. They can remove them from a particular job but not from the total organization. The incumbent's boss can fire him or her or transfer him or her. But the board makes the decision only whether to retain the individual in that particular job. Subordinates have a majority on the board. The board evaluates the job being done and makes policy but not operating decisions.

At the bottom of the organization you cannot have a group larger than can be on a board, thus, there must be 12 or fewer workers in the span of control. At the top of the organization, the board runs the corporation for the benefit of society. This happens according to Ackoff by having the corporate board composed of all of its major stakeholders, as shown in Figure 9.3. Also, employees from the bottom of the organization serve on that top board.

Any board meets two times a month for two hours each meeting. This makes a total of four hours of meetings per month. One person may serve on 11 boards. It follows that he or she would use up one fourth of his or her time in board meetings. Ackoff argues that such use of time is very efficient, as it is in those meetings that the actual managing of work is done. He also argues that in such a system, competence becomes the basis for survival.

GUIDELINES FOR DEVELOPING A POLITICAL STRATEGY

Now that the range of mechanistic to organic political strategies has been presented, we can address the issue of how to decide which strategy is appropriate.

In our Texas Instruments case, the change strategy resulted in moving the organization toward the politically mechanistic end of the spectrum. Political uncertainty was triggered by the technical shift to a radically new long-range strategic planning system.

In order for TI to move from its early 1960s state to its present state, not only the technical system had to be transformed, but also the political and cultural systems. It was the transformation of the political and cultural systems which accounted largely for the 10-plus years of time taken for this change to take effect. Politically, the change strategy included making the organization more mechanistic.

Under Patrick Haggerty, President of Texas Instruments in the early 1960s, a very tight coalition was formed at the top of TI. The political change strategy which was undertaken was rather straightforward. The managers at TI had to be socialized to manage the new system, or else they would be pushed out. Once the dominant coalition was firmly behind OST, and the supporting processes and reward systems were developed, careful attention was given to selecting executives/ administrators who politically supported the dominant coalition. Those who did not were fired. The political system here is quite mechanistic while the technical system at TI is highly organic. As will be noted in the following chapter, the cultural system is also quite mechanistic.

In the Southwest Hospital System, the political change strategy was quite different. At SHS, the desired state not only included a more organic technical system but also a more organic political system. The highly centralized headquarters management and board moved toward more participation on the part of its 12 hospital administrators and their local community boards. The local hospitals received the power of equal say in the hiring and firing of their local administrator. This was a major shift in political power. The local hospitals also had greater control over local policy, including decisions about the range of services to be offered. Such a strategic change was designed to handle the political uncertainty which erupted during the crisis when the headquarters board and administration were not only in conflict with federal funding agencies, but also with its local hospitals. The conflict was so serious that some of the hospitals wanted to break away from the chain and become community hospitals.

At McGraw-Hill, it appears that a number of the key executives have seen to it that a Machiavellian political structure operates. The political system is therefore quite mechanistic.

In contrast to all three of the above examples, Volvo has evolved a much more politically organic system in which workers, unions, and management decide democratically on many major policy issues. Most U.S. corporations fall completely in the area of purely managerial prerogatives.

The following question now must be answered: What are some guidelines for determining a political strategy?

SUMMARY

1. *Determine Level of Political Uncertainty.* The first step is to assess the level of political uncertainty in the present structure . . . and/ or how likely it is to be triggered in the desired future state. For example, at Texas Instruments, it could have been predicted that a shift in the technical system to OST would trigger political uncertainty. Likewise at AT&T, which is undergoing a major technological transformation from a regulated monopoly to an information company competing with IBM, it can be predicted that high political uncertainty exists among employees due to the technical shift.

2. *Link Political Uncertainty to the Internal and External Culture of the Organization.* Political strategies are constrained by cultural norms—both internally and those which make up the norm structure of the wider society. For example, when examining the Volvo structure, law limits the degree to which organizations can adopt politically mechanistic strategies. Workers and unions have a formal political voice through workers representatives and union participation on Volvo's corporate board. Also, the internal culture at Volvo has been one which has strong norms of participation, thus, also setting the parameters for the political strategy. In the United States, societal norms for democratization of the workplace are not comparable with those in Sweden. Therefore, Texas Instruments was not limited in its political strategy. However, societal norms exist regarding the scope of political control over people in the workplace. These norms vary in the United States among different subpopulations. The GM Lordstown plant may have been such an example. Here, younger, better-educated workers had a culture supporting more participation. Thus, boundaries existed around how politically mechanistic GM could be in that setting.

The second step in political strategy formation is to understand the parameters set by the culture for the political strategy.

3. *Link the Political to the Technical Strategy.* In addition to a cultural link, the political strategy should also reinforce the technical. There is evidence that alternative political structures can impact work efficiency and effectiveness. The now famous Lippitt and White (1958) study of democratic versus autocratic versus laissez faire leadership styles sheds light on this issue. That study showed that democratic

and autocratic leadership styles led to equal productivity when the leader was present. But when the leader was absent from the corporate scene, the democratically led group had superior performance, and the autocratically led group became an anarchy. Thus, democratic participation has been found to enhance commitment and has been shown under certain conditions to lead to greater productivity. These conditions include situations in which there is a great deal of task uncertainty which, in turn, requires high-level professionals to make complex decisions. This is the case at Texas Instruments for scientists and engineers working on R&D projects. For this purpose, the political strategy at TI is not totally mechanistic. For technical decisions, the political system is much more organic. When it comes to management procedures and planning however, the strategy remains very mechanistic. The political strategy may contain both mechanistic and organic elements. The decision should be guided by technical constraints as well as by cultural ones.

4. *Develop Image of Good Political Alignment.* By following the first three guidelines an image of an organization in good alignment will become apparent. The mechanistic-to-organic continuum (See Figure 9.2) should be considered in planning the political strategy.

CONCLUSION

This chapter presented a framework for developing political change strategies. Mechanistic, mixed, and organic political strategies were described along with guidelines for developing each. Finally, a set of guidelines for developing a political change strategy was presented.

Chapter Ten

Cultural Change Strategies

"Gentlemen, it is time for lunch, we must adjourn," announces the Anglo-Saxon chairman, in the unabashed belief that having three meals a day at regular hours is the proper way for mankind to exist.

"But why? We haven't finished what we were doing," replies, in a puzzled manner that grows rapidly impatient, an Eastern European delegate, in whose country people eat when the inclination moves them and every family follows its own individual timetable.

"Why indeed?" placidly inquires the Far Eastern representative, hailing from a country where life and time are conceived as a continuous stream, with no man being indispensable, with no life-process needing to be interrupted for any human being, and where members of electoral bodies walk in and out of the room quietly, getting a bite to eat when necessary . . .

As one or the other group persists in its own conception of the time perspective . . . mutual friction grows, murmurs of unreasonableness are heard around the room; and when the issue under discussion is an important one, overt accusations are hurled across the room of insincerity, lack of serious approach to the problem and even sabotage. (Telberg, Ina. They don't do it our way. Courier (UNESCO), 1950, 3, no. 4).

INTRODUCTION

Culture comes about as a result of members of a society and/or organization coping with their common problems, and in so doing they "try various solutions, certain of which become firmly established and are transmitted to successive generations as the culture (Kretch, Crutchfield, and Ballachey, 1962, p. 341)." The cultural system glues the organization together because it (1) provides members with cognitive maps with which to understand and influence behavior in the

253

organization, and (2) it provides a social justification for what people are doing, i.e., providing service to the customer," "making patients healthy," etc. (Katz and Kahn, 1978). A culture exists in an organization when there are norms and values which are: (1) related to specific behaviors, such as, how to treat workers or who gets consulted on what decisions; (2) accepted by the majority of the organizational members or a subgroup representing a subculture; and in which (3) individuals are aware of and are supported by the majority of organizational members (Katz and Kahn, 1978, pp. 348–395).

It has already been pointed out that major realignments will occur in technical systems during the decade of the 1980s. A major concern will be changing the cultural system. This will entail such strategic cultural changes as represented by AT&T's shift to support innovation, market competitiveness, and profit or by cultural changes which reflect new values regarding people, productivity, and quality of work life, as is also reflected in Westinghouse's productivity efforts. The loss of world competitiveness by major U.S. firms is increasingly attributed to managerial failures, especially with regard to people management and the culture of the organization. Japanese management has paid careful attention to the shaping, reinforcing and channeling of their organizational cultures to support high quality and productivity. These pressures will not subside as Lester Thurow points out:

> America is in the process of being economically surpassed by countries such as Japan, which de-emphasize individual achievements to emphasize teamwork and group loyalty . . . The United States has the dubious distinction of being the only country in the industrial world where productivity has been falling for the past three years . . . Unless American managers can find a way to get similar interest in "bubble up" productivity, the American economy will be unsuccessful no matter what is done with our laws in Washington . . . Once we are convinced that teamwork is important, we can go on to institute the changes that are necessary. Most of these actions . . . must be done on a company-by-company or plant-by-plant basis. Managers have to learn that promotions to the top jobs will go only to those who have paid their "team dues" and not to managers brought in from the outside. Team play has to become an important part of the route to the top. Workers have to learn that teamwork will pay off in higher wages and productivity bonuses (*The New York Times*, 26 July 1981).

New cultural values must be instilled in order for productivity through teamwork to occur. Organizations will have to invest in efforts to alter their dominant culture to fit the technical and political demands of the 1980s.

Obviously, although organizations have dominant sets of cultural beliefs, subcultures and countercultures may develop. For example, the subculture in research and development may be visibly different from the more staid and conservative atmosphere in the financial department. A powerful executive with an independent sphere of influence, such as John DeLorean at General Motors, may successfully develop a counterculture which challenges some, but not all, of the values of the dominant culture. Hierarchy also may affect the culture. It may not be critical for blue collar workers in an organization to share the same values and commitment as the professional and/or managerial members of the organization.

Management can simply observe or perhaps reinforce the powerful impact of the organization's culture, or it can take charge and attempt to influence the way that culture develops. Recently, more organizations have begun to try and harness the potential of culture by strategically planning cultural shifts. For example, Westinghouse has committed itself to the creation of a participative management culture aimed at solving the primary technical problem: enhancing productivity. This chapter examines two aspects of strategically managing culture: first, the content of the culture and, second, the process of shaping and altering culture.

Many discussions of corporate culture leave the uneasy impression that culture is a fuzzy or intangible concept. Some of this vagueness arises because the message has not been distinguished from the medium. That is, the content of a firm's culture must be separated conceptually from the form in which that content is presented.

The message or content of a corporate culture consists of the core values of the firm. Sometimes those core values concern technical issues, such as the shifting emphasis at Westinghouse on productivity and quality in order to survive competitively in world markets, or another firm's stress on having a long-term financial perspective. Often these core values are reflected in slogans which become important for organizational members but often sound like superficial platitudes to outsiders. Some specific examples include:

1. "IBM means service."

2. GE: "Progress is our most important product."

3. DuPont: "Better things for better living through chemistry."

4. Dana Corporation: "Productivity through people."

If the content or message of culture concerns the core values of the firm, what forms are used to transmit this information? There are two basic transmission vehicles. The first is interaction of people and is reflected in special jargon, stories, symbols, rituals, and the creation of role models. The second is reflected in, and reinforced by, management planning systems, information systems, and human resource systems.

The remainder of this chapter addresses these two issues, the content of the culture and the medium or form of transmitting the culture. Cultural alignment with the technical and political systems is then discussed and will be followed by a discussion of diagnosing and changing the culture of organizations.

CULTURAL CONTENT

The cultural change strategy is developed through two types of alignment. First, there is an alignment with the technical and political systems of the organization. Second, there is an alignment within the cultural system. Figure 10.1 highlights the content of the organization's culture in terms of its alignment on these two dimensions. It is organized according to the categories of the organization model.

Mission/Strategy Cultural Alignment

The first concern regarding culture and the mission and strategy of the organization is how to manage the influence of key individuals' values on strategic decisions. It is the values of key executives which limit and constrain the strategies of the organization.

> A corporation's culture filters top management perspectives, often limiting the strategic option they are prepared to consider seriously. Defining the cultural values of a company culture can remove old taboos that have unnecessarily constrained past strategic decision making (Davis and Schwartz, 1981).

One interesting and dramatic historical example of this is the Baldwin Locomotive Company which was the premier quality producer of steam locomotives for railroads through the 1930s and World War II. They, however, had a culture which limited their view of their mission to steam locomotives and thus missed gearing up for diesel and electric locomotives. They went out of business as a result.

Another, more contemporary example of the influence of values on strategy is illustrated by the CEO of a major money center bank who feels that the bank has a moral responsibility to society to see that money is used "constructively." Obviously the key word here is "constructively," which in this case is defined in terms of the CEO's value system. The bank is influenced by these values in considering certain strategic options, such as second mortgages. The CEO has repeatedly vetoed plans by the retail banking group to offer second mortgages. This is despite the fact that they have demonstrated through their financial analyses and data from competitors that they can make more money on second mortgages than first mortgages and that there are minimal risks involved. Thus, the technical system logic tells them to introduce the new service. The CEO vehemently says no.

Managerial Areas	Mission and Strategy	Tasks	Prescribed Network	People	Processes	Emergent Networks
Technical System						
Political System						
Cultural System	Managing influence of values and philosophy on mission and strategy Developing culture aligned with mission and strategy	Use of symbolic events to reinforce culture Role modeling by key people Clarifying and defining values	Developing managerial style aligned with technical and political structures Development of subcultures to support roles (production culture, R&D culture, etc.) Integration of subcultures to create company culture	Utilizing cultural leadership skills Matching values of people with organizational culture	Selection of people to build or reinforce culture Development (socialization) to mold organizational culture Management of rewards to shape and reinforce the culture Management of information and planning systems to shape and reinforce the culture	Fostering friendship and affective networks, coalitions, and cliques to shape and reinforce the culture

Figure 10.1

The reason for the no is cultural. The CEO states that he will not have his bank contributing to the "frivolous" use of money in society. He thinks that people who get second mortgages are not using them for constructive purposes. In fact, he considers them as contributing to this hedonistic generation which uses the money for second vacations instead of financing their children's education or improving their homes—constructive capital improvements. The more te.hnical arguments the retail banking managers provide, the more adamant becomes the CEO. The two groups are arguing apples and oranges. The retail banking people should be looking for ways of encouraging a value dialogue with the CEO. Ultimately they dealt with the value issue, by generating data that second mortgages did get used for "constructive" uses, thus, the CEO gave in to the position.

As Davis and Schwartz (1981) point out, defining these cultural values may help the organization overcome, or at least more explicitly manage, their influence on the strategic decisions of the organization. This is especially true when organizations are faced with strategic decisions that could involve major disruptions of previous policy, for example, AT&T leaving the umbrella of a regulated monopoly, or a retail-driven company such as Sears Roebuck, moving into financial, real estate, and health services. In each case, deep-seated cultural beliefs of key people are challenged and must be managed.

The second cultural mission/strategy issue is alignment of the specific content of the culture to the technical strategy of the organization. Thus, at AT&T, the change in strategy to move into the knowledge business and be competitive with IBM, Xerox, and the Japanese, will require a new set of cultural values, namely, competitiveness, profit orientation, and innovation.

Table 10.1 provides an illustration of four different company strategies and the changes each will have to make to be successful, as well as some likely cultural barriers, and alternatives for managing the culture. Thus, for hypothetical company A the strategy is "product/market diversification." The "right approach" might be through divisionalization, in which each division could be more closely focused on its own product/market niches than would be possible if the organization is highly centralized. The alternative approaches listed in Table 10.1 suggest ways of overcoming cultural barriers.

Other examples of how technical strategic shifts require strategic cultural shifts can be found at Westinghouse, which has committed itself to productivity goals of over 6% a year—up from a couple of percent a year. This is to enable it to stay competitive in world markets where its competitors are achieving 9% or greater productivity gains. The second component of the Westinghouse strategy is quality. In order to accomplish this they are stressing four areas: (1) improved materials by implementing some of the Japanese management tech-

Table 10.1 How to Manage Around Company Culture

	Strategy	"Right" Approach	Cultural Barriers	Alternative Approaches
Company A	Product/market diversification	Divisionalization	Centralized power One-man rule Functional Hierarchical	Business teams Explicit strategic planning Business measurement
Company B	Focus on marketing on most profitable segments	Fine tune reward system Adjust MIS	Diffused power Highly individualized Relationship-oriented	Dedicate full-time personnel to each key market
Company C	Extend technology to new markets	Matrix organization	Mulitple power centers Functional focus	Program coordinators Planning committees Greater top management involvement
Company D	Withdraw gradually from declining market; maximize cash throw-offs	Specifically focused organization Fine tune rewards High visibility to top management	New-business driven Reward innovators State of the art	Sell out

Source: (From Howard M. Schwartz and Stanley M. Davis "Matching Corporate Culture and Business Strategy." Copyright © 1980 Management Analysis Center.)

niques such as 100% inspection of incoming materials; (2) improved process design with heavy emphasis on automation and use of robotics; (3) improved people management with use of Japanese approaches to training around quality and quality circles; and (4) value engineering, again, highly influenced by Japanese efforts in this area. A new culture will then be required at Westinghouse. The traditional methods of catching defects in materials after the fact must change; the process design done by engineers with little contact with floor people or customers must change; viewing people as interchangeable machine parts must be changed to seeing them as part of a quality and productivity team; and value engineering must be given priority.

The whole auto industry faces a similar cultural shift. It is no longer possible to tolerate traditional quality and productivity standards and still remain competitive in world markets. Other industries, such as banking, whose strategies are changing technically will require new cultures. The entry of American Express, Sears, Roebuck, Merrill Lynch, and other nonbanking institutions into banking services, along with the trend to national consumer banking has created a need for new retail banking strategies. One important element of the strategy is to shift the traditional view of banking as built on a deep personal relationship with a bank or institution to a more consumer-goods marketing view, in which the customer has many alternatives that are not technically different. Marketing thus becomes critical. The culture must think in terms of market segments and competitive market analyses which are new to bankers, but will be necessary to align the technical and cultural systems.

Task Cultural Alignment

Strategies imply tasks. The AT&T example includes innovation as a strategic task. This, therefore, requires an articulation of what innovations the organization must undertake. The answer to that question provides the technical system content. The cultural system content is determined in parallel. It might involve instituting a receptive policy for new ideas, such as at 3M, where innovativeness is part of the culture, and shooting down a new idea is discouraged. In most organizations it is tremendously difficult to set a hearing for new ideas. One must travel through layer upon layer of approvals until, in most cases, the innovation is stifled. At 3M, most ideas are considered worthy until proven otherwise.

Other tasks, such as marketing orientation or productivity and quality improvement found in the technical system, will require congruent norms and values in the cultural system. The alignment process is interactive. The culture may ultimately limit and constrain the technical system tasks. For example, one possible scenario for Westinghouse is that their traditional culture is so imbedded around treating people in adversarial and mechanistic ways that a new technical strategy regarding people will be impossible.

The Texas Instruments case provides another example of cultural issues in the task component. The introduction of the OST process at TI required that top people carry out two separate task areas: production of current products and strategic long-term product development. These two tasks each required the development of its own culture.

Organizational Structure Cultural Alignment

One cultural issue relevant to structure is the alignment of basic structure with managerial style. This becomes particularly salient when organizations make a major switch from one type of structure to another. There are numerous examples of organizations that decided to structure themselves in a matrix based on technical system logic. The logic is that there is a need to manage simultaneously two aspects of the business with equal attention, such as product and geography, or function and product. Many of these organizations were never able to make the matrix function effectively. The reason was that a new cultural alignment was required to make the structure work. The realignment of culture will involve the following changes:

> New behaviors, new attitudes, new interpersonal skills, and new knowledge are demanded of people. Greater emotional energy is required because people must be more open, take more risks, work at developing trust and trusting others. As a functional manager once said, "You are requiring me to commit an unnatural act." He was experiencing at the time the gap between required behaviors and other's actual behavior (Davis and Lawrence, 1977, p. 108).

A less frequent occurrence, but one we may see more of in the future, is for organizations to give up their matrix structures and move to a line of business organization. This occurred recently at Union Carbide. Management felt the matrix was creating too many bottlenecks which prevented businesses from responding quickly to their marketplaces. Thus, they gave up their matrix structure and created divisions organized around lines of businesses. In order to be successful, the structure will require a new culture. Instead of managers negotiating and bargaining with other executives all over Union Carbide, division presidents are now called upon to run more self-contained businesses. The culture now needs to support more individual entrepreneurial behavior on the part of division executives. If they persist in the old culture of checking and negotiating, then a speedy market response will be lost, and the structural change will prove to be a failure.

A cultural dilemma for organizations is how to manage subcultures. As with technical organizational design, there is a need for organizations to differentiate among subcultures. There is a need for the R&D culture to be different from manufacturing or marketing. The R&D culture should support norms which encourage long-term thinking, idea generation, risk taking, innovativeness, etc., whereas these norms would hardly be desirable in a production unit where predictability, control, and concern for short-term productivity should dominate. Within an organization which has multiple lines of business, different subcultures are needed. Some companies span the spectrum from high-technology state-of-the-art products to low-technology products. Cultures must be aligned with the different business needs. The dilemma becomes one of integration. Does the company desire to have a common overarching culture. If so, how will it be accomplished?

One answer to the integration question is obviously no, don't create a common corporate culture which ties together the many subcultures. This is certainly the answer taken by conglomerate companies, such as Gulf and Western, which only integrate financially and do not attempt to create corporate cultures. This contrasts with a very diverse company such as General Electric, which is involved in such diverse businesses as financial services, consumer products, industrial products, etc. GE works explicitly at shaping and reinforcing an overarching GE culture. Other companies noted for their corporate cultures are IBM, Exxon, 3M, GM, Hewlett-Packard, and Texas Instruments.

The integrated culture is created through a development system that moves key people around. The "I've Been Moved" IBM slogan is reflective of one of their most powerful culture shaping devices. The same practice at Exxon, which moves key people every three years, accounts for the homogeneity of the culture at the top of Exxon. The integrated culture has several pay-offs for the organizations. First, it means there is increased loyalty to the corporation as a whole. This often leads to marginal decisions made in favor of the good of the organization. For example, at Exxon, it is not unusual for managers to give up good people to other parts of Exxon or to make short-term sacrifices in their own areas for the corporate good. It stands to reason that if people are primarily committed to the corporate culture, then these behaviors are more likely to occur than at Gulf and Western, where the separate businesses are related in name only. Having an integrated culture allows much more freedom of movement for key people, as they will fit culturally most anywhere in the organization. This is obviously not true in conglomerate companies.

The disadvantage of integrated cultures is that they exacerbate a core dilemma for organizations. That is, how to simultaneously have a company which produces well and also innovates well.

> Organizations that are very good at doing something for the millionth time are not very good at doing something for the first time . . . most organizations are not skilled at adapting to new ideas which are not immediately consistent with their concept of their business . . . There are several reasons for this but, basically, an establishment grows up around the current concept of a business which has been successful. This establishment is then unwilling and/or unable to see the significance of new good ideas (Galbraith, 1982).

The culture of the existing organization is generally driven by operating concerns which are short term, certain, predictable, and control oriented, whereas, the culture to support innovation must be supportive of uncertainty, risk, long-term plans, and assumes failure is good in the early stages.

One way to manage innovation is to separate it from the other parts of the organization. This allows the separate culture to exist without running up against the old culture. Experience shows that differentiation is not so easy in some companies. Exxon Enterprises, the Exxon subsidiary which has the automated office businesses of Exxon (QYX, QYP, Videk, etc.) has not been successful from a business point of view. The failure can be attributed to cultural problems within Exxon. The dominant business is oil, Exxon Enterprises makes up a mere $2 to $3 billion of Exxon's $115.15 billion-a-year sales in 1981.

It is very important at Exxon to do things the "Exxon way," that is, consistent with the Exxon culture. Exxon Enterprises was created by purchasing small, state-of-the-art, high-technology companies run by the entrepreneurial founders. Initially, Exxon wanted these founders to stay on and run their businesses. There was an immediate clash as these people neither cared about the "Exxon way" nor wanted to be controlled. As for the Exxon managers, they had trouble understanding those way-out, crazy inventor types who were losing money and didn't care about running a business efficiently. The cultural clash eventually led most of the entrepreneurs to leave Exxon Enterprises. The replacement managers were brought in either from IBM, Xerox, other high-technology companies, or parts of Exxon. The result has been a hodge-podge of cultures. The dilemma for companies like Exxon lies in managing cultural diversity to support the technical system needs of different businesses. What appears to be the outcome at Exxon is that the dominant culture will prevail, and, because of all the turmoil, most of the enterprise businesses will have fallen behind technologically. The prognosis is that Exxon will gradually divest itself of these businesses.

The interesting thing about the Exxon example and others at Sun Company and Mobil, is that the underlying problems appear to be cultural, not technical.

People Cultural Alignment

When we talk about alignment of the cultural system, we are inevitably talking about the value systems of people. Thus, in order to accomplish many of the changes presented in the previous categories of the model, it is necessary to think about changing people's values. There are two ways in which organizations change people; one is to bring in new people and the other is to train and develop existing people. When it comes to cultural alignment, selection is probably the more powerful and certainly the quicker means for culturally changing the people component.

When considering the people component from a cultural perspective, it is useful to differentiate personality attributes which are enduring and largely unchangeable from an individual's acquired, changeable attitudes. It is not always easy to differentiate between them, as some people's attitudes about interacting with other people are imbedded in their personality, whereas in others, they merely reflect the culture within which they have been operating.

A concept which has a great deal of promise is helping match people with the appropriate cultural conditions is Schein's (1978) career-anchor concept. He defines a career anchor as:

1. Self-perceived talents and abilities (based on actual successes in a variety of work settings).

2. Self-perceived motives and needs (based on opportunities for self-tests and self-diagnosis in real situations and on feedback from others).

3. Self-perceived attitudes and values (based on actual encounters with the norms and values of the employing organization and work settings) (Schein, 1978, p. 124).

This concept implies that different career anchors lead people to make different choices about their careers based on a core "concern or value which the person will not give up, if a choice has to be made (p. 128)." Thus, cultural alignment in the people component could be facilitated by matching different career anchors with different situations. One type is the technical/functional competence career anchor which implies that individuals get their fulfillment out of being constantly challenged in their work. This anchor is appropriate for project managers, researchers, members of technical staffs of R & D, etc. A second type is managerial competence which consists of analytical competence, interpersonal competence, and emotional competence. Schein found that "the person who wants to rise to higher levels of management and be given higher levels of responsibility must be simultaneously good at analyzing problems, handling people, and handling his or her own emotions in order to withstand the pressures and tensions of the 'executive suite.' (Schein, 1978, p. 138)" The other three types of career anchors are creativity, security, and independence. In each case the individual can be matched with a cultural condition that fits his or her style.

Assuming that organizations and individuals can identify career anchors it makes it possible to better align the people cultural component.

Organizational Processes and Cultural Alignment

The processes which are most central to the organization's culture are the human resource processes. The content of a culture is largely determined by the selection process, who gets hired or promoted is in part a cultural decision. The Japanese are very self-conscious about selection and culture. They have all the workers who will be working with an individual involved in the selection process. This is true for very low-level jobs so it is clear that the decision is not technical, they are not spending this time evaluating manual dexterity, etc. Rather they are seeing "how well the individual will fit in," "how consistent the person is with the culture," etc. By doing this they can select people who best fit their culture. One way to shape a culture is to prevent deviants from getting in the door. Some U.S. companies such as IBM and Exxon recruit MBAs this way. It is clear that the extensive interviewing they do is not to see if the candidate is technically competent, it is to see how well they fit in with the culture. Once the worker is on the job, development is another powerful reflector of culture. Again, the Japanese spend a great deal of time communicating and reinforcing culture through their development process. They take 3 to 4 weeks to get lower-level workers trained to work on a machine that most U.S. companies train their employees to use in a couple of hours. It is clear that they are doing more than technical training in Japan. They are doing cultural socialization, teaching about quality, cooperation, etc.

The development doesn't stop when the worker joins the work team. There is a great deal of on-the-job cultural training of imported values. The appraisal and reward systems are also carriers of the culture. A positive evaluation is not just based on technical competence, but on how well the person fits into the organization's culture. Rewards are also distributed to reflect congruence with culture.

In the United States, human resource processes have been skillfully employed to shape and mold corporate culture. Hewlett-Packard self-consciously works to ensure that the HP way is learned by all and systematically reinforced. One interesting aspect of Hewlett-Packard is that there is almost no training done by anyone but the line managers. This is for cultural reasons. If managers do the training it sends a much stronger message and reinforcement of the culture than having outside trainers or staff trainers. The appendix to this chapter presents the Hewlett-Packard goals and objectives which incorporate many of the human resource cultural content required to align the culture with the technical and political systems of the organization.

Emergent Networks Cultural Alignment

The emergent networks of the organizations play a central role in the transmission and shaping of the culture. After all, it is through interpersonal interactions among organizational members that values are communicated and shaped. As with other components of the organization, the emergent networks can be examined for their manifest or latent cultural content. For example, many organizations have an "old boy" network with a set of norms about appropriate values for those who want to get ahead. In one bank I worked for in the 1960s, it was important to be a Yale graduate with certain social ties. In any organization there will be informal clusters of individuals who represent the "old guard" or "young turks" or some other subculture. These informal clusters are often cliques and can be mobilized into coalitions for action around decisions.

Emergent networks are needed to run any large organization in the same way that prescribed networks are needed to accomplish the work. Thus, companies often invest in facilitating the development of emergent networks which support the corporate culture. The transfer of Exxon managers around the world is as much to weave an emergent network supportive of the Exxon culture as it is to develop individual skills. This is true of other successful companies including IBM and GE. They want John Smith stationed in New York to be able to call up Sam Jones in Tokyo and get cooperation and help, not because of the chain of command, but because of a shared set of values and a working emergent network.

The same differentiation and integration concerns of the prescribed network component also apply to the emergent network areas.

Cultural Form—How Is Culture Transmitted?

If the content or message of culture concerns the core values of the firm, what forms or media are used to transmit this information?

There are two basic transmission vehicles. The first is via people interactions and is reflected in special jargon, stories, symbols, rituals, and role modeling of certain people. The second is organizational systems. Culture is reflected in and reinforced by systems such as management planning, information systems, and human resource systems.

People Interactions

The following forms of cultural transmission are drawn from the research and conceptual work on culture by Professor Joanne Martin at Stanford University. Martin found that one of the most commonly used forms is a special language or jargon, comprehensible primarily to members of the organization. This jargon can be technical. For example, a sales person in at least one well-known computer firm should be able to translate the following sentence, "The heuristic scheduler in the TOPS-20 OPS make it a superior multi-user time sharing system when compared with the UMS, RSX, or IAS." Jargon can also have political, rather than technical, meaning. For example, one California business school refers to the annual performance appraisal meetings as "fireside chats" with the deans, even though the benign climate and architecture of the school make fireplaces an exceedingly rare commodity.

Another frequently used cultural form is the organizational story, myth, or legend. Such stories have starring characters, frequently the founders or top executives of the corporation. The story recounts an ostensibly true event from the company's history—one that has implications concerning current core values of the firm. Thus, organizational stories have messages or morals; they illustrate, in a specific situation, how a core value of the firm should influence employees' behavior on the job.

The focus of organizational stories can be technical or, more frequently, political. Joanne Martin's research has documented many of these stories. To give an example of a technically oriented story, members of one firm frequently tell the legend of the five-year roof. In its early years, the firm had an unusually high return on assets, attributable in part to inexpensive plant construction. Five years later the roofs on those plants began to fall apart, and the corporation had to pay dearly to have them replaced. The moral of the story, concerning the folly of a short-term perspective on corporate profitability, is clear.

Stories with a political interpretation are even more common. For example, at IBM, a newly hired, 90 pound female security guard allegedly had the temerity to stop the founding father of the company, Thomas Watson, from entering a restricted zone. He had forgotten his security pass. To the horror of his associates, she insisted he get the pass before he entered. He complied. This story has implications for top executives at IBM (they are not exempt from obeying corporate rules) and for lower status employees (they are to enforce rules, even when a high-status employee is the potential rule-breaker).

Organizational stories such as this one are shared for two reasons. First of all, such stories are inherently interesting, particularly if they concern a familiar or famous figure, such as the company founder. Secondly, and equally important, such organizational stories have a moral or message, useful because it tells employees what type of behavior is expected.

In addition to jargon and stories, Joanne Martin identifies a third form of cultural information transmission, the ritual or ceremony. Some corporations use the ritual of the annual picnic or Christmas party to communicate the message that all employees are important to the firm. Such rituals often include status-equalizing activities, such as, drinking or competing in team sports. Another familiar ritual is the retirement dinner, used to communicate the message of safe passage to a life outside the corporation. The retiring employee is assured that his contributions to the firm will not be forgotten. In addition, even in companies where the families of employees are seldom mentioned, reference is made to the employee's spouse, progeny, and the hobbies which he or she had not had time to pursue. Such references to the employee's personal situation provide an implicit guarantee that life will continue after all ties with the corporation are severed—a kind of personal immortality, or at least, a safe passage to the next stage of life.

Cultural information is often communicated in the form of a symbol. Perhaps the most familiar symbols are the executive "perks" which communicate power. These include the appropriate dress, for example, the pinstripe suit from J. Press; the location (corner) and accoutrements (original artwork) of the high-status office; access to lavish expense accounts, the corporate jet, and the executive dining or washrooms; and, last but not least, the reserved parking space. The vehemence of disputes about, for example, office size or parking space allocation are incomprehensible unless the symbolic meaning of these "perks" is taken into account. One aspect of a corporation's culture is the shared interpretation of the meaning of symbols such as these. Hewlett-Packard values egalitarianism and offers no special management incentives and minimal perks.

There are other forms in which cultural information can be transmitted, although less research on these topics has been conducted to date. One of the most important is role modeling. A manager can communicate a cultural message by modeling the appropriate behavior for his employees. For example, it is said that Dave Packard, one of the founders of Hewlett-Packard, was concerned that the firm's core value which concerned the importance of the employee's personal well-being and family life, was becoming empty rhetoric. One evening, shortly after the official close of the working day, Mr. Packard took a tour of the executive offices, telling each employee who was working late that he or she should be home, that the work could wait.

Humor is another form of cultural communication, particularly jokes that make fun of the outsider, that is, the representative of a competing firm or the employee who fails to conform to company norms. When an employee laughs at jokes such as these, he or she is identifying with the insider and is acting like a cultural initiate.

Organizational Systems

As pointed out by Thomas Peters (1980) ". . . management systems might be conceived as the carrier of an organization's language. As such they shape the dimensions of an organization's character." Thus, management meetings reinforce culture by what is given priority on the agenda and by what the top managers talk about most. Information systems collect certain numbers but not those which reflect value judgments. Management planning systems, such as MBO, reflect several dimensions of culture. First, the *content* of the objectives reflects what is deemed relevant or important. In addition, the *process* used to determine the objectives, for example, how much openness and honesty there is compared with game playing and manipulation, reflects another dimension of culture. Perhaps the most enduring and effective media for transmitting culture is the human resource system. It starts with a selection process that sorts out cultural deviants at the door: Don't hire people who don't fit with the culture. Socialization of development is the next process for molding culture. Finally, there are the appraisal and reward processes which channel and reinforce cultural values.

Cultural messages, then, can be communicated in a myriad of forms, including special jargon, organizational stories, rituals and ceremonies, symbols, role modeling, human and management systems. The variety of examples used to illustrate these cultural forms demonstrates a related point. The content of cultural messages and the forms in which those messages are transmitted vary considerably from one firm to another.

Shaping Corporate Culture

Having diagnosed the state of the current corporate culture, the next step is proactive: One must attempt to shape the evolution of that culture. This is a task which falls first to the chief executive and secondarily to the top management team. Whether chief executives intend it or not, they have a strong impact on the culture of the organization.

CEOs can role model the types of behavior they want their subordinates to exhibit. In fact, whether or not their actions are intended as role modeling, they are often so perceived. Such role modeling incidents may in fact be shared in story form by large numbers of employees, eventually gaining the status of an organizational legend. The history of the company, in particular the activities of the founder or a CEO who substantially transformed the organization, may also be a rich source of organizational stories. In a similar fashion, CEOs can invent new jargon, create new rituals, or reinstate old ones, and invest activities or rewards with fresh symbolic meaning.

Not all such efforts to influence corporate culture will be successful. Work by Joanne Martin indicates that successful cultural innovations have at least three characteristics. First, they must be credible. That is, they come from a source, such as the CEO, who has personal credibility on the issue in question. Innovations which appear to be insincere or which contradict people's beliefs about the real core values of the firm are likely to be dismissed as corporate propaganda. Second, successful innovations must be dramatic. They are inherently interesting and, with the possible exception of some rituals and ceremonies, are not boring or "hokey." Finally, cultural innovations are most likely to be memorable and believable when people have a reason to listen to them. The underlying message should have clear relevance for the on-the-job performance of individual employees, indicating, for example, what behavior is expected of them in specific situations.

In addition to the CEO, the top executive team can affect the direction in which culture develops. Indeed, the key to strategic management is to use cultural tools to reinforce the technical and political objectives of this top team. Culture has been defined as the social glue which holds an organization together. It cannot unify the organization, however, unless the technical, political, and cultural systems are consistent with each other. Only then can culture serve a unifying, rather than a divisive, function. How then can top management use cultural mechanisms to reinforce the technical and political objectives of the firm?

One set of tools the culture-conscious management can use concerns the firm's mission and strategy. Often, the relevance of cultural issues to the firm's mission is not recognized. Selecting a long-term strategy is such a complex and uncertain decision that it is often influenced as much by the personal philosophy and values of the decision makers as it is determined by technical considerations. Values and philosophies are cultural issues, yet discussions in the realm of strategy often focus predominantly on technical, and secondarily and subliminally, on value issues. If the actual source of disagreement stems from unspoken concerns with value or philosophy differences, these cultural issues need to be recognized directly. Offering technical justifications when more value-laden cultural issues are the actual concern may well be an exercise in futility.

Cultural concerns also become relevant to the firm's mission and strategy when mergers and acquisitions are contemplated. The strategies of all components of a firm must be congruent on the technical, political, and cultural levels. For example, if a firm has an overall objective of cutting costs and increasing efficiency in order to increase short-term profits, it might seem to be a good idea to seek out a "cash cow" acquisition which would provide capital for investment in new, more efficient equipment. Many cash cows, however, are at a stage of development where their culture can afford to emphasize a long-term perspective on finances and a people-oriented philosophy of management. If the culture of the acquiring firm emphasizes the bottom line more than people concerns and short-term rather than long-term financial goals, this type of acquisition, however desirable financially, may well bring serious, dysfunctional clashes on the cultural level.

Organizational structure and design decisions also have cultural implications. One aspect of culture concerns styles of management. These styles need to be aligned with the organization's technical and political structures. For example, an organization that moves from a functional to a matrix structure differs from a functional organization both technically and politically. In a matrix, power is balanced on two dimensions—such as product and function—and requires a management style of negotiated, open confrontation of conflict as opposed to a more traditional, chain-of-command management style.

A second cultural issue is the development of subcultures to support the various subcomponents of the organizational design. For example, there should be a different production culture than R&D culture. R&D should be longer term, more innovative, more supportive of entrepreneurial idea generation. Production is more cost-conscious, efficiency driven. And as a result, the organization needs to foster subcultures consistent with the subunit.

This leads to a third cultural problem. There is a need for mechanisms to integrate subcultures and create an overall company culture. If the subcultures are too strong, then R&D, production, sales, finance, etc. are each working at odds, and don't have any wider identification with the company. Some companies go to great extremes to create identity with the company, such as at IBM and Exxon, where there is a very definitive company culture that transcends any of the subcultures.

Another set of cultural management tools consists of the human resource management systems. It is in this area that Japanese management has been more attentive and sophisticated than American management. They have used the human resource systems very skillfully to shape and reinforce cultures that provide the organization with strong support for its technical objectives and political priorities. One of the most useful tools in the human resource area is the selection of new employees with a sensitivity toward how they fit with the dominant culture of the organization. Companies that use the human resource systems as a cultural tool spend a great deal of effort in this process. They involve many people in the recruitment and interview process including blue-collar workers. Applicants are screened out for cultural reasons; a technically well-qualified person, who would not fit in culturally, is often, even usually, not hired.

A second tool for shaping the culture of the organization is the way in which people are developed and socialized, and again, organizations that use the human resource systems to shape culture invest heavily in training and development. Much of it is aimed at getting people inculcated with the dominant culture of the organization.

There are two ways to accomplish this cultural indoctrination. In the United States, in culture-conscious companies, it is often done explicitly and deliberately. At IBM, for example, the values and philosophy of management are the overt focus of some of the training programs. At Digital Equipment Corporation an orientation session for new employees focuses heavily on the firm's unique culture and philosophy of management and includes a film which features the company president telling organizational stories which have relevance to current policies of the firm.

Other firms, particularly in Japan, take a somewhat different approach to cultural training and development. Much cultural information is transmitted on the job as it is relevant to the working situation. The transfer of information often takes place spontaneously, in an informal setting, in the context of face-to-face interaction with other, more experienced employees.

Recent research indicates that this latter, less planned, form of cultural education may have a stronger impact on employees' commitment to the desired values and philosophy. These research results suggest that the human resources systems may well be a powerful resource for managers, but that the process of cultural indoctrination must be handled with some subtlety (Hatvany and Pucik, 1981).

A final area in which human resource systems can be used to reinforce and shape the culture of an organization are the performance appraisal and compensation systems. Performance appraisal criteria can be designed to identify those people who fit in and support the dominant values of the organization. Likewise, promotion and financial compensation decisions can reward those who fit the dominant culture and reinforce its objectives. Thus, the selection, training, appraisal, and reward systems of an organization can be fine-tuned to provide coordinated cultural support for the technical and political priorities of the firm.

MANAGING CULTURAL UNCERTAINTY

One final strategic issue is the management of cultural uncertainty. Aside from the content of the organization's culture or how the culture is transmitted, organizations vary in their capacity for managing cultural uncertainty; that is, the extent to which they can deal with differences of beliefs, values, and attitudes of members. There are three basic options for managing cultural uncertainty.

Option 1 is to reduce cultural uncertainty. The result is a homogeneous culture. This can be done by developing ways of buffering the organization from the external environment, much in the way the Mormon community has been able to develop and maintain a very distinct culture within the wider U.S. culture. Organizations also develop unique and somewhat monolithic, homogeneous cultures. Thus when people talk about what it is like to work for IBM, Ford, GM or DuPont, they are referring to its unique culture. In addition to buffering from the environment, the organization must have means for socializing its members and insuring adherence to the culture.

Option 1 is referred to as a mechanistic culture and is characterized by:

1. Little tolerance for members who hold incongruent values/ ideologies.

2. People who fear vulnerability.

3. Relationships which are manipulative.

4. Defensive interpersonal relations.

5. Defensive norms resulting in mistrust.

6. Lack of real risk taking.

7. Conformity, external commitment.

8. Power-centered competition.

Option 2 is an organic culture. It is one with a high capacity for managing cultural uncertainty. Its characteristics are:

1. A high capacity for managing individual differences in values and ideology.

2. Orientation of people toward facilitative/collaborative relationships, minimally defensive interpersonal relationships.

3. Learning-oriented norms supporting trust.

4. Respect of individuality.

5. Open confrontation of difficult issues.

6. Risk taking and internal commitment.

Option 3 is a mixed mechanistic and organic culture. In such a culture there are certain major areas which are quite rigidly mechanistic whereas there are others which support diversity and are organic. This is the case at Texas Instruments where a great deal of cultural homogeneity exists with regard to the work ethic, the managerial philosophy, etc. However, there is cultural diversity with regard to entrepreneurial behaviors and norms dealing with products and marketing. The culture in such settings is somewhat paradoxical, and at times the result is like mixing oil and water. It is difficult to attain, and once it is done, it comes undone.

The remainder of the chapter is devoted to an exploration of these three basic cultural strategies.

Option 1: Mechanistic Cultural Strategies

Rosabeth Kanter (1977) found that the formation of closed circles in large organizations represented attempts to limit cultural uncertainty. By using certain criteria to select who was part of the "in" group it was possible to homogenize the culture. She found that social homogeneity increased the ease of communication and improved predictability of behavior due to common values of members central to the organization.

The mechanistic culture dominates much of our industrialized society. It is perpetuated by the closed circles previously described. This culture is best articulated by McGregor's (1960) Theory X assumptions. These assumptions are listed as follows, and have provided the cultural underpinnings for many of our modern day organizations. In the Theory X culture the following assumptions prevail:

1. People are inherently lazy and must therefore be motivated by outside influences, namely, economic incentives, which are under the control of the organization and are manipulated in such a way as to motivate the person.

2. People's natural goals run counter to those of the organization, hence people must be controlled by external forces to ensure they work toward organizational goals.

3. Because of their irrational feelings, people are basically incapable of self-discipline or self-control.

4. But, all people are divided into roughly two groups—those who fit the assumptions outlined above and those who are self-motivated, self-controlled, and less dominated by their feelings. This latter group

must assume the management responsibilities for all the others (Schein, 1970, p. 56).

Developing Mechanistic Cultural Strategies. The central thrust of these strategies is incorporated in the classical management principles of planning, organizing, staffing, controlling, coordinating, and leading. These principles are built on Theory X assumptions which assume men and machines are interchangeable and that a homogeneous cultural system controlled by the designers and managers of the organization is the best way to achieve efficient and effective performance. Figure 10.2 lists seven of the key characteristics of such a cultural strategy.

Option 2: Culturally Organic Strategies

Argyris and Schon's Double Loop Learning Strategy. Chris Argyris and Donald Schon (1978) developed a framework for diagnosing and changing the cultural system of an organization. Their focus is on organizational learning: how organizations learn or fail to learn. They describe organizational learning in the following terms:

> When the error detected and corrected permits the organization to carry on its present policies or achieve present objectives, the error-detection-and-correction process is single loop learning. Single-loop learning is like a thermostat that learns when it is too hot or too cold and turns the heat on or off. The thermostat can perform the task because it can receive information (the temperature of the room) and take corrective action. Double loop learning occurs when error is detected and corrected in ways that involve the modification of an organization's underlying norms, policies, and objectives (pp. 2-3).

In other words, in addition to changing room temperature, the thermostat itself may be changed in some basic way(s).

Organizational single- and double-loop learning is largely a consequence of what Argyris and Schon identify as individual's "theories-in-use" which are the theories which guide an individual's action, the set of "shoulds" and assumptions about causality. They have developed two contrasting theories-in-use. Model I, which they argue is by far the most prevalent, and Model II which is an alternative ideal. Model I corresponds to a mechanistic cultural strategy.

Table 10.2 summarizes the Model I mechanistic cultural strategy. Argyris and Schon argue that this model provides the foundation for the single-loop-learning mechanistic culture in organizations. This is because organizations dominated by Model I norms deal with error correction by making adjustments and changes

> within a constant framework of norms for performance. It is concerned primarily with effectiveness—that is, with how best to achieve existing

	MECHANICAL SYSTEMS	ORGANIC SYSTEMS
1.	Highly differentiated and specialized tasks with precise specification of rights, responsibilities, methods	Continuous reassessment of tasks and responsibilities through interaction of those involved with functional changes easy to arrange
2.	Coordination and control through hierarchical supervision	Coordination and control through network of those involved and concerned which is in frequent communication
3.	Communication with external environment controlled by top offices of hierarchy	Communication relatively extensive and open
4.	Strong downward-oriented line of command	Emphasis on lateral and diagonal consultation, advice, information giving, as source of coordination and control
5.	Insistence upon loyalty to organization and superiors	Emphasis on the task, goal achievement, and improvement of the organization
6.	High value on local knowledge and experience	High value on mission-oriented expertness, cosmopolitan knowledge of the profession
7.	One-to-one leadership style	Team leadership style

Figure 10.2 (Based on material from T. Burns & G.M. Stalker, *The management of innovation* (1961), pp. 119–125, as adapted.)

goals and objectives and how best to keep organizational performance within the range specified by existing norms. In some cases, however, error correction requires an organizational learning cycle in which organizational norms themselves are modified (p. 21).

Organizations with cultural systems dominated by single-loop learning are characterized by managers and employees striving to maximize their own incomes and avoid error to ensure survival. The result is that games are played. Examples of such games are (Argyris and Schon, 1978, p. 183):

1. Before you give any bad news, give good news.

2. Play down the impact of a failure by emphasizing how close you came to achieving the target or how soon the target can be reached.

3. In meeting with the president it is unfair to take advantage of another department that is in trouble, even if it is a natural enemy. The sporting thing to do is to say something nice about the department and offer to help in any way possible.

4. If one department is competing with other departments for scarce resources and is losing, it should polarize the issues and insist that a meeting be held with the president . . . thus they can return to their group, place the responsibility for the loss on the president . . . (p. 183).

The alternative to Model I, single-loop learning, is Model II, double-loop learning. Table 10.3 summarizes Model II theories-in-use. Double-loop learning leads to "'organizational inquiry which resolves incompatible organizational norms by setting new priorities and weightings of norms, or by restructuring the norms themselves together with associated strategies and assumptions (p. 24)." The inquiry questions the basic cultural content that the organization's cultural system is able to deal directly with value/ideological differences through problem solving. A double-loop-learning organization will (Argyris and Schon, 1978, pp. 312–313):

1. Extend the range of errors and anomalies it can detect in its transactions with internal and external environments. Because organizations' perceived tolerance for perceived error will increase, members of the organization will become more able, jointly and publically, to acknowledge the mismatch of outcome to expectation.

2. Extend the range of correctable error—that is, reduce the extent to which inaccessible and obscure information prevents members of the organization from attributing error to mistakes, incongruities, and inconsistencies in organizational theories of action . . . there will

Table 10.2 Model I Theory-in-Use

Governing Variables	Action Strategies	Consequences for Behavioral World	Consequences for Learning	Effectiveness
Define goals and try to achieve them.	Design and manage the environment unilaterally. (Be persuasive, appeal to larger goals, etc.)	Actor seen as defensive, inconsistent, incongruent, controlling, fearful of being vulnerable, withholding of feelings, overly concerned about others or underconcerned about others.	Self-sealing.	Decreased long-term effectiveness.
Maximize winning and minimize losing.	Own and control the task. (Claim ownership of the task, be guardian of the definition and execution of the task).	Defensive interpersonal and group relationship (dependence on actor, little helping of others).	Single-loop learning.	
Minimize generating or expressing negative feelings.	Unilaterally protect yourself. (Speak in inferred categories accompanied	Defensive norms (mistrust, lack of risk taking, conformity, external commit-	Little testing of theories publicly. Much testing of theo-	

ories privately.

ment, emphasis on diplomacy, power-centered competition and rivalry).

by little or no directly observable data, be blind to impact on others and to incongruity between rhetoric and behavior, reduce incongruity by defensive actions such as blaming, stereotyping, suppressing feelings, intellectualizing).

Be rational.

Unilaterally protect others from being hurt (withhold information, create rules to censor information and behavior, hold private meetings.)

Low freedom of choice, internal commitment, and risk-taking.

Source: C. Argyris and D. Schon, *Organizational Learning: A Theory of Action Perspective,* © 1978. Reading, MA: Addison-Wesley, pp. 62–63. Reprinted with permission.

Table 10.3 Model II

I Governing Variables for Action	II Action Strategies for Actor and Toward Environment	III Consequences on Behavioral World	IV Consequences on Learning	V Effectiveness
Valid information Free and informed choice Internal commitment to the choice and constant monitoring of the implementations	Design situations or encounters where participants can be origins and experience high personal causation Task is controlled jointly Protection of self is a joint enterprise and oriented toward growth. Bilateral protection of others	Actor experienced as minimally defensive Minimally defensive interpersonal relations and group dynamics Learning-oriented norms High freedom of choice, internal commitment, and risk taking	Unconfirmable processes Double-loop learning Frequent testing of theories publicly	Increased effectiveness

Source: C. Argyris and D. Schon, *Organizational Learning: A Theory of Action Perspective*, © 1978. Reading MA: Addison-Wesley, pp. 137. Reprinted with permission.

result more regularly shared awareness of organizational dilemmas . . . and acceptance of conflict among individuals and groups in the organization.

3. Become progressively more able to engage such conflicts through collaborative reflection and inquiry . . . double-loop learning.

4. Reduce the double bind experiences of individual members of the organization.

5. Increase the shared awareness of the organization's own learning system and the incidence of joint inquiry into that system.

Implementing double-loop learning begins with the top of the organization engaging in activities to change from mechanistic Model I to organic Model II theories-in-use. This is done through feedback and examination of interpersonal relationships so that individuals learn to engage in double-loop learning at a personal level. These activities are then extended to additional groups. The examination of interpersonal relationships follows the laboratory training approaches initially developed under the heading of T-groups (training). These are experienced-based learning experiences in which people learn about their own personal and interpersonal style and group dynamics via here and now examination of interpersonal and group phenomena. The T-group has led to sensitivity training and encounter groups.

The double-loop-learning culture is the most purely organic strategic culture possible, as it is built on the notion that constant adjustment in the culture is necessary and desirable.

Option 3: Developing Mixed Cultural Strategies

The alternative to either purely mechanistic or organic cultures is a mixed culture. A mixed culture has portions that are quite mechanistic while at the same time being organic for other aspects of the culture. The organization development (OD) approach is thus characterized as mixed. OD involves altering portions of an organization's culture toward becoming more organic but not to the extreme of double-loop learning which creates a culture capable of basic transformation on an ongoing basis. The Likert and McGregor characteristics of a mixed cultural strategy provide us with sets of guidelines for their design.

The mixed cultural organic strategy is built on McGregor's Theory Y assumptions:

1. Physical and mental work are as natural as play if they are satisfying.

2. Man will exercise self-direction and self-control toward an organization's goals if he is committed to them.

3. Commitment is a function of rewards. The best rewards are ego satisfaction and self-actualization.

4. The average person can learn to accept and seek responsibility. Avoidance of it and emphasis on security are learned and are not inherent characteristics.

5. Creativity, ingenuity, and imagination are widespread among people and do not occur only in a select few (McGregor, 1960; pp. 33–35).

Classic organizational development is built on these assumptions. OD has been defined as:

> A long-range effort to improve an organization's problem-solving and renewal processes, particularly through a more effective and collaborative management of organization culture—with special emphasis on the culture of formal work teams. (French and Bell, 1973; p. 15).

Such cultures are better able to manage cultural/ideological differences among members. By providing a climate which supports individual differences and explicit problem solving and discussion about norms and values the organization can manage multiple ideologies. For example, such a cultural system can manage mixed cultures, created by bringing diverse groups together, women and minorities into traditionally white male dominated jobs.

MATCHING THE CULTURE TO THE
POLITICAL AND TECHNICAL SYSTEMS

An organization's culture is both the most pervasive element as well as the least obvious. That is because culture is often implicit; people are not aware of it in the same way they are of political dynamics and technical systems. As a result, it is frequently overlooked in strategic change efforts. Or even when it is identified as important, is only given cursory attention. However, as is clear in the Texas Instruments case, it is an essential condition of strategic change, requiring major attention and accounting for success or failure of a change effort.

At Texas Instruments, the technical system was altered to be more organic and the political system became more mechanistic with the formation of a tightly knit dominant coalition backing the OST technical change. As important as these two changes was the cultural strategy.

Once the dominant coalition was uniformly behind OST and the supporting processes and reward systems were developed, the major emphasis was to develop a mixed culture (mechanistic on one hand because adherence to certain norms like work ethic, dress, and lifestyle norms were rigidly enforced while a part of the culture—technical creativity and innovations—reinforced differences and open conflict.) The major devices used to create the cultural change were careful selection of managers (people who would fit ideologically into TI) and careful termination of people who didn't fit into the TI culture. As one researcher put it: TI's culture "polarizes people—either you are incorporated into the culture or rejected. The culture tends to reject 'strange' individuals. The internal environment focused on intense loyalty to the company's goals and discipline. . . ." It is this very same culture which may have later caused TI its problems in the early 1980s.

Management of change involves the coupling or linking of the culture to the political and technical system. This is largely carried out by symbolic management. This is action aimed at providing shared meanings, paradigms, languages, and cultures to organizational members. Pfeffer (1981) argues that managers have a greater impact on symbolic outcomes (the culture) of an organization than on the substantive (technical) outcomes (profit, quantity, and quality of products and services). Weick (1979) goes so far as to argue that managerial work may be viewed as managing myths, symbols, and images, and may be more evangelistic than accountant-like. This emphasis on the control of culture by managers is further reinforced by Pondy:

> The effectiveness of a leader lies in his ability to make activity meaningful for those in his role set—not to change behavior but to give others a sense of understanding what they are doing and especially to articulate it so they can communicate about the meaning of their behavior . . . If in addition the leader can put it into words, then the meaning of what the group is doing becomes a social fact . . . This dual capacity to make sense of things and to put them into language meaningful to large numbers of people gives the person who has it enormous leverage (1978, pp. 94-95).

CONCLUSION

This chapter presented a framework for developing cultural change strategies. There are three major components of a cultural change strategy within an organization: 1) the content of the culture, 2) methods for shaping the culture and 3) ways of managing cultural uncertainty.

The chapter underscored the importance of cultural content changes in organizations necessary to successfully implement the technical and political change occurring in many organizations such as at AT&T and the productivity improvement efforts going on at companies such as Westinghouse, Honeywell and Motorola. The cultural content changes were then examined in relationship to each component of the organizational model: the mission strategy, the tasks, the prescribed networks, people, processes and emergent networks.

Once the content of the culture is decided on, then the change manager needs to develop ways of shaping and reinforcing the desired culture. A number of cultural shaping approaches were discussed including the importance of person-to-person interactions, the role of symbols, rituals and myths and the strong role of management and human resources systems.

Finally cultural uncertainty management was discussed in terms of three major approaches:

1. Reduce uncertainty via a culturally mechanistic strategy based on McGregor's Theory X assumptions.

2. Manage uncertainty via a culturally organic strategy based on Argyris and Schon's double-loop learning model.

3. Manage some cultural uncertainty and reduce some cultural uncertainty, a mixed strategy based on organization development approaches.

Finally, the chapter focused on the link between the cultural system and the political and technical systems and the role of managers for providing symbols, meaning, and the cultural fabric for the organization.

APPENDIX TO CHAPTER TEN

The Hewlett Packard corporate objectives reflect a very self conscious interweaving of the technical, political and cultural strands of the organization. It is included here as a concrete example of how important cultural values can be managed strategically.

Hewlett-Packard Results, FY 1980

Revenue	$3.1 billion
Revenue growth rate	+30.3%
Net income	$269 million
	8.7%
	+30.3% growth
Business mix	
Domestic	48.3%
International	51.7%
Computers	48.0%
ROE	
As reported	19.3%
Adjusted	27.0%
P/E early 1981	18

Objective #1—Profit. "To achieve sufficient profit to *finance our company growth* and provide the resources we need to *achieve our corporate objectives.*"

"Profit is the one absolutely essential measure of corporate performance over the long term."

"Most of profits reinvested."

"ROE must roughly equal sales growth rate." (Or sales growth rate cannot exceed ROE. *All* divisions expected to be self-financing.... Generate profit to finance own growth. If you want to grow, you must make a profit.)

"Will not rely on long-term debt. . . . Will rely on reinvested profit as main source of capital."

"Each and every product must be viewed as good value by customers and be priced for a profit."

"Need to make profit cannot be put off until tomorrow; it must be achieved today."

"Profit is the responsibility of all."

Objective #2—Customers. "To provide products and services of the greatest possible value to our customers, thereby gaining and holding their respect and loyalty."

Long-term orientation with customers.

Responsible to customers for products with:
  Superior performance,
  Superior workmanship,
  Superior service.

Necessity for cooperation among different sales teams dealing with same customer and not competing with each other.

Importance of "one company" image.

Objective #3—Fields of Interest. "To enter new fields only when the *ideas* we have, together with our *technical, manufacturing* and *marketing skill,* assure that we can make a needed and profitable *contribution* to the field."

Need for ideas and all three skills.

Key word is contribution.

Diversification generally in technically related fields, but when we diversify:
  Entry must be via something new and needed (not just another brand);
  Ideas are key but must also have marketing and manufacturing skills to execute.

Objective #4—Growth. "Let our growth be limited by our profits and our ability to develop and produce technical products that satisfy real customer needs."

"Size not important for own sake, but. . . ."

"Continuous growth is a *must* because:
   Markets HP is in are growing rapidly—must hold position;
   Growth important to attract and hold high caliber people."

Cash generation is a major factor in divisional strategic deliberations in determining how fast a division will be allowed to grow.

Objective #5—People. "To help HP people share in the company's success, which they make possible; to provide job security based on performance; to recognize individual achievements; and to help gain a sense of satisfaction and accomplishment for their work."

"Company is built around strong regard for the individual."

Need for understanding and concern by management in dealing with people with problems.

One worldwide profit-sharing program for all employees. Twelve percent of PBT divided in proportion to base pay. Typically 6½ to 9½%. Not included as pay or benefit in surveys, viewed as extra.

No management incentives. Minimal perks. Pay well.

Employees don't lose jobs due to management errors.

Layoff avoidance tactics:
   Diversification by product, customer, and geography;
   7% overtime in normal times;
   10% cut in pay and work (9 days out of 10) in extremis;
   Avoid major contracts;
   No government R&D or other direct business with government;
   15% of direct labor subcontract buffer;

Only one small layoff in HP history (20, related to acquisition).

Objective #6—Management. "To foster initiative and creativity by allowing the individual great freedom of action in attaining well-defined objectives."

Management by objectives (as we know it), with supervisory approval of the objectives.

"No management by directive."

Emphasizes importance of cooperation between individuals and between operating units.

Teams, teams, teams!

Objective #7—Citizenship. "To honor our obligations to society by being an economic, intellectual, and social asset to each nation and community in which we operate."

"Communities in which HP operates must be better as a result of HP's presence."

"Each community has a particular set of social problems. HP must help to solve those in each community."

Must be good corporate citizen in each country.

Environmental protection.

Equal opportunity.

"HP Way"

Excellent, well-paid people. Primary entry at bottom.

Employment security.

Egalitarianism:
  Worldwide uniform profit sharing;
  Homogenity of benefits and treatment for all;
  Only Hewlett and Packard have closed offices at headquarters;
  Management accessible—physically and emotionally;
  Gleaming physical environment;
  Free rolls, coffee, fruit twice a day. Management participates.

Strong climate of mutual trust.

Teams, teams, teams! "Every management team is a quality circle."

HP must win—HP objectives transcend.

Small autonomous units.

Management qualities: must have technical skills, leadership skills, administrative skills.

Heavy emphasis on equity. The function of the personnel department is to be the custodian of equity.

Other Interesting Practices

Employee benefits everywhere in world reviewed annually by executive committee for consistency with HP way.

Strong thrust toward uniform pay and benefit practices worldwide.

No hidden management agendas. The corporate goal document says it all.

Informal talent identification and placement system. All managers at functional level and above reviewed four times a year by corporate operations council.

Line management does most of the training.

Large groups of people often moved to form nucleus of new spun out divisions.

Salary administration practices wide open.

Do not believe in using tests for placement.

Eighty percent of employees participate in stock purchase plan. Up to 10% of pay allowed. HP adds one-third to employee deduction.

PART THREE

IMPLEMENTING STRATEGIC CHANGES

Chapter Eleven

Change Technologies

I have found that if you give a little boy a hammer, he will find that everything needs pounding (Kaplan, 1964).

INTRODUCTION

Hammers, like time motion studies, management by objectives, operations research, the managerial grid, job rotation, job enlargement, job enrichment, transactional analysis, autonomous workgroups, gain-sharing plans, sensitivity training, matrix structures, quality control circles, and an almost infinite list of change technologies, in the hands of managers and consultants, are often misused. These technologies are all too often touted as organizational panaceas. The 1982 top hits are Japanese management, quality circles and Theory Z. These too will be viewed as passing fads. Even though these and the earlier change technologies have their uses, none are panaceas.

Understandable pressures have created this state of affairs and will continue to do so. The pressure is on the manager to find ways of dealing with organizational problems, immediately, with minimal risk and investment. This makes the manager susceptible to overly quick actions, cure-alls, and sales pitches from consultants. (A consultant obviously has a vested interest in selling his or her services.) In earlier research, I found that when consultants carry out a general organizational diagnosis, they tend to conclude that what ails the organization is something that is treatable with their particular set of skills. Thus, an operations research consultant finds production design problems that are solvable by linear programming; a psychologist finds psychological problems that are solvable by sensitivity training, etc.

In order to avoid the pressures for panacea hammers, it is essential that change technology selection be based on: (1) a good organizational diagnosis; (2) a strategic change plan; and (3) an understanding of the variety of change technologies available and how they operate and what they can actually contribute. This chapter provides an overview of current managerial and organizational tools available to assist in a change effort as well as some newly developed social network change technolo-

291

gies. In addition, guidelines are presented for evaluating when a particular technology can be used successfully.

WHAT ARE CHANGE TECHNOLOGIES?

Change technologies are the specific tools, consisting of planned activities and procedures, for altering some aspect of organizational behavior. They include tasks which are carried out to change some aspect of organizational behavior and are related to a change strategy. For example, a change strategy may prescribe the revamping of the way an organization goes about making adjustments in its mission and strategy as the environment changes. In order to implement this strategy, specific actions are called for. An example of a change technology available for making such a change is open systems planning. This technology is briefly outlined in order to provide the reader with a better understanding of our definition of change technology.

Open systems planning involves the following set of tasks:

1. Develop an explicit, agreed upon, core mission of the organization. The key members of the organization (dominant coalition) specify why the organization is in existence. This sometimes requires negotiation among the dominant coalitions, as was the case when I was working with a large, 4,000-engineer, engineering consulting firm where some managers felt the core mission was:

> To provide consulting, engineering, construction, and project management services to the energy and energy-related industries and government agencies worldwide.

Whereas others felt it was:

> To diversify its services and aims to provide engineering, construction, and project management in the chemical process industry. These services apply to the fields of ammonia, urea, and methanol, though project management and construction services are being sought in other areas of chemical process. The focus is on the domestic market.

The two statements differ in two fundamental areas, (1) focus on worldwide versus domestic and (2) focus on energy versus diversification. These differences had to be resolved in order for the senior managers to proceed with the open systems planning task. The resolution involved both political bargaining as well as technical considerations.

2. Having defined the mission, the next step is to write a "scenario" about the present state of affairs. To do this one must first identify a series of domains that are making demands on the present system, such as:

(a) Economic factors
(b) Social values
(c) Competition
(d) Employees
(e) International governments
(f) Public image

Then for each of these domains an analysis is made of what it demands of the organization at that moment. This is specified in behavioral terms by having individuals answer the question of each domain: "What is X domain demanding of us now?" Examples include: The economy is demanding greater efficiency from us due to inflation, the public is demanding less use of nuclear power generation, etc.

3. Having defined the demand system, the present response system is defined. For each of the demands identified in the previous step, indicate what the organization's current responses are—this can range from nothing to a major organizational activity. For example, the economic demand for efficiency was responded to by a productivity program. The negative public attitude toward nuclear energy was responded to by a public relations campaign.

4. Next, managers were asked to project 3 to 5 years into the future (this can be longer). What is the relevant environment likely to be then? Specify the demands and pressure of each of the projected future domains.

5. What response mechanisms must be developed to cope effectively with the future demands and pressures (this can often include changing the external domains as well as changing the organization).

6. Having identified the necessary future responses, develop a list of activities that would have to be developed in order to achieve those desired responses.

An example of a very different change technology is the implementation of a computerized management information system to provide tighter control and coordination across both vertical and horizontal levels of an organization. This technology might be used to implement a change strategy of increased organizational integration.

CATEGORIZING CHANGE TECHNOLOGIES

In order to help understand the functioning of the various change technologies available to change managers, we have categorized them according to their major impact on the components of the organizational model. Table 11.1 relates the model categories to change strategies and in turn to specific change technologies. As can be seen

Table 11.1 Examples of Change Strategies and Technologies

Model Category	Strategies	Technologies
Input	Change the environment Anticipate environmental changes Alter characteristics of input	Interorganizational linkages Condition building Organizational set analysis Open-systems planning
Transformation process mission and objectives	Clarify Change Build ongoing mechanism for re- examining and changing	Strategic planning Goal confrontation meeting Multilevel planning
Networks Prescribed Emergent	Technical change (work flow) Social structure change Explicitly examine emergent net- works and change through new prescribed arrangements	Contingency theories of organization design, for example, differentiation integration Autonomous work groups Job enrichment Role analysis technique Sociometric network analysis
Organizational processes Communication	Change the flow Change the content	Redesign communication networks Data feedback
Control	Change the quality level of distinction Establish collaboratively designed control system Clarify standards and corrective action mechanisms	Management by objectives system Management information system

Component	Description	Technique
Problem-solving and decision-making	Develop routine and nonroutine procedures Alter decision-making structure levels, patterns of involvement	Data feedback-survey feedback Responsibility analysis
Reward system	Deal with individual differences Relate to organizational objectives	Scanlon plan
Conflict management	Alter sociotechnical arrangements Develop intergroup mechanism for handling conflict Develop interpersonal skills for handling conflict	Integrating mechanisms Organizational mirroring Confrontation meeting Role negotiation Third party consultation
Individual–group component Individual style	Alter selection and placement of individuals Train individuals Develop individuals for future	Life planning-career development Assessment center Difference selection criteria Leadership training Education: technical skills Sensitivity training Coaching and counseling
Interpersonal	Increased interaction and communication	Sensitivity training Team building Process consultation
Group culture	Change the norms and values about work and how to behave in work settings	

Source: John Sutherland (ed.), *Management Handbook for Public Administrators.* Copyright © 1978 by Van Nostrand Reinhold Company. Reprinted by permission of the publisher.

in Table 11.1, some change technologies have multiple effects, that is, technologies such as team development affect both organizational processes and emergent networks and people. An attempt was made in Table 11.1 to minimize multiple categorization.

A second dimension with which to categorize change technologies, and which is not represented in Table 11.1, is to determine their impact on the technical, political, and cultural systems. Such categorization is difficult as most technologies affect all three systems. For example, open systems planning entails making technical adjustments between the organization and its environment. However, in order to agree on the core mission and work out a future scenario, political bargaining and exchange among key players is generally required while individuals and coalitions attempt to figure out the personal implications of any future changes. Finally, the cultural system is also likely to be disrupted and changed. The organization is likely to require a new set of norms and values more congruent with the new activities.

It is not easy to categorize the impact of particular change technologies on the technical, political, and cultural systems, without knowing the organizational context within which it is to be applied. Therefore, rather than attempt to do so a priori, we will identify the considerations involved in applying a technology to help determine its application to the technical, political, and cultural systems.

CURRENT CHANGE TECHNOLOGIES

Table 11.2 presents a summary of some of the change technologies commonly used in contemporary organizations. For each technology presented, there is a brief description, a statement of its overall advantages and disadvantages, and a listing of the key conditions for its successful utilization. Some of the technologies are discussed in more detail as follows.

Open Systems Planning

Most managers in large organizations are used to planning their work against goals or objectives. When organizations become more complex and the demands of the external environment more differentiated, managers are increasingly faced with problems and budget allocations which result from competing demands for resources. The criteria for allocation of these resources tend to be based on a mixture of organizational objectives, personal priorities, and tradition and past experiences. The core mission of the organization, which is the organization's basic reason to be—"the nature of the beast"—is often not explicitly used to make major strategic decisions. This much planning allocates resources based on objectives or goals without being clear about mission priorities. The result is that the strategic decision making process is too informal or too political in a dysfunctional mode.

In simple organizations and those with "slack" resources, it is possible to have multiple "core missions" because they can all be achieved. One sector of organizations where changes have occurred is comprised of the health delivery and educational organizations. When costs were lower, research funding higher, and a balance of need and service fairly clear, the issue of whether the core mission of a teaching hospital was to train physicians and other providers or to provide quality care to patients or to service community health needs, was not a major concern of administrators. Obviously the mission was all of these. As long as one could keep the resources in some kind of balance, the problem could be managed.

With increased organizational complexity, and changes in funding practices—escalating costs of health care and increasing community pressure—this issue is more difficult for an administrator today. In fact, some member or group of the institution must set priorities against the different, possible, core missions.

The behavior of people in administrative or leadership positions is significantly affected by their concept of the mission of the institution. If their conception is not clear, others in the organization will receive mixed signals.

The process of open systems planning is for key people in an organization (or department or unit) to develop a consensus on a core mission statement and assess the current and future organizational pressures affecting the ability to carry out the proposed mission. It is a process of problem solving that can be supported and supplemented by formal strategic planning activities.

After examining the alternatives and getting a first position around the core mission, it is then desirable to "map the environment." This process involves thinking through and identifying the various institutions, groups, value systems, which are making demands on the administration of the institution or department. For example, in a hospital there might be community demands for more ambulatory care, or there might be demands in the medical school for more sophisticated equipment for specialty training. In a particular department there might be demands for more efficiency in filling beds, or a demand for limiting support staff.

Using this process, all of these competing demands should be listed. They add up to what is called the "demand system." This provides a way of looking at the core mission in the context of the open system of the organization and its environment. It is sometimes necessary to modify or revise the core mission statement after an analysis

Table 11.2 Modern OD Techniques

OD Technique	Definition	Focus	Basic Assumptions	Goals	Advantages	Disadvantages
1. Differentiation and integration	A diagnostic approach which gathers information about the interdepartmental and intergroup differences of orientation with respect to time, interpersonal relations, goals, and structure. It also identifies the integrative mechanisms for dealing with those differences in order to achieve collaboration within the total organization.	Each group, department, or unit is studied in terms of its needs and methods of meeting those needs in order to best accomplish its task. Intergroup interfaces and methods of dealing with differences are also of major interest.	Different areas of assignment within an organization need to be structured differently in order to best accomplish their purposes. Integrative mechanisms must be designed to bridge the differences and provide effective collaboration.	Identify differentiation needs, integrative mechanisms, and methods of conflict resolution. Redesign to better fit the environmental demands upon the various groups.	Helps in identifying possible intergroup problems. Very effective as a diagnostic tool. Focuses on task, structure, goals, etc., rather than personality dimensions. Useful in identifying environmental demands. Takes into account system interdependencies. Adaptable in a consistent manner to local conditions and problems. Written diagnosis is usually provided.	Extensive complex diagnosis is necessary. Minimum focus on individual problems. Depends heavily on other techniques for implementation of change. Relatively less used presently than other more common approaches.
2. Life planning—career development	A process for identifying personal strengths and success in order to establish a base for accomplishing personal, career, and organizational goals.	Personal development and increased contribution to organizational goals. Career opportunities. More creative use of individual and organizational resources.	Identifying strengths and providing relevant training does lead to a more productive use of individual resources. The organization exists for the benefit of all members. Individual fulfillment brings increased organizational effectiveness and optimizes use of member skills. Individual and organizational goals can complement each other.	Improve individual resources. Match tasks with individual strengths and resources and desires. Increase personal growth and fulfillment. Harmonize organizational and individual goals.	Career conflicts faced and resolved. Especially useful in mergers; rapid growth; acquisitions; etc. Actualization of potential of all members. Clarification of roles and expectations. Identification of personal goals and organizational goals. Team-building device for an already cohesive group. Happy, dedicated, contributing, self-actualizing employees.	May not survive change in top management. Dissatisfaction if work styles cannot be altered. Possible incongruency between reality and what one would like work to be. Conflicts between individuals' career goals. Requires great amount of flexibility on the part of management.

	Definition	Primary focus / application	Underlying assumptions	Benefits	Strengths	Limitations
3. Management by objectives	A process whereby the superior and the subordinate members of an enterprise jointly analyze their assignments in terms of reason for existence and contribution to the mission of the organization. Mutually they identify expected results and establish measures as guides for evaluation of performance. A special effort is made to focus on the desired results, not on the methods of achieving the results.	Primarily "end results," hence on "task." Key to success is when groups and individuals mesh goals and efforts to succeed in the "situation." It can apply to any manager or individual no matter what level of function, and to any organization, regardless of size.	Organization and/or individuals have, or can be given, elements of "planning" and "control" as well as the function of "doing." Reasonable and normal control over activities and results is desirable. Theory Y beliefs about people, if maximum potential of MBO as an OD strategy is to be achieved.	Improved performance of organization and individuals. Coordination of resources. Increased ownership in decisions and goals. Improved measurement of results. Clarification of responsibilities and goals.	Focuses on measurable results. Contains in its processes the traditionally recognized management structure. Gives participant responsibility for decision making. Does not limit methods—only end results.	Results focus tends to obscure process and climate issues. The tendency to "simulate" shared decision making when in reality the decisions are unilateral. Diverse misconceptions about what MBO is or is not.
4. Open-systems planning	A method of studying an organization by identifying its "mission" and analyzing all relevant variables without as well as within the organization.	All aspects of the internal and external environmental systems. The organizational processes that need to be modified in order to best adapt to environmental demands.	System has right and responsibility to make itself the way it wants to be. Organizations can to a great degree control their internal and external operations and environment. The complex organization is a set of interdependent parts which together make up a whole because each contributes something and receives something from the whole, which in turn is interdependent with some larger environment. Understanding organizations involves much	Clarify organization's mission. Make explicit the demands from other systems. Look at present organizational response to demands. Redesign of system to be more active in meeting its environment and accomplishing its mission. Directly specifying those elements important for organizational analysis. Survival of the system.	Useful when major changes are to be made such as mergers, new top management, etc. Useful when things seem too good. Useful when ability to perform is impaired by other outside groups. Useful when a group is just forming or coming into existence. Useful at regular intervals of approximately 5 years. Especially useful for organizations with "service" type technologies. Useful when organiza-	A complex and demanding procedure which entails some risk of negative outcome. Typically requires much effort in follow-through. Requires careful planning, management, and commitment. Usually requires a fairly high time commitment especially on the part of top management. Relatively new and undeveloped at present.

299

Table 11.2 (Continued)

OD Technique	Definition	Focus	Basic Assumptions	Goals	Advantages	Disadvantages
			more than under-standing goals and the arrangements that are developed for their accomplishment. Organizations are affected by what comes into them in the form of input, by what transpires inside the organization, and by the nature of the environmental acceptance of the organization and its output.		tion receives undue criticism. Useful to unite total organization to accomplish its mission. When well done, it resolves some of the organization's most difficult problems. Establishes a representative "core group."	
5. Process consultation	PC is a set of activities on the part of the consultant which help the client to perceive, understand, and act upon process events which occur in the client's environment. This process consultant seeks to give the clients "insight" into what is going on around them, within them, and between them and other people. The events to be observed and learned from are primarily the various human actions which occur in the normal flow of work, in the conduct	All interpersonal processes within the organization. All (or at least primary) relationships and procedures.	The process model starts with the assumption that the organization knows how to solve its particular problems or knows how to get help in solving them, but that it often does not know how to use its own resources effectively either in initial problem solution or in implementation of solutions. The process model further assumes that inadequate use of internal resources or ineffective implementation results from process problems, i.e., that people fail to communicate effec-	The goal of the process consultant is to help the organization to solve its own problems by making it aware of organizational processes and of the consequences of these processes and the organization to learn from self-diagnosis and self-intervention. The ultimate concern of the process consultant is the organization's capacity to do for itself what he or she has done for it. Where the standard consultant is more concerned about passing on knowledge, the pro-	Goes hand in hand with team and interpersonal relations training. Conducted on the job in the normal work setting. Effective solution of interpersonal, individual, and intergroup problems. Intended to build the needed skill in the participants to carry on, with little external contact. Participants assume full responsibility for change efforts. Organic in nature. Contributes toward ef-	Does not afford the intensive involvement offered by various forms of interpersonal relations training or team building. Takes into account only the process issues. Requires sustained involvement over a 2- or 3-year period.

	of meetings, and in formal or informal encounters between members of the organization. Of particular relevance are the client's own actions and their impact on other people.	tively with each other, or develop mistrust, or engage in destructive competition, or punish those they mean to reward and vice versa, or fail to give feedback, and so on.		cess consultant is concerned about passing on 'skills and values.	fective solutions in any and all areas involving human beings.	Often requires computer for analysis of data. Ownership of data is often difficult to achieve. Requires extensive preparation for feedback sessions in order to ensure effectiveness. Time lag between data collection and feedback minimizes effectiveness.
6. Survey-feedback-action planning	A process of gathering data usually by interview, observation, or questionnaire about important organizational or group concerns. The data are summarized and fed back to the group members and used as impetus for discussion of needed changes. Plans for action are then made and in most cases a resurvey is taken to provide a comparative measure of change before and after discussion.	Getting information flowing within the system. Work groups and their work-related concerns. Relevant issues as defined by consultant or client. Organizational climate and/or management.	Data alone will provide an impetus for discussion and solution of problems. Decision makers will accept the implications of scientifically valid data. Data-gathering methods have no disagreeable significant intervention impact upon the organization.	Providing the necessary accurate information for proper decision making to those responsible for decisions. Increasing the participation of a greater number of resource people in management decisions.	Can be adapted to any area of interest or issue relevant to organization members. Can be organization-wide or used only by those groups most interested. Provides for easy measurement and comparison of before and after any chosen intervention. Validated, reliable questionnaires already available for use in several areas of concern. May be an effective way of changing hard data indicators as well as less objective measures.	
7. Team and interpersonal relations	A method of learning and planning for change in which the participants are helped to diagnose and experience their own behavior, culture, and relation-	Interpersonal and group skills. Group expectations and goals. Intensive problem solving. Expression of feel-	The amount of work carried out by workers is determined not by their physical capacities but by their social capacities; noneconomic rewards are most important in	Increased trust, openness, and team work. Joint planning and commitment to action. Improved work climate.	Cultural and environmental change. Improved conflict resolution skills. Improved data flow within organizations. Especially useful for in-	Payoffs sometimes individually rather than organizationally oriented. Possible tendencies toward extremism on the part of some participants.

Table 11.2 (Continued)

OD Technique	Definition	Focus	Basic Assumptions	Goals	Advantages	Disadvantages
	ships. Skill exercises, simulations, theoretical discussions, and real work analysis and planning are done in a specially designed environment.	ings—emotional behavior.	the motivation and satisfaction of workers, who react to their work situations as groups and not as individuals; the leader is not necessarily the person appointed to be in charge; informal leaders can develop who have more power; the effective supervisor is "employee-centered" and "job-centered," that is, he or she regards his or her job as dealing with human beings as well as with the work; communication and participation in decision making are some of the most significant rewards which can be offered to obtain the commitment of the individuals.	Improved individual and group interaction and communication skills.	dividual growth and interpersonal skill development. Useful in establishing effective working teams. Provides opportunity for interpersonal feedback analysis of interpersonal processes. Provide opportunity for examination of the social impact and consequences of one's behavior. Builds democratic and participative norms.	Relatively high emotional demands required. Often seen as subjective rather than objective in terms of measurable results. Possible misuse as "therapy" for unstable or unproductive members in the organization.

| 8. Third-party consultation | A process of diagnosing recurrent conflict between persons or groups. Then on the basis of our understanding of the dynamics of interpersonal conflict episodes, performing a number of strategic functions which facilitate a constructive confrontation of the conflict. | "Interpersonal conflict in organizational settings," such as differences between fellow members of a governing committee, heads of interrelated departments, a manager and his or her boss. Interpersonal conflict is defined broadly to include (1) interpersonal disagreement over substantive issues, such as differences over organizational structures, policies, and practices, and (2) interpersonal antagonisms, that is, the more personal and emotional differences which arise between interdependent human beings. | The innumerable interdependencies inherent in organizations make interpersonal conflicts inevitable. Even if it were thought to be desirable, it would not be possible to create organizations free from interpersonal conflicts. The amount of emotional energy necessary to confront a conflict and resolve it is often less in the long run than the amount of energy necessary to suppress it. Indirect conflicts, have the longest life expectancy and have the most costs that cannot be charged back against the original conflict. | To develop the interpersonal skills and to create an open confrontive organizational climate conducive to effective conflict resolution. To develop capacities within or available to organizations that make it possible to resolve more of the interpersonal conflicts and lessen the costs of those which cannot readily be resolved. To increase the authenticity of the relationships and the personal integrity experienced in the relationships. | Useful on the job in the "real" work setting. Provides resolution of problems so that energies can be used for productive purposes rather than to protect or defend. Provides a balance of power for the disadvantaged. Provides a third ("objective") view of otherwise polarized issues. Provides for the "referee" function in interpersonal conflict issues. Can provide a constructive amount of anxiety; i.e., a certain pressure is sometimes necessary for resolution or confrontation of problems. | Deals with only one of many development areas. Requires a highly skilled consultant. If they are not well managed, confrontations can further polarize the individuals, increase the costs of the conflict, or discourage the principals from further efforts. As in all areas of possible high return, the risks can also be high if the proper precautions are not taken. |

Source: Adapted from Typical O.D. intervention models for planned change' ©1975 by Robert A. Baird. Reprinted with permission.

of the demands. Two case examples illustrate the application of the open systems planning process in two medical centers.

Center A is a large, prestigious medical school and teaching hospital complex in the western half of the country. The graduates represent a distinguished scientific and medical group which includes some Nobel Prize winners. The institution is also noted for the quality of its teaching in both undergraduate school and postgraduate residencies. Its faculty members have made significant contributions to biomedical research and treatment. Practically all students specialize; the facility does not focus on training general practitioners. The institution is located in a community which is well served by private practitioners.

As new pressures appeared for training more primary care physicians in medical schools and teaching hospitals, the leadership of Center A examined its criteria for allocating resources. The facts were that research grants had been sharply reduced there, as in all medical institutions. There was an indication that, if medical schools were not going to prepare significant numbers of students for primary care practice, federal funding of tuition might be cut off. There was tremendous pressure for more community service. At the same time, there was a lot of pressure from the prestigious faculty not to destroy the "elegance" of the research and training of the institution.

A series of meetings between the university leadership, medical school leadership, and the hospital leadership examined these various demands. It was decided to conduct an open systems planning exercise. After a number of meetings consensus emerged. Briefly stated, it was: "We are basically a scientific institution engaged in inquiry, and application is our core mission. To support this core mission, we wish to train qualified specialists to carry out the application of our research and clinical practice. We are not here to train doctors in the broad sense. Nor are we here primarily to service the community in which we are located. Therefore, we will focus our resource allocation on protecting our research primacy and the quality of our clinical specialty training. We see as a natural by-product high quality care for those persons who go through our system as patients."

The leadership group knew that the consequences of this decision might mean that Federal funds would be withheld or challenged; they knew that it might mean difficulties with the community. The executive management of the organization decided that these consequences would have to be accepted and managed.

In another part of the country, Medical Center B was also known for its quality care, its good research, clinical practice, and high-quality health sciences teaching program. The medical school and teaching hospitals were part of a university complex but located some distance from the main campus in a primarily rural state. Significant numbers of medical school graduates went into practice in the state, which had a great need for practitioners, comprehensive preventive care, as well as more ambulatory centers, because of the geographical distance between treatment centers and patients.

When research funding slowed down, faculty recruitment became more difficult, and requirements for increased numbers of students were placed on the institution, the dean of the school, the hospital administrator, and the university's leadership, as well as the key clinical teaching head and community representatives, examined the core mission of the medical center in the context of an open systems planning exercise.

From these deliberations came the position that "From the possible primary missions of research, teaching, and delivery of care to the community, we've determined that the delivery of care to the community is our primary reason to be. We see as part of that core mission the training of our medical practitioners to provide such care. We see the need for a good clinical teaching program in back of that good basic research, in order that the practitioners we train can provide the kind of service needed."

After that decision, they recognized that some of the faculty members whose research allocations would be cut would become discontented and perhaps leave. They also realized that their faculty recruitment problems would become more difficult. They also realized that they would probably have to increase facilities for ambulatory care in order to carry out the primary mission.

In both cases, the management of the institution, through the open systems planning process, arrived at a definitive statement of priorities and then produced specific actions. The open systems planning technology affected all three systems: technical, political, and cultural, in both of these cases. It was a major intervention.

Job Design Technologies

There are a variety of technologies available to alter the design of work tasks. One technology involves scientific management principles derived from a tradition rooted in the work of Winslow Taylor over 50 years ago and currently practiced by methods engineers, and time motion analysts, who study specific operations to be carried out by workers. Based on these studies they establish blueprints for the job which make them as simple, as standardized, and as routine as possible. The simplifying and routinization of jobs is assumed to facilitate easier selection, training, and performance. After more than 50 years, the results are quite mixed. Jobs designed with these principles have often been found to lead to dysfunctional behavior such as rate setting, sabotage, absenteeism, turnover, and alcoholism. Nevertheless, as a change technology, scientific management of job design is available and can be used quite effectively in some mechanistic settings.

Job Enrichment is another job design technology. Hackman and Oldham (1976) have one of the most comprehensive, research-supported approaches. They argue that three key psychological states affect a person's motivation and satisfaction with the job: (1) experienced usefulness: how important, valuable, and worthwhile the work is felt to be; (2) experienced responsibility: how much the person feels responsible and accountable for his or her performance; and (3) knowledge of results: how clearly and rapidly the individual gets feedback on performance.

In order to enrich a job these three psychological states must be affected. Experienced meaningfulness can be enhanced by providing greater skill variety in the task, by increasing identity with the task, and by increasing the task significance. Figure 11.1 presents some of the specific job design principles for making a change in the job to enhance experienced meaningfulness. Experienced responsibility for the outcome of work is enhanced by greater autonomy. As Figure 11.1 shows, this can be accomplished by establishing a direct relationship between the worker and the client or customer (such as when a manufacturing assembly worker is put in charge of dealing with customer repair and maintenance). This in fact happened with Corning Glass in their assembly of toasters; every toaster was identified by the name of its assembler and came with a telephone number to call for service. Vertical loading—giving planning and controlling functions to the workers—also enhances autonomy.

Knowledge of the results of work is enhanced by feedback. This can

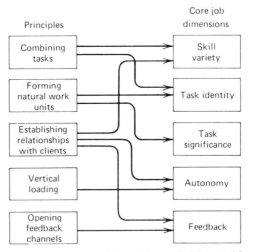

Figure 11.1 Principles for changing jobs. (From *California Management Review*, Volume XVII, 4, p. 62. Copyright © 1975 by the Regents of the University of California. Reprinted by permission of the Regents.)

come from opening up a client–customer communication channel or any of the other channels indicated in Figure 11.1.

The third technology for changing the job/task design is the autonomous work group. This was used in the Volvo-Kalmar plan described in Chapter 8.

Organizational Design Technologies

The information-processing framework for organizational design presented in Chapter 4, which helps determine "technical alignment" among organizational components, provides a set of technologies for carrying out rational organizational design changes. Figure 11.2 summarizes the steps involved in the design of the prescribed organization as developed by Tushman and Nadler (1978). The steps provide guidance for grouping tasks and identifies the integration and coordination problem.

In order to deal with the integration coordination problem, we use Galbraith's (1973) framework of integrating mechanisms to make decisions about changes. Figure 11.3 presents a set of questions used to analyze the organization's integrating mechanisms and make decisions about changes.

The procedure involves summarizing the current use of each mechanism and assessing its effectiveness. With this analysis, the change manager then begins working with the simple mechanisms and making each as effective as possible. The idea is to fully utilize the potential of simple mechanisms before progressing to more complicated ones. For example, standard operating procedures should be used as integrating mechanisms for as many routine interdependent tasks as possible. Only when it is clear that standard operating procedures are fully and effectively utilized should the hierarchy be approached. First it should be made clear which decisions are to be made at what levels. Only decisions not covered by standard operating procedures should move up the hierarchy. When the hierarchy's information-processing capacity is reached, then goal setting should be used for integrating the organization. The process of modifying the integrating mechanisms is continued up through the more complex integrating mechanisms. By working cumulatively, that is, cleaning up and adjusting the simpler mechanisms first, one reduces inappropriate spillover of problems and exceptions requiring higher level, more complex integrating mechanisms.

This technology was applied in a large engineering consulting firm which had implemented a complex matrix structure to coordinate engineering disciplines with large construction projects. The matrix did not work, and resulted in conflict, communication, and coordination problems. By first making changes in the standard operating

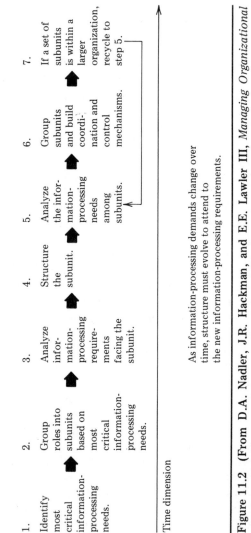

1. Identify most critical information-processing needs.

2. Group roles into subunits based on most critical information-processing needs.

3. Analyze information-processing requirements facing the subunit.

4. Structure the subunit.

5. Analyze the information-processing needs among subunits.

6. Group subunits and build coordination and control mechanisms.

7. If a set of subunits is within a larger organization, recycle to step 5.

Time dimension →

As information-processing demands change over time, structure must evolve to attend to the new information-processing requirements.

Figure 11.2 (From D.A. Nadler, J.R. Hackman, and E.E. Lawler III, *Managing Organizational Behavior*, Figure 10.10. Copyright © 1979 by David A. Nadler, J.R. Hackman and Edward E. Lawler III. Reprinted by permission of the publisher, Little, Brown & Company.)

1. *Rules and Procedures*
   Is this mechanism in use;   _____ yes   _____ no
   If yes, how effective is it?

   1   2   3   4   5   6   7
        very   not at all
        effective   effective
   Why¿?

2. *Hierarchy*
   Is this mechanism in use?   _____ yes   _____ no
   If yes, how effective is it?

   1   2   3   4   5   6   7
        very   not at all
        effective   effective
   Why?

3. *Planning*
   Is this mechanism in use?   _____ yes   _____ no
   If yes, how effective is ti;

   1   2   3   4   5   6   7
        very   not at all
        effective   effective
   Why?

4. *Slack Resources*
   Is this mechanism in use?   _____ yes   _____ no
   If yes, how effective is it?

   1   2   3   4   5   6   7
        very   not at all
        effective   effective
   Why?

5. *Self-Containment*
   Is this mechanism in use?   _____ yes   _____ no
   If yes, how effective is it?

   1   2   3   4   5   6   7
        very   not at all
        effective   effective
   Why?

6. *Vertical Systems*
   Is this mechanism in use?   _____ yes   _____ no
   If yes, how effective is it?

   1   2   3   4   5   6   7
        very   not at all
        effective   effective
   Why?

7. *Lateral Relations:*
   Integrators of Liaisons
   Is this mechanism in use?   _____ yes   _____ no
   If yes, how effective is it?

   1   2   3   4   5   6   7
        very   not at all
        effective   effective
   Why?

8. *Teams (Task Forces)*
   Is this mechanism in use?   _____ yes   _____ no
   If yes, how effective is it?

   1   2   3   4   5   6   7
        very   not at all
        effective   effective
   Why?

Figure 11.3   Organization Design Integrating Devices

9. *Matrix Structures*

Is this mechanism in use?   _____ yes   _____ no

If yes, how effective is it?

1	2	3	4	5	6	7
very effective						not at all effective

Why?

Figure 11.3   (Continued)

procedures, the use of the hierarchy and planning, it became clear that most of the problems of integration were not due to the matrix structure, but due to the fact that the matrix was built on an organization which had poorly functioning simple integrating mechanisms.

Team Development

A technology that affects both organizational processes and people is team development. Team development is based on an action research approach to change. Action research is a term coined by Kurt Lewin (1938) that refers to the orderly collection of data on real social or organizational problems for helping solve the problems. The data collection and feedback occur on an ongoing basis so that organizational members can make changes, evaluate the outcomes of changes, and then make new changes. The crucial factor of the action research approach for team development is that the consultant acts as a facilitator to enable the team to solve its own problems in a data-based fashion.

Team development is based on the following assumptions:

1. A work group is not defined as a team unless its members are actually interdependent.

2. Teams must establish explicit and shared goals which will then constitute their joint working contract.

3. Team members write role descriptions based upon the explicit goals and objectives of the team.

4. Once the goals and roles are established, the team must develop processes for communication, problem solving, decision making, and conflict management.

5. The team must develop the ability to deal with interpersonal issues brought about by interaction in the work setting.

Figure 11.4 provides a summary of the framework for carrying out team development. The objective is to impart knowledge and behavioral skills to team members so they can more effectively manage the issues outlined in Figure 11.4. Initially a team consultant works with a team in carrying out the processes; however, the consultant in collabor-

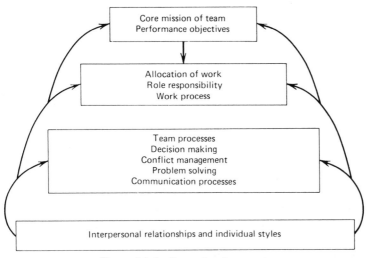

Figure 11.4   Team development

ation with the team works to institutionalize and build in the capacity for the team to carry through on the process without reliance on a consultant. In order for this to occur, normative and structural changes must occur. Normatively the team needs to develop a culture which explicitly supports the use of social interventions to regulate team processes, especially those related to decision-making communication, allocation of work, and planning. Structurally this is facilitated by formally allocating team time and resources to diagnosing and planning improvement strategies. The process entails the following sequence of activities:

1. *Mission and Goal Settings.* The team spends time collaboratively developing its core mission; the product is a written statement reflecting team consensus. This is followed by the team identifying about seven key performance objectives—measurable indicators that they will use to assess mission accomplishment.

2. *Allocation of Work.* The team members develop role statements for each other. This is done by starting with each team member listing what she or he expects to do in order to help accomplish the team's mission (each member lists on a flip chart "The following is what I expect to do, in order to help accomplish the team's mission"). These charts are posted on the wall so that all team members can view them. Each team member then reacts to the other team members' lists by either adding to the flip chart under the heading: "In addition we expect you to" or marking items which she or he feels the person should not have responsibility for doing. The result of this activity is that each individual has an indication of how much

team members agree with his or her role statement. Each team member then goes through a public session to develop an agreed upon role statement. This involves making compromises, clarifying, and changing responsibilities until the whole team agrees on each role statement. It generally takes each team member from 30 to 60 minutes of discussion to reach agreement with the team. The product is a written statement which the team agrees to (a list of concrete responsibilities).

3. *Team Processes.* The team spends time developing mechanisms for communication and handling conflict. Often a consultant works with the team to develop process skills, that is, the ability to analyze and alter interpersonal and group dynamics.

One technique for helping manage decision making and minimize conflict is responsibility charting. The team members make a list of key team decisions, such as budgeting, staffing, management of project components, etc. These are listed on the vertical axis of the responsibility chart (see Figure 11.5). Across the top of the chart are listed the members of the team. The team collaboratively decides each person's level of involvement for each decision. Possible levels are:

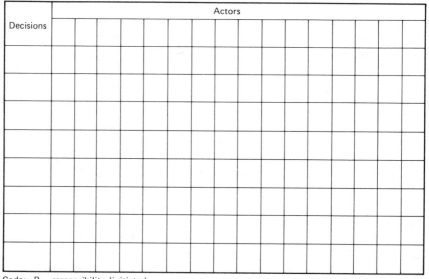

Code: R — responsibility (initiates)
       A — approval (right to veto)
       S — support (put resources against)
       I — inform (to be informed)

Figure 11.5 Responsibility chart. (From John Sutherland (Ed.), *Management handbook for public administrators.* Copyright © 1978 by Van Nostrand Reinhold Company. Reprinted by permission of the publisher.)

R = responsibility for seeing that action is taken—only one person can be assigned this level of involvement for each decision.

A = right to veto—this means that on a particular decision, this person has the right to stop the decision.

S = support—this means that the person must provide support and resources for the decision.

I = inform—this means that the person must be kept informed.

Running effective meetings is another process-focused technique provided in the team development sequence. Figure 11.6 presents the guidelines for running effective meetings. The basic points are (1) Cut down on unnecessary meetings. Only meet when the task demands it. (2) Prepare for meetings carefully. (3) Adjust the meeting's process to match the task of the meeting, and (4) Have a meeting follow-up.

4. *Interpersonal Relationships and Personal Style.* The team development process includes a variety of techniques for managing interpersonal relationships and style differences. One particularly useful technique is Roger Harrison's (1972) so-called role negotiation. The process involves a set of structured activities designed to provide team members with a tool for altering each other's behavior around getting the work done. The steps involve:

(a) Provide written feedback to all team members in the form of role messages. (A sheet is written for each team member by each team member as follows) "I (name) need you (name) to do the following in order for me to do my job better, more of: (list behaviors), less of: (list behaviors), continue: (list behaviors)."

(b) Role messages should be publicly posted on flip charts and clarified.

(c) Role negotiations should take place between all team members in a series of one-to-one meetings. The purpose of these meetings is for individuals to negotiate specific changes in behavior implied by the "more of"/"less of." Change requires an investment of energy and implies work done in return. The individuals on the team develop written agreements, "I (name) agree to produce monthly status reports on my projects for you if you (name) agree to involve me in the hiring of engineers on your staff." The contracts are signed and a follow-up review date is set to evaluate whether it has been carried out. The contract is shared with the total team for agreement regarding its workability and its ability to be monitored.

This process is a very powerful tool for enabling a team to make important changes in each others' behavior based on behavioral feedback.

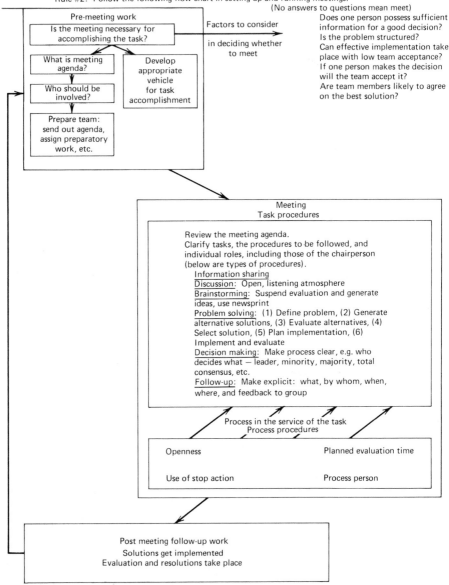

Rule #1: Cut down on unnecessary meetings. Do not meet unless the task requires it.
Rule #2: Follow the following flow chart in setting up and running meetings.

Figure 11.6   Improving team meetings

Team development as presented above represents a major group-level change intervention. All three systems—technical, political, and cultural are shifted. In general, the shift moves them all toward the organic end of the continuum.

Quality Control Circles

In the early 1980s a great deal of interest has focused on the use of quality control circles. These are generally voluntary groups of workers brought together for an hour or so a week to come up with solutions to people and productivity problems and then feed them to either the line management or some sort of steering committee. These groups are generally led by trained facilitators. The training and methodologies used in running effective quality circles are borrowed from organization development and are those outlined previously for team development.

Quality circles, like any of these change technologies, are limited tools unless incorporated into a coherent change strategy accounting for the technical, political, and cultural dynamics.

Career Development

The focus of career development is the interaction of the individual and the organization over time (Schein, 1978). Figure 11.7 presents Schein's (1978) summary of the elements of the matching process between individuals and the organization. In order to facilitate the growth and development of individuals and improve organizational effectiveness these matching processes must be effectively managed.

There are a set of change technologies designed for managing the career development process. Those discussed below focus on the portion of the system which supports the individual in his or her career development.

The approach is built on the framework presented in Figure 11.8. Four sets of factors are proposed to determine an individual's career.

1. *Competencies and knowledge* represent what the individual has in the way of job related skills. These are acquired as a result of formal education, on the job training, job experiences, and life experiences.

2. *Values and life goals* represent the individual's life aspirations and are tied to motives.

3. *Personal style, interpersonal style,* and *personality* are related to values and goals but are kept separate as they reflect how the individual relates to him/herself and to others.

4. *Knowledge of* and *access to career opportunities* represent the individual's perceptions of what is available to him/her as well as the individual's link to job networks.

The goal of a career development program is to provide technologies that further the individual's development and understanding of the four previously mentioned areas. Some of the activities and support techniques for the four areas are listed in Figure 11.8. It must be emphasized

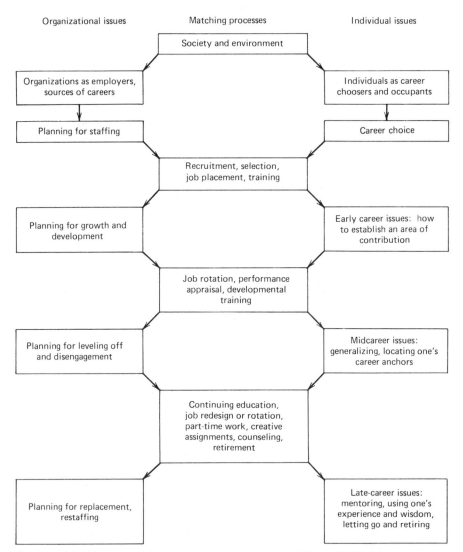

Figure 11.7 The career development perspective. (From E.H. Schein, *Career dynamics*. Copyright © 1978. Reading, Mass.: Addison-Wesley, Figure 1.2. Reprinted with permission.)

that an individual's needs for help in one area or another will vary according to his or her position in a career cycle and also to the unique aspects of each individual's situation. Some of the components of a career development system are presented as follows.

1. *Provide Career Awareness.* Individuals, especially in entry-level positions, need to be helped to see the big picture regarding

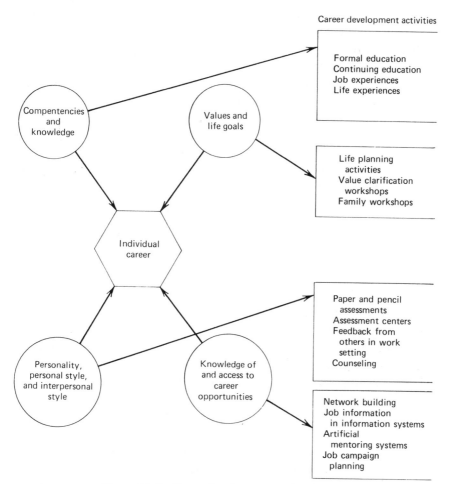

Figure 11.8   Career development technology

careers. All too often careers are limited and channeled by muddled orientation. One way to begin making the individuals more proactive regarding his or her career is to provide him or her with a conceptual map of possible career decisions. This was done in one organization by having the career development staff create a decision tree for entry-level positions for a period of several years. At each decision node, the individual is presented with a list of questions and dilemmas which should be dealt with. For example, an individual faced with a decision whether to join the line or the staff should answer a check list of questions regarding each of the categories in Figure 11.8. For example:

(a) Competencies and knowledge: What are my current competencies and knowledge, can I apply them better in line or staff?

Where will I better learn new competencies and knowledge, in line or staff?

(b) Values and goals: Given my values and life goals how do I fit with line versus staff?

(c) Personality, personal style, and interpersonal style: What is the fit between my style and the needs of a line versus staff position?

(d) Knowledge of, and access to, career opportunities: Are these my major alternatives or are there others at this juncture which could offer me greater future knowledge and access?

2. *Provide Career Assessment Activities.* The organization can provide a series of activities and workshops designed to help individuals assess and reassess themselves in work relevant areas. The management assessment centers at such places as General Electric were set up for this purpose. The workshops are designed to help individuals identify what Schein (1978) calls career anchors, which include: (1) self-perceived talents and abilities; (2) self-perceived motives and needs, and (3) self-perceived attitudes and values. There tend to be four career anchors:

(a) Technical/functional competence: The individual gets career satisfaction out of mastering the job.

(b) Managerial competence, in which the individual enjoys using analytical competence, interpersonal competence, and emotional competence.

(c) Security and stability, in which the driving career motivation is finding security and stability.

(d) Creativity, in which the career anchor is finding a regular outlet for creative needs.

(e) Autonomy and independence, the career anchor indicates that being autonomous is the most desired aspect of any job.

With a deeper self-understanding, the individual is assumed to be in a better position to make rewarding career decisions regarding development, plans for search, and plans for reassessing and replanning.

Competence development entails providing organization members with resources to continue education both through formal training and job experience. Some of the more effective methods include providing workers with sabbaticals to go work in other types of settings, or providing in-house job rotation. In-house training activities can become more closely linked with total individual development. Finally, sending people to external training events provides another vehicle for competence development.

3. *Job Search Plan.* Individuals can be helped to develop action plans for addressing issues and concerns related to each of the four areas listed in Figure 11.8. An example of such a list follows.

(a) *Competencies and Knowledge.* What: I must develop my linear programming skills to get that staff job. How: I will use the company's tuition reimbursement plan and take an evening course. When: This fall.

(b) *Values and Goals.* What: I must deal with the conflict between my career aspirations and my family aspirations as I am creating time crunches. How: I will go to a couples workshop sponsored by the company and get some marriage counseling. When: Next month.

(c) *Personality, Personal Style, and Interpersonal Style.* What: I need to assess whether my personal style fits with those of others in the new job I aspire to have. How: I will attend a management assessment workshop. When: As soon as possible.

(d) *Knowledge of the Access to Career Opportunities.* What: I need more specifics about the proposed new job—what it actually entails. How: I will make use of the computerized job vignettes in our career-development center which provide a profile of the job's tasks and interviews with job incumbents. When: Next week.

4. *Replacement and Outplacement.* The organization should provide counseling and job search services for individuals looking both within the organization and outside. Those people who are fired should be given special services to help them deal with the psychological problems of such an experience.

NETWORK CHANGE TECHNOLOGIES

This section provides examples of change technologies which are explicitly formulated in terms of social networks. They are organized in terms of the organizational model categories. As with the change technologies presented in the previous section, many of these apply to changes in all three systems—technical, political, and cultural. Table 11.3 provides a list of these change technologies.

Environmental Interface Technologies

Organizations have various technologies available for enhancing their environmental interfaces (Child, 1972). In order to monitor complex environments and gather intelligence, an organization requires external information networks (Aguilar, 1967). And in order to establish such networks, designers should understand the societal networks—social, political, and economic. If an organization can link into them, these networks can provide it with greater information-processing capacity and greater political-bargaining capacity (Blankenship and Elling, 1962). The designers should map who connects with whom, and they should assess how various types of information can be collected. One

Table 11.3 Examples of Social-Network Strategies

Model Category	Strategy
I. Environmental Interface	1. Strategic-information networks.
	2. Interlocking directorates.
	3. Identifying and working with dominant coalition.
II. Mission–Strategy	4. Use of liaisons, task coalitions, teams, and the matrix structure to combine multiple networks.
	5. Use of sociometric data to form work groups.
III. Prescribed Network	6. Network awareness and skill training.
	7. Boundary-spanning development.
	8. Role-analysis diagnosis.
	9. Career-path planning around networks.
IV. People Network	10. Coalitional organization and management skills.
	11. Reformulate traditional organizational-development communication, decision making, and conflict interventions to employ network terminology.
V. Organizational Process	12. Coalitional bargaining procedures.
	13. Transferring personnel to build up emergent information and influence networks.
VI. Emergent Network	

key lies in identifying the gatekeepers of information and influence networks: sociometric data can be employed to identify gatekeepers and to map the networks. Boards of directors afford means of linking into societal networks, as do other liaison roles.

An increasingly important set of organizational activities are boundary spanning activities (Adams, 1976; Pfeffer and Salancik, 1978; Starbuck, 1976). These are "activities which serve to relate functionally the organization to its environment (Adams, 1980)." Adams identifies five classes of boundary-spanning activities. Each is listed as follows, along with suggested organizational design strategies.

1. Acquiring organizational inputs and disposing of outputs is one activity. People who accomplish these tasks include bargaining agents, purchasing agents, sales personnel, and recruiters. The tasks, or roles, are often fraught with conflict due to the potential for mistrust on the part of people in the organization and on the outside. Adams (1980) suggests treating boundary role individuals as members of a dynamic, causally related, boundary-transaction subsystem which has its own structure, set of norms, and political dynamics. Walton and McKearsie's (1976) guidelines for effective union bargaining provide a prototype for a systematic analysis of boundary-transaction subsystems.

2. Filtering inputs and outputs is another boundary role activity. It entails the "selective acceptance or rejection of inputs and outputs

in accordance with criteria largely established by the organization . . . (Adams, 1980; p. 20)." This includes such roles as quality-control personnel, admissions officers at universities, and loan officers. There are two types of filtering errors: acceptance errors and rejection errors. The boundary-role people act as information gatekeepers and as such are prone to errors of omission, exaggeration, and selective bias (Adams, 1980; Roberts et al., 1974). An organizational design suggestion aimed at countering filtering errors is to have multiple independent sources of information on the same topic. Thus, for an important issue, the organization might build in multiple boundary roles and duplicate resources in order to avoid errors.

3. Searching for and collecting information is another boundary-role activity. The more turbulent an organization's environment is, the more valuable information concerning the environment becomes. In addition, the search and acquisition costs go up with uncertainty. However, because of the value of such information, companies such as GE invest substantial resources in the collection of intelligence about the possibility of events which might affect the organization. GE has systematically developed boundary-spanning roles that link into networks which provide information about technology, society, governments, politics, and economics. The key to building these boundary-spanning information networks is to build on the strength of weak ties principle. Grannovetter (1973) found that "an innovation is diffused to a larger number of individuals and transverses a greater social distance when passed through weak ties rather than strong ties." Thus, organizations should see that boundary spanners develop wide ranges of weak links. In addition, they should identify invisible colleges (Crane, 1972) of scholars or intellectuals working in an area. These invisible colleges are informal but stable information exchange networks.

Another set of concepts to guide the boundary spanner is the notion of a circle. Kadushin (1978) identifies social circles as the key to innovation. He argues that innovation depends on "external economies"; the parts and ideas must exist outside the focal organization, thus the boundary spanner must acquire them. Furthermore, looseness of structure seems to be a prerequisite for a nonstandard change. Circles are characterized by:

(a) Having multiple step flows of communication networks turned back on each other;

(b) Having no clear boundaries—Laumann and Pappi (1976) found that with community power there was a gradual shading between ins and outs;

(c) Having a core group yet no formal leaders;

(d) Having indirect interaction with a maximum reach of two-to-three steps.

The key organizational design suggestion is to identify and map circles relevant to the organization and then involve a boundary spanner in that circle.

Mission/Strategy Technologies

Seeking to stimulate a strategic reorientation, change managers might: (1) identify who really influences the organization's missions and strategies, (2) identify the interests of influential coalitions, and (3) assess the extent of agreement among these coalitions. If there is strong agreement about missions and strategies indicating low political controversy, then the change managers should initiate rational cooperative planning aimed at addressing the technical production problem. But if there is substantial disagreement, then the change managers should initiate political bargaining about missions and strategies on the premise that the influential coalitions desire organizational effectiveness as well as power and personal success.

An important fact to remember is that top management frequently is not equivalent to dominant coalitions. In addition, dominant coalitions have a mixture of agendas, including maintaining power bases and furthering career aspirations, as well as a desire for organizational effectiveness. Change in mission and strategy occurs through a mix of political, technical, and cultural processes carried out among dominant coalitions.

Prescribed Organizational Technologies

Porter *et al.* (1975, p.272) summarized the contingencies that should regulate decisions to create mechanistic or organic configurations. Mechanistic, heavily structured, bureaucratic configurations are most effective: (1) when members are inexperienced and unskilled, (2) when members do not have high self-esteem and strong needs for achievement, autonomy, and self-actualization, (3) when technologies are not rapidly changing, irregular, and unplanned, and (4) when environments are not dynamic and complex.

When designing a mechanistic configuration, designers should prescribe all of the important task-related networks, and they should minimize emergent networks. The traditional theories of management help to prescribe task-related networks: They advocate clarifying rules and procedures, delineating an unambiguous hierarchy of authority, creating communication networks which are consistent with task demands (Bavelas, 1951), and linking resource allocations and rewards to organizational missions so they cannot become political implements. People who communicate with each other should be located near each other; physical layouts can bring interdependent people together, regulate traffic flows, and foster affective relationships which match task relationships (Allen, 1977; Steele, 1973). Physical spaces should be the correct sizes for work groups. Channels should be created for the formal resolution of conflicts so that there are no incentives for the emergence of unprescribed relationships. In particular, people can be designated as lateral integrators who crosscut hierarchical relationships —linking pairs of departments while keeping the departments distinct (Galbraith, 1973). Task-force assignments can bring together cosmopolitans and locals, thus linking the locals to environments and binding the cosmopolitans more tightly to the organization. Similarly, rewards can encourage cosmopolitan attitudes by locals and vice versa. One very simple and important strategy is to enhance the visibility of the prescribed networks. Invisible networks lead to deviations and unnecessary trial-and-error learning, so functional or operational flowcharts should be realistic and widely distributed. Superordinate goals give people frameworks for evaluating potential behaviors and relationships, and they reduce undesirable conflicts (Deutsch, 1973; Sherif et al., 1954).

In an organic configuration, the organizational culture should support authority of knowledge and commitment to tasks over loyalties to people or to the organization. High uncertainty and irregular, unplanned technologies call for prescribed networks that are complex, not formalized, and which afford great vertical mobility. These prescribed networks should legitimate the relationships that emerge through ongoing activities; each person and work group should develop task-related networks for acquiring information and exerting influence. As Weick (1969) indicated, an organization is constantly in the business of organizing.

When designing an organic configuration, designers should specify prescribed networks that legitimate relationships which emerge spontaneously. One way to do this is to define the prescribed networks in general terms that accommodate diverse specific relationships. Another way to do this is to prescribe the relationships observable through sociometric data; such data can be gathered unobtrusively via accounting and control procedures, as by asking who was consulted informally when a proposal was being formulated.

The building of prescribed networks can be based on role analyses that proceed as follows: First, people should identify their current networks—with whom communication occurs, for what purposes, and how is influence exerted? Then, the people identify areas where they need larger flows of information, influence, or affect; also, they identify where flows are too large or inappropriate. This leads to the identification of areas requiring changes, including places where new relationships are desirable. Action plans can then be developed for altering networks.

People Network Technologies

People can be taught how networks operate, how to establish new networks, what networks already exist, how to improve existing networks, what kinds of relationships are desirable or undesirable, what rules and goals are prescribed, what norms and values are legitimate, and so on. In particular, people need special skills in order to form effective coalitions and to bargain effectively: They can be taught how to identify necessary resources, how to bring people into close contact with each other, and how to develop bargaining proposals.

Training should be integrated with career planning and recruitment. People should prepare for future jobs as well as current ones, and even jobs in other organizations. Losing people to other organizations and bringing in new ones can be highly beneficial, because an organization's networks broaden as new members bring links to new external networks. For example, governmental regulatory agencies draw some of their personnel from the regulated business firms; Chatov (1981), among others, has argued that this practice fosters cooperation between the regulators and the regulated.

Emergent Network Technologies

Burns and Stalker (1961), Hage et al. (1971), Lawrence and Lorsch (1967), and Pugh (1969) have provided evidence regarding the different networks emerging in mechanistic and organic configurations. Contrasting these two ideal types clarifies the distinctions between emergent networks and highlights a number of design issues. But the warning of Harvey and Mills (1970) should be heeded: collapsing a number of variables into an abstract one obscures the subtle differences which distinguish particular cases.

In mechanistic configurations, emergent networks should arise primarily because of inadequacies in the prescribed networks. Attempts should be made to design, plan, and prescribe roles rationally, so that the prescribed networks should account for the majority of the necessary, task-related relationships, and emergent networks should not be necessary for work. However, emergent networks are inevitable because prescribed networks are never perfect. Katz and Kahn (1966, pp. 80-81) proposed that "the inevitable conflict between collective task demands and individual needs" leads to "an informal structure among the people." This informal structure "frequently is in contradiction to the prescribing institutional paths for reaching those goals. One continuing problem for organization theory and practice is how to direct the enthusiasm and motivation of information groupings toward the accomplishment of the collective task."

Mechanistic configurations ought to spawn emergent networks primarily for expressive purposes, to fulfill the human needs suppressed by tight control and task differentiation. Communications within these emergent networks should be more affective than informational or influential. By contrast, the emergent networks in organic configurations should tend to combine information and influence related to task accomplishment. Decisions should be made by the numerous coalitions that crystallize around problems and tasks (Cyert and March, 1963; Thompson, 1967).

Organization development technologies can be adapted to uncovering and revising emergent networks (French and Bell, 1973; Huse, 1975; Tichy, 1980). For example, data can be collected describing influence, information, and friendship relationships. Sociometric data can be used to identify the people who should participate in confrontation meetings (Beckhard and Harris, 1977).

Transferring people through different assignments creates bridges between departments and work groups and adds affective relationships on top of task-related ones. Galbraith and Edstrom (1976, p.110) urged designers to use job transfers as an integrating tool: "We assumed that transfers behave differently with respect to their information collection behavior. That is, transferees communicate more often with colleagues in other units and have larger networks of contacts in the other unit." By transferring people—and thus widening their emergent network of contacts—an organization can more readily afford to have different organizational configurations and heterogeneous subcultures at different locations without losing the ability to coordinate. This approach however, is not likely to succeed merely through the transfer of people: An organization should plan transfers strategically and attend to linking the transferees into relevant networks. Much current practice regarding transfers is intuitive and the network weaving happens implicitly (Edstrom and Galbraith, 1977).

Other design strategies should be used to block the emergence of undesirable networks. Slack resources—including time and inventories—reduce needs for coordination and communication, so slack resources should be inserted where close relationships might be harmful (Galbraith, 1973). Physical distance also impedes communication; people who might engage in undesirable conflicts should be separated from each other, or people who have dangerous power should be isolated from the rest of the organization (Steele, 1973). In a mechanistic configuration, deviant power seekers who build private influence networks should be punished (Newman, 1979).

Organizational Processes Technologies

Network analysis has important potential applications to organizational change. It can be a diagnostic tool for planning changes and for measuring the effects of change efforts on both prescribed and emergent networks. Pettigrew (1975) proposed that internal change agents—and this probably applies to designers and managers in general—succeed if they can diagnose and manipulate an organization's political system.

In an organization which has sharp political controversies, designers should encourage open coalition formation, overt bargaining, and fair conflict. For example, one group of designers working with an academic medical center combined a traditional, functional structure with a matrix structure (Charnes *et al.*, 1981; Weisbord, 1974). The traditional academic departments carried on research and teaching, whereas the matrix structure legitimated coalitions for special projects and clinical training. Coalitions obtained budgets by negotiating contracts with departments and the head of the medical center, so bargaining was brought into the open. Norms of reciprocity and fair exchange were strengthened by strict monitoring of the process on the part of the dominant coalition, the Dean and department heads.

DECIDING WHICH CHANGE TECHNOLOGY TO USE WHEN

Now that some of the vast array of technologies available to the change manager have been presented, the difficult task of making a decision to use a particular technology must be faced. This section presents a set of guidelines for making informed and considered judgments on the choice of change technology.

Guideline 1—Create a Clear Link to Strategic Lever(s)

The first step in selecting a change technology is to have a clear understanding of the strategic lever for change which is the target—this refers to the particular component of the organizational model which is to be changed. Thus, if the change lever is the prescribed organization, then such change technologies as Galbraith's integrating mechanisms are appropriate. This was the situation in the SHS case where there was a need to make the prescribed organization more capable of handling greater complexity. In the TI case the OST was linked to the mission/strategy component.

Figure 11.9 provides a rating sheet for helping the decision makers in a change decision decide on the appropriate technology. The sheet forces the user to link a technology to a component of the organizational model and to indicate the change goal.

Guideline 2—Understand the Technology

The change technologies which are available to the change manager are often complex and constantly changing. It is essential that the

This sheet is to be used to record your decisions about which
techniques are best to use in carrying out a particular strategy.
In order to complete this activity you will need to refer to
the strategies which you developed in the previous activity.
Instructions:
1. Write in the goal toward which the strategy is aimed.
2. Write in the organizational model categories which would
   require change in order to carry out this strategy.
3. Decide which techniques are most likely to lead to the changes
   desired in each category. (Refer to Table 11.1 for some ideas).

Goal: *Increased Productivity*

Strategy
(Write in the name of
the category(ies) which
need to be changed to
achieve the above goal)

Techniques for creating change
(Next to each category fill
in the *one* or *two* techniques which will
most affect it.)

	1st Choice	2nd Choice

Figure 11.9   Selecting change techniques.

technology be well understood in terms of what it does, how it does
it, and the assumptions upon which it is built. In addition, each technology should be understood in terms of the following trade-offs:

1. Time it takes to use

2. Cost in dollars

3. Need for outside consultation

4. Learning contributions to the organization

5. Visible, immediate impact

Guideline 3—Clarify Depth and Target of Technology

Change technologies vary as to the depth with which they affect both individuals and the organization. A deep intervention at the individual level is one that affects not only behavior, but also attitudes and basic personality make-up. A deep intervention in an organization is one that fundamentally alters the character of the organizational components involved. A shallow, individually focused change technology would be the training of new procedures for handling a task the individual already carries out, whereas an intensive three-week encounter group with follow-up psychotherapy would be a deep intervention into individual style. Organizationally, an example of a deep intervention is the fundamental change that occurred at Texas Instruments in the mission/strategy component. This contrasts with situations in which the organization might just apply a change technology to fine tune an existing mission/strategy process.

The other aspect of depth of intervention is the degree to which the change technology alters more than just one system—technical, political, and cultural. Most have some ripple effect on the other systems, however, the judgment has to be made as to the likely size of the ripples. Obviously, change technologies that are targeted to alter all three and do so in a substantial manner are a deeper intervention into the organization than those that don't. The key is to explore these issues prior to selecting a final change technology. The change strategy should guide the decision on the desired depth of the intervention.

Guideline 4—Assess Necessary Conditions for the Use of Technology

Each change technology works well under a limited set of conditions. For example, job enrichment may not work well in a situation in which there is a high degree of management mistrust. The purpose of this guideline is to help make a systematic assessment of the organizational conditions necessary for the success of the considered technology.

Each technology considered for use should be assessed by organization members and a consultant if one is involved. The group should determine the necessary conditions for use of the technology. If those conditions do not exist in the organization, then another technology should be evaluated until one is found to be appropriate.

Guideline 5—Develop a Plan for Implementation

Finally, once the change technology is selected a specific action plan should be developed. It should state: who should participate, who is responsible for the management of the change technology, the time-table for activities, and a list of necessary special resources. This plan should be incorporated into the transition management plan which will be detailed in the following chapter.

CONCLUSION

This chapter introduced the notion of change technologies which are the specific tools available to change managers for carrying out change strategies. Change technologies were categorized in terms of their impact on the components of the organizational model. In addition, it was pointed out that special attention was required to assess the technology's impact on the technical, political, and cultural systems. A number of popular change technologies dealing with specific components of the model were presented. A newly developed set of social network technologies was also presented. These included network change technologies that focused on:

1. The environmental interface

2. The mission and strategy

3. The prescribed networks

4. The people

5. The emergent networks

Finally, a set of guidelines for strategy selection were presented:

1. Create a clear link to strategic lever(s)

2. Understand the technology

3. Clarify depth and target of technology

4. Assess the necessary conditions for use of technology

5. Develop a plan for implementation

Chapter Twelve

Transition Management

*Transition: A passing from one condition, place, activity, etc. to another (*Websters New World Dictionary*).*

INTRODUCTION

The changes referred to at AT&T throughout this book perhaps mark one of the most dramatic transformations of a U.S. company in recent history. As previously noted, the Bell system which was traditionally sheltered as a regulated telephone monopoly, began respositioning itself under the leadership of John DeButts, the chairman in the 1970s. The strategic shift was due to an analysis which led top management to conclude the long term survival and viability lay outside the telephone umbrella of a government regulated monopoly. The result was a new mission and strategy developed in the late 1970s to more broadly define the business as having a mission of being in the knowledge business, thus setting into motion a strategy which defined them as a supplier of all forms of communication systems including computerized services not traditionally related to the telephone. The strategy was articulated in the late 1970s to include: 1) a total reorganization of personnel so that there would be a telephone monopoly side of the business and a competitive "Baby Bell" side of the business, 2) total revamping of the marketing in the company, 3) plans to work with the regulatory environment to insure strategy implementation, and 4) plans to reorient the thinking of Bell employees to the new strategy and what it meant for their behavior. (*Business Week*, 6 November 1978).

In January of 1982 the above strategy at Bell was given a massive boost forward. As part of a settlement with the Justice Department, AT&T agreed to give up its 22 Bell System companies, worth $80 billion, two-thirds of the company's worth in 18 months. This leaves AT&T free to compete in the communication, data processing, and equipment manufacturing fields. At Bell, the transition is a high-stress paradoxical time. Many individuals throughout Bell experience both sides of the following emotional conflicts:

Fear	Hope
Sadness	Happiness
Anxiety	Relief
Pressure	Stimulation
Unclear	New direction
Loss of meaning	New meaning
Threat to self-esteem	New sense of value

These emotions are due to the nature of change which inevitably triggers an approach/avoidance tension. The avoidance side of the coin results in resistance to change at both the individual and organizational level. At the individual level, resistance is built upon the following: (1) habit resulting in inertia, (2) resource limitations, (3) commitment to a course of action due to sunk costs—not wanting to alter directions until the investment in old approaches is paid off, (4) threats to existing power and influence bases, (5) the pressure for conformity to norms, and (6) the lack of a climate supporting change.

Because of the inevitable resistance to change found in all organizations during times of strategic reorientation strategic change management requires a set of tools for technically, politically, and culturally managing the transition. This chapter provides such tools.

SOME CHARACTERISTICS OF CHANGE

Change requires exchanging something old for something new. It is important to recognize that all change requires exchange. People have to unlearn and relearn, exchange power and status, and exchange old norms and values for new norms and values. These changes are often frightening and threatening while at the same time potentially stimulating and providers of new hope. One must recognize the nature of exchanges: there are costs and benefits which must ultimately balance in favor of the benefits side. This can mean that transition managers have to help the balancing by reducing expected costs and enhancing expected benefits. At the simplest level, organizations sometimes provide monetary benefits for people to make changes. They also increase the costs for some by firing them.

TRANSITION MANAGEMENT

Strategic change management involves three distinct responsibilities: (1) the development of an overall strategic change plan; (2) the selection of appropriate change technologies for carrying out the strategy, and (3) the development of a transition or implementation plan. Figure 12.1 presents these three areas as the present state, desired state, and transi-

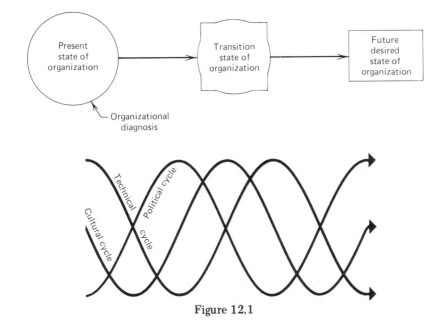

Figure 12.1

tion state. This framework is based on the work of Beckhard and Harris (1977).

The transition state consists of predicting, channeling, guiding, and altering the technical, political, and cultural cycles in order to arrive at the desired state strategy.

AT&T's hope is that their desired state strategy is implemented by the end of the 1980s, at which time technical, political, and cultural uncertainty will all be relatively low. In order for AT&T to arrive at that desired state the three cycles will have to be managed through times of high uncertainty.

Figure 12.1 diagramatically portrays the transition state as one in which technical, political, and cultural adjustments are made in the organization over time. These adjustments represent forces that carry the organization through time and are cyclical in nature. The pattern of forces varies from organization to organization. However, there are common and predictable elements: (1) they do oscillate and have a tendency to regress to the mean; and (2) they tend to set up counter-reactions, that is, an extreme technical focus represented by a peak will trigger the political and/or cultural cycle. Successful transition management requires an ability to predict, channel, and guide these cycles.

At AT&T, transition management will require change managers to, at times, be political builders of coalitions, power brokers, and influence manipulators to cope with the political cycle. At other times, change managers will be solving technical problems, relying on "scientific" data and principles to cope with the technical cycle. At other times the change manager will be a missionary introducing new values and beliefs to manage the cultural cycle. Finally, the change manager may be faced with managing all three cycles simultaneously. Therein lies the difficulty and the need for change management to be built on a deep awareness of organizational cycles.

Texas Instruments went through a similar transition state as it worked toward the implementation of its OST structure and process. Initially there was a trigger from the environment regarding technological change and competition which resulted first in a strong commitment on the part of management to deal with the production problem—making technical adjustments and developing the desired state strategic plan for OST. Soon after this technical focus there was a great deal of political uncertainty. The political cycle had been triggered and required that managerial attention and energy be devoted to the development of a monolithic dominant coalition. Anti-OST factions were not tolerated; one had to be supportive of the OST approach or else risk being fired or demoted. Once the political system became consolidated and the political cycle receded, the cultural cycle peaked. Cultural uncertainty developed because of the conflict between the traditional and emerging TI cultures. In order to alter the culture, a great deal of managerial attention centered on hiring people who fit in with TI's new culture and in socialization through training and organization development activities. The aim was to reduce cultural uncertainty by developing a culturally homogeneous work force. There was pressure not only for developing close working relationships but also for friendly relationships so as to increase the positive reinforcement of TI culture both at work and socially.

It is interesting to note that transitions are never over. TI provides a good example of this. As of the summer of 1982, TI was in the process of making changes to overcome recent business problems attributable in part to the OST system. The political and cultural systems appear to have been too mechanistic thus contributing to non-responsive and non-innovative decision making. The need is there for TI to start a new transition.

As indicated in Chapter 7, transition management is analogous to the physician working with a patient during the treatment phase. During this time, the treatment involves managing both the change in any one system—circulatory, respiratory, etc.—as well as the interdependent changes. As in medicine, the systems—technical, political, and cultural —are loosely coupled, making it hard to predict the exact nature of the interdependence or impact. Therefore, in transition management, intervention activities must proceed with an experimental orientation and a process for continual adjustment.

The guidelines for transition management are:

1. Review the current state diagnosis and the desired state change strategy to determine the technical, political, and cultural adjustments required by the change.

2. Project the sequence of cycles. When will the technical, political, and cultural cycles peak?

3. Plan for unbundling and uncoupling the three systems in order to manage the transition in each.

4. Plan for managing the transitions in each cycle—technical transition, political transition, and cultural transition.

5. Plan for recoupling the systems. How will the technical, political, and cultural systems mesh in the desired state organization?

REVIEW THE CURRENT AND DESIRED STATE

The first step in the transition management process is to develop an understanding of the technical, political, and cultural changes implied in the shift from the current to desired state.

The following changes will take place at AT&T. The technical change strategy will move from a mechanistic, stable, functional organization to an organic marketing and innovation-driven organization. There will be a great need for complex information processing as the organization competes in the marketplace and attempts to develop new products and services to meet market demand, and its major new rival, IBM. This will not be an easy task as "under a shelter of government regulation, AT&T has maintained its significant edge in size, but competition has made IBM sharper, leaner and richer (Business Week, 6 November 1978; p. 118)." In addition, AT&T will be competing with Honeywell, NCR, Burroughs, Sperry Univac, and Digital Equipment.

The technical change involves a new organizational design, a shift from a functional organization built around divisions for traffic management, plant supervision, maintenance, and installation, to one market service focused structure, one focused on business services, one on residential services, and one on network services. The reorganization is massive, it will involve giving up 22 Bell System companies, divesting itself of about 700,000 Bell employees who will go with the 22 companies.

Other technical changes will involve developing managers to have more organic styles and capabilities to fit with the new strategy. The top Bell managers will attend seminars on the corporation policy and how to manage and market in Bell's new environment.

The political change strategy involves an almost total transformation of a current state politically mechanistic system to a new desired state which will be different but also quite politically mechanistic. That is, those who controlled the goals, got promoted, and were rewarded in the past, will not, with few exceptions, be the politically dominant ones in the future. The historical track to top management at AT&T was through the operating companies. This will no longer exist. Even those who go with the new AT&T face a changed set of criteria for success. The future political strategy shows marketing and innovative types exercising the lion's share of power. As will be discussed, this political change will not be an easy trick. If it was tough at relatively tiny Texas Instruments—taking a number of years with high political uncertainty— one can imagine how much more the uncertainty will be at Bell where hundreds of thousands of people's careers are threatened. An immediate political issue is who gets to go with AT&T and who stays with the operating companies.

The cultural strategy at Bell is to replace the current homogeneous culture characterized by service orientation, tradition, regulatory conservativism, and stable financial returns with a culture dominated by market driven values: especially innovative, aggressive salesmanship and profitability. The culture will need to support a new type of managerial behavior. There will be increased conflict during the transition as the old and new culture clash.

In order to develop a new culture, the reward system will have to be altered dramatically, as will the hiring criteria and the training and development programs. This massive cultural transformation will take at least five years to accomplish.

Sequencing the Cycles of Change

Cycles are triggered by two sets of forces. First, they are triggered by environmental and technological changes, goal shifts, means of work shifts, and people shifts. Second, they are triggered by each other. As was pointed out in previous chapters, it is important to analyze which of the cycles—technical, political, or cultural—peaks first. When there is simultaneous peaking of the cycles, it is up to management to determine which to deal with first. In the SHS case, even though technical uncertainty was high, the management chose to focus on the political uncertainty.

Regardless of the level of uncertainty in each cycle, management makes a choice as to how to expend its attention and energy. Thus, the SHS managers could have spent their time attempting to fix the technical difficulties rather than bargaining for federal bail-out money. Had they done that, they might have missed getting any federal support. On the other hand, by going for the bail-out money, they ended up with an organization riddled with unfixed technical problems.

The change managers must make decisions for the transition regarding the sequence of cycles and hence the managerial attention. At Texas Instruments, the sequence was technical, political, and then cultural; this appears to be the case unfolding at AT&T.

Plan for Unbundling the Three Cycles.   For purposes of planning the transition, the three cycles should be analyzed separately and specific action steps designed to deal with each. For example, AT&T has a set of activities which are designed to deal with the technical problems of the transition—new marketing programs, new R&D efforts, redesigns of the organization which support the market focus, and others. In addition, the political cycle will require managing. This may result in such programs as outplacement work for those managers who cannot support the change. Rewards will be allocated in new ways to reflect the new opportunity structure. The cultural transition plan will involve new hiring practices, development programs, and reward and promotion criteria.

Managing the Transition

One very important way to think about transitions is in terms of their impact on social networks. Individuals are embedded in complex relational webs. The breaking of old relationships and the creating of new relationships involves a great deal of personal, interpersonal, and organizational turbulence.

Figure 12.2 provides us with an oversimplified network version of what occurred in a health center which moved from a discipline organizational prescribed network to a matrix structure. In the current state, the organization is a traditional-looking health structure with each discipline chief reporting to a director of the health center. In such an organization decision-making influence from one discipline to another had to flow through the hierarchy. The director was the integrating mechanism. Thus when the pediatricians wanted to change the way nurses did their work-ups, they had to get the director involved.

Consequently, patients are treated in a fragmented and often contradictory manner. The organization decided they would create interdisciplinary health teams. With the help of an organizational consultant, Richard Beckhard, from MIT's Sloan School of Management, it was decided that the desired state should be a matrix structure with team members reporting to their discipline chiefs (nursing, pediatrics, internal medicine, social work) for quality of care and professional development purposes and to a unit administrator for the day-to-day coordination of patient care. The desired state prescribed networks look quite different from those of the current state in Figure 12.2. In the desired state, there are direct influence links from the chiefs to all of the administrators and to all of the other chiefs—it is a fully connected influ-

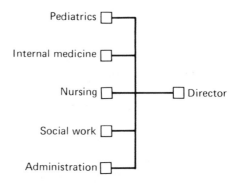

Functional organization

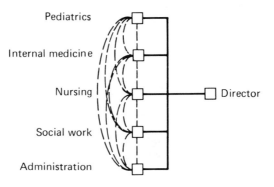

Task force organization

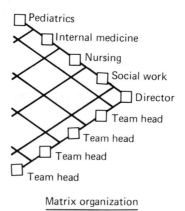

Matrix organization

———— = Prescribed influence network   — — — — = Formation of new links

Figure 12.2

ence network. The director of the health center is the tie breaker when there is an unresolved conflict, but the purpose of the matrix is to push difference management and decision making down to the team level, rather than allow it to flow up the hierarchy.

In order to move to the desired state, the organization must pass through a transition period during which new relationships can be formed and old ones ended. The transition phase included the use of task forces made up of administrators and representatives from each of the disciplines meeting regularly to coordinate their work. These task forces began the process of weaving a new set of social networks necessary for the matrix to work.

Figure 12.2 is too simplified to be of use by itself. We can begin to complicate matters by focusing on the individual level. Figure 12.3 provides an example of what the transition to the matrix might have meant for one of the participants in the process. The current state shows the individual linked to ten individuals, some directly and some indirectly. The desired state shows these same individuals linked in a totally new configuration. In order to move to this new state, the individual goes through a transition (see Figure 12.3) during which time all but one of the individual's major work relationships are changing. This means breaking old relationships with some and forming new ones with others.

This process occurred for all individuals in the health center as it moved through the transition. It means that there were literally hundreds of network linkages undergoing change during the transition. The

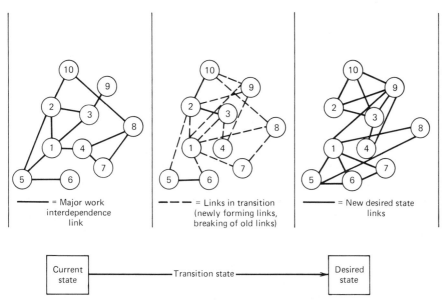

Figure 12.3 An individual in transition

picture can be complicated more when the networks are further dissected into changes in influence networks, changes in informational networks, and changes in friendship networks.

The implications for transition management are profound. Social networks make up the fabric of the technical, political, and cultural systems. The technical system is largely held together by work-related informational exchanges among members of the organization. The political system is made up of influence exchanges among members of the organization. The cultural system is held together by friendship exchanges and reinforcement of values among organizational members. In order to change an organization, the networks must be dealt with in each of these three systems.

The adjustments which take place include breaking and reforming the following network linkages: (1) information links—who I get information from and who I transmit it to, (2) influence links—whom I am influenced by and who I influence, (3) affective links—who is friendly toward me and who I am friendly toward. The major determinants of changes in information links are shifts in the task demands of the technical system. The major determination of a change in an influence network is a shift in the balance of power among organization coalitions in the political system. Finally, affective links are most affected by changes in the culture of the organization.

Network Transitions. The transition period involves the simultaneous management of maintaining certain relationships, creating new relationships, and breaking off some old relationships. To add to the complexity, the pattern of maintaining, breaking, or creating networks varies for information networks, influence networks, and affective networks.

Thus, in our health care center as it moves from a discipline structure to a matrix structure one might find a pediatrician faced with the following network transitions: First, the information exchanges with the chief of pediatrics would change. Under the matrix structure there would be little or no information exchange regarding the clinical delivery of care to a particular patient, thus, an information linkage would be broken. There would be some information exchange regarding general criteria for the quality of care and for professional development. New information links would be formed with the other members of the team, the nurse practitioner, the family health worker, and the internist, as the task demands interdisciplinary coordinated care. While the information links are in transition, so are the influence networks. The chief of pediatrics no longer has day-to-day influence over the pediatrician who now reports to an administrative unit head in charge of coordinating care and overseeing productivity. This means breaking the old link to the chief of pediatrics and forming a new link to the administrator. Also, influence links are forged laterally with other members of the team. The decision-making influence is less hierarchical within disciplines than it is lateral, among disciplines.

Finally, the affective links will change. The pediatric group's increased work interaction with the administrative unit heads will encourage cross-discipline friendships to develop.

These are the links which ideally should be altered in this transition. Changing these relationships, as was the case in the health center, is difficult and often needs to be facilitated via the use of various behavioral science team-building activities as well as the use of reward and control systems to reinforce the creation of necessary linkages. Once the new links are formed they then have to be constantly reinforced.

Figure 12.4 presents a framework for identifying the transition network changes that must be managed. The first step in developing a transition plan is to identify the network changes by answering the questions posed in Figure 12.4.

The key to mapping out the network transitions is to start with the change strategy developed in the first step of the change planning pro-

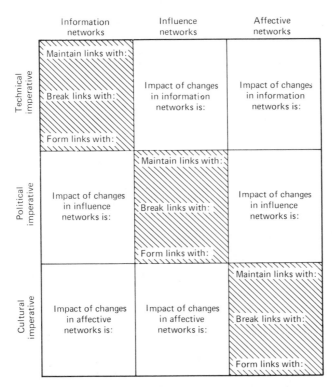

Figure 12.4 Networks in transition

cess and identify the technical, political, and cultural imperatives resulting from the change strategy. In the health center example the technical imperative was a set of networks supporting the dual authority matrix design. The political imperative was a set of influence networks to create a balance of power allowing the disciplines to be controlled by other than a discipline hierarchy. The cultural imperative was a set of influence networks to create a balance of power allowing the disciplines to be controlled by other than a discipline hierarchy. The cultural imperative was for teams to become a source of affective exchange and distinctive team identification.

The steps for using the networks in a transition framework are:

1. Identify the technical imperatives reflected in the change strategy.

2. List the key information links which need to be maintained from the current state to the desired state, the key information links which need to be broken or ended, and the key information links which need to be formed.

3. Indicate the expected impact of changes in the information networks on the influence networks.

4. Indicate the expected impact of changes in the information networks on the affective networks.

5. Identify the political imperative reflected in the change strategy.

6. List the key influence links that need to be maintained from the current state to the desired state, the key influence links that need to be broken or ended, and the key influence links that need to be formed.

7. Indicate the expected impact of changes in the influence networks on the information networks.

8. Indicate the expected impact of changes in the influence networks on the affected networks.

9. Identify the cultural imperative reflected in the change strategy.

10. List the key affective links which need to be maintained from the current state to the desired state, the key affective links which need to be broken or ended, and the key affective links which need to be formed.

11. Indicate the expected impact of changes in the affective networks on the information networks.

12. Indicate the expected impact of changes in the affective networks on the influence networks.

RESISTANCE TO CHANGE
AND TRANSITION MANAGEMENT GUIDELINES

By defining the transition state with a distinct set of organizational conditions from the current and future states, it becomes easier to think about its governance and management as requiring a special structure and system. Beckhard and Harris (1977) propose a number of alternative management approaches to the transition state. The alternatives, along with the costs and benefits of each, include:

1. *CEO as Project Manager.* The CEO becomes the transition manager with direct responsibility for coordination and implementation. The advantages of this is that it provides the necessary power and resources for making strategic changes. The disadvantage is that many CEOs are too overburdened to do the job adequately. Often the solution is to manage the transition with CEO as project manager along with other mechanisms.

2. *A Project Manager.* Another approach is to assign a project manager other than the CEO to manage the transition. This is usually a senior manager who operates out of the office of the president. The advantage is that the individual can often spend more time than the CEO can. The disadvantage is that the individual does not have the same power base as the CEO and can get caught in competitive political struggles with peers.

The project managers are then put in charge of some sort of transition structure. The alternatives include:

3. *Use of Existing Hierarchy.* Official bodies can be used to manage the transition. The advantage is that the structure exists and can often be working more quickly than other alternatives. The weakness with the use of the hierarchy is that it sets power-based negotiation, not problem solving. The hierarchy, with its direct boss/subordinate relationships, will not facilitate creative, innovative problem solving because of the inherent worries and scheming for future career mobility.

4. *Representatives of Constituencies.* Another structure for the transition is to select representatives of different types of people in the organization, such as representatives of functions, of levels, of minority groups, of union and nonunion members. The advantage of this structure is that it provides a varied and broad input into the transition management process. The disadvantage is the diversity and complexity of selecting members and deciding who should be representative of whom.

5. *Natural Leaders (Network Stars).* A committee can be created from among the network stars—those people with strong linkages to large constituencies. These are emergent network leaders who can represent large coalitions. The advantage is that this committee represents a

very important set of power figures whose support is often required to make the transition successful. On the other hand, by legitimizing these emergent leaders it creates the potential for conflict with the existing hierarchy who may feel threatened, and I might add, with good justification.

6. *Kitchen Cabinet.* This represents another version of the natural leaders, with the distinction being that this is the informal group linked to the CEO and often not representing any constituency. The advantage of using this group is that it merely recognizes the reality of who is already guiding strategic decisions in the organization. The danger is that by turning it into a committee, it legitimizes it and undermines the hierarchy.

7. *Diagonal Slice.* The final alternative is to take a diagonal slice of the organization which represents both different functions or areas and different levels. It combines the power hierarchy by having multiple levels represented, and different interest groups by having different functions and areas represented. It avoids power bargaining by avoiding boss/subordinate pairs. It works well if the selection is done in such a way that the higher level people will not stifle the juniors, and the juniors are confident enough to speak up.

The first step in the transition management process is to set up the structure using some combination of these project managers and committee structures. The next set of issues relate to how to manage the transition.

Technical Transition Management

The transition plans for coping with the changes in the technical area are designed to deal with resistances in both the individual and the organization. The individual resists change in the technical area for the following reasons:

1. *Resistance Due to Habit.* Habit and inertia cause task-related resistance to change. Individuals who have always done things one way may not be politically or normatively resistant to change, but rather, unaware of alternatives and locked into old patterns of behavior.

2. *Resistance Due to Fear of the Unknown.* Not knowing what a new job or set of tasks will entail can create anxiety and fear in some people.

3. *Resistance Due to Absence of Skills.* Individuals may resist change because they do not possess the skills required to carry out the tasks in the desired state.

The organization resists change due to the following reasons:

4. *Organization Predictability.* Organizations are generally structured to ensure predictability and reduce uncertainty: this sets into mo-

tion organizational inertia and structural habit. This form of organizational resistance parallels the individual resistance due to habit.

5. *Resistance Due to Sunk Costs.* Even when a rational calculation of the costs and future benefits of a change are worked out, organizations often get hooked on a sunk cost mentality which prevents them from cutting their losses and reinvesting in a better future alternative. Chrysler Corporation may have been guilty of this resistance in its inability to deal earlier with sunk costs in big autos.

Process Plan for Managing the Technical Transition. Beckhard and Harris (1977) present an outline for the technical aspects of a transition. The process plan includes a statement of what, when, and how to manage the transition. It is flexible and reversible. It has the following characteristics:

(a) It is purposeful—the activities are clearly linked to the change goals and priorities.

(b) It is task specific—the types of activities involved are clearly identified.

(c) It is integrated—the discrete activities are linked to each other.

(d) It is temporal—it is in time sequences.

(e) It is adaptable—contingency plans and ways of adapting to unexpected forces are developed.

(f) It is agreed upon by the dominant coalition(s).

(g) It is cost effective in terms of time and people.

Figure 12.5 presents a framework for summarizing the information network transition plan which is part of the process plan. Note that the plans's basic logic is to build off the earlier network transition framework in more detail; the major addition is a clear set of action steps.

In addition to the information network plan, the process plan includes a plan for the development of skills and resources necessary for

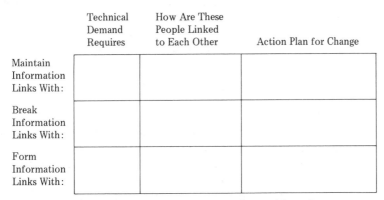

	Technical Demand Requires	How Are These People Linked to Each Other	Action Plan for Change
Maintain Information Links With:			
Break Information Links With:			
Form Information Links With:			

Figure 12.5 Information network transition plan

carrying out the new task. Therefore, resistance due to the absence of skills might be handled through skill-training programs, resistance due to the fear of the unknown might be alleviated with job preview simulations, video tape, or actual job experiences.

The technical transition plan must then be accompanied by political and cultural transition plans.

POLITICAL TRANSITION MANAGEMENT

Major structural changes, or even the possibilities of them, have political consequences. Innovations are likely to threaten existing parts of the working community. New resources may be created and appear to fall within the jurisdiction of a department of individuals who had previously not been claimant in a particular area. This department or its principal representative may see this as an opportunity to increase his power, status, and rewards in the organization. Others may see their interests threatened by the change, and needs for security of the maintenance of power may provide the impetus for resistance. In all these ways new political action is released and ultimately the existing distribution of power is endangered (Pettigrew, 1975; p. 192).

Resistances in the political area represent conflict and differences over the allocation of resources and power in the organization. For individuals, the resistances are due to:

1. *Resistance Due to Need for Power.* People vary in the degree to which they desire power as an end in itself. Often there is resistance to change due to the fear that it will mean less power to someone who strives to accumulate power for its own sake.

2. *Resistance Due to Overdependence on Others.* Change can be resisted by overly power-dependent people. Individuals can become locked into a more powerful person's orbit of influence and resist change out of fear of being set adrift. The overdependence can create problems for the more powerful person who wants to leave the low power people behind when they move to higher power positions in the organization.

3. *Resistance Due to Competition for Power.* Individuals can also resist change they perceive will unleash competition for power which they would like to avoid.

At the organizational level, resistance to change in the political area can be due to:

1. *Resistance Due to Threats to Powerful Coalitions.* The change may alter the strategic contingencies in the organization, making a new group more important to the future success of the organization and thus threatening the old dominant coalition. The old dominant coalition may resist change due to this threat of a power redistribution.

2. *Resistance Due to Resource Limitations.* As indicated in the technical area, the organization may resist change due to resource limitation. Part of this resistance may be tied with that of the technical area. It also may be tied with the political. Scarce resources result in political bargaining over who gets what share of the pie. It can also result in impasses and overall organizational resistance to change.

3. *Resistance Due to Sunk Costs.*

Managers resist strategic reorientation in order to retain power and status, and they try to persuade themselves and others that their strategies are appropriate. Crises induce skilled personnel to depart, financial backers to desert and suppliers to withhold credit. Anticipating such problems, managers may launch propaganda campaigns that deny the existence of crises (Starbuck *et al.*, 1978).

As with resource limitations, sunk costs can create both technical and political resistance to change. Politically, the dynamic created by sunk costs involves an attempt to save face and maintain political advantage. Writing off costs sunk in a new product or service leaves the individual or group open to attack that they made a mistake and thus it becomes a potential lever for undermining their power base.

Commitment Plan for Managing the Political Transition. Beckhard and Harris (1977) outline a plan for managing the political aspects of the transition. The commitment plan is a series of steps devised to secure the support of subsystems which are vital to the change efforts. The plan includes the following elements:

(a) Identify target individuals and groups whose commitment is needed.

(b) Define the critical mass needed to ensure the effective implementation.

(c) Develop a plan for getting the commitment from the critical mass.

(d) Develop a monitoring system to assess programs.

The first step is to do an analysis of key influential people. Determine their current attitudes toward the desired change. Then determine where they need to be attitudinally in order to successfully carry out the change. The gap indicates the target of your transition plan. Figure 12.6 provides a sample of how to carry out this type of analysis. Note that the third step is a network analysis of how the key influentials interrelate.

As with the technical process plan, one part of the plan is a network plan. Figure 12.7 presents the same framework now used for influence networks.

A diagnostic tool and set of action guiding principles for managing the political transition when starting an organization development (OD) effort were developed by Sashkin and Jones (1979). Figure 12.8 pre-

POLITICAL ANALYSIS FOR CHANGE

Names [Example]	Strongly Against -2	Moderately Against -1	Neutral O	Moderately Supportive +1	Strongly Supportive +2
John Doe		✓————————→ X			

STEPS: 1. Plot where individuals currently are with regard to desired change. (✓ = current)

2. Plot where individuals need to be (X = desired) in order to successfully accomplish desired change—identify gaps between current and desired.

3. Indicate how individuals are linked to each other, draw lines to indicate an influence link using an arrow (►) to indicate who influences whom.

4 Plan action steps for closing gaps.

Figure 12.6

sents the diagnostic framework. The action steps for each of the decision tree points of Figure 12.8 follow.

Decision Point 1 (If No). If the power and resources of these individuals are not supporting the transition effort, then the following actions are recommended:

Analyze why they are not supporting it. Resistance due to technical and/or political factors? Lack of knowledge of change effort? Other factors?

Develop an action plan for getting them involved and supportive; make use of the influentials who are already involved.

	Political Demand Requires	How Are These People Linked to Each Other	Actions for Change
Maintain Influence Links with :			
Break Influence Links with:			
Form Influence Links with:			

Figure 12.7 Influence network transition plan

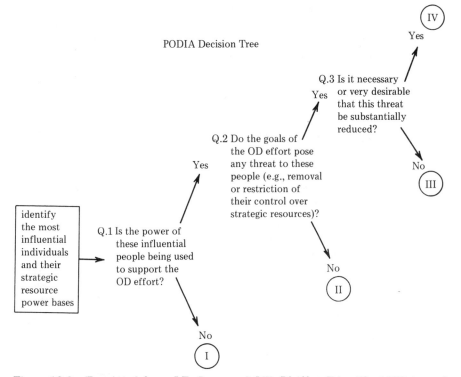

PODIA Decision Tree

Figure 12.8   (Reprinted from J.E. Jones and J.W. Pfeiffer, Eds., *The 1979 Annual Handbook for Group Facilitators.* San Diego, CA: University Associates, 1979. Used with permission.

Decision Point 2 (If No).   If the goals of the change effort do not pose any threat to the influentials then the following actions are recommended:

Analyze whether all their key resources are being used to support the change. If they are not, then develop a plan to get more commitment.

Develop ways to encourage their involvement in the change effort, including more contact with them, getting them to take actions publically, etc.

Decision Point 3 (If Decision Point 2 is Yes).   Is it necessary to reduce the threat posed by the change effort? If not, then the following actions are recommended:

Determine who else controls resources which could support the change effort.

Develop action plans for broadening the base of support by involving people with additional resources in the change effort.

Develop ways of minimizing potential interference from nonsupportive influentials by isolating them. Begin preparing countervailing forces among other influentials and developing face-saving ways for them to change their positions and support the change effort.

Decision Point 3 (If Yes). If a threat is posed by the change effort and it is important to reduce the threat or minimize the impact of the threatened influentials, then the following actions can be taken:

Analyze these individuals to thoroughly understand their position, why they are threatened, what the political balance of power is, etc.

Try to develop a cooperative approach to dealing with them. Look for ways to make it in their interest to support the change by using other influentials, altering the political stakes, etc.

Two transition management activities which help deal with political differences are Beckhard's (1969) confrontation meeting and intergroup confrontation meetings.

The confrontation meeting can be used to put problems on the table for discussion, negotiation, and action. The meeting, which generally takes a day, involves generating information about major problems, analyzing the problems, making action plans for dealing with the problems, and determining who has political responsibility for particular problems. The steps involved in the process are:

1. *Climate Setting (45–60 Minutes).* The top manager introduces the meeting by stating the goals and setting the ground rules, which include: open and free discussion, direct above-board negotiation of differences, and a commitment to action. A consultant is usually present to facilitate the meeting, although it is important that the meeting be seen as run by the top manager and that his or her power is behind it.

2. *Information Collecting (One Hour).* Small groups of individuals (five to seven) meet to generate a list of problems which are hindering the transition management. The only rule is that no boss/subordinate pairs are in the same groups. The charge to the groups is: Think of yourself as an individual with needs and goals. Also think as a person concerned about the total organization. What are the obstacles, blockages to carrying out the change strategy developed by the organization, what different conditions would make the transition effective? Each group prepares a summary report to share with the total group.

3. *Information Sharing (One Hour).* Reports from each group present the summary of its work to the total group and are posted on flip charts. The obstacles are then categorized by the leader into a few major categories, such as communication problems, resources problems, power struggles, problems with top management, etc.

4. *Priority Setting and Group Action Planning (One Hour).* There is usually a break before this step so that the top manager can categor-

ize the problems. The list of problems along with the categories is generally typed and duplicated during this break so that all members have copies. The total group is now reorganized back into work teams. Each group is headed by its real organizational boss. The groups are given the task of:

(a) Identifying the problems related to their area's difficulties with the transition.

(b) Identifying priorities for action—which blockages they can do something about—and making action plans for their group.

(c) Identifying problems they think should be dealt with by top management.

(d) Identifying problems they think should be dealt with by other groups: Why, and which groups?

(e) Identifying how they will communicate the outcome of the meeting to their own subordinates.

5. *Follow-Up by Top Management (One to Three Hours).* The top group gathers up the reports of the work teams. It meets to plan action steps for their own issues and to determine that the groups dealt with all the identified problems. This is followed by a general follow-up meeting (on another day) at which all the work teams are present. The top group reports the plan of action for dealing with blockages; it may include plans for some work groups, such as marketing and production, to meet separately to negotiate their differences.

The confrontation meeting is a relatively fast and efficient way to manage political resistance to the transition. All the problems are brought to the surface and top management exerts a great deal of influence to ensure that they are dealt with openly. This plan works as long as the political differences are not so great that making them explicit will explode the situation.

The intergroup confrontation meeting is another useful activity for dealing with political blockages of a transition. The process is designed to cut into the conflict escalating tendency of intergroup conflicts by (1) getting differences and stereotypes on the table; (2) looking for common groups; and (3) developing mechanisms for dealing with differences.

An example of such an intervention took place at Philips Industries, in Scandinavia, where I was confronted with managers from four different Nordic countries who were having trouble coordinating planning, career, and managerial decisions, due to intergroup problems related to nationality. Initially, the managers at the workshop denied holding any national stereotypes and said they were "four happy Nordic brothers." However, once asked to go off into national groupings to generate a list of stereotypes they held toward the other groups, they found it quite easy and natural to do. After sharing the lists with a great deal of tense laughter, it became clear that the four happy brothers also had to come to grips with the underlying sibling rivalry expressed in and exacerbated by the stereotypes. It was evident that staffing and career decisions at a managerial level were as much influenced by nationality as by managerial competence. The group ended up by identifying areas where stereotyping was dysfunctional for the organization, and began to devise action steps to manage these problems.

This approach is another direct, open way to handle political blockages to transitions. It is, however, predicated on the existence of a win/win solution to political differences. This is not always the case and thus there are other approaches to political transition management. If this method is not appropriate, it may be necessary to treat influentials as the enemy—that is, in a win/lose battle for control. If this is true, then Saul Alinsky's guidelines for community organizers provide action planning help:

> Power is not only what you have but what the enemy thinks you have.
>
> Never go outside the experience of your people (the result is confusion, fear, and retreat).
>
> Wherever possible, go outside the experience of the enemy.
>
> Make the enemy live up to their own book of rules.
>
> Ridicule is man's most potent weapon.
>
> A good tactic is one that your people enjoy.
>
> A tactic that drags on too long becomes a drag.
>
> The threat is usually more terrifying than the thing itself.
>
> The major premise for tactics is the development of operations that will maintain a constant pressure upon the opposition.
>
> If you push a negative hard and deep enough, it will break through its counterside.
>
> The price of a successful attack is a construction alternative.
>
> Pick the target, freeze it, personalize it, and polarize it. (Alinsky, 1971; pp. 127–130).

Alinsky's tactics are very risky, as they can turn a potentially cooperative situation into a win/lose competition. Once someone or a group is treated as the enemy they become the enemy. The process is a self-fulfilling one. Thus, the key is to make certain that all cooperative avenues have been exhausted prior to using tactics based on Alinsky's guidelines.

Cultural Transition Plan

The organization's culture is the most elusive element of the change process and often the most difficult to change. The culture embodies people's underlying beliefs, values, and norms; thus, managing shifts in culture requires tactics which alter basic aspects of the individual.

Resistance to cultural change is due to the following:

1. *Resistance Due to Selective Perception (Cultural Filters).* Change can be resisted because of the cognitive frame of reference held by people in a particular culture which prevents them from perceiving important aspects of the change. For example, in a highly authoritarian culture, the introduction of participatory management techniques may be perceived as a sign of weak, ineffectual leadership, whereas the same behavior in another culture may be perceived as a sign of strength. The transitions which are taking place at AT&T are being resisted by employees due to the cultural filters which make it hard for them to perceive innovative marketing opportunities; their culture had made them service oriented to a market that they monopolize.

2. *Resistance Due to Values and Beliefs.* The Protestant work ethic built on the Calvinistic view of hard work and delay of gratification in this materialistic world was ascribed by Max Weber (1947) to be responsible for the rise of capitalism and the drive for upward mobility. Such a belief and value system supported changes which required sacrifice and hard work. Competing value systems include hedonistic, here and now gratification of wants and desires, or humanistic beliefs in freedom, individuality, feelings, and a focus on deep interpersonal relationships. Thus, depending on how dissonant the cultural change is to the prevailing culture, there may be resistance.

3. *Resistance Due to Security by Regression to Past.* One way to cope with rapid cultural change is to regress into past cultural beliefs. Thus, one way of explaining the upsurge in fundamentalist religious movements among youth is by claiming their regression to past cultural beliefs is a way of coping with a rapidly changing culture. This can occur as well in organizations when new value systems are introduced, for example, during the introduction of an aggressive entrepreneurial culture into a traditional bank. Many of the traditional bankers regress to even more conservative "stodgy" behavior as a way of coping with the changing culture.

4. *Resistance Due to Conformity to Norms.* Change requires someone or some group to deviate from the norms and help set up a counterculture. In so doing, they must resist a great deal of social pressure to conform to the norms. Thus, when managers of Union Carbide went away to the National Training Laboratories in the early 1960s to two-week sensitivity training programs and returned to the organization with a new set of norms about openness, dealing with feelings, and providing feedback, they met extreme pressure to conform to the traditional norms of restricted openness about such matters. The change was resisted so strongly that some people lost jobs and the culture was not changed.

5. *Resistance Due to Climate for Change.* Duncan (1972) proposes three components of a climate for change: (1) a perceived need for

change among organizational members, (2) the members' openness to change, and (3) the member's perceptions about the organization's capability for change. Resistance may be due to a low rating by organization members on any or some combination of these factors.

The Cultural Transition Plan. Managing a cultural transition requires a plan similar to the political commitment plan. The elements of the plan are:

1. Identifying the cultural values and beliefs which require changing.

2. Identify the gatekeepers of the organization's culture, who are the most important guardians of the current culture, and who will be most critical in supporting a new culture.

3. Define the critical mass of the cultural gatekeepers needed to change the culture.

4. Develop a plan for getting them to feel a need for cultural change and then start working toward such a change.

5. Develop a monitoring system to support the change process.

As with the previous two plans, one part of the transition plan is the network plan. In the case of the cultural change, it is important to identify those elements of the culture that need to be maintained, eliminated, and introduced. Once this is done (see Figure 12.9), it must be decided who the key gatekeepers are for these elements. Then a specification needs to be made regarding with whom these gatekeepers must build links for changing the culture and what actions must be taken to change their values and beliefs.

Some of the appropriate cultural change techniques include the use

	Affective Demand Requires	How Are These People Linked to Each Other	Actions for Change
Maintain Affective Links with:			
Break Affective Links with:			
Form Affective Links with:			

Figure 12.9   Cultural network transition plan

of data feedback (surveys, etc.) to help create a felt need for change. For example, showing through a survey that authoritarian, nonpartici-patory managerial style is leading to high levels of dissatisfaction and turnover can be used to create a felt need for change in a managerial style. Other activities include the use of training and educational activi-ties to open people up to alternative cultural values. This has been espe-cially true in the use of human relations training, including the use of encounter groups, to help individuals experiment with new values and norms.

The explicit use of role models can also be important. If a key set of gatekeepers, such as the management committee, begins to operate with a different culture, a model is created for others in the organization.

DEVELOPING AN INTEGRATED TRANSITION MANAGEMENT PLAN

The previous section described the transition management planning pro-cess as made up of three distinct sets of activities: a technical plan, a political plan, and a cultural plan. These plans must be integrated in a real change setting, as they will be played out simultaneously. Often one area is more dominant than another, as described by the change cycles presented earlier in this chapter, nonetheless the three transition plans require coordination and integration.

Case Illustration: Pacific Mega Bank.   The first case illustration is of a large money-center bank, one of the 10 largest in the country. Pacific Mega Bank had just completed a two-year strategic planning activity which resulted in a strategic reorientation for major portions of the bank. It included strategic commitments to new markets, including a geographic expansion of major business units, and commitments to develop new lines of business. Each major business unit of the bank—retail, commercial, international, and trust—had a set of strategic direc-tions which were to be implemented. The Pacific Mega Bank had com-pleted its assessment of the current state and had developed a desired state strategic plan.

The transition planning design required the top managers, corporate as well as business, to go through a transition management training ses-sion to prepare them to develop integrated transition plans. The training was followed up by help from internal bank staff and outside consul-tants. The training design was based on the following assumptions:

1. That the organization needed to learn how to manage major change transitions in order to achieve its strategic objectives.

2. That top management had to be strongly committed to better transition management—they had to understand it and support it.

3. That corporate-level staff groups needed to coordinate efforts with a common understanding of the dilemmas of transition management and a common approach to supporting the line— this included the human resource groups, the corporate planning group, the corporate legal group, and the corporate financial group.

The design included the following components:

1. *Preprogram Work.* The top management group attends a half-day session to begin developing a transition plan for the total bank. The purpose of this half-day meeting is to get them acquainted with the ideas and the approach and to encourage them to be supportive of training for their subordinates.

Prior to the inclusion of line management groups in the training workshops, the corporate-staff groups go through the one-day training session, so that they understand the process and become committed to it. The staff design is essentially the same design as the one used for the line business units reported as follows.

Once top management and staff have completed the training, workshops are organized for each of the major business units of the bank. These business units are asked to put together groups of four or five managers who were involved in different strategy implementation projects. These groups are to select a major change problem for which they will assume responsibility. The team is told to write a one-page statement of the change problem and bring it to the workshop.

2. *Workshop.* The workshop is a one-day meeting designed to provide participants with a framework for developing transition plans and a set of guidelines for managing the transition systematically.

Introduce Workshop and Strategy Implementation Framework. The workshop begins with a brief lecture on the transition state and how it needs to be managed separately from either the current or desired state. There is a discussion of the alternative governance and management structures for the transition management followed by an outline of the day's session.

Activity I: Desired State Scenario Writing. Individuals are instructed to take their written statement and spend some time by themselves writing a scenario of the desired state. The desired state scenario should focus on what the organization would look like if the change strategy is implemented. Scenarios are to be no more than one page and as descriptive as possible. Groups meet and share their scenarios and then develop a single one to represent the desired state.

Activity II: Transition Planning Lecture. There is a brief lecture on how to plan the technical, political, and cultural transition plan. Guidelines are given for how to develop such plans.

Activity III: Groups Develop Transition Plans. Using the forementioned guidelines, each group works up a transition plan which includes a technical, political, and cultural set of actions. These plans are integrated into one overall plan for the business unit.

Activity IV: Preparation for Following Through. Participants are given a set of guidelines for determining the time and resources necessary to carry out their particular transition. Groups meet at the end of the day to assess the day and plan next steps.

Post-Workshop Follow-Up. After the workshop the internal organization development staff sets up a meeting with the top management of each business unit to help them review and assess their transition plans. Each business unit makes its own arrangements to have ongoing internal organizational development help.

Case Illustration 2: Chemical Company Z. Chemical Company Z (CCZ) is a division of a West German parent company with subsidiaries operating in the United States. CCZ is a $500 million business with 10,000 employees. CCZ had recently undergone a change in top management. The new president of CCZ was from another part of the U.S. operation of the West German company. He was a fast track senior manager with potential for a senior parent company position. When he became president of CCZ it was made clear to him that there were long-standing managerial problems, the company was not a high performer, it was behind the industry in innovation, and people seemed to be quite unmotivated. The president saw this as an opportunity to make a major impact on the company and hence enhance his upward mobility.

One of the first things he did was to administer a company-wide employee survey in order to assess the attitudes of the employees. He was expecting negative data and he got it. It was even more negative than expected. The data include such findings as: Over 40% of the employees felt the company had gotten worse since they had started work there; over 50% indicated that major changes were needed in the organization; and over 50% of the nonmanagement personnel did not trust that there would be any managerial action based on the survey. Problem areas included the promotion system, in which managerial style was punitive and nonparticipatory.

The president set up a management task force to respond to the survey results. This in turn led to departmental feedback sessions which were followed by the establishment of "peer group" employee groups to respond to the survey and make recommendations for change.

After this process was underway, the president contacted some external consultants to work with the groups. The consultants came up with the following proposal for change:

1. Change was already underway due to the administration of the survey, the feedback meetings, and peer group meetings. It was

critical that the process be managed strategically so as to lead to desired changes.

2. Change results were needed in the short run as well as the long run. Expectations had been raised that something would happen (for some there was a great deal of cynicism) therefore it was important to have some clearly visible signs of change.

3. All change activities at all levels needed to become integrated and perceived as part of the same drive to improve organizational performance via improved motivation of the work force. Thus, activities already underway to change the R&D function, to implement flex time, job posting, as well as future changes, needed to become part of an overall strategy which was clearly communicated to all personnel.

4. A long-term change strategy was needed. It must be clearly articulated and supported by the key power figures at the top and deal with the technical, political, and cultural changes.

5. There needed to be more active involvement of the total management committee in the change process as only the president and a specially selected management committee were involved up to this point.

6. The organization needed to begin developing internal capability for managing change.

General Approach to Change Process

Phase I: Developing and Launching Overall Change Strategy (4 to 6 Month Period).

1. Management Committee must meet and develop an overall conceptual framework for the change process. Prior to this meeting the consultants did interviews with each member (seven senior executives) to assess their evaluation of the survey, their evaluation of the current state of the organization, and their desired state for the organization. These data were used to discuss the current state of the organization. Once a set of core problem areas was identified the top group spent some time generating a list of potential change objectives for the desired state. They came up with:

(a) change in managerial style (more participative, improved communication and more professionalism).

(b) change in total company toward more people orientation

(c) change in organization communication (people communicate a sense of mission, openness and candor).

(d) change in organization design to one which fosters more responsibility and accountability (reduce duplication).

The group then agreed on the governance structure for the transition. The president was the project manager and the change was to be managed through the line organization. A diagonal slice advisory committee was established to help support and guide the transition. The line was used heavily because of the huge scope of the change effort.

2. The next step was a half-day meeting with the group of managers just below the management committee, this included 40 managers. This group went through a meeting to overview the proposed change process. The meeting was run by the president and the two outside consultants. The overall transition management framework was presented along with the governance structure for the change process.

3. The management committee met for a day to work out a set of change objectives for the desired state. These objectives were a further elaboration of the objectives generated at the first meeting in Step 1. These objectives became the input to a strategy planning session for the top 45 managers of the company—the president and management committee as well as the next level.

4. Strategy planning sessions for the top group to work out an overall change strategy for the organization as well as start on individual departmental change strategies. The overall strategy was built from the assessment of the current state via survey, peer group, special task forces, etc., and made use of the change objectives worked out by the management committee. These objectives were further modified by this larger group. The remainder of the two days focused on the development of integrated transition plans for the total organization.

Task groups as well as actual work teams spent time during the two days doing the following:

(a) Specifying the change strategy in technical, political, and cultural areas.

(b) Assessing alternative change technologies for carrying out the strategy.

(c) Identifying the technical, political, and cultural imperatives which would affect the transition.

(d) Developing technical, political, and cultural transition plans which dealt with major changes in the information, influence, and affective networks.

(e) These plans were drafted and submitted to the management committee for review and comment.

5. After the two-day session the management committee came together for a day to develop the overall change plan for the company by integrating the work of the departments. This plan then became the

umbrella for the departments to develop their own change plans. The consultants then worked with each of the management groups in the departments to develop change plans.

6. Review and readjust strategy—the strategy was monitored by both the management committee and the advisory committee. At the end of each six-month period a one-day session was held to review the change strategy and make overall adjustments. Departments had similar reviews for themselves.

CONCLUSION

This chapter introduced the concept of transition management: how to actually move an organization from some current state to some desired state. It was pointed out that social networks play a central role in this process as all organizational change involves breaking some networks and the forming of new ones. Transition management is viewed as the process of managing change cycles over time. These cycles refer to the areas of activity in which change is taking place, technical, political, or cultural, and the amount of energy the organization is putting into managing the changes.

Transition management plans must be developed for the technical, political, and cultural areas. Guidelines were presented for doing so, as were examples of how these three plans must merge into one overall transition management effort.

PART FOUR

MONITORING CHANGE AND THE FUTURE OF STRATEGIC MANAGEMENT

Chapter Thirteen

Monitoring and Evaluating Strategic Change

INTRODUCTION

Billions of dollars have been spent in the last two decades on management and organizational development activities purportedly designed to change organizations. These include programs to introduce management by objectives (MBO), organization development programs, the managerial grid, leadership training, strategic planning models, and, more recently, quality circles. Virtually none of these efforts has any systematic monitoring or evaluation associated with it. This leads to an unfortunate state of affairs where the waxing and waning of organizational improvement remedies are associated with limited understanding of what works and what does not and why.

Typically, once a panacea is adopted by the "right" company, other companies either try it or dismiss it on the basis of hearsay. I've heard managers say, "General Electric tried it, and it didn't work. So we aren't going to try it. . . ." Of course, what "it" consists of is never fully discussed or understood. The examples of programs listed above do not constitute what I would consider strategic changes in the context of this book. With regard to monitoring, evaluating, and understanding *strategic changes*, the systematic work is even more sparse. Before recommending some arguments for why such systematic work should be done and how it might be accomplished, I will try and explain why it hasn't occurred.

Forces Against Monitoring and Evaluating Change in Organizations

There is a set of understandable pressures that will continue to exert themselves on managers, consultants, and academicians. Pressure is on managers to find ways of dealing with organizational problems, here and now, with minimal risk and investment. This makes the manager susceptible to quick-acting, cure-all sales pitches from consultants. A consultant obviously has a vested interest in selling his or her services.

The forces against evaluation and monitoring can be looked at in technical, political, and cultural terms.

Technical Forces. Perhaps the least impactive of the three sets of forces is the technical. There are methodological difficulties in measuring change which will continue. However, the state of the art is such that there are sufficient tools to begin work in the area. The major problems of a technical nature include: (1) measurement difficulties—how to psychometrically measure attitudinal and cultural changes, how to measure performance changes and how to relate changes to aspects of the change effort; (2) role difficulties—how to develop staff and research roles with the appropriate skills to play the role of monitor and evaluator; and (3) lack of conceptual frameworks for integrating measurement of change into management's thinking about organizational performance.

The role difficulties and the conceptual framework problems deserve some more explanation. The measurement difficulties are well documented and discussed in companion volumes to this one in the Wiley Series on Organizational Assessment and Change (for example, Lawler, et al., 1980; Van de Ven and Ferry, 1980). By *role difficulties*, we are referring to the problem of who does what with whom to carry out the evaluation and monitoring. Often, for example, there are staff people in the human resource area of the organization with skills in survey analysis. Should these people be given the task of monitoring and evaluating strategic change? The answer is that they cannot be the sole providers of that service because they usually only possess some of the needed technical skills. They often lack a theory or conceptual framework for understanding and analyzing organizational change. Thus they merely possess survey methodology. The next role question is where to find the conceptual skills. This may call on the use of outside experts. Then, how do they become involved? Are they to be independent evaluation experts who help the insiders? Even if all the technical skills can be put together through some combination of insiders and outsiders, the issue of how to organize them so that they are able to produce usable information is no easy task. There are no readily workable models for the technical problems. Yet, with a fair amount of managerial time thinking the problems through, a local solution can be reached.

Political Forces. Political forces are the major forces which prevent monitoring and evaluation. The first is what Donald Campbell (1969) called the "over-advocacy trap." In order to sell a particular approach to changing an organization, it is often necessary to sell it as a sure-fire solution. Thus, the advocates of a particular strategy have to over-advocate it to get acceptance by other key players in the organization. Once this occurs, there is a clear set of political reasons for those who sold it to *not* want careful monitoring and evaluation. By overselling it, they set themselves up for failure if the approach does not succeed.

Often their own reputation, budget, career, and so on are riding on a particular strategy. In its extreme, this political situation results in loss of jobs by key people. Recently the president of a major oil company was dismissed due to his diversification strategy running counter to another strong coalition's view of what was appropriate.

Related to the over-advocacy trap is the career "time bomb" dilemma—given the short term focus of many U.S. managers who want to move quickly up the organization, there is a pressure to move on and away from one's last assignment before really knowing whether things were successful or not. This is especially true if major strategic change is underway. A manager who is given the assignment to turn around a division of a larger company and sees it as a short-term step up the career ladder is often rewarded for taking short-term expediencies, such as deferring all sorts of investments in the human and capital stock to make the quarterly and annual numbers look good. If the manager is lucky, he or she will be gone before these time bombs go off. Obviously, under these conditions it is not likely that the manager would be supportive of systematic monitoring and evaluation of the change effort.

Cultural Forces. Closely aligned with political forces are cultural beliefs which work against systematic evaluation and monitoring. The prevailing belief system of American management is dominated by a culture that Pascale and Athos (1981) sees as having a curious addiction to grand strategy:

> Our strategy fetish is a cultural peculiarity. We get off on strategy like the French get off on good food or romance. The very term stirs something within us. It evokes images of Napoleon or MacArthur masterfully turning the tide of battle with a bold vision. There's something masculine about it too—and big status. (p. 115)

This addiction to the grand strategic leap, or the home run ball, make systematic, incremental measurement alien to the organization's culture. Pascale contrasts this to the Japanese culture, which views strategy as an incremental, accommodation process. In their culture

> corporate direction evolves from an incremental adjustment to unfolding events. Rarely, in their view, does one leader (of a strategic planning group) produce a bold strategy that guides a firm unerringly. Far more frequently, the input is from below. It is this ability of an organization to move information and ideas from the bottom to the top and back again in continuous dialogue that the Japanese value above all things. (p. 116)

The Japanese culture is one which would support systematic evaluation and monitoring of strategic changes so that learning and adjustments would be guided by information.

The Case for an Action Research Culture. In order to create the conditions for systematic evaluation and monitoring, there must be a new cultural system. The case can be made in terms of a framework which divides organizational functioning into four levels. The first level is *steady state operation*. The organization operates and spends a certain percentage of its time doing such activities as routinely producing products, selling them through distribution channels, and supporting these activities with financial, accounting, and personnel services.

Unfortunately, all organizations break down and require *repair operations*. Organizations function at this second level only part of the time and must frequently deal with crises of varying magnitude. These range from responding to an unexpected rate of absenteeism one day to conflict among departments, budget crises, or union problems. Most organizations introduce new *innovative operations*, such as new technology, new management practices, and new products. This is the third level of operation.

The fourth category is *self-renewal operation*, which refers to activities, time, and resources invested in diagnosing and developing ways of improving the first three levels of operation. Self-renewal is the major factor in determining the long-term health of an organization and is characterized by a negative entropy process in which extra energy is stored and conserved (Katz and Kahn, 1966).

An organization needs to be organized and managed to facilitate all four levels. Organizations vary in the degree of how much time they should devote to each level. The key factor determining the importance of each of the four levels is the amount of uncertainty the organization faces. The greater the uncertainty, the more organization resources need to go to innovation and self-renewal.

Table 13.1 presents a summary of the conditions for effective organizational support for each level. The central points that need to be understood from the material in the table are:

1. Each level of organizational functioning requires different structural and process mechanisms for effective operation.

2. Steady state operation makes the most use of technical managerial and organizational design procedures that enable the organization to arrange itself in such a manner as to perform tasks in a maximally predictable and controlled way. Thus the tools most useful in this area are management science work flow design techniques, budget and control system design, and standing plans.

3. Repair operation requires organizational structures and processes that provide the capacity to handle conflict and to engage in nonprogrammed decision making. The crucial factor in repair operations is the ability to respond flexibly and with minimal time lag.

4. Innovative operations require structures and processes for monitoring the environment for innovations as well as mechanisms for inputting the innovations on stream. The organization must also possess risk capital or slack resources to engage in innovative operations.

Table 13.1 Levels of Organizational Functioning

Levels of Function	Conditions for Effectiveness
Steady State Operation: Ongoing regular routines of the organization, predictable, programmable, low uncertainty, low information processing requirements.	Technical system design-work flow standard operating procedures, management information systems and rules.
Repair Operation: Nonroutine problems, search for solution often unanalyzable, time pressures, often conflict, parties, and priorities.	Information search capacity, flexible problem-solving capability, conflict management structures and processes, contingency plans.
Innovative Operation: Organizationally new and novel approaches to the task, management and organizational design generally imported from the environment (new knowledge, new developments from other organizations).	Environmental-scanning capability, appropriate boundary-spanning network, to keep up to date. Managerial and organizational capacity to evaluate, decide on, and implement innovations. Existence of some slack resources generally needed.
Self-renewal Operation; Investing time and resources in diagnosing and developing improved ways of carrying out steady state, repair and innovative operation.	Value commitment to self-diagnosis and improvement (preventive medicine, orientation to organize functioning), capacity for diagnosing managerial and organizational systems and organizational change capability.

Source: From Noel M. Tichy. *Organization Design for Primary Health Care.* Copyright © 1977 by Praeger Publishers, Inc. Reprinted and adapted by permission of Praeger Publishers.

5. Self-renewal operation is based above all on a value commitment on the part of management regarding the virtue of taking time out to improve organizational functioning at the three other levels. This needs to be accompanied by specific structural and resource commitments devoted to the self-renewal mode becoming institutionalized. This must translate into political system supports for the value as represented in promotions, budget allocations, and reward allocations.

The paradox of renewal is that it requires mortgaging of short-term time and resources toward a longer-term goal of organizational health and vitality. A renewal, or action-research, orientation is the necessary condition for systematic evaluation and monitoring of strategic change. The rest of this chapter provides means of implementing such a culture but does not deal with how to create the conditions for requesting it.

Specifically, the chapter presents alternative types of monitoring and evaluating orientations, the use of diagnosis as a starting point for evaluation and monitoring, a framework for carrying out the evaluation, examples of specific models of evaluation and monitoring the ways of organizing, and managing evaluation and monitoring.

BASIC ORIENTATIONS TO MONITORING AND EVALUATING STRATEGIC CHANGE

In adopting one of the five generic approaches to evaluating and monitoring strategic change, there is a set of cultural, political, and technical trade-offs which need to be considered. Table 13.2 summarizes these trade-offs for the five generic types of evaluation. The technical dimensions run from a high level of technical research and evaluation sophistication on one end to a low level of technical sophistication on the other end. The political dimension runs from a high level of political risk, one incurring large commitments of resources, on one end to a low level of political risk and commitment of resources at the other end. Finally, in the cultural area one end of the dimension is high level of cultural commitment to evaluation and monitoring, while the other is low level of cultural commitment. This section will discuss each generic type of evaluation in terms of these three dimensions.

Basic Research and Development Orientation

This approach is one in which the organization is committed to approaching organizational change in the same way as one approaches good research and development on a product; that is, there is systematic testing and evaluation of the change as it unfolds. This includes doing experiments to determine different ways of accomplishing change goals. It might involve setting up special laboratory-like conditions to test out new concepts and ideas. An example of this might be the General Foods' Topeka plant, which was set up as a prototype or model. The

Table 13.2   Generic Orientations to Evaluating and Monitoring Strategic Change

	Trade-offs		
	Cultural	Political	Technical
Type of Orientation	Depth of Commitment To Systematic Evaluation	Risk and Commitment of Resources	Sophistication and Capability
	High	High	High
Basic research and development			
Experimental intervention orientation			
Guidance system orientation			
Managerial audit orientation			
Informal anecdotal orientation			
	Low	Low	Low

Topeka plant ended up being a very successful experiment in the short run, showing how innovative socio-technical design of new plants could lead to high productivity and high satisfaction among the employees. It succeeded technically but failed due to political and cultural dynamics. As a research and development activity, it did not contribute to strategic change at General Foods. In looking at this failure, we can better understand the conditions needed to create a basic R&D orientation in a company. From a technical point of view, the General Foods' Topeka example did work. The company had the necessary technical expertise to treat the plant as an experiment from which it could learn and derive principles for dissemination to other parts of the organization. Where the experiment ran into trouble and where it was counter to the General Foods' organization was in the cultural and political area.

Politically problems were created due to the fact that other plants and other plant managers became jealous. A disproportionate amount of attention and resources went to this plant, which made other plants feel competitive. There was pressure either to do things better than Topeka or to isolate it and make it into an aberration. The latter course was taken, thus politically preventing disruptions in other plants. The others did not have to copy the change. Furthermore, there was not political support at high levels of management for treating this as an experiment. Therefore, the plant became isolated and seen as a non-traditional and alien-type appendage.

The political problems were clearly linked to the cultural issue, which essentially reflected a culture that did not value treating organizational change as research and development activities; rather, one either made a policy to do something one way or one didn't. The result was that those who supported the Topeka plant had to over-advocate it as a panacea, thus threatening the more traditional plants. There was not a culture which enabled them to problem solve and sort out what was good, what worked, and what didn't work, and identify how lessons could be applied to other parts of the organization. As a result of these political and cultural forces, the company lost the opportunity to conduct meaningful research and development on approaches to managing plants that are in the General Foods' network.

The ideal basic research and development orientation will occur in an organization where there is the technical sophistication represented in the General Foods' example—and where there is a deep cultural commitment to conducting research and development on organizational innovations and changes and where there is an alignment of the political structures which allows people to take risks, fail, learn from mistakes, and ultimately develop new orientations. Such political and cultural orientations are very difficult to create, and to this author's knowledge there is no company that he would currently categorize as having a basic R&D orientation to organization and management.

Experimenting Intervention Orientation

The experimenting intervention orientation differs from the basic research and development approach in degree rather than substance. They both require a fairly high technical sophistication, a fairly high political risk and commitment of resource orientation, and a fairly high cultural value commitment to systematic evaluation and monitoring. The major difference is that the basic research and development orientation requires the organization to put aside separate resources and protected environments to experiment and examine phenomena related to organization and management change. The experimenting intervention orientation requires that measurement be done around actual change in the organization. That is, the change is introduced in more of an action-research mode and the organization thinks about ways of creating live experiments.

For example, the history of Volvo's efforts in the quality of work life area is an example of a company that had an experimenting intervention orientation to change. In the late 1960s there were a number of experiments done on job rotation and job enrichment, and a limited amount of team work. Each of these experiments had extensive measurement going on around them and a commitment to then sit down and say, "Okay, what have we learned at this point?" Furthermore, different interventions were tried in different groups so that they were done as quasi-experiments, with explicit methodological attention given to having some control groups. By the early 1970s the quality of work life effort by Volvo had been expanded. There was even a new assembly plant designed from the ground floor up by Kalmer, where workers, union, management, and staff people, participated in an innovative design of the production system. Throughout this effort there was an experimenting mode of work. Measurements were taken on both the people side and the productivity side as the plant was opened and the innovations were implemented. Some things were tried one way and then another way, with systematic measurement to help determine what were the best ways of proceeding. Ultimately, this line of activity including the transformation of plants like the Skovda Engine plant, and other existing plants moved Volvo toward the model of autonomous work groups and the socio-technical system as a way of life. The evolution of this approach, however, took a 10-year period in which the basic orientation of Volvo could be described as an experimenting intervention orientation.

Another example of such an orientation is currently under way in a company in which three plants are experimenting with a variety of quality of work life techniques, including quality circles. They are being evaluated over a period of several years to determine which interventions are appropriate for the company's remaining 37 plants. In both cases it is necessary to have a fair degree of technical sophistication in survey research, interviewing, and analysis of financial data so as to be able to determine the link between organizational changes and the performance of the unit being studied. In addition, it is necessary to have strong political support from the top of the organization and a value belief in an experimental approach on the part of key figures in the organization.

Guidance System Approach

The guidance system approach differs from the previous one in that systematic data are used to guide an overall change strategy, but it does not include experimental variations to learn how different things might work under different conditions. So, for example, a company that decides to undergo a major quality of work life effort might, instead of experimenting in three plants, launch it in all 40 plants, starting with a survey and some other data collection techniques, and then use the survey methodology over time to guide the change-effort to see what changes have occurred or have not occurred and make adjustments based on the data. But there would not be, from a technical point of view, an effort made to vary the types of interventions, thus having a quasi-experimental design built into the process. The guidance system approach requires a moderate degree of technical sophistication so as to be able to use tools like surveys and other systematic data collection techniques. Politically there are a moderate number of risks and commitment of resources required because with the measurement of change somewhat systematic it's easier for people to become visible and held accountable, and certainly culturally one must have an organization that values having systematic data put on the table to examine as the change process unfolds.

In many ways the guidance system approach has similarities to other control systems in organizations found in the production and financial area. There is one major cultural difference. Many of those systems are set up to catch mistakes. The guidance system approach is only workable where the predominant reason is *not* to catch mistakes and then punish for them but to catch mistakes and problem solve and learn from them. Catching mistakes and punishing for them may be appropriate in some settings where there are routine activities going on. In a strategic change activity it is inevitable that there will be many mistakes, and the issue is how we learn from mistakes. Thus, there must be a cultural value that supports the system. The system's blowing the whistle on itself is a nondefensive way of saying, "Oops, we've got to change and problem-solve." This is along the lines of the type of learning and adjustments identified by Pascale in Japanese organizations that allow them to make strategic accommodation. For example, Toyota can introduce a car, as it did in its early days in the United States, and fail, as did Datsun and as did Mazda. But the organization has the capability for learning from these mistakes, not a culture and a political system which punishe and therefore create defensiveness.

Audit Approach

The audit approach is one that is fairly common to organizations in which management makes some effort to stand back and assess what's going on or audit its own activities. An example of such an activity might be periodic review meetings where managers are asked to summarize what they are doing in a particular area and then evaluate plusses and minuses. One company has been using this approach in the quality of work life effort. The company has over 500 quality circles, gain-sharing experiments, new training and development activities, and the like going on. Periodic review meetings are held by senior management at which business managers present what they are doing in the quality of work life area, and then an attempt is made to critique what is going on. This differs from the guidance system approach, where there is a systematic measurement and evaluation process going on. Technically the audit approach requires a fairly low level of sophistication. Political risks and commitments are not that critical because the managers themselves control what they bring to the review sessions and can and usually do color them to support what the power figures want; and the cultural depth of commitment to evaluation is pretty low because there is again a great deal of distortion and the information is quite informal under these conditions.

Informal Anecdotal Approach

This approach is probably the one most frequently used in U.S. corporations where there is a low technical sophistication, that is, where information is picked up via peoples' observations—anecdotes about what is going on, very informal meetings, and so on. Secondly, there are minimal political risks and commitment to evaluation in that nothing formal is going on. This obviously is associated with a cultural value that does not place much of a premium on systematic evaluation and monitoring.

It is probably unlikely that there is a sixth generic type, namely, no evaluation and monitoring. Because we are talking about strategic change, people will form opinions and conclusions. Thus, the informal anecdotal approach is the final type available in practical terms.

It is my feeling that much is to be gained organizationally by adapting a basic research and development, or experimenting intervention, orientation to change. Often achieving this requires strategic, cultural, and political change in the organization. Getting a commitment to the required discipline in an organization may in itself be a strategic change.

Thus, we are faced with somewhat of a chicken-and-egg problem. It is a problem that at this point will be sidestepped.

A FRAMEWORK FOR CARRYING OUT THE EVALUATION

This section introduces a framework with several key factors that influence the effectiveness of an organizational change effort. There are three major variables seen as important to assess in evaluating and monitoring a change effort: (1) the environmental context; (2) the actual change effort; and (3) the outcomes.

The first set contains two kinds of *contextual factors:* (1) those external to the organization, and (2) the characteristics of the organization. The argument has already been made in this book that external political, social, and cultural forces profoundly impact the internal management of the organization. In addition, there are internal organizational factors that are relevant to a change program, and these include the nature of the product, the technology, the structure, the size, and the organization's culture. The technology of the organization is used to transform inputs into outputs and varies in terms of complexity (sounds like "routinization") and stability. The nature of this technology shapes, limits, and constrains the way in which the organization gets structured. Thus, different technologies will exert different social influences on the organization and the workers. This is also true of the organization structure. Finally, the organization's culture is also a key factor in assessing and monitoring a change program, as it may be cultural resistance that determines whether a program succeeds or fails.

A second set of factors in evaluating an organizational change effort is the nature of the intervention itself. One might envision the change effort in terms of an iceberg—with a set of concrete steps listed above the waterline and with the underlying assumptions about people and organizations reflected in an organizational model below the waterline. The iceberg analogy stresses a crucial point often overlooked in assessing change efforts. Activities depicted in the steps above the waterline grow out of peoples' assumptions and theories about human nature and organizations. These assumptions are usually implicit and therefore below the waterline or below the threshhold of awareness. Managers and consultants working to implement organizational changes should be aware of and explicit about their underlying assumptions and theories or models. For those of us who try to evaluate a change effort, it is absolutely necessary to ferret out, even if by inference, the assumptions and models that guide the program. Doing so enables us to understand the causes of success or failure and helps us in transferring an approach to other settings.

Finally, we must focus our attention on the outcomes of a change effort. Descriptions of organizational changes are often presented with little hard data on outcomes, either in terms of productivity or in other dimensions, such as worker satisfaction and contribution to organizational help. Figure 13.1 presents 20 questions that can be asked to evaluate an organizational change effort.

Twenty Questions for Evaluating Organization Change Efforts

These 20 questions provide a systematic means of examining the complex array of factors, affecting the success or failure of an organizational improvement effort.

Outcome. The first question establishes the criteria for evaluating all the other questions: What were the intended outcomes of the program and how close did the change effort come to achieving them? The success or failure of an organizational change effort is a function of the change intervention itself and the environmental context within which it occurs. Context has been divided into two sectors, the external and internal. Figure 13.1 presents questions 2 through 9 for use in evaluating the environmental context as it relates to organizational change. The external factors are important because of the issue of environmental determinism—that is, events in the environment determining the outcomes of the change effort—and because of issues of transferability in diffusion of the organizational change.

The internal environmental factors include the characteristics of the organization which have an important influence on change efforts. The recent popularity of contingency theories of organization and management reflect a growing realization that organizational effectiveness is largely a function of matching organizational structure, leadership style, planning, and control systems to demands of the organization's environment and the task or technology involved.

As technology varies in terms of the exceptions entailed and the kind of search required to deal with them, so does the kind of people best able to perform successfully, and so does the kind of structure most supportive of the work. Strategic change efforts can succeed or fail, depending on their degree of congruence with the organization's technology, structure, and people.

Organizational Change Effort. The iceberg analogy stresses the importance of underlying assumptions and models typically implicit in the guide program formulation and implementation. The success of an organizational change effort can be greatly affected by how explicit and aware key actors in the process are of these guiding assumptions. Being explicit increases the likelihood that all involved will understand the change effort and that the assumptions will be carefully examined and tested. Those of us who try to evaluate change efforts need to explicate the model whether the organization's members do or don't. Regarding the actual phases of change effort as listed in Figure 13.1, several points are worth noting. First, the phases in reality are often not distinct but overlapping. Also, some phases may never occur. For purposes of analysis and evaluation, however, it is important to make the distinction in order to identify and isolate specific factors relating to change progress. The framework and the 20 questions can be used to help guide and evaluate strategic change efforts. They are meant to be pragmatic questions for management to make use of during a change effort.

THE CASE FOR EXPLICIT ORGANIZATION MODELS FOR EVALUATING AND MONITORING CHANGE EFFORTS

As has been a major theme in this book, organizational models lie at the core of organization assessment. They provide guidelines for selecting diagnostic information and for arranging the information into meaningful patterns. This forms the basis for determining both functional and dysfunctional organizational processes in planning change action.

Researchers are in the business of using formal scientific procedures to improve existing models. The development and application of models is their stock in trade, and there is little need for educating or proselytizing members of this group about the importance of organization models. In contrast, thinking in terms of models is uncommon to the average manager or worker, who is likely to have a rather strong negative reaction to any academic researcher asking, "Tell me about your organization model." The fact is that most people outside of academia do not pay self-conscious attention to internalized models of social life that may influence their behavior.

However, they do have such models, albeit often intuitive and implicit. Managers and workers go through the same process as a researcher in evaluating their organization, although it may be less obvious and open to scrutiny. They collect data and organize the data into categories and make assumptions about causality and plan their action based on some model of organizational functioning. As Argyris and Schon (1974) point out, "human beings use micro-theories of action to inform their behavior. The theories if made explicit can be stated in formal terms."

Because organization members and researchers both employ models in their work with organizations, there are special problems and potentials that occur when members of these two groups come together for joint work. It is felt that, in order to carry out either the research or development on the experimenting intervention approaches to monitoring and evaluating change, outside researchers will need to collaborate with internal organization staff. This means that understanding each other's models becomes important.

Factor	Question
OUTCOMES	
Objectives	1. What were the intended outcomes of the change and what were the actual outcomes? It is necessary to determine why the change was initiated and its impact on "bottom line" outcomes such as productivity, turnover, absenteeism, and satisfaction.
Environmental context	
External factors	
Labor market and characteristics of workforce	2. How tight was the labor market and what were the characteristics of the available labor pool? Ascertain unemployment level and characteristics of workforce when evaluating an organizational change effort.
Social and political trends	3. Were there changes occurring in society affecting workers and the organization? The success of change may be affected by how consistent it is with certain societal trends.
Economy and market	4. What was the general state of the economy at the time of the change? Certain changes may work only in favorable economic conditions.
Environmental stability	5. How much is the organization's immediate environment changing—and is the organizational structure appropriately matched. A change may be greatly affected by the degree of congruence between an organization's structure and degree of environmental uncertainty that exists for the organization.
Internal factors	
Product technology	6. What is the product of the organization and the primary technology used to transform inputs into outputs? Ascertain the match between technology, structure, and kind of people involved and whether the change is congruent with them or tries to make them congruent with the program.
Internal factors	
Structure	7. Where on the mechanistic-to-organic structure continuum is the organization? The change should be consistent with the organization's structure or explicitly attend to changing that structure.
Size	8. How large is the organization and the plant or division within which the change is taking place? Size affects complexity of changes and the organizational resources available.
Organizational culture	9. What are the prevailing norms and values in the organization regarding involvement in organizational change efforts? Changes require changed behavior, thus changed culture—which requires attention to resistance.
Organizational Change effort	
Guiding assumptions and models	10. How explicit were the assumptions about organizations and the change that guided the effort? Being explicit about assumptions increases the chance that all involved understand the change and that the assumptions are more carefully examined and tested.

Change effort phases	
Initiation phase	11. How comprehensive and consistent with current organizational theory were the guiding assumptions and models? The success of a change effort can be influenced both by internal logic and by failure to incorporate what we know about organizations and change.
	12. What was the reason for starting the change and who was initially involved? Changes generally require a broadly shared "felt need" and involvement of affected people to succeed.
Entry and start-up phase	13. What were the initial activities at the start of the change and who was involved? Changes generally require a broadly shared "felt need" and involvement of affected people to succeed.
Diagnostic phase	14. What were the explicit diagnostic activities?
	15. What aspects of the organization were diagnosed and how? Pitfalls include the "elephant problem" (sending eight blind men out to touch the organization and try to put the separate "felt" pieces together) and the "expert" problem, caused by outsiders who do a fancy diagnosis that no one understands.
Strategy planning phase	16. How was the actual change planned and by whom? The two dimensions to assess are (1) how available resources (internal and external consultants) were used, and (2) how the diagnostic model and data were used.
	17. How explicit and detailed were the plans? Lack of planning leads to seat-of-the-pants implementation of a program.
Implementation phase	18. What was actually done, how, when, and by whom? Two pitfalls are incomplete, patchwork implementation and intervention interruptus, or failing to carry the change through to completion.
Evaluation and corrective action phase	19. Was there explicit evaluation and monitoring of the change and, if so, what was measured and how? Political pressure resulting from overadvocacy of changes sets up forces against evaluation. Evaluative measures should be directly related to intended program outcomes.
	20. What was done with the evaluation—did it result in corrective action or modification of the change? Corrective action may fail because of lack of top-level organizational commitment and/or postimplementation letdown and regression when the novelty wears off.

Figure 13.1 Questions for evaluating organizational change. (Reprinted, by permission, from "When Does Work Restructuring Work? Organizational Innovations at Vohr and GM," N.M. Tichy, *Organizational Dynamics*, Summer, 1976 © 1976 by AMACOM, a division of American Management Associations. p. 68. All rights reserved.)

377

If we assume that organizations have a large array of data that can be studied during a change effort, then organizational models guiding the choice process when there is joint researcher organization member assessment can lead to the following: (1) disagreement regarding selection of data for the assessment of the change effort; (2) inconsistent priorities in interpreting the data, and lack of shared understanding of causality, that is, how changes in parts of the organization will impact the organization in terms of effectiveness; (3) labelling problems—often the same term can mean vastly different things in two separate models and different terms can mean the same thing; (4) lack of insight—change and commitment on the part of organization members because the researcher's model which is explicit becomes predominant in the assessment but remains inconsistent with the member's model.

When people are unaware of the models that they are using and when the models remain unshared and are internally and interpersonally (between researchers and organization members) inconsistent, the likelihood of these problems occurring grows. This section argues that the management of these problems requires researcher and organization member collaboration in creating a shared organizational model. This argument is in contrast to two alternative approaches to assessing change: one, the internal audit by members of the organization, was presented earlier; the other is the evaluation based totally on outside researchers doing the assessment. We will examine these three alternative levels of collaboration and end by providing some guidelines for a joint research/researcher organization approach to evaluating and monitoring change.

Determining Level of Collaboration

The choice of level of collaboration entails consideration of a variety of issues that both parties must weigh in deciding on the appropriate level of collaboration. Figure 13.2 summarizes some of the issues involved in various levels of researcher and member collaboration. This perspective assumes that decision making influences the central variable. At the top left of the figure members have total influence. This is very much the case when members of the organization launch their own internal audit or assessment with little or no outside help. The other end of the table represents a totally research-dominated structure as might occur in a traditional, narrowly focused research effort.

There are three categories of issues associated with choosing an appropriate level of researcher and member collaboration: (1) The researchers contribute theory and research tools for dealing with complexity, whereas the members provide local knowledge. The combination of both provides greater capability for dealing with complexity. Thus both extremes, pure member and pure researcher domi-

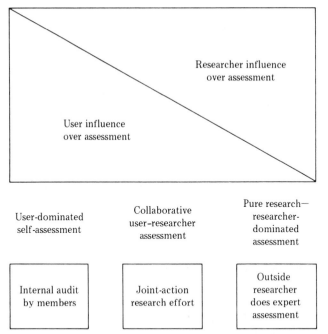

Figure 13.2   Level of researcher and user collaboration

nance, are expected to ordinarily have lower capability for dealing with complexity. (2) The means for carrying out the assessment vary with level of collaboration. Time commitment is higher for collaborative assessment due to the interaction, bargaining, and joint problem solving and decision making that take place. The use of scientific tools and knowledge is comparatively high when there is either a researcher-dominated or collaborative assessment. (3) The outcomes associated with three levels of collaboration are assumed to vary as well: Contribution to scientific knowledge is higher with researcher and collaborative levels; member ownership and commitment to use results are higher with member and collaborative levels; the member ability to carry on assessments by themselves is higher with member and collaborative levels.

Consideration of these issues results in the following suggestions for situations in which each of the three levels of collaboration are preferred.

Member-dominated asssessment is preferred when the assessment problem is not very complex, generally a concrete organization problem needing some simple yet systematic analysis, such as when (1) quick turnaround is required; (2) minimum concern exists for contributing to scientific knowledge; or (3) there is a great need for member commitment to using the results. Researcher-dominated assessment is preferred when (1) the assessment is one that can be studied without heavy reliance on organizational members' local knowledge and understanding; (2) theoretically derived propositions are being tested; (3) there is a minimum concern with member commitment to using the results or there is little concern with the member directly learning from the assessment. Collaborative assessment is preferred when (1) there is complex assessment requiring scientific knowledge and tools along with local, in-depth understanding of the organization; (2) time is available for interactive, collaborative learning and problem solving; (3) it is important for members to understand and be committed to the results; or (4) there is a desire for members to learn and continue to use concepts and techniques for self-assessment.

The third alternative, called *collaborative assessment*, is the approach built on the Lewinian (1948) action-research notion that provides the user with realistic fact finding and evaluation while providing the researcher with access to underlying social processes. Although action research has been discussed extensively in both the assessment and organizational change literature and there are many proponents of it, there are few organizational change efforts that have successfully made use of this approach. This is for all the political and cultural reasons outlined previously in this chapter. When an action research or self-renewed commitment exists, then the following guidelines should help.

Some of the elements of an effective collaborative assessment are: (1) a collaboratively developed contract that explicitly indicates how decision-making influence over the assessment will be managed (who decides what, when, and with whom); (2) a collaborative determination by members and researchers of the goals and criteria for the organizational change; (3) a joint evaluation and data collection design; and (4) joint data analysis and feedback with action planning.

The ideal collaborative process begins with an explication of individual member's models. This is followed by group consensus on a shared model, then input from the researcher on models derived from scientific knowledge and finally consensus between member and researcher on a collaborative model for the assessment that draws on all three levels of models (individual, group, and scientific).

A CASE OF ILLUSTRATION OF AN ORGANIZATIONAL ASSESSMENT APPROACH

This is the case of a company with 40 plants in the pulp and paper products business. The senior management of the company decided that, in order to stay competitive in the 1980s, they were going to have to improve productivity via more participative managerial approaches. In part this was motivated by the general U.S. management sensitivity to Japanese management approaches, including the mass media play at quality circles we are getting. Also, there were specific trends occurring in the forest products' industry in some of the leading companies along these lines. The decision was made that the basic change strategy would be to select three of the company's 40 plants and experiment for a year or so with productivity and quality of work life interventions. The overall structure for the change would be to establish a steering committee at corporate headquarters made up of the representatives, namely the general managers from each of the plants and key corporate managers. This steering committee would set policy and oversee the change effort, including an ongoing assessment and evaluation process. At the plants the name for the change effort would be "accomplishment through constructive teamwork" with the acronym ACT, and each plant would have its own steering committee to oversee the implementation of ACT groups, which in essence were similar to quality circles. Each plant would have its own consultant, whose responsibility it would be to help the plant implement the ACT program aimed toward improved productivity and quality of work life. An additional consulting unit was a team from the Institute for Social Research from The University of Michigan, which was responsible for working with the corporate steering committee in the role of evaluators and monitors of the change process.

The project was launched with surveys being conducted in each of the plants. These data were then fed back to the consultants and the plants' steering committees, who then used the baseline data to begin to plan the change strategy. Then the ISR team developed a set of research questions to be tracked, using multiple data collection methods. The framework for tracking the change effort focused heavily on the technical, political, and cultural systems, with specific questions being tracked in each system. Table 13.3 presents the research questions along with the technical, political, and cultural aspects of each of these questions. Table 13.3 also outlines the data collection modes and timing for data collection. What is unique about the process is that it is multilevel in terms of the technical, political, and cultural systems and it relies on multiple data collection modes—documents, observations, interviews, and surveys. The basic design is to start with a baseline survey, followed by a year of observation, interviewing, document collection around the research questions outlined in Table 13.3, followed by a one-year survey follow-up. These data are to be used to help formulate the strategy for dissemination of the change effort across the remaining 37 plants and take corrective actions in the three pilot plants.

Such a design has the benefit of providing the client organization with guidance data, as well as providing useful academic research on the management of change.

Table 13.3   An Evaluation and Monitoring Plan for Accomplishment through Constructive Teamwork (ACT)

Research Questions	Three Perspectives on Questions			Data Collection Modes	When
	Technically	Politically	Culturally		
1. What is corporate role? (a) Pilot phase (b) Future dissemination	Providing technical help and structure	Power and influence ACT	Corporate norms versus ACT	Documents Observation (field notes) Interviews	Ongoing Ongoing Spring 1982
2. What is plant manager role?	Tasks associated with ACT	Influence and power *vis a vis* ACT	Value shaping role (own value shifts)	Consultant observation (field notes) Mini-interviews (telephone) Interviews Observation	Monthly Jan/Mar/June Jan/Mar/June
3. How do outside influences affect ACT?	Economic and market factors	Political	Societal norms and values	Documents Mini-interviews Interviews Observation	Ongoing Monthly Jan/Mar/June
4. How does the organization structure relate to ACT?	Formal and informal task structure	Formal and informal power structure	Norms and values of different groups in the structure	Documents Mini-interviews Observations	Ongoing Monthly Jan/Mar/June
5. How do consultant approaches differ?	Task and technology mix	Use of influence and power	Value shaping (role making, reinforcing, and so on)	Documents Mini-interviews Interviews Observations	Ongoing Monthly Jan/Mar/June Jan/Mar/June

No.	Question	Task	Power, influence role	Value shaping role	Methods	Timing
6.	What is: (a) Corporate steering committee's task role? (b) Plant steering committee's roles?	Task	Power, influence role	Value shaping role	(a) Documents, Observations, Interviews (b) Observation, Documents, Mini-interviews, Interviews, Observations	(a) Ongoing, Spring 1982 (b) Ongoing, Monthly, Jan/Mar/June, Jan/Mar/June
7.	How do personnel systems relate to ACT?	Nuts and bolts systems	Political dynamics of selection, development, appraisal, rewards	Value shaping role	Documents, Mini-Interviews, Interviews, Observations, Observations	Spring 1982, Monthly, Jan/Mar/June, Jan/Mar/June
8.	How do ACT groups function?	Around task	Influence power	Norms	Documents, Mini-interviews, Interviews, Group Process Survey	Ongoing, Monthly, Jan/Mar/June, Monthly
9.	What are the conflicts, and how are they managed?	Over technical matters	Over power, rewards, status, prestige	Over values, style, norms	Documents (memos, and so on), Mini-interviews, Interviews, Observations	Ongoing, Monthly, Jan/Mar/June, Jan/Mar/June
10.	What are the relationships between ACT and unions?	Around task accomplishment	Power relations	Culture and values	Documents, Mini-interviews, Interviews, Observations	Ongoing, Monthly, Jan/Mar/June, Jan/Mar/June

Table 13.3 An Evaluation and Monitoring Plan for Accomplishment through Constructive Teamwork (ACT)

| | Three Perspectives on Questions | | | | |
Research Questions	Technically	Politically	Culturally	Data Collection Modes	When
11. How do consultants including ISR relate to each other?	Task relationships	Power relationships	Style and value shaping role	Documents Mini-interviews Interviews Observations	Ongoing Monthly Jan/Mar/June Jan/Mar/June
12. What are the ACT outcomes?	Bottom line	Power shifts	Value changes	Documents (Production, financial data) Mini-interviews Interviews ISR survey	Spring 1982 Monthly after March June interviews Sept. 1982
13. What are the role shifts related to ACT?	Task related changes	Influence, power shifts	Norms about relationships	Documents Mini-interviews Interviews Observations	Ongoing Monthly Jan/Mar/June Jan/Mar/June
14. How do people learn and master ACT process?	Problem solving and task process	Influence processes	Value and norm shifts	Documents Mini-interviews Interviews Observations	Ongoing Monthly Jan/Mar/June Jan/Mar/June
15. How is Institute for Social Research data used?	For task purposes	For political purposes	For cultural purposes	Documents Mini-interviews Interviews Observations	Ongoing Monthly Jan/Mar/June Jan/Mar/June
16. What are people's expectations about ACT?					

SUMMARY AND CONCLUSION

This chapter has argued that for primarily political and cultural reasons most organizations do not engage in systematic evaluation and monitoring of strategic change efforts. However, when this does occur, such as in the case of Volvo, it can have a very beneficial effect.

The chapter did not provide guidance on how to create the political and cultural conditions for systematic evaluation and monitoring; rather, it focused on how to implement such a process.

1. Having an explicit organization model;

2. Having an outside research role for technical and political reasons;

3. Having an agreed-upon set of research questions and methodology for data collection;

4. Having a feedback and problem solving-process for using the data.

Chapter Fourteen

Strategic Change in the Future

INTRODUCTION

Everywhere in the countries shaped by Western civilization, the amenities of existence are threatened by environmental nausea. Mounting material and psychological problems create the impression that humankind has lost control of its affairs. The deteriorating conditions of our cities, our adversarial relationship with nature, the futile occupations that waste our days, are—unnecessarily and unconsciously—determined more by technological imperatives than by our choice of desirable human goals. (Dubos, 1982).

This view of life and world conditions can lead to a fatalistic passivity which helps feed a self-fulfilling prophecy. As Dubos (1982) stated, "A key to overcoming the passivity born of pessimism is to remember that the really important problems are not technical. They originate in our thoughts, our uncertainties, or our poor judgment concerning parascientific values."

This final chapter attempts to balance the severity of the very real problems of the world, society, and organizations with a challenge to renew and reenergize rather than give way to pessimism.

The objectives of this chapter are the following:

1. To view strategic change management in the context of world and societal pressures.

2. To discuss responses to these pressures and identify emerging change strategies for managing these problems.

3. To propose future steps for theory and research work on organizational change.

TRANSFORMING ORGANIZATIONS IN TURBULENT TIMES

In May of 1982 the Falkland Islands were still being held by the Argentines. The British Navy was engaged in battle to repossess them so that the British could then negotiate a face saving solution giving the islands to the Argentines. Poland was fraught with tremendous internal unrest; the Russians still occupied Afghanistan and had indicated their support of the Argentines. Central America was in turmoil. The Mideast remained a hot spot. The U.S. economy was in a deep recession, with high unemployment, a prime rate in the high teens, and no prospect for a quick turnaround. Whether these particular problems persist over a long period of time or not, we will continue to face serious problems of this nature for the foreseeable future. The basic forces or conditions creating the 1982 problems will be with us for at least a decade. We are in a time when there will continue to be turbulence in the technical, political, and cultural systems on a worldwide basis. Individuals and organizations will increasingly need to learn to manage under these conditions.

Table 14.1 identifies some of the external pressures that will affect organizations. There is bitter irony in some of what is occurring. For example, in the United States we are rapidly advancing with technological change, increasing the development of very sophisticated systems, and moving into the age often characterized as postindustrial

Table 14.1   Environmental Forces in the 1980s for U.S. Organizations

Technical Pressures	Political Pressures	Cultural Pressures
Falling U.S. productivity	Problems of worldwide distribution of wealth	Decline in work ethic, pressure for fulfillment at work
Intense world competition	Lack of integrative mechanisms for worldwide disputes	Entrepreneurialism and risk taking less evident
Inflation/disinflation uncertainty	Pluralism (the haves vs. have nots)	Demographic changes An older work force Expectations of World War II baby boom
Interest Rates	Government policy and regulations conflicted	
Low capital investment in the United States	Democratization of the workplace	
Low R & D investment in the United States		
Shift to service economy		
High technology changes (communication and computers)		

with complex interdependencies and symbolic transfers more important than material handling. The irony is that, in the face of this opportunity, the United States is actually moving backward, not forward, in dealing with its economic problems. Before addressing the proactive process of how organizations can deal with these pressures, I will discuss some of the pressures in Table 14.1.

Technical Pressure

The world is changing quickly. For the first time since World War II, the United States is losing its claim to the highest standard of living in the world. In the matter of a few years it slipped from first to fifth place, and in early 1982 it fell to eighth place. Under the burden of exorbitant energy costs, double digit inflation, and declining world competitiveness in world markets of autos, steel, consumer electronics, machinery, and recently computer memory devices, the United States faces great challenges.

It is beyond the scope of this book and my own personal competence to explain the causes and consequences of all of these phenomena. Thus, this discussion will be brief and admittedly superficial. Nevertheless, there is one insight I feel it is important to share: the systemic and hence self-reinforcing or self-perpetuating nature of many of these fundamental problems. To illustrate this point, I will present an analysis of the declining rate of productivity growth in the United States that was developed by Charles Fombrun (1982) at the Wharton School. Figure 14.1 diagrams the problem.

After reviewing the current litany of reasons for productivity decline in the United States he came up with the following explanations:

Reduced capital-to-labor ratio, brought about by the increased participation of women and the entry of the post-World War II baby boom workers who are less experienced, and by falling expenditures on R&D, has lowered the growth in productivity.

A shift in the percent of GNP from the private to the military sector has reduced productivity (argues Seymour Melman).

The increased alienation of the worker has led to such productivity decline behaviors as greater absenteeism, production slowdowns, and sabotage activities.

The increased stress on our resources has resulted in waste as we live beyond our means and get diminishing returns on labor, land, and even knowledge.

Fombrun states that:

The corporate response has been paradoxical. As productivity growth declines, executive officers are pressured to show effective coping by taking measures which will offset the decline. Clearly, however, their primary concern is with results which will be manifest in the course of their terms as

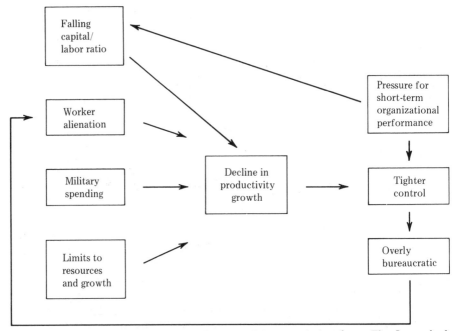

Figure 14.1 Productivity problem. (Reprinted by permission from *The Journal of Business Strategy*, **3(1), Summer 1982. Copyright © 1982, Warren, Gorham and Lamont, Inc., 210 South Street, Boston, Mass. All rights reserved.)**

corporate officers. Since most CEOs are approaching 60 and will only be in their role for about five years, declining productivity growth is therefore followed by the imposition of tighter control systems. Expenses are more closely monitored. Compensation systems are geared to reward individual measurable and quantifiable goals, the kind which tend to involve only the short run. The failure of productivity to grow therefore promotes more bureaucratic control over worker behavior, compounding worker alienation. At the same time, it raises the inertia level within organizations, making it increasingly difficult for future adaptation to take place.

Thus, the cycle diagrammed in Figure 14.1 is self-perpetuating. It becomes necessary to apply major surgery to get long-term change. The cycle must be revamped to stress long-term performance with a shift in compensation for key managers to reward for longer-term productivity growth, organizational changes to deal with worker alienation, and changes in the capital-to-labor ratio. Rather than tighter error avoiding control, where everyone is watching out for Big Brother, there should be a dramatic increase in error embracing control which aims to solve problems and increase productivity. The extensive use of quality circles by the Japanese represents such an error embracing control system, which in turn reduces worker alienation and hence improves productivity growth.

In all of our technical, cultural, and political problems we find self-reinforcing cycles which we have to revamp in order to get change. The medicine is not to apply more pressure to an already self-defeating process, which occurred when W.T. Grant went bankrupt by driving a self-destructive system harder.

Political Pressures

The world political scene is troublesome; almost a decade ago Robert Heilbroner (1974) warned us:

> The long era of industrial expansion is now entering its final stages and we must anticipate the commencement of a new era of stationary total output and if population growth continues or an equitable sharing among nations has not yet been attained, declining output per head in the advanced nations . . . leading to convulsive change.

His scenario for world political adjustments is very violent; he argues that we do not have the processes in place to resolve political differences. The events since 1974 when Heilbroner wrote this have pretty much followed this scenario. Furthermore, the conditions needed to change are not in sight. Thus, organizations can expect to have to function in a volatile world where political risk analysis is as important as economic risk analysis when conducting multinational operations.

A less negative political trend is one occurring in Western countries, the democratization of the workplace. In Europe this is reflected in several decades of laws enacted around codetermination which have resulted in workers on boards and a move toward union ownership of significant voting shares of companies in such countries as Sweden. The same trend toward more democratization in the workplace is evidenced in the United States, yet the path taken is and probably will continue to be distinct.

> What is happening in the United States, in sum, is wholly different in character, in nature, in form, in language, and to a considerable degree, in union and management intent, than what has happened so fast in the Europe of the 1970s. Missing from the American response to what seems to be a worldwide phenomenon of workplace democratization are government intervention, workers on boards (actual or sought), works council structures, increased union influence in management decision making, and (as in Sweden particularly) huge expansion of the areas permissible for collective bargaining.
>
> Present in the American response, and largely missing in most of the European "advances" . . . is focus on worker (as distinct from organization-wide) decision making, the notion of union-management cooperation on a voluntary basis, and especially a pragmatic, uniquely American sense of evolutionary, trial and error growth without legal prescriptions. . . . The American approach has been defined as "faith in human nature, faith in human intelligence, and the power of pooled and collective experience." It's not belief that these things are complete but that if given a show, they will grow and generate the knowledge and wisdom needed to guide collective action. (*American Center for the Quality of Work Life*, 1978, pp. 27–28)

Whether the shift toward more politically organic workplaces occurs in a trial and error revolutionary fashion or moves with the revolutionary pace evidenced in Europe does not alter the strong indication that this will continue to be a major force in the 1980s. As such it is an opportunity for organizations who are willing to get ahead of the wave and manage it.

Cultural Pressures

The cultural environment is undergoing change. It is not entirely clear what all the shifts mean, what are actual trends, and what are aberrations. Much is said about the declining work ethic, hedonistic trends, changing sexual and family mores, new definitions of equity, and other changes. One popular and somewhat utopian view of the cultural shifts occurring in the United States is Alvin Toffler's:

> ... [We are] creating a new civilization in our midst with its own jobs, lifestyles, work ethic, sexual attitudes and concepts of life ... if we begin now we and our children can take part in the exciting reconstruction not merely of our obsolete political structures but of civilization itself. ... (Toffler, 1980)

Whether one accepts the utopian view presented by Toffler or some other less positive view, we are still faced with new cultural pressures.

One set of pressures can be attributed to the post-World War II baby boom cohort just beginning to have its impact on the work force. In 1982 the leading edge of this group is 36, it trails off at age 18. This large group has been reared in an affluent environment, is highly educated, has high expectations about what it can achieve in terms of career, salary, and life-style. This group is ideally suited for a fast-growth economy where there is a tremendous amount of opportunity. Instead they face a slow-growth economy with limited opportunities fanned by the intense competition of their peers who are equally talented and also have high expectations. Members of this group, who were trained to be leaders, will end up stuck on the lower rungs of many corporations as followers. If this problem is not managed, the result will be unmet expectations leading to disillusionment, frustration, and dissatisfaction. The cultural pressure is built into the demographics and will exert itself throughout most of the 1980s.

Shifting values and norms in society is a very complex and subtle process which provides very slippery ground for making generalizations and predictions. Nonetheless we must try. One area that bears discussion is the extent to which the Protestant work ethic has given way to what Lasch termed "the culture of narcissism" (1978). He provides a view of individuals obsessed with the superficial, external trappings of life who cannot deal with tomorrow and hence focus on today's gratification.

In this case, work becomes a means to a superficial end and the content of work is secondary. Everything is done to gratify oneself in the present. Fombrun (1982) points out:

> What these attitudinal trends spell out is consistent with the demographic patterns which are taking shape. As organizations move through the 1980s and 1990s, the changing nature of the workforce will call for detailed attention to problems that motivate achievement, reward success and cope with failure. The danger is that organizations may choose to do nothing, a disadvantage for both organizations and society because it would only be a short run solution to what is a fundamental problem.

The Technical, Political, and Cultural Dilemmas

The three strands are interrelated in society just as they are in organizations. The dilemma for society is to evolve a more satisfactory weaving of these three strands. It will not be easy as we are increasingly having to do this in the context of a zero-sum economic setting. In the past we had an expanding economy that allowed us to use money to solve our problems. We don't expect to have this luxury in the near future. Thus we are faced with the dilemma described by Lester Thurow (1980):

> Slow growth and declining productivity, energy shortages and overregulation, chronic inflation and persistent poverty—the problems are all too visible and so is our inability to solve them. As the rest of the world begins to overtake us in real economic growth and productivity our society seems paralyzed, unable to act or even to agree on what action is necessary . . . none of the problems that bedevil us—whether it be energy or inflation or technological innovation—can be solved without making many Americans worse off, even though society as a whole might gain.
>
> The problem is that in our democratic system these minorities have the power to veto solutions they do not like. . . . The result has been paralysis and drift. Today, as never before, all policy solutions involve some degree of redistribution of income and wealth. And until we face up to this painful reality and learn as a society to agree on who should bear what costs, economic growth will continue to elude us.

The challenge is clearly before us. The pressures on organizations are also clearly evident.

BACK TO BASICS

Managing in turbulent times requires that organizations go back to basics and face squarely the task of reweaving the strategic rope. The fundamental character of the technical system will need reexamination in many companies and will result in dramatic transformations such as are occurring at AT&T. The political strand will be central to much of the change in the 1980s as more and more key executives' jobs will be put on the line and as the rewards of organizations are adjusted to new realities, whether in terms of more performance-driven rewards systems, more long-term driven reward systems, or a renegotiation of power and rewards with the unions, such as the changes started with the United Auto Workers and the auto industry. The cultural strand is perhaps the most complex, subtle, and most pervasive influence on organizational effectiveness. It will require concerted effort to manage it in these turbulent times.

In order to work on these three strands of the strategic rope, management will have to be explicit and get the dialogue out in the open. Trial and error and back room politicking will not do the trick. Thus, in the coming years methods will be needed for helping management as part of the strategic management process of the firm work on these issues.

This book focuses on the use of these concepts as a process for managing strategic change. Implicit is the notion that it is for extraordinary times and hence attention is not given to incorporating these concepts and procedures into the ongoing management process of the firm.

In the future, TPC theory should have a more central role in the ongoing strategic management of organizations. I am already working with several companies that are beginning to incorporate some of these concepts into their strategic planning processes. Thus, management can continue to be confronted with such basic questions as: What business(es) are we in? Can we be joined by . . . ? Who reaps what benefits from the organization? What are appropriate norms and values for people in the organization to have?

Figure 14.2 presents a management exercise which is one of the early steps in strategic planning. It is intended to focus attention on the nontechnical aspects of strategic planning and the interdependence of the three strands. Once the individual managers have drawn their cycles, a group is brought together to agree on a common scenario. This dialogue forces a great deal of back-to-basics work. People must share normally implicit assumptions about the future, especially with regard to political and cultural issues.

The second step in the process is to make the picture a bit more complex. Rather than present them with the total organizational matrix developed in this book, which is constructed by crossing technical, political, and cultural systems with the six categories of the network organizational model, a simplified three-by-three matrix called the strategic management matrix is used.

Strategic Management Matrix

The strategic management matrix focuses on the three systems and on three sets of managerial tools used to align the three systems. The

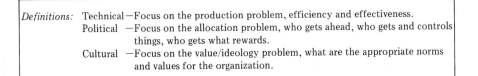

Definitions: Technical—Focus on the production problem, efficiency and effectiveness.
Political —Focus on the allocation problem, who gets ahead, who gets and controls
things, who gets what rewards.
Cultural   —Focus on the value/ideology problem, what are the appropriate norms
and values for the organization.

Procedure: 1. Draw cycles (label each—technical, political, and cultural) to indicate
what must happen for the company to be successful.
2. Say what events and issues will be associated with each cycle.

High

Uncertainty
and
managerial
attention

Low

1983   Time   1990

Figure 14.2   Plotting organizational cycles

three tool areas are mission and strategy, organizational structure, and human resource management. Mission and strategy entail setting goals and developing strategy, including all of the managerial processes necessary to realize the goal. Structure is broadly defined to include the tasks of the organization, how people are grouped and coordinated to accomplish the tasks, as well as the managerial processes of control, information, and so on needed to make the structure work. Human resource management tools include staff selection and placement of people, from both outside and inside the organization; development of people for performing in their current as well as future jobs; appraisal of performance, potential, and both financial and nonfinancial rewards.

Managers are given the task of deciding where their organization needs to invest its limited senior management time by rating each of the nine cells in Figure 14.3 according to the amount of change required for the firm's success. This is the same activity outlined in Chapter 7 to develop a change strategy. The difference is that it is simplified and incorporated into the regular strategic planning process. In order to prepare managers for this task they are given the following background on the strategic management matrix.

Technical System. Managers are told that the technical row in

Managerial Tools

Managerial Areas

	Mission and strategy	Organization structure	Human resource management
Technical system	Assessing and defining what business we are in and determining the business strategy [1] [2] [3] [4] [5]	Defining reporting relationships, and groupings of people and departments, to meet business needs [1] [2] [3] [4] [5]	Methods of staffing, development, and assessment of people [1] [2] [3] [4] [5]
Political system	Who gets to influence the mission and strategy of your organization [1] [2] [3] [4] [5]	Distribution of power in your organization, both across the organization and up and down the organization [1] [2] [3] [4] [5]	Managing the politics of succession, reward system, and appraisal [1] [2] [3] [4] [5]
Cultural system	Developing a culture, or set of values, to support business strategy [1] [2] [3] [4] [5]	Developing managerial style and culture to fit your organization [1] [2] [3] [4] [5]	Selection, development, and rewards to support your organization's values and culture [1] [2] [3] [4] [5]

Figure 14.3 Strategic management matrix. (*Procedure:* For each cell on the matrix, indicate the amount of change you feel is required over the next five years for your organization to be successful. Circle the number below each box to indicate: [1] no change required, [2] some, [3] moderate change required, [4] more, [5] a great deal of change required.)

Figure 14.3 is representative of much mainstream management training and writing. It represents tasks that management spends considerable time working on. The first managerial tool is mission and strategy, where we find such traditional management tasks as assessing the environmental threats and the opportunities facing the organization, assessing organizational strengths and weaknesses, and defining a mission that fits organizational resources. The strategy identifies how the major resources fit together to accomplish the mission.

The second managerial tool area is organizational structure. Here management faces the traditional organization design dilemma of differentiating within the organization, that is dividing the organization into work roles such as production, marketing, finance, and R&D and then, once there has been a division of labor, integrating the organization, that is, finding mechanisms to combine the roles into departments, divisions, regions, and so on. Another organization design issue is how to align the structure or design of the organization to the strategy of the organization. For example, functional organizations fit best with single line businesses.

The third tool area for dealing with the technical system is the use of the human resource management system. This involves the proper match of people and jobs, the specification of performance criteria for different organizational roles, means of measuring performance (appraisal systems, etc.), and approaches to staffing and development to fill the roles in the present and in the future. All of these tool areas—mission and strategy, organization structure, and human resource management—combine in most organizations to solve the technical problem.

Political System. The political row of Figure 14.3 is the least talked about, yet frequently the major absorber of senior management time and resources. It may not be the topic for management committee meetings, but it is certainly the major topic of lunches, cocktails, and private discussions in individual offices. In these discussions there is plenty of time spent on who's going to be promoted to what position, what group is in power, who's going to get to influence the strategic decisions, how the budgets are going to be allocated across businesses or divisions, what the balance of power between different functional areas is, and the political nature of the allocation of bonuses and rewards. The problem is that in most organizations to *call* these decisions political is to be guilty of heresy. In reality, these are all allocation decisions, hence, political. The real issue is not whether we call them political but whether they're made in a way that is perceived as fair and considerate of the larger needs of the organization. Examples of specific managerial tasks associated with the political system are presented in Figure 14.3.

The first managerial tool applied in working with the political system of an organization is mission and strategy formulation. In this area there are at least two major tasks. One is determining who should influence the mission and strategy of the organization. Technical textbooks and consulting groups often lay out descriptions of how to do strategic planning, but they don't specify how to allocate power vis-à-vis the actual strategic decision making process. It's not clear what levels of the organization should be involved; for example, should all division presidents have equal power? Should the chairman make the strategic decision by him/herself? Thus, there are a set of decisions about who gets to influence the mission and strategy. The second set of political tasks regarding mission and strategy is the management of coalitional behavior around strategic decisions. No matter what the strategic decision is, inherent in it is a set of political outcomes that results in the creation of coalitions; that is, decisions to enter new businesses or markets, to invest more in a starting up a business, or to sell a dog business will impact adversely on some careers and further others. These decisions imply the movement of resources and budgets and inevitably result in coalitions taking different positions. Therefore, the management of coalitional behavior around strategic decisions is a critical political system activity for management.

The second area in which managerial tools are used to manage the political system is the design of the organization or the organizational structure. The technical issues are how to rationally differentiate and integrate the organization. The political issue relates to the distribution of power across the role structure. That is, how much power should a department or division head have in relation to his or her subordinates? What should the allocation of power across the organizational structure be? This can be reflected in the scope of decision making authority individuals have regarding budgets and in how much power they have over people's careers further down in the organization. A second organization design political issue is how the balance of power takes place across groupings; that is, what's the relative power of sales and marketing, of production and R&D, of the controller and the human resources group. These decisions are political as they balance the allocation of power in the organization and, often, the allocation of money across different parts of the organization.

Finally, human resource systems in the political system area need to be adjusted. The first issue is managing succession politics. It must be decided who gets ahead and how they get ahead. Any time there is a succession issue, given the pyramidal shape of organizations and the fact that organizations tend to produce more candidates than there are positions, there are going to be win/lose decisions. Therefore, there will be succession politics. Organizations vary greatly in how they handle this. On one end of the spectrum are fairly strong and institutionalized practices, as represented in General Electric's slate system, where a strong human resource staff works with line management to establish a slate of candidates for positions among the top 600 people in GE. Managers can fill those positions only with someone who is on the formal slate. This is in marked contrast to the majority of U.S. corporations where there is a very informal process of choosing candidates and there's a great deal of informal political behavior to move your person or to politically maneuver so that you can get a shot for a job. Generally missing are a formal system to identify candidates for key positions and a political system that sees to it that formally identified succession candidates are actually appointed.

The second political human resource issue is design and administration of reward systems—who gets what and how they get it. Again, there are many variations in reward systems. One example of a political issue that needed to be resolved was a plastics company where the lion's share of the bonus was being allocated to the top three executives. This created a very unhappy senior management group below that level. They began to exert political pressure on the top three to open up the bonus system to people further down in the organization.

Finally, an important political issue in organizations, because of its centrality in decisions that regard pay and promotion, is the managing of the appraisal process. Who is appraised by whom and by what criteria? Here is an interesting conflict between the logic of a political system and the logic of a technical system.

In appraisal research, it's been found that, from a technical point of view, subordinates and peers have a better and more valid understanding of an individual's performance than his or her boss. This dates back to a line of research started in World War II where peers were better able to predict who would be successful pilots than the instructors. This finding has been replicated in a variety of ways in industrial settings where peers and subordinates provide a better indicator of actual and potential performance than a boss or a supervisor. However, 99% of U.S. corporations politically could not tolerate having peers and subordinates appraise their bosses, even though, from a technical point of view, it provides better data. This is an example of political logic overruling technical logic and represents a dilemma that has to be managed in the politics of appraisal.

Cultural Systems. The third system that needs to be managed is the cultural system, and, as with the technical and political systems, there are four categories of management tools for addressing the cultural system.

The first management tool area is in the mission and strategy area. There are two issues management needs to attend to here. One is the influence of values and philosophy on the mission and strategy of the organization. Because of the uncertain and complex nature of business strategy and deciding on the mission of the organization, it is greatly influenced by the personal values of the key decision makers.

As a result, entering certain markets or businesses is often as much influenced by a value position as by a technical analysis of whether it would make money or be a successful business venture. One task for management is to recognize value positions and develop ways of addressing them as value instead of technical issues. Running technical analyses when someone is arguing against something because of a value position is arguing apples and oranges. The second mission and strategy task related to culture is developing a culture that accords with the mission and strategy of the corporation. That is, in order for a company to be successful, its culture must support the kind of business the organization is in. For instance, in the AT&T example the changed mission and strategy which moved them from a solely regulated telephone monopoly to a competitive information business will require a culture that supports innovation, competition, and profit.

The second area that needs to be addressed to manage the culture is organizational structure and design. Here the paramount issues are the development of managerial styles aligned with the technical and political structures of the organization. For example, an organization that has moved from a functional organization to a matrix organization requires a very different managerial style. These organizations are very different, both technically and politically. Power is balanced on two dimensions—such as product and function—and requires a management style of negotiated, open confrontation of conflict, as opposed to a more traditional chain of command management style. A second cultural issue is the development of subcultures to support the various subcomponents of the organization design. For example, the production culture should be different than the R&D culture. R&D should be longer-term, more innovative, more supportive of entrepreneurial idea generation. Production is more cost-conscious, efficiency-driven. As a result, the organization needs to foster subcultures consistent with the subunit. This leads to a third cultural problem; the extent to which there are mechanisms for integration of subcultures to create a company culture. If the subcultures are too strong, then R&D, production, sales, finance, and so on are working at odds and don't have any wider identification with the company. Some companies go to great extremes to create identity with the company; for instance, at IBM and Exxon there is definitive company culture that transcends any of the subcultures.

The final area for managing the culture is the human resource management system. It is in this area that Japanese management has been more sophisticated and attentive than American management. They have used the human resource system very skillfully to shape and reinforce cultures that provide the organization with strong commitment to the technical outcome of the organization. One of the first tools used to accomplish this in the human resource area is the selection of people, specifically, the selection of people who are sensitive to how they fit in and reinforce the dominant culture of the organization. Companies that use the human resource system as a cultural tool spend a great deal of effort in the selection process. They involve many people in the interview process and screen people out for cultural reasons; that is, the criterion is how a person will fit in. This is true in Japanese firms, where workers have a large role in the selection process, as well as in U.S. firms that Ouchi would characterize as applying Theory Z.

A second tool for shaping the culture of the organization is the way in which people are developed and socialized. Again organizations that use the human resource system to shape culture invest heavily in training and development. Much of it is aimed at getting people inculcated with the dominant culture of the organization. So, for example, if you review many of IBM's training programs you will find that a very explicit goal and a very explicit part of the program deals with IBM values. This is done in Japanese firms as well, where they put a high premium on development, much of which is on-the-job and aims at getting people to internalize values important to the culture of the organization. Finally, the management of rewards obviously can be used to shape and reinforce the culture of the organization—promoting and compensating people who fit the dominant values of the organization. Using the human resource system to reinforce the people around the culture is a very powerful tool for aligning the culture system with the technical and political systems.

The analysis of the strategic management matrix leads to a better understanding of the basics of management. The strategic task now becomes more than merely talking about a portfolio of businesses and the strategies for the strategic business units, it focuses on managing the nine cells of the matrix as a dynamic jigsaw puzzle that requires ongoing attention and adjustment. How much adjustment depends on some of the turbulent environmental pressures outlined earlier in the chapter. The strategic plans then should include the strategies and technologies presented in this book.

Over the next several years research and the application of this approach to strategic management will be carried out. It is already becoming apparent that the area that will receive the most attention by many organizations is human resource management. It is the most underdeveloped and least strategic of the three management tool areas and, as a result, is not contributing technically, politically, or culturally in a manner necessitated by the pressures in the 1980s.

THE FOCUS ON HUMAN RESOURCE MANAGEMENT

The technological, economic, and demographic changes occurring in the 1980s are pressuring organizations to use more effective human resource management. While sagging productivity and worker alienation have popularized management tools such as quality circles and profit sharing plans, the long-run competitiveness of American industry will require considerably more sophisticated approaches to the human resource input that deal with its strategic role in organizational performance. Thus, the three human resource management cells in Figure 14.3 warrant a great deal of attention.

The 1980s is a decade when TPC theory will have increasing relevance to human resource management issues.

Beyond Operational Services for Human Resource Management

Effective human resources management means designing organizational systems that address the human resource dimensions of the firm's strategic, managerial, and operational tasks. Most personnel functions in American industry provide highly sophisticated human resource support for operational tasks. However, managerial and strategic tasks are largely driven by unsystematic, idiosyncratic, and frequently conflicting systems.

While this is partially due to the complex and changing nature of human resources, it is reinforced by a perspective that views human resources management as a staff function rather than an integral part of line management. It is my position that it must be a responsibility built into the management process.

Figure 14.4 diagrams the relationship between business functions that have to be performed and corresponding human resource tasks. Two critical questions must be addressed: (1) What are the specific human resource activities that are required to support the business at each level? (2) What is required to forge the link between the business functions and the human resource function at each level?

At the operational level the business side is concerned with the execution of day-to-day tasks, the ongoing production process. On the human resource side the concern is ensuring that employees come to work, perform, are evaluated, rewarded, and have the job skills they need to do their work. The operational link is the interface between the day-to-day activities of the business and the human resources system designed to facilitate this process. In order for this link to be effective it is necessary that:

1. The line have good technical human resource systems.

2. Middle and first line supervisors know how to make effective use of the human resource system at their disposal (selection/staffing, compensation and benefits, appraisal and development).

3. Competent human resource generalists be developed who can monitor the overall use of the human resource system by the client managers.

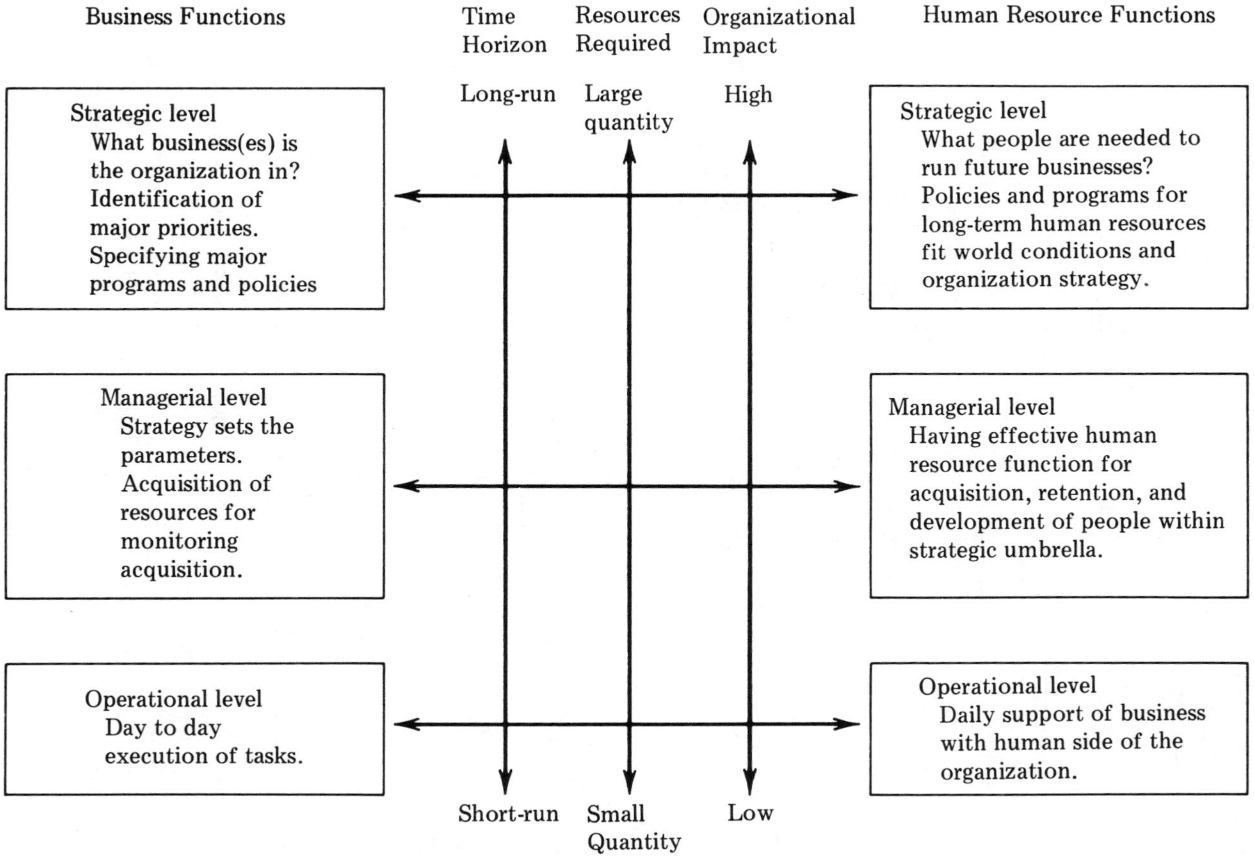

Figure 14.4 The link between business and human resource functions

403

4. An organizational culture exists that recognizes the importance of human resource tools for enhancing overall organizational performance.

5. The political system supports and rewards good use of operational human resource management systems.

At the managerial level, the business side is under the umbrella of the strategic thrust of the business. The major focus is on the acquisition of resources for carrying out the strategic plan and the development of procedures for measuring and monitoring performance. On the human resource side the concern is with developing an effective and efficient human resource system for acquiring, appraising, rewarding, and developing human resources to achieve the strategic goals.

Building a managerial link requires dialogue around such issues as: Do we hire or go outside to develop the human resources needed in the medium term? How do we meet the needs of the internal markets for human resource services? What are the strategies for each of the subfunctions, such as staffing, compensation, appraisals, and development?

For an effective managerial link to emerge, the following conditions must be met:

1. Senior human resource staff must take on a strong staff role with the full cooperation of line executives.

2. Internal marketing data are needed regarding the specific human resource services required to support managerial activities.

3. Accurate data bases must be available on the internal labor pool, its current capabilities, and its potential.

At the strategic level the business side is concerned with determining what business(es) the organization is in or should be in; choosing objectives and reviewing them; identifying major priorities; and specifying major programs and developing policies to achieve them. On the human resource side, the key issues are determining the kinds of people needed to run the business in the long term; specific policies and programs for the long-term development of human resources and an appropriate social and cultural context within which the objectives are likely to succeed.

The strategic link calls for dialogue between business and human resource concerns. This dialogue is reflected in the establishment of boundaries around the human resource strategic planning, that is, deciding what the human resource pool will consist of in the long term for this particular organization. In addition, the strategic link discusses the trade-off between the human, financial, informational, space, and other scarce resources and the implications of alternative commitments of the organization.

For the strategic link to emerge, the following conditions must be met:

1. Senior line management must give these concerns their attention. There must be a strong commitment to treating human resource issues with the same level of attention given to other major factors such as financing, marketing, and production.

2. There must be effective environmental scanning on the part of the human resource staff to anticipate changes and provide good labor market and relevant social trend data to senior management.

3. A comprehensive and valid internal and external labor market data base must be on hand to provide data that are readily translatable into quantifiable reports for use by senior management in strategic decision making.

4. It is necessary for the organizational culture to value the human element in strategic decision making. The political system must reinforce this value via rewards to key executives (bonuses and promotions that take into account the priority managers give to human resource issues).

Table 14.2 presents a framework that illustrates the range of human resource activities associated with each of the four generic human resource functions: staffing, appraisal, rewards, and development at the strategic, managerial, and operational levels.

The Human Resource Management Cube

Our work with human resource management and TPC theory has led to a three-dimensional framework presented in Figure 14.5. Each of the human resource functions (selection, reward, appraisal, and development) can be viewed from a technical, political, and cultural perspective and sliced strategically, managerially, and operationally. The goal of an effectively managed organization is to manage the whole cube. Most organizations are only working on the technical and operational human resource issues, thus undermanaging the vast majority of human resources.

If human resource management is to move out of the doldrums of operational servicing, if it is to survive in the strategic arena, actually deliver in new areas of the human resource cube, and perform when challenged, senior executives must begin to recognize and understand the managerial nature of its activities and their importance for managerial effectiveness. The steps we are currently taking with several organizations in this area are listed below (Tichy, et al., 1982).

1. *Design a Corporate Philosophy/Culture.* Decide what the critical thrust of the strategic plan will be and what kind of organiza-

Table 14.2 Human Resources Functions

Level	Employee Selection/Placement	Rewards (Pay and Benefits)	Appraisal	Development	Career Planning
Strategic	1. Specify the characteristics of people needed to run business over long term. 2. Alter internal and external systems to reflect future.	1. Determine how workforce will be rewarded over the long term based on potential world conditions. 2. Link to long-term business strategy.	1. Determine what should be valued in long term. 2. Develop means to appraise future dimensions. 3. Make early identification of potential.	1. Plan developmental experiences for people running future business. 2. Set up systems with flexibility necessary to adjust to change.	1. Develop long-term system to manage individual and organizational needs for both flexibility and stability. 2. Link to business strategy.
Managerial	1. Make longitudinal validation of selection criteria. 2. Develop recruitment marketing plan. 3. Develop new markets.	1. Set up five-year compensation plans for individuals. 2. Set up cafeteria benefits packages.	1. Set up validated systems that relate current conditions and future potential. 2. Set up assessment centers for development.	1. Establish general management development program. 2. Provide for organizational development. 3. Foster self-development.	1. Identify career paths. 2. Provide career development services. 3. Match individual with organization.
Operational	1. Make staffing plans. 2. Make recruitment plans. 3. Set up day-to-day monitoring systems.	1. Administer wage and salary program. 2. Administer benefits packages.	1. Set up annual or less frequent appraisal system. 2. Set up day-to-day control systems.	1. Provide for specific job skill training. 2. Provide on-the-job training.	1. Fit individuals to specific jobs. 2. Plan next career move.

Source: Devanna, Fombrun, and Tichy "Human Resource Management: A Strategic Approach" *Organizational Dynamics*, Winter 1981.

HUMAN RESOURCE FUNCTIONS

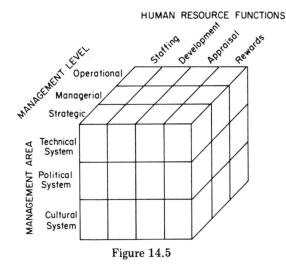

Figure 14.5

tion should follow. Whether the critical values the organization will adhere to involve product quality, growth, customer service, or employee satisfaction, they should be specific enough to represent an organizing set of cultural principles for the company.

2. *Design Human Resource Systems that Reflect the Corporate Culture.* If the corporate culture involves treating its employees like members of a family, then job security should be a key reward for performance. Such a value should be reflected in all of the human resource systems; it should be stressed as a recruitment criterion, tied to compensation, and built in as an assumption of development programs.

Another important reason for a clearly articulated corporate culture is to insure consistency across the human resource functions so that staffing, appraisal, reward, and development activities are mutually reinforcing. The kinds of individuals recruited and the basic stance the organization takes to the retention, use, and development of its human resources stem from a basic set of values, which in most organizations remain implicit. Whether implicit or explicit, it is this culture that provides the cohesion between the four generic human resource systems.

Perhaps one of the most striking examples of the integration of culture with business objectives and human resource activities is that of Hewlett-Packard. Woven together are seven objectives for profit, customers, fields of interest, growth, people, management, and corporate citizenship. Associated with each objective are clearly articulated policies which reflect what is known as the "HP way." For example, when it comes to customers the "HP way" stresses cooperation among the different sales teams dealing with the same customer. This is not a mere platitude but a deeply held value in the HP culture. Growth is considered vital at Hewlett-Packard because of a belief that growth is essential to attracting and retaining high-caliber people.

The most interesting objective from a strategic human resource point of view is their people objective: "To help HP people share in the company's success, which they make possible; to provide job security based on performance; to recognize individual achievements; and to help gain a sense of satisfaction and accomplishment for their work." This translates into such practices as a single worldwide profit sharing program for all employees which is 12% of profits divided according to base pay. There are no special management incentives and few perks. Clearly, Hewlett-Packard is a company in which the corporate culture and the political system is closely and explicitly woven together with the technical system.

3. *Make the Management Process the Target.* The objective of injecting human resource management into the strategic arena is not to enhance the status of traditional personnel staff. Rather, it is to alter the way managers set priorities and make decisions. Thus, the major change must be in the behavior of line management, getting them to consider human resource issues as they plan and implement future strategies. The first step in developing a strategic human resource function, therefore, calls for a careful analysis of the management process of the company to understand the interplay between marketing, financial, technical and human resource inputs. The change strategy obviously involves new technical skills for managers as well as a new set of cultural values and a political system to back them up.

4. *Identify the Portfolio of Human Resource Activities.* Determine the appropriate operational, managerial, and strategic level human resource activities for each of the human resource areas. Tasks are determined by an analysis, with line managers, of business needs at each of the three levels—operational, managerial, and strategic—and of how they can be facilitated by different human resource services.

The analysis includes an audit of what the company is currently providing in the way of services at each level and in each human resource area as well as what is needed. At the operational level, the managers are presented with a variety of diagnostic questions, samples of which are presented in Figure 14.6. These questions attempt to determine how well business operation activities are supported by the human resource systems. Managers are then asked what changes would provide more support.

A similar process is undertaken at the managerial and strategic levels. Figure 14.7 illustrates some diagnostic questions for the strategic level of analysis.

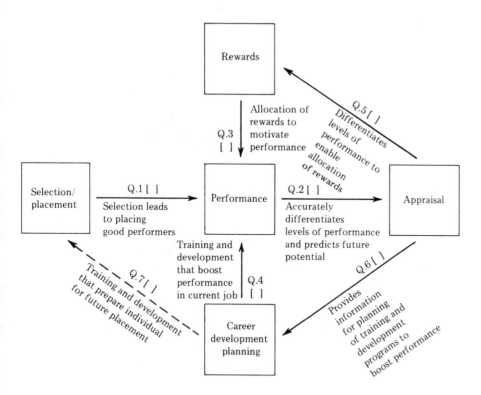

Using the scale to the right as a guide, indicate your response to each question listed below by *writing the number* of your answer in the brackets [ ] shown *in the diagram above*.

	Not at all effective				Very effective
	[1]	[2]	[3]	[4]	[5]

Q.1. How effective is the selection process in assuring that people are placed in appropriate positions? Explain.

Q.2. How effective is the appraisal process in accurately assessing performance? Explain.

Q.3. How effective are rewards (financial and nonfinancial) in driving performance? Explain.

Q.4. How effective are the training, development, and career planning activities in driving performance? Explain.

Q.5. How effective is the appraisal process in differentiating performance levels for justifying reward allocation decisions? Explain.

Q.6. How effective is the appraisal process in identifying developmental needs of individuals to guide training, development, and career planning? Explain.

Q.7. How effective are the training, development, and career planning activities in preparing people for selection and placement into new positions in the organization? Explain.

8. Overall, how effectively are the five components integrated and mutually supportive? Explain. [1] [2] [3] [4] [5]

Figure 14.6 Operational level human resource management

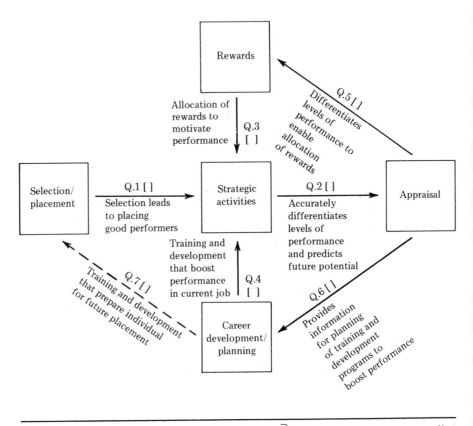

Using the scale to the right as a guide, indicate your response to each question listed below by *writing the number* of your answer in the brackets [ ] shown *in the diagram above.*

	Very little		Moderate		Very great
	[1]	[2]	[3]	[4]	[5]

To what extent. . .

Q.1. Are key people selected for their positions based on their ability to act strategically? Explain.

Q.2. Are key people evaluated on their strategic activities? Explain.

Q.3. Are key people rewarded for their strategic activities? Explain.

Q.4. Are key people trained for their positions to function strategically? Explain.

Q.5. Does the appraisal of strategic activities affect the rewards key people receive for strategic performance? Explain.

Q.6. Does the appraisal of key people's strategic activities affect the training and development they receive for strategic performance? Explain.

Q.7. Does the training, development and career planning key people receive prepare them for placement into their positions and the strategic activities required in it? Explain.

8. Overall, is the human resource cycle—as an integrated unit—supportive of strategic activities? Explain.   [1]   [2]   [3]   [4]   [5]

Figure 14.7   Strategic level human resource management

5. *Design Targeted Information Systems.* A sure way to remain operational and irrelevant in the human resource management area is to develop sophisticated computerized systems without involving the line. Management must begin by identifying, in cooperation with the human resource management staff, the type and format of the human resource data they need for strategic decision making. The human resource function needs to be prepared with some basic data and analyses which are not excessively complex, but simple and pragmatic.

6. *Grow System Over Time.* The organization should start by modifying and developing only some rudimentary strategic human resource systems. These should only be expanded and made more complex as management demands. This is because the human resource systems must be incorporated into the cultural and political systems of the organization in order to work. They are not plug in appliances. Developing them slowly allows for the management of cultural changes and political dynamics, such as resistance and sabotage. The system should expand as they clearly demonstrate utility in the strategic arena and new needs can be met.

7. *Design the Corporate Human Resource Strategy.* The final part of the process is to figure out the organization strategy, structure, and internal human resource systems for the human resource function. The most fundamental change involves cultural change on the part of both line management and the human resource staff. Line management must stop thinking about personnel as "green eyeshades" or "bean counters" and begin to look at them as valued members of the management team instead of second class citizens. At the same time, the human resource staff has to stop thinking reactively. The human resource executive must become a general manager. He or she must think of running a service organization with a definite marketplace, namely, the various managers and employees. This general manager orientation leads to a focus on the development of strategies for the marketplace, distribution mechanisms to use, organizing the function to deliver these services, and staffing the function for effective delivery. Because most human resource staff grew up on the staff side of the organization, it is unusual for them to think like general managers and act in an entrepreneurial mode.

To change this orientation, a combination of development and selection is called for. Moving some key executives with line experience into the human resource function promotes change and has been an increasing trend for a number of companies, including Citibank, Aetna, and Hewlett-Packard. This stands in stark contrast to the days when human resources was used as a dumping ground for line managers who could not make it elsewhere. Now high potentials are being rotated into the function.

Another way to alter the function over the long term is from the input side. Several companies, such as Pepsico, Citibank, and Exxon, are now hiring MBAs from the better business schools to staff their personnel function. This will fill the pipeline with more managerial professionals.

Developmentally, a number of activities can be undertaken. The first involves training human resource managers. Many have not been taught about strategic planning and are weak in their understanding of the financial, marketing, and production dimensions of the business. They also need concepts and tools for looking at their own function. General Electric began an aggressive training effort for its personnel managers several years ago to give them a more strategic outlook on the business and their role in it. There is a need to help the personnel staff think entrepreneurially about their function.

The process of working through these seven steps involves the application of a great deal of the TPC theory outlined in this book. First, the technical system must be totally redesigned for human resources to be strategic. Second, the political dynamics are fierce as strategic human resource issues get to the heart of the political system. For instance, human resources aims to change the way key people are selected, promoted, appraised, and rewarded. The forces around these issues do not easily bend to rational technical arguments. The cultural system is also fundamentally altered as most organizations have not managed people strategically. It requires changing priorities and elevating people issues at the expense of such issues as finance, production, or marketing.

The change process takes about three years but, if successful, results in a major organizational transformation. I took time in this last chapter to describe the seven steps and discuss the use of TPC theory as it relates to human resource management issues in order to present a current application of TPC theory and to foreshadow my next major effort to academically and clinically expand the boundaries of change management.

THE FUTURE OF TPC THEORY

As pointed out in the introduction, TPC theory is not a formal theory but a meta-theory. It is based on an analysis of organizational problems or dilemmas and treated in terms of an integrated conceptual scheme. Ultimately it will become more formal, more empirically based and probably substantially transformed. The future should see more attention being given to some of the following issues, which need further development.

Macrolevel Issues

TPC theory has face validity when applied to society-level analyses. In analyzing U.S. society in 1982 it is apparent that there is a great deal of technical uncertainty (a messed up economy) and a growing degree of political uncertainty triggered by the lack of success of Ronald Reagan's supply-side economics. This political uncertainty will increase as we draw nearer to the 1984 election and certainly if the economy does not turn around. There has been increasing cultural uncertainty in the country for the past decade and a half. The same issues discussed in the previous chapters of this book apply to our society-level analysis, that is, how do we develop a strategy to manage uncertainty within each of the three areas, and then how do we develop an integrated technical, political, and cultural strategy. The mechanistic and organic concepts also appear to apply.

It may be possible to develop TPC theory into a macro and micro systems theory along the lines of social network analysis which has been applied to small face-to-face groups as well as the analysis and study of societies. In the coming years I hope to pursue some empirical and conceptual work at a more macro level.

Organization-Level Issues

One area for greater conceptual clarity and hence more operational definitions is in determining the bounds of the technical, political, and cultural problems. Talcott Parsons (1960) presented what he considered the functional imperatives of social systems, four problems in organizations, each of which developed coping mechanisms. These were the "value system, the adaptive mechanisms which concern mobilization of resources, the operative code concerned with the mechanisms of the direct process of goal implementation, and finally the integrative mechanisms" (p.57). Parsons's work provides many useful insights into the nature of social systems and the functions needed to deal with different problems. TPC theory needs a similar type of conceptual clarity so that the subdefinitions of the three concepts can be articulated to show how they are reflected in organizational structure and process.

Another interesting sociological area for exploration is in developing organization typologies. Etzioni's (1961) typology of compliance types—utilitarian, normative, and coercive—appear to align with the technical, cultural, and political, respectively. Theoretically this was never the intent, yet there is enough face validity to warrant further analysis along these lines.

Uncertainty as a concept and as a variable for empirical measurement is in need of further conceptual development. Even though it is a concept that has been studied in the technical sense for several decades, it is still dealt with in less than satisfactory terms. Political uncertainty is a new concept in organizations. There is a great deal I feel needs to be drawn from political science to further the development of this concept. Finally, cultural uncertainty is the least developed.

The cultural area, in general, needs the most work as it has been dealt with in some confusing ways. First, it will be necessary in the future to be able to specify some hierarchy of cultural values. It might be useful to draw upon Rokeach's (1970) multilevel analysis of values, attitudes, and beliefs. He proposes that we have only a few core values, upon which we base a large number of values and many beliefs. The argument can be made that in a culture there may be a few core values, a larger number of cultural attitudes, and then a large number of superficial cultural beliefs. The change theory implication is that, in order to get at the core of a culture, it is necessary to identify and try to change the core values. Working on beliefs is superficial and at best effects marginal changes in a culture. Analyses of organizational cultures need to be conducted to test this multitiered notion.

Individual-Level Issues

The material in this book skims over the psychological aspects of change and TPC theory. Ultimately any theory of change needs to include a set of psychological constructs. It is interesting to do a comparison of some concepts about personality in terms of the technical, political, and cultural problem areas.

The technical area seems most related to McClelland's (1961) need for achievement concept. One would expect high need for achievement individuals to be most attracted to work on the technical problems in the organization. Carl Jung's (1933) thinker and intuitive type personalities fit best in the technical system where rational, logical, and abstract processes predominate. Finally, the technical system might correspond to Freud's rational problem solving ego.

The political area is most aligned with McClelland's need for power personality and Jung's sensor type, who is always looking for action, and what Freud identified as the id, which wants immediate gratifcation.

The cultural area divides into two subcategories. McClelland and Jung have concepts that describe the people orientation of an individual. McClelland speaks of the need for affiliation while Jung refers to feeler-oriented people. The second cultural area relates to higherorder values and is reflected in Freud's concept of the superego.

Of these three theories the one that best fits TPC theory, in terms of both content and the dynamics of personality, is Freudian theory.

This is because Freudian theory is dialectical, deals with interaction among the three levels, and handles paradox as an inevitable part of the conflicts among the levels. Furthermore, the individual's psyche is always in flux as is true of organizations managing technical, political, and cultural dynamics.

Obviously these short and superficial linkages to psychological theories are not meant to draw any conclusions but rather to indicate that much work needs to be done in this area. The last few pages are meant to encourage work on the theoretical and research issues needed to carry TPC theory to its next stage of development.

Of greater importance is a call to action that encourages the clinical use of the framework. Etzioni's (1968) call to action is well suited to TPC theory and is a fitting end to this book:

> An active orientation has three major components; a self conscious and knowing actor, one or more goals he is committed to realize, and access to levers (or power) that allow resetting of the social code. . . . Without consciousness, the collective actor is unaware of his identity, his being acted upon, his ability to act and his power; he is passive, like a sleeping giant. Without commitment to a purpose, action lacks direction and merely drifts. Without power, the most incisive and sharply focused awareness or the firmest commitment will not yield more action than a derailed train. To be active is to be aware, committed and potent (4-5).

REFERENCES

Ackoff, R.L. *Redesigning the future: A systems approach to societal problems.* New York: Wiley-Interscience, 1974.

Adams, J.S. The structure and dynamics of behavior in organizational boundary roles. In M. Dunnette (Ed.), *Handbook of industrial and organizational psychology.* Chicago: Rand McNally, 1976.

Adams, J.S. Interorganizational processes and organization boundaries activities. In L.L. Cummings and B. Staw (Eds.), *Research in organizational behavior,* Vol. 2. Greenwich, CT: JAI Press, 1980.

Aguilar, F.J. *Scanning the business environment.* New York: MacMillan, 1967.

Aldrich, H. *Organizations and environments.* Englewood Cliffs, NJ: Prentice-Hall, 1979.

Alinsky, S. *Rules for Radicals.* New York: Random House, 1971.

Allen, T.J. *Managing the flow of technology.* Cambridge: M.I.T. Press, 1977.

Alsop, R. More firms are hiring own political analysts to limit risks abroad. *Wall Street Journal,* March 30, 1981, Vol. CXCVII, No. 61.

American Center for the Quality of Work Life. *Industrial democracy in Europe: A 1977 survey.* Washington, DC, 1978.

Argyris, C. *Interpersonal competence and organizational effectiveness.* Homewood, IL.: Dorsey Press, 1962.

Argyris, C. *Intervention theory and method.* Reading, MA: Addison-Wesley, 1970.

Argyris, C. and Schon, D. *Theory in practice.* San Francisco: Jossey-Bass, 1974.

Argyris, C. and Schon, D. *Organizational learning: A theory of action perspective.* Reading, MA.: Addison-Wesley, 1978.

Arnold, J. The chin down manager. *Fortune,* 1974, **90**(1), 98–99.

Baldridge, J. *Power and conflict in the university.* New York: Wiley, 1971.

Bavelas, A. An experimental approach to organizational communication. *Personnel,* 1951, **27**, 366–371.

Beckhard, R. *Organizational development strategies and models.* Reading, MA: Addison-Wesley, 1969.

Beckhard, R. and Harris, R.T. *Organizational transitions: Managing complex change.* Reading, MA: Addison-Wesley, 1977.

Behind AT&T's change at the top. *Business Week,* November 6, 1978.

Bennett, R.A. Is one stop banking next? *New York Times,* December 28, 1980, p. F20.

Bennis, W.G. *Organizational development: Its nature, origins and prospects.* Reading, MA: Addison-Wesley, 1969.

Blankenship, L.V. and Elling, R.H. Organization support and community power structure: The hospital. *Journal of Health and Human Behavior,* 1962, **3**, 257–269.

Burke, W. *Organization development: principles and practices,* Boston, MA: Little, Brown and Co., 1982.

Burns, T. and Stalker, G. *The management of innovation.* London: Tavistock Press, 1961.

Campbell, D.T. Reforms as experiments. *American Psychologist,* 1969, **24**, 409–429.

Chandler, A.D., Jr. *Strategy and structure.* Cambridge: M.I.T. Press, 1962.

Charns, M.T., Lawrence, P.R., and Weisbord, M.R. Organizing multiple-function professionals in academic medical centers. In P.C. Nystrom and W.H. Starbuck

(Eds.), *Handbook of organizational design*, Vol. 1. London: Oxford University Press, 1981.

Chatov, R. Cooperation between government and business. In P.C. Nystrom and W. H. Starbuck (Eds.), *Handbook of organizational design*, Vol. 1. London: Oxford University Press, 1981.

Child, J. Organization structure, environment and performance: The role of strategic choice. *Sociology*, 1972, **6**, 1–22.

Coch, L. and French, J.R.P., Jr. Overcoming resistance to change. *Human Relations*, 1948, **1**, 512–533.

Cohen, C. and March, J. *Leadership and ambiguity*. New York: McGraw-Hill, 1974.

Corporate culture: The hard to change values that spell success or failure. *Business Week*, October 27, 1980, pp. 148–158.

Crane, D. Social structure in a group of scientists: A test of the "invisible college" hypothesis. *American Sociological Review*, 1969, **34**, 335–350.

Cyert, R.M. and March, J.G. *A behavioral theory of the firm*. Englewood Cliffs, NJ: Prentice-Hall, 1963.

Dahl, R. *After the revolution: Authority in a good society*. New Haven: Yale University Press, 1970.

Davis, S. Trends in the organization of multinational corporation. *Columbia Journal of World Business*, 1976, 25–34.

Davis, S. and Lawrence, P.R. *Matrix*. Reading, MA: Addison-Wesley, 1977.

Davis, S. and Schwartz, H. Matching corporate culture and business strategy. Concept Paper Series, Cambridge, MA: Management Analysis Center, 1981.

Dearborn, D.C. and Simon, H.A. Selective perception: A note on the departmental identification of executives. *Sociometry*, 1958, **21**, 140–144.

Deutsch, M. *The resolution of conflict*. New Haven, CT: Yale University Press, 1973.

Deutsch, M. and Krauss, R. *Theories in social psychology*. New York: Basic Books, 1965.

Devanna, M.A., Fombrun, C., and Tichy, N. Human resource management: A strategic approach. *Organizational Dynamics*, Winter, 1981.

Dubos, R. Reason for optimism. *United Nations Magazine*, April, 1982.

Duncan, R.E. Characteristics of organizational environments and perceived environmental uncertainty. *Administrative Science Quarterly*, 1972, **17**, 313–327.

Edstrom, A. and Galbraith, J. Transfer of managers as a coordinating and control strategy in multi-national organizations. *Administrative Science Quarterly*, 1977, **22**, 248–263.

Etzioni, A. *A comparative analysis of complex organizations*. New York: Free Press, 1961.

Etzioni, A. *The active society*. New York: Free Press, 1968.

Fombrun, C. Towards the active society. Unpublished working paper, 1982.

Fombrun, C. Environmental trends create new pressures on human resources. *The Journal of Business Strategy*, Summer, 3(1), 1982.

Fombrun, C. and Tichy, N. The link between strategic planning and human resource management: at rainbow's end. Ann Arbor, MI: Working Paper Series, Graduate School of Business, University of Michigan, 1982.

Forrester, J.W. *Urban dynamics*. Cambridge, MA: M.I.T. Press, 1969.

French, W.L. and Bell, C. *Organizational development*. Englewood Cliffs, NJ: Prentice-Hall, 1973.

Friedman, T.L. Autos: Studying the Japanese. *New York Times*, February 27, 1982, pp. 29, 31.

Galbraith, J. *Designing complex organizations.* Reading, MA: Addison-Wesley, 1973.

Galbraith, J. *Organization design.* Reading, MA: Addison-Wesley, 1977.

Galbraith, J. Designing the innovating organization. *Organizational Dynamics*, Winter, 1982, 5-25.

Galbraith, J. and Edstrom, A. International transfer of managers: Some important policy considerations. *Columbia Journal of World Business*, 1976, XI (2), 100-113.

Galbraith, J. and Nathanson, D. *Strategy implementation: The role of structure and process.* St. Paul, MN: West Publishing, 1978.

Granovetter, M.S. The strength of weak ties. *American Journal of Sociology*, 1973, 78, 1360-1380.

Grossman, J. and Rockart, J. A managerial perspective on information systems in medical care organizations. *Advances in biomedical engineering*, 1976, 6, 158-208.

Gyllenhammer, P. *People at work.* Reading, MA: Addison-Wesley, 1977.

Hackman, J.R. and Oldham, G. *Work redesign.* Reading, MA: Addison-Wesley, 1976.

Hage, J., Aiken, M., and Marrett, C. Organization structure and communications. *American Sociological Review*, 1971, 36, 860-871,

Harrison, R. When power conflicts trigger team spirit. *European Business*, Spring, 1972, 57-65.

Harvey, E. and Mills, R. Patterns of organizational adaptation: A political perspective. In M.N. Zald (Ed.), *Power in organizations.* Nashville, TN: Vanderbilt University Press, 1970.

Hatvany, N. and Pucik, V. Japanese management practices and productivity. *Organizational Dynamics*, Spring, 1981, 5-21.

Heilbroner, R. *An inquiry into the human prospect.* New York: W.W. Norton, 1974.

Henderson, B. The experience curve—reviewed. Boston Consulting Group Paper, 1974.

Henderson, B.D. *Henderson on corporate strategy.* Cambridge, MA: Abt Books, 1979.

Herzberg, F.B., Mausner, B., and Snyderman, B. *The motivation of work*, 2nd ed. New York: Wiley, 1959.

Hickson, D.I., Hinings, C.R., Lea, C.A., Schneck, R.E., and Pennings, J.M. A strategic contingency theory of intraorganizational power. *Administrative Science Quarterly*, 1971, 16, 216-229.

Hrebiniak, L.G. *Complex organizations.* St. Paul, MN: West Publishing, 1978.

Huse, E. *Organizational development and change.* St. Paul, MN: West Publishing, 1975.

Janis, I. and Mann, L. *Decision making.* New York: The Free Press, 1977.

Jaques, E. *A general theory of bureaucracy.* London: Heinemann, 1976.

Jay, A. *Corporation man.* New York: Random House, 1971.

Jung, C. *Psychological types.* New York: Harcourt Brace, 1933.

Kadushin, C. Introduction to macro-network analysis. Unpublished working paper. New York: Teachers College, Columbia University, 1978.

Kadushin, C. Small world—How many steps to the top? *The Detroit News*, September 17, 1978, 19A.

Kanter, R. *Men and women of the corporation*. New York: Basic Books, 1977.

Kaplan, A. *The conduct of inquiry*. San Francisco, CA: Chandler Publishing, 1964.

Katz, D. and Kahn, R.L. *The social psychology of organizations*. New York: Wiley, 1966.

Kahn, R. Field studies of power in organizations. In R.L. Kahn and E. Boulding (Eds.), *Power and conflict in organizations*. New York: Basic Books, 1964.

Katz, D. and Kahn, R.L. *The social psychology of organizations*, 2nd ed. New York: Wiley, 1978.

Khandwalla, P.N. *The design of organizations*. New York: Harcourt Brace Jovanovich, 1977.

Kohlmeier, L. *The regulators*. New York: Harper & Row, 1969.

Kotter, J. *Organizational dynamics*. Reading, MA: Addison-Wesley, 1978.

Kretch, D., Crutchfield, R.S., and Ballachey, E.L. *Individual in society*. New York: McGraw-Hill, 1962.

Lasch, C. *The culture of narcissism: American life in an age of diminishing expectations*. New York: W.W. Norton, 1978.

Laumann, E.O. and Pappi, F.U. *Networks of collective action*. New York: Academic, 1976.

Lawler, E.E., III. *Motivation in work organizations*. Monterey, CA: Brooks/Cole, 1973.

Lawler, E.E., III, Nadler, D.A., and Cammann, C. *Organizational assessment: Perspectives on the measurement of organizational behavior and the quality of work life*. New York: Wiley, 1980.

Lawrence, P.R. and Lorsch, J.W. *Organization and environment: Managing differentiation and integration*. Homewood, IL: Richard D. Irwin, 1967.

Leavitt, H. Applied organizational change in industry: Structural, technological, and humanistic approaches. In J.G. March (Ed.), *Handbook of organizations*. Chicago: Rand McNally, 1965.

Lewin, K. The conceptual representation and measurement of psychological forces. *Contributions to Psychological Theory*, 1938, 1(4).

Lieberson, S. and O'Connor, J.F. Leadership and organizational performance: A study of large corporations. *American Sociological Review*, 1972, 37, 117-130.

Likert, R. *New patterns of management*. New York: McGraw-Hill, 1961.

Lippitt, R. and White, R.K. An experimental study of leadership and group life. In E.E. Maccoby, T.M. Newcomb, and E.L. Hartley (Eds.), *Readings in social psychology*, 3rd ed. New York: Holt, 1958.

Lohr, S. Overhauling America's business management. *The New York Times Magazine*, January 4, 1981, 33-118.

March, J.G. The business firm as a political coalition. *Journal of Politics*, 1962, 24, 662-678.

March, J.G. and Simon, H.A. *Organizations*. New York: Wiley, 1958.

McClelland, D. *The achieving society*. New York: VanNostrand Reinhold, 1961.

McGill, A. The top 47 who make it happen. *The Detroit News*, September 17, 1978, 1a, 22a.

McGregor, D. *The human side of enterprise*. New York: McGraw-Hill, 1960.

McMurray, R. Power and the ambitious executive. *Harvard Business Review*, 1973, 51,(6), 140-145.

Merry, U. and Allerhand, M.E. *Developing teams and organizations*. Reading, MA: Addison-Wesley, 1977.

Merton, R.K. *Social theory and social structure*, rev. ed. Glencoe, IL: Free Press, 1957.

Mintzberg, H. Planning on the left side and managing on the right. *Harvard Business Review*, 1976, **54**(4), 49-58.

Mintzberg, H. Strategy-making in three modes. *California Management Review*, 1973, **16**(2), 44-53.

Mintzberg, H. Policy as a field of management theory. *Academy of Management Review*, 1977, **2**, 88-103.

Mulder, M. Power equalization through participation. *Administrative Science Quarterly*, 1971, **16**, 31-38.

Nadler, D.A., Hackman, J.R., and Lawler, E.E. *Managing organizational behavior*. Boston: Little, Brown, 1979.

Naylor, T. *Strategic planning management*. Oxford, OH: Planning Executives Institute, 1980.

Newman, W. Company politics: Unexplored dimensions of management. *Journal of General Management*, 1979, 5(1), 3-11.

New York Times. Thesbald next Citicorp chief. March 12, 1982, 29, 34.

Nord, W. Dreams of humanization and the realities of power. *Academy of Management Review*, 1978, 3(3), 674-678.

Ouchi, W. *Theory Z*. Reading, MA: Addison Wesley, 1981.

Parsons, T. *Structure and process in modern societies*. New York: The Free Press, 1960.

Pascale, R.T. and Athos, A.G. *The art of Japanese management*. New York: Simon and Schuster, 1981.

Pateman, C. *Participation and democratic theory*. Cambridge, England: Cambridge University Press, 1970.

Peters, T. Management systems: The language of organizational character and competence. *Organizational Dynamics*, Summer, 1980.

Pettigrew, A. Towards a political theory of organizational intervention. *Human Relations*, 1975, 28(3), 191-208.

Pfeffer, J. *Organizational design*. Arlington Heights: AHM Publishing Company, 1978.

Pfeffer, J. Management as symbolic action: The creation and maintenance of organizational paradigms. In L.L. Cummings and B.M. Staw (Eds.), *Research in organizational behavior*, Vol. 3. Greenwich, CT: JAI Press, 1981.

Pfeffer, J. and Salancik, G. *The external control of organizations: A resource dependence perspective*. New York: Harper & Row, 1978.

Pondy, L.R. Leadership is a language game. In M.W. McCall, Jr., and M.M. Lombardo (Eds.), *Leadership*. Durham, NC: Duke University Press, 1978.

Porras, J. and Berg, P.O. The impact of organization development. *Academy of Management Review*, 1978, 3(2), 249-266.

Porter, L., Lawler, E.E., and Hackman, J.R. *Behavior in organizations*. New York: McGraw-Hill, 1975.

Price, J.L. *Handbook of organizational measurement*. Lexington, MA: Heath Co., 1972.

Pugh, D., Hickson, D., Hinnings, C.R., and Turner, C. The context of organization structure. *Adminstrative Science Quarterly*, 1969, **14**, 91-114.

Roberts, K., O'Reilly, C., Bretton, G., and Porter, L. Organization theory and organizational communication: A communication failure? *Human Relations*, 1974, **27**(5).

Roethlisberger, F.J. and Dickson, W.J. *Management and the worker*. Cambridge, MA: Harvard University Press, 1939.

Rokeach, M. *Beliefs, attitudes, and values*. San Francisco: Jossey-Bass, 1970.

Salancik, G.R. and Pfeffer, J. A social information processing approach to job attitudes and task design. *Administrative Science Quarterly*, 1978, **23**, 224-253.

Sashkin, M. and Jones, J. Power and OD intervention analysis. In J. Jones and J. Pfeffer (Eds.), *1979 annual handbook for group facilitation*. La Jolla, CA: University Associates, 1979.

Schatzman, L. and Strauss, A.L. *Field research: Strategies for a natural society*. Englewood Cliffs, NJ: Prentice-Hall, 1973.

Schein, E.H. *Process consultation: Its role in organization development*. Reading, MA: Addison-Wesley, 1969.

Schein, E.H. *Organizational psychology*, 2nd ed. Englewood Cliffs, NJ: Prentice-Hall, 1970.

Schein, E.H. *Career dynamics: Matching individual and organizational needs*. Reading, MA: Addison-Wesley, 1978.

Seeger, J. First National Bank Operation Group (A). Harvard Business School Case 9-474-165, Intercollegiate Clearing House, Soldiers Field, Boston, 1977.

Sherif, M., Harvey, O.J., White, B.J., Hood, W.R., and Sherif, C.W. *Experimental study of positive and negative intergroup attitudes between experimentally produced groups*. Norman: Univeristy of Oklahoma, 1954.

Somebody called Ford. *Fortune*, August 14, 1978, p. 13.

Starbuck, W.H. Organizations and their environments. In M. Dunnette (Ed.), *Handbook of Industrial and Organizational Psychology*. Chicago: Rand McNally, 1976.

Starbuck, W.H., Greve, A., and Hedberg, B. Responding to crisis. *Journal of Business Administration*, 1978, 9(2), 111-137.

Steele, F.I. (Ed.) *Physical setting and organizational development*. Reading, MA: Addison-Wesley, 1973.

Steers, R.M. *Organizational effectiveness: A behavioral view*. Pacific Palisades, CA: Goodyear, 1977.

Steiner, G.A. The changing role of tomorrow's corporate planner. International Conference on Corporate Planning, Montreal, 1972.

Taylor, F.W. *The principles of scientific management*. New York: Harper, 1923.

Telberg, I. They don't do it our way. *Courier (UNESCO)*, 1950, 3(4).

Thompson, J.D. *Organizations in action*. New York: McGraw-Hill, 1967.

Thompson, J.D. and Tuden, A. Strategies, structures, and processes of organizational design. In J.D. Thompson et al. (Eds.), *Comparative studies in administration*. Pittsburgh: University of Pittsburgh Press, 1959.

Thurow, L.C. *The zero-sum society*. New York: Basic Books, 1980.

Thurow, L.C. Where's America's old team spirit? *New York Times*, July 26, 1981, p. F3.

Tofler, A. *The Third Wave*. NY: William Morrow & Co. 1980.

Tichy, N.M. Agents of planned social change: Congruence of values, cognitions, and actions. *Administrative Science Quarterly*, 1974, **19**, 163-182.

Tichy, N.M. How different types of change agents diagnose organizations. *Human Relations*, 1975, **28**, 771-799.

Tichy, N.M. When does work restructuring work? Organizational innovation at Volvo and GM. *Organizational Dynamics*, 1976, 5(1).

Tichy, N.M. *Organization design for primary health care: The case of the Dr. Martin Luther King, Jr., Health Center*. New York: Praeger, 1977.

Tichy, N.M. Current and future trends for change agentry. *Group and Organization Studies*, 1978, **3**(4), 467–482.

Tichy, N.M. A social network perspective for organization development. In T.G. Cummings (Ed.), *Systems theory for organization development*. New York: Wiley, 1980.

Tichy, N.M. Networks in organizations. In P.C. Nystrom and W.H. Starbuck (Eds.), *Handbook of organizational design*, Vol. 2. New York: Oxford University Press, 1981.

Tichy, N.M., Fombrun, C., and Devanna, M.A. Strategic human resource management. *Sloan Management Review*, 1982, **23**(2).

Toffler, A. *The third wave*. New York: Morrow, 1980.

Tushman, M. and Nadler, D.A. Information processing as an integrative concept in organizational design. *Academy of Management Review*, 1978, **3**(3), 613–624.

Urwick, L.F. *The elements of administration*. New York: Harper, 1943.

Van de Ven, A. and Ferry, D. *Measuring and assessing organizations*. New York: Wiley-Interscience, 1980.

Vandivier, K. The aircraft brake scandal. *Harper's Magazine*, 1972, **244**(1463), 45–52.

Wall Street Journal. "Labor relations changes in the auto industry" April 24, 1981, p. 1.

Walton, R.E. and McKersie, R.B. Behavioral dilemmas in mixed-motive decision making. *Behavioral Science*, 1966, **11**, 370–384.

Wanted: A manager to fit each strategy. *Business Week*. February 25, 1980, 166–173.

Webb, E., Campbell, D., Schwartz, R., Sechrest, L., and Grove, J.B. *Nonreactive measures in the social sciences*. Boston: Houghton Mifflin, 1981.

Weick, K. *The social psychology of organizing*. Reading, MA: Addison-Wesley, 1969.

Weick, K. Educational organizations as loosely coupled systems. *Administrative Science Quarterly*, 1976, **21**, 1–19.

Weick, K. Cognitive process in organizations. In B. Staw (Ed.), *Research in organizational behavior*, Vol. 1. Greenwich, CT: JAI Press, 1979.

Weisbord, M. A mixed model for medical centers: Changing structure and behavior. In J.D. Adams (Ed.), *Theory and method in organization development: An evolutionary process*. Arlington, VA: NTL Institute for Applied Behavioral Science, 1974.

Wieland, G.F. and Ullrich, R.A. *Organizations: Behavior, design and change*. Homewood, IL: Richard D. Irwin, 1976.

Wrapp, E. Good managers don't make policy decisions. *Harvard Business Review*, 1976, **45**(5), 91–99.

Zutty, N. The new way of life! Caring with change. *American Paint Journal*, August 18, 1980, 15.

Author Index

Ackoff, R. L., 215, 243, 247-248
Adams, J. S., 320, 321
Aguilar, F. J., 319
Aiken, M., 324
Aldrich, H., 118
Alinsky, S., 352
Allen, T. J., 323
Allerhand, M. E., 47
Alsop, R., 230
Argyris, C., 7, 44, 180, 275, 277, 284, 375
Arnold, J., 147
Athos, A. G., 118, 365
Auerbach, N. E., 32

Baird, R., 303
Baldridge, J., 69
Ballachey, A. L., 253-254
Bavelas, A., 322
Beckhard, R., 12, 46, 163, 325, 333, 347, 350
Bell, C., 282, 329
Bennett, R. A., 4
Bennis, W. G., 9
Berg, P. O., 47
Blankenship, L. V., 319
Borucki, C., 50-68
Bretton, G., 321
Bulchard, W., 227
Burns, T., 42, 46, 234-235, 259, 324

Caldwell, P., 19, 20
Cammann, C., 364
Campbell, D. T., 163, 364
Carnegie, A., 26
Chandler, A. D., Jr., 18, 81
Charns, M. T., 326

Chatov, R., 322
Child, J., 319
Coates, W., 50-55
Coch, L., 44
Cohen, C., 237, 239
Crane, P., 321
Crutchfield, R. S., 253-254
Cummings, L. L. (Ed.), 283, 320, 321
Cummings, T. G. (Ed.), 70
Cyert, R. M., 47, 80, 128, 129, 325

Dahl, R., 242
Davis, S., 203, 216, 256, 258, 261
Dearborn, D. C., 40
Deutsch, M., 327
Devanna, M. A., 164, 405
Dickson, W. J., 43
Drucker, P. F., 26, 29
Dubos, R., 387
Duncan, R. E., 353
Dunnette, M. (Ed.), 320

Edstrom, A., 324
Elling, R. H., 319
Etzioni, A., 14, 161, 413, 415

Fayol, H., 42-43
Ferry, D., 364
Fombrun, C., 164, 389, 393, 405
Ford, H., 21, 69, 137
Ford, H., II, 19-20
Ford, W. C., 20
Forrester, J. W., 117
French, J. R. P., Jr., 44
French, W. L., 44, 282, 325
Freud, S., 414-415
Friedman, T. L., 254

Galbraith, J., 118, 126, 172, 177, 190, 212, 263, 307, 323, 325, 326
Granovetter, M. S., 321
Greve, A., 347
Grossman, J., 173
Grove, A. S., 28, 30
Grove, J. B., 163
Gyllenhammer, P., 217

Hackman, J. R., 15, 88, 220, 306, 322
Hage, J., 324
Haggerty, P., 249
Hammar, F., 222, 226-229
Harris, R. T., 12, 325, 333, 343, 347
Harrison, R., 313
Hartley, E. L. (Ed.), 250-251
Harvey, E., 324
Harvey, O. J., 323
Hatvany, N., 272
Hayes, R. H., 27, 33
Hedberg, B., 347
Heilbroner, R., 391
Henderson, B., 3, 90, 209
Herzberg, F. B., 15, 44
Hickson, D. I., 230
Hinnings, C. R., 230
Hood, W. R., 323
Hornstein, H., 41
Hrebiniak, L. G., 223
Huse, E., 46, 325
Hutchinson, J., 211

Iacocca, L., 19-20, 69, 137

Jacques, E., 15, 242, 243
Janis, I., 148
Jay, A., 132, 235
Jenkins, D., 246
Jones, G., 229
Jones, J., 351
Jones, R. H., 23, 27, 227
Jung, C., 414

Kadushin, C., 69-70, 321
Kahn, R. L., 134, 163, 232, 243, 254, 324, 366
Kanter, R., 240-241, 274
Katz, D., 134, 254, 324, 366
Khandwalla, P. N., 90, 171, 174, 221, 224
Kohlmeier, L., 131
Kotter, J., 118
Kretch, D., 253-254

LaFley, A., 222
Lasch, C., 392
Laumann, E. O., 321
Lawler, E. E., 15, 86, 88, 220, 364
Lawrence, P. R., 84, 216, 261, 324, 326
Lea, C. A., 230
Leavitt, H., 31, 118
LeBrecque, T., 227
Lewin, K., 43, 310, 380
Lieberson, S., 78
Likert, R., 44-45, 281
Lippitt, R., 250-251
Lohr, S., 22
Lombardo, M. M. (Ed.), 283
Lorsch, J. W., 84-85, 324

McArthur, J. H., 33
McCall, M. W., Jr., 283
McClelland, D., 15
Maccoby, E. E. (Ed.), 250-251
McGill, A., 70
McGraw, H., 228, 229
McGregor, D., 274, 281-282, 284
MacGregor, 90
Machiavelli, 235-240, 249
McKersie, R. B., 320
McMurray, R., 236
Mann, L., 148
March, J. G., 14, 31, 47, 80, 118, 128, 129, 235, 237, 239, 325
Marrett, C., 324
Martin, J., 267-268
Maslow, W., 15
Mausner, B., 15, 44
Melman, S., 389
Merry, U., 47
Merton, R. K., 43
Mills, R., 324
Mills, T., 246
Mintzberg, H., 11, 17, 19, 37, 47, 73
Morita, A., 23-27, 78
Mulder, M., 244
Murphy, T. A., 26
Murrin, T. J., 50-55

Nader, R., 23
Nadler, D. A., 88, 118, 220, 307, 364
Nathanson, P., 118, 177
Naylor, T., 208
Newcomb, T. M. (Ed.), 250-251
Newman, W., 325
Niskanen, W. A., Jr., 30

Nord, W., 230, 232-234
Noyce, R. N., 28-29
Nusberg, J., 41
Nystrom, P. C. (Ed.), 326

O'Connor, J. R., 78
Oldham, G., 306
O'Reilly, C., 321
Ouchi, W. G., 31, 35

Packard, D., 268
Pappi, F. U., 321
Parsons, T., 413-414
Pascale, R. T., 365, 371
Pateman, C., 242
Pennings, J. M., 230
Perrow, C., 83
Peters, T., 269
Pettigrew, A., 325, 346
Pfeffer, J., 20, 78, 129, 283, 320, 347
Pondy, L. R., 283
Porras, J., 47
Porter, L., 15, 88, 321, 322
Price, J. L., 163
Pucik, V., 272
Pugh, D., 230

Roberts, K., 321
Rockart, J., 173
Roethlisberger, F. J., 43
Rokeach, M., 414

Salancik, G. R., 78-79, 129, 163, 320
Sashkin, M., 347
Schatzman, L., 163
Schein, E. H., 14, 15, 17, 47, 264,
   315, 316, 318
Schneck, R. E., 230
Schon, D., 7, 275, 277, 284, 375
Schwartz, H., 216, 256, 258
Schwartz, R., 163
Sechrest, L., 163
Seeger, J., 137
Seidler, L. J., 27
Sevan-Schreiber, J., 22

Sherif, C. W., 324
Simon, H. A., 11, 14, 40, 235
Sloan, A., 32
Smith, A., 15
Snyderman, B., 15
Spencer, W., 4
Stalker, G., 42, 45, 234-235, 259,
   328
Starbuck, W. H., 320, 326, 347
Staw, B. M. (Ed.), 283, 320, 321
Steele, F. I. (Ed.), 325
Steers, R. M., 74
Steiner, G. A., 206
Strauss, A. L., 163
Sutherland, J. (Ed.), 295, 312

Taylor, F. W., 42-43, 305
Telberg, I., 253
Thompson, J. D., 18, 78, 82, 130, 154,
   171, 232, 325
Thurow, L. C., 22, 130, 254, 393
Tichy, N. M., 8, 9, 40, 50, 70, 77, 104,
   140, 164, 192, 218, 325, 367, 405
Toffler, A., 30, 392
Tuden, A., 130
Tushman, M., 118, 126, 127, 307

Ullrich, R. A., 18, 236, 240
Urwick, L. F., 42-43

Van de Ven, A., 364
Vandivier, K., 133

Walton, R. E., 320
Watson, T., 267
Webb, E., 163
Weber, M., 42, 353
Weick, K., 80, 148, 187, 283, 323
Weisbord, M. R., 326
White, B. J., 323
White, R. K., 250-251
Wieland, G. F., 18, 236, 240
Wrapp, E., 235-236

Zald, M. N. (Ed.), 324

Subject Index

Absenteeism, 8, 152, 155, 219, 250, 305
Aerospace, 86
Aetna, 411
Alignment, 100, 118, 137-138
  analysis of, Texas Instruments, 201-202
  cultural, internal, 132-137
  diagnosed degree of, 168
  people, 222
  political, internal, 128-132
  reduction of uncertainty, 129
  strategic, 124-125
  of subsystems, 111-114
  technical, internal, 126-128
  technical environment, 204-207
  temporary phenomenon, 125
  test for, 129
Allocation:
  budget, 296
  power, 20, 130
  prestige, 130
  resources, 12, 113, 118
  rewards, 230-231
  time, 193
  work, 311-312
American Center for the Quality of Work Life, 391
American Express, 260
American Motors Corporation, 80, 124
American Paint Journal, 204
American Telephone & Telegraph, *see* AT&T
Approach to change:
  audit, 372, 378-380
  experiment orientation, 370

guidance system, 371
informal anecdotal, 372
research and development, 368-370
Assembly line, 82, 85, 87, 218
AT&T, 12-14, 76, 81, 130, 248, 258, 260, 283, 331-333, 335-336, 353, 393
Authority structure, 39, 43, 90
Automation, 4, 51, 77, 127, 260
Automobile industry, 4, 8, 14, 19-20, 30, 35, 51-52, 79, 80, 82, 93, 124, 230-231
  competition, 124
  Volvo, 217-220

Baldwin Locomotive Case, 256
Bankers Trust Company, 130
Banking Industry, 4, 31, 81, 85, 130, 222, 227, 256, 353
Bankruptcy, 394
Bargaining, as change activity, 49, 131-132, 225
Behavioral emphasis, 75, 162
Blue-collar worker, 82, 134, 218
Bonus, 25
Boss-worker relations, 35
Boston Consulting Group, 208-209, 221
Budget:
  allocation of, 296
  control of, 9, 136-138
  integrated, 190
  Westinghouse Case Study, 50
Buffer:
  for management, 151-152
  work areas, 218
Bureaucratic personality, 43

Burroughs, 335
Businesses, basic types of, 208-209
Business Week, 132-133, 167, 222, 229, 331, 334

California Management Review, 306
Capital spending program, 28, 31, 347
Career development path, 190, 315-319
"Cash cow," 209, 221, 273
Centralization, 4
CEOs, 20, 132-133, 137-138, 168, 227, 230, 256, 270
Change lever, 6, 330
Change manager, 40, 164, 193, 201-202, 333-334
Change process:
  activities, 49, 164, 190
  cycles, sequence of, 356-357
  defined, 17, 185
  planning for, 190
  successful implementation, 20-21
  technology, 185-187
Change strategy:
  components, 197-207
  cultural, 253-288
  political, 227-251
  technical, 203-229
  test for adequacy, 202
Change triggers, 152-154, 157, 194-196, 201
Chase Manhattan Bank, 85, 167, 222, 227
Chase Manhattan Bank case:
  emergent networks, 228
  environment, 228
  people, 228
  prescribed organization, 228
Chemical industry, 120-122
Chief Executive Officer, 20, 132-133, 137-138, 168, 227, 230, 256, 270
Chrysler Corporation, 14, 124
Citibank, 4, 137, 227, 412
Cluster, 69, 72
Coalition, 7
  change trigger signal, 153
  continuous adjustments in, 129
  Detroit, 70
  formation of, 47, 326
  relationships in, 70
  struggle for control, 47, 153
  transition in, 354

Communication, internal, 45, 53-54, 70, 223
  distortion-free, 91
  qualitative elements, 91
  timeliness, 91
Communication industry, 14, 107-109, 110, 133, 332
Competition, 3, 35, 254
  Europe, 51, 124
  Japanese, 51
  semiconductor industry, 195, 204
  Swift Engineering, 112-113
Computer-based planning model, 208
Computer industry, 28-31, 51
  Japanese threat, 120
  rapid pace, 12-14, 34, 195
Concorde, 27
Conoco, 121
Consciousness-raising, 136
Consultant, 20
  data collection by, 162
  development process, 47
  operations research, 291-292
  Richard Beckhard, 142
  Swift Engineering, 94
  use of, 181-183
Control:
  coalition, 47
  external, 124
  organizational process, 91-92
  struggle for, 47
  worker teams, 219
Coopers and Lybrand, 32
Corporate authority, 31, 90
Corporate paternalism, 25
Cost of living increase, 125
Crisis-oriented operation, 207
Cultural system, organization as, 7-8, 16, 70
  alignment, 132-137
  change strategy, 253-288
  counterculture, 133
  implications for diagnosis, 180
  incongruence, management of, 134-135
  informal structure, 70
  Intel, 29-31
  mechanistic, 273-275
  mixed, 281-282
  organic, 273, 275-281
  overemphasized, 9
  pervasiveness, 132
  problems in, 6, 10, 49, 73

strategic changes in, 122
subcultures, 117, 120
transitions in, 350
uncertainty, 118, 134-135
Volvo, 219
Cycles of change, sequence, 336-337

Dana Corporation, 231
Data:
  access to, 179
  competition, 200
  diagnosis for change, 156-162, 192
  feedback mechanism, 354-355
  method of collection, 95, 162-165
  organizational conditions, 55-56
  sociometric, 323
  summary of, 404
Datsun, 93
Decentralization, 4, 121, 241
Decision-making, 30
  employee participation, 53
  hierarchy, 85
  long-term view, 122
  mechanistic, 92
  organic, 92
  process, 69-70, 92, 225
  statistically-based, 32
  values, 122
Decision network, 69
Democratic management, 35
Development system, 3
Diagnosis:
  application of strategy, 169
  dysfunctional, 148-149, 375
  guideline for final assessment, 166-168
  impact of, 194-195
  in-depth, 156-168
  management of, 148
  Southwest Hospital System case study, 169-175
  technical process, 148-149
  Texas Instruments, case study, 175-178
  types, 154-166
Digital Equipment Corporation, 335
"Dog," 209, 221
Dow Chemical, 203

Economic requirements, 20, 130, 390
Electronic industry, 4, 29-31, 52-53, 79, 126, 169

Emergent networks, 7, 70, 93-94, 328
  alignment with culture, 270-271
  change process, 164-165
  Southwest Hospital System, 173-174, 192
  Swift Engineering, 90, 98-100, 109-112
  Texas Instruments, 190-191
Employee:
  job security, 54
  level of education, 34
  management of, 33, 35
  motivation of, 14
  participation, 53
  tools, 52
  training, 53
  work arrangements, 70
Energy crises, 4, 5, 26, 124, 130, 148
Engineering industry, 54-55, 228, 307
Entrepreneurial management, 26, 35, 77, 122, 222, 271
Environmental impact:
  concentration of power, 78-79
  conflict, 80
  energy, 4, 5, 26, 124, 130, 148
  interconnectedness, 79
  interdependence, 79-80
  limitations, 5, 122, 157, 405
  uncertainty, 80
Equal Employment Opportunity legislation, 130
Evaluation for change, 373-380
  case study, 380-385
  collaborative assessment, 375, 380
Exchange relationship, 14
Expectancy theory of motivation, 86-90
Expertise, technical, 131
External pressures:
  economic, 34, 76, 203, 390
  energy, 26. *See also* Energy crisis
  environmental, 4, 157. *See also* Environmental impact
  national culture, 33
Exxon, 261, 263, 265, 271, 400, 412
Exxon Enterprises, 263, 265

Federal Bureau of Investigation, 133
Federal Communications Commission, 3
Federal funding, 75, 132, 138, 304-305
Financial analysis, 256, 395, 407

Ford Motor Company, 19-20, 30, 69, 80, 137, 231
Fortune, 20, 147
Fujitsu, 52
Functional structure, 4, 84-85, 203, 210, 271
Funding issues, 75, 138, 169, 296, 304

General Electric, 4, 23, 27, 130, 203, 222, 398-399
General Foods, 368-369
General Motors, 4, 26, 32, 35, 80, 133, 231, 255, 261
  Brookhaven plant, 35
  Lordstown plant, 8, 251
Geography, organization by, 47, 84, 203, 210
Goal optimization, 74, 161
Goal-setting, 9, 46, 81
  concerns, 228
  core goals, 132, 296-298, 311
  funding issues, 74
  nongoals, 74
  political, 129
  research, 74
  service, 74
  supporting objectives, 133
  teaching, 74
  trade-offs, 74
Goodrich, B. F., Company, 133
Governmental regulations, 127, 131, 186
Grant, W. T., Company, 92, 150, 391
Graphic depictions of models, 62, 66
Group dynamics, 47
Growth share matrix, 208

Harvard Business School, 23, 27, 33
Hawthorne studies, 43
Health, Education, and Welfare, U.S. Department of, 8-9, 143
Health delivery services, 75-77, 206, 228
  case studies, 77, 304-305
  goals, 132
Hewlett-Packard, 35, 261, 266, 268, 284-288, 407-408, 411
Hierarchy management:
  as barrier, 30, 240
  effect on culture, 134, 255
  integrating device, 214
  structures, 35, 215
High technology, 28-35, 263, 267-269

Hiring criteria, 5
Historical aspect:
  cultural cycle, 78
  economic context, 78-81
  political context, 78
  role in network model, 94
  technical cycle, 78
Honeywell, 283, 335
Human resources, 267-268, 400, 401-412
Human resources organic model, 43-47

IBM, 4, 231, 261, 263, 265, 267, 271, 400-401
Incentive system, 4, 25
Industrial revolution, second, 27
Inflation, 230, 389
Influence networks, 7, 338
Informational exchange model, 70-72, 267
Information collection and processing, 94, 127, 148
  capacity, 204, 212, 230
  enhancement of, 128
  Swift Engineering, 105-107
  technical change strategy, 203
  see also Communication, internal; Data
Information processing industry, 14, 28, 30, 80, 82, 85, 121, 127, 267, 335. *See also* Communication industry
Input to organizational model:
  environment, 75
  history, 73-76, 93
  resource, 75
Integrating mechanisms, 212, 307
  complex, 85, 213-214
  intermediate level, 85, 213-214
  lateral, 215
  simple, 85, 212-214
  vertical, 214-215
Intel, 28-31, 35
Interlocking directorates, 131
International business, 5, 22, 33, 203
Investment, 4, 32, 75, 254-255
Iron law of oligarchy, 232

Japanese:
  auto industry, 93
  challenge, 31, 120
  culture, 369

industry, 22, 24-26, 74
management style, 30-31, 265, 271-272, 366
productivity success, 52-54, 390
quality success, 52-54, 91, 258, 370, 390
training and development, 272
Job design technology, 305-307
Justice, Department of, 331, 335

Kalmar, 8, 217-220
Korea, as competitor, 51

Layoff, 14
Leadership, 19-21, 86, 90, 222, 250, 343, 363
Learning curve, 209
Long-term strategy, 50, 93, 206, 390-391
Loop-learning strategy, 275-286

MacDonalds, 76, 85
McGraw-Hill, 228, 229, 232, 249
Machiavellian management, 235-240, 249
Management of conflict:
  mechanistic processes, 225
  organic processes, 225
Management by crisis, 147
Management information system, 105, 119, 190
Management by objectives (MBO), 363
Management strategy, 6, 8, 9, 94
  environmental context, 78-81
  intuitive, management strategy, 90, 133, 379
  myths, 37-39
  participative, 240-241
  professional techniques, 90
  rotation of managers, 193, 222, 261
  seat of the pants, 90
  tools, 119
  trial and error, 90, 133
Management style, 37-39, 222
  conceptual framework, 40-41, 64, 364
  congruence with task, 222-223, 263-265
  decision-making, 151-152
  hands-on, 121
Management system:
  change strategy, 12, 189-190

design of, 9, 35
hierarchical, *see* Hierarchy management
personnel, 33
Managerial failure, 23-24, 148, 206
Managerial mobility, 78
Marketing research, 70
Market share, 190, 208, 209
Martin Luther King, Jr. Health Center (MLK), case study, 138-144
  cultural cycle, dominance of, 139
  information processing, 141-142
  mission strategy, 139
  organizational cycle, 139-140
  political cycle peak, 141
  start-up phase, 139
  technical cycle, 142-143
Masters in Business Administration (MBA), 32-33, 265, 411
Matrix structure, 4, 39, 47, 84-85, 203, 210, 213, 395-400
Matsushita, 52
MBA, *see* Masters in Business Administration
MBO, *see* Management by objectives
Measurement:
  change, 42, 370-371
  organizational effectiveness, 63
  product-defect ratio, 53-54
  Swift Engineering, 113
Mechanistic-to-organic continuum, 202, 204, 215
Mechanistic strategies:
  configurations, 324
  political, 235
Merrill Lynch, 260
Miller Brewing Co., 17
Mission/strategy, 6, 81-82, 96, 117, 200
  alignment, cultural, 256-258
  core, 257-258
  democratic, 131
  facilitation of, 93
  mechanistic-organic continuum, 42-47, 128, 131, 202, 221
  political, 47-49, 131
  strategic change plan, 1, 164
Model, organizational:
  exercise in building, 55-66
  generation of, 40
  implicit, 39-41
  simulated, 210
Montefiore Hospital, 138

Morale, 39, 229
Motivation, 44-46, 86-89, 219
  equation for determining, 88
  expectancy application, 87
  expectancy theory, 86-87
  Swift Engineering, 107
Motorola, 28, 52, 283
Multinational corporation, 5, 22, 23, 203
  environmental impact on, 234
  market characteristics, 34-35, 203
  structuring of, 210

National Semiconductor, 28
National Training Laboratories, 353
NCR, 339
Negotiation, as change activity, 49, 225
Network structure, 69-115, 323-325
  analysis of, 325-326
  configuration, 94, 324
  influence, 320
  transitions in, 340-342
New markets, 3, 34
New York Times, The, 4, 22, 237-238, 254
New York University, 70
Non-oligopolistic markets, 79
Norms, 7, 16, 72, 123, 326
  conformity to, 353
  congruency of, 296
  cultural system, 134
  shifting, 128, 332
  traditional, 137

Office of Economic Opportunity, 143
Oil embargo, 26
Oil industry, 26, 79, 120-121, 132-133, 137, 168
Oligopolistic market, 79
OPEC, 79, 121
Open systems planning, 296-305
Organic strategy, 193, 206, 241-248, 374-375
Organizational chart, 70-71, 83, 159
Organizational climate, 220, 224
Organizational cycle, 11
Organizational design:
  boundary roles, 320-321
  configuration, 159
  desired, 6, 18, 45
  initial, 117, 125
  interactions, 45, 65
  organic, 215-216, 217

problems, 155
redesign, 117, 144, 186
structural change, 121
Organizational effectiveness, 74-75
  assumptions, 72
  key variables, 63
Organizing dimensions of large businesses, 84, 121
OST, 207, 249, 282-283, 326, 334
Outplacement, 323

Pacific Mega Bank, case study, 355-360
People, 7, 45-47, 96, 131
  cultural alignment, 264-265
  formal structure, 70
  informal structure, 70
  trigger for change, 135
  see also Coalition
Pepsico, 414
"Perks," 252
Philip Morris, 17
Political analysis for change, 348-352
Political cycle, 77, 132, 397
Political design, 71-73, 83-85
  alignment, internal, 128-132
  problem, 10, 73, 137
  resistance to innovation, 121
  uncertainty management, 118
Political entity, 7-8, 16, 117, 397
  controversies, 130-132
  diagnosis, 180
Power, 16, 31, 48-49, 78, 232-234, 241, 243
Predictability, organizational goal, 75, 83
Predicting organizational behavior, 76
Prescribed network, 70, 71-73, 83-85, 98-100, 189-200
Presidential viewpoint, 19-20, 30, 120-122, 217
Prestige, 14-15
"Problem child," 209, 221
Problem-solving, 6, 12, 30, 40, 83, 118-119, 179, 215
Production, 12, 33-34, 76, 152, 200, 219, 271
Productivity, 5, 8, 24, 26, 47, 52, 74, 121, 139, 251-252, 293, 300
Product line, organization by, 39, 84, 121, 203, 209-210
Profitability, 6, 54, 74
  long-term, 50, 93

margins, 121
pretax, 28
short-term, 24, 28, 50
Profit impact marketing strategy
    (PIMS), 53, 210
Promotion, 3, 87, 92, 121
Psychological factors, 8, 14, 43-44

Quality awareness, 51
Quality circles, 51, 91, 315, 363, 370,
    390
Quality control, 8, 24, 32
    detection of errors, 54, 91
    game-playing, 91
    Japanese, 52-54, 91, 248
Quality of work, 4, 244, 258
Quasar, 52

Radar scan diagnosis, 154-155, 168
Rate of industrial growth, 347
Reagan administration, 34
Recoupling, 188, 329
Religious movement, 131, 137, 232,
    273, 353
Reporting structure, 29, 127
Research and development, 28, 72, 81,
    85-86, 156, 200, 207, 223, 266,
    271, 366-367, 400
Resources, 81
    allocation of, 81
    control of, 47
    financial, 70, 74, 208
    people, 265-266
    scarcity of, 79, 366
Reward system, 3, 14-16, 44-45, 92-
    93, 86-87, 272-273
Robotics, 51, 260
Role negotiation, 313

Salary increase, 87
Sales volume, 190, 208, 209
Sears Roebuck, 4, 260
Self-esteem, employee, 14-16
Sensitivity training, 133
Service organization, 69
Service-oriented, 6
Short-term perspective, 77, 365
Silicon Valley, 23, 120
Sloan School of Management, 142
Social networks, 69-115
    role of, 69-97
Social welfare, 77
Sony Corporation, 23

Southwest Hospital System, case study,
    169-175, 192-193, 196-202, 207,
    212, 249, 326
Sperry, 333
Stanford University, 31, 33, 267
"Star," 209, 221
Statistically based decision-making, 32
Steel industry, 79
Stock market, 31
Strategic change, 6, 11, 18-20, 82,
    147-165, 187-188
Strategic portfolio model, 208, 209
Strategic rope, 10-11, 188, 397
Stress, 148-150
Swift Engineering, case study, 94-115
Symptom-focused diagnosis, 155, 164
Systems perspective, 75-77, 137

Task component, 96
    alignment, 226
    interdependency, 127, 307-310. See
        also Task interdependence
    nature of, 127
    nonroutine, 127
    predictability, 87
    priorities, 225
    strategic, 118, 119
    Swift Engineering, 98-100, 101
Task Force, 86, 213
Task interdependence, 83, 127-128,
    138
    on culture, 260-261
    pooled, 83
    reciprocal, 82
    sequential, 83
Task uncertainty, 87, 126-127
Team building, 47, 218-220, 310-315,
    365
Technical cycle, 77, 132
Technical design, 49, 117
    change strategies, 203-229
    internal alignment, 126-128
    strategy development, 226
    uncertainty in, 118
Technical perspective, 7-8, 16, 70, 73,
    132, 179, 330
Technology, impact on organization,
    19, 132, 195
Test-marketing, 29
Texas Instruments, 28, 51, 207, 249,
    251, 261, 262, 268, 326
    case study, 175-178, 189-191, 195
    cultural uncertainty, 282-283

product customer center (PCC),
    189-190
objectives, strategy, tactics (OST)
    organization, 189-191, 334
reinforcement of innovation, 191,
    198, 202
shift to organic configuration, 200
T-group, 47, 136, 281
Theory X, 44, 90, 274-275
Theory Y, 44, 90, 281
Theory Z, 31, 291
3M Corporation, 260-262
Time, managerial, 151-152, 207,
    364
Time bomb, 77-78, 137
Time dimension, 127, 132
Time-trap, 151-152, 310-315, 365
Toyota, 51-52
Trade-offs, 187, 210-211, 327, 368
Training:
    of employees, 30
    of managers, 121, 363
    mechanism, 355
    sensitivity, 47, 136, 281
Transactional content, 71
Transition management, 12-13, 186,
    331-360
Triage systems, 151, 207
TRW Systems, 47
Turnover, 155
Type A, 31
Type Z, 31, 35

Uncertainty, 126-127, 143, 152-154
    cultural, 283-284
    management of, 118, 283-284
    political, 231, 241
    technical, 126

Union Carbide, 203-204, 261, 353
Unit cost, 209
United Auto Workers, 394
United States:
    adoption of Japanese techniques, 91
    business policy, 25
    chemical companies, 120-121
    cultural diversity, 25-26
    economy, 34-35, 130
    Justice Department, 331, 335
    unemployment, 130
U.S. Army, 18
UNIVAC, 335

Values, 7
    competing systems, 353
    congruence, 296
    cultural, 72, 123, 270
    ideological issues, 241-242
    shifts in, 135-136
Vigilant change diagnosis, 151-152
Vigilant decision-making, 193-194
Volvo, 91-92, 128, 250, 370, 385
Volvo-Kalmar, case study, 217-220

Wages, 14, 25, 125
Wall Street, 27, 32
Wall Street Journal, 230, 231
West Germany, 31, 34
Westinghouse Corporation, case study,
    50-68, 254
Win-lose strategy, 46
Work group, development of, 44-45,
    311-319, 343
Work satisfaction, 44
Work setting, 87

Xerox, 263